P9-CLB-818

THE
FORTUNATE
ONES

THE FORTUNATE ONES

A NOVEL

Ellen Umansky

wm

WILLIAM MORROW
An Imprint of HarperCollins*Publishers*

This book is a work of fiction. References to real people, events, establishments, organizations, or locales are intended only to provide a sense of authenticity, and are used fictitiously. All other characters, and all incidents and dialogue, are drawn from the author's imagination and are not to be construed as real.

HarperCollins books may be purchased for educational, business, or sales promotional use. For information please e-mail the Special Markets Department at SPsales@harpercollins.com.

FIRST EDITION

Designed by Bonni Leon-Berman

Library of Congress Cataloging-in-Publication Data has been applied for.

ISBN 978-0-06-238248-1

17 18 19 20 21 LSC 10 9 8 7 6 5 4 3 2 1

In memory of my mother, Gloria Mark Spivak,
with deep, abiding love.

And for Dave, Lena, and Talia, always.

THE FORTUNATE ONES

COMFORT

VIENNA, 1936

OMA WANTED TO SEND A telegram to Papi in Paris, but Mutti said no. "He will be back in three days. He will know soon enough," Mutti said from the cot in the little room that would have been the nursery. She had moved in once the pains began. ("It's too early!" Rose had heard Mutti cry out.) The doctor had come and gone, the sheets had been changed, the blood scrubbed away. Without any evidence, it almost seemed to Rose as if it hadn't happened.

"She will be fine, won't she?" Rose asked Gerhard.

"Of course," he said. "She has been those other times."

"What other times?"

Gerhard shook his head. He had little patience for his younger sister. "She will be fine," he repeated.

They were seated at one end of the long dining table beneath the brass chandelier, eating apricot dumplings with cinnamon. Cook seemed to have forgotten that they had had strudel after lunch. Rose had already polished off her serving, but her brother had about half left. Between small careful bites, he turned to a composition notebook by his side, studied a list he'd written.

"What's that?" Rose asked. Normally she tried not to ask Gerhard too many questions. Her brother loved nothing more than to lord his knowledge over her. But right now she would do anything not to think of her mother lying pale down the hall.

Gerhard considered for a moment. "I am working out how to sell tickets to the Dianabad pool," he surprised Rose by answering. "Near the wave machine."

"But the Dianabad is public, and the season doesn't open for two more months," she felt compelled to say. "No one owns those spots."

He let out an exaggerated sigh, but it was no match for the glow of satisfaction lighting up his face. "You can sell anything, if you know how."

Rose heard steps and Bette's fair head appeared. "Gerhard, I could use your help." He got up and Rose did too, following them down the long hall, away from where Mutti was lying, and into their parents' bedroom.

The brocade curtains were drawn, the embroidered coverlet on the bed smoothed back, the pile of silk pillows just so. The room was chilly, and all the exactitude made Rose uneasy. "Why are we here?" she asked.

Bette sighed. "You don't have to be," she said, and to Gerhard: "She wants the painting of the boy."

"The painting?" Rose said, as surprised as if she had been told that her mother had arisen this morning and announced she was joining a nunnery.

Gerhard and Bette were already tugging at the gold frame. "She said she sleeps better with it nearby. And we are not to question her. Do you hear?"

Rose nodded. She couldn't imagine questioning her mother, today of all days.

Bette, thin-shouldered, only a few years older than Gerhard, strained as she tilted the heavy picture, scraping the plastered wall. "Gentle, gentle," she cautioned as Gerhard helped her heave it off.

Rose joined them as they carried it down the hall, and she considered it a victory that Bette didn't shoo her away.

Inside the little room, Mutti lay against white pillows on the cot. She wore a white nightgown, but the darkness of her hair, piled up on her head, stood out in contrast to all that white. Rose decided it gave her face definition. She was still reassuringly herself, beautiful. The room was cozy, the porcelain *kachelofen* chugging away, Mutti's brass lamp with the pink glass shade casting a warm glow. Bette must have moved it in, Rose realized.

A cane-backed chair sat close to the cot, and Bette and Gerhard angled the painting to rest on it. "Thank you," Mutti whispered. Her dark eyes fell on the picture, and Rose followed her mother's gaze. The boy in the painting was not pretty. He was too skinny in his red uniform, his face pasty and elongated. The paint was thick, thrown on; it looked as if the painter couldn't be bothered to slow down and pay attention. Rose didn't understand why her mother loved it so.

"Children, you are here." She said it wonderingly, not at all the sharp Mutti Rose knew, and it made Rose wish she had stayed at the dining table and not followed her brother in. Mutti motioned for her to come close, she laid a hand on Rose's head. Rose saw that the bedsheets were Mutti's favorite, edged with crochet. "My little *mausi,*" she murmured, and Rose felt chastened.

"Beef broth, ma'am?" Bette said. "The doctor said you must eat."

"I could use a touch of something," Mutti said, and leaned back against the pillows.

Bette curtsied, and signaled to the children. "Come, let your mother rest."

Back in the drawing room, Gerhard picked up the volume about the Kaiser that he had been reading, sank into the wingback chair near the windows.

"Why does she like the painting so much?" Rose leaned against the chair behind her brother, playing with the fringed edges of the

Persian throw that covered the top of the cushion. Across the room, a glazed porcelain vase crowded with roses occupied a spot on the mantel. Why hadn't her mother asked for flowers instead?

"I don't know," Gerhard said, and he didn't look up from the book. "She does."

"Well, I think it's ugly."

"Of course you do. You're too young to understand it."

"I know *you* don't either," she said, coloring. And from the way Gerhard pushed his nose into the book, peered at the pages more closely, Rose could tell that she was not wrong, and it irked him.

"Who is the boy in the painting?" Rose ventured. "Does she know him?"

"No. She bought it in Paris on a trip with Papi, years ago," Gerhard said, not looking up. "You were just a baby. You don't remember."

Gerhard was right. She didn't remember. The painting of the boy had always been in their flat, along with so many other things. Rose loved the tapestry of the peacock with its lustrous blues that hung near the swords that had been her grandfather's, the velvet jewelry case with the silver clasp that had been Oma's, the small landscape of a waterfall that if you were attentive and looked behind the copse of trees (which Rose always did), you could detect the shadow of a bear.

But her mother doted on the painting of the boy, took considerable comfort from it. It disturbed Rose. "I wish it were gone," she said with coarse agitation.

1

LOS ANGELES, DECEMBER 2005

LIZZIE MADE HERSELF LOOK. The pine casket was descending, the sun playing against its surface, metal railings guiding it into the ground. A knot of cemetery workers stood nearby, shovels in hand. She gazed past them toward a trio of slender cypress trees cutting sharp against the resolutely blue sky. It was not yet noon but already hot. Out of the corner of her eye, she registered smudges wheeling and darting. Hummingbirds? Possibly. They used to flit around the twisted vines of scarlet bougainvillea out by her father's pool. She could remember her father pointing to the tiny birds when she and Sarah first moved to L.A. "Hummingbirds don't hum," he had said. "Hear that? It's more of a *scratch-scratch*. No poetry there."

Now Lizzie squinted behind the oversized sunglasses that she'd purchased last summer on Canal Street, played with her father's watch. The Rolex was too big and loose for her wrist, but it was his. She looked again in the direction of the cypresses, but whatever birds had been there were gone. Or maybe they had never been there at all. She heard the rabbi chanting. She grasped her sister's hand.

This was a mistake. It could not be right. How could that be her father in there? How was that possible?

Lizzie had last spoken to him four days ago. She had left work that Thursday at a decent hour and was negotiating the crush of people on Sixth Avenue when he had called. He was telling her about a few trips he was planning. Next month to Iceland: he was talking about Reykjavík and eating fermented shark and how the first lady was Jewish, Israeli-born. The following spring he wanted to go to Seoul. Lizzie was only half listening, her mind focused on getting on the subway downtown so she wouldn't be late. (Another online date, another evening for which she was trying—unsuccessfully—to keep her expectations low.) Still she couldn't help but say, "So many trips. I thought you were concerned about money."

"No," he had said. "*You* think I should be concerned about money."

She half laughed, half snorted. "I do not," she had said, but that was the way it had always been between them. She was thirty-seven, and little had changed since she was seventeen.

An hour later, Lizzie thought her date was going fine, but after one round he stuck out his hand and said, "Good luck with everything!" (A banker and former ZBT brother? Just as well.) She went home, poured herself a glass of wine, settled on the IKEA couch that she kept telling herself she had to replace, and chanced on *WarGames* on TV. She reached for her phone and pecked out a text, all thumbs. "The only move is not to play," she typed. "Bullshit eighties propaganda. I'm jealous," Claudia soon responded, and Lizzie laughed, feeling better already.

The first two calls didn't wake her, but the third did, and Sarah's voice sounded high-pitched and strange: "There's been an accident, a car accident." Lizzie got on the first flight the next morning. She took a cab to JFK well before dawn and landed in L.A. just as the sun was coming up, the dishwatery gray of the sky turning a lurid orange. As she barreled over skeins of freeway to UCLA, she chanted to herself: *He'll be fine, he has to be fine*. But he never regained consciousness.

Now the rabbi motioned for the sisters to stand. Angela, on Sarah's other side, stood too, her arm around Sarah's shoulders. Lizzie clutched her sister's hand. She wished she were standing in the shade of those cypresses. She could hear the rush of cars on the nearby freeway, sounding like water. An unspeakable thought intruded: *What if the doctors had been wrong? What if for one moment when they unhooked the machines and covered him up, what if he had still been alive?*

The rabbi gestured for them to come forward, toward the fresh mound of soil beside the gaping hole. A shovel pierced the dirt, stood upright.

Lizzie remembered little of her mother's funeral, but she recalled that hill of dirt. She had been thirteen then. Lynn had been sick for about a year (and surely long before that, Lizzie realized after she died). During that year, while her mother got sicker and sicker, Lizzie and her sister continued to go to school and Hebrew school, taking ice-skating and clarinet lessons—pretending, fruitlessly, that everything would be fine. Their grandmother moved in. Joseph stepped up his visits, coming once a month. (She overheard her mother on the phone with her father: "No, no, Joseph, that's ridiculous. You need to be out there, working. I am *fine*.") He took them to the Ground Round and to Friendly's for Fribbles as he had when he and Lynn first split up and he'd moved into a rental in the city, before his friend convinced him to join his ophthalmological surgical practice out in Los Angeles, before there was the slightest inkling of Lynn's cancer.

During their mother's illness, Lizzie was the one heating up cans of Chef Boyardee for herself and Sarah, forging their permission slips, lugging up loads of laundry; she was the one who went to Sarah's soccer games. (Except for those times that she didn't, using the money her mother gave her for snacks to play Ms. Pac-Man at the arcade, slamming wrist against joystick and gobbling up those dots and cherries as if her life depended on it.) She always thought her additional domestic duties, emotional and practical, would be temporary.

She was twelve years old. Things would change. Never did she think they would change because her mother would die.

Sarah squeezed her hand, and the warm pressure of her palm, the tightness of her fingers, somehow enabled Lizzie to move forward. She took a step, stumbling slightly, but she righted herself when she took hold of the shovel's metal handle. It was heavier than she thought, but she pressed down and succeeded in flinging down a paltry patch of dirt. The hollow thump of the soil making contact with the lid of the coffin—a *pling*, really—was a harrowing, haunting sound.

Where was her father?

AFTERWARD, THEY DECAMPED TO AN art gallery at Bergamot Station. The long narrow space filled up quickly. The air grew warm. So many people, from so many different parts of her father's life: med-school classmates and cousins and ex-girlfriends and former patients and neighbors and the caterer who was also the mother of Sarah's friend from middle school (she and Joseph had probably dated, Lizzie realized with a start). Her father would have loved this. It almost felt like he was here. Max, Joseph's good friend, offered her a drink. She shook her head. "Coffee," she said. "Please," her voice sounding tinny in her ears.

Lizzie thought she spotted Claudia, but as she fought her way through the tangle of hips and elbows, the crowd closed in, tightening. It felt less like a memorial than an art opening. The space was so hot and packed; the loud voices seemed to warble, ricocheting against each other. She stood, uncertain.

"Oh, Lizzie. Oh, oh." Before Lizzie knew what was happening, a soft rotund woman rushed up and threw her arms around her. "I'm so so sorry about your father," she said. "He was wonderful."

"Thank you," Lizzie said, her cheek pressed into the woman's wiry earring. She smelled of baby powder. Who was she? And then it clicked: her father's former secretary Pat. She had worked for him for a year, maybe two, tops, ages ago. It was during the time when his practice was booming, when Joseph issued limos to bring patients in for their cataract surgeries. All the Beverly Hills ladies loved him. He was raking in the profits and was eager to spend—on trips to Hawaii and Morocco, two-seater Italian convertibles, artwork that he liked to show off during dinner parties. All Lizzie remembered about Pat was that she was a rabid Clippers fan and lived with her brother. In fact, Lizzie now recalled, the brother started coming into Joseph's office, hanging around until his sister got off work. *The patients don't like it,* Lizzie could remember Joseph complaining. *I don't like it.* Pat was still hugging Lizzie, an awkward intimacy. But Pat felt strongly about her father, and Lizzie held on.

"I hadn't seen him in months," Pat said, finally pulling back. "Maybe even a year. What kind of person am I? It had been so long. Why hadn't I made plans?"

"It's okay," Lizzie said. "I'm sure he felt the same way." She added this even though she couldn't remember the last time her father had mentioned Pat.

"But I should have known better. I *knew* better. And now he's gone. It's too late. I can't believe he's gone." Pat's voice trembled.

"I know," Lizzie said. She couldn't bring herself to say anything more. *Remove yourself,* she could hear her father say. Where was Sarah? Claudia? She wanted a rescue.

"He was still young. And now he's gone, just like that. I can't believe it. You poor girls." She gave Lizzie's hand a squeeze. "I'm going to miss him so much."

"Thank you," Lizzie managed, "I have to—" and with her sentence unfinished, she fled.

At the back of the gallery, she stood against the wall, praying that it was close to five P.M. They had called for the memorial to end then. There were fewer people back here, no one who seemed to recognize her, and that enabled her to breathe. It was hard to be around people. But she did not want to be alone. She gazed at a large photograph of a man's torso, elongated and stretched thin.

"There you are," Claudia said. "I've been looking all over for you."

"Found," Lizzie said as she threw herself into her friend's arms, desperate for solidity.

After a moment, Claudia pulled back, cocked her head to the side. "How are you doing?"

Lizzie touched the back of her head. Her hair felt frizzy, her body unclean, her eyes itchy from lack of sleep, all the coffee she'd been drinking. She kept waiting for Joseph to emerge from the crowd. "I'm okay," she said.

Claudia looked at her steadily and didn't say a thing. Finally she said: "Have you eaten? I have to say, the food is shockingly good. Your father would be proud."

"All Angela's doing." Lizzie's sister's girlfriend was the one who had reached out to the gallery owner, an old friend of Joseph's; Angela had set up the caterer, she hired the bartender and arranged for the chair rentals too. "I feel like I should be doing more," Lizzie confessed.

"Are you kidding me? Today, of all days?"

"I know," Lizzie said. Still, it made her uneasy.

"That's Angela. She's probably making you feel that way."

"I don't think so. She's been great."

"Uh-huh. I spoke with her earlier, and she seemed as prickly as ever."

"You're terrible," Lizzie said, laughing. It felt good to laugh.

"I'm right. You know, it stems from insecurity. She's just afraid your sister's going to leave her for a doctor or a lawyer."

"Angela *is* a doctor," Lizzie corrected her. "An anesthesiologist, remember?"

"Oh yeah. Well, then, a doctor with a dick," Claudia said, unperturbed. She chewed on a strawberry. "You didn't answer me: Have you eaten today?"

"A little," Lizzie lied.

"Come on," Claudia said. "Let's get you some food and libation."

Soon Lizzie was biting into a bagel that Claudia had loaded up, eating it for her friend's sake. She truly wasn't hungry. The bagel itself was dry, but the lox was fantastic, not too salty, buttery—where was it from? she found herself wondering. Then she realized her father would wonder. She turned to the lukewarm Chardonnay. Last night, despite the Ambien, she'd woken up in a sweat around four in the morning in her sister's guest room, her heart galloping, not remembering where she was or what was so criminally wrong. A maw of fear overtook her. Oh God, her father.

Claudia fished through her bag. She picked up her buzzing phone, rolling her eyes. "This had better be crucial. I told you I'm at a fucking funeral," she said. "Uh-huh, okay." She mouthed to Lizzie, *I'll be right back*.

Lizzie nodded but she felt a flip of panic. She couldn't handle another conversation like the one she had with Pat. Where was her sister? She eyed the narrow room. The crowd had thinned. She didn't see Sarah. She went to the bathroom, found the door locked.

As Lizzie waited against the wall, she looked at a nearby canvas: A large-scale painting, depicting a couple sitting on a boat-sized couch, watching TV. The man's feet were propped up on an ottoman, the woman sitting up straight, only inches apart, but a discernible distance. Sunlight spilled in from a window but their eyes remained on the glowing screen. They paid no mind to the largest object in the room: an elephant, standing to the right of them.

The elephant in the room. Lizzie let out a snort. It was funny, but it was more than that. The painting itself was beautiful: the elephant's leathery wrinkly hide, the polished elegance of his curved tusks. And it was this gorgeously rendered specificity, the fact that the painter was willing to bestow such attention, that made her think of Ben. He would like it too.

Did he know about her dad? She wanted him to know. And yet

she didn't feel like she could call him. It had been nearly three years since they had broken up. She still sometimes wondered if she had made a mistake.

The bathroom door opened, and an old woman Lizzie didn't recognize came out. She saw Lizzie looking at the painting. "What do you think?" she asked, her hands on her hips like a general.

"I like it," Lizzie said. "You?"

"Not really," the woman said. She was tiny, in a dark tailored suit with a brightly colored scarf at her neck. She spoke with a gravelly voice that made Lizzie think of peeling paint. It carried a hint of an accent—British?—that she could not place.

"You don't?" Lizzie asked. What was there not to like?

"She's not working hard enough. I'll bet you she's capable of more. At the end of the day, what are you left with?"

There was more to it than that. The joke was only the start. She could hear her father say, *Tim-ing, now that is everything.* But Lizzie only said: "I always thought being funny could get you fairly far."

The woman looked at her, her thin mouth expanding into a smile. "It's nice to finally meet you. I'm Rose Downes." She held out a hand. "I'm so sorry about your father."

Oh God, was she supposed to know her? Lizzie could be terrible with names. "Thank you. It was nice of you to come today." She hesitated. "I'm sorry; how did you know my father?"

Rose touched the silk at her neck and smiled inwardly. "You probably know me better as the woman whose family used to own *The Bellhop.*"

Lizzie couldn't have heard her right. "*The Bellhop?*"

"Yes."

"My Soutine?"

"Well," Rose said, and drew her lips in. "Some might argue it's *my* Soutine. It was my family's. But yes, that painting."

"And my father knew this?" Lizzie said thickly.

"Yes, of course he knew," Rose said with a touch of exasperation. "That's how we met."

"I'm sorry," Lizzie said. "I didn't realize—" She couldn't finish her thought.

Lizzie first saw the painting on the day she arrived in L.A. after her mother died. She hadn't been to her father's house in close to a year. He opened the front door and she was hit by the light, a blinding California light. The floor-to-ceiling windows in the living room were like a taut glass skin—a country of it, everywhere you turned. She walked to the windows, stuck her face up against the glass, and peered down into the mouth of the parched ravine, the yawning canyon far below. The depth to which she could tumble filled her with a bruising, voluminous peace. It was larger than her mother's cancer, bigger than moving across the country to live with a father she didn't really know.

She turned around and, with her fingers still pressed up against the glass, she saw him. Across from the fireplace hung a painting of a man. A young man, dressed in a uniform, a fancy red uniform with gold buttons. His face and limbs were elongated, his ears elephantine. His nose was crooked, as if someone had slammed a fist into it. His stance was awkward, his head too large for his body. He didn't seem to know what to do with his hands. But the colors! His face was a riot of swirls: when she went closer to the canvas, she discovered other hues in his uniform, dips of blue and white, streaks of gold and black and purple, as if whoever had painted it couldn't contain himself, as if he were unleashing all the pigment he had at his disposal. It was angry and ugly and dizzying and beautiful, all at once.

"You like that?" Joseph asked. "It's pretty nice, isn't it?"

She shrugged. "It's okay," she said, and sat down below it. All that red!

He cleared his throat. "For someone not interested, you're paying a lot of attention."

Lizzie gave another shrug, stayed silent. She made her father nervous, she was realizing, and she found, to her surprise, that she liked this feeling, the tart taste of power like a cold marble in her mouth.

"It's by a guy named Soutine. He was a French Expressionist. Which can refer to many things, but expensive is one," Joseph continued. "I first saw it years ago, in New York." He paused. "With your mother. She liked it too."

Rose, eyes narrowed, was looking past Lizzie at the elephant in the room. "I thought your father told you, but perhaps I misunderstood," Rose said. "I truly liked him. My condolences to you and your sister." She nodded quickly.

"Your family owned the Soutine," Lizzie said, her mind too awhirl to settle on a question.

"We did."

"Where? Where are you from?"

"Vienna. My mother purchased it in Paris, in the twenties, and brought it back home."

"Oh," Lizzie said. The accent fell in place. "And then?"

"It was stolen. When the Germans came."

"Oh," she repeated. She did the math in her head. She understood. "I'm sorry."

Rose nodded. "I know it was taken from you too. I met your father, afterward. I read about the theft in the newspaper. There was a small item in the *L.A. Times*—"

Lizzie felt a familiar tightness in her stomach. She remembered reading that article months later, before she left for college. She was looking for stamps on her father's mess of a desk when she came across a short clipping from the paper, and the memories from that night came flooding back as surely as if she had been slapped. *Why was he saving it? Why was it here on his desk?* She crumbled it up, buried it deep in the wastebasket. But within the hour she stole back into his study, fished it out, ironed out the wrinkles as best she could, and placed it back where she had found it, feeling guilty once again.

"My husband read it," Rose was saying. "I couldn't believe it—*The Bellhop*, here, in Los Angeles! I hadn't seen it since I left Vienna as a child. I got in touch with your father. In the beginning, we met to talk about the painting and the theft. But—well, through the years, we just kept meeting. Not often, but we'd go to lunch or maybe an exhibit together. He always drove. I abhor driving. And he took me places I hadn't been."

"Really?" Lizzie asked, the tightness beneath her ribs easing up. She could imagine it, her father with Rose. "Where would you go?"

"Different places. The Bradbury Building, for one."

"Oh, I love that building." Her father took her there after she watched *Blade Runner* in her high school film class. She could remember the moment of stepping past the plain façade into the sun-soaked interior, all that gorgeous wrought iron. *It's even better in person, isn't it?* her father had said, and there was such delight in his voice; even if she hadn't liked it, she would have agreed.

"It's overrated," Rose said with a shrug. "Too much going on. You know the architect famously claimed he got a message from a Ouija board as to how to design it. It looks that way."

Lizzie let out a snort of a laugh. She couldn't help herself. She liked this woman.

"We went years ago," Rose continued, unfazed by Lizzie's laughter. "And to Grand Central Market afterward. This was before it was cleaned up, fancified. We tried four different kinds of *mole*, and all were delicious."

Lizzie could picture it precisely—her father leading past stalls filled high with dried chilies and avocados and mangoes, past the lunch counter with its neon sign advertising chop suey. The thought gave her a lift, made her, for a brief moment, happy. "I wish I could have been there."

Rose gave a hint of a smile. "Yes," she said, and they both fell into silence. Rose glanced toward the front of the room and Lizzie followed her gaze. The gallery had emptied out; Lizzie saw the bartender stacking glasses into an orange plastic crate. "I have to get going," Rose said. "My condolences again." She nodded seriously.

"No, you haven't met my sister yet—"

"Another time."

"Only if you mean it. I really would like to talk to you more."

"Of course."

But Lizzie couldn't shake the feeling that if Rose left, she would never see her again. She could just hear Sarah: *You met who? She claimed to have owned what?* And this fear lent a particular urgency. "You said you were born in Vienna," Lizzie said. "During the war—where were you?"

Rose touched the bright silk at her neck. Her eyes in her lined face were like polished dark stones. "I was in England," she said.

She said it so simply, seemed so matter-of-fact about it that Lizzie decided to add: "So you got out."

"My brother and I did," Rose said. "My parents did not."

"Oh," Lizzie said. It was terrible, what Rose was saying. She didn't have to say more. "I'm so sorry."

"It's happened," Rose said firmly, as if Lizzie were trying to convince her otherwise.

2

VIENNA, 1938–1939

THEY WERE NEARLY PREPARED. BETTE had filled the wooden bucket halfway with water and set it next to the tiled stove. A cast-iron ladle leaned against the bucket, and a collection of small tin balls nestled in a snowy dishcloth, as if preparing for the alchemy that lay ahead. Rose had purchased them earlier in the week with her own money, from the bounty of the two shillings that Oma had given her for her eleventh birthday last month, forgoing a chance to see *One in a Million* at the UFA movie house. When she slid her coins over the counter, the wizened shop clerk had cracked a lopsided grin at her. "And a happy new year to you, young lady." Rose pocketed the tin balls with a smile, feeling giddy and shy with belonging.

Now she fingered a pellet and rolled it around in her palm. It was light, to be sure, but it still felt substantial, hard. She liked the feel of the cool metal against her skin. "Are you sure it will melt?" she asked.

"Of course I'm sure. I've been doing it as long as I can remember," Bette said, and she punched the heel of her palm into the dough. "It's heat to metal; it's what happens."

Bette was from the country, nearly half a day's train ride outside of Vienna—a village where chickens ruled the dirt streets, water was drawn from a well, and a movie house was an inchoate fantasy. Rose thought of herself as having a good imagination, but when she tried to picture herself living in such a place, the movie in her mind simply stopped, unspooled itself off the reel.

Rose moved closer. "When can we start?" She felt itchy in the woolens that her mother made her wear, her feet sweating in her thick black boots.

"I need to finish my work first."

And my parents have to leave, Rose thought, but she knew it would annoy Bette if she said it. After Rose had bought the tin balls, she tucked them deep into her knapsack, never mentioning her purchase to her mother. *Lead pouring is an old wives' tale,* she could hear Mutti say. *That's what they learn in the country.* But how would Rose know it wasn't true unless she tried? Everyone else was having fun on New Year's Eve—Gerhard was staying at his friend Oskar's for the weekend, her parents were going to a party at Tante Greta's—why shouldn't she too?

Rose watched Bette's slender fingers ribbon the edges of the dough, the smell of the yeast tickling her nostrils. "Heinrich says too much bread isn't good for your constitution," she said.

"Is that so?"

Rose nodded. "He says in the future we'll probably swallow a pill instead of taking meals." She dipped her fingers in the water of the bucket and swished them around. She had just reported the entirety of one of her conversations with Heinrich. They had had two in total. She had met him last summer at the holiday camp she had attended at the foot of the Alps. He was a reedy redhead a year her senior who spent most of his time ferreting out shade to read Jules Verne. When she saw him crossing the grounds, holding his book like armor to his concave chest, such a fluttery feeling arose in her stomach—Rose had never felt something like that before.

"Only people who have an excess of food would complain about it," Bette said when: *brrring!* The bell sounded. Rose started. "Let's go see what the missus wants," Bette said, wiping her floury hands against her apron and heading toward the door. Rose followed. "Not *you.*" Bette let out one of those thin knowing laughs Rose hated. "She rang for me, not for you. I'll be back soon."

After Bette left, Rose tried to amuse herself by attempting to toss the tin balls into the bucket. But each time she failed. Finally she decided to go to her parents' bedroom, see what Bette had been summoned for.

She took the long hall—still harboring a new-paint odor—past the pantry and laundry and turned down the second hall that led to the drawing room and her father's study, guarded by the double swords her grandfather had purchased in Constantinople. In their old flat, the swords had hung in the drawing room, but her mother had argued that the new home demanded a new start. Nothing was where it used to be. The one exception, Rose thought as she cut through the sitting area to knock on their bedroom door: the portrait of *The Bellhop.* In the bedroom it remained, despite her father's objections. ("I should be the only man in here," he said.)

"Come in," Mutti called. For Rose, the shift was as great as stepping from the darkened movie house into bright afternoon sunlight. She registered the smell of lilies and the rustling sound of silk before she could take in the dazzle of her mother in her entirety.

Charlotte was giving her nose a final pat of powder. A smooth lock of hair dipped down below her left eyebrow, giving Rose the unsettling impression that Mutti was winking. She wore a navy silk gown that made her pale skin look paler, her dark hair darker. Her beauty made Rose feel light-headed and envious and wistful and proud, all at once.

"Where's Bette?"

Mutti tsked. "Manners, child. What kind of greeting is that?"

"I don't know," Rose said, and looked down at her toes. Her feet felt even sweatier, entombed in her boots.

"An honest one," Papi said. Wolfe was short but nimble, always in motion. He fiddled with his tie. "We should go."

Mutti shook her head—at Rose or Papi, Rose wasn't sure. "Bette is fixing the fastener on my cape. It should only take a moment."

Her father frowned. "We'll be late. We're expected at Greta's in less than an hour."

"And it will take us less than half an hour to get there. We're not in the nineteenth district anymore."

He looked away from her, gave his tie one last decisive tug. "Indeed we are not."

Her mother had pressed hard for the move to this apartment, Rose knew, to this neighborhood in particular. Now they were close to the embassy quarter, within walking distance of Ringstrasse and the Opera—her mother's dream. No one else had seen the point in moving. So what if some rooms in their old flat were forever hot and others forever cold? Who cared if their stretch of Liechtensteinstrasse was thick with leather and machinery shops? The man in the shop on the corner always gave Rose peppermint candy when she passed, and she loved playing in the walled garden of the hospital two blocks away. But her mother persevered—she always did.

"If we're late, maybe we'll miss Karl's speechifying," Wolfe said. "He makes it sound as if Schuschnigg is already at the gate, waiting to swing it open for Hitler."

"No politics," Charlotte said. "Not tonight."

Rose had studied the Great War in school. She knew that Papi had been a foot soldier in northern Italy, but he didn't like to talk about it. She heard him once telling Gerhard, "I fought a war so you don't have to."

Bette came in, holding Mutti's wool cape in outstretched hands. "Ma'am," she said, and offered it to Charlotte.

"Perfect," Mutti said. "Thank you." Bette gave a little curtsy and bob of her head and left. "I'm glad I noticed it before we left," her mother said.

"Yes, can you imagine? Someone might have said, 'Your cape fastener is loose. Horrors!'" Her father widened his eyes at Rose, who giggled.

Charlotte pursed her lips. "Someone should look presentable, don't you think?" She touched Rose's head. "You're a good girl."

"Thank you, Mutti," Rose said. "Good night."

"We'll see you next year," Papi said, and he too touched her head and they were gone.

SHE *WAS* A GOOD GIRL, Rose thought as she ran a hand over the polished brass handles of her mother's inlaid dresser. But not *that* good. She sat down on her mother's settee and yanked off her black boots and woolens, liberating her sweaty feet, the air delicious between her toes. Then she went over to her mother's closet, running her hand against her dresses—silk and worsted wool and light cotton.

She paused at a peacock-blue dress, linen with an Empire waist and beautiful white piping. Mutti had worn the dress at Bad Ischl last summer, when they ate pink ice cream in the café. Rose remembered how after the ice cream, they ran into Herr Schulman, her mother's piano teacher, near the river. When Charlotte's hat blew off, Herr Schulman leaped after it, retrieving it with speed, heaving, and handed it back to her with such a grin on his face, as if he'd won a grand prize. Now Rose tugged off her own dress and slipped into her mother's. It was enormous—the square neckline slipped off her shoulders—yet it felt wonderful, like sipping from a big glass of lemonade in the shade of summer.

Rose wound a long string of her mother's pearls around her neck, dusted her face with powder. She added her favorite scarf of her mother's, blue-and-purple silk with a pattern of birds perched on branches, others with wings open in flight. The material felt fine and elegant against her neck. Rose assessed herself in the mirror and spoke: "Why, thank you, Heinrich, I would love to dance." She gave a curtsy and held out her hands. She pictured Ginger Rogers and Fred Astaire. She spun in a circle. Once, twice.

When she stopped, she was in front of *The Bellhop*. The boy in the painting gazed at her. How many times had she looked at the picture? She knew Mutti had bought it on a whim in a Parisian gallery for far too much money—so said Papi. It had been painted by a man named Soutine, who was Jewish, her mother liked to say, as they were. (But *Ostenjuden*, her father would often add, not like us—an immigrant, from the east.) Rose had not changed her mind. She still thought the portrait ugly, but she couldn't stop looking at it.

The boy in the painting stood awkwardly in his red uniform, gold buttons glinting, a matching red triangular hat perched atop his head. His hands rested on his hips, legs straddled open so wide he looked as if he might topple over. His pale face was impassive, his dark eyebrows shot up high. There was a resentful look in his eyes, as if he didn't trust the painter, the endeavor altogether. The paint itself was so thickly piled on that Rose had the feeling it had been created in the middle of an argument—she heard shouting, she saw the flinging of color onto the canvas.

But now, none of this mattered. He did look awkward and unpleasant, but he was a boy only a few years older than herself, a boy who wanted more than anything to escape: his uniform, his life, his own skin. He didn't want to be unpleasant, Rose was convinced. She longed to help him.

"I'm sorry," she said. "I didn't mean to be rude." She curtsied and said, "Yes, I would love another dance."

Bette's high pitch cut through Rose's imagining. "Rose, where are you?"

"Coming," Rose called as she stepped out of the dress and left *The Bellhop* behind.

BETTE WOULDN'T LET HER HOLD the ladle. "You're my responsibility," she said, tossing her thin braid back. "Heaven forbid you burn yourself." But she did hand Rose a ball. "Now roll it around tightly, and shake well. My *oma* always said that this gives them your strength, your print."

Rose made a fist and shook. Then she placed the ball in the cast-iron ladle. Bette positioned the ladle on top of the stove's front burner. She held it with a steady hand over the flames. Every few seconds she angled the ladle from side to side, a graceful balletic move. Soon the lead ball was shuddering under the heat, no longer a ball but a silvery amoeba-like creature, slithering to spread to the edges of the spoon. Rose, peering close, thought of the fat caterpillars she and Gerhard spotted down by the marshy banks of the Danube. "Is it ready?"

"Almost," Bette murmured.

Rose felt the heat. The ball had lost its color altogether. It flashed iridescent, something otherworldly, like something out of Jules Verne.

"Okay," Bette said. "Now." And Rose didn't know how she did it, but Bette managed to keep the ladle steady and guided Rose's hands to her own too. "You slide it into the water," Bette said. "My *oma* says it's part of the fortune."

Although her stomach was careening, Rose obliged. She could feel an emerging, nearly drowsy sensation that took her a few beats to recognize as calm. Bette transferred the ladle to Rose, but kept her hands on Rose's, and it was this warmth too, this feeling of support and connection, that Rose cottoned to, would remember for years to come when Vienna seemed like a dream.

"Now!" Bette ordered, and Rose released the bubbling metallic mass. A bright, tinkling noise sounded as the hot metal hit the water. Though there was little splash, Rose tipped back. She wiped her sweaty forehead and peered over the pail. The metal had hardened immediately. She couldn't discern its shape. She was almost afraid to look. Over the past week, she had listened attentively as Bette described the possible shapes and their corresponding fortunes: Would they see a ship, which would indicate travel in the next year? (Rose very much hoped this would be the case.) A ball could mean that luck would roll your way. If the metal resembled an anchor, that meant that you must help someone in need; and a cross . . . "Well, let us hope we don't see a cross," Bette had said, making the sign of a cross.

But all Rose could make out was a bubbly surface: "That's money! That's definitely money," Bette said with true excitement, but Rose was looking down farther—more money would mean more movies, it would mean more travel too, wouldn't it? But then, oh, there was something else, a small little something, a thin piece of metal no wider than her thumb.

"Do you see that? What's that little piece, there?" Rose pointed.

But Bette had already turned, she had pulled out the spoon. "I saw it—that doesn't count—let's try again."

IN FEBRUARY, BETTE'S MOTHER FELL ill and she went home to take care of her younger brothers and sisters. In March, Chancellor Schuschnigg opened the gate for Hitler after all. Now instead of shillings and groschen, there were marks and pfennig. There were German soldiers in uniform on the street saluting one another. They spoke in funny accents, which Papi imitated with gusto at home, but fell silent when outside.

The Vienna spring of 1938 was unusually balmy. The lilac bloomed early, the chestnut trees preened with their gaudy pink blossoms, and the park benches sprouted new signs: NO JEWS PERMITTED TO SIT HERE.

In school, Rose and her Jewish classmates were moved to the back of the room, six of them occupying the last row, separated from the Christian students by two empty rows. They were a world apart now, the Jewish students. Rose hated sitting in the back. She hated class. And to make matters worse, Gerhard didn't have to go to school anymore. The new restrictions said that Jewish children the age of fifteen or older didn't have to attend. It was so unfair, Rose thought, why couldn't she stay home like her brother?

By June, Bette was no longer allowed to work for them. Wolfe's importing business—which Rose's grandfather had started when he was a young man living in Constantinople decades earlier—had been repatriated. Papi disappeared for hours at a time into his study, barricading himself behind the tall thin pages of the *Neue Freie Presse*. But more distressingly to Rose, nearly as significant as Bette's departure, was this: Rose wasn't allowed to go to the movie house anymore.

"I can't go to *any* movie?" she asked. For a moment, she could imagine a dividing line: *Snow White*, yes; anything with Deanna Durbin, no.

"It's part of the restrictions," Papi said. "Those are the rules."

They were sitting at the dark oak dining table after dinner, drinking coffee and eating tiny delicious choux pastries with cream filling that Tante Greta had brought over. Mutti kept the bell to the right of her, as if a new unnamed maid might miraculously appear if she rang.

They had been talking about visas. They were always talking about visas, Rose thought, tired. They weren't going anywhere. Tante Greta had come for a visit while Onkel George went to the American embassy. Everyone said there were no American visas available until 1950, but still, they went to put their names on the list.

"Can Ilse still go to the movies?" Rose asked.

"Of course. She's not Jewish," Gerhard said, waving a spoon at his younger sister. "Idiot."

Rose waited for her father to admonish her brother, but Wolfe only lifted his eyes skyward. Rose followed his gaze up to the plaster ceiling.

"She's a child," Charlotte said to her husband, plainly enough for everyone to hear. "You think they would bother a child?"

His dark eyes became slits. "Do you really want to find out?" he snapped.

Mutti shook her head, gaze averted. Rose shot a look to her brother, but Gerhard bent over his plate and ate uncharacteristically fast.

Papi looked at all of them, into that great bowl of silence. When he spoke again, his voice had dropped. "My apologies," he said. His strangled voice was far worse than his yelling. He pushed his chair back, hurried out of the room.

For a moment, there was only the sound of scraping: Gerhard's spoon against china, as he took great care to chase down every last morsel of whipped cream. Then Tante Greta spoke: "And, Charlotte, Rose should get rid of her movie-stub collection too; it's unhygienic to have all those old tickets lying around."

Rose stared at her plate, blistered by her fury. She hated every single member of her family, but her Tante Greta most of all; she truly did.

A WEEK LATER, ROSE, MUTTI, and Gerhard decamped from Vienna to spend the summer months with Charlotte's parents in the country in Parndoff, and for a while everything seemed normal, good even. Every morning Rose helped her grandfather tug his apartment window open and lower a string down to the street. Within a few minutes a boy would yell out, "Ready!" and Rose's grandfather, with her assistance, would haul the string back up, the day's newspaper attached.

Rose spent countless afternoons swimming in the Danube with Gerhard, who liked to ignore her but never said no when she tagged along. Rose would lie on the marshy banks, pushing her toes into the warm squishy mud, the sunlight against her bare arms a reminder that no, she hadn't fallen asleep. She wondered if Heinrich had gone back to the holiday camp. She listened to the drone of insects, she tried to ascertain the shapes of the gunmetal clouds scuttling above. She decided that the country was better than the city after all.

One afternoon she and Mutti went to the grocery store. As they were about to walk inside, Charlotte recognized a stout, redheaded woman fishing a triangle of cheese out of the wooden barrel out front. "Gertrude?" she said, "Gertrude Bieler?"

The woman looked up.

"It's Charlotte Zimmer. How nice to see you!"

With seeming ease, the fat woman spit at Mutti—a great hurl of saliva. Rose saw it darken a spot on her mother's lovely cotton blouse.

"What do you people want?" Frau Bieler hissed. "Why are you still here?"

Charlotte stood, a smile cemented on her face. She smiled and she didn't say a word.

"*Juden.*" Frau Bieler spit again, this time at her feet.

It was Rose who tugged at her mother's hand, Rose who sprang back to life first. "Mutti, Mutti," she said, the words tumbling out of her.

FALL, BACK IN VIENNA. THE days growing shorter, the sky paper white. Rose attended an all-Jewish school deep in the nineteenth district. It took more than an hour to get there by tram. There was discussion of keeping her at home. But for the time being, she continued to go. Everything, it seemed, now fell under the category of "for the time being."

Each day, a different embassy. This was how her parents spent their days, waiting at consulates for hours at a time—Canada, Argentina, Paraguay, Uruguay, Ireland, Cuba, China, it didn't matter where—lines snaking around corners, switchbacking up the sidewalk. A new dialect sprang up at home: Words like *affidavits, baptismal certificates, exit* and *entry visas* dominated the conversation. It was all the adults talked about: Try the Bolivian embassy in the late afternoon; avoid the man with the leathery face.

Wasn't there anything else they could discuss? Rose didn't want to hear their strained voices, the urgency with which they spoke. She missed Bette.

And Gerhard wasn't around to distract her. Her brother would disappear for hours at a time, sometimes saying he was going to meet Oskar, other times just slipping out without warning. They all knew he was going to see Ilse. "At least he doesn't look Jewish," Rose overheard her mother say to her father. It was true; Gerhard was rangy and blond, and at sixteen he had a good couple of inches on their father, hitting six feet. Rose knew that Gerhard's looks brought her parents no small amount of comfort as they thought about him on the streets alone. She tried not to think about her own dark complexion.

In early November, a Jew murdered a Nazi in Paris. School was let out early, and Rose was told to hurry home, avoid the main thoroughfares and the trams. In the flat, they gathered around the wireless, glued to the broadcasts. Her parents wouldn't let her go outside for days.

There were so many stories swirling: her mother's old piano teacher, Herr Schulman, had been arrested and was being held in Dachau. The Begeleisens had had their apartment repatriated—soldiers had come in the graying hours of dawn—and had been forced to move into a flat with three other families. Rose hadn't liked Peter Begeleisen; he had told her that witches like to yank teeth out of the mouths of little girls in the middle of the night, but still she felt bad for them. The Volkmans had managed to get out last week, their visas came through for Ireland. The husband had been able to land work as a machinist for a clothing factory outside of Belfast.

Their friends the Klaars had taken out a small classified advertisement in the *Jewish Chronicle,* seeking work in London, and Rose's parents decided to follow suit. They fought over the language in the ad. They fought a lot those days.

Wolfe wrote: "Would noble-minded people assist Viennese couple, capable of every kind of housework, knowledge of English, French, and Italian? Exemplary references upon request."

"No one cares what languages we speak," Charlotte said to Wolfe. He was sitting in the velvet wingback chair near the window, trying to balance the writing tablet on his knee in the watery light of the late afternoon. He now avoided his study.

"What do you suggest?"

Charlotte took the writing paper out of his hands. Wolfe played with the loose ivory threads from the Persian throw covering the velvet head cushion. His wide face looked slack, jowly.

She wrote: "Married couple, cook and footman, Jews, seek position in household."

"Everyone knows we're Jews," he said bitterly. "Why else would we be looking for work?"

"Then we shouldn't hide from it, should we?" Her mother said the words with such sharpness that Rose half expected blood to bloom.

ONE DAY IN JANUARY, ROSE came upon her mother in the kitchen. Charlotte wore Bette's old apron, which was too long on her. A jumble of pans and bowls and piles of snowy flour crowded the table. "What are you doing?" Rose asked.

"What does it look like? I'm baking." Charlotte pushed a strand of loose hair out of her glistening face with the back of her hand. "A poppy-seed cake."

"You bake?" Rose wouldn't have been more surprised if her mother had donned a pair of ice skates and broken out in song.

"Of course I bake," Charlotte said. "I do lots of things that you don't know about."

The next morning, Mutti dressed in her best suit, a houndstooth pencil skirt and flared jacket that Rose loved, with a creamy blouse with a scalloped neck. She looked like Greta Garbo. She muttered something about visiting Tante and rushed out the door, the poppy-seed cake held carefully in both hands. Rose watched her hurry down the street; the bare crooked fingers of the chestnut trees sliced the putty sky.

A week later, Rose found out where she had really been. The Kultusgemeinde, the city's Jewish community organization. Onkel George had a cousin who had a fiancée named Edith who worked for it. And because of this connection, Mutti said brightly, stooping to meet her daughter eye to eye, you're going to England!

They were in the drawing room, her father in his wingback chair, not saying a word.

"What?" Rose asked, blankly.

"You are going to England, where the queen lives with her two little princesses," Charlotte told her. "Remember Mutti showed you the pictures of the little girls in their beautiful dresses who live in castles?"

Rose stared. Her mother was speaking as if she were a baby, a girl of six years old, and not eleven. She wasn't making sense. England? How could she go to England?

But what she said was this: "Are you coming?"

Her mother shook her head, soundlessly.

"I'm going alone?"

"No, no, not alone," Mutti said quickly. "Of course not! Gerhard is going too. Along with hundreds of other children. It will be a great adventure." She straightened the hem of Rose's middy blouse, flattening down the sailor collar.

"Where am I going to live?"

Mutti's eyes were glassy bright, her cheeks aflame. "You," she said, "are going to live with an English family. A *lovely* generous English family," she emphasized.

"Who are they?" Rose asked, her insides slickened with a hideous sickly sensation. She hadn't known this was possible, but now she realized that it was everything she feared.

"They are good people," Mutti finally said. "They are *very* good people. I know this, because they've agreed to take care of you."

"No," Rose said. "I won't go."

Her mother must have answered, Rose knew she did, but the roar of her fear descended and tore through her, like a train bulleting ahead. Mutti had done her best to comfort her, but try as she might, Rose could never recall what she had said.

3

NEW YORK AND LOS ANGELES, 2006

HER DAYS WERE STULTIFYING AND long. The nights were longer. After she went home to New York, Lizzie took a week off from the new firm (she still thought of it that way, even though she had been there close to a year). Her senior partner didn't encourage her, but he didn't argue either. Those first days were a disaster. She picked fights—with the sweet Croatian owner of her dry cleaners when her cardigan wasn't ready, with a taxi driver for deciding to take Broadway downtown in the midafternoon. Small kindnesses could be her undoing. Her college boyfriend sent her a short e-mail saying how sorry he was, and there she was, weeping over her laptop. One evening after she came back from the bodega with beer, the nighttime doorman said, "Nice guy, your dad. I remember him helping you move in." And it was true, she remembered with a faint smile, Joseph had been there—directing the movers, saying to her, "You could have lived in a place with an elevator; why didn't you like that apartment on Ninety-Sixth Street?" The doorman said: "I'm sorry. My mom died five years ago and I still don't believe it."

She thanked him tearfully, hurried up the stairs. She didn't believe it either. Nothing made sense to her. Not lying on the couch watching reruns of *Freaks & Geeks*, not meeting a law school friend for lunch, not talking to Sarah or Claudia on the phone or pounding on the treadmill or downing cup after cup of coffee. The feel of the raw winter air against her face—that was the only thing that felt close to right.

One night, she was on her couch wearing a thin V-neck of her father's, leggings, and a pair of his wool socks, eating pad thai from Saigon Grill and watching *Double Indemnity*. She loved the movie, had seen it numerous times: she loved Barbara Stanwyck, who managed to be both steamy and coolly intelligent, and she loved poor hapless Fred MacMurray, who was no match for Stanwyck. Lizzie appreciated the ratatat dialogue and seeing Los Angeles as a city of noir, where nothing was as it seemed. But tonight, watching MacMurray race through the downtown L.A. streets, drive up to Stanwyck's house high in the Hollywood Hills, not the same hill where she'd grown up but not unlike it either, those spindly palm trees looking even more surreal and strange in black and white—she felt unnerved, seeing the city she knew so well, a city that wouldn't be the same for her ever again. Los Angeles was achingly far away.

Had her father ever seen the film? She switched the TV off. She called Sarah, but it went to voice mail, and she hung up before leaving a message.

Lizzie grabbed her coat, hat, and scarf from the hook, stuffed her keys, phone, and some bills into her pockets. Outside it was cold. The streetlamps threw out pools of anemic yellowish light. The moon was nowhere to be found. She began walking down Broadway, her gloveless hands clenched in her coat pockets, head down. She made her way past a pair of teenage girls wearing long thick sweaters, maneuvered around a stoic dog walker who held the leashes to four yelping, straining creatures. She passed newsstands and the little French bistro where her father and Sarah had taken her to celebrate the end of her first year of law school and the Starbucks that had been a Love's Pharmacy that had been—she had seen pictures—a butcher's shop.

And the pet supply shop that had been a video store where Claudia flirted with the teenage clerk, and she and Ben fought about which movies to rent.

She didn't know where she was going until she saw it. There was little inviting about the boxy Cuban diner, its fluorescent lights, but Lizzie went inside.

The waitress ushered her to a booth toward the back, but Lizzie shook her head. "Can I sit here?" She motioned toward a table by the door.

The waitress shrugged. "You'll feel the wind every time the door opens."

"That's fine," Lizzie said resolutely, and she slid in.

She had last sat at this table with her father. It had only been a few months ago, a quick weekend trip in October for the wedding of someone Lizzie barely knew, the son of a medical school classmate of Joseph's. The skeletal trees along Broadway she stared at now had been full and resplendent. He had ordered the bistec, a charred sirloin loaded with garlic and onions, and ate it with gusto, grousing about going to a wedding solo and asking her about dating. ("Are you using OkCupid? I love it; I've met lots of—" "Dad, please. Can we talk about something else?" "But OkCupid was started by Harvard students!") Now she ordered bistec, her second dinner of the night. When it arrived she ate and she ate. She scraped her plate clean, thinking of her father all the while. She never felt full.

As she was paying, feeling wobbly from all that food, she remembered her father telling her about a cousin of her grandfather's who had gotten off the boat from Poland, thinking he was in New York and only later realizing it was Havana. Joseph had called her after Castro had transferred power to his brother. "We should make plans to go to Cuba; it won't be long before Fidel is gone." She heard the tenor of his voice—it sounded so clear and distinct in her head—and something inside her cracked open. She attempted to zip up her jacket with trembling hands.

"You okay?" the cashier asked.

"I'm fine," Lizzie insisted as she pushed open the door. The brutal cold was a comfort as it hit her hot face, stung her lips, her skin.

The next morning she was up at sunrise, and for the first time in a week her mind felt sharp. She was at her office by seven thirty. An hour later, Marc, her senior partner, strode in.

"What are you doing here?" Marc said. "You look—" He paused. "You do not look good. Go home."

"Please," she said. "I need to be here. Please."

By the following week, she hit upon a viable angle for the Clarke appeal. Marc thought it was a solid approach, and even Clarke, who wanted to know every last detail in his weekly calls from prison in Otisville, chortled and said, "This might actually work." Lizzie should have been happy. But it felt beside the point.

Then Ben called, nearly three weeks after Joseph died. "I'm so sorry. I just heard," he said. It was so good to hear his voice, so specifically good, that Lizzie started talking—she told him about the blind curve on Mulholland and the SUV that Joseph never saw coming. ("It wasn't his fault," Lizzie said, "it wasn't anyone's fault.") She told him about the funeral and how she feared she didn't do her father justice with her eulogy, and then, she said, there was the woman who came to the burial in flip-flops. "Who goes to a cemetery in flip-flops?" she said.

He cleared his throat, didn't answer.

"You know, that was a rhetorical question," she said, feeling self-conscious, and tried to laugh.

"I'm just so sorry," he said. "I wish had known—"

"I should have called and told you."

"No, no, it's okay. I just—" He paused. "I liked him a lot. Your dad. He was a good guy."

"He liked you too," Lizzie said, and it was true. Joseph had been so disappointed when they broke up. She fought to keep her tears at bay.

She and Ben had met in law school, and moved in together after graduation; both landed jobs as associates at big, white-shoe law firms. It was as exhausting and all-encompassing as everyone had warned her it would be—there was nothing in her life but work—but she kept her head down; she was good at working. And she was pulling in so much money—she had gone from making zero to $175,000 a year. (She stared at that first paycheck, the march of digits incomprehensible.) Over her second year at the firm, though, something shifted. Her exhaustion metastasized into something darker, an anxiety that became her most voluble companion. Her senior partner now yelled at a new associate, and even this Lizzie took as a sign of failure. "Maybe you'd be happier at a smaller firm," Ben said. She made a face. What? Like she couldn't handle the work?

Their sex life sputtered out. They fought about the most superficial things. The way he would sometimes empty only the bottom half of the dishwasher made her want to scream. But they got engaged. She neared thirty-four. (As her grandmother loved to remind Lizzie, "When your mother was your age, she already had two children." Lizzie considered it a triumph that she didn't respond: "Yes, but she was also on the cusp of divorcing.") Then one sticky August night when Ben was out of town for a friend's bachelor party, she exited a bar through the back door and made out with a cocky summer associate in an alley off Baxter Street redolent of warm asphalt and garlic. She left his third-floor walk-up before dawn, feeling as if she had to vomit. Who had she become?

After Ben moved out, she walked around their apartment in a fog, feeling stunned and ashamed and small. How did she let this happen? She wasn't a dramatic person. She wasn't messy. Until she was.

Now Ben was talking about the time her dad insisted on taking him to the L.A. Auto Show, despite Ben's lack of interest in cars, and the spectacular dinner he took him to afterward in a tiny, eight-seat sushi bar that lacked a name on the thirty-seventh floor of a downtown office building. There Joseph held forth on the artistry of Vin Scully and his profound disappointment that Ben did not know him.

"How can you not know who he is? How is that possible?" Ben bellowed, imitating Joseph. *"He is not 'just a baseball announcer.' He is a master storyteller. He is a master of life."*

The lights in her apartment were low. "Where was I during this dinner?" she asked. What she meant was: *Please keep talking.* Ben knew her father. No one would ever know him like Ben did.

"Oh, I don't know; gossiping with your sister, scowling at me."

A heaviness descended upon Lizzie. "I didn't scowl at you all the time, did I?" she asked softly.

"No, you didn't. I'm sorry I said that," he said, but he hesitated—Lizzie was certain—God, she had been awful to him.

"I'm really sorry," she said. "About everything."

"Listen, I did some scowling too. Stealthily, but I did."

"I fucked everything up, didn't I?"

"Oh, Lizzie."

She should stop. She didn't trust what she was feeling. But the more intensely she felt, the more convinced she became. She had messed up one of the only good things in her life. "I miss you," she finally said, alone on the couch that she and Ben used to share. "I probably shouldn't say that, but I do."

He didn't answer, and his lack of a response fed her conviction. "Come over," she whispered.

"Lizzie," he said, a plea airlifted with regret.

"I'm sorry," she said, speaking toward the ceiling. "I'm sorry for so much."

"It's okay. I'm sorry too."

"You have nothing to be sorry for."

"Not true." He let out an odd warble of a laugh.

"Let's both not be sorry," she heard herself say with sudden conviction.

"Okay," he whispered.

She closed her eyes. "Come over."

He didn't answer. She was too agitated to fill the silence.

"Okay, then," he finally said.

His hair was thicker than she had remembered and he was wearing that orange T-shirt that she loved, and the combination of new and old, rawness and comfort, felt so inevitable and right. When he fumbled with a condom, she said, "No, just let it be," because she could easily imagine it happening; she *wanted* it to happen. But he flashed her a hard, desperate look. "No," he said, and he tugged it on.

Afterward, they lay together, still. He was brushing her hair back from her face with a tenderness that made her ache when he said, "You know, I have to tell you something."

"What do you have to tell me?" she said teasingly, thinking, *He's a good man, a kind man.*

He shook his head. His gaze was fixed beyond her: on what? Did it bring him comfort to see that the window blind was still broken? Did he look at her clothes strewn on the wingback chair and think with satisfaction that she wasn't as neat as she liked to claim? Or was he thinking of the times he had pulled her into his lap on that chair? They had been happy then, hadn't they?

"I'm seeing someone. But you knew that, right?"

She closed her eyes. Even the air felt heavy, a trap.

"I should have said," Ben continued, "but, I—well, I didn't. But you had heard that, hadn't you? You knew."

"Yes," she said. "Of course. I know." And now she did.

ON ONE OF THE MANY nights that Lizzie couldn't sleep, as the delivery trucks rumbled down Broadway and the sky lightened to the streaky, cement-colored dawn, she watched bundled-up figures hurrying down the street, and she thought about Rose Downes.

Lizzie could remember asking her father all kinds of things about *The Bellhop* when she was a kid: *Was he famous? Was the man who painted him famous? Who picked out the frame? (You're a funny kid,* she could remember Joseph saying; *what kind of kid wonders about frames?*) But she couldn't remember asking him why he'd bought it.

Why hadn't she asked him? And she couldn't recall ever thinking about the other people who might have owned it before.

She decided to write Rose a note. She found a card she had bought at the Frick aeons ago, featuring an Italian Renaissance portrait of a young man against a sumptuous green background. It was easy enough to locate Rose's street address online. She wrote: "It's not our Bellhop but I've always liked him. I hope you do too. It was lovely to meet you. I'll be in L.A. in three weeks; coffee then?" She signed it with her name, her e-mail address, and all three numbers—cell, work, and home.

THREE WEEKS LATER, ON A Thursday, she took the last flight out of JFK to LAX, and she spent much of it working, reviewing a stack of cases she'd printed out from Westlaw and Lexis. She arrived after one A.M., flying in a cab over wide stretches of freeway to arrive at Sarah's house long after she and Angela had turned in for the night. Lizzie's body was jangly, buzzing with restlessness, in full-throttle protest. The next thing she knew, Sarah was standing over her, already dressed. "It's almost ten," she said. "We need to go."

Lizzie's left cheek felt as if someone had jabbed it with a stapler. She had fallen asleep on her laptop. "Okay," she said, rubbing her cheek, running her fingers through her knotty hair. "Just give me a few minutes and I'll be ready."

Sarah assessed her. "You look exhausted. You sure you're okay?"

"I'm fine!" Lizzie said loudly, which did nothing so much as prove Sarah's point.

MAX RAN HIS OWN SMALL law office from a Spanish stucco overlooking the thin ribbon of park on Ocean Avenue. For years, their father's friend had focused on criminal defense, but his current practice mostly consisted of longtime clients, many for whom he now settled business disputes, the occasional DUI, and even rarer, estate planning. Inside his office, Lizzie downed her second cup of coffee and picked at a cranberry muffin as Max went over the steps in painfully simple detail—filing the will with probate court, making an inventory of the estate's assets, paying off the estate's debts and taxes—yes, yes, she knew all this.

"Everything okay?" Max asked, as if sensing her impatience.

Lizzie felt chagrined. "Yes," she said, "of course."

"You know, your father chose me to be the executor because the laws in California differ significantly from those in New York, and more important: he knew it would be burdensome. He didn't want you—either of you—to have to deal with this."

"I'm so glad," Sarah said.

"Me too," Lizzie said, a lie. She didn't know why she cared about being executor. She didn't want to deal with Joseph's estate. It was likely a mess. And she wasn't expecting much. Joseph mocked cushions, 401(k)s, Roth IRAs, most fiscal plans that smacked of—well—planning. He had made a small fortune with his surgical eye practice, but the Joseph she knew was a spender through and through; he lived off the money's exhaust.

Still: when Max spoke about the second mortgage on the house (taken out, Lizzie realized as he went over the details, when she was in law school), she felt a flicker of unease. Then Max mentioned a real estate deal Joseph had made years earlier, a shopping mall in the Central Valley that had gone belly-up. The value had taken a nose dive when Joseph needed the cash the most, so he had to unload it with the mortgage underwater. It went into foreclosure. Max said there was little in terms of liquid assets.

How were his finances really that bad?

"There's still the house," Sarah was saying. "We can pay off what we need to with the profit from the sale."

"Yes," Max said as Lizzie looked at her sister anew. They would sell the house? Of course they would. Still, the thought of it gone made Lizzie feel hollowed out. She glanced out the window. A stone fountain dominated the courtyard, four muscular fish holding up a conch shell. Even the fishes' mouths looked parched.

She thought of all that money he had made through the years, so much earned and blown. Why hadn't he said anything? She could have helped. At least she should have pushed him harder to sock some away for himself (and yes, maybe a little for her and Sarah too). Lizzie had chosen to become a lawyer in part so that she could take care of herself. She did not suffer from want. Still, she sat in Max's office, feeling bereft, and thinking: *There wasn't anything?* She asked: "And the insurance money from the paintings?"

"That was quite a while ago," Max said, but his light-colored eyes settled on her face. There was sympathy in his gaze, an odd intimacy. She flushed, looked away.

Max went on to say that Joseph had requested that his possessions be split evenly between the two girls, with a few exceptions: He wanted Max to have the Ortiz collage; Lizzie the Julius Shulman photograph (he remembered how much she loved it, and this thought brought her back to herself, gave her a shot of pleasure); Sarah the Sugimoto seascape; and the West African funeral masks to Rose Downes.

"Rose?" Lizzie echoed.

"Who?" Sarah asked.

"The older woman I told you about, from the memorial?" Lizzie turned to Max and said, "I don't understand. They weren't close. Why give her the masks?"

Max shrugged. "Perhaps because of *The Bellhop*. It was stolen under his watch, after all."

"My watch, actually," Lizzie muttered. And after that, she didn't ask any questions.

IN FEBRUARY, THEY PUT THE house on the market. In less than a week, during a snowstorm that pummeled New York, they got an offer. The buyer was a Paramount exec around Lizzie's age—ob-gyn wife, two young kids—with the sort of swaggering verve that Joseph would have admired and made Lizzie annoyed. ("I want this house, I love this house," their broker reported him as saying. "I'll pay ask, all cash. The offer's good for forty-eight hours. After that, it goes down twenty-five thousand each day.")

A month later, she was flying out again. She and Sarah had to do a final cleaning to empty out the house. It made Lizzie feel queasy to contemplate, but she tried to remain pragmatic. Max had recommended an estate sales firm and she and Sarah lined it up. "Trust me, everything has value," Miller Perkins, the head of the firm, had said. "There's a buyer for it all."

At work, Lizzie learned that a similar case to Clarke's was being argued in front of the Third Circuit. Oral arguments were scheduled for the day after next. "You should go down to Philadelphia," Marc said. "Hop on the Acela and turn around the same day."

"I'm supposed to leave for L.A. tomorrow."

"Ah," he said, considering. Then he brightened. "Well, Kathleen can go instead." Kathleen was a hard-charging associate three years behind Lizzie. She was supposed to report to Lizzie on cases, but Lizzie often found her talking to Marc instead.

"Kathleen can go to L.A.?" Lizzie offered sweetly.

"She probably would, if we told her to," Marc said. "She'll be fine in Philly. She can be your ears."

"I don't need extra ears. Let me figure it out. There might be some wiggle room."

When Sarah picked up, Lizzie plunged forward: "I'm really sorry, but I can't come out tomorrow."

"What? Why?"

"Work." Lizzie let out a big exhale. "My boss is insisting that I go hear a case being argued in Philadelphia." Sarah didn't respond, and Lizzie added: "An important case. I don't really have a choice."

"Well then," Sarah said coolly. "Fine."

"I'm sorry," Lizzie said. "But I have an idea." She tried to lift her voice enthusiastically. "We're so rushed; what about postponing and getting a storage space? Then we'd have time to go through everything when we can." She had been thinking of the time she and Ben had gone to his parents' storage space on the Upper East Side. Lizzie and Ben had visited it to collect his tent for a July weekend in the Catskills (camping, Ben's idea). But camping seemed steadfastly beside the point once she stepped into Manhattan Mini Storage. So clean, so quiet, such a blessed rush of air-conditioning. Forget about North-South Lake or wherever they were headed, Lizzie had said, they should spend the night here, watching movies in the unit among the bank boxes of tax returns, ski equipment, Ben's clarinet from junior high, a Pack 'n Play that his sister's baby had used: all of it safe, untouched, waiting, for the future, for life to begin again.

"That's ridiculous," Sarah said. "Perkins is already on board. He's started getting the word out—"

"I'll pay for it," Lizzie said. "I don't mind."

"What? No. It's not about the money. I don't want the stuff in storage. I want to get it over with. I want it finished."

"Okay, then, okay," Lizzie said, regretting that she had ever brought up the idea. But when she actually forced herself to picture emptying out the house, getting rid of all her father's things—the thought made her break into a sweat. How could anything to do with their father be finished?

LIZZIE WENT TO PHILLY, WHERE, during court breaks, she would call Sarah back, steel herself to answer her questions. (*Yes, let's sell the side tables. No, hold on to his medical textbooks.* "You know, I could answer much faster if you could text me," Lizzie said. "It takes me forever to text," Sarah said, "all that up and down with my thumbs. Why can't I just call?") From Philly, Lizzie flew Denver to L.A. By the time she made it to Sarah's house in Los Feliz, Sarah and Angela were long asleep. Her sister had left the kitchen light on and a note on the counter. "Welcome," it said. "There's pasta if you're hungry."

Lizzie was. For the first time in a great while, she was ravenous. She opened the fridge. Inside were yogurts and bright juices and fresh berries nestled in bowls; two kinds of water (seltzer and flat) and two kinds of milk (almond and regular), and yes, pasta too, some olive, tomatoey thing. Lizzie, cowed by the bounty, ate standing—delicious, even cold. She should have put it in a bowl and heated it up, eaten like the grown-up she was. But she couldn't be bothered.

Wine, on the other hand, she could use. She opened cabinets, searching. Sarah and Angela had renovated this Craftsman house high in the hills when they moved in about a year and a half ago. For months, it was all Sarah could talk about: her sister, a social worker at a halfway house for girls, who used to rail against skyrocketing recidivism rates and people's idiotic notions of mental illness and psychopharmacology, now all she could talk about was baseboards and backsplashes.

Lizzie had taken to grousing to Claudia about Sarah's endless renovation talk, pointing out that this was a house Sarah never could have afforded on her own social-worker salary. "Being with a doctor must be pretty nice," she had said.

"You could have a nicer place," Claudia said.

"What's wrong with my place?" Lizzie said. She loved her apartment, even though it was tiny, with the kitchen the size of a TV, as Ben used to say, and only one true closet. But it was rent-stabilized and had been her home since law school. Why should she spend more? "You have no idea how crazy real estate is in New York."

"Uh-huh," Claudia said. And then: "Maybe Sarah's house will be annoyingly *Architectural Digest*."

Her friend looked at *Architectural Digest*? Did she know anyone anymore? "No, it's going to be beautiful," Lizzie said with uncontained wistfulness.

And it was. As she opened the white cabinets that only looked expensive ("IKEA!" Sarah had crowed), Lizzie admired and felt envious of it all: the dark-stained floorboards, the brushed-nickel pulls on the drawers that opened so smoothly, even the poured-concrete countertop, which Lizzie had secretly thought (hoped?) might be sterile, but turned out chic.

Behind the slim bottles of oil (olive and walnut and almond too) she finally spotted wine. She pulled out a Malbec. After she filled a glass, she kept opening cabinets in her sister's indisputably lovely kitchen, no longer sure what she was looking for. On a shelf above the sink, she saw squat bottles of medication and vitamins. There was the lithium that Sarah had been taking for nearly twenty years—"I'm a goddamn poster child for it," she'd say, sounding like their father—there was red yeast rice and folic acid and a prescription bottle for Clomid. Made out in her sister's name.

Lizzie stared at the label for the Clomid as if it would transform itself. She knew what it was. Claudia had been taking it for months ("popping it like candy," she had said) since she married Ian last spring. What would Sarah be doing with it?

She turned back to the Malbec and downed two more glasses in quick succession. Sarah didn't want a baby; Lizzie was the one who was supposed to have a baby. She climbed into the bed in her sister's guest room, unnerved and exhausted, trying not to dwell on it, wishing she did not feel like crying.

THE SUNLIGHT IN THE KITCHEN hurt her eyes when Lizzie padded in, wearing a worn T-shirt of Ben's and sweats she'd cut off at the knees. Sarah was washing strawberries; Angela, pouring coffee into a travel mug. Angela was already dressed in heels and high-waist trousers. She looked taller, more imperious, than usual. Lizzie was suddenly aware of her ratty T-shirt. She wished she had put on a bra.

"You got in okay?" Angela asked. There was a touch of bristle to her voice, as if she suspected Lizzie were about to complain.

"Just fine, thanks," Lizzie said with caution. She turned to her sister. "Hello, you," she said, brushing her cheek with a kiss, trying to be casual about her studied glance. Did her face look rounder? Was she hiding anything beneath her loose, striped T?

"I see you made yourself right at home," Sarah said, nodding at the not-quite-finished bottle of wine, perched alone on the gleaming counter. Someone had cleaned around it, Lizzie realized, and decided to leave it there.

Lizzie blushed. "I'm sorry. I meant to clean up."

"It's fine," Sarah said, and her clipped tone only confirmed her annoyance. "Perkins called me yesterday and told me to leave the cookbooks behind. Apparently there's even a market for those old microwave ones."

"Thanks so much for taking care of it all, Sarah, seriously."

"I'm glad to have done it. You should have seen me; I turned merciless, really."

"Do not tell me that," Lizzie said, half laughing. "I don't want to know." And it was the truth, she didn't. She felt a sludge of panic. "The masks, for Rose Downes? They were put aside?"

"Yes, of course."

"You sure?"

"Yes, of course I'm sure; we put them downstairs," Sarah said, doing little to disguise her irritation. "Along with everything else that we're keeping."

Lizzie nodded, but she was having that familiar sinking feeling, without edges or borders, that she had lost something again. She had written Rose that postcard, and she had never heard back. "You know, maybe I'll just go up there and check things out. The sale doesn't start for another hour, right?"

"That," Sarah said, "is a terrible idea. Everything is fine. And Perkins said owners should stay away."

"I'll go in and out. I just need to make sure."

Sarah shook her head and pulled her hair back, tying it up in a knot in one clean sweep, such a familiar gesture, Lizzie felt her stomach contract. "Because no one else can do it right but you."

"That's not true," Lizzie said, but she could barely get the words out. Their mother used to do that with her hair, in the days before she got sick. Lynn would pick them up from school in her banged-up Dodge, the radio turned up too loud, and she would be lighting a cigarette in one moment and tying her hair up in the next, her skinny freckled arms in motion, yelling at the girls to sit down, sit down and stop arguing! Lizzie saw it so clearly: the sticky black vinyl interior, the brown-orangy shine of her mother's lipstick, Sarah's tiny perfect feet.

"It would be so much easier if you simply admitted how controlling you are," Sarah was saying. "If you just acknowledged it, it would be much easier to take."

Lizzie heard her sister, but her words echoed like faraway street noise, worlds away.

HER FATHER'S SHORT DRIVEWAY WAS thick with cars. A string of bright blue flags stamped with *Westside* snapped in the wind. Inside, the rugs were already gone, as were the Barcelona chairs and the leather couch and the mahogany side tables. The air carried a slight candied smell. There was space galore, great empty pockets, yet the house looked smaller, not her own.

Come back! her father used to call her to say in college. *Come back.* But once she left, she left; she never lived here for more than a few weeks again. Sophomore year, her boyfriend at the time, an econ major from Montreal with a penchant for pot, landed a summer job in the William Morris mailroom. "We should spend the summer in L.A. together," he'd said. "I can't believe you're from there and actually choose to live here." *It's too much,* she'd said, describing the artwork, the glass-and-steel house cantilevered over the canyon, Joseph's cars. "He has more than one?" he had said. She'd simply sighed.

Now a slight guy with thick sideburns in a Westside Estate Sales T-shirt approached her. "Can I help you find anything?"

"I'm looking for Miller Perkins," Lizzie said. "I'm Lizzie Goldstein. This was my house." And it was only then that she realized she was shaking.

"Oh," he said, his face more alert. "He's downstairs. I'll get him for you."

"Actually, I want to find something down there—"

"No, no, please." He touched her forearm, a light touch, but clear enough. "Let me." A braided velvet rope cordoned off the stairs. He ducked beneath it, disappeared down the stairs.

Lizzie waited. She had talked to Miller Perkins on the phone a week earlier, but she began to nurse an odd, dislocated feeling that he wouldn't appear. Maybe the estate sale was a ruse—she and Sarah wouldn't see a cent. She watched a squat woman inspect a trio of sea-green metal canisters: *Flour, Coffee,* and *Sugar,* each stamped in a skinny midcentury font. She remembered that her father had brought them home from a flea market in Pasadena years ago, and filled them with the flotsam from his desk. "The veneer of organization," he would say as he lobbed another uncapped pen into the flour can. "It's all that matters."

She had always liked those canisters. She should have claimed them. She could picture them on the shelf above the stove in her kitchen, or in her bathroom, maybe, one holding makeup, the other a jumble of hairbands.

Near her was a sturdy oak jewelry case, courtesy of Westside Estate Sales, inside of which was a cache of cuff links and a Hamilton watch that Joseph had worn for a time years earlier. Her father's Rolex was squirreled away in her nightstand back in New York. Wasn't it? A man with a bulbous nose tried on the Hamilton and she stifled an urge to grab that too.

The day remained cloudy, but a steely light streamed through the enormous windows. Lizzie watched a little girl squirm and dance.

A lithe woman in a sundress grabbed the girl's hand, hissing, "Not here, Zoe!"

The mother returned to shopping. The girl made her way to the windows. She gazed down into the mouth of the canyon, pressing her palms against the glass. Lizzie had done the same thing when she was younger. She remembered pressing hard, testing the strength of the glass, testing herself, when all the light and airiness flooding this house only seemed to add insult to the fact that such a world could exist when her mother had been taken from her. She had been terrible to her father then. And now he was gone too.

Lizzie returned to the kitchen canisters that the short woman had left behind. She picked up the sugar can and slipped it into her leather shoulder bag. Her bag was big, but not that big. The leather bulged with effort.

"Is that you, Ms. Goldstein? Miller Perkins, at your service." A short man in a flash of color headed up the steps, hand extended, an exuberant smile on his broad face. He wore a navy vest with big silver buttons, a lime-colored shirt, bejeweled rings on numerous fingers. "I am delighted to meet you, of course, but—" His voice was silky, Southern smooth. He wagged a playful finger. "*What* are you doing here? Didn't I tell you and your sister to stay far, far away?"

"Yes, I know, I'm sorry. But a pair of masks is supposed to go to a friend of my father's, and I wanted to make sure they weren't inadvertently sold."

"Oh, my dear, you're worried. Of course, you're concerned. But you know you shouldn't be." He steered her by the elbow, away from the others. He had a surprisingly strong grip. "The masks are downstairs, sequestered away, as we had agreed. I myself have been keeping a careful eye. I *can* handle things. You know, I've been doing this for more than twenty years."

"I'm sorry. I just wanted to check. It looks like it's going well."

"Oh, it is, it is! It reminds me of the Thomas sale, last year. Did I tell you about it? Frank Thomas, one of Disney's most renowned animators? Really, I was so honored to be a part of it. I was just telling Max—"

"Max?" Lizzie asked. "Max is here?"

"Yes, yes, he's downstairs. Didn't you know? He too wanted to keep an eye. We could have a tea party with the principals at this sale!" Miller gave a shot of sharp laughter. "I can take you downstairs, if you'd like. I prefer to wait until everything is over, but if you'd like to see what's sold, we can go over inventory. Perhaps something to drink? I have some sparkling water, my secret stash of Pellegrino."

"Oh no, that's not necessary," Lizzie said. The faster he spoke, the more tired she felt. Maybe she should go downstairs, lie down on the sleeper couch in her old room, close her eyes for a while. (Was the couch still there?) She watched a Perkins employee bang Joseph's exercise bike up the stairs. "I'm sorry for barging in like this."

"No, do not be silly! This is your house; these are *your* things. I take my stewardship very seriously." He patted her bag and lowered his voice. "And you know, you can always change your mind."

She blinked. "I'm sorry?"

He leaned in conspiratorially. "The canisters." He gave her bag a firm tap. "Would you like the whole set? They're yours, after all. I would hate for you to feel as if you were reduced to the role of petty thief."

"Oh." She felt her face redden. "This? It's just—"

"Please, there is *no* need to explain." Perkins flashed her a well-practiced grin. "I'm going to get back to it. I'll give you a call later, if you're not still here!"

"Okay," she said. She felt less embarrassed than deflated. She didn't want the sugar canister after all.

Perkins headed down the stairs and squeezed past the employee with the exercise bike. He took care not to come into contact with his employee or the customer trailing him, a rangy man in fraying jeans and orange flip-flops who had a tenuous grip on the bike's back wheel.

At the top of the stairs, the man let go of the wheel with a thump. Lizzie felt her heart thump with it.

She knew that man. She knew that head of rich dark curls. She knew that lanky body.

For a fleeting moment, she thought of not saying a word. But how could she not? "Duncan Black," she said, tapping him on the shoulder as if asking for directions.

He gave her a slow smile, then a look of dawning recognition spread across his face. "Lizzie Goldstein? Is that you?"

"Indeed," she said, and she couldn't help but laugh.

"What are you doing here?"

"This is my father's house," she said, oddly confused. Did he really not recognize it? "What are *you* doing here?"

"You know, I thought it might have been the same house, and then I thought, no, it couldn't have been. But I was driving up the hill, and I thought—swear to God, I thought, 'Lizzie Goldstein used to live in a house just like this.' Sometimes, I have the worst memory."

She smiled ruefully, and it was like being back in high school, where a decent memory was a liability, proof that you thought too much, had too much time on your hands. "You just came for the sale?" She gestured at the bike. "A burning need to exercise?"

He flushed slightly, bobbing a bit, he still had that loose fluid way with his limbs. "The bike's for my dad. He's wanted one for months now. I got a great dinette set at a Westside sale in Hollywood last month." He was still attractive, emphatically so, but he also looked worn; his face was sharper than in high school, a fine web of wrinkles fanned off his eyes. He looked as if he'd spent too much time on the beach over the last decade, and she tried to recall what she had heard about him through the years—playing for a band in Ashland? Working for a tech company in the Bay Area? No, no. "My wife thinks it was a terrible idea," he continued. "The table is a beautiful marble and she thinks the kids are going to scratch it up."

Of course. She felt a faint sting, but she smiled and said: "How old are your kids?"

"Five and three. Zoe and Marlon. Zoe's around here somewhere, with my wife." He swiveled around. "Jo," he called loudly. "Jo!"

A couple of heads turned in their direction—none Jo, from what Lizzie could see, and she said, "It's okay." He didn't seem at all self-conscious that other people were looking at him. She remembered that from high school, the principal reason she was drawn to him. Duncan Black was more comfortable in his skin than anyone else she knew.

"No, no. Hold on, she's here, somewhere." He called her name again. The slim woman in a sundress with the blond girl Lizzie had seen earlier now emerged from the hall. "I thought you guys had abandoned me, alone on this mountain," Duncan said.

"No such luck," Jo said. She had a surprisingly deep voice and a delicate face, dark hair, pale skin. Her coloring was not unlike Lizzie's, but she was taller, more graceful.

"This is a friend from high school," said Duncan. "Lizzie Goldstein, this is my wife, Josephine Black."

They shook hands, Josephine smiling easily. The little girl tugged at her mother's dress. "Can't we go? I'm bored."

"Zoe," Duncan said sharply. "Please."

Lizzie stooped down, thinking of how Zoe had played against the windows in the living room. "It's nice to meet you. I knew your father a million years ago, when he wasn't so much older than you."

The girl stared. "So?" she said, then ran off.

"I'm sorry," Jo said. "Manners: we're working on those." She went after her.

"She can be a handful," Duncan said to Lizzie.

"It's okay."

"You don't have kids?"

"No, I don't," Lizzie said, and she blushed. Was it obvious? Was she that awkward with them?

She asked where he was living, he spoke about Culver City, its schools, how he had always wanted to try New York. "It's nice to see you, really," Duncan said. "Maybe we could have you over for dinner one of these days."

"That would be great. We'll figure out a time," Lizzie said. She made a gesticulation, first at her watch, then in the other direction, as if there were this thing, a great unnamable *thing,* that threatened to claim her if she did not leave.

Duncan cracked two of his knuckles, a dull pop. "I just wondered, about your father—Joseph, right?"

Lizzie shook her head, wanting to shake away the question that he couldn't seem to bring himself to ask. "He died," she said. "Two months, nearly three months ago." It felt strange to put a time frame on it. But in nine days, it would be three months. She knew, of course.

"Oh, Lizzie. I thought that might—" His lean handsome face darkened. "But I hoped—I don't know—I'm so sorry."

"Yeah, well," she said, and she felt the tears start up. "It's okay."

He bit his lip. "How?"

"Car accident."

"Jesus, Lizzie." He pulled her into a hug.

"Oh," she said, taken aback. Her head was against his chest, and the pungent smell of his sweat mixed with something sweeter. It had been nearly twenty years since she had last touched him. But his ropy arms felt familiar, her head resting against his chest.

They had first gotten together at the party she had thrown during her senior year of high school. Her father was out of town, a medical conference in Boston. She was supposed to be at Claudia's, and Sarah at a friend's, but Lizzie had taken advantage. This same living room had been dark and loud and roiling, with the sweat of bodies, the sweet smell of pot, the pulse of music, the clink of bottles being opened. Lizzie was floating among her many guests, feeling good, when Duncan finally appeared and, unbelievably, sought her out.

Lizzie was seventeen years old. She couldn't remember a time when she hadn't had a crush on him. Duncan maintained a deadly combination of nonchalance and assurance that should have been patented; he did more looking than talking; he had the pale, elusive gaze of the misunderstood, a fragile, Byronic look that surely translated to depth. (Didn't it?) The air, increasingly choked with smoke and sweat, tasted honeyed. He asked her if she wanted to go outside and her heart darted about like a quicksilvered fish. Out by her father's pool, he plucked a tiny brass pipe from his pocket and they got high, dipping their bare feet in the heated water, the air cool, the sky a band of black. They kissed for the first time, messy, sloppy kisses that left Lizzie breathless and hungry for more. When they finally went back in, Duncan had stood up and offered her a hand, a courtly gesture she never would have expected from him.

She had led him down the stairs and into her bedroom. Even now, twenty years later, she could recall her amazement. He was so beautiful. *Duncan Black,* she yearned to say over and over again. She had wanted him for so long. It didn't feel good. But she was prepared for so much worse. And it was this fact, coupled with the finality of it—her virginity, out the window, spirited away by Duncan Black—that allowed her to feel a certain elation, a pleasure that wasn't at all sexual.

But that elation hadn't lasted. Hours later, she awoke, and her world was never the same.

Now she was sniffling against Duncan's thin T-shirt. This boy who had been her first was now a man, a married man at that. He was rocking her gently. It felt nice. It felt more than nice. She tried to ignore it but she felt a rising heat. She wanted to taste the sweat on his neck. She wanted to taste all of him. Never mind that he had a wife; never mind that that wife and daughter were only feet away. She could unhook Miller Perkins's velvet rope and lead him downstairs. In the name of sympathy and mourning, she could.

After a moment, he pulled back. "Well," he said. "I really am sorry."

"Thank you." She nodded, tried to affect a smile. Had he sensed what she'd been thinking? Was he slightly tempted too?

They exchanged numbers. Lizzie was saying she really would like to see him again, she hoped his father loved the bike, when he asked: "Whatever happened to those paintings? The ones that were stolen the night of the party. It was a Picasso and a Modigliani, right?"

"Soutine," she said. She wished it surprised her that she had to correct him. She looked past him into her father's living room that was emptying of his possessions by the minute. "A Soutine portrait and a Picasso drawing."

"God, remember how the cops were all over everyone? I heard that Cori Carpenter started crying and confessed about the time she bought pot at a Tears for Fears concert. They never turned up, did they?"

Lizzie shook her head.

"Of all the things to steal. You can't fence famous artwork. The paintings are too recognizable. Anyone who knows what they're worth will know that they've been stolen. Well, you can only hope that the fucker who took them had the decency not to shred them."

She was too flustered to speak. Maybe *The Bellhop* was rolled up in an airport locker somewhere, a bank vault in Grenada, hanging on the walls of a garish villa in Dakar or Patagonia. But destroyed?

Duncan, his easy talk of the paintings, her father's empty house: it all felt wrong. For a brief moment, she imagined walking off, leaving Duncan without a word and climbing into her rental car, taking the turns of the hill that she knew so well.

But soon they were hugging again, awkwardly this time. (Why? As if bodily contact, twice in nearly twenty years, might prove to be their downfall?) Soon she was watching him hoist the bike onto his shoulder, press his way out the door.

And then the living room flooded with brightness. Lizzie shielded her eyes. For a second, she didn't know what happened, so quick was the shift—but squinting, she saw that it was just the sun, fisted clouds finally loosening their grip, bathing the room in abundant California light.

She felt a pressure on her arm. A voice, Max's voice, quiet. She hadn't seen him approach, had forgotten he was there. "Let's go. I'm taking you to lunch."

THEY TOOK HIS CAR. DOWN to Santa Monica, to a little Spanish café on Ocean Avenue a few blocks from his office. They didn't talk much. She was glad to have him drive.

The hostess seated them outside on the terrace. The afternoon remained gorgeous, cool but not cold, the sky scrubbed free of clouds. As they looked over the menu, Max told her that a friend of a friend owned the café. He was full of suggestions: sangria, Manchego, the grilled calamari and mushrooms too. Soon he was pouring sangria; he was passing her tiny ceramic plates piled high.

Lizzie ate olive after olive as Max told her about the restaurant's owner. He had been a bond trader, working fifteen-hour days, traveling half the month to meetings in Santiago and Dublin, rarely seeing his family. Then his youngest got sick with Hodgkin's, and the man swore if his kid got better, he would change everything.

"So, the boy got better and the father opted out of the rat race." Lizzie rolled an olive pit between her finger and thumb.

Max gave her a small smile. "His son went into remission, Marco opened the restaurant, and now he works as much as before—making one-tenth of the money."

"That's terrible," she said, laughing, "and completely unsurprising."

"Some habits are pretty deep-seated," he agreed. "At least for Marco."

"I don't know; it's not just him. I mean, who really changes?"

"You believe that?" His tone was easy enough, but his eyes settled on hers.

"Yes," she said, and she found she was serious too. "I do." She was the same as when she had been a kid. The reliable child who stuck

Stouffer's lasagnas in the microwave for herself and Sarah for dinner, who kept track of her sister's orthodontist appointments, who made sure that someone stopped at Vicente for milk in the morning. She was the same girl who followed the rules, who liked having rules, the type of kid who got high and got the munchies for *salad,* of all things. She had a hard time forgiving herself, then and now. ("So you fucked up," Claudia would say with a shrug. "Who hasn't?") Being here in L.A., her father's death, hurtled her back to being seventeen and the one mistake she felt like she could never undo. For years as she ticked off each accomplishment—graduating from a fine college, getting into a top law school, landing an associate position in the appellate department of a reputable firm—she felt like she was trying to prove, to her father and to herself, that that one night didn't define her.

It tired her, this realization. And it made her feel, for reasons she wasn't quite sure she could articulate, lonely. She hung a shrimp by its tail, dragging it through a glistening pool of oil. "You obviously feel differently, though."

Max didn't answer for a moment. "Yes, I do," he finally said. "Partly it's my line of work, and partly it's a question of age. I believe you can make mistakes. Everyone makes mistakes—"

"Of course—"

"But sometimes making such a mistake—an irrevocable mistake, with true repercussions—is what makes you change. You see the way things might have been, and they're not like that, because you messed up. Undeniably. I've seen it with clients. Things that you thought might not be such a big deal, things that you thought you might be able to explain away, loom large. There's nothing you can do about them." He played with the lip of a squat unlit candle in the table's center. "And maybe it's regret like that that fuels change."

"Of course," Lizzie repeated. "But as long as you're not talking about mass murder . . ." It was a lame stab at lightness, and the second she said it, she regretted it. He had defended murderers. He knew about regret.

Or he could be referring to his divorce, the wreckage of his marriage. He had a stepdaughter, Lizzie remembered, a shy little girl she met years ago at Joseph's house, poolside. What was her name? She must be close to college age now, Lizzie thought.

She sipped her sangria. "Sometimes I think I regret too much," she said.

"What do you mean?"

"Well, in some parts of my life, I have a hard time letting go. I wish I could just make a decision and not look back, move on." It was strange to hear herself admit this, and so freely too. Had she ever spoken to Max for more than ten, fifteen minutes at a time?

"Who does?" Max looked at her with his eyes grayer than blue, the color of rushing water.

"Most of the world, apparently." She was thinking of Claudia and her sister when she said this, wishing she could be more like them.

"You don't really believe that, do you? If it's something truly important?"

"No," she said. "I suppose not." He was still watching her, and she hoped what he was seeing did not disappoint him.

She looked past Max, beyond the restaurant patio. Out on the sidewalk, a man in a dirty puffy parka rattled a shopping cart crammed with objects. She spotted a desk lamp, a sofa cushion. The air was growing cooler, the day shifting. Lizzie could see across the street a strip of park lined with prehistoric palms. Beyond it she could make out the rising lift of fog. The water and the sky seemed to commingle, bleeding together in the same implacable color of bone.

"You know, your father used to tell me what a good lawyer you were," Max said. "He was very proud of you."

"Thank you," she said a little too quickly; the mention of her father cracked something open in her. She liked to think Max was right. She could remember the evident pleasure etched across her father's face that warm May day when she graduated from law school.

They stood on the corner of Amsterdam and 116th, among a sea of graduates in shiny blue robes, and he kept grabbing her hand as they tried to catch a cab down to Jean-Georges. She thought of the time they went to the fish market on Wilshire last summer. When it was finally their turn, her father introduced her to the young fishmonger plunging his hand into a vat of raw shrimp. "Ed, this is my daughter, the lawyer from New York," Joseph told him, and Ed looked up and barely muttered hello to Lizzie, but there was no denying the pride in Joseph's voice.

Did her father know how much she adored him? He did, didn't he?

The terrace was nearly empty. An old couple was barely talking, and at a round table sat a trio of young women, lipsticked and bright-eyed. One kept repeating loudly—"So I said, 'just leave your pants on! Leave them on!'"—as her friends hooted and guffawed. How was it possible that all these people were here and her father gone?

"Tell me something else about my dad." Lizzie, her voice shaky, turned back to Max. "Tell me something I don't know." She picked at the Manchego.

"Let's see, a story about Joseph," Max said. "Well, you know how we met."

"My father started coming into your parents' gallery."

"Yes, I was working there during law school, helping my parents who were helping me. It was at the start of your father's collecting frenzy, and he was"—Max paused— "immeasurably proud of his recent endeavors."

"So he offered you some ridiculously low price on a Modigliani sketch," she guessed, "thinking he knew more than you did, and you refused."

"Not quite. He came in carrying a painting that he had found at an estate sale. A Utrillo. He had been very happy with his purchase." Max fell silent for a moment, and gave her a small smile. "And I had the distinct pleasure of telling him it was a forgery."

"Really?" How had she never heard this story before? "He must have hated that," she said, but it pleased her, the thought of this unlikely start to their friendship.

Max grinned. He cupped hands around the fat unlit candle. His fingers were long and slender and tapering. Even the few unruly black hairs that sprang up close to his knuckles seemed elegant. His mouth was generous, his lips full, and Lizzie realized, with the shock of tasting sugar when you expected salt, that she thought he was beautiful. "I can't believe he continued to talk to you," she said, returning to the here and now, trying to brush aside her thoughts.

"Well, it wasn't as if we became such good friends then and there. But he kept coming back into the gallery. I think he was glad somebody caught it before it became a significant embarrassment." His craggy face carried a frank, gentle expression. He dipped the heel of the bread in the speckled oily puddle that was all that remained of the olives. "He grew to trust me enough to buy work from us. We sold him the Soutine."

"*The Bellhop?*" The painting had come from New York; her parents had first seen it together. Lizzie knew this. "But he saw it in New York."

"He did," Max said, nodding. "It had been in a show at the Marlborough on loan from my parents' gallery. He purchased it from them, years later."

Lizzie remembered when her parents first saw the painting. She had been eight years old. Her parents separated six months later, and that evening was etched in her mind, one of the few memories she had of them married. Lizzie was supposed to be asleep when she heard her parents' heated voices rising up the stairs. "Why would I want to own a third-rate sketch from Manet when I can spend the same money and buy something I truly love?" Lynn had said.

"Because it's a fucking Manet! Because he's one of the masters of the art world!" Joseph exploded. "And he's dead, so he's not making any more masterpieces, which means the value is guaranteed to rise."

"Nothing is guaranteed. And it's art. It should be something you love. Like that Soutine."

"Why can't it be love *and* an investment?" A pause. "I'm on your side, you know."

Her mother didn't answer for a long time. Finally she said with a flatness that left Lizzie cold, "Who said anything about sides?"

That was the last Lizzie heard of Soutine until she arrived at her father's house. In those first few awful months in L.A., she would lie on the carpet stomach down and gaze at it. *The Bellhop* was also a stranger in California. It was only paint thrown on a canvas, but the portrait made her feel less alone.

For Rose Downes, there was no such comfort, Lizzie thought. She had lost everything—her home, her parents, her country. It had been weeks since Lizzie had written her. Maybe the address she had found was an old one. She resolved to look again.

Now Lizzie said to Max: "Do you know where your parents got the Soutine?"

"No. Their records were spotty. But I'm sure they had no idea it was stolen during the war. They would have been aghast, like your father was. In those days, people weren't as assiduous about checking the provenance as they are today."

For a moment, neither spoke. Then Max said: "You know your father was very good to my parents." Lizzie nodded, though she hadn't known.

"Especially my father," Max continued. "I can't imagine anyone having been better to my father. When he started getting sick—it was Alzheimer's, but it took us a long time to realize that—the gallery became a mess, but he wouldn't give it up. The more paranoid he got, the more his memory slipped, the more difficult he became. Joseph used to come by, chat with him, listen to the same stories over and over, convince friends of his to buy some pieces. He used to say that my father demented was more interesting than ninety-nine percent of the rest of the world. But really, he saved him. I know he saved me."

Lizzie was nodding hard. This was the father she knew. She kept nodding, as if that alone might stop her tears.

"Oh, I'm sorry—" Max said, as if just now realizing her distress.

"No, no, it's okay. I'm glad you're talking, please keep talking. It's good to hear these stories, you have no idea."

"I think I do," Max said, and he reached across the table and touched her hand. It was a light, evanescent touch. By the time she registered it, he'd lifted his fingers. But she felt jolted by it all the same.

Max cleared his throat. "You know I'm here for you, for you and your sister. If I can help in any way, about anything—please, tell me."

"I know. Thank you." She tried to bat away the tap of disappointment she felt when he said "*for you and your sister.*" What did she expect? He was her father's friend.

Then she felt her phone buzz. She dug it out, and saw a 310 number she didn't recognize. Her sister? Miller Perkins? "Hello?"

"Lizzie? Is this Lizzie Goldstein? It's Rose Downes."

"Rose!" Lizzie exclaimed. "I was just thinking of you."

"You were?" Rose's voice was wary.

"We were talking about the Soutine, Max and I," Lizzie said, then stopped. What could she say? How could she explain? "You got my letter," she settled on saying. "I'm glad you called."

"Yes, you sent it, and I received it. That's the way the postal system works. I'm sorry I didn't get in touch earlier. Are you still in town?"

"Yes, for a few more days."

"Can you meet for a walk tomorrow?"

"I would love that," she said. She felt Max watching her, and sitting outside in the cool dying light of a March afternoon, Rose in her ear, Lizzie was startled to feel a charge of expectation. There was so much she wanted to know.

4

LEEDS, 1940

ACTING THE PART WASN'T HARD. Rose had all the props: a cup of milky tea that Mary had brought sat untouched on the night table next to Mutti's silk scarf with the birds, numerous woolen blankets under which she lay mummified. "I'm not feeling well," she said from the depths of her bed, only her eyes and nose exposed to the damp air.

"You haven't been feeling well these past three Saturdays," Mrs. Cohen said. She attempted to strike a stern tone, but it came out beseeching. She stood in the doorway of Rose's room, her sharp frame encased in a scratchy brown tweed suit with deep ruby buttons catching what little light there was. "The stitching is fine enough," Rose's mother would say. But it would be the jeweled buttons she would linger over, in a hungry manner Rose told herself she remembered well. *The buttons are nothing,* she wanted to tell Mutti.

Rose bit her bottom lip and didn't answer Mrs. Cohen for several beats. She had been living in the Cohens' house in Leeds for nearly a year now. She didn't like to think about how much time had passed. Here she had turned twelve years old; she had seen the calendar, incredulously, catapult into a new decade altogether. But it had only taken her about a week with the Cohens to realize that silence was her most effective weapon. Finally she said in a thin watery voice, "It's my stomach." And in truth, it was. Her stomach was aflutter, leaping and pirouetting. *Hello!* her insides seemed to be saying. *When are we getting out of here?*

Mrs. Cohen nodded, adjusting the tan feather tucked into the ribbon circling her chocolate-colored velvet hat. (Brown, brown, brown, Rose thought, picturing her mother's blue linen dress, her purple silk wrapper. Why must everything be brown here?) Mrs. Cohen moved closer, looking down at Rose. "It couldn't hurt you to come." Her eyebrows were thinly plucked, sharp like the rest of her.

Rose didn't answer, her gaze falling on the teacup by her side. She detested the milky tea, but the cup was her favorite. The creamy porcelain was etched with a portrait of the young princess Margaret Rose, a garland of flowers framing her face. The handle was chipped, the princess's cheek marred by a smattering of cracks, but she held her neck high, her features fine. Rose felt a kinship with the princess, only a few years younger than herself, with whom she shared a name.

Mrs. Cohen leaned down and, clearing her throat, said: "We're going to the Rosenblatts' for lunch after *shul*. I'll make sure Mary brings you some broth." The cadence of her voice was uncharacteristically soft, her smell clean and lightly sweet. Rose felt a stab of anxiety. She wriggled down, burrowing farther under the sheets. "Thank you," she said. But her words were muffled, and Mrs. Cohen, with an aggrieved sigh and a click of her heels, murmured, "You're a funny one," and took leave of the room.

Within minutes Rose heard Mr. Cohen bellow, "My overcoat, Aida!" Mrs. Cohen's high voice cried, "Ah, Mary, Mr. Cohen's overcoat, please!" She heard the sounds of footsteps in the stone front hall, the creak of the front door opening and closing, and then, finally, mercifully, silence.

She had managed to avoid synagogue for weeks now. The place

gave her the creeps, with its dank smells, its gloomy light, and the Hebrew she didn't understand. From the women's balcony where they sat, Rose watched the men below, huddling under voluminous prayer shawls, bowing and bending like bugs unused to the light. The last time she'd gone, she sat silently next to Mrs. Cohen, who was sitting next to Mrs. Appelbaum, who was gossiping about someone's daughter. Mrs. Cohen tittered in response. The very air in the synagogue was so thick and foreign it seemed nearly unbreathable. Rose thought, longingly, about how her family never went to temple in Vienna. And Gerhard didn't have to go in England either. Once more Rose thought of the unfairness that her brother was lucky enough to live with a boisterous Christian family in Liverpool, while she had been forced to be in Leeds with the Cohens, a childless Orthodox couple who insisted that they wait three hours after beef stew for a slice of buttery cake, who ferreted out any leavened products with a feather before Passover, who swung a chicken over their heads during the Jewish new year, who were the most aggressively un-English family she knew.

THOUGH IT WAS INDISTINCT, ROSE thought she could make out the sounds of Mary's brush attacking the pots in the kitchen sink. Mary took her work seriously, as if she were the true owner of the house and the Cohens long-term tenants whose presence she humored, barely. She wasn't like Bette; she paid little attention to Rose, and when she did, she was dismissive: yet another decorative, questionably useful object that required dusting. But there was something about this lack of attention that made Rose like her all the more.

Rose heard Mary move into the parlor—there was the creak of the floorboards settling under her formidable weight, there were the pings as she ran her rag over the keys of the grand piano. Rose jumped out of bed, wriggling into her pants, pulling a second jumper over her first. She arranged the flat pillows in the center of the bed, pulled the sheet over them, and made a halfhearted attempt to plump them up.

It looked more like a lumpy raincoat than the shape of a girl, but Rose couldn't afford to waste time. Down the rambling Victorian hall, she passed the lavatory, and Mr. and Mrs. Cohen's bedroom, Mrs. Cohen's brown-hued sitting room. ("*England is done up in browns,*" she had written to Mutti when she first arrived, and was she ever proud of the observation. "It makes me appreciate the colors of your pretty scarf all the more. The birds on it keep me company.") At the far end, opposite the square window that looked over the garden that had seen better days, Rose pushed open a wooden door without a handle, slipped into the darkness of a tight corridor.

Two baby steps forward, one hand on the dirty brick wall guiding her, reading the mortar like braille. It was cooler in here, the air dank. The steps plunged down. Rose closed her eyes, taking a deep breath and coaxing herself to get moving, *faster, faster!* She knew the servants' staircase well. Mary had been the one to show it to her, saying, "*I go up the front stairs, and so do you.*" But three months ago, after the war began and the char had been dismissed and the cook and gardener too, Rose began to think of the stairs as her own. In this cloistered darkness, everything dropped away: England and Austria, the perplexed looks and sighs of Mrs. Cohen, the letters she received from her parents, and the clamoring silence that took the place of those letters since the war began. Here, as she sank into darkness, the pain in her chest that was her most constant companion—it gave her life contour, even as she tried to ignore it—eased a little. She could be anywhere and everywhere at the same time.

Rose made her way down, her hands scraping against the crumbling wall, skipping the creaky seventh step, knowing to step to the right on the thirteenth to avoid a loose board. At the foot of the stairs, the door leading to the cellar had been propped open, and Rose stooped down to remove the wad of newspaper that she had placed here the day before—she could be a planner, when she needed to be.

She was breathing heavily when she emerged from the cellar to the quiet street, the pavement shiny damp. The sun looked small and discarded, an orangy scrap low on the horizon. But Rose eagerly took it all in. She yanked at a low-lying branch on the giant horse chestnut tree on the corner, making the blossoms dance and shiver, a rain of petals on her skin. She passed the Harveys' house, their Austin Six on blocks in the front yard. A few houses down was the Convoys', whose wrought-iron gate had been largely dismantled, only the far two posts remaining, the rest of the metal given over for the war effort. There on the corner Rose spotted the T of Margaret's back, her shoulders slouching in her dark wool coat, her single fair braid running down her back like a beacon on this gray day.

Rose hurried to her, skipping. "Hallo!" she cried out, expelling the word like a breath.

"Hello." Margaret turned, far more subdued. Her small blue eyes scanned Rose's face. "You're dirty. Look at your hands!"

Rose tried to wipe her palms on her friend's jumper, but Margaret squealed and pulled back. "I'm early. It was easy." Rose did a little jig for Margaret, her arms flailing about, compelled to entertain. Around Margaret, her body had a mind of its own. Back at the Cohens', she would recall her dancing and cringe.

"You're hopeless," Margaret said, but she said it companionably, agreeably. "Come along." Rose was happy to fall in line as Margaret took the lead.

ABOUT A MONTH AFTER ROSE arrived, Mrs. Cohen took her to Woolworth's, or Woolies, as everyone in Leeds called it. Rose was spending most of her time hidden in the darkness of the servants' staircase or beneath the piano in the drawing room. The afternoon when Mrs. Cohen had invited over a pair of sisters around Rose's age, refugees from Germany who had arrived on a train a few months before Rose, did not go well. (The older sister wanted to talk only about hairstyles; the younger sister barely spoke, and all Rose could think about was the unfairness that they had been placed together, while she and Gerhard had been split up. "It's a big expense and responsibility to care for a child," Mutti wrote. "We are very fortunate that two families agreed to take you both in.")

Perhaps a trip to Woolies would prove a useful distraction, Rose heard Mrs. Cohen say one morning to Mr. Cohen as he was nearly out the door. Off to Woolies they went. Rose was examining a display of notebooks, trying to decide what to buy, when a young blond girl peered over from the inkwell section and said, nearly bored: "You want the lined one." As Rose soon would learn, Margaret was six months older, and having lived in Leeds all her life, she seemed to know it all.

They tried to see each other every weekend, Rose skipping synagogue when she could. Today they went to the cinema, and using the sixpence that Mr. Cohen gave to her on Sundays, Rose paid to see *Intermezzo* for the second time. Sitting on the back steps of the post office afterward, digging their hands into the grease-stained bag in which Margaret kept the sourballs and jelly babies that they bought weekly with their ration stamps, Rose found it difficult to care who might walk by and spot her.

"Leslie Howard is the perfect gentleman," Margaret proclaimed. "I'm going to marry someone like him."

"Me too." Rose could picture it. She too would marry an Englishman. He would be tall and fair, with light-colored eyes like Margaret and Gerhard, and even the slightest bit stoop-shouldered like Margaret's father, a doctor, his steps heavy with the gravity of his work.

Margaret said that she had read that in his next film Leslie Howard was going to play a pilot; what could be grander than that?

"Mmm." Rose was focused on breaking a sourball into two. She tried biting it, gnawing on its underside, but nothing was working. The tips of her fingers became sticky and discolored with sugary purple.

"He's very active in the war effort, you know."

Rose nodded. She did know, but she did not want to think about the war effort. Studiously she concentrated on the marbleized fissures in her sourball. The sourball looked so easy to crack, and yet, she was getting nowhere. "What movie is coming next—did you ask Mr. Early?"

Margaret shook her head. "My dad says that it's because of men like Leslie Howard that we're going to get rid of Hitler." She bit off a licorice end, chewing thoughtfully. "He'll be gone, the war will be over, and then you can go home again."

Rose nodded mutely, her throat tightening. *Home.* The very word filled her with such a gust of icy hollowness, one whoosh and her insides were emptied out. "Yes, of course," she finally said, trying to be the good English girl she told herself she was. When she thought about leaving, all she could remember were the reasons she wanted to stay: Margaret and the movies and Woolies and the scrapbook she was making of the royal family.

"Then my brothers will come home," Margaret said. "Can you imagine, the war over?"

"No," Rose said, putting the sticky-wet sourball back into the paper bag. In her mind's eye, she saw her beautiful Mutti, her slender neck bent over the piano keys, intent on practice. She remembered the heavy smell of Papi's leather case and the way he used to let her sit on his lap when she was little and stamp his correspondence. It had been hours since she had thought about her parents. What were they doing now? What would her mother think, if she could see Rose, ignoring the Cohens' rules, stealing off to go to the cinema, laughing with her friend?

Rose stood, unsteady on her feet. "I should get home," she said. All that sugar was unsettling her stomach. "I don't feel so well after all."

WHEN SHE RETURNED TO THE Cohens', she didn't bother climbing up through the cellar, but opened the front door slowly, resigned. There was Mary in the entry hall, her stout body down on her knees, furiously brightening the brass inlay of the umbrella stand. She looked up at Rose, her little blue eyes set deep in her pale moon face, a face that inspired equal amounts of fear and admiration. "Child."

"I went outside," Rose said.

Mary looked at her, but didn't respond. She rubbed the clawed foot of the umbrella stand, and then swatted at it for good measure.

"I shouldn't have."

Mary snorted. "Not my house, not my business."

Rose was feeling too miserable to answer. She felt another twinge in her stomach. Was this God's way of punishing her for skipping out on synagogue, lying to the Cohens? She wished it was Mary's business, she truly did.

"You've got a letter," Mary said. "I've laid it on your bed."

A letter? Rose's stomach flew up to her throat. She hadn't gotten a letter in months. What if it were bad news? After all this time, it could only be bad news. "Oh," she said.

"Go upstairs, read it. Get back into bed." Mary touched the tiny silver cross that nestled in the hollow of her neck. "Or Mrs. Cohen is liable to blame all your nonsense on me, just like everything else."

Rose nodded, swallowed. She pictured the letter upstairs, waiting for her, lying on her tan coverlet—whatever news it contained, it existed, it was not something conjured up by her imagination. She turned to Mary, as if to speak, but no words came out. She wheeled around and tore up the front staircase to the third floor, where she was told she belonged.

IN THE BEGINNING, SHE LIVED for letters. She would ask Mrs. Cohen, by the fire in the drawing room in the morning, from the safety of her perch beneath the piano in the afternoon—how long does it take for a letter to travel from Vienna to Leeds?—so persistently, so often, that Mrs. Cohen threw up her hands, exasperated. "Several days, as I've said many a time before. It takes what it takes, child. What more can I say?"

Rose got through those first dizzying weeks, when she felt as if she were sleepwalking round the clock, when her English was nearly nonexistent, when she was too numb to cry, by imagining what she would write home. From the fat committee ladies who greeted her and Gerhard when they came off the boat in Harwich to Mrs. Cohen, who said to her, "there, there," even when she hadn't been speaking, from the disgusting kippers—and why would anyone ever put milk in tea?—to Mr. Cohen, whose wire spectacles were small and eyes even smaller and whose favorite sweater was a scratchy red cardigan, *the exact red of Herr Soutine's bellhop's uniform,* Rose wrote about it all. She hoped Mutti would be pleased that she remembered the painter's name.

Those first letters she got back, plain pale envelopes filled with tissue-thin purple stationery—a burst of color in this world of browns, a vital heart—these letters written with her father's dark fountain pen in her mother's elegant hand, meant everything to her. "*Ah, my beautiful Rose,*" her mother wrote, "*Papi and I are so glad to hear that you are settling in so nicely. Have you seen any black cats in Leeds yet? Here at home, everyone asks after you and Gerhard. How we all envy your England adventure!*" She went on to tell her how Swibber the butcher had broken his arm and now cut meat in the most awkward manner, and how Oma had moved into the flat too, so they were all cozy and together for the winter. "*Mr. and Mrs. Cohen sound like fine people, and you must remember to show your gratitude and be obedient every day, as I know you will.*"

Rose wrote back immediately, told her mother about Margaret and school and the English poetry she was learning. She said Leeds was nothing compared to Vienna; she wrote that she slept with her mother's scarf every night and she couldn't stand the full skirts that were all the rage among the girls.

February brought a deluge of rain, a request from Mrs. Cohen to be called Auntie Aida that Rose pretended she didn't hear, a card from Bette saying she had married a boy from Munich, and a letter from Mutti telling Rose they had moved again. Now she and Papi, along with Oma and Tante Greta and Onkel George, were sharing quarters with the Fleishmans and the Weitzs from downstairs. "*Do you remember the Fleishmans? Their Walter was in Gerhard's form. Mrs. Fleishman is hard to forget. She is a big woman with snapping dark eyes. She used to be a dancer when she was young and is still very vain and particular about nearly everything: her corsets must be washed out twice before wearing; we should not ingest meat during a full moon (as if there were meat to be had) or drink water during our meals as it impedes digestion! Whenever I find her too draining, I remind myself that you and Gerhard would get a great laugh out of her.*"

In March, Rose won third place in the annual Tennyson recitation at school. In April, as if to celebrate the lengthening days, she began dreaming in English. The gaps between the letters she wrote home widened. She was so busy in school, she told herself, but she was also venturing forth. Sometimes she would ride the bus alone into town to Schofields on the Headrow. The department store was nowhere near as grand as the Gerngross back home, but she still loved exploring it. In the ladies' department, she would quietly take note of the inventory, thinking, *Mutti would admire that shimmery blouse with the bow. She would despise the checkered skirt.* One time, she wandered into the café and saw ladies in evening gowns and elbow-length gloves sashaying and weaving among the tables. "Bloody fashion show, gets in my way," a waitress whispered to Rose. Then she added: "But it can be quite grand, I will say." *Not as grand as some things I know,* Rose was tempted to say.

June brought a letter from her mother talking about quotas and gardens and admonishments. "*I walked by the walled garden behind the hospital the other day and spied in. It was bursting with color. I could see all the berries—goose, currant, even your favorite, straw.*

"*We haven't heard from you in three weeks, my sweet little mausi. Your father and I hope that means you're focusing on your SCHOOLWORK. Your last description of Mary made me laugh, and made me hungry for more. Is she really as menacing as you say?*"

And then, in September, war was declared, and the letters stopped arriving.

MARY WAS WRONG. IT WASN'T a letter but a postcard this time, dated "Sept. 5, '39," more than three months earlier. "*My dearest mausi,*" her mother began, "*please know your Papi and I are well. I fear that with the outbreak of the war we will not be able to write for some time and so I am routing this letter to Cousin Hedy in Holland with the hopes that she can get it to you. We hope to join you and Gerhard before long, but until then, we will be thinking of you constantly and always. You have done all you could. We are very proud of our brave girl.*"

Rose lay back on her bed. She clutched the card in her sweaty right palm, and balled up a fistful of Mutti's silky scarf in her left. Her head felt prickly, her eyes achy hot. Her mother was wrong. Rose hadn't done everything that she could. Gerhard had; her brother had bicycled to some of the larger estates in the county, presenting himself at the front door and asking if the household could use a hardworking married couple. Rose was terrified by the prospect, but she promised that she too would ask. Then she had an idea.

"Let's go to your house," she said to Margaret one Saturday after the cinema. "You have the latest *Peg's Paper,* don't you?"

Once there, Rose excused herself to go to the toilet. But instead, she took the stairs down to Margaret's father's study. She knocked, timidly at first, then harder.

"Yes?" The voice sounded exasperated, but Rose couldn't back out now. She opened the door to find Margaret's broad-shouldered father behind his desk. "Margaret is upstairs."

"I know," she said. She dug her fingernails into her palm. "You know my parents are still in Vienna." She flung the words out, her eyes trained on the ocean of papers in front of him. "They would do anything to be here, with us. But they need to be sponsored—"

"Rose," Dr. Bradford said, removing his thin glasses.

"There is so much they could do. My mother," Rose said, trying to imbue the words with confidence and ease, "is a fine cook. The cakes she makes! And my father is a whiz at numbers. His books are impeccable. Might you know of any positions that could be suitable for them?"

"It's an awful situation. Simply horrid."

"Or any positions, suitable or unsuitable. Any positions at all," she said. She feared she sounded desperate, but she *was* desperate. Dr. Bradford knew so many people. He must be able to help.

"It's more complicated than that. But there might be"—he paused—"a possibility. I will ask around."

"Really?" Could this be? She imagined telling Mutti: *I was terrified to talk with him, but then I did.* She felt a smile tugging to lift the corners of her mouth.

"I don't want to say any more, not yet. Don't get your hopes up," he cautioned. "But I will try. Now go on, I have to get back to work."

"Thank you, Dr. Bradford," she said, wild with happiness, and spirited up the stairs to Margaret.

That was the last Rose heard about it. She felt as if Dr. Bradford looked at her differently from then on—there were moments over the next few weeks when she was certain he was about to speak—but a month after she approached him, the war started, and the borders closed for good.

Although there wasn't a tinge of criticism in the words her mother had written, Rose had the most horrible feeling that her mother knew Rose hadn't done all that she could. She sensed that Rose had waited too long to ask Dr. Bradford about sponsorship; why hadn't she asked anyone else? Mutti knew that Rose was impertinent and lied to Mrs. Cohen; she deduced that Rose had secretly gone to church with Margaret last month; she sensed that on the day that war broke out and all the adults at the Cohens' were crowded around the wireless in the drawing room, Rose crouched in the corner away from the others, immobilized by fear, but still she wondered what would happen on her birthday, which was the following week. She was a terrible daughter.

Rose remembered some things from that cold awful night she left Vienna. Walking from the tram with her parents and Gerhard, Mutti in her navy wool coat with the rabbit-fur collar, her face flushed. She wasn't wearing gloves, and neither was Rose, and Mutti gripped Rose's hand in hers, her fingers sweaty despite the chill in the air. Rose could remember her mother chatting about incidental things—a black cat she'd spotted in the neighborhood, Rose's coat that was too big now but was sure to fit snugly next winter if Rose took good care of it. She remembered arriving at the field behind the train station, where the children were supposed to gather.

But Rose did not remember saying good-bye to her parents. She could not remember leaving the field and walking to the train platform. Did she say good-bye in the field? Did they come to the platform with her? What did Mutti say? Rose didn't know. When she thought of that night, her mind snapped shut, leaving a shameful void. Why couldn't she remember?

Her stomach was truly hurting her, fisted and knotted up. She resolved to go to synagogue. She would call Mrs. Cohen Auntie, if she still wanted. Rose would do anything to set things right again.

She felt shivery. The cramps were getting worse. She got up to go to the toilet, and as she was scurrying down the hall, she felt between her legs a small but definite leak. She shifted, and there it was again. A wetness to her underwear, against her inner thigh. She rushed into the bathroom, aghast, slammed the door shut. How could she have had an accident? She was twelve years old. She took care of herself. She hung her head in her hands but she didn't cry. She didn't cry anymore; she wouldn't cry now.

It was only after she had been sitting on the toilet for a minute that she looked down at her underwear. There, instead of a yellowish hue, was a strip of stain winking back up at her, a shock of living, thick red.

All Rose could do was stare. She knew what it was. But knowing didn't help her believe it. Her mind began tumbling: Margaret, a year older at thirteen, hadn't gotten her monthlies yet. Her cousin Kaethe didn't get them until she was nearly fifteen! (Rose remembered the sturdy belt, the thick woolen napkins her cousin paraded in front of her like a prize.) Was this too early? She took her index finger and tentatively touched the rust-colored blood. It smelled dank, earthy. How could she be sure it was her monthlies? How could she know that something wasn't wrong with her?

Panicking, she tore off her wool pants, hopped out of her underwear. Still wearing her thick socks, she examined the damage. Her knickers were woefully stained, and she saw to her horror that a patch of blood had seeped onto her trousers too. Clutching them under the faucet, rubbing the material together, she thought how furious Mrs. Cohen would be if she found out. "We all have to do our part for the war effort," she often declaimed. Their part included using only the allotted pat of butter for tea and not asking for meat or too much soap since they were rationed.

The soap and water were doing little to ameliorate the stain on her pants. Rose feared she was only making it worse. She scrubbed harder, splashing water onto the toes of her thick woolen socks. Finally she stopped. This wouldn't do. She thought for a moment, and began searching the vanity. In the uppermost drawer, she found what she was looking for: scissors.

She sat back down on the toilet, grasped her pants, and was surprised to find that her hand was steady as she cut, then ripped, a tiny hole along the bloodied seam. She would say that she got caught on the gate outside of the Mullroys' house. A tear was much better than blood. A tear was something that was understood.

Rose's head ached and her chest felt both cold and hot at the same time, but she felt better, calmer, as she padded her damp underwear with a wad of toilet paper, put her ripped trousers on. Back in her room, she changed once more, pulling off the ruined knickers in exchange for clean ones. She balled up the dirty ones, looking around her room, hesitating. The pants she could explain away, but her underwear? She needed to get rid of them. But where? She couldn't use the trash or stuff them in the back of a drawer; Mary would surely discover them. But Mary had turned over her mattress just yesterday and given it a good cleaning; she wouldn't be there again for a while. Rose stuffed the product of her shame beneath her mattress.

As Rose was shifting the makeshift napkin between her legs once again, she heard a knock on her door.

"Just a moment—" Rose said, swiveling the pad around.

Another knock. "Please open up." Mrs. Cohen's voice.

"Coming," Rose called, pulling her pants on.

"Rose, now!"

She opened the door to face a shaking, flushed Mrs. Cohen.

"What were you doing?"

"Nothing, I—"

"You seem to have recovered well from this morning," Mrs. Cohen said in a tight voice. "I heard you went out earlier."

"I am sorry," Rose said, sliding away from Mrs. Cohen, onto the edge of the bed.

"You are often sorry, Rose, but that is not the answer."

"Mrs. Cohen, I truly am sorry, truly." Rose lowered her eyes. The room felt warm, murky. Rose thought she could detect the dank traces of her blood in the air. Could Mrs. Cohen smell it too? And what about the postcard? Was it hidden beneath her pillow? She didn't want Mrs. Cohen reading her mother's words, all that Rose sensed from the short card that Mutti couldn't bring herself to say. Mutti's hand had formed the beautiful cursive in black ink, her skin had touched the paper, and Rose couldn't bear for Mrs. Cohen to see it. "I was just getting dressed, and in Vienna," she tried, "at home—"

Pink blotches bloomed on Mrs. Cohen's cheeks. "I know, I know. You do everything differently at home. I am sorry this is not like your home." She turned her head away. "I am trying to do well by you.

Mr. Cohen and I both are trying to do well by you. But you act as if the world were against you, as if *I* were against you."

Rose didn't answer her, and the silence grew thick, ungainly. "I don't mean to," she finally said. But too much time had gone by; the words hung in the air, prickly short.

"Yes. It does seem to be beyond your control." Mrs. Cohen reached over and picked up Mutti's scarf. She examined the wrinkled silky material, casting an eye on the scarf's purple parrots, caught in flight. *Put it down,* Rose pleaded in her head. But she said nothing as Mrs. Cohen pulled on the material, revealing her slender bone-white wrists, hands not much bigger than Rose's own. "This could use a good cleaning," Mrs. Cohen said. "I'll give it to Mary."

"No!" Rose said, and snatched it back, buried her nose in its silkiness. She was convinced the scarf still held traces of Mutti's smell; her mother had packed it herself. Hers were the last hands to touch it, besides Rose's. Who knew what would happen if it were cleaned? But Rose could feel Mrs. Cohen's reproachful gaze on her, and finally she looked up from the scarf. "I'm sorry," she said, and the words felt stuck in her throat. "I like it this way."

"That is *exactly* the type of unacceptable behavior I'm talking about," Mrs. Cohen said. "Some would consider you a very fortunate girl."

"I know I am," Rose said quietly into her lap.

Mrs. Cohen sighed again. "Of course," she said, and then she was gone.

ROSE WOKE UP EARLY THE next morning, determined to do better. A steady rain was pelting the eaves as she squirreled away her makeshift napkins in a bag beneath her bed, went down to the breakfast table, and asked Mrs. Cohen how she could help. Soon she was perched next to Mrs. Cohen in her sitting room, her arms held wide for the skein of navy wool Mrs. Cohen was using to knit scarves for Margaret's brothers in the service.

Not long after the rain stopped and a grainy light speckled the room, Mary appeared. Handing Mrs. Cohen a sheaf of letters that had arrived by post, she announced: "I'd like to take the child for a walk."

Mrs. Cohen looked at Mary. "A walk?"

"A turn in the park."

Mrs. Cohen glanced from the resolute expression on Mary's face to Rose, who, too excited at the possibility, snapped her gaze down. Mrs. Cohen pursed her lips, considering for a moment. Finally she said, "Ah, yes, a turn in the park," as if the idea had occurred to her. "The fresh air might do her some good."

The cool air outside felt like a relief. Then Mary took a right instead of a left at the street lined with horse chestnut trees. Rose became confused. The park was the other direction. They were walking toward town. Mary hadn't spoken a word, but seized Rose's hand and walked at too fast a clip, her bag thumping at her side. Rose struggled to remain apace.

The streets became narrower, the houses smaller. After a bend in the road, they passed a newsagent and a pub with lace curtains. A man clutching a little girl in a camel overcoat by the hand said, "Why, hello, Mary." Mary didn't reply.

"Where are we going?" Rose asked.

"You'll see soon enough," Mary said, not breaking her stride.

Now Rose was growing scared. Mary continued to grip her hand; they walked farther. Maybe she was being kidnapped! Maybe Mary was snatching her away from the Cohens because she couldn't stand that Rose was being raised Jewish! Rose's breath picked up speed. Could that be it? How would she ever alert Gerhard? Could she get word to Margaret? What about her parents? Would they ever know?

And just as Rose was growing misty-eyed about the Cohens—it would be written up in all the papers, they didn't deserve this fate—Mary made an abrupt left, pulling Rose past some scraggly hedges into the tiny back garden, more gravel than grass, of a low-slung brick home.

"Sit." Mary ordered Rose onto a chilly stone bench by a trio of bicycles and answered the unasked question forming in Rose's eyes. "This is where I live."

Rose was too stunned to do anything but comply. Mary removed a small tin bucket from beneath the bench and then opened up her bag, revealing the crumpled paper bag that Rose had placed under her mattress hours earlier. "How did you get that?" Rose asked, astounded, her cheeks spotty and hot.

"Do you have to ask?" Mary snorted. "It's your bag, you take out the remains." She pointed for Rose to place the soiled napkins in the can. "I've got proper napkins for you inside. And I'll get you one of these to keep at the Cohens'. You're to tell me whenever you need to use it."

"Does Mrs. Cohen know?" Rose whispered, too embarrassed to meet Mary's eye.

"Please." Mary snorted again. "You think she notices anything?" She stooped her considerable girth low over the tin bucket, trying to strike a match. It didn't take. The second one sputtered aflame and died out. "This dampness is the devil itself," she said as she cupped her hands and the third caught and cast a weak glow.

As Mary poked inside the bucket with a stick, Rose stole a glimpse at her surroundings. The house was modest, more like a cottage, with gingham curtains lining the windows and a handful of stone, rain-streaked bunnies lining the walkway. She thought she heard the tinny sound of a dance number coming from inside. That didn't seem like the Mary she knew. But maybe she didn't know her, Rose thought, and for the first time in a great while, the realization of not knowing didn't fill her with dread, but rather a quiet, rising expectancy.

Rose couldn't detect any flames, only smoke clouding the can. The air felt cool against her cheek. She pulled her jacket tighter, but she tasted the char in the back of her throat and it warmed her, reminded her of a time long ago, falling asleep in front of the great tiled stove fed by coals—the *kachelofen,* it was called—at her *oma*'s house, wanting, more than anything, to stay tucked in the tiny chair by the fire.

As Mary urged the flames on, Rose felt light-headed, heady with the knowledge of a secret that women like Mary carried around with them. She wondered if her mother too burned evidence of her monthlies. Rose couldn't picture it, couldn't see Mutti kneeling over a dirty can like this, couldn't imagine where in their high-ceilinged apartment she would do such a thing.

Then a reckless thought came to her. It didn't matter what her mother did. Rose felt iciness hollow out her insides; it seemed a horrible betrayal. Rose thought of the postcard, she thought of all those letters from her mother written on tissue-thin purple stationery (stored in a biscuit tin with a royal seal in her wardrobe), she saw Mutti putting on a pair of chandelier earrings, tightening her jacket with the rabbit-fur collar the night she left. Rose, turning away from Mary and the bucket and the smoke, thought about how she too was becoming a woman. But she was not becoming her mother. She never would be. This thought filled her with such a strange, sad, tangled mixture.

Would Rose burn her napkins twenty years from now? When she was grown up, when she was already old and married, with kids of her own, was this what she would do? But the questions made the iciness inside gust upward. How could she answer? For so long she told herself that she was going back home. But now?

Her parents would come here, she told herself with renewed resolve. They would all be here. They would make England their home. She was still a stranger, and yet the place and its ways were not unfamiliar. She hadn't wanted to belong here, but here she was.

One day this would all seem like a long time ago—Mary, the Cohens, the strangely damp taste of smoke against her lips, the drumbeat of dislocation, this newer feeling of being on the cusp of something. She would tell Mutti about it. This afternoon would exist as a memory, a story she might tell.

Rose peered over the side of the bucket. The mashed papers were sooty, gone hoary gray with ash and burns, turned into something else entirely.

"It's even harder with proper napkins," Mary muttered, peering into the can. "But this is what we do here in England."

Flush with the possibilities of what was to come, Rose barely registered her words.

5

LOS ANGELES, 2006

ONE MID-OCTOBER AFTERNOON, NEARLY TWO years after Lizzie arrived in L.A., some kids at school noticed a pallid cloud hovering over the ridge. It was thick, but diffuse somehow. It seemed not to move. The air was uncommonly warm and restless, the Santa Anas in full blast.

"It's fog," someone said. It was lunchtime, and the school alley was choked with everyone buying Mountain Dews and Fantas and chips and quesadillas off the taco truck.

"It's smoke." Duncan Black rolled his eyes. He lived in Malibu with his father and considered himself an authority on such things.

"It's past Temescal. It's at Will Rogers."

Another boy was talking about how in the last big fire, his best friend's cousin's house burned down. "He says it was one of the best things that ever happened to him. They stayed in some sweet-ass hotel down on Wilshire, then he got everything new—*everything!*—clothes and skateboards and a new set of Blue Öyster Cult records and even some dumb baseball cards he'd had since he was, like, seven. It was sweet, man. Insurance paid for everything."

No one paid attention. Everyone was looking up at the grayish yellowing cloud, which was unmistakable but not necessarily unusual—it looked more like smog than anything else.

"Where are the flames? You can't see the flames," Cori Carpenter said.

"Dumbfuck, of course you can't see the flames yet. It's not some fucking *movie*," Duncan said with disgust. "Trust me, it's smoke and it's coming this way. We'll be out of school in two hours, tops."

Kids were filling the air with questions—*Is PCH closed down? What about Topanga? How is my mom going to get here?* They were nodding and talking and pushing closer to each other, a moving cloud themselves. All Lizzie could think was *My house, my things*. She thought of her photos and letters and the Mel Gibson collage that Claudia had made her for her fourteenth birthday and her mother's Connecticut College sweatshirt and the old *Mademoiselle* that featured a picture of her mother from the summer Lynn worked there, and *The Bellhop*—oh God, *The Bellhop*. Lizzie was feeling that familiar sickly sensation; nothing was under her control. Where was her father? *No*, she whispered to herself.

It took less time than Duncan had predicted. Within the hour, they were gathered in the school gym, told about mandatory evacuations. They were awaiting parents, awaiting friends, held captive until an adult came to claim them.

When the gym was nearly emptied out, Lizzie remained huddled in a corner, convinced that she was going to spend the night on this spongy flesh-colored floor that emitted a weird gaslike odor. She would never see her house or her family again. Then a distracted-looking Max hurried in, Sarah rushing to keep up with him.

Max had picked Sarah up at her elementary school first. He was taking them back to his house in Venice in his battered VW Bug. Joseph was up at the house packing and "watching things," Max said as he jammed the car key into the ignition, the engine sputtering to life. "He'll meet us soon."

In the backseat Lizzie opened the triangle window, nervously scanning the sky.

As Max drove, he tried to distract them, talking about the old amusement park, the Venice of the West, it was called. One hundred years ago, there were gondolas for the canals and dance halls and arcade games and a huge swimming pool with a mechanical wave machine. Lizzie nodded, though she couldn't picture it. *Just let my father be safe,* she repeated to herself. They got to Max's house and Max convinced her and Sarah to go down to the boardwalk. It was hot and crowded with roller skaters and skateboarders and bodybuilders and people eating *churros* and corn dogs on sticks, people who seemed to have no idea about the fire less than ten miles away. Max bought them ice cream—strawberry in sugar cones—and despite her initial reluctance, Lizzie devoured hers.

It was this taste of cold sweetness that Lizzie distinctly remembered years later, a delicious evanescent treat laced with an unspeakable fear. She remembered Max's small house situated on the edge of the dank canal—his cottage, he called it. She remembered feeling safe in that house—Max ordered pizza and installed Lizzie and Sarah on the couch with multiple blankets despite the day's heat, told them they could watch whatever movies they chose. ("You sure *Godfather II* is okay for Sarah?" "It's fine!") She could recall all this as well as the conviction of her feeling: her house would burn. She would never see her father again.

But when Lizzie woke up the next morning, her father was sitting at Max's tiny metal kitchen table. He was filthy in his old NYU Med sweatshirt, sweat-stained and dirt-streaked, but his eyes were bright. Lizzie could see white in his hair, what she would later learn was ashes.

Joseph hugged her tightly, and Lizzie could smell the smoke and sweat emanating from his clothes, his skin. "The wind," he kept saying, "the wind." The fire had barreled through the mouth of the canyon, edged past Sullivan, and Joseph and his neighbors were ordered out of their houses, off the roofs they were trying to protect by hosing them down. But the wind abruptly changed course, and their houses were spared. Lizzie could remember her father laughing and shaking his head. "I'm a lucky man, Lizzie. I don't know why, but I've always been incredibly lucky."

She remembered Max vividly from that time too. He was younger than her father. Lizzie remembered thinking that he was still old, though, close to forty, she had guessed. She remembered the way the reddish hairs in his beard would catch the light and gleam. He spoke to her like she was a real person, not a kid. And she remembered telling him: "You're very different from my dad."

"Is that so?"

"Yeah," she had said. "You're much quieter."

"I talk," he said, with a sly smile, but then, as if he couldn't help it, he fell silent.

HE WAS A LISTENER THEN and he was a listener now. Because here Lizzie was, back in Max's house, the Venice canal nothing more than a silvery streak out the window, a trick of reflection. Here were his nimble hands, exploring the territory of her body. He was a detailer, that Max, a recorder, a collector; he brought fierce attention to whatever task was at hand, unwrapping the cellophane of a cigarette pack, unwrapping her. Lizzie lay back on his couch and looked up at the wood slicing the living room ceiling, those same thick roughhewn beams that she'd slept beneath on a night more than twenty years earlier when she feared she was once again losing all that mattered. Max had taken care of her. Now he brought the same steadied attention to the tracing of her.

And my God, did it feel good. How in the world could something feel this good? She was dizzied by her desire, under a spell. The only part that made sense was that something that made so little sense was transpiring. She and Max shouldn't be happening. If her father were alive, they *wouldn't* be happening. This, she tried not to dwell on.

She called her senior partner. "I think I need that bereavement leave after all," she said. She told him that her father's estate was a shambles, her sister a wreck. "I need to be here," she said in a gust of prevaricating self-righteousness. "I'm sorry, but I do."

Marc agreed to two weeks. "Thank you," she said. "That's all I need." She thought to herself: *Two weeks, and I'll figure it out.*

But what needed figuring out? She knew, even if she couldn't admit it to herself, even if she hadn't said a word to Max, she wanted to stay here in this delicate bubble, an unreal time that wasn't the past and wasn't the future but a surreal melding of the two.

Her life was like this: during the day, she went for runs in the morning and then read for hours at a time. Max would come home from work, and they would open a bottle of wine and make do with whatever was in the refrigerator, quick cobbled-together meals—pasta and sausage, a frittata with onions and cheese—as if it didn't occur to either one that supermarkets and gourmet shops and dozens of restaurants were just around the corner, provisions theirs for the asking.

While Max cooked, Lizzie asked questions. They both drank. They didn't talk about their shared profession. They rarely spoke about Joseph. Lizzie learned that Max had lived in Australia for a year after college. His mother never tired of telling him that she had wanted a daughter, and barring that, a doctor for a son. Max had been a pudgy kid, looking out at the world from behind thick-lensed glasses. He worried about his ex-stepdaughter, a cool, distant seventeen-year-old named Kendra, whom he tried to see once a month. He was a quiet, relentless competitor, a marathoner who only gave up racing a couple of years ago when his knees gave out. He said he loved going down on her.

They brought glasses of wine to his bed, and she was eager for him to indulge. Max's chest hair had turned mostly white, with some patches migrating to his shoulders. At fifty-five, his stomach was ample, soft, and there was something slightly comical about the way it looked, perched atop his still-muscular runner's legs. But Lizzie couldn't remember ever feeling this hungry for someone's touch. Their time in bed was marked by an urgency, shorn of any niceties, a tumbling down into what felt like her own true hard self. *It won't last,* she told herself. It couldn't.

Could it?

HER FIRST MONDAY, AFTER MAX went to work, she spent the morning examining his prodigious shelves, crowded with art books—Courbet and Ellsworth Kelly and the architecture of the desert—and European histories and biographies and many a volume on the Civil War. She pulled down the doorstopper of *The Power Broker,* which she had always wanted to read, but New York and Robert Moses's machinations felt far away, and after several pages she lost interest, was back inspecting the shelves. Closer to the window, she spotted the creamy spine of *The World of Yesterday,* by Stefan Zweig. Years ago, a boyfriend of hers had thrust the xeroxed pages of a short story of Zweig's into her hands with the fervor of a convert. She could remember little about the story's particulars, only that it took place on an ocean liner and followed two men who played chess. But she had been compelled, she recalled, gripped by a story about a game that she cared little about.

Zweig was Viennese-born and Jewish, like Rose Downes. Lizzie moved to the window seat with coffee and Zweig's memoir in hand. She began to read. Zweig called the period in which he grew up before World War I in Vienna "the golden age of security." Politics took a backseat; theater, music, and literature were revered. Zweig wrote of once passing Gustav Mahler on the street and boasting about it for months. As a student, he took part not in political rallies but in demonstrations that protested the tearing down of the house that Beethoven had died in. Lizzie read about the pleasures of the Viennese coffeehouse, where not only Austrian but also French and English and Italian and American papers and magazines were on offer. This dreamy, intellectual world that Zweig was describing would not hold, Lizzie knew, and she read the nostalgic passages with growing dread.

What happened to Zweig? Lizzie skipped ahead in the book to find out, and read the publisher's note at the end. After Hitler overtook Austria, Zweig had fled, first wending his way to France, then England, then New York, eventually landing in Brazil. Despondent over his exile and the state of the world, he and his wife committed double suicide in 1942.

Lizzie shut the book, shuddering. Zweig had gotten out—he was, in a sense, lucky—and still he had ended his life. And he had killed himself in 1942, before the world knew about the concentration camps, before the full extent of the terror was understood.

But Rose had lived. For decades afterward, however painful it might have been, she had decided to live. Through the window Lizzie saw a snowy egret wade into the shallow waters of the canal, peck at a bobbing yellow something, far too brightly colored to be natural. She stared at the bird but it barely registered.

Then she heard a noise: her phone, vibrating against the glass of Max's coffee table, Sarah calling. Oh God, Lizzie had forgotten all about lunch with her sister.

"SORRY, SORRY," LIZZIE SAID, SLIDING into her seat across from Sarah on the café's patio, her hair still damp from the shower.

Sarah waved off the apologies, kissed her. "It's fine. I ordered myself some courage while I was waiting." She nodded at a frothy, milky glass in front of her.

"Your drink has courage?" Lizzie asked. It felt surreal to be sitting across from her sister now, blithely chatting. Sarah still thought she was staying with Claudia.

"It's called 'courageous.' I don't know if that means it encourages courage. Or contains courage. Either way, it is seriously foul."

A willowy waitress with a buzz cut handed Lizzie a menu. She was wearing a button that said, *What Fulfills Your Heart?* Lizzie scanned the menu: "pure," "openhearted," "radiant." "I'll get the breakfast tacos," she said, and pointed to the item, unable to bring herself to say "superb," the dish's name. "And coffee, please."

The waitress nodded stonily. "Anything else?" She gestured at Sarah with her chin.

"I'm good with my 'courageous,'" Sarah said, smiling sweetly. "Thank you."

The waitress left. "I hate this place," Sarah said.

"So what are we doing here?" Lizzie said. It had been Sarah's suggestion. When Lizzie had looked up the café online and read that it had a motto—"stay, acknowledge, be"—she thought: *Of course. This is exactly what Sarah would choose.*

Sarah shrugged. "Its pretentions are only matched by how good it is. They hand-hull the nuts for the almond milk. This drink probably has more nutrients in it than everything else I'll ingest this week." She downed the remains like a shot.

"Do you need a lot of vitamins these days?" Lizzie said.

Sarah studied her, her eyes narrowing. "Excuse me?"

Lizzie blushed. The words had popped out. "Nothing," she muttered, and she played with her fork.

"You are a liar." Sarah let out a snort. "You've always been an awful liar. It's like that time when I told Dad I was at Amelia's—"

"You were fourteen! You guys wanted to go to Tijuana. I wasn't a bad liar; I just wouldn't cover for you."

"Don't change the subject," Sarah said, and she sat up straight, like the actress she had once wanted to be. She folded her hands, her long tapering fingers—their mother's, not the stubby ones of their father's that Lizzie had inherited—on top of each other. She fixed those deep hazel eyes of hers on her sister. "I know you."

"When I was staying at your place," Lizzie admitted, "I saw something, a prescription bottle, for Clomid—"

"What? You knew about the Clomid? You knew and you didn't say!"

Lizzie nodded, embarrassed. "I didn't know what to say," she finally said, and that admission felt like a small but essential truth.

"I know. It must have been a surprise. It's not like I talked about wanting kids. I never thought I did." Sarah ducked her head, her dark hair curtaining off her face. "But I don't know—Angela and I kept talking about it, and something just changed. Once it shifted, that was that. I'm excited; I really want this." She looked back up, her fine features settling, growing serious. She reached for her sister's hand. "It scares me, being this excited."

Sarah's fingers were cool to touch. Lizzie understood, she wanted to say. She knew that fear. But it was thrilling too: her sister, a mother. Then she felt something burble up, an unsettling sensation—she was forgetting something. There was something she needed to do.

"Dad," Lizzie said to her sister, on the edge of tears. "You should be telling this to Dad."

"I know," Sarah said, squeezed Lizzie's hand, bit her lip. "I was thinking that too."

For a moment, neither of them spoke. Then Lizzie heard herself say: "I have something to tell you too. I haven't been staying with Claudia. I've been with Max."

Lizzie pulled her hand back, reached for her water. She glanced at her sister, but Sarah's open, expectant expression hadn't changed. "Max . . . ? Max Levitan?"

Lizzie nodded, unable to speak. Was Sarah disgusted?

"You and Max, what?" Sarah said, uncomprehending.

"We've been—seeing each other," Lizzie finished. For a wild moment, she thought: *I'll call it off now. I will.*

"Wait, you and Max, together?" Sarah did look truly surprised, her mouth open, her big eyes growing bigger. "How? Wait, forget that," she said, waving off her own question. "I mean, how long has this been going on—since before Dad?"

"God no," Lizzie said, horrified. "No, not long at all. But, it's happening."

"Oh, I didn't mean it like that; I was just—not expecting it. But of course, it's fine; it's great!" Sarah said, recovering. "Not that you're asking for my approval. But it's not all that surprising. I had a crush on him when I was a kid too."

"Well, I didn't," Lizzie said weakly. Her words sounded small, ungenerous, which wasn't what she had intended. She had only meant this: what had happened with Max had surprised her like nothing else. And of course she wanted her sister's approval.

"Sure you did," Sarah said, waving her off. "All our secrets are coming out now, aren't they?"

AFTER MAX LEFT EARLY THE next morning, Lizzie decided to go for a run. She was meeting Rose in the early afternoon but the day seemed too open. She wished she had arranged to meet her earlier. She followed a path alongside the canals, and tried to imagine what it must have looked like a hundred years ago, when the waterways first opened as a resort, with bona fide gondoliers brought in from Italy. But she kept thinking about the first time Joseph had brought her to Max's little house by the water. She couldn't have been older than eleven. It was their second or third trip out to L.A. after Joseph had moved. Lynn was still alive. Max took Lizzie and Sarah for a ride in a canoe while Joseph stayed behind. The canal's water was dark and unimpressive—she remembered plucking out a slimy green soda bottle, its label too worn to identify. The canal smelled of nothing good. She turned to Max: "Why would you defend a murderer?" she asked.

He looked at her. Everyone knew about the Cohen killings. There had been a storm of press coverage, thanks to the family's Hollywood pedigree. (Just the year before, the father, the sole survivor, had won an Oscar for best director.) The son, who had killed his mother and brother, had gotten life imprisonment, not the death penalty, thanks to Max. And she wanted to know: How could he fight for him? It seemed unquestionably wrong.

"Everyone deserves an advocate," Max said. "If I don't do it, who will?" They drifted close to the mossy edge of the canal, and Max let go of the oar, which clattered against the flooring of the boat's aluminum hull, and pushed off with his hand. "Besides, things are often more complicated than they seem."

"He killed his mother and his brother," Lizzie said, unsatisfied. "What's complicated about that?" Still, she could remember how much she liked being in that canoe, rowed by Max, the distinct feeling of being quieted by the boat's rocking.

She ended her run at the boardwalk and crouched down, panting. A shirtless guy, his torso a coil of muscles, was palming away on the bongos. A woman lifting a headless mannequin clad in a G-string came out of a shop. Displays were being set up at rickety stalls with T-shirts and nose rings and candles and Guatemalan woven shirts, a table manned by Lyndon LaRouche supporters. A middle-aged man in bright Lycra wove unsteadily by on his bike and there was something about the shape of his shoulders, the determined thrust of his neck and head that gave Lizzie a chill of recognition. For a moment she thought: *That's my father.* It brought her comfort, how her body was charged to try to find him. *I'm sorry for your loss,* people said to her, and in these not infrequent moments she felt as if her father were not dead but truly lost, able to be found if she searched for him hard enough.

She turned away from the boardwalk, away from the homeless with their rattling carts and the shiny Rollerbladers, all the cacophony of Venice, and looked out over the broad expanse of beach, a dirty pale carpet of sand. The morning was stubbornly overcast, the sky anemic, the ocean a shade darker. Lizzie headed toward the water, watching the waves careen and heave onshore. The wet sand grew firmer beneath her feet. The wind kicked up, ocean spray mingling with her sweat. She sat down, pulled off her sneakers and socks, and gazed out over the grayish-greenish water. Her eyes burned. The day after tomorrow was the twenty-second, exactly three months since he had died. Last month on the twenty-second, she had gone to

Barney Greengrass for an early breakfast and ordered the most expensive sturgeon on the menu. "Dad would have loved that," Sarah said, and it pleased Lizzie to hear Sarah say it. The twenty-second wouldn't always feel so fraught, Lizzie suspected, and the prospect of that dissipation served up its own fresh sadness.

Lizzie found herself saying, "Hey. I miss you, so much. I promise I do." She felt self-conscious, but it was a relief to say it out loud.

She sat for quite a while. When she rose and started for Max's, she saw something she hadn't noticed before: a synagogue next to the lingerie shop—a whitewashed stucco building with sky-blue accenting its windows. THE SHUL ON THE BEACH, a sign read.

She was gazing at it, surprised she had missed it before, when a short, round-faced man in khakis and a baseball cap approached. "Can I help you?" he asked. "Are you Jewish?"

Once or twice a year, a pair of dark-suited young men, looking as if they were twelve, would approach her in Midtown. They would climb out of a van with the words MITZVAH-MOBILE festooned across its side or hurry down the sidewalk and ask her the same question, thrusting Hanukkah candles her way, the ceremonial fronds for the holiday of Sukkot. Lizzie would pick up her pace, ignoring them altogether.

But now she looked down at her sneakers. "My father just died," she said.

"I am so sorry. May his memory be a blessing," the man said. He didn't avert his eyes as some people did when her father's death came up. "I'm the rabbi here. Morning services are about to start. Would you like to say kaddish?"

Lizzie had last attended services with Ben and his family on Yom Kippur a couple of years earlier, an unpleasant hour at his parents' synagogue in the Garment District with the rabbi using his sermon to rail against Palestinians. "I don't know how," she said.

"I'll explain," he said. "You'll try."

Inside, the sanctuary smelled dank. It was spare, the white walls unadorned, the back lined with books, a low wooden banister separating the room. The rabbi, the baseball cap off and a crocheted yarmulke affixed in its place, gave her a booklet with transliterations along with a lace head covering and bobby pin, and pointed her to the left side of the room. Lizzie sat down behind two older women, the only people on this side of the room, stunned that she was here. She draped her sweatshirt first over her bare legs, then over her shoulders and short sleeves, uncomfortable either way. On the other side of the low partition were about a dozen men, most old and in suits, a few bushy-haired and T-shirted.

The service began. Most of it was in Hebrew, and although she didn't understand it, she found the sounds comforting. What would her father think of her being here? He had never been much of a synagogue-goer himself. But on Yom Kippur he would fast, and he used to insist that they watch Laurel and Hardy movies together on that day. He probably wouldn't be impressed with this synagogue. "What, you couldn't say kaddish somewhere in Brentwood?" she could hear him saying. But he would not be displeased.

The rabbi was saying something in Hebrew, looking her way. "The Mourner's Kaddish," he said in English, nodding at her. She scrambled to her feet. *"Yitgadal v'yitkadash sh'mei raba,"* she read out loud from the transliteration: *Glory and sanctified be God's name.*

Her heart seized. Her parents were gone. She wanted to shake off that fact, she wanted to escape it; she wanted more than anything for it not to be true.

She went on chanting. She ignored the English translation. She didn't want to know the meaning of the words. It was the sounds that mattered, the sounds that were offering her solace. She was here, standing, for him. She was his daughter, still. A raspy voice had joined her, a male voice—another mourner, she realized.

There were probably fifteen people present in a room that could hold a hundred, but when the others joined in to read the last line in unison, to say amen, it was the first time in months that Lizzie felt the weight of her loss ease a little.

After, the rabbi approached her. "You see? You were able to say it. May God comfort you among the mourners of Zion and Jerusalem, and may your father's memory be a blessing."

It shouldn't have felt like such an achievement and yet it did. "Thank you," she managed.

BY THE TIME SHE GOT back to Max's, she was running behind. She had been looking forward to seeing Rose all week. Now she would be late. She showered quickly and downed a yogurt and got in her rental car. They were meeting at the small park tucked behind Wilshire in the shadow of the La Brea Tar Pits. It had been Rose's suggestion; she lived nearby. "First the May Company moved out and then Bullock's too," Rose had said to her on the phone. "Now it's just me and the dinosaurs."

Lizzie made surprisingly good time from Venice to mid-Wilshire, and made it to the meeting spot about five minutes late.

Rose was waiting. She wore a long tailored white shirt, a chunky amber necklace, looking more chic and younger than Lizzie had remembered. "Shall we?" she said. There was a note of imperiousness in her tone. Without waiting for an answer, she began down the path at the park's edge. Lizzie scurried after her.

"Sorry I'm late," Lizzie said as she hurried. "Traffic." Rose's fast pace surprised Lizzie. She was tiny, a good several inches shorter than Lizzie herself.

Rose didn't respond. When she finally spoke, her tone was softer. "I try to walk every day. After I retired from the school, I was driving Thomas, my husband, crazy, moping around the house—a common enough story—and these walks, they're such a small thing, but they saved me." A thin, rolled-up circular sat in the middle of the path; she kicked it out of her way.

"You're married?" Lizzie asked. She didn't know why it hadn't occurred to her that Rose might be.

"I was, for a long time," Rose said. "More than fifty years. But Thomas died nearly two years ago."

"Oh, I'm sorry," Lizzie said as her image of Rose shifted again: she had been married for more than half a century; she was a woman who had also experienced a big loss.

Rose gave her a curt nod.

"Do you have any other family, kids nearby?" Lizzie asked.

"No," Rose said. "No kids—nearby or elsewhere."

"I'm sorry," Lizzie said. "I don't know why I asked that." She hated it when people made assumptions about her. She had only meant—she was thinking of how difficult it must be to lose someone after all that time—she only hoped Rose wasn't alone.

"It's fine. Not everyone is made to have kids."

"Yes," Lizzie said, still feeling chastened but slightly relieved. "Absolutely." Maybe she was one of those people.

"We were very happy together, just the two of us, Thomas and I," Rose said plainly. She was walking briskly when she said it, didn't look at Lizzie.

"That's wonderful to hear."

"Are you married?"

"No," Lizzie said. "Not married, no kids." She tried to say it airily, but even she could hear her plaintive undertone.

"How old are you?"

"Thirty-seven."

"Still young yet," Rose said.

Lizzie gave a half smile. She did the math in her head all the time: *If it works out,* she might think on a promising first date, *then I could get pregnant in the next year.* Or even if it didn't work out. She had been thinking this with Max. *Would it be so bad if I just got pregnant?*

"You have no idea if you're going to get married," Rose said. "But the world is teeming with all that we don't know. It doesn't mean that you won't."

"True enough," Lizzie said. She was relieved that Rose didn't start naming random single men—the nephew of her mah-jongg partner, that chatty dentist who was quite attractive—that she could set Lizzie up with. Even Claudia—Claudia!—who had been involved in a ménage with her married landlords postcollege, who used to flit from partner to partner like the sun might not rise tomorrow—was now married and talked to her as if she were doing something wrong. "Maybe you need to be a little more open," she had said after Lizzie called to chat after a disastrous blind date. *More open?* Lizzie had just gone out with her friend's mother's oncologist. ("He's *very* sensitive and empathetic," her friend had said. *And arrogant,* Lizzie thought within minutes of meeting him. *And most likely gay.*) Not open? What was Claudia talking about?

At the corner, Rose turned down a smaller, residential street. They passed modest stucco Spanish-style houses built close together, yellowing pocket-sized lawns. The sidewalk was empty of people. Was one of these houses Rose's? Lizzie could imagine passing it, and Rose not saying a word.

"So you used to be a teacher?" Lizzie asked.

Rose nodded. "English, junior high school English, for more than thirty years. Much of that time at Eastgate, when it was still all girls. Such a mistake to merge with Wilton. Come," she said, and they crossed the wide stretch of Third Street, cars flying past.

Ah, Eastgate. Lizzie smiled in recognition. Of course. The illustrious school Joseph had hoped she would attend, but there were few spots the year they moved and Lizzie didn't get in. The high school she went to was more progressive ("ragtag," Joseph had called it). "I went to Avenues."

"Now, that makes sense."

Was that a touch of sarcasm in her voice? "What does *that* mean?" Lizzie asked.

"Nothing," Rose said. "I only meant: you seem more, I don't know, artistically inclined."

"Please, I was the least artsy person there," Lizzie said. She added: "Lawyer," with a gesture toward her chest with her open palm.

"So I heard from your father," Rose said. "Wise."

"I don't know about that," Lizzie said, although she continued to love her work, the precision of the law. But she was thinking of all the books she had been reading at Max's—it had been years since she had read that much. "I always loved English class, and reading in particular," she said to Rose. "It must have been fun to teach."

"I don't know if *fun* is the word I'd use, and reading is the least of it. But it was a wonderful career."

"I was reading a book yesterday that you probably know. By Stefan Zweig," Lizzie said.

"Of course."

"That chess story of his—"

"*The Royal Game.*"

"It's wonderful, don't you think?" Lizzie said. "Yesterday, I read a lot of *The World of Yesterday*. The way he describes living in Vienna before the wars—"

"Actually, I'm not a fan," Rose said. "Zweig's writing is too mannered, too sentimental, especially in *The World of Yesterday*. Not everything was so wonderful before the wars as he claims it to be."

"Oh," Lizzie said, deflated. Sentimental? "I see what you mean; it felt nostalgic, but I kept imagining him fleeing Vienna, being forced to move from one place to the other, then down in Brazil . . ." She trailed off, feeling self-conscious. Had she offended Rose?

"And that double suicide," Rose was now saying. "I am sorry, but suicide is always a coward's way out. Such a selfish act."

Lizzie nodded, reluctant to argue. But what if a person were gravely ill, with no hope of living? What if she were truly suffering?

"I had a cousin, my father's first cousin, although he wasn't all that much older than I, who took pills when he was basically still a child," Rose was saying. "Eighteen, nineteen. A brilliant, sensitive boy. There were rumors that he was gay, though no one called it that. His mother never got over his death, of course. She had an opportunity early on to get to France, but she wouldn't leave Vienna, said she would wait until the family could all go together. Everyone said it was because she wouldn't leave her son's grave."

"That's awful," Lizzie said. "I'm so sorry." Her mother was buried in Westchester, in a large Jewish cemetery that stretched over a series of gentle hills. She hated how far away she was from it when she moved to L.A., hated thinking of how barren the grave would look in winter. "I'll take care of it," her grandmother had told Lizzie without specifying what she was referring to, but Lizzie knew exactly. "How old were you when you left?" she asked Rose.

"Eleven."

"It must have been so hard." When Lizzie was eleven, her mother was newly sick. A revolving mix of sitters—it was hard to distinguish them apart, they turned over so often—picked up Lizzie and Sarah from school, took them to skating and ballet lessons. They were often late. Once, one never showed. After waiting more than an hour and calling home and getting no answer, Lizzie caught a ride with an older male cousin of a classmate. She didn't know the guy but he had been waiting around school ("sometimes I help out with soccer practice," he said) and he offered. Her mother went ballistic when she found out. Then her grandmother moved in. "For the time being," Lynn had said.

"My brother and I were put on a train, together, to England in the winter of 1939," Rose was saying. "After the Anschluss, after Austria was annexed by Germany. I should like to say that Austria was invaded, but it was decidedly not."

The slight wind felt welcome against Lizzie's warm face. She had read about those trains, seen a documentary on PBS about them, maybe. Trains filled with Jewish children, ferrying them out of Nazi-occupied Europe. "*Kindertransports,*" she said.

"Yes," Rose said, "that's what they're called now. At the time, there was no name for it. They were just trains that we were put on."

"Of course," Lizzie said. Rose had said this nonchalantly, but Lizzie felt as if she had blundered.

"I'm not blaming you," Rose said with little hesitation, her fingers at her necklace's amber beads. "You didn't name them."

Lizzie let out a nervous burst—part cough, part choked laughter. "No, I certainly did not," she said, and realizing that Rose might take her laughter the wrong way, she added: "I'm sorry; I know it's not funny."

"That's quite all right. You can be funny." Rose did not seem thrown by Lizzie's unease. Disagreement seemed to enliven her. The wind ruffled the loose white hairs haloing her sharp, finely lined face. There was something striking about her, not one thing in particular, but the way she carried herself, the sum of her parts. "You do remind me of your father, you know."

"I do?"

"Yes, you're quieter than he was, more controlled—"

"Controll*ing*, he'd say."

"But just as smart, just as interested in the world," Rose continued. "And curious about others around you."

"Thank you," Lizzie said. "That's nice to hear." It was more than nice. "I bet it would make him happy that we were together. And talking about him—he would *love* that we were talking about him."

"Yes, exactly." Then Rose added: "I don't know why he didn't tell you about me. He spoke about you and your sister all the time. He told me that he wanted us to meet."

"I don't understand it either," Lizzie said, but she had her guesses. Neither she nor her father liked talking about the stolen painting; it had been such a painful time. She liked to think that Joseph didn't tell her about Rose because he wanted to spare her the reminder. But she feared there was a darker impulse at work: he hadn't mentioned Rose because despite everything, Joseph still blamed Lizzie.

Rose reached the corner before Lizzie. There she gazed over the intersection, hands on her hips as if surveying hostile territory. "We'll turn here," she called over her shoulder, and waited for Lizzie to catch up. "Though I was touched that he left me the masks."

"He must have known how much you admired them."

"No, not really. I've only seen them once, at his house, many years ago, when we first met. But I think it was a nod to the Soutine. African art was all the rage in Paris at the time Soutine was painting. He and his contemporaries turned to African art for inspiration. Obviously it's clearer with Modigliani, but it was true for Soutine all the same."

"I can't help but wonder if my father left you the masks because he couldn't give you the Soutine back." It was hard for Lizzie to say but it was, after all, the truth.

"Something like that," Rose said. Now she was the one looking away.

They walked on in silence. They were passing a large brick apartment building with a colonnaded front, unusual in this neighborhood of small, one-story houses, when Rose said, "Do you know what aggrieves me? This apartment building. It offends my sensibilities, and it has since it was built. Why the columns? If you're doing something in brick, leave it brick. If you want to go rococo, then by all means do that. But the two together, in this instance especially, do not work. It's like crossing a giraffe with a monkey. Why try to be something that you're not?"

Lizzie started to laugh. *They would be friends,* she thought. They would be.

"I am serious," Rose said.

"I know you are," Lizzie assured her. She imagined standing in Max's kitchen tonight, glass of wine in hand, telling him, *She's not like anyone else I know.*

"I'll tell you what I want right now," Rose said. They were nearly back at Third Street, back where they started. "Coffee. How does that strike you?"

"Like a seriously good plan," Lizzie said.

THE CAFÉ WAS A CONFECTIONER'S fading dream. Pink vinyl booths, pink cushions, heart-shape–backed chairs, scalloped wainscoting on the walls, a countertop made out of some fake substance that didn't look like marble but didn't look unlike it either. "It's been this way for decades," Rose told Lizzie, "ever since Thomas and I moved into the neighborhood. If they ever renovate, I will take my business elsewhere."

The restaurant was nearly empty, a few metal chairs upturned and resting on tables. They slid into a booth up front. "The pink is altogether too much, I know," Rose said. "But there's always a seat and the coffee is hot and still less than a dollar, as it should be."

"I love it," Lizzie said. It reminded her of Café Edison around the corner from her old firm, where on those rare days when she actually had time to leave her desk, she would go and order a bowl of matzo ball soup and eat it slowly, imagining the soup dissolving the hardened knot that had taken up residence beneath her rib cage. "You okay?" she remembered a waitress once asking her as she gave her the bill. "I'm fine," Lizzie had said, handing over a crisp twenty, winding her scarf around her neck, thinking of a citation she forgot to include on the draft of the brief; she'd add it once she got back to her desk. The waitress gave her an inquiring look as she took the money in her palm. "You're crying," she had said.

Now the waitress brought two coffees, and Lizzie tipped in milk and sugar.

"You know what you can do for me?" Rose asked.

"Name it," Lizzie said, stirring.

"I'd like to see the reports from the investigator your father hired years ago."

"The investigator?"

"The one he hired after the paintings were stolen."

Lizzie didn't remember hearing of an investigator. Was this something else Joseph hadn't told her? "I'll look for them," she said. "What was his name?"

"You know," Rose said after a pause. "I can't recall. This is what happens now. I hate that this happens."

"I'm sure it won't be hard to find," Lizzie said. "If I can't come across it, I'm sure Max will know."

"Max?"

"My father's friend," Lizzie said, nodding forcibly. "He's the executor of the estate."

"Ah, yes," Rose said. "Max. I've heard of him. Another thing I forgot." Her hands were wrapped around the coffee mug. Her nails were manicured, painted a lovely taupe color, and her fingers were short, stubby, not unlike Lizzie's own. She wore a gold wedding band on her left hand. "It's good to have someone helping you," Rose said. "It's good to have someone like that."

"It is," Lizzie said, and she heard her voice carry. The place was cavernous. Past Rose, a lone man was reading the paper at the lunch counter, his plate of eggs untouched. Lizzie did not want to talk about Max. Toward the back, a busboy filled saltshakers from a pitcher. Were they the only other customers here? The emptiness made her lean into Rose, made everything seem more intimate. "You said your mother bought the Soutine in Paris. At a gallery? From Soutine himself?"

"A gallery. My father had business in Paris—he was an importer, and he bought clocks, I think, in France—my mother rarely traveled with him, but she did on that trip, and she spotted the Soutine. It wasn't all that long after Dr. Albert Barnes, who was on a buying spree for the collection he would eventually amass for his Barnes Foundation, outside of Philadelphia, bought a large number of Soutines. That purchase made Soutine's career."

Lizzie nodded. She had taken a trip down to Philadelphia to the Barnes Foundation when she was in college, not long after *The Bellhop* was stolen. She had gazed at the other Soutine portraits—a baker's boy dressed in white, a thin, heavily browed man in a sea of blue—knowing that she wouldn't see *The Bellhop,* wishing for it to appear nevertheless. She asked: "After you left Vienna, what happened?"

"Our apartment was seized—my parents were still living there at the time. My brother and I only learned this after the war, from friends of theirs. Our parents were writing us daily at the time and never said a word. The Nazis took everything of value from the apartment, and there was a lot: jewelry and paintings and knickknacks, my mother's furs, the silver service. *The Bellhop* too, of course."

Lizzie was nodding, thinking of when *The Bellhop* was stolen from her house. To think that everything had been taken from Rose's family, every last possession of value, and how possessions were the least of what Rose had lost. "I'm so sorry," Lizzie said.

"My parents were ordered to Theresienstadt," Rose continued as if Lizzie hadn't spoken. "That's where I thought they were through the war. But we never learned—anything more."

"I'm so sorry," Lizzie repeated, wishing there were something else she could say. The clatter from the kitchen sounded. And then stupidly—Lizzie would later think, here was the moment where she should have stopped talking: "Did you ever file a claim against the Austrian government? You know you can, right?"

"I do know," Rose said. "And no."

"I could help, if you needed it."

"I don't want their money."

"But it's not theirs, really," Lizzie said. "It's compensation for what's rightfully your family's."

"Please," Rose snapped. "Let me be clear: I don't want that money. It's blood money. It makes what happened about property, and it most certainly is not. Besides, I'm not the victim here; my parents are."

"Of course—" Lizzie said in retreat. It was not hers to decide. Why hadn't she stopped talking?

"I am not a victim," Rose repeated, her voice emphatic. "I don't need anyone to feel sorry for me. Do you understand? I don't want their money."

Lizzie nodded. Later recalling the moment with a sting of embarrassment, she would think: *I just thought I could help.* "I do understand," she said, though *understand* was not exactly the right word. "It's none of my business. It's unimaginable, what happened. Of course you're handling it as you see fit."

"It might seem unimaginable, but it did happen," Rose said.

"I know," Lizzie said, miserable.

Rose downed her coffee. When she spoke again, her voice was firm. "I'm sorry. This is my problem, not yours. Let's not talk about the war or *The Bellhop* or what Austria might owe me. I'll tell you what I do want to talk about: your father."

"My father?" Lizzie said.

"He was a good friend. I bet he was a better father."

"Well, I don't know about that," Lizzie said immediately. "But he was a great father." *The best,* she could hear him saying in her mind. *Why can't you say I'm the best? Why can't you be unabashed, wholly enthusiastic for once?* She shook her head, thinking. "Did he ever take you to dim sum?" she finally asked.

"No."

"He used to take us all the time. My favorite was this place downtown, four flights up, no elevator—with sticky noodles and lotus leaves and purple taro and fried chicken feet—so many new weird foods, it terrified my sister. He could be a pain in the ass about it. 'Just try,' he'd say." It made her happy to recall. "The waiter would tally up the check at the end by counting the number of plates on the table, and my dad used to joke that they should hide plates under the table to lower the bill. There was that time he flew us up to San Francisco for the day—via charter plane—just to try out a dim sum place that a patient of his swore was the best."

"He chartered a plane just for the family?"

"Yes, I know," Lizzie said, reddening. "It was too much." She wished she had left that detail out. "But it wasn't long after we moved to L.A., and in retrospect, I think he was trying to impress us. Our mother had just died. I did not want to be living with him. I think he was trying to make us happy."

"You were fortunate to have him."

"Very," Lizzie agreed. She began stacking sugar packets atop each other, thinking: it had been so hard, but she and Sarah were lucky. Once Rose left Vienna, she was alone.

"So what happened on that trip up to San Francisco for dim sum?" Rose asked. "Did he impress you after all?"

"Not exactly. The flight was bumpy and loud—it was a tiny plane, and it was nerve-racking. And then it got worse when we arrived. Sarah complained of stomach pains, and we spent the first part of the day in the lobby of a Union Square hotel where she locked herself in a bathroom stall. Finally my father insisted we take her to the doctor. So we ended up going to the emergency room in San Francisco, and they checked her out. Turned out that she was just—well, seriously constipated."

"Oh my."

"Yes," Lizzie said with a chortle, shaking her head. "It was a disaster. But he tried. He tried a lot. And I didn't give him credit for it."

"He knew," Rose said.

"I'm not so sure." The sugar packets had become an unwieldy tower. "So he talked about us?"

"He did. He talked about you a lot. He used to say you were like him, you know. He told me that once. 'Determined,' he called you."

Lizzie so wanted this to be true. She gave an odd, contorted smile. "That was code for '*pain in the ass*.'"

"I don't think so," Rose said soberly.

The waitress approached, asked if they needed anything else. Lizzie, following Rose's example, shook her head. The waitress slid the bill on the table. Lizzie reached for it, but Rose was faster. "Please, do not insult me," Rose said. "This is on me."

"Fine," Lizzie said. "This time. Thank you. I wish . . ." She trailed off, that sibilant sound—*sshh*—lingering. There were so many things she wished for. "I wish my father had told me about you."

Rose took bills out of her long zippered wallet. "You know what? I don't."

"You don't?"

"No." And Rose smiled here, as if she knew she was about to bestow a treat. "I'll tell you why," she said as she reached across the littered Formica table and took Lizzie's hand. "Because meeting this way, this has been such a pleasure."

6

LONDON, 1945

AMID THE GIDDY CAROUSING ON that warm May night, Rose and Margaret picked their way through the packed streets, Union Jacks fluttering, bunting spilling out of windows, bonfires ringed by children and adults dancing, faces pink and slick with perspiration. Now and again fireworks shot up; a Roman candle whizzed through the air. They passed a piano that had been dragged out onto the sidewalk, draped with people singing "Roll Out the Barrel." A stranger thrust a glass of lemonade and a slice of apple cake into Rose's hands.

It took Rose several beats to realize why it was so bright, to understand that the blackout curtains had been yanked away, and several more minutes before it occurred to her: she had never seen London lit up at night before.

All the light was unquestionably beautiful. And yet it made Rose feel off-kilter. It illuminated things better left in the shadows: a gaping pile of rubble where a trio of terraced houses had once stood, the dinginess of her thin white cotton dress (despite the red, white, and blue ribbons that Margaret had braided around her waist tonight, and her own too). The light couldn't do anything about that smell, the taste of dust in the back of her throat that she couldn't manage to swallow away.

But none of this mattered. She would see her parents soon. This knowledge was like a strand of silk thread that they used in the factory: barely visible, yet material you could rely on. She would go home tonight and write to her parents. She had an address through the Red Cross. They would surely receive letters now. They would come to England—she would be seeing them soon.

How long would it take? Two weeks, a month? Longer? What would that be like, seeing them again? That last night, on the way to the train station, Mutti wearing her navy wool coat with the rabbit-fur collar, her hands sweaty despite the winter chill; Papi, telling her not to worry, she shouldn't worry, Gerhard would watch out for her. Rose had been eleven then. Now she was nearly eighteen. It had been almost half her life since she had seen them. Would she recognize them? Would they know her?

It was over. All the waiting, over. She grabbed Margaret's hand and jumped up and down, as she used to do when they were kids. "Come *on*. What are we waiting for?"

Margaret's mouth, reddened by beetroot juice, widened into a smile. She had only two inches on Rose but seemed taller, more comfortable in her enviably curvaceous body. "Since when are you in a hurry for anything?" she said, but she picked up speed. They cut through the thicket of revelers. "To Trafalgar we go! We are celebrating—finally!"

Finally was the only word to describe it. The night before, a thunderous rainstorm had woken Rose up. Her body was primed for that shuddering sound, the vibrations that meant a rocket. She looked over at Margaret's sleeping form in her own narrow bed, thinking she had to wake her up, they had to rush down into the shelter. But then she remembered: the war was over.

Trafalgar Square was raucous and crammed with people banging on dustbin lids and singing, bodies pressing up against each other—

Rose barely cleared five feet, so her view was of shoulders and chins, the backs of heads, arms swinging, jostling. "There's Fred!" Margaret yelled, though they were standing right next to each other. "Fred!"

It took Rose a moment to remember who Fred was. Yes, the lumbering American MP that Margaret had met at the Rainbow Corner a few weeks ago. With Margaret these days, there was always a boy. None lasted. (You wouldn't know from the way she went on and on about them that she was one of only a handful of women in her first year at the London School of Economics.) Margaret slipped off to Rose's left, the crowd swallowing her up. Rose tried to follow, but she no longer could see Margaret, and she didn't see Fred. A serviceman shimmied up a lamppost, whirling off his jacket. A girl in a yellow dress clambered up to the fountain with two officers and danced between them.

Rose stepped back, her ankle hitting something hard. It was only then that she realized she was standing at the bottom of the marble steps leading up to the National Gallery. Floodlights blazed, casting the building in an amber glow.

In the eight months that Rose had lived in London, she had been inside the National Gallery once, the same week she had moved, after Margaret had offered to share her London room and enabling Rose to leave the Cohens'. Margaret was registering for classes at LSE and Rose—well, she was supposed to be looking for a job. "Perhaps you can tutor," Margaret had offered, not unkindly. "You can tutor *and* go to school."

"We'll see," Rose had responded, not wanting to spoil the pretense. They both knew she needed a dependable paycheck that tutoring wouldn't offer. But first Rose had come to the National Gallery and queued up. She had heard all about Myra Hess's lunchtime concerts—in the papers, and on the wireless—a friend of the Cohens' had attended one and said it was too wonderful to describe.

It took nearly two hours to get to the entrance, where she dropped her shilling into the box and stepped inside. The walls looked so strange with all those empty frames, no art inside (with the exception of the picture of the month, the gallery's collection was squirreled away in a wartime hiding spot—where exactly, no one knew). Rose bought a raisin-and-honey sandwich from Lady Gater's canteen and ate it at the counter, quickly and quietly, as if someone might spot her and tell her to leave. But no one said a word and she made her way into the packed area beneath the gallery's glass dome, and when she realized that all the seats were taken, she stood along the side and Miss Hess came out—smaller and rounder than Rose would have thought—and she played Bach with such ferocity and perfection that all Rose could think was, *I will tell Mutti all about it. One day I will bring her here.*

Now here was Margaret, pulling her hand, her face shiny, her blond hair still neatly gathered in its roll at her neck and a big man in uniform at her side. They pulled her into a line of people dancing, Rose behind Margaret behind Fred, who wasn't lumbering but graceful on his feet. Another American soldier, a handsome navy man in spite of his odd cap and tie, took his place behind her. It was easy to move, *shuffle shuffle shuffle, kick, kick,* to be pulled along—and she liked being a small part of a larger something. Rose marched, *one-two-three, kick, kick. The war is gone,* she thought. *Kick, kick . . .* she thrust out her legs, one after the other, exhilarated: *no more war.* Her hands slipped down Margaret's waist.

"Help," the navy man behind her said. He nearly shouted to make himself heard.

"Excuse me?"

He gripped his hands on her waist. "My dancing. I need guidance." He swiveled her around. She was right; he was handsome, tall with bright eyes.

"Hardly."

He repositioned his hands on her waist. "But I can think of more fun things than this dancing."

"Now I know you're not in your right mind." Rose tried to say it tartly, but it didn't come out that way. She turned back, hurried to catch up with the line, concentrated on Margaret's backside, the slight way she was swiveling her hips to and fro.

He tottered, grasped at her waist. "Come *on*," he said, and he pulled her off the line. "I'm Paul."

"Rose."

"I'm going home soon."

"Everyone is coming home to me." She liked saying that out loud. The more she said it, the more deeply she believed it. She'd gotten her last letter from Gerhard about a month ago, when his troop was on the outskirts of Berlin. It won't be long, he had said.

"I'm going back home to Maryland, to work with my father." He leaned close, played with the ribbon hanging from her dress.

Her heart sped up. He was so good-looking. She didn't know where in America Maryland was—America was America—and she didn't ask. She thought of the silk factory on Tottenham Court Road. Rose hoped to quit before long. Her parents would be horrified to learn that she had been working in a parachute factory—Mutti especially—but she would show them the hard-earned money she'd saved. She earned five pounds a week; that wasn't nothing. "It was all worth it," she would say.

"You're beautiful," Paul was saying now. He pulled off his cap, nuzzled her neck, his mouth languorous.

She stiffened. "I'm not," she murmured, but she didn't move. Except for a chaste awkward kiss by Phillip Trumbell, a friend of Margaret's second-oldest brother, no one had ever touched her before. And certainly not like this. Was this the way it happened? Rose looked around, her heart careening this way and that, but no one seemed to be paying them any mind.

She tried pulling his head up to meet her lips, but his mouth was exploring her neck, her ear. She felt his tongue darting about. "No, not here," she whispered, but he didn't seem to hear. Tentatively she tried kissing him back, dropping a quick succession of pecks on the top of his head, her palms cupping his ears. They felt delicate, strangely separate from the rest of him.

But the more she tried to slow down, the more he sped up. He leaned over, clutched at her waist. His hands moved up.

"No," she said, but the word was like a gelatinous thickening in her throat. "Paul." That was his name, wasn't it? She tried coaxing him up. She wanted him, but not this, not all of this.

"What?" He breathed out the word, the sound stretching thin, but his hands became all the surer. Before she knew it, he had lifted the hem of her dress and grabbed her backside as if it were simply his for the taking.

"No. Please," she said—she could only manage that. She tried to push him off, but it was no use. Now he was pressing her up against something—a wall? He was so much larger. She went flat with fear. For a moment, she couldn't hear a sound. It reminded her of the dreadful silence that punctuated her past year in London, the envelope of quiet before the *chug chug* and the awful splintering that sounded like a motor spinning out of control, and then a deafening rattle. It happened in seconds. Silence and then the unearthly noise: a rocket, exploding.

But Paul had pulled away. "I'm not going to make you," he said, disgusted.

Rose felt even shakier, more muddled. "I'm sorry," she said. It would be years before she wondered why she was the one who apologized.

She didn't look for Margaret. She kept her head down, hurrying through the throngs, through the relative darkness of Lincoln's Inn Fields. There were celebrators there too, whooping it up and setting off firecrackers, but fewer of them, and no one seemed to register her. She was grateful for that, for the darkness that engulfed her.

When she got home, she drew a bath (lukewarm and no more than the requisite five inches—it comforted her tonight to follow the rules). The water didn't cover her stomach or her breasts, but she lay there a long time. Finally she climbed out, her limbs heavy. What had she been doing out? She needed to write to her parents.

AFTER THE TWO-DAY NATIONAL HOLIDAY that Churchill declared in honor of victory, Rose put on her overalls and pulled her hair back and returned to the factory, which remained open. ("'Course," said Mrs. Lloyd as she took a drag on her cigarette. "Who do you think is sewing the parachutes for the Pacific?") Just as she'd been doing for months, Rose took her seat on her stool, stared at the bright white silk under the lights, and guided the material through the machine. Big-band music on the BBC poured from the loudspeakers, but it was no match for the voracious clatter of the jittering machines. It was hard to focus, and Rose needed to focus (there had been awful accidents; girls' hair got caught in the wheels). But all Rose could think about was where she would go at half past four when she clocked out and her day would truly begin.

She usually went to the Bloomsbury House first, that massive stone building in the West End that she felt a kinship to long before she set foot in it. Bloomsbury House was not a house at all but a multifloored administrative building that held a number of Jewish refugee organizations. Bloomsbury House was the place that brought her to England.

The actual offices were of little interest to her now. There were lists on the walls. There were names. Typed up on thin onionskin paper, tacked up in the crowded halls, the lists were not dated or alphabetized. There were so many names sounding achingly familiar to Rose—Solomon, Karl, Eva, Trude, Lore, Kurt; Singer, Weinstein, Porges, Schwartz. These were Jewish names, people she grew up with. The experience of reading the names made her feel vertiginous. She hadn't seen her parents' names. She didn't recognize anyone on the wall. But there were new lists going up all the time, and this meant that every viewing, every new day, held a flush of promise.

After Bloomsbury House, Rose visited the Red Cross and the

UN Relief Agency. In the crowded hallways of the summer of 1945, people talked: Did you try the World Jewish Congress? Did you hear that the American army has its own lists up at Rainbow Corner? The Jewish newspapers—the *Jewish Chronicle*, the *Tribune*—ran columns of names in their back pages. People were being found. New names were going up every day.

It was a laborious, imperfect process, and the people who crammed into these offices alongside Rose were not quiet about their complaints. But Rose for one was grateful for the queues, for the maddening slowness of information trickling out. Shadows meant that there were still facts that had yet to be unearthed. Uncertainty, by its definition, included a thin, silvery shot of hope.

She had heard, of course. Horrible, unspeakable things. Buchenwald was the first camp she had learned about, back in April, when Allied troops were closing in on Berlin and Stalin was taking no mercy. Even before VE Day, there had been reports. She knew: at some point the lists of survivors that she studied so vigilantly would be replaced by lists of the dead. But that hadn't happened yet. For now, there were still survivors. She continued looking.

London in the summer of 1945 was heavy with grime and rubble and shrouded in bad smells—burning newspaper and old frying oil and urine. The lights that so struck Rose on VE Day now flickered—in shops, the underground, the factory. Outages were common. Rations were still in effect. But for some illogical, unnamable reason, Rose felt hopeful. She had purpose. She would ride the Tube after leaving Tottenham Court Road on her way to look at the lists, holding a pole with one hand, the other clutching a fat novel of Margaret's that she felt too impatient to read, the light dim (or sometimes out altogether, when someone pilfered the bulbs from behind the seats). But she felt as if something still *might* change. It was a time when fear and frustration and doubt still commingled with the slightest leavening, the most tenuous and fragile hope, of possibility, that all this might one day recede safely into the past.

How strange it would be if her parents did indeed walk through the door. What would Mutti think of her little girl who was now grown up? Would they recognize each other? What would they talk about? Would Mutti tell her that she needed to wear a coat or who to date, or yes, she was right, *It's That Man Again* was a truly awful show?

She kept searching.

"I DON'T KNOW WHY YOU'RE not coming out." This from Margaret as she sat on the edge of her bed, clad in her robe, legs stretched before her. She was applying a sponge to her calves, dabbing gravy browning to her legs, changing their color from pale to tanned. "I have twenty quid from my father! Tomorrow it will be gone."

Rose shook her head. "You know I can't. I have to be up early."

"You work too hard." Margaret pressed a thumb against her calf and inspected it. "I wish you didn't have to work so hard."

Rose shrugged. "It's fine." She gestured with her chin at Margaret's legs. "I don't know why you bother with that."

"I don't either," Margaret muttered, head down as she blew on her legs. "Takes too bloody long to dry." Then she looked up, her eyes fixed on her friend. "It doesn't have to be this way," she said, and Rose knew they were no longer talking about the gravy on her legs.

"I need to work. You know that." Rose flushed, and focused her attention on smoothing out the thin coverlet on her bed. Their beds sat side by side, with a thin gully of space in between. There wasn't much else; a chest of drawers pushed up against the wall near Rose's bed, a crate beneath the only window where Margaret kept her schoolbooks.

"I know. It's just that you're so smart," Margaret said, and touched Rose's shoulder. "It's not my business, but I wish you had a job where you could use your smarts."

Rose pulled back. Margaret was right; it wasn't her business.

Rose was being churlish, she knew. Margaret was only trying to help. "It's only temporary. And there are loads of smart girls on the floor with me," she said. Rose was taking care of herself. When Mutti and Papi arrived, they would need as much money as she could offer. But she knew it wasn't so simple; she wasn't proud to don those overalls every day and stitch together pieces of silk for hours at a time. She feared Mutti's disapprobation when she learned that her daughter worked in a factory. *But you have to understand,* Rose wanted to tell Mutti and Margaret both. She was doing what she could. Of course she was capable of more.

"I know," Margaret said. "I know it's temporary. But I was thinking: What about asking the Cohens again?" She took a thick pencil from atop the shared bureau and sat next to Rose. "Just think: if they relented, you could work part-time, make money, and go to school."

It frustrated Rose to hear Margaret articulate this scenario, as if anything were that simple to attain. She couldn't ask the Cohens. They did not owe her. Rose glanced at the mushroom-colored window curtain that looked like it could fall down at any moment. The room was too small, Margaret, with all her good intentions, too close. "But they're not relenting," she said. "And I won't ask them again."

"They care so much about you, Rose. I know you don't always feel it, but they do." Margaret leaned in. "I know they told you they would only help with nursing. But if you went up for a visit, and truly explained to Mr. Cohen, I don't believe he wouldn't help. It's worth a try."

Rose shook her head. "I can't," she said. Mrs. Cohen had been emphatic. Nursing was a practical profession, a noble one. And if she didn't want to do that? Well, when she was eighteen she was expected to join the ATS. "You should be grateful," Mrs. Cohen had said. "This is the best way to pay back your country."

"All right," Margaret said. "It was only a suggestion." Rose could tell she wanted to say more, but Margaret took the pencil and began drawing a thin dark line from the back of her left ankle up her calf, imitating the seams of the stockings that neither of them could afford.

Perhaps Margaret was right. Perhaps Mr. Cohen would acquiesce. Every month, she got an envelope from him with two crinkled pound notes inside—not that much more than he used to give her as pocket money when she was twelve. And yet, every month the envelope arrived. "For Rose," he wrote in his spidery handwriting, nothing else. That card never failed to deliver a pang. She kept Mr. Cohen's money in a separate envelope and used it to buy small purchases, one more unnecessary than the next—black currants that she spotted in October in a shop in Notting Hill, a slim leather volume of Hopkins's poetry, a tin of marzipan from Selfridges that she ate furtively, not sharing with Margaret, the almond taste taking her back to her family's flat on Liechtensteinstrasse.

"Thank you for suggesting it," Rose said as politely and with as much dignity as she could muster. "But you have to understand, it's different for me." Besides, she couldn't change course, not now. How could she make any decisions until she heard from them?

ONE THURSDAY IN LATE NOVEMBER, nearing clock-out time, a white-coated inspector stopped in front of Sylvia, a small, serious girl from Prague who sat next to Rose and was deft with the massive spools of thread. It was then that Rose realized Sylvia had stopped working. "That's the second needle you've broken this week, Miss Strauss," the inspector said. "It's coming out of your wages."

Sylvia nodded. "It won't happen again, sir."

He strode off, and Rose leaned over. "You all right?"

Sylvia nodded, turning back to her buzzing machine with renewed intent.

"She cut her finger the other day," said Mrs. Lloyd, Rose's other neighbor. "It's swollen up to something awful. It's got septic." Mrs. Lloyd's husband, as she often reminded them, had been a pharmacist before the war.

Rose glanced back at Sylvia and saw that she kept her small left hand in her lap. "She has to go to hospital. She shouldn't be here," Rose said. "Come, Sylvia; let me see." But Sylvia didn't move.

"Infection or no, she's relying on this week's wages," Mrs. Lloyd said. "She's not going anywhere."

"I got back my letter," Sylvia said. She did not look at Rose as she spoke. "It says they were deported."

"Which letter?" Rose asked, but she knew.

"My parents. It came back. On the back it says 'deported to Auschwitz.' And there is a date, the tenth of November 1944."

Rose nodded dumbly. She had never spoken to Sylvia about her parents. They hadn't talked about their families at all. Rose realized she held a hand over her mouth. It felt essential to do so, to keep all that was loose inside of her contained.

"But there are so many people in those DP camps," Sylvia said, "They couldn't have registered them all yet."

"That is right, that is absolutely right," Rose said with a conviction that she did not feel.

IT WAS COLD BY THE time Rose made it to the flat on Catton Street that night. The two sweaters she wore under her overcoat did little to keep out the bitterness. Daylight was long gone, though it was a clear night, the half-moon just clearing the tops of the worn brick apartment buildings across the road. Soon it would be December, the first holiday season after the war.

She was rummaging for her key when she registered an officer in uniform, standing past the laundry on the corner, smoking against the peeling trunk of the plane tree. She paid him little mind. Then she heard: "Why, *mausi*. You're not going to say hello?"

She screamed.

AFTER SIX MONTHS STATIONED IN Minden, Germany, Gerhard had been granted a leave. He had five days in London, and he had just dropped off his bags with Charles, the brother from the family he had lived with up north. "I came straight here," he told her as she led him up the three dank flights to the flat, put the kettle on in the kitchen nook, and pulled down the tin of biscuits that she thankfully had not finished.

"You should have written—or called. But am I happy to see you," she said. "Would you like biscuits? Or, I have a tin of corned beef somewhere. I could fix you a sandwich. Or an egg? Margaret has an egg and I'm sure she won't mind us using it on this fine occasion. Or what am I thinking? Perhaps you want to shower?"

"*Mausi*, stop. Would you, please? I'm fine." He said it with such recognizable, familiar brotherly annoyance that it made her want to nail him to the spot, never let him go.

She squeezed his arm, moved to pour the kettle. Had his eyes always been that vivid shade of blue? They were the same color as the birds on Mutti's scarf.

"I'm a lieutenant now," he said with a wry little grin.

"A lieutenant? That's wonderful. You must be important." Rose handed him a cup.

"Not really. They need translators."

"Really? And how is your German?" Rose asked in English. They always spoke in English now. Papi was going to be appalled by how little she remembered, her vocabulary stuck back in grammar school.

"*In Ordnung*," he said. *Okay*. That she remembered. "They are desperate to get things in order," he said. They were perched side by side at the foot of her bed, balancing cups on their knees. "Little chance of that happening anytime soon. It's a mess over there. Bloody Jerries. They deserve every last bit of horror that comes their way." He sipped his tea, took another mouthful of the biscuit with evident pleasure. "These are delicious."

"They're stale," Rose said. "Now I know how they treat you." She took a sip of her own tea. It was tepid, and she suspected it had never been warm. "Have you found out anything new? Everything is so slow here—I haven't been able to learn anything." She stirred her tea as she said this, her eyes fixed on the metal spoon, the way it looked bent beneath the surface of the hot liquid, another trick of the eye. If she couldn't find Mutti and Papi, maybe she could find someone who knew what had happened. She had started looking for the Fleishmans, the family that had lived with her parents for a time after she and Gerhard had left. She had tried to find Bette too, had written to the last address she had for her in Munich, but nothing. "I know what you said in your letters, but you've found nothing on Mutti and Papi since then?"

Gerhard shook his head. "There's another Jewish lieutenant originally from Freiberg, and we have a system set up to check the DP lists—nothing." He looked at her steadily. "But I was in Vienna."

She was sure she hadn't heard him right. Vienna? Their city? "When?" she finally made out.

He lit a cigarette. "About two, nearly three weeks ago. We had been told that we would be interviewing officials." Without asking, he lit another and handed it to her. She took it gratefully, and brought over Margaret's ashtray from the windowsill. "You know, men real close to the top. They needed a team of us, they said. I was boiling over for it, gunning for it—but it wasn't at all like I thought. They were just small-timers. One was a mayor of a small village called Fiestel, and yessed me about everything—'Did you know the butcher, a Jewish man called Weiss? Did you work with so-so, who was a Nazi official?' Yes, yes, yes, he said. It turned out that he had a sick wife. He would have agreed to anything to get back home to her." Gerhard paused. "I hated him for that too."

Rose was listening, she was trying to understand, but she didn't think she did. What did a Nazi's sick wife have to do with anything? She sucked in smoke. "What did the apartment look like? Is it all right? Did you go inside?"

"I didn't go to the apartment."

"You didn't go to the house?"

"I was there for so little time, and working for all of it. We were quartered outside of town. You don't understand; it was so strange, being there, like this"—he gestured down to his uniform—"with all the other men. It didn't feel like a city I knew, let alone where I grew up."

"But it would have been different if you had gone to our street," Rose said, as if she could still convince him to change course. How could he be there and not go? What if their parents had been there? What if someone had talked to them?

Gerhard was shaking his head. He jammed the tip of his cigarette into the ashtray. "You don't know what it was like," he said. "It is not the same. It's just another bombed-out city."

"That can't be true."

"It is. The opera house burned down. The Burgtheater too, and the roof on St. Stephen's Cathedral collapsed—damaged by a fire that had been lit by looters, Austrians"—he shook his head—"not our men. It is not the same place. That city is gone."

"But Mutti and Papi," Rose willed herself to say, battling the terrible emptiness inside. "They could go back there, somehow."

"No, Rose." He stubbed out his cigarette. "I don't think so."

"You don't know. You can't be sure." She could barely get the words out, her throat so tight, the pressure behind her eyes spiky hot.

"I do," Gerhard said with roughness. "I'm afraid that I am. In Minden, where we're stationed, the town was destroyed—the town hall, the cathedral, all bombed. But people are coming back. One day, we were handing out blankets, and I met these boys, Jewish boys, two brothers, Samuel and Martin, and a friend of theirs, Oskar. They had been in Birkenau together, and they came back because Oskar's father had owned a house outside of Minden—there had been Jews there since the thirteenth century. They didn't know where else to go—"

"You see," Rose said, "that's what I mean. *Of course* they went back to where they're from; that's what people do—"

He put his hand on hers. "Would you let me finish, please? God, you are like Mutti. Always have to have it your way."

The mention of their mother, the pressure of his hand, stunned Rose into silence.

"I'm telling you, the way they looked, the stories they told . . ." Gerhard's voice trailed off. "They're not coming back," he finally said.

"You don't know that," she cried. All she wanted was for him to be wrong. "You don't know that at all."

"I didn't want to know it. I never wanted to know anything like this. But I do," he said, shaking his head. "They're not coming back, Rose." He stood, walking his cup to the tiny sink, twisting on the water.

"Gerhard, please," she said, and she grabbed his arm to stop him. Washing up? *Now?*

He pulled her into a hug. "*Mausi*, we're here. We're still here," he kept saying into her hair.

THAT NIGHT, SHE WALKED. SHE walked away from Holborn and her room on Catton Street, away from Soho, where she knew Margaret was meeting friends, and Clerkenwell, where Gerhard was staying with Charles. She walked as if she had a purpose, as if she knew where she was heading.

She didn't bother putting on a jumper beneath her overcoat. Where was she supposed to go? Tonight, next week? Next month? It was unimaginable, the future.

She ended up at the Embankment, at the foot of the Waterloo. The bridge had taken a hit early on in the war, and over the last few years it had been rebuilt—she'd heard that so many women worked on it that it was called the Ladies' Bridge. Here was yet something else that had been devastated and was rising again, and she hated the bridge as surely as if it had stolen something from her.

She took the steps up. She began walking across. The Thames was a carpet of black. Out in the open, the cold rose. The air whipped across her cheeks, her fingertips grew prickly. Lights necklaced the river; there was Westminister aglow, and St. Paul's beyond.

Rose looked away from the vast city lights and down toward the water. It coursed fast, dark silvery movement that she could sense more than see. She felt a thrumming inside of her. Her hands gripped the icy railing.

Her parents were dead. She knew this to be true. But how could there be no evidence? How could she possibly live in a world where there was no proof? And if no one knew about them, what would happen to her? Her life here in England wasn't meant to last. It wasn't meant to be permanent. What would she do now?

Her head felt too heavy for her body, and she wanted to rid herself of this weight, this awful heaviness. Why was it better that she had survived? Rose thought of the soldier from VE night, the way he had touched her, as if she were his for the taking. She wished he had. She wished he had done every unseemly thing he had wanted. Her tears stung her raw cheeks and she thought, no, no, she didn't want him to touch her at all, she didn't want anyone to ever touch her again, she couldn't help her parents, they were dead, she knew that Gerhard was right, but he was so wrong. She and Gerhard didn't deserve to be here. How could they be here, with bodies to enjoy and lives to live?

The water glittered and beckoned, strangely inviting on this brutal night, and even the thought of falling seemed tempting—tumbling, erasure, blackness. But Rose's hands remained curled on the cold railing. She knew she could never do such a thing, even though she hated herself for it. Why did she deserve to live? she asked herself as she walked off the bridge, steadily, quietly, alone.

"YOU'RE ILL," MARGARET CLUCKED AT her the next morning. "You stayed out too late," and Rose did not disagree. Margaret kept the kettle on. Margaret made her cup after cup, and they listened to *It's That Man Again* on the BBC. By the afternoon, Rose was feeling, if not better, then at least more like herself. She got dressed. Gerhard had called on the shared telephone line and asked to meet her for supper at the White Tower in Fitzrovia. It was his last night before the army would claim him again. And who was she to say no?

"The White Tower, it's supposed to be one of the best restaurants around," Margaret said as she helped her get ready, crimping her hair, applying beetroot juice on her lips for color.

"You look quite becoming," Margaret said. Rose considered the phrase. She was nearly eighteen. What was she becoming?

BY THE TIME ROSE REACHED the end of Charlotte Street and hurried inside the White Tower, unspooling her scarf, it took her a beat or two to spot her brother, though the restaurant, with its green walls and red-beaded lampshades, was less than half full. Gerhard was seated with a woman that Rose did not know, a young fair-headed beautiful woman.

"Hello," Rose said, and Gerhard popped up out of his chair, nearly knocked it over.

"Oh, hello!" he said with nervous energy, as if her presence were a surprise. He reached for her, stuck out his hand, laughed again, and clasped her shoulders in an awkward hug. "So nice to see you!"

Rose stared. Why hadn't he told her? Why was he acting so strangely?

"May I introduce you to Isobel. Isobel, this is my sister, Rose." Rose could have sworn Gerhard blushed while saying it.

"Rose," Isobel said, extending a slender hand. "It is ever so nice to meet you. I've heard so much about you."

Rose nodded dumbly. Isobel wore a dark wool skirt and a pink sweater with black silk trim. Her shoulder-length hair was tousled but shiny, a slight messiness that managed to signal expense.

"Do you love Greek food?" Isobel said as they took their seats. "I adore it. Absolutely adore it. We both do." She turned significantly to Gerhard.

"I've never had it before," Rose said truthfully, looking at her brother. *He liked Greek food?*

"Moussaka, that's what you must have," Isobel said. "You simply must."

Rose nodded. Whatever moussaka was, she would have it. The portraits of mustached soldiers, staring grimly down at her from the walls, were no match for the force of Isobel's words.

Isobel said she had grown up in Yorkshire, but didn't speak as if she were from the north. She was an only daughter after a trio of boys. "Even my father—or especially my father—was relieved when I was born." She asked Rose about her flat and Margaret, living in London. She didn't bring up the factory. She smiled easily. She touched Gerhard's hand often.

Rose asked: "How long have you two known each other?"

"About a year," Gerhard said.

"More than a year," Isobel said with unmistakable pride. "Sixteen months, nearly a year and a half."

"I see," Rose said as she forked off some of her dish. Was that aubergine? It was too soggy to identify, too laden in sauce. "Most of the time while Gerhard was away?"

"Yes," Isobel said quickly. "I'm so proud of him. My officer." She laughed, as if she had made a joke.

Rose continued to pick at her dish, saying nothing.

"Gerhard says that you live in Holborn," Isobel said. "How do you like it?"

Rose shrugged. "It's all right."

"She and Margaret are wonderful roommates together," Gerhard said. "I wouldn't be surprised if they lived together for years to come."

"Well, there's a lovely thought," Rose said, shaking her head at Gerhard.

"One of my brothers lived in Holborn for a time. On Macklin. I quite liked it. It has its charms."

"Yes," Rose said. "I suppose it does." She wound a strand of cheese on her fork, drew it through a puddle of tomato sauce.

"If you'll excuse me for a moment," Isobel said, and pushed back her chair. Gerhard jumped up to help her.

As Isobel walked away, Gerhard leaned down to Rose and whispered: "Why are you being so curt with her? Would it kill you to be kind?"

"You could have told me she was coming," Rose said, her eyes remaining on Isobel, watching her navigate between tables to the back of the restaurant.

"I'm sorry," Gerhard was saying. "I was nervous." And that's when Rose realized: Isobel was wearing real stockings. They were perfect, the seams beautifully straight, not a darn in sight. When she saw the real thing, it made her despair. What was the point in trying to imitate them? She could never come close.

"How does she have money for real stockings?" Rose asked.

"What?" Gerhard shrugged uneasily as he sat back down. "She's wearing real stockings?"

Rose shook her head, exasperated. Of course he hadn't noticed. And that's when she understood that Isobel came from significant money, and it was nothing Gerhard would talk about it.

"Who cares about her stockings?" he continued. "She's a wonderful person. You have to give her a chance. Please." He said this with un-Gerhard-like eagerness. "I really like her."

"You never mentioned her before. Not yesterday, not in any of your letters. Why didn't you tell me about her?" How could he like Isobel so much and not tell her? Did he have any idea how alone she felt? How could he not feel the same way?

"I don't know," Gerhard said, and his face grew serious. "I'm sorry for that. I should have." He turned to his plate, chased down the last morsel of moussaka. Only a reddened stain remained. He had polished off his entire plate while Rose hadn't noticed. "It makes me nervous, I suppose. We are very serious. I feel—well, I want to marry her. I'm going to. You'll like her too, you'll see. She's unlike anyone else. And I want to start my life. I'm ready."

Marriage? Now? Already? Gerhard deserved happiness, of course, but all Rose could think was: *Your life? You want to start your life? How do you feel like you have a life? Mutti and Papi—*

But no. There was no finishing the thought.

The beads on the red lampshades shook and shimmered, throwing off dapple and shadow. "I am happy for you," Rose whispered.

7

LOS ANGELES, 2006

ALL ALONE, IN A COUNTRY that wasn't hers. Lizzie was thinking about Rose as she and Max finished dinner on his small brick patio that overlooked the canal. The darkening sky still bore traces of violet, the air turning rapidly from cool to cold. Lizzie always forgot this about L.A., how swiftly temperatures could drop, how quickly conditions could change.

"Do you know the name of the investigator that my dad hired after the paintings were stolen?" Lizzie asked Max as they cleared the table. He carried the plates and platters, she had the glasses.

"No," Max said, and he held the door open for her. "I didn't know he hired one. Why?"

"Rose Downes asked me."

"Ah." Max took the wineglasses from her, heading toward the sink.

"I was going to do those," Lizzie said.

"I've got it." Max said this easily enough, but he made it clear: he would wash them. It was only in the last day or two that she had come to realize that his solicitousness masked a more exacting part of his personality. She watched him wash the delicate glass under the faucet's stream. He did this deftly. She would have taken more time. She knew she could be clumsy. But also: the glasses weren't hers.

"Did you check your father's papers?" he asked.

"No," Lizzie said. "I need to." The thought made her tired. She and Sarah had taken a storage unit after all, moved Joseph's papers there along with some things that Lizzie wanted to ship back to New York eventually—from the intricately carved Chinese set of drawers that she'd always loved and her childhood books (*All-of-a-Kind Family* and *Summer of My German Soldier* and the Trixie Belden mysteries) to her father's medical textbooks and the framed 1930s photograph of the boxer Barney Ross that had hung in the hall outside her father's room for as long as she could remember.

"We should have Rose over for dinner."

"What?" Lizzie said, taken aback. She had heard him. But they hadn't gone out with anyone yet, not Sarah, not Claudia.

"We should have Rose over for dinner," he repeated with a self-effacing smile. "You're spending a lot of time with her; I thought it would be nice."

"It would be," she said, surprised, pleased. She and Ben used to have the dumbest arguments about their friends: he thought Claudia self-involved and dramatic; she found his best friend to be loud and shockingly confident, given the banal things he had to say.

"As far as I'm concerned, the more friends you have out here in L.A., the better," Max said.

Lizzie bit her top lip, less from nerves and more to keep herself from smiling too broadly.

LIZZIE COULD GET USED TO this life. She arrived at the Dish before Claudia, took a spot on a stool at the U-shaped counter. A compact man with smoothed-back graying hair and a trim mustache manned the grill. He nodded at her. "Hickory, no cheese, cream soda," he said gruffly.

"Yes, please. But wait on the burger. My friend should be here any minute." Lizzie loved this place, with its old-fashioned counter and wood-paneled walls. She'd been coming here since she was a kid, continued to stop in whenever she was in town. She loved the charred smells and scraps of conversation and the sputtering sound of fat on the grill. The screen door banged open and shut, customers coming and going.

The grill man nodded again, slid a soda can and a full cup of ice toward her. "Haven't seen you in a while."

"Busy," she only said. He had worked the grill since she was in high school. She was fairly certain he thought she still lived in L.A. She had no desire to correct him.

"You." She heard Claudia's voice behind her.

"Hello, you," Lizzie said, twisting around, kissing her friend. Claudia was wearing a short leather jacket that Lizzie had never seen before and a shirt patterned with tiny roses, looking stylish as usual.

"Hickory, cheese, fries," the grill man said to her in greeting.

"Actually, grilled cheese and fries," Claudia said. "And a slice of banana cream. Thanks."

"Grilled cheese and pie?" Lizzie asked, looking at Claudia. Was it the shirt or were her breasts fuller too? "Is there something you have to tell me?"

Claudia shook her head, her face tightening. "Nope. Got my period yesterday."

"Oh, Claude." Lizzie gave her friend's hand a squeeze. "I'm sorry."

"Yeah, well," Claudia said. "I'm having terrible cramps, and I think the Clomid is making them worse. Pie is the only remedy."

"It will happen, I'm sure it will." Claudia and her husband had been trying for several months now.

"I'm not so sure anymore," Claudia said. "But I'm still trying."

Soon the grill man slid a burger and a grilled cheese nestled in wax paper toward them, a mound of fries on a separate paper plate. "Okay?" he said. They nodded back. The ceiling fans clicked and whirled overhead.

"What's going on with you?" Claudia asked.

"Me? I have turned into a lady who lunches."

"A lady who lunches on burgers and fries," Claudia clarified, biting into her grilled cheese.

"I only meant it's strange, not working. I feel like I'm skipping out on something."

"It's good for you to relax."

"I'm not relaxing."

"My point exactly," Claudia said, her mouth full. "How's Max?"

"Oh," Lizzie said, dragging a french fry through a puddle of ketchup. She felt a smile unbidden, forming on her lips. "He's good." She still couldn't quite believe it. "He's really good."

"Well," Claudia said. "That is good." The grill guy delivered her pie. She pulled it closer to her, forked off a dollop of cream. "Want some?"

Lizzie shook her head. "I'm not a fan," she said. Her father had loved the banana cream. She remembered the first time she'd come here, during that initial year they lived in L.A. She and Joseph had ordered burgers; Sarah, nearly eleven years old then, had announced that she was a vegetarian. She was unhappy with the menu options. Finally she ordered the grilled cheese.

When it showed up, Sarah took a tiny bite, made a face, and then pulled at the hardened cheese along the crust. "It tastes funny," she'd muttered unhappily to Lizzie, who was polishing off her burger.

"Just try to eat some," Lizzie whispered back. Sarah's pickiness had gotten worse after their mother died. "Here," she said, reaching to tear off a bite for herself. "I think it's good." She tried to say it encouragingly, but Sarah shook her head.

"What's wrong?" Joseph said.

"Nothing," Lizzie said.

"I'm asking Sarah," their father said. "Sarah?"

"I don't like the cheese," Sarah said. "It's too cheesy."

"The cheese is too cheesy?" Joseph repeated. "But it's grilled cheese. That's what it is."

"I'm sorry, Daddy," Sarah said, faltering.

Lizzie turned to her father and tried to catch his eye. So she didn't like it. Couldn't he be nicer about it? Their mother would have been. Sarah was close to tears.

"Fine," he said, but it was clear he didn't mean it, and no one spoke while Lizzie finished her burger and Joseph did too.

"What do you want for dessert?" he asked Lizzie.

"What about Sarah?" Lizzie said.

"She can have dessert when she finishes her sandwich."

"But she's not going to finish it," Lizzie insisted as her sister hung her head.

"It's dessert," Joseph said. "It is not a God-given right."

"That is really mean," Lizzie said. Why couldn't he make Sarah feel better? She was trying. It was just a stupid sandwich.

Joseph ordered a slice of banana cream. "When you're a parent, you'll make the decisions," he said. Infuriated, Lizzie pulled her straw out of its paper encasing, and folded and crinkled the wrapper to make it as small as possible. Her father had no idea what to do with them. Lizzie could probably make better decisions than him. She sucked up droplets of water in her straw, dropped them on the crinkled-up wrapper, and watched it spasm and elongate; for a brief hapless moment, it seemed alive.

"What do you know about being a parent?" Lizzie said.

"What?"

"You know what I mean; you left."

Joseph let out a strange sputter of a laugh. "Do not test me. Do you understand?"

"Yes," she muttered. She shouldn't have said it, but she was not sorry. Her anger had been hardening for months now, ever since she arrived. How much longer could they dance around what they all knew to be true? She and Sarah didn't want to be here, and Joseph wanted them even less.

"Can we please go?" Sarah implored, her eyes enormous, glassy with tears. "Please." She tugged on her sister's sleeve. She sounded younger than her ten years.

Joseph swung back toward the counter. "No," he said. "Not yet. I am finishing my dessert." He bent over his plate.

She despised him, she really did, she couldn't imagine that her mother had ever loved him. Divorcing him had been the smartest thing she ever did. Lizzie had been young but not stupid. Her father working late, never around. Maybe it had been that part-time bookkeeper at his office, maybe it had been someone he knew in the city, but he'd had an affair with *someone*. She had distinct memories of her mother from that time, always whispering on the phone, pulling the curled telephone cord taut, behind closed doors. She must have known too.

"If you two want dessert, you can have it," Joseph muttered. "Sarah, a milk shake?"

"Yeah," Sarah said tentatively, the beginnings of a smile forming on her teary face. "Chocolate, please."

"Good," he said, grinning. "A milk shake's got milk. Lizzie?"

She shook her head. "No thank you," she said clearly, seething. So he had changed his mind; now he was a hypocrite who couldn't stand by his convictions. She wanted to hate him. She had to.

"You're missing out," he said tightly. "It really is delicious." And he'd polished off the pie, hadn't left a crumb behind.

"HOW GOOD IS GOOD?" CLAUDIA was saying.

"What? What's good?" Lizzie echoed. It must have been so hard for her father back then. She had only made it harder.

"How good is Max? Maybe stay-in-L.A. good?"

Lizzie smiled sadly. "I don't know."

"Why not?"

"What do you mean? You know: my whole life is in New York." She said this as much for herself as for Claudia. "And this thing with Max—it's only been two weeks."

"So? I knew I would marry Ian the first night we got together."

"That's you. I'm not like that. You know I'm not."

"Okay," Claudia said. "But why wouldn't it work?"

"Oh, come on, there are so many reasons."

Claudia folded her arms across her chest. "Name them."

"Okay, it's not just that he's so much older." Eighteen years, to be exact. Permutations of that number kept running in her head. In five years, he would be sixty. Would she still be attracted to him in a few months, let alone a few years? And that was the superficial side of the equation. No one stayed healthy forever.

"Irrelevant," Claudia was saying.

"Not irrelevant—"

"Okay, but definitely not a deal breaker."

"Okay," Lizzie said. She knew the principal cause for her reluctance, the reason she felt she could not trust herself. Would they be together if she and Max weren't both grieving for her father? Wasn't it an unseemly way to mourn? "He was my dad's best friend," Lizzie said.

"Also not a deal breaker," Claudia said.

"Come on. It's weird," Lizzie said. When would she stop being embarrassed about it?

Claudia shrugged. "I can think of weirder."

"Of course *you* can." She took up the last of the fries. "And you know I want to have kids." It was hard for her to admit, even to Claudia, this elemental desire.

"And do you know that he doesn't? Do you like him? Do you?"

"Yeah," Lizzie said. For all of her caveats and concerns, she *knew*. "Fuck, I really do."

"You should embrace it. For once, you should embrace something. Take it. The Cossacks aren't chasing you."

"That," Lizzie said, "is exactly what I was worried about here on the Westside."

ON WEDNESDAY NIGHT, MAX BROUGHT home a gift for Lizzie, a gorgeous wrap dress in an eye-popping pattern of greens and blacks. "I saw it in the window of a shop on Abbott Kinney, and I thought it would look great on you."

"Wow," Lizzie said. "It's beautiful. Thank you." No man had ever bought her clothing before. When Ben considered her gifts, he often brought her by the store to get her approval beforehand. At the time she said she liked the practicality of it. But this gave her a rush, imagining Max walk into a boutique and imagining her size, picturing her body in the dress.

She tried it on. "It fits perfectly. I knew it would," he said from the edge of the bed. He gestured for her to come to him. Soon he was running his hands along her back. "I thought you could use some new things. You have so few clothes here."

"That I definitely could," she said, leaning in to kiss him. Her wardrobe these days consisted of the few things she had brought with her on what she thought was going to be a quick trip—her good jeans and old boots, a demure A-line skirt that she usually wore to work, packed expressly to wear to the initial meeting she and Sarah had with Max (nearly two weeks ago, she thought with amazement), a couple of tops, a pair of running shorts, along with a few things of her father's—an old Dodger-blue T-shirt that she liked to sleep in, a thin rust-colored V-neck she was convinced he wore the last time he'd visited her in New York. She liked to think that the speckle of discoloration below the V was the result of the grease from their La Caridad meal. "It's funny, but I don't miss my stuff," she said. "Do you ever feel that way, that it's a relief not to be surrounded by your possessions?"

"No." Max gave her a bewildered smile. "I don't."

"Of course not," she said. "Everything here is gorgeous." Even incidental objects in his house—the cloth napkins he used at nearly every meal—seemed uncommonly lovely.

"What's wrong with having nice things?" He said it mock-serious, but there was a touch of defensiveness to his voice that reminded her of her father. When Joseph had first seen her walk-up apartment on 105th Street, he had been appalled and pushed a plan to buy a place in Midtown. An investment, he had said, a two-bedroom, "one bedroom for you and a guest room—I could stay there when I visit. In a doorman building, with an elevator." But she wasn't interested. "I like being close to school," she said, already feeling hemmed in by the prospect of such an arrangement. Joseph let it go, but not before telling Lizzie: *There's nothing shameful in living somewhere nice.*

"I love your things," Lizzie said now as she was thinking: *Max is different.* "I wish I had an eye like you do. I have a hard time spending money on things—well, some things," she qualified, thinking of the $700 Isabel Marant leather skirt she'd bought (on sale!) just before her father died. She had more than enough money. She had gotten used to the numbers on her pay stub. But she still lived like she was in law school, socking the lion's share of her money away. Who knew when she might need it? Who knew when it might all vanish? This thought ballooned, filling her with a queasy sense of unease. "It's just—everything costs."

"Well, of course. But not everything is expensive."

Once again, she heard Joseph in her head. He used to say at the Dish: *If I could have a hickory burger every day, I'd be happy.*

"And I like wanting things," Max was saying as he touched her wrist lightly, the dress's silky sleeve. "I don't believe we're that different."

"You haven't seen my apartment." She made a face, a preemptive gesture, designed to ward off disappointment. She found it hard to think of Max in her apartment, sitting on her IKEA couch, scrounging for paper napkins after they ordered in from Saigon Grill.

"I would love to see it," he said. "But it's hard for me to imagine it, when all I can think of is how fantastic you look in that dress."

Lizzie raised her eyebrows, shook her head. She'd never been good with a compliment. When she was younger, she could remember her grandmother gazing at Sarah, her huge eyes, her enviably straight hair. "That one is such a stunner," her grandmother said to Lynn. Then she saw Lizzie watching. "You'll be pretty too when you grow up," she said, patting her arm.

Max traced Lizzie's jaw with a solemn expression etched on his well-lined face. "You're so beautiful, you know that? It breaks my heart, a little."

"Now, why would that be?" He was being earnest, she could tell, and it made her nervous.

But his seriousness would not be deterred. "I dread the thought of you leaving. You have to know that." He pulled her hands down, gripped them tight, a look of urgency in his eyes.

"Max," she murmured.

He was still pressing her hands against his. "You could move in tomorrow, permanently."

Her stomach coiled up, a contortionist's trick. Did he mean it? He couldn't mean it. "No joking about that," she said, and now she was the one being serious.

"I'm not."

She pushed him back on the bed. She could hear Claudia in her head: *Here it is, yours for the taking.* Her arms up around his neck, fingers inching up the base of his skull; she delighted in the stubbly feel of his shaved head. *I want this,* she thought as she climbed atop him, hiking up the dress, straddling his hips.

"Come meet me for lunch tomorrow; wear this and nothing under," he commanded, his hands tunneling beneath the silky material.

"Tomorrow? I can't," she said, but she was already working her underwear down one leg, following at least part of his instructions.

SHE AND ROSE HAD PLANS to go to the Huntington. The library's immense grounds were glorious, and here in the late-morning sun, miles inland from the foggy shroud of the ocean, everything popped: the faraway red pointy roofs of the Chinese garden's pavilions, the white dogwoods and the bright coral trees blooming with such confidence. Even the craggy snowcapped San Gabriel Mountains looked purple-hued in the distance.

Rose took charge at the entrance desk, showing her driver's license for the senior discount and taking a while to fish out a card for one free admission from her bag. ("I can pay for us," Lizzie had said. But Rose insisted: "It's the principle of the matter.")

"Come. Let's go to the herb garden," Rose said. "Sometimes, with all these sights, it's smells I like to immerse myself in."

The herb garden held little appeal for Lizzie, but Rose was asking—or rather, instructing—and Lizzie was glad to comply. She had a poor sense of smell (*nonexistent,* Ben used to tease her, after he once again fished out moldering cheese from their fridge). She came from a long line of nonsmellers. She could even remember her mother saying, *Consider yourself lucky. It only changed for me when I was pregnant with you and your sister.*

Rose and Lizzie stepped around a gaggle of schoolchildren, two teachers facing a losing battle trying to quiet them. The garden was nearly empty save for a pale thin man being pushed in a wheelchair by a bored-looking attendant. "You know, the woman responsible for much of this estate, Huntington's second wife, was also his aunt, the widow of his uncle," Rose said.

"Is that legal?" Lizzie said, putting her nose to a woolly mint plant. HOREHOUND, a small sign said.

"Biblical, perhaps. And prudent, actually. Think about it: it cuts down on alliances. Your entire estate would stay within the family."

"That's because you wouldn't *have* any new family," Lizzie said. "That can't be good for the genetic pool. Were you and Thomas secretly second cousins or something?" she added teasingly.

"Ah, no; nothing even nominally salacious, I'm afraid. Thomas and I were nothing alike, in terms of our background, our families, our constitution. People always thought that because he was an engineer, he was the practical one, but he was a dreamer and a romantic, and a far far better person than I." She said these last words plainly.

"Come on, I doubt that," Lizzie said. "How many years were you married?"

"Fifty-one, nearly fifty-two."

"A half a century of breakfasts with the same person, a half a century of dinners together," Lizzie said. The monotony sounded appealing.

"Well, sometimes we let each other out for good behavior," Rose said dryly. "But yes, mostly."

"It's amazing that you were together that long," Lizzie said as they rounded a corner. She detected basil—even she could identify the clean, foresty smell.

"Well, you're young yet; I'm sure you'll meet someone. But it *is* luck. I turned Thomas down twice, you know."

"You did?"

"I did," she said slyly, with a gleam in her dark eyes.

"Why? Because you weren't sure?" Lizzie wanted to know. "Because he wasn't Jewish?"

"Not Jewish?" Now Rose looked annoyed. "I didn't care about that. No. I was very young. I had just learned about my parents. And marrying, believing in the future—it didn't feel right."

Rose couldn't have been much older than a child herself when she found out that her parents had been killed. Lizzie's mother's death had detonated her, twenty-five years ago, and Lizzie felt so unmoored now, as a fully formed adult nearly forty, with both parents gone. It was unimaginable to think of what it must have been like for Rose to have lost her parents, her home, her country, forced to take care of herself when she was not yet twenty.

Lizzie could hear the schoolchildren in the distance, shouts and giggles and teacherly admonishments. Rose was looking at a low bed of herbs. TUSSIE-WUSSIES, a sign explained, *small handheld bouquets of scented flowers and herbs that have special meaning for the recipients;* delicate purple borage meant *bluntness,* while the tiny white flowers of sweet alyssum signified *worth beyond beauty.*

"I remember hearing about tussie-wussies from Mrs. Cohen," Rose said, and her voice had regained its cool tones. "They're a romantic Victorian tradition." She stretched out the first syllable of *romantic* with significant arch.

"Mrs. Cohen?" Lizzie ventured.

"The wife in the house I lived in."

"Oh," Lizzie said. Rose had never mentioned where she had lived in England. "Well, they do sound romantic. A bouquet that tells a story."

"That's what she used to say. It's from the Victorians, and the Victorians had manners, they knew how to live. She was quite an old-fashioned lady, I suppose. But if you ask me, people should say what they mean."

Then you'd lose out on a whole lot of intrigue, Lizzie was half tempted to say, but the man in the wheelchair was slumped over, chin at his chest, the attendant pushing his chair talking on her cell, Lizzie didn't feel like joking. "What happened to Mrs. Cohen, the family you lived with?" she asked.

"The Cohens?" Rose looked at Lizzie with surprise, as if she had conjured them out of nowhere. "They're both long gone. Mr. Cohen died of cancer in the fifties, not long after I moved here, and Mrs. Cohen passed away a few years later. They never had children. They were good to me, Mr. Cohen in particular."

"I'm glad to hear that," Lizzie said, and she truly was. It wasn't hard to imagine a horrible story, with many an ugly permutation. Lizzie had read about a pair of *Kindertransport* siblings who were forced to work as servants in England. They never wrote to their parents to tell them for fear of upsetting them. And what recourse would the parents have had, from so far away?

"He was kind to me, even after I left Leeds. I wish I had been more grateful," Rose said. "When I lived in London, he used to come into town for work, and I—well, I rarely saw him." She paused. "Can you smell that? Lavender, I think."

Lizzie nodded, though she didn't detect it herself. She wanted to hear more about Rose and London and Mr. Cohen, but she didn't dare ask.

Rose straightened. "I wish I had been more generous toward him," she said. "But it wasn't a time in my life where gratitude or kindness came naturally."

"I understand that," Lizzie said. She was in her father's house, a kid again, ignoring Joseph, staring at *The Bellhop*, thinking, *How did I get here?*

"I know you do," Rose said. She stooped to examine a plant with prickly leaves. "Your father loved you very much," she said.

Lizzie felt a chill out in the bright Southern California sun. "Thank you for saying that," she finally said. "I loved him too." She was afraid that if she looked at Rose, she would start crying.

"He knew. He really loved you. I didn't know him all that well, but I know that."

"Thank you," Lizzie said, nodding fast.

"It's the truth," Rose said. "You need to remember." She tucked the loose end beneath the rest of her scarf, and gestured down the brick path. "Shall we?" They picked up the pace in silence. Then Rose spoke: "I heard you were once engaged." She said this as if passing along a small piece of useful news.

"You did?" Lizzie said as heat rose to her cheeks.

"Your father mentioned it. You're surprised."

"A little," Lizzie said. It both gladdened and unnerved her, to think of Joseph talking about her and Ben. "What did he say?"

"Only that you had been engaged and that you had ended it."

Rose spoke the words so evenly that Lizzie became convinced she meant something else entirely. Did she think Lizzie was the type who couldn't make a commitment? Did Joseph tell her that he thought his daughter was being unrealistic? That was the gist of what he'd said to Lizzie. *Oh,* he said, *I knew things were hard, but I had no idea it was that bad. Are you sure? Because no matter who it is, you'll always have to compromise.*

It hadn't been one of her finer moments; she'd turned it back on him. "Is that what you did with Mom, compromise?" And they were off to the races. *You have no idea what happened with your mother,* he said. *You have no idea what I think about anything!* Lizzie could remember shrieking, fourteen again.

"I do remember him saying that he was glad you had called it off beforehand, glad that you hadn't decided six months after the fact that you'd made a mistake. But he was disappointed."

"He liked Ben," Lizzie said. It was such a simple, innocuous statement, and yet her throat tightened up. "Everyone liked Ben."

"But not everyone was marrying Ben," Rose said pointedly.

Lizzie nodded. She was convinced Ben was going to marry the woman he was with now—once Ben was in, he was *in*. Their mutual friends hadn't told her much: Long Island–bred, Michigan grad who worked in advertising. "She's *organized,*" their friend Jen sniffed, and if that was the worst she could come up with—well, then. Lizzie should be happy for him. She had cheated on him; she had orchestrated their relationship's demise (it had taken her a while to admit that to herself). Even she was impatient with her own regret—and yet she still wondered if she had made an irrevocable mistake. Though, as Claudia had pointed out, it seemed to be the irrevocability that she focused on, and not Ben himself.

"Are you seeing anyone now?" Rose asked.

It was sweltering out here, in the noonday sun. "Well," Lizzie said as she shed her jacket, "no one special. And you?"

Rose shook her head. "No one special either."

Lizzie gave a light smile. They walked on in silence. Then Lizzie said: "Can I ask you a question? You turned Thomas down at first. I know you said it had to do with your parents, but I'm wondering: How did you know?"

"Know what?" Rose said, but she said it with warmth and a distinctly raised brow.

"How did you know that you could be happy with Thomas in the long run?" As she said this, Lizzie thought: *Rose must have met and married Thomas in her twenties.* Lizzie was already fifteen years older, at least. Time was barreling by.

"It's a good question," Rose said. "Honestly, I don't know. Or rather: I wasn't certain. But I wasn't *not* certain either, and that was enough, at some point. I liked him quite a lot. He made me happy—so little then made me happy. But I wasn't certain, not at all. Sometimes you have to jump."

It was, in a sense, standard advice, but coming from Rose, it felt like advice that Lizzie might be able to follow. "I hate jumping," she said. "I loathe heights."

Rose laughed. "Your jump can be from the smallest step. Heights might not be involved at all. And you know, marriage can be quite difficult. Don't let anyone tell you otherwise."

"So I hear," Lizzie said. But her newly married friends didn't like to talk about it—or if they spoke of it, it was to each other, not to her. "Did you ever hear the story of my grandparents?" she asked. Rose shook her head, and Lizzie continued: "Years and years ago—my father must have been in college—my grandparents were having breakfast, and my grandfather, who was a really quiet, taciturn type, said, 'I'm going out for oranges.' He got up, left the table. He never came back. A week later, she got a postcard from him from Florida, which said, 'I'm sorry. The oranges are better here.'"

"My goodness," Rose said. "And that was that?"

"That was that. They never divorced, but they never lived together again," Lizzie said. "So you see: my family does not have the marriage gene."

"Now, that is a cop-out if I've ever heard one."

"What?"

"A cop-out," Rose repeated with impatience. "Blaming circumstances, evading responsibility."

"No, I *know* what 'cop-out' means; I just didn't expect you to use that word."

"Why? Everyone thinks it's slang, but it's 'cop' as in the verb meaning 'to take,' and not as in the police sort of 'cop,' although the two share commonalities."

Lizzie laughed.

"What?" Rose said irritably. "What?"

INSIDE THE AMERICAN WING, THEY admired a small Mary Cassatt painting of a mother and child. (Rose spoke of the composition—"Do you see the diagonals formed by the child's legs?"—while Lizzie noticed that the mother looked so wistful, and wasn't looking at her child at all.) They saw Edward Hoppers and high-kicking dancers carved out of wood and many a landscape. After negotiating the knot of people in front of Gainsborough's *Blue Boy* (he looked so insolent, resplendent in his silvery-blue clothing, so self-satisfied, Lizzie thought), they stopped at the museum's café, and sat in plastic chairs on the shaded patio, overlooking the immense gardens. It was midafternoon but Lizzie had skipped lunch. Now she bit into her dry chicken sandwich and said to Rose: "Did your family have a lot of art besides the Soutine?"

"Not really," Rose said. "There were objects galore—vases, music boxes, silver swords that had been my grandfather's, a landscape that I think had been a wedding present. But my parents weren't art collectors. It was strange, the way my mother fell in love with *The Bellhop*. Even now I remember the way she looked at it."

Lizzie nodded. She didn't think it was strange, but Rose's face was veiled in contemplation. She didn't say anything for a moment and neither did Rose. "Do you collect any art?" Lizzie asked timidly.

There was a shift in her look; Rose, returning to herself. She scoffed. "Oh no, I would never spend the kind of dollars on art that you need to."

Lizzie smiled. "So you're not a spender."

"Most definitely not. It used to drive Thomas crazy. 'A yearly trip to Hawaii won't be the end of us,' he'd say, and he was right, but it made me nervous nevertheless."

"Now, *that* I understand," Lizzie said. "We're alike in that way. And unlike my father. You know for my sixteenth birthday he offered to buy me a piece of art. Anything I wanted."

"Anything?"

"Well, he knew I wouldn't have picked anything outrageous. At first I started haunting these galleries on Melrose, and then, one day, I walked into a vintage clothing store, of all places." She remembered the day perfectly. "I saw a photograph from the sixties, a black-and-white shot of two chubby young girls, sisters. One sat on the couch, clutching a doll in one hand and a kitchen knife in the other. It looked like she was about to slice the doll's hair. The other sister sat below her on the floor, staring at the camera, legs spread out, holding a toy grenade. The girls terrified me. And I just knew that my dad would hate it. There was one other obstacle."

"It was thousands of dollars."

Lizzie shook her head. "Nope. It wasn't for sale. But I brought my dad down to the shop anyway." She had declined to tell him the photograph wasn't available. "The shop was dark and cluttered, lots of velvet and mirrors. I brought him in, and he said, 'This is what you want?' and started muttering about Cindy Sherman knockoffs and the overweight girls and tired Appalachia narratives. But he kept staring at it. Finally he said to me, 'I don't like it, but I understand why you do.' He turned to the saleswoman and asked the price. She told him it wasn't for sale, that it was the owner's. And my dad looked at her with a little smile and said, 'Everything has its price.' I remember him saying that so well. He wrote out his name and number and told her that the owner should call. And within a week, the photograph was hanging in my bedroom."

Lizzie remembered feeling astounded by its arrival. How had he done it? What would it be like to never take no for an answer? Joseph paid whatever he paid for it, fought with whomever he fought with, on her behalf.

The embarrassment didn't come until later, though it was the more lasting, saturated feeling, the one that stayed with her, blanketing the episode in her mind, the feeling that fueled her to take down the picture two years later while in college and never put it up again, the one that made this a story she rarely told. She did not want everything to have a price; that wasn't the way she was going to live her life.

Rose stirred her iced tea, squeezed a tiny triangle of lemon. "That doesn't surprise me in the slightest," she said. "He could be persuasive, your father."

"I know. I shrugged off the gift." Lizzie picked at a sliver of pale tomato; it was tasteless, a simulacrum of the real thing. "As if I expected it." Her voice caught. Her sixteenth birthday. A lifetime ago; it didn't matter anymore. But she wished more than anything that she could tell her father how much she appreciated all he did. "I was lucky," she said now. "And I couldn't see it."

"You were a teenager."

"I know, but I could be so nasty to him." It was terrible to recall. Had Joseph thought of it as typical teenage behavior? Was he able to shrug it off? "I don't even know what he spent on it. He shouldn't have been spending money on something I didn't need, especially then."

"What do you mean?" Rose asked. "'Then'?"

Lizzie paused. She hadn't meant to say that; why had she said that? On the other hand, why should she be secretive about it with Rose now? "Just, that's when he was having those problems with his practice. His office manager ripped him off. She was messing with the billing, big-time. She was charging patients the full amount, recording smaller amounts in the books, pocketing the difference. He didn't discover it for months. I don't know all the details, but I do know that he lost a lot of money over it, and that threw everything into a mess. He never liked the business side of things." Lizzie picked at the remnants of her roll—chalky, stale.

"That's terrible," Rose said. "He never said a word to me. We weren't such good friends, but still."

"I don't remember the exact timing. It might have been before you met him. He had stopped buying art then." Lizzie felt herself edging close to the story that was so hard for her to tell. Here, with Rose, she didn't want to stop. "My sister got sick not long after. The night the artwork was stolen, Sarah—"

"I know."

Lizzie nodded, feeling her breath quicken. How much did Rose truly know?

The night of the party, Sarah had been antsy, waiting for a boy she called James P to arrive. James, at seventeen, was two years older than Sarah, a seemingly genial enough (or boring, Lizzie thought to herself) junior who went to a different high school but worked in the same darkroom as Sarah. When he gave her a ride home, she was euphoric for days. A conversation in which he mentioned another girl could send her into a tailspin for a week.

James eventually did show up—Lizzie caught a glimpse of her sister chatting with him in a large cluster—but when Lizzie went downstairs with Duncan, there was Sarah in a heap on the carpet, head down, arms around her knees. "Sarah?" she asked, exasperated. What was it this time?

Her sister lifted her head. She looked pale in the low light, her heavy mascara and liner raccooning her eyes. "I fucking hate him, I can't believe how much I hate him."

"Who?"

"James P. Who else? Did you see that girl he came with, the one with the red hair? That's his girlfriend—his fucking girlfriend! How can he have a girlfriend? How can he do this to me?"

Lizzie got down on the thick creamy carpet and wrapped her arms around her sister. Out of the corner of her eye, she saw Duncan hanging back. What would he think, seeing her mess of a sister? Lizzie tried to tug Sarah up. "You don't know what's going on between them; you don't—"

"Her name is Charlie!" Sarah skirted back from Lizzie. "How ridiculous is that? Carlotta, really—a lame old lady's name. She goes to Eastgate and she's a swimmer and they spend their summers in Europe—"

"Shhh, it's okay." Lizzie saw the desperation etched so plainly on her sister's face, and for a moment, she was afraid.

"No, it's not! It's most definitely *not* okay. James P told me all of this! He's all impressed, he's all, like, proud! I felt so stupid I wanted to die."

"Look, maybe he didn't know how you felt. Maybe he has no idea."

"God, you don't know; you really don't know, do you?" Sarah was weeping now. "I just want to die." She buried her face in her hands, her sobs loud, extravagant.

"Do you think she wants some water?" Duncan asked softly. "Maybe she'd feel better if she drank something."

"No," Sarah had said with disdain. "I do not"—*beat, beat*—"want something"—*beat*—"to drink." She had glared at Duncan. "I want to talk to my sister, okay? I need to talk to my sister."

"Hey," Lizzie said. "He was just trying to help."

"It's okay," Duncan said.

"No, it's not." She was not going to let Sarah fuck this up, not this time. "Just a second," she said to her sister. And to Duncan: "Come."

She led him down the hall as Sarah cried out: "Lizzie!"

"Just a sec!" Lizzie called back to her sister more sharply this time. "Wait for me," she said to Duncan when they reached her room. She kissed him, determined that this moment, her moment, would not slip away.

When she returned, Sarah's crying had slowed. "I'm so sorry, L," she said, hiccuping the words out. Her face remained strained, her pupils enlarged, otherworldly. "I just—I don't know what to do anymore."

Lizzie was tired of all of it, her moods and neediness, her dark beauty and apologies. "You know what? Go to sleep. Or don't. I don't care." Sarah would just take, take, take until there was nothing left of Lizzie. She was newly fifteen, two years older than Lizzie had been when their mother got sick, when Lizzie was heating up dinner for them both, her mother asking her to make sure that Sarah had snacks in her backpack for after school. She did not need a protector anymore.

Sarah's face crumpled. "Lizzie . . ." She could barely get her name out, and covered her mouth with her hands. "Don't say that."

"No, I don't want to hear it. I'm sick of this, okay? You'll be fine in the morning."

And with that, she went to Duncan, left her sister in the hall alone. A few hours later, when Lizzie awoke, Duncan was pressed against the wall, as far away as her twin bed would allow. The house was quiet. She got up, pulled on a T-shirt and underwear, feeling strangely alert. In the hall, a pile of earth-hued bottles and a shiny flattened bag of Doritos greeted her. She found a garbage bag, and began cleaning up.

When she first spotted her sister, it was Sarah's foot that Lizzie noticed. Lizzie had gone into her dad's bedroom, praying that it wasn't a mess, when she remembered thinking matter-of-factly: *That's Sarah's foot.* It was a bare foot, peeking out through the frame of her father's bathroom, not moving.

"Sarah?" Why was her sister lying there with her foot at that weird angle? How could she be sleeping, lying like that? Lizzie's breathing sped up, her heart scuttled about. But she could remember thinking clearly: *This does not make sense.* "Sadie?"

Now Lizzie peered around the corner. Sarah was facedown on the bathroom tile, and there was something about the odd shape of her body—head slumped to the right, legs akimbo—that made Lizzie understand even before she could articulate it, even before she spotted the empty bottle of Valium by her sister's outstretched hand. Lizzie touched her sister, lightly at first, then more aggressively. Sarah didn't move.

The screaming that Lizzie heard—and it was an awful shriek, an inhumane rattling sound—it had come from her. By the time Duncan rushed in, she was cradling her sister's unresponsive body, wiping the saliva that had dripped from her mouth, rocking her. "Please breathe, oh God, please please breathe," she was saying.

It must have taken close to fifteen minutes to reach the ER at St. John's in Duncan's car, fifteen inexorable minutes in which lights must have turned red and cars had to be passed and several miles of Santa Monica streets needed to be traversed. But Lizzie didn't remember any of it. She would remember the soury-sweet smell of vomit, she would remember using her fingers to prop and massage her sister's mouth open, she would remember barely taking in air herself. She would remember the double-wide doors of the emergency room swinging open like a grinning mouth, easing Sarah inside. "I'm her sister, I'm her sister," Lizzie kept saying, as if that would explain everything.

Hours later, after Lizzie had insisted that Duncan go home, a petite doctor in scrubs and orange clogs came out and said that they had talked to Joseph in Boston, pumped Sarah's stomach, and were keeping her under watch. There was nothing more for Lizzie to do. She should go home, get some rest, and come back the next day.

Lizzie hurried out of the emergency room, freshly ashamed, and into a blazing Southern California day. She took a cab home, feeling haggard and more exhausted than she'd ever known. Lying on the couch, she remembered looking up and thinking: *The walls are so dirty. How come I never noticed how dirty they are before?*

That's when it hit her. The Picasso sketch and *The Bellhop,* her *Bellhop,* were gone.

TWO DETECTIVES RESPONDED TO LIZZIE'S phone call: a tall black man with a shadow of a mustache who quietly asked Lizzie about the artwork, and his partner, a ruddy-faced woman with a tight short perm. She was the one who asked Lizzie to make a list of the names of everyone who had been at the party. "It wasn't all that many," Lizzie said warily. "Uh-huh," the female detective said, amused.

There were no signs of a break-in. No clues of any kind. "Whoever took them knew exactly what they were looking for," the male detective said.

The party had provided the perfect cover. Lizzie was haunted by this thought. If she hadn't thrown the party, if there hadn't been so many people, they never would have come inside. It made her skin crawl to imagine someone inside the house, grabbing the painting that she loved, touching all of their things. She had left the door open, and the paintings were the least of it. If she hadn't thrown the party, if she hadn't left Sarah alone to be with Duncan (it disgusted her now, her desire for him; she avoided him at school, ignored the few messages he left on the answering machine), Sarah would have been fine. If Lizzie had only remained with her, done something as easy as sit with her, listened to her tape of *The Queen Is Dead* on repeat or convinced her to watch old episodes of *Who's the Boss?* on VHS, a show that Lizzie thought was stupid but Sarah inexplicably loved; if she had just paid attention to her, taken care of her as she had done so many times in the past, if she hadn't been so fucking stupid and selfish, then her sister wouldn't have done what she did. Lizzie's world would not have imploded.

And she wasn't the only one who felt this way. "A party, Elizabeth, a fucking party?!" her father had screamed at her when he arrived back home from Boston hours after Lizzie had called him from the hospital. "You weren't supposed to be here! Your sister—" He had shaken his head, opened and closed his hands as if he wanted to grip something, but came up empty.

"I'm sorry, Daddy," Lizzie cried, over and over again that first hideous day. But nothing she said made a difference.

"I counted on you. You lied to me! I trusted you. And you lied."

It didn't matter what else she had done in her life, how good a kid she had always been. It was as if this was who she was, selfish and uncaring and a fuckup, every one of her numerous faults on display. She knew it and her father knew it too. The guilt pressed against her and became her most voluble companion. *You were* never *a good sister,* the voice told her. *Your father knows it and your mother knew it too.* "I'm sorry. I'm so sorry," she said to little avail.

About a week later, her father apologized, telling her: "I had no right to say those things to you. I was out of my mind with worry."

"I know," Lizzie said. It was easier to acquiesce, to simply agree. But she could not stand being here, in her skin. His apology could never take away what they both knew to be the truth: she had been the one to set those awful events in motion.

"I don't think you do," he had said. "It wasn't your fault." She remembered him saying this. They were in the living room, the Lakers game on low. She stood there in agony, watching James Worthy tip the ball with enviable ease into the basket. "You didn't steal the paintings. You didn't take those pills. You need to know that I know that. Come *here*. Please."

He looked so wretched, pleading. Her father was not a pleader. She moved closer. He squeezed her arm. "I'm so sorry you got caught up in this. It was like—a car accident," he said. "And you were a passenger. You had nothing to do with it. Okay?"

"Okay," she said, and she even managed a tight little smile. But she never did believe him.

"They discharged Sarah from the hospital the next day," Lizzie said now to Rose. "She was contrite, so apologetic, kept swearing that she would never do anything like that again. So we brought her home. The doctors basically chalked it up to teenage moodiness and drinking. But the next week she started acting weird again—staying up until two, three in the morning, calling her friends in the middle of the night, asking them to pick her up, not saying where she wanted to go, only that she had to. My father insisted that Sarah had to get another evaluation—I remember call after call, appointment after appointment. He made a big stink, the way only he could." She took a deep breath, remembering.

Sarah would be fine, Lizzie could recall thinking. She had been an intense little kid and was developing into an emotionally volatile teenager; none of this was surprising. Sarah had been hung up on a boy and did something stupid. And now she was being moody and regretful. That's all this was, Lizzie wanted to believe.

But Joseph was convinced there was more, and he was dogged on Sarah's behalf. When Lizzie looked back on that time, she recalled her father installed behind the closed door of his bedroom, his voice rising, needling. It was only then that he sounded like himself. In Lizzie's presence, even after the apology, he rarely spoke. He seemed numbed to everyone around him. She swore she could see him stiffen when she was present. So she tried to be present as little as possible.

"My dad called all these doctors," Lizzie continued. "He eventually got her in to see this child psychiatrist at UCLA, an expert who was doing research into girls and suicide attempts and he had Sarah admitted to the inpatient unit. She spent a few weeks there. It was awful. But she finally got her bipolar diagnosis. They started her on lithium. And finally it was okay."

Lizzie remembered waiting in those red plastic molded chairs in the waiting area at UCLA, not wanting to be called through the excruciatingly heavy locked double doors. When inevitably she and Joseph were, they would find Sarah at the art therapy table, her face heavier, wearing sweats and canvas sneakers without laces. Lizzie hated those un-Sarah-like sweats and sneakers with an abiding fierceness. She would thrust a mess of magazines at her—*Popular*

Photography, People, Seventeen. "Thanks," Sarah would mutter, eyes averted. Lizzie hated everyone there—the competent, omnipresent nurses, the few doctors, the other patients, her sister, her father. She hated them as if hating could actually accomplish something.

"He took care of her," Rose was saying now. "He did everything he could."

"Yeah, he did," Lizzie said, and she bit her lip. She had never needed her father's care like that. Sometimes she wished that she had. "I never gave him enough credit for it. But he did."

LATER THAT NIGHT, LIZZIE LAY next to Max, her foot hooked around his ankle. "Did you know that Huntington was married to his aunt?"

"No," he said. She turned on her side and closed her eyes as he traced the knobby route of her spine. "I did not."

"It just got me thinking. There are stranger beginnings than ours."

"Yes," he said, and he kissed the top of her head. "There are."

She pulled her arms into her chest, curling up. "Maybe we could do this." Her afternoon with Rose had had a strangely buoying effect on her. She thought of Rose telling her that sometimes you have to jump. *This,* she thought, *this is what I want.*

"Maybe we could," he agreed.

She put a hand on his chest, a tangle of matted hairs. It was warm, and she could feel his heart. The steady beat of that thick bloody muscle gave her courage. "The other day, you said you wouldn't mind if I moved in with you," she said. "What if I did?"

"For all intents and purposes, you have."

She shook her head. She could make a joke about it—she could pretend—but no. She meant it, and she wasn't going to feign otherwise. "You know what I mean."

"You wouldn't go back to New York." He said the words slowly. "You'd move here?"

Did she detect a note of incredulity in his voice? Lizzie told herself not to be so sensitive. Give him a chance. "Well, I'd have to go back, for a while anyway: my job, my apartment, everything. But I could come back, network, eventually take the bar. People do move, and I've got family, good friends here. It's not like you're the only one." She tried for a playful tone, but couldn't quite pull it off. "What I want to know is: Would you want me to?"

He didn't answer for a beat. "These past two weeks have meant everything to me," he said, and the meaning hit Lizzie at once. She thought, wildly, *What a fool I am*. "Your dad—"

"No," Lizzie said. "This can't be about him. God, this can't be about him."

"It's just moving so fast—"

"Forget it," Lizzie said. She should have known better. She *did* know better. Why was she trying to change? "I shouldn't have said anything. I'm sorry; I'm not myself these days."

"Please don't apologize," Max said, touching her hair, looking at her when all she wanted to do was escape his gaze. "I care about you so much."

"No," Lizzie said sharply. "Do not." She was done talking. Why was there always so much talking? And with that, she rolled over.

8

LONDON, 1948

"CONSIDER IVAN'S WORDS TO ALYOSHA," Professor Hillman was saying. "'I don't want harmony. From love to humanity, I don't want it. I would rather be left with the unavenged suffering.'"

Rose wrote down "unavenged suffering" in her notebook, struck by the phrase. She loved the Russians, and Dostoyevsky in particular.

"Later, Ivan says, 'One reptile will devour another,'" he continued. Rose liked Professor Hillman. He had a plump, kind face that contradicted the stiff striped ties he wore. He was soft-spoken outside of class, seemingly embarrassed if you did as much as say hello, but in class, while lecturing about his beloved Russians, he commanded. She had heard that he had a samovar in his office that he brought out on special occasions for prized students, but although she was doing well in his class, she had never seen it. "What does Dostoyevsky mean by that?" he asked.

Rose, in the front row, shot up her hand. She saw Professor Hillman's eyes register her, then glance away as he scanned the lecture hall. Rose strained her arm higher, but she knew it was hopeless. Half the time he didn't call on her. So she raised her hand often? She knew the answer. Shouldn't that be rewarded? Rose sighed, lowered her arm, and gazed around. The delicate wainscoting of the light blue walls and the ornate marble fireplace that Professor Hillman stood in front of seemed at odds with lecturing. Bombs had demolished a good part of the Bedford College campus during the war, and the university had rented this row of Regent's Park mansions until rebuilding was complete. Rose imagined dances taking place in this ballroom, dances not unlike the ones described in such vivid, blood-quickening detail in the Russian novels she was reading.

"Miss Gissing?" Professor Hillman said. "Why do you suppose Ivan thinks that reptiles will devour each other?"

Eva Gissing sat one row behind Rose. Rose twisted around to see her blush. "I don't know," Eva said. Rose raised her hand again. "I suppose all reptiles devour each other, don't they?"

"I meant in the context of the text, Miss Gissing," Professor Hillman said. "You must return to the text." He nodded at Rose. "Miss Zimmer?"

"Dostoyevsky says that we all have dark, murderous impulses. We all would eat each other if we could. It's prescient, in a sense, as later—well, when the father is murdered. It's the irrational side of us that reigns." Rose didn't need Dostoyevsky to tell her that, but she found his insistence on the ugliness of the human condition comforting. It made her feel, in no small part, understood.

"Indeed," Professor Hillman said. "Part of celebrating the Russian soul is celebrating that darkness. We are now fortunate as Englishmen to have access to these great literary powers. Other writers do no more than play at the feet of the giants that are Tolstoy and Dostoyevsky. For next week, reread the 'Grand Inquisitor' section. And your essays are due next week as well," he finished as the bell rang.

Books and notebooks were scooped up, scarves and coats gathered. When Rose was at the door, Eva caught up with her. "Do not tell me that you've read the entire book," she said with a theatrical exhalation. Eva, like Rose, was small and dark-haired and fair-skinned; but unlike Rose, she was chatty outside of class, tentative in.

"Then I won't," Rose said.

"You know why Dostoyevsky's novel is so bloody long, don't you?"

"Why don't you tell me," Rose said easily enough. It was hard to take Eva seriously, but knowing this made Rose feel more kindly. They headed together down the marble hall, passed a carved depression in the wall where an organ used to reside in the building's grander days.

"Serialization." Eva drew the word out. "If I got paid by the installment, I'd write a long novel too."

"I'm sure you would," Rose said.

"Lore and I are going for coffee," Eva said as they neared the building's entrance. "Come."

"I can't," Rose said, and she injected a note of remorse that she didn't quite feel into her tone. "Too much to do." She gestured down at the load of books she carried.

"You don't have to actually read *everything*," Eva said, as if reading books in their entirety was a sign of silliness, something a child might do. Rose tightened her grip on her books. It wasn't worth the effort to argue, with Eva especially. She remained astonished and grateful to actually be here at the University of London, doing nothing but studying literature, *reading*, which she would frankly do on her own. She hadn't worked at the silk factory on Tottenham Court for almost two years now and still she would sometimes glance at a clock and think: *It's nearly time for elevenses, the shift half over.*

The girls walked outside. A light drizzle was falling, the sky pebbly gray and vast, the new green leaves budding bright on the thick-waisted plane trees across the street in Regent's Park.

"One of these days you should join us," Eva said. "The coffee is strong, like back home, and there are loads of nice boys there."

"That sounds splendid," Rose said, and she opened her umbrella and shifted her books into her other arm. Students streamed up the paths in sandy-colored mackintoshes, their dark umbrellas unfurling. Rose looked for Harriet. She would be easy to spot, what with the purple scarf she always wore loose around her shoulders. But she didn't see her. She felt dampness at her collar and she sighed, fingered the material beneath the rib of her umbrella. There it was: a tear. "Another time, I'll join you," she said.

Eva had said this before to her—*back home*—and though she knew she was being ungenerous, Rose felt an urge to say, *We don't share the same home*. Eva was from Bavaria. At the onset of the war, she and her parents made it to Basel, and managed to make their way to Spain and then to Lisbon, where they waited it out. They were relatively new to England. The first time Eva and Rose chatted outside of class, Eva spoke to her in German. Rose answered in English. She rarely used her German now. Eva's father had settled in Golders Green, where he taught at a Jewish school. Eva kept inviting Rose over for a Shabbos meal, "or any time at all," she'd say, but Rose kept finding excuses not to go.

Lore, a few years older, came from a town near Prague, and like Rose, she and her brother had come over on a transport. She didn't talk about her parents either. She had lived with a family in Manchester's Cheetham Hill, and then joined the ATS and drove cars for the service during the war. One time early in the year, they had left class together—Eva was sick—and run into a friend of Lore's, a young man named Walter from Berlin. He invited them to tea. Walter was exceedingly tall with a mop of hair, and a great talker. He joked about England's incessant dampness, the lack of meat on the black market, the way his landlady had a habit of coming downstairs in her too-short robe. "Oh! So sorry. I keep *forgetting* there are men in the house," he imitated her with gusto.

"Walter," Lore said with a snort and a hand to his forearm. "You are too much."

Rose smiled faintly. "How do you two know each other?"

"Oh, Lore and I go way back. I was her brother's keeper for a time. We bunked together on the Isle of Man."

"The Isle of Man?" Rose repeated.

"You know," Lore said. "When the men were interned—"

"Less than a year after I arrived," Walter broke in. "I was eighteen, just made the cutoff. Lucky me." He grinned, but Rose wasn't smiling. Now she remembered: the government had rounded up all men from German-speaking countries and held them in an internment camp. Gerhard had been fortunate, on the other side of that cutoff.

"I'm sorry," Rose said.

"Oh, it was fine." Walter waved her off. "The boredom was the worst of it. Such a bloody waste of time. And good thing people are so much clearer now on our loyalties. You know I went for an interview the other day and I was told that I had great ability, but 'so sorry, the firm already has our fill of foreigners. Cool your heels and maybe a spot for your kind will open up soon.'"

"That's awful. And I hear it's gotten worse since last summer." Lore didn't have to explain. The troubles had remained mostly up north, but they had all heard. In Cheetham Hill, where Lore's foster family lived, shop windows were smashed, bricks thrown from cars, the main synagogue vandalized. It was reprisal for the two British sergeants who had been killed in Palestine by Jewish underground fighters. People ascribed the violence in Manchester to a small, bad element—hooligans, they called them. They're not coming to London, everyone said. But Rose thought: *Wasn't this how it began in Germany?*

"It's not happening here," Walter said.

"No?" Rose said, alert, eyes on him, not doubting for a moment that he had surmised what she had been thinking.

"No. England is different. And we're pushy people, or so I'm told." He gave her a shadow of a smile. "We won't let it happen again."

Lore later told Rose: "Walter likes you. He said he wanted to come round again."

"Really?" Rose said, dubious. Didn't he like Lore? He seemed far too confident and attractive to be interested in her. Boys made her more anxious than excited. She had never had anything close to a boyfriend. But maybe things were changing, she thought nervously. She had liked talking to him. Maybe Walter would be the one.

He never came around again, and though she was disappointed, Rose never asked Lore why. It confirmed what she already knew. Rose was at a loss around boys. Sometimes she wondered: What would Mutti have told her? Would she have been more assured, growing up under her wing?

But school was something that Rose understood. In her studies, she excelled.

"I'm off," Rose said now to Eva. She felt droplets collecting on her neck; the drizzle was increasing. The figures hurrying along the paths were no more than smeary dabs. Harriet was nowhere to be found.

"To reread the 'Grand Inquisitor' section," Eva said.

"Yes," Rose said. Eva might be trying to mock her, but here was the trick: Rose didn't care. She felt a small but heady rush; Rose knew what she wanted, and what she wanted was tantalizingly, incredibly hers.

AFTER HER COMMUTE BACK TO South Kensington (two different lines, half a mile's walk), Rose let herself into Mrs. Deering's with her own key. She had begged Margaret not to leave London, she thought it was a big mistake to follow her beau back to Leeds. But if Margaret hadn't left, then Rose would have never ended up at Mrs. Deering's. Her attic room wasn't much to look at, but it had a bed and a gas ring on which she made tea, and a washbasin and, if she craned her neck, a slight view of the walled garden below. She shared a bathroom down the hall. Mrs. Deering wasn't exactly warm, but she was organized and she ran a good house. She rarely saw Mr. Deering, who had been blinded at Dunkirk, and stayed in the two rooms on the parlor floor that he and Mrs. Deering claimed for themselves. Rose liked the seamstress Mrs. Karlkowski on the third floor, who wore bright lipstick and rouge no matter if she didn't leave the house, and most of all she liked Harriet, a clever broad-shouldered blonde from America who was studying science at university and talked less about her family than Rose did. One night, over gin and lemon, she had mentioned a former husband back home outside of Philadelphia. "Technically, he is still my husband. But the things he did," Harriet had said, and stopped.

"What?" Rose breathed.

Harriet shook her head. "He is not a man; only a boy would do such things. I am fortunate that my father finally agreed." She would say no more. "It doesn't matter," she told Rose. "It's in the past. We are very lucky to be on our own." And they clinked glasses, drinking to it.

Rose entered the carpeted hall and walked past the umbrella stand and coat hooks and small curved table that held the communal telephone. Mr. Lewis from the second floor was polishing the banister with fervor.

"Hello, Mr. Lewis," Rose said.

"Oh, hello, Miss Zimmer," he said, and clutched the rag behind his back. "A fine afternoon, isn't it?" A purplish hue bloomed on his thin cheeks.

"Yes," she assured him, taking care not to focus her gaze on him, especially not on the rag she could still partially see. "An absolutely fine afternoon."

Mr. Lewis wasn't supposed to be cleaning the common areas. This everyone knew. But Mr. Lewis, a timid bookkeeper from Wales who so disliked attention that he blushed whenever spoken to, was a firebrand on the topic of cleanliness. He would tiptoe around the house—collecting towels for washing, wiping down the kitchen counter and the telephone with a heady-smelling concoction of disinfectant that he mixed himself. ("Oh no, you cannot rely on store-bought," he would say, shaking his head mournfully.) His cleaning enraged Mrs. Deering, who felt that his dusters and disinfectants were not removing contaminants from her house but adding others that marked his territory.

Now Rose heard a creak, and she and Mr. Lewis both glanced up to see Mrs. Deering making her way down from the second landing. A deep pink flamed across Mr. Lewis's face. "Well, I'm off to the post office," he announced, and scurried away.

"Miss Zimmer," Mrs. Deering said before she reached the floor. "Just the person I wanted to speak with. You are a good tenant."

"And I like living here," Rose interjected, feeling uncertain, as if this were a test.

"I am glad to hear that. But, as I have already informed the other tenants, there will be an increase in rent as of two months from now."

"An increase?" Rose repeated. Gerhard had given her a monthly sum for tuition and board after he had calculated her expenses with precision. There was scant extra.

"You are paying thirty-two shillings weekly. It will be increasing to two pounds."

"Two pounds?" Rose said, aghast. "For my room?"

"Yes, for your room." Mrs. Deering's voice rose indignant too. "Ask around. You will find that's what most rooming houses are charging, or more. What with the housing shortages around here—"

"I cannot afford it." She thought about the leather-bound volume of Gogol's stories on Charing Cross that she had spotted the other day. Twenty-eight pence. She wanted it badly. But she hadn't bought it. If she couldn't afford a book, how could she manage such an increase? She hated to take money from Gerhard in the first place. She couldn't ask him for more.

"I'm sorry, Miss Zimmer. But I am running a business here—it is my home but it is a business, the only business my husband and I now have. And what with all the doctors, and all the medications—" She stopped herself. "Let me know what you decide. But the rent will be increased in two months' time."

"And if I can't pay it?"

Mrs. Deering's voice got softer. "Then you'll have to make other arrangements."

ROSE'S ARMS ACHED BY THE time she made it to Gerhard's in Hampstead. She carried a string bag heavy with three loaves of bread and a fragrant bouquet of purple and white hyacinths that had been a last-minute purchase when she had gotten off the Tube. (She told herself not to think about the fifteen pence that she spent on them.) She walked up Holly Hill, past the white-stoned façade of St. Mary's, the streets much cleaner and quieter than in South Kensington.

When Mrs. Tompkins opened the door to her brother's flat, Rose detected the slight but stubborn odor of new paint. "Miss Zimmer," Mrs. Tompkins greeted Rose. "Mrs. Zimmer is resting in the drawing room."

"No, I am here, I am here," Isobel called as her fair head peeked into view. Her belly was straining against the ribbon that held her silk wrapper closed. Still she managed to look beautiful, her tousled hair shiny, her full lips fuller. "Hyacinths?" she exclaimed. "Oh, Rose, they are too lovely."

"I saw them and decided you must have them," Rose said, and promptly reddened.

"They are positively gorgeous, and perhaps they'll cut that awful new paint smell. It is horrid, isn't it?"

"I barely smell it."

"Oh, you're a liar," Isobel said with a laugh. "I love you but you are a terrible liar."

"Ma'am, let me put these lovelies into water," Mrs. Tompkins said. "Miss Zimmer, I'll take your things as well."

"Thank you, Mrs. Tompkins, and I picked up some loaves as well," Rose said, wriggling out of her coat, handing the string bag over.

"You must stop going to the bakery and standing in that queue for us," Isobel protested. "It is wholly unnecessary."

"You say that every week," Rose said.

"And every week it is true. Come. Let's go into the drawing room."

"How are you feeling? You look bigger than you did last week. Lovely," Rose said, catching herself, "you look lovely."

"Oh, I'm fine," Isobel said dismissively. "Quite fine. No problems at all." And she did look more than fine. No one Rose knew had had children yet, but Isobel looked as if her pregnancy was only one of her many activities. She could fit childbirth in while moving to a new flat while planning a dinner party while arguing that yes, the summer Olympics would be a boon for London.

The late-afternoon light filtered in through the bay windows, and it created honey-colored pools on the maple floorboards. "Look at this." Isobel gestured to a chair by the fireplace. "What do you think of it?"

"Is it new?" Rose said, hesitating. The chair was made of pale wood, austere but sinuous too. The wood bent this way and that. How did it do that and not break? It looked like nothing she wanted to sit in.

"Yes, I bought it the other day. It was designed by a husband-and-wife team who teach at Croydon. Isn't it wonderfully fresh?"

"Wonderfully fresh and wholly uncomfortable," Gerhard called as he came in. He carried a cigarette case in one hand and wore a crisp brown suit. Rose look down at her own skirt and noticed with renewed consternation the wrinkles she'd shrugged off when she pulled it on this morning.

Isobel sighed. "No one is asking you."

"Rose is sensible. She will agree with me." He leaned in and gave his sister a brush on the cheek. "Right, *mausi*?" Rose thought her brother looked bigger—broader in the shoulders, more imperious. But perhaps it was the fine wool suit, perhaps it was impending fatherhood.

"Are you saying I'm insensible?" Isobel asked. "Never mind, I don't care if you think I am." In fact, Rose thought Isobel probably preferred Gerhard to think of her that way. "Come here, Rose." She patted the cushion beside her. "Come talk to me. Sit here: it's a highly comfortable, old-fashioned settee, with tea rose fabric and all. Your brother's favorite." Gerhard snorted, and she continued: "Exams are soon, aren't they? How are you faring?"

"They are. I'm doing all right. It should be all right. I like my Russian literature class," she said with what she hoped was a confident, easy, Isobel-like air. "We're reading Dostoyevsky."

"Dostoyevsky?" Isobel said, twisting to puff up the pillow behind her back, frowning as she did so.

"Yes, *The Brothers Karamazov*."

"Oh yes," Isobel said. "Are you reading Miss Garnett's translation? An astonishing woman. Do you know that she learned Russian when she was confined to bed during a difficult pregnancy? And then she had the child, left him with her husband, and went to Russia for several months—"

"Don't get any ideas," Gerhard said.

Isobel shook her head at him. "She met Tolstoy and stayed with him at his dacha. Then she came back to England and spent decades translating the Russians. I met her once, in Kent, not long before she died. She wasn't well, she was on crutches then, but we had a great chat about Newnham."

"Hold on," Gerhard said. "Did you meet her through that White Russian of yours?"

Isobel sighed. "He was *not* a White Russian. He was a nobleman with the heart of a revolutionary."

"Who preyed on young, idealistic English girls," Gerhard said.

"There was no preying to be had," Isobel said. "But your jealousy is quite sweet, really." She laid a hand on his forearm, cocked her head at Rose. "Pay your brother no mind. It was quite an honor to meet Miss Garnett. Without her, we would not have access to those great Slavic minds."

"Yes," Rose said, still feeling confused. Her sister-in-law had met Constance Garnett, the great translator of Tolstoy and Dostoyevsky? She had read the Russians too? Was there nothing she couldn't do?

Isobel, Rose was sure, would be trotting out unexpected facts about herself well into her eighties.

"I'm so very glad you're enjoying your classes. Everyone should have an education. Particularly women—"

"'Particularly'?" Gerhard asked, opening his cigarette case, taking an ashtray from the mantel.

"Especially," Isobel said. "Especially women. And especially you, Rose. It's criminal to think that you of all people wouldn't have an education."

"I'm grateful to you," Rose said quickly. "To you and Gerhard. I am so grateful."

Isobel waved her off. "Oh, the thought that you would still be in a factory; what a waste, what an absolute waste!"

"People do have to work in factories, Isobel," Gerhard said as he drew in smoke. "That is how things are made. I should only be so fortunate—if the business takes off, then we too shall have a factory." Gerhard had opened a greeting-card business with Isobel's sister's husband in the past year. Sales were brisk, the cheerful, preprinted cards far more popular than Rose would have ever guessed, but a factory?

And yet, look at him, resplendent in his Savile Row suit with his gold cigarette case. "My brother, the industrialist," she had described him to Harriet with more than a little vinegary bite. But certain facts were unassailable: Gerhard had achieved. What she had deemed as his foolish outsized optimism had fueled his success, transformed his daily existence. Yes, he had gotten his start by marrying Isobel, but he had also prospered. He never again would have to fret whether he could spend the money to purchase a book; he never would worry about a rent increase. Oh, how she yearned, in that particular moment, to be more like him. What would it be like, to feel as if success, not the past, lurked around the corner? Sometimes Rose imagined talking to Gerhard, really talking to him, alone, and he would reveal himself: *The dreams I have,* he would say. *You have no idea.*

"Well, yes, people do work in factories," Isobel was saying. "But your sister doesn't. You don't."

"I would if I needed to," he said roughly. And if it hadn't been for Isobel and her money, he easily might have.

"Oh, Gerhard, really," Isobel said with a slight toss of the head. "We are not going down that road, please."

"And which road—"

"I have something to ask," Rose interjected, more out of a desire to stop them than any thought-out plan.

"Of course," Isobel said, but she was still scrutinizing Gerhard as she said it. Then she swiveled back to Rose. "Yes?"

"Well . . ." Rose hesitated. Could she ask Mr. Cohen for the extra money? Margaret? "My landlady told me that the cost of my room is going up," she confessed. "I'm afraid I'm going to need more money for the rent."

"How much more?" Gerhard asked with a bluntness that Rose wished surprised her.

"It doesn't matter," Isobel said.

"Isobel, please—"

"Twenty shillings more weekly," Rose answered, undercutting the figure by ten—too ashamed to say the full amount. She could make up the difference out of her pocket money; she was certain she could.

"That's quite a jump," Gerhard said.

"I know," Rose said wretchedly. "That's what I told her."

"For God's sakes, Gerhard," Isobel said. "Of course we'll give her the money."

"That's not the point. We—and she—should know the details. Perhaps Deering is taking advantage of her. Also, we do have an abundance of room here. And with the baby on the way, she could be useful—"

"Me? With the baby?" The words fell out of Rose's mouth, she didn't have time to scrub them free of her distaste.

"I'm not saying you should," Gerhard said, "only that we should discuss it as a possibility."

"You don't have to," Isobel said quickly.

"No, it's just that—you're so far from school—"

"Not that much farther than South Kensington," Gerhard pointed out.

"Gerhard," Isobel chided.

"What?"

Rose could barely hear them. This was what she had been afraid of from the moment they offered to pay her expenses. She wasn't herself on these weekly visits. The thought of living here made it difficult to breathe. Maybe it wasn't absurd to ask Mr. Cohen for the money. Mrs. Cohen still made it clear that she thought literature an impractical pursuit for a girl like Rose, but several months ago, Mr. Cohen had come to London on business and he called on her. She hadn't seen him in well over a year. The last time he had been in town, she was still employed by the factory, and she avoided him. He knew where she worked but that didn't mean that she had to talk about it. Rose was grateful that the Cohens had taken care of her, resentful that she needed such care. Often there was an air of stiffness to their conversations. But this time proved different. Mr. Cohen waxed nostalgic about reading Kipling and Tennyson during his own school days. "You've turned into quite the young lady," he said as he shook her hand upon leaving. He undoubtedly approved of her studies. She could ask him for a temporary loan to carry her for a few months. Rose could get a job, something part-time, so she could continue at school. She would figure out a way if need be.

"It's—how much is the increase?" Isobel asked.

Rose hesitated. "Thirty shillings more a week," she eventually said.

"You said twenty before," Gerhard said.

"I made a mistake," Rose said, appealing to her brother. He had to understand how difficult this was for her. "It's thirty."

Isobel said: "That's less than fifty pounds yearly. You know, my family doesn't have so much money . . ." Rose gaped at her, baffled. Isobel had more money than anyone she had ever met. ". . . But we have enough. We certainly have more than enough for you not to worry about such things."

"Thank you," Rose managed. Thank God. "Thank you, Isobel."

"We are glad to help," Isobel said, and she stood up, leaned her heavy frame against Gerhard. Rose watched them, relieved. She was always surprised to see how much shorter Isobel was than Gerhard, and she wasn't more than a few inches taller than Rose herself. "I want you to think of it as your money too."

Rose nodded. "Of course," she murmured. But that was like imagining a London without the war ever happening: such an exquisite thought, but altogether impossible.

"MISS ZIMMER," PROFESSOR HILLMAN SAID. HE gestured toward the seat close to the door with his chin. He had a pronounced chin, Rose thought now; she had never noticed it before. She tried to focus on this detail and his receding hair, and not the fact that she had been called in to speak with him. She had thought her paper on *The Brothers Karamazov* was all right. Was it her best? No. But she hadn't been sleeping well. It was difficult to concentrate. Although Isobel said they would cover the difference in her rent, Rose still feared that it wouldn't happen, that her brother would become even more attracted to his idea that she move in with them. Isobel—and indeed her brother—had given Rose no reason to believe this. Still she worried.

Professor Hillman's office was tiny, the bookshelves hulking. There was no samovar. Rose positioned herself at the edge of the chair, kept her moist hands folded in her lap. It was hot in here; she had an urge to pull at the collar of her jumper, allow in more air, but she didn't dare.

"Your paper was intriguing, but undisciplined, for you. I thought your structural point on how Dostoyevsky was playing with time, flattening it in the first half of the book, was well taken. And more than that, original."

"Thank you," Rose said, for that was a compliment mixed into the criticism, wasn't it? It was exceedingly difficult to think straight.

"But it wasn't carried forth throughout the essay. You dropped it quite suddenly, as if you forgot about it. And I expected you to touch more on the theme of suffering you had discussed in class."

"Oh," she said, and she could not look at him. He was right. She too had thought about the notion of unavenged suffering, but when she thought of exploring it, truly articulating what she thought Dostoyevsky meant by it, she felt overcome, panicky with emotion. There was only so much she could say on the subject. Now she simply felt ashamed. She hadn't wanted to do the hard work that university required. Professor Hillman was right. It was a shoddy paper, and it was all she could do not to leap across the desk and grab it and tear it up into minuscule pieces.

"You are a clever girl, Miss Zimmer," he said. "I am telling you this precisely because you are clever. This paper is acceptable. If another student had written it, it might be quite fine. But you can do better. I've seen you do better."

"I understand, Professor Hillman," she said, and even she could hear the quiver in her voice. He was saying something kind, but how could she believe him? She had a hard time believing people, trusting the most basic of facts.

"I called you here for another reason too. Have you thought about your plans after you obtain your degree?"

She shook her head. Of course she had, but only hazily. A job in publishing, perhaps, or a position at the Home Office. These were things she had to consider, she knew—Gerhard and Isobel would not fund her indefinitely, nor would she want them to. But it unnerved her, to think of a time after school, when she would have to get a job again, when she would have someone tell her what to do.

"I hope you will consider teaching. You would make a fine teacher."

"What?" It was something she scarcely allowed herself to imagine, too heady was the possibility. Teaching! "You think I would?"

"Yes, I most certainly do." He reached for a thick catalog on his desk. "It takes work. You must earn an additional certificate through the education department, but you are up to the task. Certainly for secondary school—and there is still a great need, after the war—but I could see you, if you continued on this path, continuing your studies and remaining at a university level too. Not many women have the fortitude, but I believe you do."

"Thank you, Professor Hillman," Rose said, and couldn't help flashing him a pleased grin. To be a teacher would be an honor and responsibility. It would give her security, a clear career path. She feared she wouldn't be up for the task; she would work harder than ever to make it so.

But doubt crept in: Would Mutti have seen it this way? She respected teachers to be sure, but a career? She would want Rose to get married, have a family of her own. This was what mattered most to her. At twenty-one years old, Rose knew she should already be thinking of these things. But she felt so much older than her years, and sometimes she wondered if, after everything she had been through, meeting a boy was a step she had inadvertently bypassed, something that she was simply not destined to do.

"I appreciate all your guidance," Rose said, more muted this time. "Thank you."

Professor Hillman held out his hand and grasped hers with a firm shake that surprised her. "It is I who am honored to teach you."

"YOU'RE QUIET TODAY," ISOBEL SAID to Rose as they neared the end of Sunday dinner.

"I'm tired," Rose said, and it was the truth. She had stayed up late reading the night before. It had been four days since she had met with Professor Hillman, and every night she stayed up hours past the other residents at Mrs. Deering's, poring over her books. She wouldn't let Professor Hillman down again.

"Well, I read the most amazing item in the paper today," Isobel said. "I've told you that when Grandpapa was in Sydney, he had a partner, haven't I?"

"Perhaps," Gerhard said with a little smile directed at his sister. "But the details on Grandpapa's concerns have always been mysterious to me."

Rose couldn't manage a smile back. She forked off another morsel of Mrs. Tompkins's roast. Rose knew that Isobel's grandfather had gone to Australia as a young man and bought dozens of properties. The investments had paid off handsomely and provided the foundation from which Isobel's large family had drawn for decades.

"Yes, well, Grandpapa's ways were mysterious to all of us," Isobel said. "But his partner was a man called Henry Cooper, and Mr. Cooper's family and ours remained close. His grandson Douglas Cooper and I spent summers together in Wales, and he was at Trinity while I was at Newnham. Then he went off to the Sorbonne and Freiburg—and when he returned, he opened an art gallery. He always had such a critical eye. He could be a bit of a rogue, but my parents adored him. In fact, when I came home and announced to my parents that I was besotted with your brother and they were not at all pleased, they trotted out Douglas's name."

"Your father should have known better than to raise objections about a foreigner to you," Gerhard said, raising an eyebrow, dabbing a corner of his mouth with his napkin. Had Isobel ever liked an Englishman? Last year, when she was reading Browning, Isobel told her about a northern Italian boy she had met during a sojourn to Lake Como. "He came from a banking family," Rose remembered Isobel saying, "but he had the soul of an artist." Her brother, Rose thought, was Isobel's perfect match: a foreigner, which of course pleased her, and a man who seemed English to the core for her parents.

"Mrs. Tompkins," Gerhard now called. When the housekeeper emerged, he said: "Delicious, as usual. My whiskey now, please." He turned back to Isobel. "But why were you not enticed by the estimable Mr. Cooper?"

"So many reasons," Isobel said. "Foremost I was not available, but had I been, Douglas Cooper does not like the female persuasion."

"Ah," Gerhard said. "And why are we speaking of him now?"

"Well, I knew from Mama that Douglas was in Europe, but what I did not know was that he became a British officer specializing in art. Tracking down lost art from the war. Douglas Cooper, can you imagine that? In a position of importance and authority!"

"What do you mean?" Rose asked, suddenly alert. "Lost art?"

"That's what the item in the paper today was about. During the war, so many things went missing—'looted' is the better term, of course. And apparently Douglas Cooper was sent to Switzerland a few years ago, and in just a few weeks he was able to turn up dozens of pictures and valuables that had been stolen from their rightful owners and sold by the Nazis—many to people who claimed, cravenly, that they had absolutely no idea what the Nazis were doing. The paper called him a British hero. Douglas Cooper! I tell you. I never would have guessed it. Thoroughly astounding."

"That does sound astounding," Rose said. Gerhard was sipping his whiskey, leaning back in his chair. Was he not going to say anything? His ice cubes clinked, he drained his glass, silent.

Isobel was still speaking. "How amazing: to find a canvas that had been missing for more than five years. The paper said that France has set up a commission to find the art too, and all that they do find they store in the Jeu de Paume until they find the owners. Has either of you ever been there? Oh, Gerhard, we must go one day. It's such a lovely little museum, right on the edge of the Tuileries."

Rose heard Isobel but her particular words did not register, because she felt a flare of possibility. *Everything was gone,* Gerhard had told her, *Vienna was not the same*. Perhaps, just perhaps, he wasn't right.

Now Isobel was talking about the Rothschilds, and how the patriarch of the family, now living in Toronto, had tracked down his Vermeer, which had been sold to a dealer in Lucerne. A woman had gone into an antique shop here in Knightsbridge and spotted her mother's Limoges sixty-piece dinner service, hand-painted with her family's initials.

"You know, Isobel," Rose started to say, her heart resounding, "our family owned some pictures. One in particular that our mother loved very much. By a painter named Chaim Soutine."

"But we aren't Rothschilds, and that's not a valuable painting," Gerhard said.

"Why does that matter?" Rose retorted.

"Really, Gerhard," Isobel said. "There might be something we could do. Why would you not tell me such a thing?"

"It's in the past," Gerhard said. "So many things, they're in the past."

"But that doesn't mean they have to remain there." Isobel said this firmly, but Rose wasn't sure she heard her correctly. She felt a quickening, a fluttering rise. In her mind's eye, she saw the red of the Bellhop's jacket, the thickened paint strokes, she saw her mother, seeing those things.

"Could you write to Douglas for us? Could you ask him about the Soutine?"

"Why, it's not a question. Of course I will."

"It's a waste of time," Gerhard said. "You don't know." His voice deepened, but the words sounded brittle. He grabbed his glass and stalked out of the room.

Her brother's anger only fueled Rose's certainty. Isobel poured herself water and spoke: "You shouldn't mind him. But I suppose you know that better than I."

"I don't mind at all," Rose said. She was somewhere else entirely. It was *The Bellhop* she was thinking of, those dark eyes that gave nothing away. *I will find you,* she thought. And for the first time in years, she felt as if it were a promise she had a chance of keeping.

9

LOS ANGELES, 2006

LIZZIE HADN'T ASKED ROSE FOR her approval. She told herself that she didn't need it. She was gathering facts. What was the harm in being informed?

Plenty, she could hear Rose retort. But Rose was full of protestations. She couldn't always mean them. This was what Lizzie thought as she read online about the 1999 Washington Conference on Nazi-Confiscated Art and the Holocaust Art Restitution Project and the Conference on Jewish Material Claims Against Germany. It was easy to pretend, as she kept scrolling, that *The Bellhop* was like the other artwork in question, languishing in a private collection or a museum somewhere, its provenance suspicious and light on details. But *The Bellhop* wasn't missing because of the Nazis. Lizzie imagined Rose saying, *That's precisely why you want to know about restitution: so you can forget that night.* Still she kept searching.

On a Harvard law school syllabus, she read the language that the Nazis had used to codify the seizure of artwork. They had gone to the trouble to make it legal. The law, established in 1938, stated that "products of degenerate art that have been secured in museums or in collections open to the public . . . may be appropriated by the

Reich without compensation." Lizzie read about New York's 1963 *Menzel v. List* case that had established the demand and refusal rule, which stated that the limitations period begins once the owner makes a demand for the return of the property in question. She read about battles over Monets and Matisses, the stonewalling by prominent museums that insisted there was no plundered artwork hanging on their walls; she read many a reference to Klimt's *Portrait of Adele Bloch-Bauer.*

"The prospect of attempting to claim seized art is daunting, arduous, expensive, and byzantine at best," an attorney by the name of Michael Ciparelli was quoted as saying in one news account. His name sounded familiar. She looked him up. He was an expert in the field of art restitution, and she saw that he had been an associate at Paul, Weiss years earlier, as had her boss. Perhaps Marc could put her in touch. *What's he going to tell you?* She could imagine Rose scoffing. *We don't know where* The Bellhop *is. How can it be claimed?*

I don't know, Lizzie told Rose in her head. *That's why I'm going to ask.*

NONE OF THIS SHE TOLD Rose that afternoon. The plan had been for another walk. But after they left Rose's apartment in the late afternoon, the wind kicked up—it was cooler than either Rose or Lizzie had expected—and the streets felt emptied out, desolate. "I could use some coffee," Lizzie offered, but as they headed to the café, Rose looked at her watch: "Corman!" she declared happily.

Corman apparently meant Roger Corman, which apparently also meant the Los Angeles County Museum of Art. The nearby museum was hosting a retrospective of the director's work ("He's that B-movie guy, right?" Lizzie said, and Rose threw her such a look of disdain. "If that's the way you want to think of one of the most influential directors and producers of the twentieth century, then so be it.") This week his Edgar Allan Poe adaptations were being featured,

Rose explained as she led Lizzie the several blocks to the museum, with more alacrity to her step than she'd had moments before.

They made it with fifteen minutes to spare, and they had their pick of seats in the small screening room. Soon they were watching *Tomb of Ligeia*. It was a hot, gothic, campy affair: a loner of a man (Vincent Price, looking younger than Lizzie had ever seen him) obsessed with his dead first wife, a crumbling abbey, a deranged black cat, hints of necrophilia. The plot was overstuffed but Price hammed it up, and the scenes filmed outside in the English countryside were gorgeous. It seemed to be more concerned with romantic obsession than an attempt to frighten, and it reminded Lizzie of *Jane Eyre* and *The Woman in White*, two books she loved. ("The script is by Robert Towne, who also wrote *Chinatown*," Rose leaned over to whisper.)

As Vincent Price was fighting with the spirit of his first wife, who now took the form of a cat, Lizzie felt her phone buzz. She looked down to see a text from Max ("Miss you," it said. "See you for dinner?"). She turned back with renewed determination to the screen.

The film ended a little after six P.M. It was already dark when they left the theater, Lizzie's thin jacket no match for the dropping temperature. They headed back to Rose's apartment, where Lizzie's car was parked.

"What did you think?" Rose asked.

"It was fun," Lizzie said. "Vincent Price especially."

"You know Robert Towne didn't want to use him. He thought he was too old. But Corman insisted. He made Price wear a wig and layered on the makeup."

"See, there are solutions to everything."

"I would say that it's essential to stick to your guns."

Lizzie laughed; she read it that way too.

"Food. Shall we order in for dinner?"

"Yes," Lizzie said. "Please." She still hadn't answered Max's text. She'd gone to the bathroom, started to peck out a response, then stopped.

Earlier that morning, she had pretended to be asleep when he left, keeping her eyes faux-shut when he brushed his lips across her forehead. After he'd gone, she got up and headed out with her laptop, spent the morning at a nearby café. She came across a long thread in her work e-mail about the Clarke appeal. Kathleen, the associate, reported to Marc that Clarke had complained in a call that they were being too deferential to the lower court in the brief. ("They're wrong; that's what the appeal is based on. Why fuck around?" Kathleen reported Clarke as saying.) But that would be a mistake, Lizzie thought, and she wrote both Kathleen and Marc, furiously tapping out her response. A few minutes later, she sent Marc a separate e-mail about Michael Ciparelli, the lawyer who specialized in restitution cases. "Of course I know him," Marc wrote back. "Sharp, smart. I'll put you two in touch." Lizzie felt a flash of pleasure. Maybe Rose would listen to Ciparelli, if not her.

Now Rose was talking about the dearth of decent Chinese food in her neighborhood as they rounded the corner and reached her building, a stucco four-story fronted by a shallow rectangle of yellowing grass and a forlorn palm tree. A man stood on the steps of the concrete walkway. "Rose! There you are!" He took the stairs purposefully. He was a bear of an older man, clad in a dark blazer and jeans. "I was beginning to worry."

"You were?" Rose said, sounding annoyed. "Why?"

"Porter's—for dinner." He reached Rose and kissed her on the cheek. He dwarfed her. "Don't tell me you forgot." He had a deep, authoritative voice; it assumed people paid attention.

"So then I won't," Rose said. Lizzie was watching and listening to all of this, taking in Rose's irritated tone, the man's clear affection for her. Who was he? She had a sense but she didn't dare ask.

"Come on," he said, head to the side, but he didn't seem annoyed. "Aren't you hungry? I for one am famished." He turned to Lizzie. "I don't believe we've met; I'm Bob Fisher." He gripped her hand in greeting.

"I'm sorry," Rose said. "Lizzie and I were at the movies. Lizzie is the daughter of an old friend of mine. And Bob is—a new friend of mine."

"Not all that new," Bob said.

Rose shrugged.

Lizzie wanted to catch Rose's eye and raise an eyebrow, knowing she would be furious if she did. Rose had a boyfriend!

"Lizzie and I were just talking about dinner; she'll join us," Rose said.

"For dinner?" Bob said. He looked at Rose, then to Lizzie, then back at Rose again.

"No, no," Lizzie said. She wasn't going to intrude. "I'm fine."

"I know you're fine," Rose said. "But you're coming. Do not tell me you have plans. You didn't have them five minutes ago." She turned to Bob. "I took her to a horror movie—the least I can do is feed her."

Bob gave Lizzie a declarative nod. "Of course, join us. I hope the film wasn't too bad; Rose is always trying to drag me to the worst movies." He reached for Rose's hand, grinning.

"It was *Corman*," Rose muttered, but she allowed him to take her hand.

Watching them together, Lizzie felt a quick joyful current. "She does have very particular taste," she said to Bob. "And thank you, I will come."

"Oh, please, what's wrong with my taste?" Rose asked, but Bob was already on his phone calling the restaurant to change the reservation, and Lizzie was texting Max back. "I'm so sorry; I won't be back for dinner," she typed with a strange shot of giddiness. "But I won't be back late." And for the first time that day she truly missed him.

THREE PEOPLE, TWO CARS, LESS than half a mile's drive. In no time at all, Lizzie pulled up at Porter's on La Cienega, Bob and Rose behind her in Bob's boat of an old Mercedes. The steak house was more Austrian ski lodge than L.A.: darkly but invitingly lit, wood beams crisscrossing the high ceiling, wide-mouthed fireplace crackling, leather-bound books for menus.

"They have boar here, and it is delicious," Bob told Lizzie as they were ushered into a leather booth.

"I am not ordering boar," Rose said, nose to menu.

"You don't have to, but it is an option."

"I like options," Lizzie said.

Bob suggested manhattans, he highly recommended the strip steak and creamed corn too. Lizzie took him up on all of it. Rose stuck with water while Lizzie was soon draining her drink and eating a warm roll and oysters (when had Bob ordered those?). And then the steaks arrived—charred at the edges, tender, delicious.

Bob was talking and talking—about being a salesman for a medical equipment company ("He's being modest," Rose added. "He's a salesman and a vice president.") and his boat that he liked to sail out to Catalina. "Have you ever seen the wild pigs out there?" he said. "They'll eat anything, including each other." He asked her about living in New York and how she decided to go into appellate work (he knew what appellate law was; not everyone did). And after ordering a bottle of Merlot, he said: "Here's the thing you need to know about me—and Rose is coming to terms with it—I am a Springsteen fanatic."

"Okay," Lizzie said. She waited. Was there more to it than that?

"What do you think about Bruce?" He was looking at her with such intent, nearly grimacing.

"I think he's fine. I like him fine." The truth was, Lizzie didn't have a strong opinion about Bruce Springsteen. On the musical front, she was a hanger-on, usually decades behind the times.

"I would respect you more if you hated him," Bob said.

"Oh, please," Rose began. "Do not start."

"Why? You hate Springsteen, and I adore you," Bob said. He leaned over, his enormous face intent on Lizzie's. "I've seen him dozens of times. God, Staples Center, 1999, the reunion tour: Those opening cords of 'Jungleland.' And the Big Man on the sax, and then Bruce yelling, 'Is there anyone alive out there?' And it's a good question, don't you think? It's the most important question we should be asking, all the time: Is there anyone alive out there?"

Lizzie was already woozy but she took a long pull on her wine. "You're right," she said. In the middle of the clinking glasses and clatter of dishes and conversation and smoky smells and rush of waiters and all of the rich abundance, gustatory and material, it felt like a striking, profound question. All she could think of were her parents: her father, dead in a nanosecond, her mother's agonizing demise encircling her childhood. *Is anyone alive out there?* Was she? "I should see Springsteen in concert," she said, and her voice turned hoarse with emotion. "I will."

A slow smile flitted across Bob's face. "I know you will," he said with a gravelly satisfaction. "And you will not regret it." He stood, wiped the corner of his mouth with the napkin with a surprisingly delicate gesture. "Now, ladies, if you'll excuse me a moment." He wove past the other tables and the fireplace and disappeared from view.

"Why the Springsteen obsession," Rose said. "I do not know."

Lizzie leaned across the table, touched Rose's wrist. "I love him," she proclaimed. "I do."

Was Rose blushing? "He can be a handful, but I am fond of him," she admitted.

"He is besotted with you," Lizzie said. "As well he should be."

"Yes, well," Rose said. "I'll tell you what I'm besotted with—these rolls." She broke one in half, spread on a thin layer of butter. "It seems easy to do a nice hot roll, but it isn't, and it shouldn't be overlooked; it should be taken seriously and celebrated."

"I'll celebrate that," Lizzie said as Bob returned. The waiter came by and offered more wine, which Lizzie gladly accepted, despite what she suspected was a look of disapproval from Rose.

"Remind me how you two know each other?" Bob said.

"Lizzie's father was the one who owned my family's painting."

"Oh yes. The one that was stolen from the house. The painting by—what's his name?"

"Soutine," Lizzie and Rose said nearly in unison. Lizzie blushed.

"Chaim Soutine," Rose amended. "You would find him interesting. If not as a painter, then as a person. He was a character, a hypochondriac who lived in fear of going bald. He loved his friend Modigliani and the Old Masters like Rembrandt." Rose hadn't told Bob about Soutine before? For a moment, this surprised Lizzie, then she thought: *Who did she talk about Soutine with?*

"And boxing," Rose continued. "Apparently Soutine used to say that if he hadn't been an artist, he would have liked to be a boxer. The writer Henry Miller was his neighbor for a time and they used to go to matches together."

"Really?" Lizzie said. She didn't know that Henry Miller had lived nearby. What else did she not know? Her head was so fuzzy. "You like boxing?" she said to Bob.

"I do. I used to box myself, years ago. I know what people think of it, but they're wrong. It actually taught me to be more patient. I learned that if you swing at an opponent's face, he'll hit right back. It taught me to hold back a bit, to be more controlled."

When the waiter came over with dessert menus, Bob told him: "We'll have the chocolate cake. One slice, three forks."

"We will?" Rose said.

"It's the only thing to get here," Bob said. "Hot molten chocolate cake. It's delicious." Lizzie was already so full, but when did she ever say no to a few tastes of sweetness? "So the detectives never came across any clues?" Bob added.

"No," Rose said.

"There were no signs of a break-in," Lizzie said. "It happened during a party—a party I threw." She managed to say this in a steady voice.

"And they don't think one of the guests took it."

"In the beginning, yes, they thought it might have been a prank, but the artwork—there was a Picasso drawing too—they were the only two things taken. Whoever stole them knew exactly what they were looking for. And all my friends were in high school. None of them knew anything about art."

"That must have been terrible," Bob said. "Being there at the time, knowing that it happened."

"Yeah," Lizzie said. "It sucked."

"'Sucked'?" Rose repeated.

Lizzie blushed. "You know what I mean," she muttered. "It was horrible."

The waiter delivered the cake with a flourish, placing it in the center of the table—round and dark and dusted with powdered sugar. Bob cut into it, and melted chocolate oozed out, darkening the plate. "Delicious," he said. "Have some." When neither Rose nor Lizzie reached for it, he added, "The detectives must have talked to everyone, including your father."

"Yeah, they did," Lizzie said. "He was in Boston when it happened."

"Oh," Bob said, and he gave the one syllable force. His forearms were planted on the edge of the table, and Lizzie was struck by how large his hands were—boxer's hands. "And the paintings were insured, weren't they?"

"Of course," Rose said. "Why?"

"I just wonder how much they were insured for, how much they were worth at the time. The art market is famously volatile. It's interesting."

"How do you know about the volatility of the art market?" Rose's voice was sharp. "And nothing is just *interesting*. Things are upsetting or wonderful, stupid or delightful, charming or beautiful or terrible. What do you mean, 'interesting'?"

A flicker of uncertainty crossed Bob's face. Lizzie saw it, a sudden shift. "I used to have a neighbor who worked as an investigator for an insurance company," Bob said. "He was always talking about the fraudulent claims he uncovered."

"No," Rose said. "Do not. Joseph wanted to get them back. That's it, end of story."

Lizzie felt caught behind a thick distorting pane of glass. What was Bob saying? Rose was sitting up straight, her body tight with anger.

"You're right, I'm sorry," Bob said.

"Of course I'm right. He worked for years to get them back. Do you want to accuse a dead man of anything else, while his daughter is sitting here?"

"I don't understand," Lizzie said.

"I'm sorry," Bob said softly, turning to her. "I'm sure the police cleared it up. I don't know why I said that."

"It's okay," Lizzie stammered. Nothing was making sense. Bob was suggesting—what? That her father had something to do with the stolen paintings?

"No, it is not *okay*." Rose was livid. "How dare you?" She grabbed her blazer, fumbled putting it on. "Who do you think you are, saying such things to us? Impugning my friend like that—a dead man who cannot defend himself. Come, Lizzie, we're going."

"No, Rose; wait, please," Bob said, reaching for her. "It was stupid; I didn't mean it."

But Rose shook him off. "Let's go."

"I'm sorry," Lizzie said to Bob.

"Why are *you* apologizing?" Rose cried.

"You can't leave me here alone," Bob said. "There's still cake." He tried to laugh.

"It looks," Rose snapped, "like a pile of shit."

LIZZIE, BEHIND THE WHEEL OF her car, was shocked into sobriety as surely as if she'd downed a pint of burned coffee. Rose sat beside her, fuming. "I am absolutely appalled. The nerve to suggest such a thing. Your father hired an investigator at his own expense when the police turned up nothing. Years! Decades! All on your father's dime."

"I know," Lizzie said. "I know." A strand of hair fell across her cheek; for a moment, nothing had ever felt more irritating. She yanked at it, clutched the steering wheel with the other hand.

"Bob gets these ideas in his head and he just says them—he'll say anything that comes to mind. He is seventy-three years old and he has absolutely no idea how to behave. I am sorry."

"It's okay."

"It's not."

"It is." Lizzie rolled down her window. "Please."

"It's rather cold, don't you think?" Rose said. "Do you need the window open?"

"I do, yes," Lizzie said. "The fresh air is helping me, sorry." She turned on the heat.

Within minutes, Lizzie had pulled up in front of Rose's building. "You know, I bet my father would find it kind of funny," she said as Rose unbuckled her seat belt.

"What? No."

Lizzie was too worn out to explain. She only meant that her father wasn't easily insulted. He was more confident, more certain of himself than anyone else she knew. She would call Sarah; she would tell her the story. She could hear her sister's response: *Oh, please,* she'd snort. *As if the police didn't consider that on day one.*

"Let's talk tomorrow," Rose said, and gave Lizzie a stern nod. *Chin up,* Lizzie felt she was saying. She nodded in return.

Leaving Rose's, she turned onto Fairfax, heading back toward Venice. After a few blocks, she pulled over and called her sister, who picked up right away.

"The strangest thing happened tonight. I was having dinner with Rose," Lizzie began.

"Yeah?" Sarah asked.

Lizzie hesitated. Why would she tell her the story? What did she think Sarah would say? She remembered that first night in the hospital, the V of Sarah's thin gown puckering, the fluorescent light giving her skin a greenish cast, tubes snaking up from her hand taped to a pole; she heard the clicks and whirls of machines. It had only happened that once. Sarah had been stable for years and years now.

Still. Lizzie took a deep breath. She loved her sister. And the story she was thinking of telling now felt like a burden. "Rose has a boyfriend," she said.

"So? That's the strange thing?"

"Yeah," Lizzie said. "I had no idea she was seeing someone."

"Why shouldn't she?" Sarah said. "Because she's older? Sometimes you suffer from a lack of imagination."

"That's the truth," Lizzie said, trying to blink away all that couldn't be forgotten.

10

LONDON, 1950

ROSE DIDN'T KNOW WHY SHE had settled on this particular antique shop, only that she had. For the past two months, the shop off Old Bond Street was the only one she visited. The smells of dampness and benign neglect made it seem more approachable than its price tags might suggest. Its poor lighting allowed her to examine merchandise in relative seclusion. But those weren't the only reasons; so many of London's shops were dimly lit and dusty. There was something about the heaviness of its furniture—much of it black oak, chairs covered in velvet, chaise longues formidable as stone—the knickknacks, the oil paintings in their ornate frames, and the trove of porcelain vases. Walking into the shop gave her a strange, unsettling sensation. It reminded her of home.

Today the salesgirl was busy helping a flaxen-headed boy who seemed to be far too young to be contemplating the brooch before him. It took Rose's eyes a few minutes to adjust to the light. She saw a large bronze peacock flecked with mottled green and purple that hadn't been there the week before. She gave a marble chessboard and a jewel-encrusted cigarette case little more than a quick, practiced glance.

Rose had no intention of making a purchase. She finally had landed a position—as a secretary, not exactly the teaching job she had been searching for since getting her degree, not exactly well paying, but it was a position nevertheless. She paid her rent, she covered her expenses, and then: well, there was little left. Still, she was glad to be on her own, no longer taking money from Gerhard and Isobel. After she had started working for Mr. Marks, Rose found an apartment in Belsize, a tiny two-room flat at the top of a perilously uneven staircase. The halls smelled like wet wool and she regularly heard the shriek of the baby next door, but the place was all hers. She had a minuscule breakfast table that she was able to situate beneath a small but perfectly suitable window, and an old pair of club chairs that Gerhard and Isobel had given her when they redecorated. It was in one of the armchairs that she would have her tea, balancing a cup and saucer on her knee, even if she was alone, as was most often the case. (Last week her tea offerings vastly improved when she received a small box from Leeds containing a tin of chocolate biscuits, a collection of jellies, and, most wondrously, a small crock containing four eggs nestled in straw. "From the Cohens," the card said, but Rose immediately recognized Mary's hand.) What Rose had these days was a surfeit of time, as Gerhard pointed out far too often. For the past month, as the days shortened and edged closer to winter, she had been drawn to this shop week after week, as surely and as inexplicably as the queues that still crisscrossed the city, nearly five years after the war.

Isobel had been true to her word. She had written her childhood friend Douglas Cooper, and he in turn had guided them. Austria had enacted laws on restitution at the end of the war, the so-called Rückstellungsgesetz, which said that all victims were entitled to list and report the loss of property. Gerhard and Rose wrote to the Austrian Federal Monuments Office with a record of all the valuables they could recall from their parents' home. Months went by, then a year; finally they received word: no matches. The Austrian government was holding thousands of seized artworks in collecting points throughout the country: in a monastery in Mauerbach, in salt mines near Salzburg, storage rooms in the Finance Ministry in Vienna itself. "There are lists," Douglas had written, thousands upon thousands of items on those lists. "The Austrian government claims the work is heirless; they say they are working on returning what can be returned. They are not releasing the lists." But Douglas had seen some, and there were no Soutines, nothing that fit *The Bellhop*'s description.

"But they could be wrong," Rose said.

Isobel sighed. "They probably are," she said. "Unconscionable—ignorant, murderous Krauts."

"Isobel," chided Gerhard.

"What? They are."

Douglas told Isobel of a lawyer, a Franz Rudolf Bienenfeld, a Jewish emigré from Vienna, who worked on such issues in London. They met with him. He was a small middle-aged man in a well-cut suit. "There are possibilities," he said. "We could apply for restitution for interrupted schooling. For both of you."

"No," Rose and Gerhard said. On this they agreed.

"They can keep their money," Gerhard said, arms folded over his chest.

"I want my mother's painting," Rose said.

Bienenfeld's eyes squinted behind round wire spectacles. "It is owed to you," he said. "It is not their money."

"I don't want it," Gerhard said. Rose stole a glance at her brother. It wasn't as if she weren't tempted. But the notion of filing a claim felt like acquiescing. She imagined it displeasing both her parents. So she said nothing at all.

Rose continued to look. The trick was not to narrow one's focus. Expectations couldn't be tamped down entirely—that wasn't realistic, and Rose was, if anything, a realist (even within this fool's errand). But it was a nameless, shimmery expectation, so light and gossamer thin that it existed as sensation only. She thought about searching when she was taking dictation for Mr. Marks. It was on her mind when Mr. Cohen wrote to her to say that he would be in town on Saturday and was she available to meet for tea? "I'm busy," she wrote back, thinking of the shop on Old Bond. She thought about looking while swaying in the dim light of the Underground, listening to people grouse about Korea and the National Health Service. I have this, she would think. Searching gave her purpose.

Every item was defined by its negative—the ivory handles on the pair of swords hanging opposite the clocks were too intricate to be the ones her grandfather brought back from Constantinople. The rococo mirror she spotted last month was too small and bright to be her mother's. Now she turned over a midnight-velvet jewelry case, but this had a soft gold clasp, not silver, and its underside wasn't nicked as her grandmother's had been.

She remembered what Isobel had read in the paper: how a former cook of one of the Rothschilds had started a new position and was astounded to see the Vermeer from the *baronne*'s dressing area hanging in her new employer's drawing room. In the past two years, Rose had gathered stories from the papers on her own. A Mrs. Arnold had spotted a set of mother-of-pearl nesting boxes inlaid with her mother's initials in the window of an antique dealer in Paris. Nathan Rosenberg went into a Zurich picture dealer and saw one of his family's eighteenth-century portraits hanging on the wall. These things did happen.

Rose had reached the far wall of the shop, on which a select number of pictures were hung. Within a beat, she had her answer—registered by the drop in her stomach before her mind could articulate why. There were pastoral scenes—a brook, a picnicking group—and pictures of horses galloping and boys diving. But no portraits.

"That horse couldn't win a pigs' race, I tell you." The fair-haired salesgirl was standing beside Rose, contemplating a picture with her narrow blue eyes.

"I'm sorry?" Rose asked. She was trying to remember when she had last come in: last week or the week before? Had the landscapes been here? Maybe they hadn't gotten any new paintings in. She should inquire, but she didn't like to ask questions.

"I'm telling you, look at his legs, yeah? Too short and stocky, out of proportion."

Rose looked. "Yes," she admitted. She hadn't noticed. She had barely registered the horses at all.

"I'm Julie," the salesgirl said, extending a hand, her small features composed into a genuine smile. Rose had been in the shop enough to know that she smiled often. Even so, Rose was taken aback. She didn't expect a smile from her—or from most people, really.

"Rose," she said, and took the girl's cool hand.

"Nice to finally make your acquaintance," Julie said. "I told Mr. Bradshaw the picture was no good but he didn't care. If he could, he'd turn the entire shop into an equestrian palace. What are you looking for? I know it's something in particular. You'd think I would know by now, but I haven't a clue."

"Nothing," Rose said, blushing. Clearly a lie. Embarrassed, she shifted her gaze to the chess set. It was made out of two different shades of marble, one honey-colored, one dark. Someone had spent a good deal of time carving it. Papi had played chess, hadn't he? Did he have a chessboard? She couldn't remember.

"If you tell me," Julie said, "I could keep an eye for you."

"I appreciate it, I do, but I'm simply looking." Rose tried to smile but it felt forced, nothing like the genuine warmth on the salesgirl's face. "I should get going."

In the front of the shop, the boy was still contemplating jewelry. As Rose tried to brush past him, he spoke: "Sorry, but may I ask you a question? I'm buying something for my mum. But I don't know which." He pointed at two brooches on the counter. Rose registered that the boy had dark, liquid eyes, just like Dirk Bogarde, that movie star that Margaret used to go on about, a similar Brylcreemed wave to his straw-colored hair. "I don't know anything about these things," he confessed. "But she's dark-haired, like you, with a similar complexion."

"You should try them on!" Julie said with enthusiasm, now beside them.

What? Rose almost scolded her on behalf of Mr. Bradshaw. She almost said, *I'm not the buying type. He isn't either. Can't you see?* It was exhausting, Rose thought, all that people couldn't see, right in front of their faces. "So sorry, I can't," she said, but nevertheless she lingered.

"I'll take this one," he said, and pointed with authority to a sterling brooch in the form of a sunburst, tiny red stones winking at its center. Looking at him up close, his thin face, the set of his jaw, she realized that he wasn't a boy at all.

"So lovely!" Julie said. "That was my choice too." She wrote out a ticket, copied the number into a ledger, then took the pin and wrapped it in a dark cloth with a purple ribbon—wrapping that looked more sumptuous than the jewelry itself. "What a good son. My first sale of the day and a lovely story at that! You would think this would make Mr. Bradshaw very happy. But he'll say something like: 'I don't know the point in making more money. It'll all go to Atlee's government men anyway.' Just you wait."

"All right," the boy said as he slipped the small package, the velvet now twice covered in butcher paper, into his pocket. "We will." He directed a shy smile at Rose. He had a long but friendly face, with a sharp nose, not unlike hers. His eyes were not dark brown as she had first thought, but a lovely striated green. "We will."

Wordlessly, she followed him outside. The air was warmer than she had thought. The rain had ceased. They passed an elegant but worn town house, its façade pocked with shrapnel. At the corner, they slowed. The sun hovered low in the pale afternoon sky. The light above the chemist's shop flickered.

"I don't know why I bought it," he said.

"You're a good son," Rose said. She was only repeating the words that Julie had said, but they seemed hollow leaving her mouth, nearly querulous. *Try to be nice,* she told herself. Why was it so hard to be nice? She imagined the room in which such a gift would be offered. She saw a tea trolley in a richly appointed drawing room, a platinum bowl filled with delphiniums.

"I'm not," he said, and he let out a low mangled laugh. "But she always wanted one. And now she's sick. She's dying."

"Oh," Rose said, less a word than an exhalation. The flickering chemist light caught a wave of his blond hair, and for a moment his curl turned silver. She saw a darkened spot of stubble along his jawline that he had missed shaving. He was skinny and slight, not more than a few inches taller than she. And whatever she had thought was so young about him before dissolved in the face of his proximity. "That's very kind of you," she said.

He thrust his hands in his pockets—his mackintosh was too big on him, its sleeves spoiled and loose with unraveling threads. "I don't feel kind. I'm Thomas."

For once she didn't hesitate. "Rose," she said, and her name seemed to glide out of her mouth.

Thomas smiled. "Do you want to walk, Rose?"

It felt too improbable to be real. "Yes," she breathed.

"IT'S RAINING AGAIN." EVA SIGHED. "I *cannot* believe it's raining again." She had grown fleshier in the years since they had studied together at university, and now her sighs were voluble, full like the rest of her. "When I first came here, I thought it was nonsense—it can't truly rain *all* the time—but no, it does. It's England, and it rains." She leaned against Rose's desk and admired her left hand, on which a tiny diamond caught light. "Edgar says New York isn't nearly as gloomy."

"Is that so?" Rose murmured. She knew far too much about Edgar, Eva's USAF officer, for someone she had never met. She had been typing up letters all morning, and now she was supposed to finish hand-copying the long list of suppliers to another list, but she had hardly made a dent. "I don't mind the rain. It's bracing, natural." This, despite the fact that she feared the rain would mar her blouse when she stepped outside for lunch. She was wearing her best one today, her navy silk, purchased six months ago when she was offered this position, a job she had learned about because of Eva, whose mother had a cousin who knew Mr. Marks. Everyone in the office was an immigrant, including Mr. Marks himself. (He liked to hire his own, he said.) "Perhaps it takes some getting used to. You've been here, what? Five years?"

"Just under," Eva said with a smile.

"I've lived here for more than ten years, nearly half my life. I'm practically English."

"You?" Eva looked amused.

"Yes, me. I'm more English than most English people." Rose prided herself on her degree in English literature and her diction scrubbed free of any German. She was grateful for her ration books, for the fact that there were rations to be had, and she liked watching *Kaleidoscope* and relished the smells emanating from the cafés along Haverstock Hill and taking turns in Belsize Park.

Eva laughed. "That's the problem. No one English tries so hard."

Rose cringed, and Eva's words reverberated, as much as she tried to swat them away. Did she try too hard?

Soon it was half past twelve, lunchtime. Mr. Marks was yelling again. His girl was out but Rose suspected he left his door open on purpose; he wanted the office to hear every word. "Do not tell me that we'll cross that bridge when we come to it. I am so tired of hearing that phrase. Let me buy the casings now!" He slammed the phone down. "*Schwachkopf*. Stupid bridge crossers."

Rose had finally finished the forms and was straightening her desk—she worked hard, she was no bridge crosser—when Eva appeared. "Come now, Claire and I are off to look at all we can't buy at Derry and Toms."

"I can't," Rose said. "I promised my sister-in-law I'd pick things up for Sunday supper."

"Oh, Rose. How will you ever meet a chap in a grocery queue?"

"She's eight months' pregnant. And I am interested in things well beyond chaps," Rose said as briskly as she could manage.

"Of course you are," Eva murmured, and freed a few of her abundant curls from under her wool collar. Rose watched her file out of the office and waited a few crucial minutes, telling herself not to rush. Then she took her coat and went outside.

Near the newsstand, Thomas's face lit up when he spotted Rose. "I've been waiting," he announced with mock seriousness, "four and a half minutes. Four and a half minutes is too long for Miss Rose Zimmer to appear again in my life."

"Hush," she said, laughing, looking around. It had been a little more than a month since they had first met. She still found it shocking that he rang when he said he would, that his interest in her seemed to grow instead of abating. "How was your interview?"

He took her elbow, guiding her past a phone box. She hurried to keep up with him. "You worried someone might think you're with me? Like that coworker of yours that just left?"

"Eva?" Rose looked down the street, trying to spot Eva's full figure, those dark curls that looked wet even when dry. "No."

"The infamous Eva! She turned at the newsstand. Now, why wouldn't you introduce me?"

"I don't know. We're not close."

"But she's a part of your life."

"In the broadest definition of the word. Come now, where are we dining and on what?" She tried to grab the paper parcel from him, but he held tight.

"I'm serious," he said. "I'm serious about you."

She nodded, her eyes averted. It made her anxious, being this serious with Thomas. She felt her face grow slack.

"You know, you tug on your left earlobe when you're nervous." And then, more gently: "Are you nervous? Do I make you nervous?"

Yes, she almost admitted. But her throat felt constricted, hot. "You don't know me," she said, although she knew it wasn't true. But the prospect that he did know her made her feel so vulnerable; where would she go when it fell apart?

Thomas's eyes were on her face—she could feel them. He didn't argue. He didn't seem frightened by what he saw. "Okay, then," he finally said, and his voice was even, as if she had simply suggested toast instead of biscuits for tea. "But perhaps I will get to."

The day was damp but not too cool, the type of overcast afternoon in which it felt that the sun simply needed a little encouragement to shine. They walked to the Embankment, crowded with other dayworkers from Westminster, but managed to find a bench for themselves. Thomas spread his mackintosh and they sat upon it underneath a low clay-colored sky and ate sandwiches that Thomas had made himself. The bread was tough but oozed mayonnaise, the pickles pleasantly sharp, the cheese tasting like a treat.

"Tell me something," Rose said. She was looking at all the boats and ferries crawling up river, an army of them, crowding the water the same oyster hue as the sky. "How is your mother?" A pair of gulls swooped low over a barge.

"She's all right."

"Has the doctor been by?"

He shook his head, and Rose wasn't sure if that meant the doctor hadn't, or if the news was too terrible to convey. He said airlessly: "She's feeling all right."

"I'm glad," she said. She took a bite of her sandwich, concentrated on chewing. She shouldn't have asked. But how could she not? Still, his reticence was something that she, of all people, should understand. When she told him how she'd gotten out of Austria, he nodded, asking, "And your parents?" She only shook her head.

"You didn't tell me about your interview," she said now.

He didn't answer, and for a moment she wondered if she had said something else to upset him, but he leaned down to pull up his trousers, revealing thick, crimson socks. "Do you like them?"

"Your socks? They're very red."

He nodded. "They match my tie, see?" And he pulled back his crumpled suit jacket for confirmation.

"So they do," she said. They were a lovely red, actually, a brilliant vermilion when she least expected it. They were thick and they were heavy, practical despite their rich hue. Her heart scudded and it took her a moment to realize why. They reminded her of *The Bellhop*.

Something welled up inside of her and she tried to swallow it down. It felt like an ambush, the recollection. She spoke: "Were you wearing those for the interview? It seems an awfully bold choice for a junior engineering position."

"Bold, yes; that was my thought." He rummaged in his suit pocket, pulled out his cigarette pack, and offered her one. She took it, and he lit it, cupping it protectively before lighting one for himself. "I thought it would make me stand apart from other candidates."

She took a drag. "And?"

"One of the partners asked me: 'Why are you wearing so much red? Is there a political statement to your choice of color?'"

"What did you say?"

"I said, 'Of course not.' If I had wanted to make such a statement, I would have sewn on a hammer and sickle."

"Thomas! Goodness. You didn't say that, did you?"

"No," he said, leaning forward on the bench, inhaling deeply. "I'm terrible at sewing. But I could have drawn one. Not all engineers are decent draftsman, but I am. Do you know that about me?"

She gave him a little smile, but shook her head nevertheless. "This is not a joke," she said, and handed her cigarette back to him. He stubbed it out on the bench leg. "You know these things aren't jokes. Of course they wondered. Why would you give them any doubt?"

"I didn't give them any doubt. They made their doubt. Bloody Tories. All anyone cares about is the Eton-Harrow match and they act as if a revolution is going on."

"Oh, come now." She brushed the few crumbs off her lap. An old man in a great overcoat was sleeping one bench over, his broad, ravaged face tipped up to the sky. Whatever little warmth or sun was on offer, Rose thought, he was determined to catch it.

"It's five years after the war and it feels like nothing has changed. Everything is still so difficult." Thomas flicked his cigarette filter to the ground.

"I know." All Rose wanted to do was teach, and where was she? Stuck as a secretary for Mr. Marks. But still, she wouldn't complain. "It's getting better," she said.

"We won the war." He let out a sharp laugh. "You would have no idea from the looks of it that we *won*. And now with my mum . . . But it's not just her. I want to leave. I could. An old schoolmate of mine just got a job at Grumman in New York. And Lockheed out in California is hiring loads of engineers too."

"America? You want to go to America?" It was less a question than an echo. She was here, in London, with Thomas. Thomas was talking about leaving. She repeated these basic facts to herself in her head, as if recitation would lead to understanding.

"I don't know," he said, and he squeezed her hand. His fingers were warm, oily from the mayonnaise. "I really don't. But I do want to know this: Would you ever come with me?"

"Come with you?" she repeated. *But I barely know you,* she thought. And yet that was not true. She well knew what was happening. It rattled her, this certainty, this feeling that could be only called happiness. She didn't deserve it. She looked back at the sleeping old man on the neighboring bench, as if he might offer her some hard-won wisdom. But Thomas was trying to catch her eye, Thomas, with his kind expectant face, a face that was equal parts enthusiasm and determination. She liked that face. She trusted it. Him. And she was saying, softly, "Maybe."

He kissed her. "A maybe is nearly a yes."

She laughed. "Maybe," she said again. Together they headed back to Westminster, walking side by side, fingers so lightly entwined that Rose was left not knowing where her hand ended and Thomas's began. She couldn't remember what they talked about, but she would always remember the pulse of happiness she felt, her fingertips abuzz as they brushed against his in the afternoon's mercurial light.

Back at Mr. Marks's office, she spent the afternoon in a trance at her desk, copying more numbers onto more lists, thinking about that *maybe*. Not quite believing that she had meant it, knowing that in fact she had.

Mr. Marks left in a huff around three. Soon afterward, Rose turned to Eva and said, "I'm not feeling well. I think I need to leave."

"Oh, you poor thing. Is it your stomach? Edgar had a touch of upset earlier in the week. Go home and I'll cover for you."

Rose complied. And she felt as if she were still complying, still following someone else's explicit instructions as she went down into the Tube station, got on the train, and held on to the strap and swayed.

She managed to exit at Piccadilly, make her way to Old Bond Street. The pharmacist's sign pulsated like a beacon. Stepping through the antique shop's peeling doorway, she felt soaked with its familiarity, a distinctive relief.

"Hello, you!" said Julie, for of course she was there. "It's not even the weekend!"

"I want to tell you about the picture I'm looking for," Rose said. Julie's eyes widened as Rose spoke of the Bellhop's crimson uniform, tarnished gold buttons, the declarative shape of his thin hands planted firmly on his hips. "It isn't a pretty picture," she added. She tried to describe the thick strokes of paint—the swirls of red and gold and blue, so many colors! She knew she was talking too quickly. She looked down at the glassed-in jewelry counter, the same counter where Thomas had been standing—incredibly, a stranger to her, just a month ago.

As she spoke, as *The Bellhop* took shape by her words, she realized that her fear of talking about the painting had been wrong. She had been afraid that describing it, coming clean, would remind her of its painful absence, dilute her memories. But instead it burnished them. She saw the painting in her parents' room in the flat on Liechtensteinstrasse, its heavy gold frame; she saw her mother playing Chopin on the piano while her father kept trying to persuade her that perhaps they should go somewhere besides Bad Ischl this summer, Gerhard arguing that he was absolutely old enough to go to the UFA by himself for a matinee. Bette rang the bell for dinner, and Rose saw her mother pass by *The Bellhop*, swiping a speck of dust off the frame with her pinkie. All this did not just exist in the hazy firmament of Rose's memory. It had been real. It was.

"It sounds just like a picture Mr. Bradshaw was telling me about," Julie said. "I swear, a hotel worker or a waiter of some kind. He most definitely said expressionistic. *And* valuable. It's not here yet, but he said he'd bring it in tomorrow." As her own words sank in, Julie's tone grew elated. "It does sound like that painting; I knew it! It does!"

Rose looked into the girl's eyes. Could it be? It seemed impossible that *The Bellhop* would be here, in a small shop that she had chosen for reasons she did not understand. And yet. Maybe.

Rose thought of her lunch with Thomas by the river: she saw movement; she felt possibility. She wanted Julie to be right. Every fiber in her body leaped at the possibility. But she also wanted to remain here: no one telling her yes, no one telling her no.

THE FOLLOWING AFTERNOON, SHE RETURNED to the shop. Julie ushered her into the back. A skinny stooped gentleman in an ill-fitting suit stood waiting beside a small drafting table, canvas in hand.

"Mr. Bradshaw, this is Miss Rose Zimmer."

He looked nothing like the debonair antiques dealer she had imagined. She tried not to be disappointed, told herself that it had no bearing on the possibility of *The Bellhop*'s presence. "It's very nice to meet you," she said with renewed vigor. "I adore your shop."

"Why, thank you," he said. "I hear that you're quite excited about a certain portrait that I have here."

"That's right," Rose said as he began to unroll it, her stomach taking root in her throat.

The canvas was only half-visible when she knew. It was thickly painted, like *The Bellhop*, but the coat that the man in this portrait wore was of a darker red, wine-colored. There were no buttons in sight. The background shimmered, a swirl of oceanic blues and greens. The man's face was painstakingly detailed, his pink lips even held the the beginnings of a remote smile.

"Thank you," she managed to say. "But that's not my painting."

"Oh," Julie said, her face falling. "I'm so sorry."

"I'm sorry," Rose said, ludicrously.

"You're certain?" Mr. Bradshaw said.

"Very certain," Rose said. "Quite." She felt unsteady. She wanted to weep. "So sorry," she said as she fled the shop. She would never find *The Bellhop*. It was nowhere to be found.

She began walking, she had no idea where, and her despondency curdled into anger. This was her fault. Why had she pinned her hopes on finding it? Why did she ever think that recovering that stupid, ugly painting would make a difference? She hated that her mother had loved it. She hated that it ever mattered. She passed a deep hole of rubble sandwiched between two standing houses, a burst water pipe still trickling. Past a "Get Your Own Back" war savings banner plastered against a wall, faintly visible in the meager light. She kept moving. Darkness descended. The night was damp.

There were few streetlamps. A lorry rattled past. She thought of that night five years ago, when she had stood at the railing of the Waterloo Bridge, unable to envision a future. Five years had gone by and what had changed? She neared Bethnal Green and she felt so despondent, so unbelievably useless. It was too late for her to be out here at night by herself. She was nowhere where proper girls went by themselves. But she wasn't proper—she had done everything wrong. If she truly had been good, she wouldn't have gotten on that train. She would have done more to get her parents out. They would be here today. It felt like an articulation of everything she had long feared and yet tried to avoid. She bore responsibility. Why did she pretend otherwise?

HARRY WAS A DICTATOR: RUTHLESS, vicious, unrepentant, two years old. Rose was supposed to be keeping an eye on him and his baby brother, in the room that her nephews shared. The boys' nanny was ill. The cook had her day off. Isobel was in the kitchen. Harry kept tossing items into the playpen, dangerously close to his little brother's head—a comb, a rattle, a tin cup. Rose was doing nothing to stop him.

She should, of course. But she didn't have the energy. Or, in truth, the volition. Rose was in a foul mood. She thought: *Harry is a terror but he is a terror that Peter must live with. If I step in then Peter won't fend for himself. If I interfere, how will Peter ever learn?*

Rose had offered to handle supper, but Isobel refused. "I would so much rather be in front of a stove than mind those two horrors," she said with a laugh, though they both knew she wasn't entirely joking.

"Everything all right in there?" Isobel called now.

"Oh yes, fine." Rose took a book of Harry's from atop the bureau and was thumbing through it, a story about a plucky orphan who grew up in his village's parsonage. She looked up from the pages to see baby Peter slowly but determinedly pulling himself up by grabbing the bars of the crib. He weaved, unbalanced, but then—triumphantly—he stood on his own, grinning wildly.

Rose watched Harry take this success in, assessing Peter's presence, his achievement. Harry affixed his gaze on his brother, leaned over the rail of the crib, and slapped his head so hard Peter fell back down with a thump.

"Harry!" Rose yanked her older nephew aside. She scooped Peter up. He didn't seem truly hurt, but he was wailing and blinking furiously. She wheeled around to Harry. "What did you go and do that for?"

Harry stared at her, considering. "I don't know," he said, and he too burst into tears.

Isobel appeared in the doorway. "Harry! What happened?"

"Peter pulled himself up and Harry couldn't stand to see him succeed," Rose explained. "He hit him."

"Has the devil gotten into you?" Isobel slapped Harry's bottom, pushed him on his bed. "Someone needs to knock some sense into *you*! Wait until your father hears this. You stay here. Understand?"

Harry nodded as his face crumpled up, crying.

"Lord help me if this one is a boy too," Isobel said as she rose from the bed.

Rose, still clutching her whimpering nephew, trailed Isobel down the hall. Peter was heavier than he looked, his breath fast and shallow, his rosebud lips warm against her chest. Rose readjusted him in her arms and steadied a hand against the wall covered in a flocked print of tiny gray-green flower buds. Rose had admired the new wallpaper, but today it conspired to make her feel claustrophobic, nothing she desired. In the kitchen she went, with Peter straining in her arms. "I think he wants you."

"He always wants me," Isobel said, not turning around, one hand on her lower back. (She still had a month left to go with her pregnancy; she was already so big. How on earth would her body get bigger?) She handed Rose a bottle from the counter. "And he has to get used to not having me."

Rose nodded, lowered herself into the cane-backed chair, balancing baby, bottle, and herself. She tipped the bottle into his mouth and he sucked at it vigorously.

"Thank you," Isobel said, and the force of her voice couldn't cover up its underlying unsteadiness. Rose looked at her sister-in-law, still beautiful even in her swollen state, her face flushed, her forehead shiny. "Thank you for coming out all this way today to help me," Isobel said. "Truly."

"Of course." Rose had been glad to get Isobel's phone call. Her exhaustion was only trumped by her desire not to be alone.

"I am in no shape for this at all." Isobel's voice cracked a little.

"It's all right," Rose said, wanting to comfort her, uncertain how. Isobel was so rarely rattled. "It's going to be all right. Look, he's asleep." Peter's eyes were closed and he was emitting shallow moaning sounds. She shifted, surprised that he could remain asleep in her arms. She liked his slightly sour smell, the breathy weightiness of him.

"For five minutes, maybe," Isobel said. "And then? I can barely manage to make it to the toilet."

"It'll be all right," Rose repeated again. And it had to be. Three young children did seem an awful lot, but if Isobel couldn't get through motherhood—capable Isobel, who made everything seem stylish and effortlessly smooth—then what chance did anyone ever have? Rose pressed Isobel's damp hand to her own. "I know it will."

Isobel squeezed back. "Thank you. I'm glad one of us is convinced," she said. She heaved herself out of the chair. "How is that new beau of yours? You're bringing him to supper next week?"

"I was planning on it," Rose said, and but today she wasn't sure. She was so tired, and being tired made her feel pessimistic. What was wrong with Thomas? Something had to be wrong with him if he were so unerringly certain about her. "Perhaps we should put it off, until after the baby is born; maybe that would be better."

"No, no," Isobel said. "We cannot wait for that. Who knows what sort of state I'll be in then? And I refuse to wait that long to meet him." She opened the refrigerator. "I still can't get over that we have eggs again. Do you realize it was a decade ago that we could last buy them?" Her voice had regained its brighter tones. "Now, if we could just get sugar—oh, and butter. How I dream of butter. That and sleep are the things of my dreams these days. It's maddening, how boring I've become." She shook her head.

"Please, Isobel, you're one of the least boring people I know," Rose said. "Who else among your friends has talked Russian translations with Constance Garnett?"

Isobel smiled sadly. "I wish I could be reading them and chatting with her now. Three under the age of three. Damn your brother."

As if on cue, Rose heard the door whine open. "Hello," called Gerhard from the hall. He came in, set the string bag on the table, kissed the top of his wife's head. "Did you get the milk?" she asked.

"'Course I did. You asked me to." He cocked an eyebrow at his sister with a half grin, and Rose saw him as he had been when they were kids, her fearless brother who would pull their grandfather's swords from the wall and swoop them through the air, shouting, *This is for the Kaiser!*

Peter had awoken, whimpering. "There, there," Rose whispered, trying to push the nipple back into his mouth. "You want more?" But he batted the bottle away. "Your son is crying for you," she said, holding Peter toward Gerhard.

"Ah, not for me, never for me." But he picked him up and swung him around. "Oh, hello, little man. You're a sweet one, aren't you?" Peter crowed with delight.

"I spoke to Jenny earlier today," Isobel said, easing herself back into the chair. "She and William really are going. This summer."

"Are they, now?" Gerhard said, and he handed Peter to his wife. William was Isobel's eldest brother. Rose knew that Gerhard had asked him to invest in the business early on and William had refused.

They had remained amiably chilly ever since. Gerhard opened up a pack of cigarettes, drew one out, and tapped it against the table.

Isobel brushed her lips across Peter's head. "They've decided upon Toronto. Everyone is leaving, it seems."

"Not everyone," Rose said. Just last week, Margaret had written her that her husband Teddy's brother was moving to Calgary and perhaps they too would follow suit. Thomas had mentioned America, but there were engineering positions in Canada too. Did it matter? The New World was all the same to her: shiny, optimistic. Not England.

Gerhard took his time lighting the cigarette, inhaling with evident pleasure. "We're not. We're doing very well. The business is doing well. Why would we go?"

"We'll be the only ones left."

"That's not true."

"It *might* be true," she said, and took his cigarette from him.

"Why must you be so negative about everything?"

She sucked in smoke, drew her arm over her belly. "I don't know, Gerhard. Why do you think?"

"Perhaps I should go check on Harry," Rose said. "He's awfully quiet."

"I'll come with you," Gerhard said. In the hall, he whispered: "You mustn't mind her."

"I don't," Rose said. "*I* don't mind her at all."

Gerhard exhaled, opening the door to the boys' room. It was strangely silent inside. Harry was . . . where? Then Rose spied him, lying on the rag rug facedown—one leg to his chest, the other splayed out akimbo, arms above, framing his head. Nothing about the position looked comfortable, but he was steadfastly asleep. "He looks so peaceful," she said.

"Probably cried himself to sleep," Gerhard said matter-of-factly. He knelt down and scooped the boy up. Rose was surprised when he didn't wake up, but Gerhard seemed to take it for granted. He sat down next to his son's balled-up sleeping form, patted the plaid coverlet beside him. "How's your new Englishman—is he for God and love and country?"

"Thomas?" she asked, though of course that was who he meant. "He wants to leave too."

"Screw the whole lot of them."

"Indeed." Here, in the moment with her brother, her ally no matter how great their differences, she meant it. "I'm not leaving England."

"Now, that's good to hear." Gerhard leaned back on his elbows against Harry's bedspread. He looked like a giant, Rose thought, a blond English giant. "But you're not really finished with him, are you? I hear you're bringing him to supper next week. I want to meet this man who has captured my sister's heart."

"I don't know," she said. She was so worn out. "Captured my heart is not exactly the way I'd put it."

"I didn't ask how *you* would put it," Gerhard said, and gave her an appraising look. "You're going to marry him. I know it."

"How can you say that?" His certainty rankled her. "You haven't met him. You don't know if you like him, or if he's good for me."

"But you like him," Gerhard said, unfazed. His hand was on Harry's small back. She watched it rise and fall with every breath. They both did.

His calm conviction infuriated her. She had vowed not to say anything to Gerhard, but now the words tumbled out: "I thought I had found Mutti's picture. I thought I had, but I didn't."

"What? What picture?"

"*The Bellhop,* Mutti's *Bellhop,*" she said softly.

Gerhard's confusion turned to irritation. She could see it, plain on his broad face. "Why in heaven would you think it was here in England, of all places?"

"It has to be somewhere."

"No, it doesn't. Good Lord, *mausi,* you've been searching for it?"

She didn't answer, and he stood. The mattress shifted with the lessening of weight, and Rose reached out, hand on the bed, steadying herself.

"Why not?" she said, looking down at her chapped hands, nothing like the slender long-fingered hands of her mother. "What's wrong in thinking that we might find something?"

"It's *over,*" he said roughly, with sudden force. "That life, it's gone."

She shook her head. She was staring at the bureau, at the leather-bound book of Harry's she'd been reading before, written in a language that she worked so hard to claim as her own, when she repeated: "*Gone?* They didn't vanish. They were stolen. They could be anywhere—houses, basements, museums, collecting points. But they didn't *disappear.*"

Gerhard emitted a strange, horrible laugh. "Fine. But they're gone."

Rose shook her head, trying to rid herself of his words. How could he? Didn't he realize how ugly this sounded, what a betrayal it was?

All she wanted was proof. All she knew was this: February 1942, their parents had been sent to Theresienstadt. In January 1945, most of the camp's prisoners were sent east. In May 1945, when the camp was liberated by Russian troops, their parents were not among the survivors. Had they died in the chaos of the brutal winter of '45? Were they shot on the march east? Did they stumble into a ditch somewhere? Were they together at the end? All she wanted was proof of their deaths. She who didn't pray prayed for corroboration.

"Things do not disappear. People don't disappear." She was shocked to hear that she sounded—not *un*calm. She wanted to hit her brother, do him true bodily harm. He had a body; how dare he not recognize what a gift that was. How dare he not feel, as she did, that their parents' paths had been *their* paths. There was no godly reason they had survived and their parents hadn't. Didn't he feel, as she did, like a ghost? "They were killed. Murdered," she said softly. "They did not disappear."

Gerhard looked at her with a gentleness she was startled to recognize as pity. "I know that. You think I don't know that? But it's over. For your sake—and mine—it's enough, Rose. Enough."

"You are wrong, so very wrong," she said, and she was crying openly now. All she could think was, *I need to leave right now.* Because the truth of what he was saying would destroy her. She thought this, and she realized: it already had.

11

LOS ANGELES, 2006

WHY COULDN'T SHE STOP THINKING about it? Why couldn't she let go? Lizzie awoke alone and headachy in Max's lovely, low, king-sized bed. Light was bleeding in along the edges of the heavy curtains; the day had long begun. She was feeling the detritus of last night, the booze and so much food and all that was said. She pulled on the jeans she'd worn yesterday and the first T-shirt she could find, made her way into the kitchen. It took her a moment to realize that Max was seated at the table, already dressed and groomed.

"You came in late last night," Max said.

"Not that late. I was back by ten. You must have fallen asleep early."

He got a mug and went to the carafe to pour, the coffee already made.

"I can do it," Lizzie said. Even she heard the bristle in her voice.

"Sure thing." He made a show of backing off. "If you want."

"Don't," she said, shaking her head. She was too tired.

"Lizzie, I'm sorry."

She focused on her tasks: milk, sugar, stirring. "I really cannot talk about this now."

"Okay," he said. "But we need to, at some point. I mean, I want to."

She glanced at the digital display on the stove. "I need to get going, actually."

"Where?"

She was still so angry at him, she couldn't believe how angry. "Are you surprised that I have places to go?"

"No, not at all. Come on."

She blew into her mug, cooling it down, trying to calm herself down. She took a swallow. "I'm sorry. I'm going to synagogue," she said, though it had only occurred to her in the last few moments to do so.

"You are? Why?"

"I went last week," she said, aware she wasn't answering his question.

"You didn't tell me."

She shrugged. "I went to say kaddish."

"Oh," Max said, and that tiny word seemed to hang in the room, heavying the air. "That's good," he added.

"It made me feel better," Lizzie said, although *better* wasn't quite the right word for it. She thought of that worn bare room, the dankness, the sound of the voices chanting. She remembered the feeling of standing for the prayer. It seemed impossible to rise to her feet, but when she did and saw the few others around the congregation standing too, it felt like a bodily acknowledgment of all that she wanted to forget. Her father was gone. There was no pretending. But she was here. She was his child, and she would endure.

"Well, then you should go again." Max had waited awhile before responding, but he said it firmly. "I want you to know something, though: I've been thinking about what you said yesterday, and I'm sorry."

"Max—" She didn't want to hear explanations, not today.

"No, let me finish." He was wiping off the counter, though to her it looked perfectly clean. "You were right. I care about you so much. I want to try this."

"Wait," Lizzie said. "What?" Had she heard him right? Were they talking about the same thing? "You do?"

"I do." A small smile tugged at the edges of his beautiful mouth and his eyes crinkled. He nodded at her with intent, and she felt a rush of happiness. "Truly," he said. "I was being foolish, but I am not a fool." His voice was scratchy, low near her ear.

"Is that right," she said, and now his lips were grazing her neck and she was laughing a little, amazed. She did not care that he was her father's best friend, she did not care about the age difference. Why did she ever try to deny her feelings? For once she did not doubt herself. She only wanted to be here, with him.

He took her by the hand, led her toward the bedroom. "I can't," she said.

"Sure you can," he said, and he gave her that slow smile that would be the end of her, and soon her synagogue plan was all but forgotten.

AFTERWARD, SHE SAID TO HIM: "Can I ask you a question: Do you still have records from your parents' gallery?"

"Some," he said. "Why?"

"I just wondered; I've been thinking about how *The Bellhop* got here, from Europe. Do you have any idea who your parents bought it from?" Lizzie was out of bed, retrieving her scattered clothes as she spoke. She had wanted to ask Max this for a while, but after last night—well, she wanted to think of something other than what Bob had said.

"No," he said. "Not really. But there's a decent chance they bought it in New York. They purchased a lot of artwork there, in the early years of the gallery, the fifties and sixties, and I do know that they held on to the Soutine for quite a long time."

"Why?"

"They did that sometimes. With lots of pieces," Max said, maddeningly vague.

"You know, I really would love to know who they bought it from," she asked again. She didn't want to be a nudge, but who could she ask, if not him? She pulled her shirt over her head. "Where are these records?"

"I have a few boxes in the garage. But don't hold your breath. They weren't so great on the record-keeping front, especially early on. But I could look."

"Would you, please?" Maybe the answer was right here, in Max's house. Why had she waited so long to ask him? She leaned over, gave him a deep kiss at the edge of the bed.

"You realize that even if we do have a record, it'll only be a name," he said softly into her hair. "That's all it's going to tell you."

"That'll be enough."

"Will it?"

"Yes," she said guardedly. "What do you mean?"

"I just mean—the painting was stolen twenty years ago." He gave a twist of an uneasy smile. "I wish you could put it behind you."

Did he not think that she wanted to? What did he know about that night? She stood, arms across her chest. "I have," she said. "I mostly have. Why would you say that to me?"

"I don't know. I shouldn't have," he said softly. "I know how much you loved the painting. Come here." He pulled her into an embrace. "Forgive me."

She let him, but reluctantly, her arms at her sides. Did he really think there was something wrong with the fact that she couldn't let go? "I'm not the only one with questions," she said, pulling back.

"Yes?" He said it lightly enough, but he tightened his lips and for a moment he looked like no one she knew.

"Last night, I was having dinner with Rose and a friend of hers, and—" She stopped. What was she trying to protect him from? It felt wrong to go on, disloyal to even give rise to the suspicions, but stranger not to. "When the paintings were stolen," she continued, "do you know if the police ever questioned my father?"

"Of course. Many times," he said evenly enough. "Most of the information they had came from him."

"Was ever he considered a suspect?"

"A suspect?" Max said, scooping up his keys, his phone, his money clip from his bureau—the armaments he needed for the day. "A person of interest, sure. He was at first. It's the obvious choice. But that doesn't mean it's the right one. They spoke to him at length, and then they moved on."

"To what?"

He sighed. "I don't know, exactly. They spoke to dozens of people. There were so many possibilities. There still are. Your father, bless him, was not exactly modest about his possessions. He was proud of the art he owned; he told lots of people. And so many people came through your house; think about it. Just those dinner parties alone: guests and friends of guests and the caterer and the waiters and bartenders. All those people in and out. Someone could have been casing it, saw the party, jumped on the opportunity. To say nothing about all those babysitters and drivers you guys had to take you girls around; or more probably, the boyfriend of one of those people, or, most likely, an art thief you did not know at all."

Max was right; there were so many people in Joseph's orbit, any one of them could have done it. But that familiar feeling of unease slid over her. There must have been something she could have done.

"You know what I've learned as a defense attorney?" Max was still talking. "Guilty clients always have an alternative story, but the innocent ones? They never do. They're hard to believe because they don't know who did it. You know why? Because *they didn't do it*. How would they know what happened? An absence of evidence doesn't point anywhere. You know that."

"I know," she allowed, and the sickly feeling was receding, she already felt on more solid ground. "I know; it was just this friend of Rose's, he said it so easily, tossed it out as if it were obvious—"

Max shrugged. "Of course. Twenty years after the fact. Colonel Mustard in the library. What was Rose's reaction?"

Lizzie allowed herself a small smile. "She nearly ripped his head off."

"Ah," Max said. "A woman after my own heart."

WHEN MAX LEFT, LIZZIE NOSED around online. She looked up an old law school classmate, Jonathan Bookman, who she knew had moved to L.A. She saw that his firm had a small appellate department. She was thinking of writing him, to see if he wanted to meet for coffee, when her phone buzzed.

"It's a miracle that I can even call you," Rose said. "My phone has been tied up all morning. Bob: calling and calling."

Bob. His name alone put Lizzie on edge. "What did he say?"

"I don't know," Rose said. "I haven't been inclined to pick up the phone and speak with him."

"You should, you know," Lizzie said, breathing a little more easily.

"In due time. First, I wanted to apologize to you."

"You don't need to." It wasn't Rose's fault, but still, it was reassuring to hear.

"Well, he was my guest. It was my fault that he was there. What he said was unconscionable and presumptuous, not to mention awful. He cannot blithely throw out theories like that." Rose's gravelly voice slowed. "I am sorry. It must have been very painful for you. But I am also calling to ask you a favor," she added after a beat.

ROSE BARELY SAID HELLO TO Lizzie after she opened the door, and climbed on the stepstool in the hall. She stretched to adjust a thick strip of blue painters' tape.

"What are you doing? You're making me nervous," Lizzie said. "Why did you ask me here if you're just doing it yourself?"

"I'm putting up the tape; you're doing the hard work of hanging the masks. I've never fallen yet."

"That," Lizzie said, "is not particularly reassuring."

Soon enough Lizzie was the one climbing up, and before long her father's masks were affixed to the wall. They looked good: the smaller one was a half bird, half reptile made out of a chalky-white wood. The larger one was also carved from wood, but a richer, darker color, and had a more stylized look, with an elongated nose and sidelocks hanging down (*peyot,* Joseph called them) where ears should be. Lizzie had paid little attention to the masks when they had been at her father's house, and was dismissive of them when she had (*Of course the only pieces of non-Western art he has are African masks,* she could remember telling Claudia, *such a cliché*), but now she was struck by their delicate artistry.

Soon Rose made strong coffee that she topped off with cream. She served it in finely etched, pale green porcelain teacups that seemed at odds with the more utilitarian surroundings of her small living room. "Thomas bought them for us," Rose said, even though Lizzie hadn't asked. "They reminded him of home."

"They're beautiful." And they weren't the only beautiful things Lizzie noticed today. Above the club chair where Rose sat hung a framed stretch of silky blue-and-purple material. It featured a lovely pattern of birds, some perched on branches, others swooping through the air, wings outstretched.

"Not that he had china like this at home," Rose was saying. "He didn't come from money."

"Where was Thomas from?"

"Brighton," Rose said. "Do you know it? A seaside town, famous for its pier and promenade. His father worked for years maintaining some of the rides on the palace pier. He could be difficult. By the time I met him, his wife—Thomas's mother—had passed away. He wasn't particularly happy that Thomas was dating a Jewish girl. I remember he was trying to buy something on the black market, a television maybe, and he couldn't get it. He blamed the Jews, of course. Everyone used to say that the Jews—Spivs, they called them—controlled the market. 'You people love your money, don't you?' I remember him telling me the first time we met."

"Wow," Lizzie said. "A real charmer."

"It wasn't all that unusual then, his dislike of Jews. The fact that people get nostalgic for the time after the war amazes me. I love England, but it was a tough time, all around."

"I would have just thought, after the war—" Lizzie didn't finish. How could people blame Jews then, after everything they had been through? It wasn't so long ago, and yet it felt light-years away from the world that she had grown up in. On the Westside, even her non-Jewish friends knew about seders, held forth on their favorite bagels and Woody Allen films. Whatever anti-Semitism there was (and she wasn't naive enough to think there wasn't any), was rarely spoken out loud, at least not directly to her. "So what happened when you got married?" she asked.

"What do you mean?" Rose asked, frowning.

"I just meant—in terms of holidays, that sort of thing," Lizzie said, already wishing she hadn't. "Did you celebrate Jewish stuff, or . . . ?"

"I barely celebrated Jewish holidays with my family in Vienna. Marrying Thomas, a lapsed Anglican, didn't change that. And you?"

"Me?"

"What are your religious beliefs?" There was decided arch in Rose's tone.

"Oh. Well. We were major-holiday Jews: You know, Rosh Hashanah, Yom Kippur, Passover. My father loved the seders. That was about it," Lizzie said. She thought of the synagogue on the Venice boardwalk, the comfort she found there, but she couldn't imagine telling Rose. How could she explain the consolation she felt? *A prayer did that for you?* she could imagine Rose saying.

"Have you gone through his things?" Rose was now asking. "That's one of the hardest parts."

"It was hard. I couldn't—my sister did most of it."

"And he had a lot of stuff," Rose looked at her and there was sympathy in her gaze.

Lizzie took a long pull of her coffee, trying to steady herself. "Yes; we're lucky, though. We have so many great things. He left me a Julius Shulman photograph—do you know his stuff?"

"Shulman! Of course. One of his nieces was a student of mine, years ago. Is it the photograph of the Case Study house?"

Lizzie shook her head. She knew the Case Study house, of course: Shulman's most famous photograph, a nighttime shot of two well-dressed women coolly chatting inside a brightly lit modern house, cantilevered over the dark spread of Los Angeles below. Up until several years ago, you could still buy prints of it, but Joseph hadn't been interested. *Why would I want something that everyone else has?* Lizzie could remember him saying. "No, it's of downtown, the old Department of Water and Power building." Less known but no less gorgeous: a haunting black-and-white photograph of a reflecting pool beside the office building, the sharp lines of downtown reflected in the water, the sky a moody knitted collection of clouds. It reminded Lizzie not of the L.A. that she grew up in, but something more classical, distant. "He bought it years ago, from Shulman himself."

"Really?"

"Yeah." Lizzie smiled, drained her cup. "It's a classic Joseph story. Back in the nineties, he found out from his friend Judy, the woman who owned the gallery where we held the memorial actually, that Shulman liked visitors. And that he would sell prints to anyone who asked. It was Judy's assistant who had told him, a gorgeous young arts student—"

"Oh no, I can see where this is going," Rose said with a touch of a groan.

"Maybe," Lizzie said. "Maybe not. Anyway, this young art student had been to Shulman's house in Laurel Canyon. She said that Shulman liked visitors of all kinds, particularly women, and particularly those who came bearing single-malt scotch. So my dad got the address and showed up at his house, and the old man opened the door, and my dad laid it on thick: 'You're a brilliant photographer,' he said. He gave him the scotch, and Shulman sniffed and said, 'No, it's tequila that I like.' And my dad said, 'You want me to run out and get some? Because I will.' And Shulman waved him off and invited him in and my dad kept praising him, telling him how much he loved his pictures of Neutra's work. 'That guy was a nutjob,' Shulman said. 'But he could build a building.' Shulman must have been charmed because he pulled out a bottle of tequila and the two drank. Shulman had been born in Brooklyn, like my dad, and they talked about that, and the store that my grandparents had owned. It turned out that after Shulman moved to L.A., when he was a boy, his parents ran a general store too, in Boyle Heights, and Shulman used to sell pickles out of barrels to immigrants from Japan and Mexico."

"So at some point, during all this carousing, your father bought the print from Shulman."

"I wouldn't call it *carousing*, but yes, I think it was the second time he went by, my dad said to him, 'You know, Julius, how much I respect you as an artist.' And Shulman said: 'Come now, don't bullshit a bullshitter. Just ask.' So my father did. He asked to buy a print. 'I've got loads lying around here,' Shulman said. 'Take one.' And he did."

"Wait, Joseph didn't pay for the print?"

"No, no," Lizzie reassured her. "Of course he paid for it."

"How much?"

"I'm not sure, exactly," Lizzie said, although that wasn't true. She was growing uncomfortable. The story she had told many times before, her father drinking and charming a famous photographer, seemed to be shifting under Rose's attention.

"Come now. How much?"

"I think it was two hundred for the print."

"It was probably worth ten times that even at the time, if not twenty, at least. He ripped him off. He took advantage of a lonely old man."

Lizzie reddened. She had doubled the amount. "Shulman knew what he was doing. He was famous, even then. He was giving them out, left and right. He *liked* my father," she protested. "Plenty of people visited him and did the same thing."

"Really? That's your excuse?" Rose let out a snort. "Other people behaved poorly? Your father had ulterior motives. It wasn't an original sin, but let's at least acknowledge that."

"I'm only saying," Lizzie said, and stopped. What *was* she saying? She could see what Rose meant, but she also knew that Joseph genuinely liked Shulman, he enjoyed talking to him. It wasn't so simple. "The Getty acquired Shulman's collection before he died. It's worth millions. He did quite well for himself," she said.

"That's not the point and you know it," Rose said, rising. "I need more coffee."

Lizzie got up too. But Rose picked up her cup and commanded: "Stay: I've got it."

If her father were here, he would explain himself, Lizzie thought as she regarded the framed wall-hanging of the birds above the couch. Looking closer, she saw that it was silk, the edges finely stitched, even the birds' feathers painstakingly detailed, elegant. There was discoloration in the lower right corner; it looked like it had been used.

Rose came back, handed Lizzie her cup.

"This is beautiful," Lizzie said to Rose, nodding at the frame.

"It was my mother's," Rose said. "Her favorite scarf."

"Oh," Lizzie said, and she felt an urge to touch Rose's hand, but she held back. "It's beautiful," she repeated. "I'm so glad you have something of hers."

"She gave it to me the night I left. It's one of the only things of hers that I do have."

"Oh," Lizzie said again. It was unbearable, what Rose had gone through, and the pain never stopped, did it? Lizzie thought of all her father's things that she had, her mother's too. Even incidental objects—maybe especially those, like her mother's copy of *Valley of the Dolls* that Lizzie had always wondered if Lynn had kept as a joke—comforted Lizzie through the years. "I wish you had more," she said softly.

"It's gone," Rose said crisply, and Lizzie knew Rose well enough now to know that the sharpness in her tone was only a small part of the story.

"I know you might not want to hear this," Lizzie decided to begin. "But the other day, I realized that I had a connection to a lawyer who is an expert in art restitution."

"Okay."

"Michael Ciparelli. He used to work with my boss, who says he's a good guy and an excellent attorney. I think it's worth talking to him."

"I don't think so."

"Just hear me out. He's hugely connected and has a wealth of expertise in this area. He's been doing this for decades."

"Lizzie, it's not for me," Rose said, and moved to the edge of her chair, sitting taut and straight. "You have to stop trying to convince me."

"But why?" Lizzie asked. She couldn't shake the belief that she could make things better for Rose. "I know that it's not my place, it's your decision, but I feel like there are things that can be done—"

"You're right, it's not your place," Rose snapped. "You don't understand. This didn't happen to you. I don't know how to make you realize that. As sorry as you are, as horrified as you may be, *this did not happen to you*. So, please, stop acting as if it did."

"I know it didn't," Lizzie said quietly. Did Rose really think that she presumed it had? "I never meant to suggest that it did."

But Rose was shaking her head. "I'm friends with a man, a former German professor. A few years ago, his granddaughter took a school trip to the Museum of Tolerance. Like all the students, his granddaughter was given identification when she walked in. The ID was circa World War II, and it featured a child. The girl on her paper happened to have the same last name," she said. "She walked through the interactive exhibits—full of video and buttons you can press. At the end, she and her classmates found out the fate of the children on the papers they carried. My friend's granddaughter learned that the girl on hers had died at Auschwitz. She went home with the paper, showed it to her parents. Her father told his father. 'That was my sister,' my friend said."

"That is awful," Lizzie said. "That is so awful."

"Do you understand? Rose said. "This might be a game to you, but it's not for me. Losing the Soutine was the least of it."

"Of course, I know that." Did Rose really think she thought it was a game? Is that what she thought of her? "I don't think that; I never have. And I know our histories are different. What I went through was nothing compared to you—"

"I do not want to talk about this." Rose tore off each word.

"I'm so sorry." Why had she ever spoken up? If she were Rose, she would despise her too. Maybe she should leave. "I didn't mean to be presumptuous. I'm so sorry," Lizzie said. "I just wish there were something more I could do."

"Do you? Do you really?" Rose said, and dropped her cup back on the coffee table with a clatter. "You say that, but sometimes I wonder. Because there is more you could find out. But you have to want to know."

12

LOS ANGELES, 1958

EASTLAKE SCHOOL WAS HOUSED IN the sprawling Spanish-style former residence of a silent movie star. It was a warm midafternoon in February, the sky cloudless and bright. Rose was walking toward the administrative offices to take a call from Thomas when she heard the rise of giggles, a braiding of voices. "Tennyson," she thought she heard a female voice say.

Then she spotted them. Gathered on the administration steps, a knot of long-limbed girls in uniforms of pale blue pleated skirts and white collared shirts. They were thirteen, fourteen, on the cusp. The burnished coins in their loafers glinted in the sunlight. "Tennyson," she heard again. The speaker was Helen Peale. "You *must* admire him." Helen dropped her usually tentative voice low and guttural. "You have altogether no choice in the *matta*." Her friends giggled again as she turned *matter* into a hammer of a word, losing the *r* entirely.

That was her, Rose thought, stock-still. Helen was imitating her. She stood on the path and watched Helen laugh. She needed a haircut, Rose thought. Her limp brown hair was too thin and those bangs altogether unflattering.

It was then that Helen noticed Rose. "Good afternoon, Mrs. Downes," she stammered.

Rose gave her a curt nod. She continued up the steps of the administration building with deliberation. So Helen Peale was a mimic. Rose could be teased for far worse. Most teachers were. Helen was one of the few boarding students here at Eastgate, an only child whose father traveled constantly for work and whose mother chose to accompany him. She had few friends—even Rose knew this. She was doing what she could to fit in.

And yet Rose still felt a tightening within her chest as surely as if Helen had followed her home and spied on her and Thomas alone in their bedroom.

Nearly three years earlier, they had moved to Los Angeles. Thomas landed a job at Douglas. The aircraft industry was booming, everyone focused on Boeing up north. It was no longer a question of if, but when, and which company would first succeed with a commercial jet. Rose didn't have such employment luck. But one night about two years ago Thomas came home late and said, "I've found you a job, a teaching position."

They stood shoulder to shoulder in their tiny aqua-tiled bathroom. He was brushing his teeth. "A teaching position?" she repeated incredulously.

He spit in the sink, looked at her reflection in the mirror. "Potentially," he amended. "At a very posh school. Someone quit midyear and they're looking to hire immediately."

"How in the world did you hear of it?" Rose had long given up on teaching. In England, there were no positions, nor had she seen any here. She had been circling ads in the paper for secretarial work—had been on a few interviews so far, two for real estate companies, one for advertising—but nothing.

"From Reynolds, who heard it from Douglas's secretary. His daughter goes there. Eastgate. A girls' school near Beverly Hills. It's been there for years. And it's quite the place, apparently: horses, tennis courts, an outdoor and indoor swimming pool."

It sounded like a resort, not a school, Rose was tempted to say, but the possibility of teaching here, in America, even the slight possibility, gave her a thrill. "Are there classrooms too?"

He regarded her image in the mirror. "I believe there are, yes."

"With one or two Jewish teachers at the helm?" She tried to ask this with a lightness that she did not feel.

"That I do not know." He picked an errant hair from the wet sink, dried his hands thoroughly on the towel. "Believe it or not, the faith of the instructors did not come up."

She fixed him with a look. "You know what I mean."

"I do," he said. "I did not ask. Best to simply apply."

There weren't many Jewish teachers on staff among the L.A. private schools, she had heard. (*It wasn't that they refused to hire Jews,* the well-meaning wife of a colleague of Thomas's had told Rose soon after they moved, *it was just that they* didn't *hire them.*) But the world was changing, Thomas liked to say. Not fast enough, Rose thought. Her religious beliefs had not shifted since she had been that unhappy child made more unhappy when the Cohens tried to take her to synagogue and required her to keep the laws of kashrut. But she was all too aware that wasn't the way the world saw her.

"They should seek out Jews. In the nineteenth century, every truly educated soul knew Hebrew," Thomas was saying now.

"Ah, yes, the halcyon days of the nineteenth century," Rose said.

Thomas laughed. "So you'll write Eastgate tomorrow. Tell them that you know Mr. Douglas."

"But I don't know Mr. Douglas."

"Ah, but your husband does. And he told me to tell you to do so." He tapped her backside with affection. "Silly Rosie. Why must you make everything harder on yourself?"

She made a face at Thomas, asserted it wasn't so, but a week later, behind the wheel of her neighbor's Buick (they had barely scraped together the funds for Thomas's clunker of a Chevy, let alone a car for her), Rose wondered if Thomas was right. Did she make everything harder on herself? Her anxiety was mounting: What made her believe she could get a teaching job? She had spent eight months student-teaching at a second-rate vocational school in Croydon six years ago. Her students were sixteen-year-old boys who would have rather eaten their fingernails for supper than recite a sonnet. Why did she ever think she could land a job teaching at an illustrious school in Los Angeles? ("Mr. Douglas told me that Shirley Temple went to Eastgate," Thomas said last night. "You are not helping," she barked at him.)

She took Beverly Glen past Sunset, maneuvering the unfamiliar car up the curving, darkly paved road, past the high hedges that obscured the homes behind them. The lots were big, the houses had to be grand. She was glad in her agitated state not to see them.

The Eastgate parking lot was filled with gleaming Cadillac coupes and Ambassadors with oversized fins. Rose locked the car, and, walking slowly to the main building, passed a gorgeous flowering tree with the most striking bluish-purple blossoms. A jacaranda, she would learn later.

A secretary brought Rose through an arched doorway down to the headmistress's office, Rose's heels making far too much noise against the polished stone. They passed through a corridor lined with framed photographs of Eastgate graduating classes, grave-faced girls dressed in white, clutching single lilies in their hands. Rose realized that Eastgate, for all its luster, was a young school. Forty years at most—laughably short by English standards. Gerhard had recently written her about a construction site down the road from him at which workers had unearthed in the mud a handsome marble bust, shockingly well preserved. It was of a Roman god, and soon it was discovered that the site had been the grounds of a two-thousand-year-old temple. Rose came from a place with true history. She, not Eastgate, embodied tradition.

"Mrs. Downes," said the headmistress as Rose was ushered inside her office. Miss Monroe was a thin, silver-haired woman with a penetrating gaze. "How nice to meet you." Her voice was warm enough but rapid, only a hint of a smile on her remarkably unlined face. She picked up the letter Rose had written. "As you must have heard, we are in a bit of a bind."

"Yes, I heard," Rose said. "Mr. Douglas told my husband, who told me," she clarified.

"Ah, yes," Miss Monroe said. Yes to what? Rose thought in a panic. "A wonderful family, the Douglases." She rubbed her thumb and forefinger of her right hand together—a gesture that seemed to betray her lack of interest in what Rose was saying. "So tell me about your experience. You've recently moved here, isn't that right? From England? And you studied there?"

Rose nodded. "I did. I received two degrees, one in literature and the other a teaching certificate. At the University of London, Bedford College." She spoke rapidly herself. She felt acutely aware that her time was limited. Still, she couldn't help adding. "I don't know if you're aware of Bedford, but it has quite a history; it was the first college for women in Great Britain."

"No, I'm not familiar with it. I know Oxford and Cambridge, of course."

"Of course," Rose echoed. Was she only interested in teachers with degrees from Oxford?

"But I must say I was glad to see that you studied in England. When I was at UCLA, I studied math with a Scottish professor. 'We're too soft in America,' he used to say, and he was not wrong. Here at Eastgate we are rigorous. More so than our brother school down the road, I would say."

"Indeed," Rose said, sensing an opening, "rigor is key. But so is engagement, particularly with younger students. At my last teaching position," she said, and she saw no reason to point out that it was her only teaching position, "I was at a boys' school and they were a rather challenging group of young men, shall we say, so I had to come up with unorthodox assignments to engage them. To trick them into learning, whether they wanted to or not."

"And you did this, how?" Miss Monroe asked, elbow on her desk, chin resting on her hand. For the moment, she seemed legitimately intrigued.

"A number of different methods. I had them write loads of reviews," Rose explained, feeling more confident. "Films they had seen, meals at the pub; one time I assigned them to write a critique of the coach's direction of their football team. That inspired more paragraphs of opinion, more actual writing, than I had seen before." Miss Monroe smiled lightly, perhaps too lightly? "But that didn't mean we steered away from the classics altogether," Rose added hastily. "I took them to see performances, *Tamburlaine the Great* and *Twelfth Night* at the Old Vic. I had them reciting poems weekly. I had a list of words—'the forbidden twenty,' I called it—if any word on that list was misspelled on a quiz or paper, the student received a failing grade. The students thought it draconian, but by the end of the term no one confused the possessive 'its' with the contraction of 'it is.' I don't imagine here that your students need such enticements."

"You would be surprised," Miss Monroe said. "'The forbidden twenty,' I like that. We here at Eastgate place an emphasis on educating our girls on all fronts—how to be strong wives, mothers, citizens in a democracy."

"Of course," Rose said, quickly, "the art of letter writing—"

"But sometimes we do so at the expense of rigor," the headmistress went on. "We could use more of that rigor here." She rose. "I'll introduce you to two of our English teachers, who have some questions for you. But first, may I ask: Downes is your married name?"

"Yes, it is," Rose said. She tried to say this with a smile. The interview had gone well. Hadn't it?

"It's only that your accent is unusual. You weren't born in England, were you?"

"No, I wasn't. I grew up in England," Rose said, considering. "But I was born in Vienna. Perhaps that's what you hear, my German, seeping through."

"During the war, you moved to England?" Miss Monroe's voice wasn't warm, exactly, but there was a newly tentative quality to her words that made Rose conversely feel in control.

"Just before. I'm Jewish," Rose said. "It wasn't safe. My brother and I got out."

"Ah," the headmistress said. "I see. You know, the only time I have been to Europe was in '35, before the war. We spent several days in Munich. It's strange, what you recall. We had gone shopping and we were at a large department store where I was admiring a music box, a beautiful enamel box out of which a silver bird popped. It even flapped its wings, and sang. I was so engrossed in the box that I didn't see several men in brown uniforms appear. They escorted a man out. They were saying—well—anti-Jewish things. It was terrible. A shameful time."

Rose nodded, tense. How many more teachers did Miss Monroe say she must speak with?

"We have a music teacher here, a lovely man, a Mr. Goldstein. Originally from Europe too. He plays the cello. And he plays it so wonderfully, with such a mournful soulfulness; I sometimes find myself wondering where that feeling comes from."

It was too much for Rose, the sympathy, the attention for all the wrong reasons. This woman thought she knew Rose, but she didn't. "It comes from the music," she said, the words out of her mouth before she could consider them.

Miss Monroe looked at Rose in surprise. Rose gazed down at her feet, pinched in pumps she rarely wore. She had spoken rashly. She had botched her one chance.

But here was Miss Monroe, holding out a cool hand and murmuring, "Yes, the music; how right you are." A week later, Rose was hired.

A FEW HOURS AFTER ROSE overheard Helen Peale, Helen entered her classroom uncharacteristically boisterous, chatting with Susan Smith about someone who had been on *Ed Sullivan* the night before. Rose waited for an embarrassed half smile of acknowledgment, a tacit apology of some sort. But nothing. Susan let the door slam shut behind her, and a puff of chalk dust kicked up. Teaching was less about instruction and more about exerting control. "Take out a sheet of paper. We're having a pop quiz," Rose decided to say.

"But we had one last week!" Susan said. "That's not fair, Mrs. Downes."

"That, Susan, is the nature of a pop quiz. You never know when you'll get one," Rose said, still working out what she would test them on.

"Mrs. Downes, I need to go to the bathroom. Can I have a bathroom pass?"

"'*May I* have a bathroom pass,' Linda," she said wearily. "And no, you may not."

More groaning, more litanies of "it's not fair." It was maddening, really, the number of times these well-fed, well-dressed daughters of privilege complained. Helen was quiet, pencil in hand, readied over paper. She gazed at Rose. Was that a hint of challenge in those solemn, dark eyes?

"You're in luck, only one question," Rose said. It came to her in an instant. "We've spent a great deal of time on poetic form. Tell me what form our country's most valuable document is written in."

"Excuse me?" Susan said, openly annoyed. "What document are you talking about?"

"Well, then, it's a two-part question, isn't it? A document that has to do with our country's founding. There is your clue—a big one. And the form it takes is a poetic one."

"We haven't gone over this," came a mutter from the back row. It was Annie, a voluble girl who rarely passed up a chance to complain.

"No, we have not, but you will be in a great deal of trouble if all you can do is parrot back what I've told you." A few minutes passed: several girls, hunched over their desks, wrote down answers; others, including Helen, stared off in the distance. The lack of trying irritated Rose more than anything else. "Helen, please come up here," she said.

Moving slowly, Helen complied. "Write down the first line of our founding document," Rose said.

"I—I don't know what you mean, exactly." Helen blinked, her soft mouth open.

"So you didn't even hazard a guess. You didn't put in any effort."

"Well, that wasn't it—"

"No, I don't want to hear it," Rose said. "Listen: 'We hold | these truths | to be | self-ev | ident.'" She was tired of excuses. She didn't want to hear any. How could it be that she, the foreigner, was the only one who knew this? "I am quoting the Declaration of Independence. I trust you've heard of it?"

A few girls tittered. "Quiet down or you'll come up here too," Rose said. "Helen, please write it."

Helen copied the words in big, flowing letters on the blackboard. She had beautiful penmanship—Rose had to give her that.

"Iambic pentameter, the most popular metrical line in the English language." Rose said, the quiz wholly forgotten. "It helped form the stately prose of this country's founding—our country," she said, though she herself was not yet a citizen. "The least you can do is know it."

FOR THE FIRST TIME IN what felt like weeks, Thomas was to be home for supper. Rose decided to ignore the pile of papers that she had to grade. She stopped at the butcher on Robertson and picked up a roast. They ate it with potatoes and cream and drank red wine and opened the windows, the faint chlorine smell of the courtyard pool that no one ever swam in wafting in. There was something wonderfully dissonant about their heavy meal in contrast to the tropical warmth eddying about. Rose leaned across the crowded linoleum tabletop and deposited a kiss on Thomas's lips. "And what did I do to deserve that?" he asked, delighted.

"You married me. Thank God." It was a sentiment that she thought often, if expressed less. Rose was not given to flights of fancy, but she was convinced if she hadn't gone into that antique shop on Old Bond, if she hadn't been searching for *The Bellhop*, she would still be working for Mr. Marks, still living alone in her tiny Belsize flat, never knowing that she was in fact capable of such happiness.

"Well, Mrs. Downes, it remains my pleasure. Again and again and again." Thomas kissed her back. "I have you and my beautiful new teacups; what more could I want?"

She laughed a little, shook her head. "Is that your way of saying you'd like a cup?"

"Yes, please," he said, and she put the kettle on. The week before, Thomas had a cavity filled, and afterward, he and Rose walked back to the car parked on Beverly Drive. Across the street from Nate 'n Al's, Thomas stopped in front of a tiny antique shop that featured a full suit of armor in the window. "I've always wanted one of those," he said, his words slurry from the Novocain.

"You are not in your right mind," she had said, but it was with affection. Inside the shop they went. And Thomas was oohing and aahing over everything within reach—the armor, a bronze elephant, a silver tea cart—Rose declaring that the drugs had gone to his head, when he spotted the teacups in a glass-fronted case. Even Rose had to admit they were gorgeous, hand-painted a pale green with a spray of yellow and blue flowers, gold leafing on the delicate handle. "They're

Minton," Thomas said, reading the tag. "Bone china, from the late 1800s. My mum always wanted a Minton tea service."

"Let me see," she said, for the tag also listed the price: one hundred and twenty-five dollars for the set. A ludicrous amount of money for six cups, entirely frivolous. Thomas gave Rose such a solemn look—"I want them," he said—that all joking about drugs was pushed aside. She nodded in assent and soon he was writing a check.

"We should use them often," she said now. "That is the only way I can explain away the wild expense." She might tease him now and again, but they reminded him of his mother. She of all people never would have said no to that.

"Ah, Rosie," he said. "Every once in a while we can afford something frivolous. They make me happy. What could we buy you to make you happy?"

"More time," she said as the phone rang.

"Downes residence," Rose answered, holding the receiver, spotted with grease, away from her ear.

"Is this Rose Downes?" a bubbly voice asked.

"To whom am I speaking?"

"Oh, am I glad to talk to you! I called earlier and got no answer, and I thought, 'Poor girl, she must be so busy, so *terribly* busy, and just having moved here and not knowing anyone.' But now here we are, speaking!"

"Yes, we are," Rose managed to say, too confused to dispute this characterization—*newly arrived? Poor girl?* "I'm sorry, who are you?"

"Oh, did I not say? Forgive me! I'm Dotty Epstein, Kurt Epstein's wife, formerly Dotty Gimbel, of the Philadelphia Gimbels, not the New York Gimbels—but the same extended family, those are my cousins." She spoke gaily, rapidly, as if any minute another voice—another friend or another cousin—would join in. "And you *are* Rose Downes, Gerhard Zimmer's sister, are you not?"

"I am," Rose said. "But I'm sorry, I don't know you." Gerhard? What did Gerhard have to do with this?

"Did your brother not tell you?"

"Tell me what?"

"Oh, this must be so absolutely bewildering to you!" She said it with such merriment that Rose felt like any objection, even the most clear-eyed of objections, would be taken personally, ruin all her fun. "My husband, Kurt Epstein, and Gerhard went to school together in Vienna. A lifetime ago, *of course*. Is his name familiar to you?"

"What? No." Rose felt an intense need to sit down. She steadied herself against the refrigerator door. Kurt Epstein? Who? The thought of someone from Vienna here in Los Angeles filled her with a strange expectant dread.

"Well, he says he remembers *you*, from when you were a tiny little thing. Anyway Kurt was across the pond for work—he's a filmmaker, you know." Dotty dropped her voice, as if she were bestowing a most delicious secret. "And he was in London and ran into your brother. They hadn't seen each other since they were children, *practically*. When he learned you had *just* moved to L.A.—"

"Two years ago," Rose cut in, "not *just*."

Thomas, scraping food into the trash bin, raised a questioning eyebrow at her. She waved him off, turned away. She couldn't begin to explain.

"We've been here for more than a decade, and we know so many others from Vienna. You must come over. We're in Brentwood. Where are you?"

"Mid-Wilshire," Rose answered, feeling relief that they were in different neighborhoods, a thirty-minute drive from each other.

"Ah, close to Wilshire Boulevard Temple! Lucky for you."

"Yes," Rose said, not sure what she was saying yes to, exactly, but finding it impossible to say no.

"Are you members yet?"

"What? No."

"Well, you must join. I'll introduce you to Rabbi Magnin. He's wonderful and charming and—urbane—not like most rabbis. We go far back, my family and his family knew each other—the retail business, *you know*. But why am I speaking of Rabbi Magnin? I am calling to invite you over this Sunday afternoon. We're having some friends over, fellow expats, for coffee and cake. You'll come over and it will be lovely."

"That does sound lovely," Rose said, "but we can't." She worked to sound regretful.

"Oh," Dotty said. "But you must. Kurt will be terribly disappointed, as will I."

"We cannot, not this week anyhow," Rose said. "But I thank you for the invitation." The more tense she felt, the more prim she acted. She didn't want to be rude, and she was sure that Thomas would tell her she was being silly—*aren't you just the slightest bit curious? Maybe you would recognize him when you saw him*. But whatever curiosity she felt was trumped by her unease. Why did people think that simply because she had been born in a particular city to a particular set of circumstances, she would want to socialize with others who shared those circumstances?

"You'll come another time," Dotty said. "They are wonderful get-togethers, I promise you."

"Yes, another time," Rose said, and soon hung up.

"Who was that?" Thomas asked.

"That," Rose said, "was a force of nature. A woman by the name of Dotty Epstein. She says that her husband, Kurt, might have known my brother back in Vienna."

"Might?" Thomas asked.

"Did," Rose corrected herself, smoothing out a tea towel on the kitchen counter. "He *did* know Gerhard. Apparently they ran into each other in London recently. I don't know why Gerhard didn't mention it to me in his last letter. It's so like him not to mention it."

"So these Epsteins live here in L.A. and invited us over. Why did you say no? We're free this Sunday."

"I don't know," Rose said. She continued to smooth out the towel, folding it into thirds. "I didn't want to."

"Why not? It might be fun."

"I simply didn't want to," she said querulously. Of course Thomas would think that it might be fun, Thomas, who saw the world's ugliness but didn't shirk away from it, managed to come out as an optimist, merely glad to be on the other side. She was not like him. She imagined meeting people from Vienna, being asked which school she had attended, which neighborhood her family had lived in, and though these questions were innocuous enough, the simple possibility of them felt like something hostile. She had been eleven when she left, not a small child, but there was little she remembered. She had one photograph of her family, taken a few summers before she and Gerhard left. They stood on a footbridge over the river in Bad Ischl, her father looking at something outside the frame. Her mother gazed directly at the camera, one hand resting on Gerhard's shoulder (he was nearly her height then) and the other on Rose's small kerchiefed head. Rose was the only one smiling, grinning, really. There were many reasons Rose could hardly look at the picture, but chief among them was this: She didn't recognize that little girl.

Now Rose folded her arms across her chest, trying to bat back her tears. Thomas knew that gesture, and he said, "Oh Rosie," and took her in his arms.

"I'm all right," she said. "I really am." And she was, here with him.

He breathed into her hair: "All right, then."

LATER THAT NIGHT, IN BED, when Thomas reached for her, she pulled back. "I'm going to the doctor on Friday to get my new diaphragm—remember?"

"Well, there are certain things we can still do," he said, and bit her bottom lip teasingly. She tasted the smokiness of his scotch. He was small but lithe; they fit each other well.

She closed her eyes. Thomas had always been able to make her feel good. She felt greedy when he touched her, looked forward to her mind quieting.

But now she spoke into his chest: "Thomas. We can't."

"I know. I was only—" and he pulled away, lay on his back. "Did you think I would?" he said to the ceiling. "Like that? After all these years?"

"No," she said. "I don't know. I wanted to be sure."

"Yes," he said flatly. "You can be sure."

They had agreed. Before they got married, they had agreed. Rose had made sure of that. When she told him, when it became finally clear that her *I-can't-have-children* meant, in fact, *I won't have children,* when she tried to explain, she started talking about going to the cinema. She loved movies. She loved so much about them—the immense screen, the velvet seats, the expectant hush as the lights dimmed and the music kicked up. And yet nearly every time she went to the cinema, sat in a crowded darkened movie house filled with strangers, she felt a volley of panic, fought an urge to leave. Why was everyone sitting here, together, so close, so calm? What enabled them to do that? Wouldn't someone somewhere do something terrible?

Thomas had listened. He had let her speak, didn't ask any questions. She loved him for that.

"I feel so fortunate with you," she had said then. "So uncommonly lucky." She felt something spiky lodged in her throat, and try as she might, she couldn't swallow it down. "I'm afraid of ruining it." That was the closest she came to articulating the question that terrified her: How in the world can you protect that which you love?

He knew that too, of course. "But you go to the cinema," he said softly. "You don't avoid it altogether."

She dropped his hand. "I'm not talking about the cinema," she said. They were back in her tiny room in Belsize. She remembered concentrating on the clank of the radiator, trying to focus on that and not Thomas's words.

"Sometimes I think that you think you don't deserve this. But you do," he said. "You have a life. We can have a life together. You have to try."

"I *am* trying. I just don't think I want children. I don't."

"But I think I do," he said, and with that he left. She spent nearly a week catatonic with fear. But he came back. "I love you," he had said.

Now, more than a decade later, she touched her husband, a body that she knew as well as her own. She wanted to climb inside of him, to feel completely surrounded. "I love you," she said now, reaching for him, but Thomas rolled over.

"Love you too," he said. "I have a long day tomorrow," and he clicked off his bedside light. Rose was left alone in the dark, a loneliness all the more acute because she knew she had brought it upon herself.

TWO DAYS LATER, THE RAINS began. A relentless rain, a rain that seemed otherworldly in force. The city was not built for such deluge: Olympic and Pico flooded, rocks tumbled, mudslides ensued. PCH was shut down. Much of this Rose and Thomas read in the paper or saw on the news, grateful for their dry second-floor apartment near Fairfax.

That morning, when Rose left for work, she passed the building's super, Mr. Osaka, in the lobby. "You really driving in this mess, Mrs. Downes?" Mr. Osaka said as she darted through the lobby back out to the uncovered parking lot. The driving rain made a racket on the roofs of the cars, pelted against her umbrella. She could hardly see. Just as she was trying to manage both her umbrella and the key (she and Thomas had bought a used Chevy after she began teaching at Eastgate: "A two-car family," Thomas had said. "Now we're truly Angelenos"), something caught her eye. It was a shadowy something. Discarded piping from one of Mr. Osaka's projects? The piping began to move: a snake, glistening among the deepening puddles, pocked by the raindrops. A moving living snake. It was coppery brown, undulating through the shallow waters with ease.

Rose stared, stiffening. Her back was getting wet, her ankles dampened by rain, but she barely noticed, stunned by fear. She had never seen a live snake before. It wasn't small. She watched it oscillate beneath a neighboring car. Then she ran back through the puddles of the parking lot and into the lobby.

The super was still inside, now atop a stepladder, replacing a light bulb.

"Mr. Osaka, there's a snake out in the parking lot."

"Oh?"

She nodded, breathing audibly. She rubbed her damp cheek with her hand. "Whom shall we call? Who removes snakes in these situations?" She tried to laugh.

"He'll go away on his own. Sometimes they come out in the rain," Mr. Osaka said, shrugging. "Other times heat, the dryness, brings them out."

This was Los Angeles to Rose. A surreal landscape, whether it was the rains, the Santa Anas, the coyotes that roamed the jagged canyons, the brush fires, the cactus flowers that inexplicably bloomed from dust and rock. Even on its many gorgeous days, the beauty of Los Angeles had an underlying hardness. There was nothing soft about it, and she loved this—the city's sharp lines and wild heart even when it tried to disguise them. Los Angeles had made itself. Everything was imported—the water that was pumped in from the north, the palm trees for which the city was celebrated. Everyone and everything here came from somewhere else.

When she managed to drive through the churn that Sunset had become and at last arrived at Eastgate, only five students were in her second-period class, four in her third. By noon, the administration had moved to shut the school for the afternoon. The classroom was chilly, the radiator barely emitting heat, seemingly resentful that it actually had work to do. But Rose decided to stay for the hour to catch up on papers she had to grade, go over lesson plans. She was dreading the drive home.

At two o'clock, ten minutes after sixth period usually began, Rose heard footsteps, a knock at the open door. She looked up to see Helen Peale, clad in a soaked yellow plastic poncho.

"I know I'm late," Helen said.

"Didn't you hear?" Rose asked. "Class is canceled."

"I know," Helen said. She remained in the doorway, the plastic crinkling as she moved, forlorn in bright yellow. "But I'm here at school. So here I am." In the poncho, she looked closer to ten than her fourteen years.

"Well, then," Rose said, sighing. "Take that wet thing off; you're dripping all over my classroom." Helen hung the poncho up, and went to her usual spot, but Rose gestured to the front row. "Come, to Susan's seat. No reason to hide back there. Bring your *Versification* book and turn to page ninety-three."

Helen's expression was solemn as she studied the book. "Robert Frost's 'Fire and Ice.' It is a compact poem, but it is not small," Rose said. "Scholars say that Frost had Dante's *Inferno* in mind when he wrote it."

She asked Helen to read it aloud. The sound of Helen's clear girlish voice reciting Frost's words, the rhythmic patter of rain against the roof, combined to make Rose feel warmer. They were the only two in the classroom; were they the only people left in the building?

"How do you think the world will end?" Helen asked when she finished.

Such a terrible question, but Helen posed it with forthrightness. Rose could remember sitting on her bed in Leeds, waiting for letters that never arrived, thinking, *I am supposed to go to school and study? I am supposed to go to the cinema and enjoy it?* "I have no idea," Rose said.

Helen didn't say anything, and then: "My father died."

"What?"

"My father died." She repeated the words patiently. "Two weeks ago. A boating accident, in Hawaii."

"Oh, Helen, that's awful. I'm so sorry." Rose moved close to the girl, bent down so that she was at eye level. She wished she had known; why hadn't the administration told her? It made her angry that she hadn't been told.

"It's okay," Helen said, chewing on the end of a limp strand of hair, not looking at Rose. "I'm okay. I hadn't seen him in so long anyway."

"Where is your mother?"

"Still in Hawaii. She's staying there for now. She doesn't want to come back. She doesn't want me."

"I'm sure that's not true," Rose insisted, despite what she knew of the family.

Helen shrugged and smiled, the sort of sweet-sad smile that children give adults who lack understanding of the situation, a look that Rose could recall employing herself. "She hasn't come back. And I'm still here."

"Well, I'm here too," Rose said. An absurd thing to say, because where was she but in a chilly classroom with a dusty blackboard and wrinkled likenesses of Dickinson and the Brontës and spelling lists tacked up on the walls? What did she have to offer? *She needs her mother,* Rose thought, infuriated—if she knew anything, she knew this to be true. But here they both were. Rose herself might have been a paltry substitute for what Helen needed, but she hoped in the moment for her presence to be enough.

THAT NIGHT, AT HOME, TWO aerograms awaited Rose. The first, from Mrs. Cohen, contained not unexpected news: Mr. Cohen had passed away two weeks earlier. He had been ill with lung cancer for more than a year. "The funeral was simple, as he would have liked," Mrs. Cohen wrote. "He remembered you fondly, and I hope you will do the same for him."

"I should have gone back," Rose said to Thomas. "I should have seen him more often." Why couldn't she have been kinder, after all he had done?

"He knew how you felt," Thomas said.

"I'm not so sure." With a sigh, she turned to her brother's letter. Gerhard spoke about meeting with distributors in Edinburgh and his hopes that the crocuses in his garden would be blooming before long. "Isobel wants me to tell you she is horrified by what she reads about the South, and Harry wants to know when he can come to California to meet Betty Grable," Gerhard wrote.

"The other day at Kings Cross, I had the most extraordinary experience. I saw a thin middle-aged man staring at me. I kept thinking, why is that old gentleman looking at me?, when he turned and I saw that he was my age—not old at all—and he said my name." Gerhard went on to say what Rose already knew: that Kurt Epstein lives in Los Angeles, that he works in the entertainment industry. "I told him you were there and he immediately asked for your telephone number. He claims to remember you from when we were children. How surreal and wonderful it was to see him again. Like time collapsing on itself. I do hope he calls."

"What does Gerhard say?" Thomas asked.

"He wrote about his garden," Rose said. "He is so focused on his crocuses."

A week later, when Dotty Epstein called, talking about the Sacher torte she made and a well-known actor who would be coming by this Sunday, and how Rose must join them, Rose answered right away. "We will be there," she said, thinking of both Mr. Cohen and Helen Peale.

KURT AND DOTTY'S HOUSE ON Cliffwood looked like a smaller version of the main Eastgate building—Spanish style with red roof tiles, creamy stucco, flowers spilling over the brick walkway. Rose and Thomas headed to the front arched door, nearly twenty minutes late. Traffic had slowed them down, but really Rose's own tardiness was to blame. She had taken longer than usual to get ready, finally settling on a tweed pencil skirt and a cream-colored sweater set.

"I bet not one person here has read Thomas Hardy, except for you," Thomas said, squeezing Rose's hand reassuringly. Just last night he had said to her, *If you don't want to go, you don't have to.*

"You haven't read Hardy."

He grinned. "Exactly."

The door swung open. "Rose Downes! Thomas Downes! Come in, come in!" Dotty Epstein was even bigger and more declarative in person—her voluptuous frame, the colorful pattern of her dress, the large sunglasses in her hand. She gave Rose a noisy kiss on the cheek.

"You look positively darling. What a charming skirt and top." Dotty's tone indicated she thought Rose's outfit sweet in much the same manner that a child wearing bloomers was sweet—charming in its oddity, its essential irrelevance. They passed a blur of rooms—"billiards, study, living room," Dotty said, ticking them off with her well-manicured hand. "Powder room on the left. We are going outside because today is beautiful and I will not be denied."

Rose and Thomas followed Dotty through the sliding glass doors and out into the rich sunshine. Rose hadn't brought her sunglasses—it hadn't occurred to her that they would be outside—and she stood blinking, her eyes adjusting before she could make out in detail the white gazebo situated by the kidney-shaped pool, the water silver in the dazzling light. A dozen or so people milled about, men in light-colored suits and women in bright full-skirted dresses that rustled with the slightest movement.

"Kurt must be around here somewhere," Dotty said. "Kurt?"

A man emerged out of the cool shadow of the gazebo, a tall but narrowly built man in a pale summer suit. When he saw Rose, he clapped his hand to his mouth. "Gerhard's little sister! Is that you?"

"It is indeed," she said. It was odd; he was no one she recognized, but she felt a little woozy at the sight of him. He had thick brows accenting his expressive dark eyes, a chipped front tooth that only seemed to add to his allure. He was handsome, undeniably so, nothing like the few boys she remembered from her Viennese youth.

"Ah, you don't look like your brother—lucky for you—but I swear, I remember your face. I haven't seen you in more than twenty years, but I do remember your face!" He laughed as he said this, grasping her right hand between his two. They were cool, despite the sun.

"I find that hard to believe. I was eleven when I left."

"There are many things that are hard to believe," he said, letting go of her hand. He smiled at her then and there was something intimate about that smile, directed just at her, that made her say: "I'm afraid I don't remember you." She knew she sounded prickly, but she felt the need to defend herself.

"You are forgiven," Kurt said, and laughed again. "The world is a small place after all."

"Kurt, this is Mr. Thomas Downes. He is an engineer at Douglas. Aviation." Dotty paused meaningfully. "A top engineer. Working on jet travel."

"Is that so?" Kurt said idly.

"Not *top* engineer," Thomas said, coloring, "not top at all."

"Don't sell yourself short," Dotty declared. "We will have none of that in my house." Rose couldn't remember telling Dotty where Thomas worked, let alone that he was an engineer. How did she find that out? "And my Kurt is an acclaimed screenwriter," Dotty said.

"Acclaimed," Kurt repeated, lifting a bushy eyebrow, "is one way to put it."

"It's my way," Dotty said, and laced her hand with his.

"What films have you written?" Rose asked.

"Have you seen *The Thing*?"

"The Thing?" Rose asked, puzzled.

"Yes, the *Thing* movies: *The Thing Escapes*, *The Thing Returns*. Now I'm working on *The Reign of the Thing*. Have you seen any of them?"

Rose shook her head. "I don't believe so, I'm sorry."

"Don't be," he said. "I would be more surprised if you had."

"Why is that? They're witty, *wonderful* films," Dotty said.

"You know, I did see one, years ago," Thomas said. "It was quite entertaining. It truly was. Well done."

"Thank you," Kurt said with a little bow.

"What is the Thing?" Rose asked.

"What do you mean?"

"Is the Thing a person? A monster, a figure of the imagination?"

"We don't know," Kurt said with a wry little smile. "That's why he keeps coming back."

"Now we could talk about the Thing all day, but come now," Dotty said. "Let's get you some food."

Under the gazebo, oh, the sweet abundance: Such an array of desserts—dark chocolate Sacher tortes, as Dotty had promised, and poppy-seed cakes and a platter of almond cookies dusted with sugar and elegant petits fours in the form of tiny purple flowers. There was a large silver coffee urn surrounded by rows of china teacups stacked on top of each other and several pitchers of water accompanied by tall glasses to help wash down the treats just as, Rose unexpectedly remembered, her father liked to do.

Soon Rose was settled on a lounge chair balancing a plate that held a slice of the Sacher torte, and drinking the strong coffee and listening to a composer ("very accomplished," Dotty had ducked down to whisper) talk about the Vienna Opera House and the mournful cries of the coyotes he heard at night from his house in the hills. Thomas was engaged in a conversation with a portly man about air travel while his stunning wife tried not to look bored ("his third," Dotty informed Rose).

"Did you ask your analyst?" Rose heard a mustached man ask Dotty.

"Oh, he would *never* answer," Dotty said.

"That is why I go monthly to Menninger in Kansas," he said. "To have an analyst with such an astute, incredible mind, it is worth journeying."

The composer said to Rose: "Have you been back to Vienna?"

"Me?" She shook her head. "No." After a moment, she asked: "You?"

"No," he said. "Why would I ever go back? It's just as Wilder says: 'The Austrians have managed to convince the world that Beethoven was Austrian and Hitler a German.' You cannot trust them."

"No," she said quietly. "You can't." Rose felt hot in her tweed skirt. Her head hurt. She shouldn't have had that second cup of coffee. She made her way around the pool, toward the house. Inside it was thankfully cool, enveloping. She found the bathroom again, but it was occupied. She waited. A moment later, the door opened and Kurt stepped out.

"Well. Hello." A smile lit his handsome face. He had a hand against the doorframe. "Enjoying yourself?"

"Yes, very, thank you." She gestured at the door. "Excuse me—"

He moved closer. They were neither in the bathroom nor in the hall. "I was hoping to see you alone. You have a look about you. Your eyes—they're beautiful. They remind me of Adele's." His voice was gentle.

Who was Adele? "I'm sorry—" Rose stuttered. Kurt kept his gaze trained on her. She shifted uncomfortably. Thomas must still be outside. She shouldn't be reminding Kurt of anyone.

"It is the most uncanny resemblance," Kurt said. A light smokiness emanated from his clothes. She could have moved past him, but she didn't. "You're lovely like her. Not of this world, like her."

Rose was too stunned to say anything. Finally she murmured: "I have to—I should go."

"Of course." But he leaned in and she didn't move. He grazed his lips across hers. They felt cool and dry. It was quick and then it was over.

"No, don't," she said after the fact.

He looked at her, smiled, shrugged. And then he was gone.

Rose had no idea how long she remained in the bathroom, trying to slow her flailing heart. *It doesn't matter,* she told herself sternly, except that was a lie. She splashed water on her face, once, twice, smoothed her hair, stared at herself in the mirror. Thomas would take one look at her and know. Eventually she walked out. In the hall, she heard: "Rose?"

Dotty was in the kitchen, cutting oranges into quarters and adding them to a glass pitcher with lemons already crowding the bottom. "Sangria," she explained. "It can't be coffee and Sacher torte all the time." Inside, with her hat and sunglasses off, without an audience, she seemed smaller. "I am glad you are here. Was that Kurt you were speaking to in the hall?"

Rose nodded.

"Is he okay?"

"Yes," Rose said quickly. "Of course."

Dotty's hand guided the knife, *chop, chop chop*. "Did you know Adele growing up?"

"Excuse me?" Rose blurted.

"Adele. Did you know her?"

Rose shook her head. Was she too quick to answer? Why would she know her? "Who is she?"

"His wife," Dotty said, funneling sugar into the pitcher, a white snowy path. "His first wife."

"Oh," Rose only said. She wasn't sure she wanted to know the rest.

Dotty stirred the contents of the pitcher. She didn't look up. "They were childhood sweethearts in Vienna. I thought maybe you knew her; I'm certain your brother did. She and Kurt were madly in love. They married, in the camp. They were nineteen. And then she caught pneumonia. Died."

"I didn't realize," Rose said. It was inconceivable. All of these stories were: Kurt's, her parents', so many stories, each ghastly in its own particular way. "That's terrible."

"It is," Dotty said. Only then did she stop mixing. "It is terrible. He yells out in his sleep sometimes: 'Adele, Adele!' He has a Ouija board. I know he tries to reach her. But he won't talk to me about her." She turned back to the sangria, gave it a vigorous stir. "I tell myself it's over, but it's not. When will it be over?"

Rose looked at the pitcher filled with fruit, such a bright, optimistic bounty, and she was back in those bleak days in London after the war. "Dotty," she asked in a voice far gentler than her own, "what can he possibly say?"

MONDAY MORNING, THE HEADMISTRESS'S SECRETARY came to Rose's classroom with a note. "You'll be getting another student for sixth period next week, possibly two. Helen Peale has left."

"What?" Rose could only say dumbly. "When?"

"Her mother came and took her this weekend. Quite right; it's about time."

When her students filed in for second period, Rose took attendance and had to be reminded of the presence of two students, whose names she overlooked. She told the class to take out the *Versification* book. They were reading Frost again today. She had them turn to "The Road Not Taken." Rose couldn't focus. What was the rhyme scheme again?

Elicit and evoke, an old teacher of Rose's used to say. Now she tried; she asked about Frost's intent. Only two hands went up. She called on a chatty girl named Annie. "We should take chances," Annie said. "We shouldn't be frightened by what is less traveled on, what we don't know."

"Don't let the last stanza fool you. Read the poem again. From the top." Rose missed Helen.

Annie did, more hesitant than the first time, and Rose pointed out that Frost called the other path "just as fair," and how both paths had been worn "about the same."

"Frost made it tricky, but the evidence is there. It doesn't matter which road you take; you take one or the other. But you must take one."

"Of course it matters," said Susan Smith. "How can you say that our decisions don't matter?"

"I didn't say that. And that's not what Frost is saying. At the end of the poem, he talks about how he'll tell the story in the future, with a sigh. He is talking about years from then, is he not? When he returns to that moment, when he revisits that decision. You must make decisions with incomplete information, with what you know at hand. That's the way life works. Even if it's paltry."

"No," said Susan. "It's not right."

"Actually, it is," Rose said sharply. It was lost on them, this feeling of darkness. Of course it was. When had they ever felt true discomfort? When had any of them been in a situation with only terrible choices? Escape a war. Leave your parents behind. "That's what the speaker is sighing over, years later. He had to convince himself that one was better. But he had no idea which road to take. This is the lesson. You must pick. Stop your hand-wringing. You must decide." Her voice was louder than it needed to be.

The young faces looked at her. Annie was scared, Susan sullen, resentful. A few others gazed out the window, doodled in their notebooks, paying little attention. But Rose, feeling the white heat of her own anger course through her, did not care. She folded her arms over her chest. "Any questions?"

13

LOS ANGELES, 2006

LIZZIE DIDN'T KNOW HIM BUT she did. Her recognition registered as sensation, a whistle of breath when the door to the forlorn Hollywood coffee shop opened. In came Detective Gilbert Tandy, the same detective who had shown up at her house the morning after the paintings were stolen, twenty years ago.

The small coffee shop was nestled at the far end of a strip mall next to a cell-phone store at the intersection of Sunset and El Centro. Lizzie's booth seat was crisscrossed with electrical tape, the worn carpet sticky in spots. Tandy had suggested meeting there.

The detective was a stocky black man with a wide pleasant face. Lizzie had remembered him as much taller. He had a deliberate walk and wore baggy jeans and a pink short-sleeved collared shirt, attire that made Lizzie feel less panicked. Just minutes ago, before he walked in, she'd stared at the front door, stomach lodged in her throat, thinking: *I can just get up and leave*. But how terrible could it be if he was wearing pink?

"Lizzie Goldstein," she said, rising to her feet and offering a firm hand.

"Of course," he said, sliding in across from her. "I remember you. You look the same."

"Well, that's nice to say, but I hope not," she said. "My hair was huge then."

He didn't crack a smile. "I'm glad you called. And thanks for meeting me out here. You're on the Westside?"

"I'm staying there, yes," she clarified. "I live in New York now."

He nodded, ordered coffee from the passing waiter.

"I can't believe how much this neighborhood has changed," Lizzie said, feeling the need to fill the air. "I just passed Hollywood and Vine and saw condos going up. When I was in high school, I had my car radio stolen a couple blocks from here, on Gower near Melrose. I remember driving around here then and seeing all these women on corners, beautiful women in heels and microskirts leaning into cars, and I remembered thinking: 'They're so friendly, giving directions.'"

"Yes, it's different, at least on the surface," Tandy said. "But expensive condos just mask crimes of another kind."

She nodded, her hands nesting the coffee cup. Of course; he was a detective, he probably saw crime everywhere.

"You said on the phone you wanted to talk," he said.

"I did," she said, and the air felt warmer. "My father died several months ago."

"I heard. I'm sorry."

She nodded. She bunched up her napkin in her lap. "Thank you."

"Did you come across anything?" He asked this gently.

"What?" Lizzie was still looking down at her napkin. Even that little question made her recoil.

"Did you come across anything that seemed unusual, any payments, any correspondence, anything that you were wondering about?"

"What? No." A prickly heat coated her neck. She had been dreading such a question long before Tandy had walked in. But she had been expecting it too—she had initiated this meeting, after all, she had chosen to be here—and that only made her want to reject it more forcibly.

"The artwork is still missing; you know that. It's still an open case."

"Of course I know that."

"May I ask you—" And then: "Why did you call me?"

How could she answer that? No part of her wanted to. What was she doing here? Lizzie looked past him toward the front, where an old man in a beret was trying to get himself settled on a stool at the counter. "You want the cottage cheese, Murray?" the waiter asked. "But of course," she heard the man say.

"So he was a suspect," she heard herself say, eyes still fixed on Murray.

"He was a person of interest—yes. We were very interested in his story."

She swung back toward Tandy. "And what about the private investigator? What did he say?"

"What investigator?"

"The one my father hired."

She felt his eyes on her. "He told you he hired a PI?"

"I heard that he did. To help find the paintings."

"That would surprise me, immensely," he said slowly. He sipped his coffee. "I am highly skeptical that he hired an investigator on his own."

She shook her head, confusion and terror mixing into a new terrible feeling. "I don't understand," she whispered. She wanted so badly not to.

"What I'm telling you," he said, "is what I know: your father did not hire an investigator to look into this case." There was kindness visible on his face, in his steady gaze, but Lizzie felt herself falling, and that kindness registered as an assault.

"You're wrong."

"Look, I'll tell you what I know. In 1986, your father lent the Picasso drawing of the bull and the Soutine *Bellhop* to the San Francisco Museum of Modern Art for a show," he said. "Museums usually insure loaned works under a blanket policy, and no one at the museum appraised the paintings. Goldstein had purchased the Picasso in 1979 at the Phoenix Gallery in New York for a hundred and forty-three thousand dollars. He bought the Soutine three years later from the Levitan Gallery for a little over seventy thousand. In 1986, they were worth about close to a million, combined, but he was allowed to file his own estimate of their value for the museum's insurance purposes: four million. The museum drew up a loan agreement, stating the value provided by Goldstein. And Goldstein took that agreement and got a new insurance policy based on that inflated amount, underwritten by Lloyd's of London and a German company, Nordstern. About a year after that, the art market fell, the work was worth even less, and the painting and the drawing disappeared."

Lizzie was no longer in her body. Someone else was seated in this booth, trying desperately to hold on to that cup of coffee, nodding at the detective, thinking, *It all fits.*

Tandy was still talking. "Goldstein's insurers denied the claim, saying that he had deliberately overvalued the artwork. He sued, alleging bad faith and demanding the four million and then some—he asked for another million in punitive damages."

"My father sued?" How did she not know that?

He gave her a little hard smile. "He did. Rather than risk losing in front of a jury, the insurers backed down. They paid him the full amount."

"You think he set it up."

"I'm telling you the facts as I know them," Tandy said. "And where the facts lead."

"But that's what you think."

He gave the smallest of nods. "Yes."

"So then he destroyed them," she heard herself say coldly, as if she were talking about a stranger, a defendant whose case she'd taken on. "He had to get rid of the evidence."

"I don't know."

"But it only makes sense." That's what she would do, she thought wildly. If she had done something insane like this, she would follow through. "You get rid of them, you destroy the evidence. You can't fucking sell them; everyone's on the lookout, who would buy them? If you're doing something as horrible as this—if you're letting your kid take the fall, you destroy them, don't you?" Her voice had grown shaky. She slid out of the booth, stumbling. What had she been thinking, meeting with this man?

"I'm sorry," he said, his mouth a hard line. "I'm sorry for us all."

"Don't," she said as she flung a ten-dollar bill on the table. "Don't for one moment pretend that we are in this together."

KEEP MOVING. THAT WAS HER instinct, the only thing clear in her mind. She got on the freeway heading east and kept going, flying beneath those immense green signs that announced directions and destinations in what now seemed like a strange, foreign shorthand, not built for human scale. She passed the trickle of the concreted Los Angeles River and the Staples Center and glittery tower of the Bonaventure. The multiple lanes of freeway knotted up, traffic barely moving, and still she urged herself on.

Her mind was caught in an endless loop: her father and *The Bellhop, The Bellhop* and her father. She remembered how he had laughed and mussed up her hair when she had asked if the man in the painting was famous. "In our house he is," she remembered him saying.

Did he hire someone? Did he not go to Boston at all?

All those years she had blamed herself. And he let her.

She sped up; she slowed down. No, it wasn't true. Her hands remained tight on the steering wheel, she drove as if she had a plan. She switched the radio off, but within minutes clicked it back on. The silence was worse, shrill.

He had been ripped off by his office manager right before the paintings were stolen. His practice took a beating. And there had been that real estate deal that went bad. He stopped buying art. She knew he had expenses. Hefty ones. But this? Surely this wouldn't have been his solution. There was that time in high school—it must have been before the paintings were stolen, it was definitely before the paintings were stolen—when Joseph had floated the idea of their moving. Friends had gotten a condo off of Olympic. A much smaller place than their house. "It's great!" Joseph had said. "A shared pool and you girls could walk places, even to school. What do you think? Don't you ever get tired of the hill?"

"No," she could remember harrumphing, aggrieved. "I don't."

Her mind sputtered, flayed about. She remembered her first summer as an associate, when she had been doing research and came across a decision from the Second Circuit that seemed to go against the case they were building. She brought it to the senior partner, proud of herself. But the senior associate had thrown the decision back in her face. "What am I supposed to do with this?" Lizzie stammered something about how the facts didn't match the case. "No," the partner said, "you've got it wrong. You *use* the facts. You anticipate how others will use them. They don't use you."

Lizzie passed West Covina and Pomona, the sky giving in to a grayish, almost yellow tint of late afternoon. She dimly registered hunger, her gas meter dipping lower than a quarter of a tank. It was only then that she realized she was heading out into the desert.

She remembered the vastness of the desert from when she was a kid, Joseph's small car careering along the ribbon of concrete, no match for the enormous stretch of sky and the sun-bleached ground and the snow-tipped mountains in the distance that seemed like a trick of the eye. She remembered the wind turbines, a gorgeous manmade orchard of tall sleek slices of metal, spinning, spinning.

But now the city had taken over, the Angeleno sprawl had spread. Now there were endless subdivisions and malls with Outback Steakhouses and Starbucks and Targets and Noah's Bagels. Nothing was the same.

Lizzie drove and she drove and she thought: *It's not true. It can't be. He had money; he did. And even if he had been in trouble, he loved the Soutine. He never would have done something like this. Not to me.*

But the jagged details came careening back: her father's face blotchy, hair matted down with sweat, as if he had flown back from Boston powered by his own vitriol and fear. *A party, a fucking party, Elizabeth?! You lied to me; I trusted you and you lied.* Those weeks of ugly silence: Sarah in the hospital, the two of them in the house, weary, embattled, alone. For years Lizzie's own guilt had impelled her, shaped her.

She was crying now, her hands shaky on the wheel. He had orchestrated this. He had set it up. All those years—all those times she had wished she could go back, undo the damage she had caused. *He* had done this.

Somehow she managed to switch lanes, get off the freeway. She pulled onto the shoulder, glanced at her gas gauge: nearly empty. She was going to stall out here in this no-man's-land of Walmarts and In-N-Outs and Wendy's.

Lizzie twisted around, looking for a station, and it was then that she saw the dinosaurs: two gigantic prehistoric sculptures that commanded the desert, shadowing a low-roofed diner and a gas station too.

Lizzie had forgotten all about the dinosaurs. How could she? She circled the service road that followed the curve of the larger dinosaur's slender neck and took her into the gas station. She got out of the car, her legs unsteady. The warm air was fragrant, a heady scent of flowers and gas and oil-soaked fry. She paid for a tank, downed a bag of oatmeal raisin cookies and a bottle of seltzer. A sign read WORLD'S BIGGEST GIFT SHOP INSIDE A DINOSAUR! She made her way over to the door cut into one of the dinosaurs' tails.

She'd been inside this gift shop before. It was before her mother had died, when her father was working so hard to impress—an antic tap dance of plans and sights and attractions—bumper cars and corn dogs at the Santa Monica Pier! Lunch at a movie studio! Guess jeans and Kork-Ease and satin jackets and anything she and Sarah wanted! Sunbathing in the desert in January—can you do that in New York? Can you?

But this particular outing had not gone well. Neither she nor Sarah would try a date shake at Hadley's Farm (*but they're sweeter than sweet!* Joseph had said) and then there was Sarah's meltdown about the lack of a miniature personalized license plate; they didn't have her name (inexplicably they had *Sara,* but no *Sarah.* "Who cares?" Lizzie could remember saying. There was no *Lizzie* or *Liz* either. "It's not like it goes on a real car"). Their father had tried to tell them about the man who had built the dinosaurs. He had spent years working on them, using concrete and steel left over from the construction of the freeway she had just gotten off. *Everyone thought he was nuts,* she remembered Joseph saying. *But he didn't care.*

She walked in. The gift shop occupied a small dark space, filled with rickety displays of dinosaur kitsch. But the back wall held a different type of attraction: INSTITUTE OF CREATION SCIENCE, a sign read. *Primordial soup to the zoo to you; is evolution true?*

Apparently not, according to the display, which talked about how early humans coexisted with dinosaurs ("just like the one you're standing in!") and how the earth ("in all its splendor and diversity") was created in six days. A painted bust of a Cro-Magnon man, looking like a hirsute Jon Voight, sat next to a sign arguing against Darwin's theories; a clay diorama of Noah's Ark showed two dinosaurs next to a duo of giraffes.

"I don't understand," Lizzie said to the young girl behind the register. "Since when is the gift shop a creationist museum?"

"We're just offering information," the girl said coolly, and returned to her book.

"Well, it's insulting to both scientists *and* dinosaurs," Lizzie said, but she said it as she was nearly out the door, a coward's retort. Outside, she leaned against the dinosaur's tail, pulled out her cell phone.

What was she doing? She felt a heaviness slowing her breath. Still she dialed. "Do you know there's a creationist museum in the dinosaur gift shop?" she said. "A fucking creationist museum—how crazy is that?"

"Lizzie? What are you talking about?" Sarah said. "Where are you?"

Lizzie looked around. In the pale crepuscular light, everything winked and glowed—the nearby Burger King, the dinosaur belly, the cluster of desert city lights in the distance. "I'm in Palm Springs—well, almost in Palm Springs. Remember the giant dinosaur sculptures? I'm there. I'm here; I'm getting gas."

"What are you doing there? Are you with Max?"

Lizzie shook her head. *Max,* she thought. "No," she said.

"What are you doing there?" Sarah repeated, more forcefully this time.

Lizzie shook her head again. "I don't know," she whispered. And then, "I saw the detective. It's a mess." She was crying now. "I'm a mess."

"What detective? What are you talking about?"

Lizzie didn't answer; how could she answer? She gripped her phone close to her ear, suddenly precious, the only thing securing her to this world.

Sarah's voice sounded tinny and far away. But she did not hesitate. "Just stay where you are. I'm coming."

WAS IT MISFORTUNE OR GOOD luck that one of the few rooms available was a luxe villa at the Grove on Palm Canyon Drive—a midweek special, theirs for the night for a mere $600. By the time Sarah arrived, Lizzie was already checked in, ensconced on the big private patio, listening to the hum of the few golf carts still traversing the green, the light clicking of the sprinklers, when her phone rang. Max, she saw. She let it go to voice mail, looking past the sand traps and the fourth hole at the marbleized surface of the craggy mountains in the distance, inured to the bite in the air. She had taken only a cursory glance at the sumptuous king-sized bed, the deep soaking bathtub that could hold a party. *I earned this luxury,* she thought, pulling a bottle of Côtes du Rhône from the minibar, feeling as tender as a bruise. *Every moment of this, I deserve.*

When Sarah rushed out onto the patio, they hugged and hugged, and for once, Lizzie wasn't the first to let go. "Dad did it," she kept saying.

Sarah shook her head. She poured herself a glass of wine and motioned Lizzie to sit beside her. "Tell me."

Lizzie recounted what the detective told her, the free fall in the art market, the fact that the artwork was insured for far more than the current value. She told Sarah about the PI Joseph had supposedly hired and how that wasn't true. She reminded Sarah about the business manager who ripped Joseph off, and the real estate deal that had soured. "It all fits," she said to her sister.

"It doesn't," Sarah said firmly. "I don't believe it."

"I do," Lizzie said. She was worn out, exhausted and depleted, and yet she felt a smooth glide of a sensation that she recognized as truth. "It makes sense. No one broke in, they took the most expensive art and didn't touch anything else. He was stressed about money and then he wasn't. It all makes sense."

"But none of that means he did it. Where is the evidence? Where is the proof? The fact that I can't prove to you that he didn't doesn't mean that he did."

"If you had talked to Detective Tandy—"

"I don't *want* to talk to him."

"I know," Lizzie said softly, miserably. "I know, I'm sorry."

"No, you're not," Sarah said, looking out at the lights spotlighting the fourth hole of the golf course, the ground's bright, unearthly green. "You think the worst of him; you always have."

Lizzie shook her head. "That's not true," she managed.

"Of course it is." Sarah said it so gently Lizzie started to cry. "He tried, you know. It couldn't have been easy, but he tried."

"You think I don't know that?"

"I wonder sometimes. And it's always been about the painting for you. I don't know why you're so hung up on the painting. Why does it matter? He loved you. He loved you, no matter what."

"I know," Lizzie whispered.

"No, he really loved you. Can you imagine?" Sarah said with a volley of insistence. "A single parent of two little girls? His ex-wife dead? He tried his best."

"I know," Lizzie said, and now she was pleading, out into the night, the tiny white lights that necklaced the patio. "But you know, he didn't always try." She looked back at her sister, her pretty face striking even in the low light, a face she knew almost as well as her own. "You were so young when they were still married. But things were tense; he was never around."

"I remember," Sarah said. "I remember more than you think."

"She wanted—I don't know—she wanted more."

"*Please.*" Even in the fuzzy light, Lizzie could see that Sarah's mouth was firm. "Yeah, she wanted more."

"What does that mean?"

Sarah shook her head. "Nothing," she muttered.

A rudimentary fear rose inside of Lizzie. "Come on. What did you mean?"

"Why do you think you know their relationship? How could you possibly know what happened?"

"I was eight years old; I saw things."

"Yeah, well." Sarah reached for her wine. "I remember that time before their divorce pretty well. And I know you think he was the one who had an affair, but he wasn't. It was Mom."

What? No. Lizzie was shaking her head, warding Sarah off. "That's absurd. You were five, six years old. How would you know?"

"I just do." Sarah said it with such finality that for a heart-stopping moment, Lizzie believed her. "I saw something. Someone. There was this guy: tall, bearded. He came by a bunch. You must have been in school. He called me Sarah Sue. One time Mom was supposed to take me to ice-skating lessons and instead we took a drive to his house; it was on a kind of farm, or at least, there were chickens there, and some turkeys too. I remember this drafty, messy kitchen, lots of dirty dishes and pots, a big sink. I asked for something to drink, and Mom made him clean the glass twice before giving it to me. I remember her laughing. And then he filled it up with chocolate milk and it was really good."

Lizzie studied her sister, her disbelief morphing and twisting. "That's it? You had chocolate milk from some hippie and now Mom had an affair?"

"I know what I saw," Sarah said. "My therapist," she said, and stopped. "What?"

"Nothing," Lizzie muttered. Of course this came out in therapy.

"And anyway, that doesn't even matter. I asked Dad."

"You asked Dad?" Lizzie said with unvarnished surprise.

"Yeah. He confirmed it. He said he didn't blame Mom, and I shouldn't either. He said people make mistakes. He said they both had been at fault, that he hadn't been home, and when he was around, he wasn't *really* around."

Lizzie stared at her sister, who was gazing out into the cool desert night. "Why didn't you tell me before?"

Sarah exhaled. "I thought about it; I wanted to. But, I don't know. So then you could think worse of Mom too? She wasn't around to defend herself or explain. It didn't seem right."

Lizzie shook her head. She was thinking of her mother, her beautiful mother, her warm eyes and her crooked half smile and that laugh that had made Lizzie feel more loved than anything else in the world. She was thinking about those afternoons when they would go alone into the city for what Lynn called L time (*just the two of us*) to lunch in Little Italy, where the food wasn't much better than the pizza place in town, but they called Lizzie signorina and they had chocolate chip cannolis and it was only two blocks away from the arcade in Chinatown where you could put in a dime and watch a live chicken dance in a cage. Lizzie had always thought of those afternoons as their time, together, but maybe they were an escape for her mother, to get out of Westchester, if only for the afternoon. She saw Lynn in her jeans and boots and her suede coat with the big buttons, her hair frizzing this way and that, just a touch of lipstick, astonishingly beautiful and alive, walking in the city she loved, and Lizzie thought: *Of course someone fell for her.*

But when Lizzie thought of how vibrant her mother looked on those afternoons, striding down Canal holding her hand, another, less pleasant memory forced its way in: the errand they ran after their Little Italy lunches. The storefront in Chinatown had windows lined with rows of dusty unmarked glass jars filled with dried purple and blackened herbs. The store smelled something awful, but her mother took no notice. Lynn handed a slip of paper to a short woman at the counter who measured out the herbs, gave them to Lynn in a series of clear-faced envelopes with no explanation. Lynn swiftly paid, deposited them in her purse, and took her daughter's hand. "Youth potion," she said, and outside Lizzie gulped down the exhaust-tinged air of Chinatown as if it were the freshest she had ever tasted, too afraid to ask any questions.

Lizzie told herself she didn't want to remember stopping in that shop—it was awful to contemplate; what were those herbs exactly? Had they done more harm than good?—but it wasn't wholly true. Lizzie longed to remember it all.

"It's hard for me to picture her face," she confessed to Sarah. "I mean, I know what she looks like, but I can't see it anymore in my mind."

"I don't know if I ever could."

Lizzie grabbed her sister's hand. Neither spoke for a long time. "It's going to happen with Dad too," Lizzie said.

"Yeah, it will." Now Sarah was the one tightening, holding on. "But we'll be okay."

"I don't know about that," Lizzie said. She could barely get the words out. "I loved them both—so much." How could it be that she would never see them again? How was that possible?

"I know, I know," Sarah murmured. "But you've got me."

"Thank fucking God." Lizzie let out a weird hiccup of a laugh. When had Sarah become such a stalwart, so steady and calm? With one hand, Lizzie wiped away snot and tears, sniffling, unseemly; with the other she gave Sarah's hand a little squeeze.

"I'll tell you what I need," Sarah said, rising. "Food. I bet you this place has everything." She took Lizzie's glass and filled it up, took a swig. "Maybe we need another one of these bottles too."

"Hey," Lizzie said, for it just dawned on her. "You're drinking."

"I am." Sarah met her gaze. "It didn't happen this month."

"Oh," Lizzie said. She had truly thought it would. "Sadie, I'm sorry."

"It's okay. The doctor says we just need to be patient. But I'm not exactly the patient type. We Goldstein girls aren't."

"'We'? I'm so patient and laid-back."

"Ha." Sarah said, and she swatted at Lizzie. "Ha, ha. Ha. What did Max say?"

"Max? About what?"

"About the detective."

"Oh," Lizzie said, and her stomach contracted. The detective, Max. She couldn't handle thinking of either. "I haven't spoken to him."

"Why not?"

"I don't know." That wasn't exactly true. She thought back on the other day, when he was so adamant. "I didn't think it through. I wanted to talk to you."

"Ah. So you ran away." Sarah grinned, which was both irritating and comfortingly familiar. "You ran away like you often do."

"Come on, that's not true," she said, although the second Sarah said it, Lizzie was supplying her own examples: she had run away from Ben; she had fled California and her father; she had hightailed it out of L.A. after meeting with Tandy. She ran away as if leaving the scene of the crime would negate it—which it never did. "Jesus, do you ever let up?" she said with affection. Her sister had driven a hundred miles, just for her.

Sarah shrugged. "Not really," she said, grinning again.

THEY ATE FRIED CALAMARI AND tuna burgers sandwiched in sweet buns and slathered in tarter sauce and all that richness didn't come close to filling Lizzie up. They curled up on the giant bed, flipping through the channels until they found Gene Hackman in *The Conversation* (Sarah: "I always thought he was sexy." "You think a lot of men are sexy," Lizzie said, which made Sarah laugh.) Lizzie called Max, leaving a message on his cell phone, saying, "I'm out with my sister, and I'm drunk. I'm staying with her tonight," which was, at least, part of the truth.

They pulled back the comforter and climbed beneath the sheets, so soft they made Lizzie want to cry. "You're always looking for answers, you think every situation *has* an answer," Sarah said after they turned off the lights. "Maybe there isn't one here; did you ever think that?"

"No," Lizzie murmured honestly. "I didn't." She rested her head on her sister's shoulder. She was so tantalizingly close to sleep. She had a flash of flying back and forth from New York to L.A. when they were kids, Sarah's head damp with sweat as she slept against her, shuttling between their parents' homes, thousands of miles up in the air. They weren't their mother's or their father's then, but each other's. Here was the best thing their parents had ever done.

THE NEXT AFTERNOON, THEY TOOK to the road, and before Lizzie knew it, she was back in Venice. There was Max, swinging the door open before she rooted out her key. "I thought I heard you," he said, leaning in to kiss her. "I just got home a few minutes ago."

In an instant, she was taking in his watchful eyes, the lanky height of him. She felt her heart lurch, a gawky, clumsy step. "You look tired," she said, following him in. If anything, she knew she was the exhausted-looking one. But his eyelids did seem heavier, the lines gullying his mouth sharper, more pronounced. He seemed, if only for a second, not just older but old.

"I stayed up late last night—too late. But I still can't believe I found it," he said with a sly smile.

She looked at him, not comprehending. "Found what?"

"Didn't you get my message?"

She shook her head; she had never listened to the voice mail he left last night.

"The gallery records," Max said, gesturing toward a pair of open boxes by the sofa. A cloth-covered book lay next to the glass bird sculpture and a bottle of scotch on the coffee table. Max picked up the thick book. "I found it on my first try," he said with a melancholic stamp of pride. "See?" He pointed at a swollen page. The entry, written in florid cursive, was divided into columns and filled with numbers looping and dipping across. Lizzie felt dizzy, as if she too were swimming off the page:

Chaim Soutine (1893–1943)
The Bellhop
signed "Soutine" (lower right)
oil on canvas
26 1/8 x 20 1/8 in.
Painted c. 1921

"My parents purchased it on September 12, 1971, for fourteen thousand seven hundred dollars. They bought it from a Jack Mendor.

I went online," Max was saying. "And I found this obit." He handed her a printout. She read: "John ("Jack") Thomas Mendor, of Fair Lawn, N.J., passed away on November 29, 1989, his beloved wife, Maggie (Ingoglia), by his side. A World War II veteran, he proudly served his country during three major battles in the European theater, including Normandy and the Battle of the Bulge. After returning from war, he gained employment at the Joseph Kurzon Electrical Supply Company as a salesman, and worked at the company for twenty-nine years, rising to become an executive. He leaves behind his loving wife and two sisters."

"I'll bet you he bought the painting while he was in Europe during the war," Max said. "Doesn't that make sense? It all fits."

It all fits. That's what Lizzie had told herself when she was speaking to Tandy, that's what she had said to Sarah earlier. "Yeah," she said faintly to Max now. A GI brought *The Bellhop* back to America, to Jersey? An electrical supply salesman?

"I looked up his wife too. She died in 2002. They didn't have any children. I wish there were more to learn," Max said. "But now we at least know who my parents bought it from and how it probably got here."

"Yes, thank you," Lizzie said automatically. "Thank you for going to the trouble for finding this." Her mind was skittering about: a vet grilling in his Jersey backyard, boasting about the painting he had bought for pennies in Europe; *I'm telling you where the facts lead,* Detective Tandy was saying. Lizzie put Mendor's obituary and the gallery book on the coffee table, next to the bottle of scotch. It was open, she saw. "You've been drinking," she said.

"My company while you were gone. I've gotten used to having you around."

She nodded, looking out the window at the strip of muddy canal.

"You okay?" he asked.

"I saw the detective yesterday." Her voice sounded hoarse.

"What detective?"

"Gilbert Tandy."

"I don't know who that is. Should I?" There was no look of recognition on his face—his gaze remained steady, maddeningly difficult to read. Could he really not know?

"The detective investigating my father's stolen artwork."

"Oh," he said, and she could have sworn that he pursed his lips. "And how did that come about?"

There was no turning back now. "I called him."

"And? Did you learn anything?" He folded his arms over his chest, but his voice stayed infuriatingly calm.

"He said; he said . . ." The words felt bony, useless; she had to force them out of her throat.

"What?" And there was something—a shadow crossing his face, a crack of hesitation. She hadn't imagined it, and now she felt a terrible fear.

"You have to tell me. Please tell me," she said.

He shook his head.

"I'm asking you, Max," she said, quiet but no less desperate, her heart a knotted collision. "You."

Max tented his hands over his nose and mouth. "He didn't want to," he finally said. "It was just an idea." He was staring beyond her. "He needed money. I told him no, I said it was crazy, but your father—he could be persuasive."

"Persuasive?" Lizzie said with incredulity. That was his explanation? She had lived her entire life with her father's persuasions, his appetites; she had been cowed by them, shaken them off, been defined by them. But she had been a child. *Persuasive* was all it took to convince Max?

"Lizzie—" He reached for her arm, but she wheeled around, bumped against the coffee table; the glass figurine teetered and fell, its delicate beak cracked.

Max bent to pick it up. "You okay?" He tried to touch her, but again she shook him off. What was she doing here? She would drown in the warm sea of Max's explanations.

"You were there that night, weren't you?" she said in an anguished rush.

"No, no, Lizzie, you don't know—"

"No, I don't," and she was crying openly now. "I have no fucking idea. But he let me take the blame. You both did. You let me think it was my fault, all these years."

"Lizzie, please, you don't understand. He never meant for it to be permanent. I've wanted to tell you, I've wanted to say something for so long. It never should have happened; I should have stopped it from happening. It was a mistake, a huge, monumental mistake, and all I've ever wanted to do was make it up to you."

"My God. *That's* what this was about?"

"No, no; I love you, I do. You know that, don't you? I love you, and I'll do anything not to lose you—"

"No," she said. She backed against the bookshelf and slid down, making herself as small as possible. "You have to stop. No more talk." She said this into her knees. "Please."

"Oh, Lizzie." He spoke in a raspy, choked voice. "Oh God." He was sobbing. Making awful sounds, his body shuddering. "You have no idea how sorry I am. If I could take it all back, if there was some way I could go back in time, I would; you don't know what I would give to make this right for you, for all of us."

"You helped him, didn't you?" she heard herself ask.

"I only told him, I only gave him a name. No one was supposed to be there that night, you girls were supposed to be staying with friends—"

"Jesus, I *know that*. Do not tell me that. This had nothing to do with me or that fucking party." She had scrambled to her feet and hurtled the words at him. She had blamed herself for so long. "What happened to the paintings? Tell me. You have to. Where are they now?"

Max shook his head. "Gone," he said softly.

"What do you mean, 'gone'? Did you—get rid of them?" Lizzie saw *The Bellhop* in her mind's eye: his hardened mouth, the glossy dark eyes, the oversized ears, the tilt of his head that seemed like posturing. That first night at her father's after her mother died, she had laid eyes on *The Bellhop* and she had thought that he would keep her safe. But no, she had been foolish, so unbelievably wrong; that was never *The Bellhop's* job. Lizzie was crying, sobbing, as terribly as Max had been. Her father.

"Lizzie, please stop," Max was saying. "Oh God, please." He kissed the side of her neck. *No, no,* she wanted to say. But she was drowning and his lips felt soft and she was desperate to hold on to something. Soon she was doing the only thing she knew to do with Max; she was tugging at his clothes. Soon she was matching his greediness with her own.

LATER, THEY LAY ON HIS Turkish rug, limbs entwined. Lizzie's unhooked bra hanging limply at her chest. Her thighs were cold. Max's pants and boxers were pooled at his ankles.

"He let me take the blame," Lizzie said quietly.

"He never meant to. You have to believe me; that was his biggest regret." Max smoothed back her hair with the palm of his hand, kissed her brow with what struck Lizzie as an unmistakably paternal gesture. "Come," he said, shifting his legs, pulling up his boxers. "Let's go to bed."

Lizzie shook her head. It was like that first night out in California when she was thirteen, when her motherless world was not one she could bear to inhabit. She didn't want anything to do with a reality that insisted, *All this is true.* She couldn't stay. But how could she leave?

14

LOS ANGELES, 1968

NEARLY NOON AND HARRY WAS still sleeping. It was the fourth day after his arrival in Los Angeles. "Maybe he is ill," Rose said to Thomas. Her own stomach had been bothering her of late. "This can't still be jet lag, can it?"

"He isn't sick. He's lazy," Thomas said.

Where had this handsome, dark-eyed man come from? The last time Rose had seen her nephew he was a slightly built fifteen-year old with wispy facial hair and a head that seemed too large for his body. Now Isobel and Gerhard's eldest stood more than six feet tall, with dark curls, a strong jaw, and an olive complexion all his own, confident as only a twenty-year-old could be.

Harry had recently dropped out of the University of London ("I am *not* pleased," Gerhard had said on the phone, and Rose could hear his disapproval surging through the transatlantic crackle). He was here to try his hand at acting, a plan eventually approved by his mother, grudgingly tolerated by his father. But as far as Harry was concerned, there was no trying: "I'm an actor," he'd maintained when Thomas asked him what he'd be doing for money. "I'm going to act." Rose and Thomas had agreed to put him up in their small study for the month. "Then you must promise me you'll kick him out," Gerhard said to Rose. "He needs to learn to take care of himself."

"Oh, we will," Rose said into the phone, and rolled her eyes at her husband. Gerhard and Isobel paid for everything.

SATURDAY MORNING, EDGING PAST TEN. Thomas had to work for a few hours. No sound from Harry. Finally Rose opened the door to the study. Harry's suitcase still lay open and unpacked on the floor. Was that a dirty sock draped on their Smith Corona on the desk? "It is long past time to get up," she said to the figure under the sheets. "What are you going to do when you have auditions?"

"Oh, Auntie." Harry sat up, rubbed his eyes. "I'm acclimating. My body's adjusting—just like the astronauts. You can't rush these things."

"In fact, you can," Rose said. "And you will."

Within the hour, they were on the road. First stop: the Griffith Observatory. They took her Impala, Harry slumped down in the passenger seat, sunglasses on. "You know the '68 model comes in a convertible," he said. "Simply gorgeous. And it's not all that much more money."

She laughed. "How in the world would you know how much money it is?"

"I'm hardworking," he said. She laughed some more. "I am. When I set my mind to something, I most certainly am." He rolled down the window, fiddled with the radio dial. Someone was singing about a beautiful balloon. "God, I adore this place," he said, fingers trailing in the warm air.

At the observatory, Harry bounded about, paying little attention to the magnificent views, all of Los Angeles fanned out below, talking about *Rebel Without a Cause* and soon enough, his hunger. "Absolutely *famished*," is what he said. "Is Schwab's anywhere near here?"

She exhaled. "Schwab's is a tourist trap and Lana Turner wasn't discovered there anyhow. I'll take you somewhere better." They drove back down the hill into Hollywood proper, to Carolina Pines Jr.'s. It was just a diner, nothing fancy about it—but she loved the futuristic swoop of the roof, the large glass windows that looked out onto the bustle of Sunset, the warm cinnamon rolls topped with the perfect amount of icing.

A young copper-haired waitress took their order. Rose asked for a cinnamon roll and a cup of coffee. Harry ordered coffee too, and a steak sandwich. And fries. "Wait," he said as the waitress was turning away. "Can you add a side of chili too?"

She smiled at him, revealing a sweet gap between her top teeth. "'Course," she said.

"Are you certain you'll eat all that?" Rose said. "That's quite a lot."

"That it is. I'm a hungry boy."

Rose shook her head while the waitress laughed, twirled her pencil between thumb and forefinger. "You look familiar," she said. "You've been here before?"

"No," Harry said, and he sat up straight, folded his hands like a schoolboy. "But I'm an actor."

"Really? Maybe I've seen you in something."

"I don't think so. But you will." He said it so seriously; in the moment, Rose nearly believed him.

When the food arrived, Harry tucked in. He ate and he ate, chased the last slivers of onion from his sandwich. After he finished nearly everything on his plate, he tore off some of Rose's cinnamon roll and dunked it into his coffee. Rose watched, astounded. Her brother had always been a careful and appreciative eater, even before the wartime years; her nephew ate as if he might never fill himself up.

Harry drained his cup of coffee, leaned his long torso back. "You were right; that was good. And now?"

"I thought we'd go by the County Museum. It just opened last year." She told him about the plaza out front, the Rembrandt portrait that she admired.

Within the hour, they were heading up the stairs from Wilshire to the museum, Harry taking them two at a time. "Oh, it is lovely," he said. A trio of austere white buildings aproned the plaza, rising up and cutting against the cloudless sky. "When you and Uncle Thomas get sick of me, perhaps I'll pitch a little tent here."

Rose didn't answer. She was staring ahead, shading her eyes. Could the sun be playing tricks on her?

"Auntie?"

Rose was walking toward the museum entrance, feeling light-headed, paying Harry no mind. There was a poster hanging by the entrance, an abstract swirl of a landscape in a blaze of colors—yellows and greens, roiling in movement: CHAIM SOUTINE RETROSPECTIVE, MARCH 3 TO APRIL 18, 1968.

There was such a pounding in Rose's ears. A Soutine exhibit, here? Opening in less than a week? Harry was saying something—she couldn't hear him, she couldn't hear anything—she nodded mutely. He disappeared. And soon Rose was standing alone in front of the admissions desk.

"May I help you?" asked a fleshy woman with glittery cat-eye glasses.

"I'd like to know about the Soutine exhibit," Rose said. Here she stopped. What did she want to know? "Are there portraits in the show?" she finally asked, feeling a profound sense of anticipation and unease.

"I believe so. There are lots of paintings, close to one hundred, I think."

"Is there a list?"

"A list?" The woman behind the desk looked perplexed.

"Of the paintings in the show."

"No. I'm sure someone has one, but we don't have it. We're just volunteers. Come back next week; it's supposed to be terrific."

Rose nodded, made her way to a nearby bench. She was sitting there when Harry emerged from the restroom. "You ready?" he asked. "Let's go see that Rembrandt fellow everyone raves about."

"Actually, I'm not feeling well; let's go home."

SHE DIDN'T TELL THOMAS. WHAT was there to tell? She had known about other exhibits of Soutine's work through the years—significant ones. A show at the Museum of Modern Art a few years before she moved to America, and a show in London at the Tate after she had left. The Barnes Foundation outside of Philadelphia boasted of many Soutines in its collection. She had written to the museums and galleries, requested and received (at no insignificant expense) catalogs of the exhibits, lists of paintings with their provenance included in their collections. *The Bellhop* had never been among them. What were the chances that it would magically resurface now, at a museum a mile away from her home?

Still Rose felt a low-grade nausea, a blanket of queasiness wrapped around her. The day the exhibit opened, she felt worse. She told Thomas she had a stomach bug and called in sick. She went back to sleep, and by the time she woke up again, even Harry was gone. She finished the dishes and made her bed and tidied up the study too, but all this seemed to be staving off the inevitable.

When she arrived at the museum, there were few people in the exhibit's three rooms. Rose's heart resounded so loudly, she felt as if it might crash out of her ribs; she half expected one of the elderly women milling about to hear its beats, look askance, shuffle away. Instead she heard one woman say: "Van Gogh's work is *much* more precise, don't you think?"

Rose looked and looked. Ninety pieces of Soutine's work were gathered here ("the largest ever exhibition of his in this country," the curator noted in an introduction mounted at the show's entrance). She moved past so many—steely faces of waiters, forlorn brides, dizzying landscapes with windswept trees, silvery herrings about to be pierced by forks, skinny, headless, nothing chickens, swaying in front of brick walls.

Then her heart contracted. On a canvas in front of her was a boy in a red thickly swirled uniform. Rose's cheeks flamed hot, her hands went cold. But no, this boy's hands were at his side, not on his hips; his eyes were wider, his face paler and pancaked white. He didn't look as constricted, as sullen, as she remembered *The Bellhop* being. Rose looked at the card. It was called *Page Boy at Maxim's*, painted in 1925. It wasn't hers.

She kept looking. Ghostly sting rays, their faces eerie and yet humanlike, portraits of a baker's boy and a man in blue. Huge sides of raw beef, splayed open, entrails exposed with such furious brushstrokes that Rose had to avert her eyes, nearly mistook the paint for blood.

She reached the end of the show. Her inevitable disappointment overcame her like a warm murkiness, a thickness to the air. Everything slowed. She looked at the last picture. A distorted landscape of a country road beneath a vast swirling sky, a pair of children holding hands—were they siblings?—faces blurry, unclear. *Two Children on a Road*, it was called, painted in 1942.

She knew how Soutine's story ended. By 1942, the painter was living in the French countryside, moving from village to village, trying to avoid detection by the Gestapo. He suffered from ulcers. A particularly ugly bout left him writhing in pain, bleeding. His girlfriend urged him to return to Paris to see a doctor. They took a circuitous route to evade officials. The trip took more than twenty-four hours. By the time Soutine arrived, his condition was dire. He died on the operating table.

Rose's breath felt shallow, not at all sufficient for her body. She shouldn't be here. There was nothing to find. Why did she ever think otherwise?

She hurried back through the exhibit, past a black-and-white photograph of Soutine himself, smoking, taken in profile, handsomer than his self-portraits would suggest.

Then she saw another portrait that she had somehow missed; she slowed down. The painting was of a woman, an elegant, sharp-eyed woman, her dark hair cut in a fashionable bob. She wore a sumptuous red dress, and a fur cloaked her shoulders. The woman's legs were stylishly crossed at her ankles, her fingers lightly touching in her lap. There was a wryness to her gaze that made Rose think she was tolerating the painter, humoring him. She had better places to be. *Portrait of Madame Castaing,* the card said; she was a patron of Soutine's. Rose had seen reproductions of it before. But now, seeing it in person, Rose's skin went icy. There was something in that knowing gaze that Rose recognized. She couldn't shake the thought: it reminded her of her mother.

A great swell of nausea overtook her. Rose hurried out of the museum into the bright California light. She blinked and took in the fresh air, but she felt a bilious heave, a sour, metallic taste curdling in her mouth. She leaned into a nearby bush and vomited what little food was in her body.

"Love, you all right?" She heard a woman with a thick Scottish accent behind her.

"Yes, thank you." She tried to sound convincing. Rose thought of the Scottish woman who used to man the tea counter near her apartment in Belsize, and this reminder of England brought her to the brink of tears. She wiped her mouth on the cotton sleeve of her dress, trying to rid herself of that awful metallic taste.

"Oh, dearie, you most certainly are not." The woman handed Rose a handkerchief, produced a cup of water from who knew where. It tasted deliciously cool and sweet.

"I'm fine," Rose said, "I'm fine." And this little kindness from a stranger made it so.

ROSE WAS ON THE COUCH when Thomas came home that night. "How you feeling?"

"Okay," she said. Thomas studied her. "Not great," she allowed.

"Poor thing." He brushed a kiss against her forehead. "Still the stomach?"

She nodded. "It's nothing. I'll be fine by tomorrow."

"I'm going to put the kettle on; want some?" She shook her head. Speaking made her feel more nauseated. "Where's the boy?" Thomas asked.

"Out."

"May I ask you a question? Has he actually been on any auditions?" He said it lightly, but Rose knew where it was leading.

"I have no idea," she said with considerable effort. She had little interest in monitoring her nephew's whereabouts when she was feeling her best, and absolutely none now.

"I never realized how low the ceilings in our apartment were until he moved in. How long did we say he could stay?"

"A month," she said. "And it's been two weeks. Please don't start." They had the extra room. Harry went to the grocery store for her, he took the bus down to the mechanic's on East Vernon the other day to pick up her car without complaining. She liked having her nephew around. How much of an imposition was he on Thomas?

"I'm not starting." He sat at the edge of the couch, played with the crocheted throw at her feet. "What can I get you? Maybe a scramble? Have you eaten anything all day?"

She shook her head. "I don't want anything." The nausea, which had retreated, had snuck back with force. She despaired that she might remain on the edge of vomiting for a good while. When she called in sick, the school secretary had told her that three girls were out with the stomach flu.

"It's not good for you not to eat," Thomas said.

"I know. In a bit."

"If you feel this rotten tomorrow, you should see the doctor."

"It comes and it goes. There's a virus going around at school. There's no need."

"So he'll confirm it. You always put it off, going to the doctor; then you go, and you feel better."

The thought of going to the doctor made her feel worse. "I was feeling better earlier," she decided to say. "I went to the County."

"Museum? When you were feeling this ill?"

"I was feeling better then. There was an exhibit." She paused, looking up at the ceiling. "A Soutine exhibit." She pulled the blanket off, swung her legs over, sat up. It took significant effort. She walked to the sink, slowly.

"I'm confused. An exhibit of his paintings opened? How did you know?"

"I saw something. In the paper."

"Why didn't you tell me? I would have gone with you."

"I know." She filled a glass. Tepid water. Maybe that would calm the upset. She shook her head, took a sip. "*The Bellhop* wasn't there. Of course."

"I'm sorry," Thomas said with a hand to her shoulder. Gingerly she walked off, made her way back to the couch, water in hand. It made him nervous when she spoke about the Soutine. Thomas knew that the missing painting, and all it represented, made her unhappy, and he knew he couldn't fix it. Rose understood that he wished more than anything that he could, but he couldn't. It was Thomas's frustration that he couldn't make her feel better, Rose had long decided, that wedged between them, and not her past itself.

She reached the couch. She felt as if she were moving through sludge.

Thomas came over. "Are you okay?"

"No," she said to the ceiling. "I am not. I feel awful. On many levels."

"I'm sorry," he said. "It must have been disappointing."

"It was. And it was strange. Awful and strange."

"I wish I could have been there with you."

"I know, but it doesn't matter."

"Don't say that. It does matter—to me, at least. And I hope to you."

She nodded, took his hand. She held it, felt the rise of his knuckles, bone, the pulsating warmth of his skin.

"You do things on your own," Thomas said. "But then you're upset that you're on your own."

"I know," she said, feeling worse than before. "But not today. Please. No lecturing, not now." She stood, uncertain.

"What?" Thomas said.

"I have to—" She pushed past him, nausea overtaking her.

BY THE TIME ROSE GOT out of bed the next day, Thomas was long gone. He had left a note by her bedside: "You have an appointment with Dr. Cohen at three o'clock. No skipping it."

Rose pulled on her bathrobe, went into the kitchen. Harry was there, in jeans and a flannel shirt, long legs stretched out beneath the breakfast table, a copy of *Variety* along with a crumbled pack of cigarettes on the table, spooning peanut butter out of the jar into his mouth. He sprang up when she entered. "Hello, Auntie."

Rose motioned for him to sit, turned on the kettle. "You're up early."

"Yes. Well, you're up late."

She took a spoon from the drawer, took the jar of peanut butter from him, and carved out a generous spoonful. She had awoken with the nausea mostly gone. She was starving.

"Today is my first elocution class," Harry said. "I'm gonna learn to speak like an American." He said this last part with a deliberate twang.

The kettle whistled. Rose poured tea for herself; Harry declined. He reached for the jar of peanut butter, spooned out more. "Peanut butter is a very strange substance, don't you think?" he said. "I remember it from my trip here when I was fifteen. I was repulsed by it—the stickiness, the flavor, all of it. But I was also determined to like it. I thought it would make me American."

Rose let out a rueful laugh, sipped her tea. "I hated it too, when I arrived. But nothing makes you American. One day you wake up, and you simply are. The moment has passed, and you didn't even see it happen."

"I should only be so lucky." Harry pulled a cigarette out of the pack, and only then, while tapping it on the table, said, "Do you mind?" Rose shook her head. He lit it, took a long drag.

"May I have one?" Rose gestured at the pack.

Harry offered it to her. "I didn't know you smoked."

"I don't."

Harry smiled, lit a cigarette for her. She hadn't smoked in years. She had never been a heavy smoker, but she had liked a cigarette at night, after supper. She had quit along with Thomas not long after they moved here. The last time she could remember having a cigarette was at the Ambassador; she and Thomas had gone to celebrate her getting the Eastgate job. In the ballroom's low light, the fake palm trees that fanned the perimeter of the crowded dance floor looked disarmingly real—papier-mâché coconuts and mechanical monkeys climbing the trees, their yellow electric eyes blinking and following her every move. She and Thomas drank and smoked and danced—Thomas was a good dancer, agile on his feet, more graceful than she—and the place felt silly but wonderful too. She had not wanted to leave England, but now that they were settled here, it was difficult to recall the particulars of why.

Rose sucked in smoke, felt the rush go to her head. "Now, why did I ever quit?"

Harry let out a low laugh and tapped off ash into a gold-rimmed ashtray that Rose realized wasn't hers—Harry must have picked it up somewhere. She was about to ask him where when he said: "May I ask you something, Auntie? The other day, when we were at the museum, you got upset."

Rose drew in and held the smoke in her lungs. She tapped the cigarette against the ashtray. This was another reason she had liked smoking: it gave her something to do with her hands. "I wasn't feeling well."

"I know," he said. "But it was more than that, wasn't it? I saw the poster too."

"What?" she asked thickly.

"I saw the poster for the Soutine exhibit. That's what you were looking at, wasn't it?"

"How do you know about that?"

His prominent unlined brow now furrowed. "You mean the Soutine? My dad told me."

"He did?"

"'Course. He told me that your mum had loved the painting and that the painter was well known. He must have told me when I was a little kid. He told me that your flat had lots of beautiful things. That your mother had a good eye."

"Of course," Rose echoed as she ground her cigarette down. She was trying to take all of it in. Her brother, the same one who told her to forget it all, was telling his children about the Soutine? He was proud?

"He doesn't talk about Vienna much, but he'd tell us stories now and again: like how your mother used to ask, 'Are they fine people? Or are they not so fine?' about anyone she would meet. And how frugal your father could be, how he refused to smoke an imported cigar because he thought it was as unnecessary extravagance, instead smoking whatever the government issued."

"'Just like Franz Joseph.'" Rose heard herself quoting her father automatically. She hadn't thought about that in thirty years. She remembered her father smoking, that stale woodsy smell from his study—was that the smell of a cheap cigar? She hadn't remembered her mother's focus on 'fine people,' but she could so easily hear Mutti saying that. What else did Gerhard remember that she did not? They rarely talked about their childhood.

"The painting wasn't at the exhibit, was it?" Harry asked.

She shook her head.

"I'm sorry."

She nodded again. "As am I," she managed to say.

"But you still find yourself looking for it, even when you're not looking."

"Yes," she breathed.

"I do too." His voice was low. "I don't even know what it looks like exactly—but I do too."

Was he truly looking for it? For Gerhard? For himself? Rose couldn't bring herself to ask. The kitchen was warm. She was aware of small noises floating about: the ticking of the electric clock, the wheeze of the ice-maker. She touched Harry's wrist. *Thank you for saying that*, she wanted to say, but she said nothing, afraid the words might have proved her undoing.

THE DOCTOR'S WAITING AREA WAS stifling. Even the ficus in the corner looked dejected. Rose's queasiness had returned. The exam room she was ushered into felt twenty degrees colder. The nurse instructed her to change into a gown and then Rose waited some more. She pulled her knees to her chest. Why such thin gowns? Why didn't they provide something with a little more protection?

Finally Dr. Cohen walked in. "Good afternoon, Mrs. Downes! I haven't seen you in a while. Too good for me these days?" Dr. Cohen sported a thick, snowy-white mustache and a jovial demeanor. While she complained about his style to Thomas—she half expected him to say one day, *Hello, Mrs. Downes, I'm here to tell you that you have shingles!*—she found him surprisingly reassuring. *It could be worse*, he was fond of telling her, and most of the time, she had to agree.

He took her temperature, asked her if she was still teaching at Eastgate, checked her throat, ears, and nose, pronounced all normal. Then he examined her abdomen, pressing down with his thumb and forefinger. He asked about her symptoms again, nodding all the while.

"When was your last period, Mrs. Downes?"

It had been some time. She struggled to remember. A month and a half? Maybe longer? It hadn't alarmed her. After all, she was nearly forty-one. "They've been irregular as of late," she said. "I'm not quite sure."

"Well! I believe a blood test is in order. I would not be at all surprised."

"What?" she asked dumbly.

Beneath that great brush of a mustache, Dr. Cohen's mouth turned upward into a grin. "All your symptoms point to a pregnancy. You should make an appointment with your gynecologist."

"No, it can't be," Rose said. "Can't you check? I don't want to see another doctor. It cannot be." She was shivering audibly. "I'm forty."

He sighed. "Mrs. Downes, you have to follow up. It absolutely *can* be," he added without any gaiety or adornment. And it was his serious tone that made her believe him.

SHE TOLD THOMAS THAT SHE had to go back, Dr. Cohen wanted to run some tests. "Tests for what?" Thomas asked, looking concerned.

"Nothing," she said, "it's nothing."

She went to her gynecologist. Four days later, after she returned home from school—Thomas still at work, Harry, who knows where—the nurse called. "Congratulations!" she exclaimed. Rose was nearly three months' pregnant.

"All right, then," she said, though she had no idea why. It was certainly not all right. Pregnant, after all this time? What in the world was she going to do?

She filched a cigarette from Harry's room. Out on their tiny balcony, she perched on the edge of a plastic chair grimy with dirt and lit the cigarette, inhaled deeply. The nicotine enveloped her. Even with the smoke, Rose could still make out the odor of chlorine drifting up from the courtyard. The pool water was a murky grayish green, a scrim of leaves laced the edges. They had taken the apartment in part for the pool, but even when it had been in good condition, they had rarely gone swimming.

She could get rid of it. She knew enough to know that it wasn't the way it used to be. She was friendly with a math teacher at school; Joan was an Isadora Duncan devotee at least fifteen years Rose's junior who was teaching herself German and lived on a diet of nuts and honey. Rose felt certain that Joan would know where to take care of it. Thomas wouldn't need to know.

But how could she not tell him? They almost never spoke of it anymore—his desire for children, her desire not to have them. She had thought and thought about it. She had believed herself to be right. For years she had told herself: not everyone was made to be a mother. It was easier to believe that than reckon with the more pointed question that often came to her at night: How could *she* be a mother? What did she know about taking care?

Whenever she thought about it, Rose felt like a child herself. She was back in the flat in Vienna, watching Mutti, dressed in silk, give her nose a final dusting of powder. The Mutti in the letters that Rose treasured was warmer and chattier than the elegant, distant mother she recalled from her early years. When she considered being a mother, all Rose could think about was the pain of separation, of being left behind.

Rose liked to think that not having children was not a tension in her marriage, but what had begun as a question between them had morphed into a sadness, a particular sadness for both of them, with a presence all its own.

And now? Now she was at sea with no idea of which way to turn. She hadn't wanted this. They hadn't been careful of late, but they had been careful for so long. How could it have happened?

That wasn't the point anymore. What if for all these years, she had been trying to protect herself against something that could not be protected? The growth inside of her felt violent, a disturbance, disrupting everything that she had insisted upon. Nothing was the same. Her body was telling her so. And, perhaps, Rose tried to tell herself with a calm that she did not feel, it was time for her to quiet and listen.

THAT NIGHT, IN THEIR TINY windowless bathroom with the turquoise tiles that Rose had thought about replacing for a decade now, Thomas brushed his teeth methodically, keeping an eye on his watch as he always did, timing himself.

"I have to tell you something," Rose said, looking at her husband's reflection in the mirror.

He held up several fingers—three more seconds—and spit into the sink. "Mmm?"

She had a hand on the edge of the wet sink, leaned on it for support. *Just say the words,* she told herself. "I'm pregnant," she finally said.

He stared, his thin lips whitened by toothpaste, his cheeks drained of color. She would never forget how in that moment he was a stranger. "What?" He said it so sharply that Rose could only hear disappointment.

She swallowed. She wasn't sure she could work up the courage to speak again. "I'm—"

"I heard you," he said. "My God, did I hear you?" He clapped a hand over his mouth. "You're pregnant?"

She nodded, grabbed his wet hands with her own. A sob ripped through her.

"Are you sure?" He was crying now, but also—she was sure of it—laughing. "You're certain?"

She nodded again. "You're happy?"

"I'm delirious." He pulled back, scrutinizing her. "And you? What about you?"

"I'm scared," she said, and she was crying now too.

"Do you—do you want this?"

She gripped him hard—she was that frightened. But she made

herself say the words. "I think I do. I do. But, Thomas, we will be so old; people will think we're the child's grandparents."

He kissed her damp cheeks, one after the other, laughing all the while. "I do not care," he said. "Do you hear me? I do not care at all."

THE NEXT DAY WHILE ROSE was teaching fourth period, a junior came to her classroom. "There's a call for you, Mrs. Downes," she said. Rose hurried to the office. What was wrong? Thomas only called if it was urgent.

But it was her nephew on the line. "I got a callback!" Harry said joyously. "For the doctor role."

"Oh, Harry," she said, irritation mingling with relief. "I was in the middle of teaching. You worried me."

"So sorry, Aunt Rose," he said, not sounding sorry at all, "but I got a callback! They want to see me again. This afternoon." His voice dropped. "But I'm not at all prepared."

"But you are," she told him.

"You don't know that."

"I do. You are only scared because you care so much." She believed this, didn't she?

ON SATURDAY, ROSE RETURNED TO the Soutine exhibit, Thomas and Harry in tow. This time, she felt prepared, happy even, her nausea abated, glad to have her men by her side. Today the gallery rooms were crowded, and Rose elbowed her way to show Harry the *Page Boy at Maxim's,* the portrait in the show that had reminded her of *The Bellhop.*

Harry, attentive, eager, was taken with the still lifes. He kept bounding between them and Rose and Thomas—"that bloody side of beef," he said. "It's unseemly and awful and fantastic." A few minutes later, he came back. "I just read an amazing story in the catalog; did you know that Soutine hauled an actual side of beef up to his studio, and kept buckets of cow's blood by its side and doused it whenever it started to turn gray?"

"I did know that," Rose said. It was an oft-told story about Soutine and she had wondered if it was true. She loved that Harry was taken with it.

"The smell and flies got so bad that the police were called," Harry continued. "And apparently Soutine said, 'What does sanitation matter when compared to the sanctity of art?'" He chortled, and off he went again.

Thomas stayed by Rose's side, a hand on the small of her back, walking where she led them. She pointed out the portraits; she told him that Madame Castaing reminded her of her mother. "She's beautiful," he said. He cast a sideways glance at his wife. "Like you."

She shook her head at him, gave him a grateful smile. The waistband of her dress felt tighter. She could take this one out, but soon she wouldn't be able to wear her regular clothes.

They paused in front of a Soutine self-portrait, his ears and nose exaggeratedly large, his misshapen body adorned in a garish yellow-green jacket. "Now, that is positively monstrous," Thomas said. "Why in the world would someone depict himself that way?"

"He was not a happy man," Rose said.

"That's one way of putting it. But look: there aren't any hands in the portrait. He cut off his own hands. Why would he do that?"

"Apparently hands are hard to paint," Rose said. "And it's probably harder to paint them when you're using them *to* paint."

"Maybe," Thomas said. "But I think it's awful. He needs his hands, and now they're gone."

That wasn't the way Rose thought of it. But standing next to her husband, seeing it through his eyes, she did not disagree.

FOUR DAYS LATER, AS SHE was teaching sixth period, the cramps started. *It's nothing,* she told herself. They continued through the day and intensified on the drive home. But by the time she managed to get up the stairs and inside her apartment, the bleeding had begun. She fought her way to the toilet, doubled over, sweating, terrified. She held on in desperation as her insides knotted up, the pain ballooning. Nothing was anchored, nothing safe. Eventually she forced herself to stand: dark purplish swirls of blood, clots that Rose couldn't bear to look at, filled the bowl. She grabbed towels, staggered to her bedroom—the phone was in the kitchen, miles away—and there Thomas found her two hours later, curled up, soiled towels beneath her.

"It's over," she said to him. "Thomas." She said his name again as she wept. Mutti, this had happened to Mutti too.

"No, it's not," he said. "It can't be." But when they got to Dr. Cohen's that night (he had returned to the office to see them, a kindness she would never forget), he shook his head, confirmed what Rose already knew.

THE HOSPITAL SET IN STUDIO 43 in CBS's Television City was smaller and more makeshift than Rose had envisioned. Harry had landed the part of a newly arrived, mysterious foreign doctor: "No one quite trusts him, but few can resist his charms," he had told them.

"Now that sounds like a stretch," Rose had said. But when she called Gerhard and Isobel, she boasted of how much the producers loved him; three weeks in, the role had already been expanded.

Thomas and Rose watched him stride onto the set—the ceiling a forest of lights and girders and beams and cameras—in his white doctor's coat, then turn his face toward the makeup girl, who sponged on some lurid-looking cream.

"I hope that looks better on camera than it does in person," Rose couldn't help but say.

"Let us hope," Thomas whispered back. And then: "Harry George is an inane name."

Rose shrugged. "The producers didn't like Zimmer," she said. She agreed with Thomas, but it was hard for her to get worked up over the name change. It was hard to get worked up over much these days. The last month she had felt so tired, too tired to object.

"He might actually become something," Thomas whispered.

"I believe he already has."

He smiled, sidled up closer. In her heels, they were about the same height. "You are looking particularly lovely today, Mrs. Downes."

She was wearing one of her favorite dresses today. It was a simple cotton A-line in periwinkle with pearl buttons that flashed against the blue. It fit her well again. Most of her clothes did, a fact that unnerved her, made her slow as she was buttoning up in the morning. "Why, thank you," she said. Her eyes remained on her nephew. He truly was handsome, and though he looked nothing like Gerhard, she saw something familiar in the shape of his mouth, his prominent brow—Papi, she thought now.

She heard Thomas's voice, close to her ear. "I want to try again."

Try again? she nearly asked, but she knew. She couldn't bring herself to answer.

The pregnancy had been a fluke. Rose's gaze remained on her nephew. "It's too late," she said, her voice catching on something nubby in her throat.

"It's not. It happened once. It can happen again. We just need to try." He wove an arm around her waist. "Hard work, I know, but please say you'll try."

She rested her hand on top of his. It *had* happened. And if for a moment she could scrape away the terror and doubt, ignore the constant churn of sadness, she could admit this, if only to herself: she *had* been happy.

Here was Thomas asking; she wanted simply to feel his hand on her, steadying her.

"Yes," she said even if she didn't quite believe it. She turned to him, allowed herself the tiniest of smiles. "Yes, I'll try."

IT HAPPENED AGAIN AND FAST, not three months later. It wasn't like the time before. Rose knew right away. It felt like a thrum, this pregnancy, quieter, but more insistent. By the time Dr. Cohen confirmed it with a due date of September 15 (*three days after Mutti's birthday,* Rose thought but did not say), her stomach already felt swollen, her body readying for action. She was less queasy this time, and that made her nervous; she was vigilant about tracking every twitch and wave of nausea. One night, long after they both had gone to sleep, Rose woke up with a start, convinced that she had felt blood. In the bathroom, she checked and checked. "Everything is fine," Thomas murmured when he found her there, his words blurry with sleep.

"You don't know that," she said with equal parts fury and despair.

She realized she was miscarrying a second time when they were seated in a front booth at Carolina Pines Jr.'s, eating a celebratory breakfast in honor of Thomas's forty-third birthday. As Thomas sped them in their car down Sunset to the doctor's, Rose wincing with every cramp and turn, she thought, *How could Mutti have withstood this? How did she ever keep going?*

They ceased talking about it. They never did stop trying. A year later, as Rose neared her own forty-third birthday, her period was late. She didn't tell Thomas. *Wait,* she cautioned herself, *simply wait.* But there was little private joy. When eight weeks later, her period arrived, Rose felt more resignation than sorrow. She had known that her body was broken for decades, even if she couldn't have articulated it before. There was relief in acknowledging what she was, if only to herself. She could remember sensing it when she lived alone in London after the war. *Ghosts can't give birth,* she thought.

Ludicrous, Thomas would say. *You are here, living. You are simply afraid.*

But she never did give him the chance to respond.

15

LOS ANGELES, 2008

"ARE YOU SURE YOU'RE UP for this?" Sarah whispered to Lizzie.

"Of course," Lizzie said, lowering her voice to match her sister's.

"He fell asleep in the car on the way over," Sarah said as she wheeled the stroller into Lizzie's apartment. "By some miracle, I was able to transfer him. If you're lucky, he'll sleep for a couple of hours." Oscar was ten months old, a grave-faced child with a scattered patchwork of pale downy hair. For the first few months of his life, Lizzie privately thought he looked like a tiny old Southern senator in baby garb. But now his body was filling out, and when he laughed, often unexpectedly, she felt like she caught a glimpse of the boy he was becoming.

"There are more diapers and wipes than you'll ever need," Sarah said, unclipping the bag from the stroller. "A bib, a couple of binkies, his bottle. I stuck in two changes of clothes, just in case. He has a slight runny nose; he seemed fine, but he might drink more milk because of it. Just heat up half at a time; my supply is getting low."

"Got it," Lizzie said with what she hoped was a confident expression. She had taken care of Oscar before, but never for this long. "It's going to be fine."

"I know; thank you so much. And it's good training for you, right? If you're unsure of anything, just call. If I have to step out of the event, it's not a big deal. Angela's got a few procedures today, so she'll be harder to reach."

"I've got it. You're coming back in a few hours, right? He's not staying for the month."

"You never know," Sarah said. "If I get a taste of freedom, I might run off." She leaned down, kissed her son's sleeping head. "I would never do that, monkey," she murmured. She threw her arms around her sister. "Thank you. I'm so so glad you're here." And soon the door clicked behind her.

Lizzie had moved back to L.A. nearly six months earlier. In many ways, it felt longer. After she and Max had ended things, she went back to New York, tried to throw herself into work. But as she elbowed her way down the packed subway steps in the morning, she would find herself picturing the canyon behind her father's house, the steep drops and sun-bleached terrain, and the clusters of poppies in February. When, amazingly enough, they won the Clarke appeal, Marc took her and the other associates out to a boozy, celebratory meal. Lizzie tipped back oysters and glasses of Prosecco, pleased that their strategy had done the job, but she was thinking: *Now what?*

Her mother's birthday passed. Then it was her father's. That summer, Sarah got pregnant. November marked the first anniversary of her father's death, and Lizzie, felled by a mean virus, was glad for an excuse not to leave her apartment for days. Her life felt full of ghosts, her dreams often sharper and more vivid than her waking life. And then Oscar was born and she flew out to meet him, and holding that tiny, wheezing alien being tight against her chest, she thought, *What are you waiting for?*

Miraculously, she quickly landed a job in L.A.: directing a family foundation, of all things. A former client was on the board, and he called her when he heard she was on the hunt for work. *I don't know anything about running a foundation,* she was about to say. But even as she thought it, she was typing the name of the foundation into Google with nervous excitement, and she heard a voice in her head—an undeniable mixture of Claudia's and Rose's—that made her sit up. *Don't run away,* this voice ordered her. *You are stronger than you know.*

Now Lizzie turned to her sleeping nephew, wearing striped shorts that ballooned over his knees. Though he was snugly buckled into his stroller, his head lolled askew. Delicately she tried to straighten it. His head was warm, moist. Snot was encrusted around a nostril. He smelled yeasty sweet. Within a second, his head had toppled back down to the same awkward angle. "Okay, okay," she said. "If that's what you want."

She headed into the second bedroom that she was using as a study, still lined with boxes. She hadn't been inclined to take the apartment until she walked into that second bedroom. It was tiny but overlooked the courtyard and was suffused with sunlight. As she stood, looking down in the courtyard, the Realtor impatient behind her, an unexpected feeling came over Lizzie: *I could be happy here.* The master bedroom was dark, some of the cornflower-blue tiles in the shower were cracked; the common hallway carried a faint mildew smell. It was well within her newly diminished budget, though, and the balcony was big enough to fit a two-person table, and she loved that second bedroom. But it was probably the way it reminded her of Rose's home—the balcony, the stucco, the utilitarian feel—that convinced her most of all.

They hadn't spoken in more than a year. Rose had called Lizzie a few times after that day, but Lizzie, embarrassed, ashamed, hadn't returned her messages. She thought of her all the time, when she was driving down Wilshire and passing the La Brea Tar Pits, when she caught a mention of Roger Corman on the radio. There was a new tearjerker of a Holocaust film about the daughter of a Danish fisherman who tried to ferry Jews across the narrow strait to Sweden during the war. It was hugely popular, despite critical grumbling, and Lizzie knew that Rose would have much to say about it, little good.

She wanted to reach out to her, but the more time went by, the harder it had become. What could she possibly say?

Lizzie went to her laptop and returned a quick e-mail to a board member. When she went back into the living room a few minutes later, Oscar was staring at her from his perch in the stroller. "Oh, you're up," she said. "Hello."

He considered her gravely. Then he began to howl.

"No, no," she said, hurrying to unbuckle him. "No, no, baby." He was screeching and he was squirming—she couldn't believe how much he could squirm. What could possibly have gone wrong so quickly? How did he already know that Sarah was gone? Finally she got him out, plopped him onto the floor. "Maybe you just need a minute."

He eyed her. "Meh," he yelled. But the sound of it wasn't as guttural and intense, and for a moment he fell silent.

Lizzie let out a breath. "You better?" she said, and allowed herself a tentative half smile.

"Meh!" He swatted at the air.

"I'm sorry, no smiling. But I don't know what you want," she said. "What do you want?"

Oscar grunted and crawled on his belly, commando-style, toward a trio of boxes in the corner. He grabbed hold and began to pull himself up.

"No, no," Lizzie said, and swooped him up. He screamed as she carried him into the kitchen. Screamed as she heated his milk. He batted the bottle away. Was he going to scream for the next three hours? Is this what she had signed up for?

"What about a peach?" She grabbed a perfectly ripe one from the bowl, washed it off. He followed her movements with his eyes, too distracted, it seemed, to cry. She sped up, sliced the peach fast. Any minute that ungodly screaming would begin again. The peaches were only a part of the bounty she had purchased yesterday at the Santa Monica Farmers Market. She had been contentedly walking among the stalls alone, tasting samples of pluots and apricots and tiny strawberries grown in Oxnard, still feeling amazed by the gorgeous abundance of produce in February. That's when she saw him.

It's someone who looks like Max, she first thought as she stared at the back of a lanky man in a gingham shirt several paces ahead on his cell phone, standing near the oranges. She still saw versions of her father all the time—men younger than him, men with more facial hair, a man at least six inches taller but with a similar determined step in his walk. She would feel a drop in her stomach, the ground unstable. Was it him? It wasn't him.

But no, this man in the gingham turned and it was decidedly Max, baseball cap visoring his roughly handsome face, sleeves rolled up to reveal his sinewy arms. He was ending his call, looking around; he was chuckling. She ducked near the almonds. He looked tanned, relaxed. Her heart jackhammered. And she simply knew: *He's seeing someone,* she thought.

He inspected a handful of satsumas, paid the cashier, and walked off. The bags didn't seem to weigh him down. Lizzie observed all these details with prickly astonishment, waiting for him to notice her, waiting to hear herself call out his name. *I've never said anything to anyone about the paintings,* she wanted to tell him. But she said nothing, her insides wrenched. Was he leaving? Could she actually let him go? She felt drunkenly off balance, as if one of her legs was heading off without her. The crowd had swallowed him up; for a moment, she strained in the bright sunlight and could see a spot of royal-blue check, a flash of shoulder. And then that too was gone.

Now Lizzie cut tiny pieces of the peach, sticky and dripping. She handed them to Oscar. "Meh," Oscar said crossly, and dropped them on the floor.

"My sentiments exactly," she said. All that sweetness, and she was left wanting too.

Her phone rang, a 213 phone number she didn't recognize. Sarah? She picked up.

"Ms. Goldstein?" the male voice said. "Elizabeth Goldstein?"

"Yeah," Lizzie said. He sounded vaguely familiar. She opened up a bottom drawer filled with Tupperware, and gave two pieces to Oscar to play with.

"This is Detective Tandy. From the LAPD."

Detective Tandy. Her stomach lurched.

"We found the paintings, Ms. Goldstein."

"Excuse me?" she asked, though there had been nothing unclear about his words.

"Your father's artwork. The stolen Soutine and Picasso." She detected a shred of impatience.

"I'm sorry," she said. The paintings? Her mind couldn't take anything in. "You found *The Bellhop?*"

"We found the artwork holed up in the garage of a house in the Valley; Reseda, actually. A ranch house in miserable condition, falling apart."

"Jesus," she said. "The paintings—are they all right?"

"Yeah, unbelievably, they're all right."

She closed her eyes, woozy. Could this really be? Rose; she had to tell Rose. And her sister. She heard something slam and opened her eyes: there was Oscar, banging away happily on the Tupperware lids, drooling. She sank down beside him.

Tandy was still speaking. "No thanks to the person whose care they were in. The house is owned by a Jane Reynolds. The mother of Desdemona Reynolds, the ex-girlfriend of Sean Malone. Do any of those names ring a bell? Did your father ever mention Malone to you?"

Lizzie shook her head. "No," she whispered. Who were these people?

"Sean Malone's a former cop who contracted services to Kruger and Dunn, where Max Levitan worked before he started his own practice. Levitan and your father enlisted Malone to take the paintings—"

A hot viscous sensation heaved up, flooding Lizzie's insides. "You know that?" she asked. "You're sure?"

"Yes," Tandy said, and the single drop of the word sounded gentle. "Malone will testify to it. His girlfriend too; she was privy to conversations. There is significant evidence."

Lizzie nodded, but didn't say more.

"There were disagreements afterward," Tandy continued, his voice warming up. "Malone wanted a larger take, saying he hadn't gotten paid enough for the job, that there were complications."

"The party I threw," Lizzie choked out. Oscar was trying to climb into her lap now, his tiny sticky fingers clawing at her hair.

"Yes. So he held on to the paintings, refusing to turn them over. He wasn't exactly quiet about it. He told his girlfriend, bragged about it. Everyone seemed to know about the goddamn paintings." For a moment, he sounded strangely like Joseph. "Years went by. Desdemona was pushing Malone to get married. Then she caught him screwing her best friend, and she decided that she'd had enough of him. She went to the cops—turned out he was dealing opiates, big-time, in cahoots with a doctor in Woodland Hills. And she told the police all about it, and then said, maybe you'd be interested in some old artwork too? It's a miracle those paintings survived. Desdemona's mother had built an aviary in her garage, metal cages filled with birds—all different kinds—and let me tell you, birds are nasty creatures. Dirty and mean. She had decided to raise the birds as part of her retirement plan—she had some crackpot scheme to breed them."

"And the paintings?" Lizzie broke in. "What about the paintings?"

"The paintings were holed up on a top rack of a shelf, surrounded by that squawking mess, a carpet of bird shit and seeds. I never knew birds smelled that much. They were in metal canisters. Desdemona had told her mother that it was a drawing and a painting of hers from high school; can you believe that? Her mother didn't have a clue that they were worth millions."

"Of course she didn't," Lizzie said, and she felt a strange rush of feeling. Poor Mrs. Reynolds and her birds.

"All the work we had done through the years didn't mean shit," Tandy said, and Lizzie could tell he wished they hadn't found the paintings this way—he viewed it as cheap, lucky—he almost wanted the mystery back. "It's always the girlfriends. They'll turn on a dime."

Lizzie pulled Oscar tighter. She started to cry. Oscar pushed a wet fist into her mouth, rooting around for her teeth. Now she was laughing and crying.

"We'll need you to come in and identify them. You and your sister," Tandy was now saying. "There are details to be worked out, of course; but the important thing is we've got them back."

"We'll be there," Lizzie said.

16

LOS ANGELES, 2008

Rose remembered when she and Thomas were waiting, grimly, for the first biopsy report. "We need to prepare ourselves," she recalled him saying. "If it looks like a horse and acts like a horse, it's probably a horse and not a zebra."

"But I want a zebra," she said to him. "I demand a zebra."

By the time the pancreatic cancer was diagnosed, metastases had already taken root in his liver and lungs. He was gone within nine months, an awful, harrowing time. And yet Rose would gladly relive any one of those days to have him again. Nearly fifty years they had been together. She had been uncommonly lucky. When Thomas died, she told herself that it was a gift to have his body at all, a luxury to be able to decide where to bury him, to have a burial, a headstone, a spot of her own choosing, one that she could visit, that would be tended to, not vandalized or ignored.

But she wanted more. After all those years of feeling as if she didn't deserve happiness, that she was snatching bits of goodness wherever she could, that one day she would be punished for surviving—after all of that, she was left wanting, wishing for more.

Getting older meant facing loss, over and over again. Its presence was not limited to one's spouse. People got sick; they suffered; they died. Turn left, turn right; there was a former colleague of Thomas's, murdered in his Laurel Canyon home by a meth addict; Rose's dentist, guffawing at her last cleaning, asking about her summer plans, nearly mute six months later when he told her his seven-year-old had lymphoma; five Amish girls shot and killed in their school by a truck driver; hundreds dead from a heat wave in India.

Rose, of all people, understood that devastations occurred all the time. But that didn't mean you got used to them. Or accepted them. Almost four years after Thomas's death, his plastic reading glasses remained on his nightstand. She still couldn't sleep on his side of the bed. As Rose got older, she was surprised less by tragedies than by the absence of them. Life was fragile—what else was new?

But what to do with an actual astonishing turn, something that presented indisputably good news? "They found *The Bellhop,*" Lizzie said on her voice mail, and it took Rose three more vertiginous listens, rewinding and replaying with shaking hands, to come close to understanding.

She called the detective Lizzie cited in her message. He told her about the former cop who had once worked with Joseph's friend Max, how he had been hired by Joseph to steal them. "Not unlike what I had always thought," the detective offered. "The deal went bad from the beginning."

"Can I see it? When can I see the painting?" The details he was telling her were not insignificant, but for now, she only cared about one thing.

"Why don't you come tomorrow afternoon with Ms. Goldstein?" He gave her the address and she repeated it back to him twice, still in disbelief that any of this was happening.

She called Gerhard. "That's not possible," he said.

"But it is," she said, laughing a little. "It's in police custody. Here in Los Angeles. You should come. You need to." If there were ever an instance where he would hop on a plane a day later and fly the more than five thousand miles between them, shouldn't this be it? "I can see it tomorrow, but I will wait if you can come. We can see it together."

He signed. "I can't leave Izzie. And she can't fly."

Then Isobel got on the phone and, lowering her voice, said, "I wish I could be there, but I can't leave your brother. And he simply isn't strong enough for the long flight."

But Harry, who was wrapping up a film in Vancouver, was ready and willing. "I always *knew* it would be found," he declared. "I told you last year, when I read that script involving Modigliani, that it meant something. I had this *feeling*—"

"You were right, Harry, absolutely," Rose said. Even she couldn't deny him his flights of fancy that day.

Harry drove them downtown in Rose's car. As traffic slowed on the 101, Harry kept chatting, about his current director's penchant for multiple takes—"he thinks he's Kubrick but he's not"—his ex-wife's refusal to support their daughter taking a year off from college to teach English in Guatemala. (On this, he sounded very like Isobel: "She's nineteen, for God's sake! Why shouldn't she explore?") At the LAPD's glass tower in the Civic Center, she and Harry passed through security, stepped into a lurching elevator. As she pressed the button for the seventh floor, Harry was still talking: "It is such a crazy story; if only the canvas could talk—"

"Harry, can you please be quiet?"

Out of the elevator, Rose knocked on the door to suite 703, and a short young man opened it. "I'm looking for Detective Tandy," Rose explained.

"Tandy!" he yelled.

Detective Tandy, wearing a brightly colored shirt and no tie, appeared. "It's good to meet you both," he said, and ushered them inside. The large office thrummed with activity: people milling about, odd assortments of furniture—scratched-up file cabinets and desks, a battered refrigerator, green and red tinsel twisted limply above a whiteboard filled with scrawl—"57?" It was a corner space filled with light, but the windows had gone gray with grime.

"Rose," she heard a familiar voice. There was Lizzie near the file cabinet with her sister. It was unquestionably her, but she looked different, Rose thought, her hair longer, spilling past her shoulders. Despite the tailored blazer she was wearing, she looked younger, and for a brief disorienting moment, on the cusp of seeing *The Bellhop,* Rose thought, *Time is going backward.*

"Lizzie," Rose said, and she was pulling Lizzie into a hug.

"Rose," Lizzie said, her voice cracking. Rose felt her limbs stiffen, then undoubtedly loosen. Rose held on tight.

After a moment, Tandy cleared his throat. "It's a small space; I'll take you in two by two."

Lizzie pulled back, wiping her eyes. "You go first," she told Rose.

Tandy led Rose and Harry through the maze of his office into another room guarded by a man in uniform, who handed Tandy latex gloves. He snapped them on. They made his hands look bulbous, fishlike.

Rose and Harry followed him into a tiny, low-lit, windowless space dominated by a large industrial table ensconced in plastic. The air felt thin, stripped of oxygen. Rose grabbed for the edge of the table. "Auntie?" Harry said as he steadied her elbow. For a moment, she thought she might pass out.

There he was, *The Bellhop,* lying unadorned on the table, the boy in red on the flat canvas, just as she remembered, with his gold buttons and strange surly face and stretched-out limbs. It was him, absolutely.

But gazing at him for the first time in more than sixty years, Rose felt a dark expanding swath of fear. The thick swirling redness, his tiny mouth, dark eyes, the way he positioned himself at an angle against the rich background: the boy didn't want to be here. She hadn't remembered that about him. He stared resentfully. He didn't want to be here at all.

Time folded in on itself, snaking, contorting. She saw *The Bellhop* in their Viennese flat, hanging on the wall in her parents' bedroom, Papi complaining about it ("I should be the only man in here"). There was Mutti, at the piano, practicing a spirited Shubert concerto in the drawing room with the red velvet chairs and Herr Schulman by her side, murmuring, *gut, sehr gut,* watching her with hooded eyes. Rose remembered dancing alone in front of *The Bellhop* on New Year's Eve when the lead-pouring went awry and Bette sensed the ugliness of the year ahead. She could hear Gerhard arguing with Mutti and Papi: *The soldiers aren't going to bother me. I'm going to see Ilse. I am.* There they were, gathered around the dark oak dining table beneath the massive brass chandelier, Mutti and Papi and Onkel George and Tante Greta arguing about the wait at the American embassy. Mutti wanted to put their name on all the lists. *We are not going to Argentina,* she could recall Papi saying. *Why not?* Mutti demanded.

Rose remembered when she was younger, Mutti in the cot in the tiny room that was to be the nursery, her cries of pain, the doctor rushing past, Bette cleaning up the blood. Mutti asked for *The Bellhop*—that's what she wanted, not Rose or Gerhard, but *The Bellhop,* by her side.

"Let's go," Rose said to Harry in a gravelly voice she did not recognize.

"But that's it, isn't it?" Harry said. Tandy too was studying her. "That's the painting?"

Rose nodded, turning away from them, eyes back on the canvas. Here it was, after so many years, and all she felt was sorrow. She was an old woman. Her parents, so many people she had loved, had suffered. They were murdered. They had been dead for decades now. *The Bellhop* was paint covering a surface; that was all. "Let's go," she said to Harry, her voice barely above a whisper. She hurried out of the small room, past Lizzie and her sister, waiting beside the door.

"Rose?" she heard Lizzie call. "Rose?"

"I'm sorry," she muttered, head down.

"SHALL WE STOP FOR COFFEE? Is that pink palace of yours still in business?" Harry asked, back behind the wheel of Rose's car.

"No, I want to go home."

He cast a glance at her. "I know that must have been overwhelming, Auntie, after all these years, but—"

"Harry, *please:* I do not want to talk about it."

He nodded. "It is good news, Auntie, unquestionably. After all of these years, you and Dad are getting the painting back!"

"It's not ours anymore," she said, and it was too painful to say anything more. "Technically, it's the insurance company's."

"The lawyers will take care of that," he said. "It's very clear."

She shook her head, slumped in her seat. She and Gerhard had already spoken about it. They would hire a lawyer here in the United States. But hiring a lawyer was the least of it. Cases like this could drag on for years. Rose was so weary, she wasn't sure she had the fight in her. (*Yes, you do,* she could hear Thomas telling her. *Of course you do.*) Why in the world had she cared so much? This was what she had said she wanted for all of those years: *This?* A painting? After the murder of her parents, a painting was what she had focused on?

Even Gerhard had said to her, *Mutti's* Bellhop, *your* Bellhop! *You can have it back.*

I don't want it, she thought petulantly. The image of *The Bellhop,* lying flat on the table in police custody, made her seize up with shame. It wasn't the painting she had wanted.

HARRY DROVE ROSE BACK HOME and clucked around the apartment, checking, Lord help her, if the milk in the refrigerator had not expired and turning up the heat ("Why is it sixty-five degrees in here? Why are you denying yourself the bloody comforts of the contemporary age?"). "Harry," she said, "I like it this way. I am seventy-nine years old, not ninety-nine. I can still do things for myself."

"It's called concern, Auntie," he said, and leaned down to give her a slide of a kiss. "Shall I order us dinner?"

"Bob is coming over. I'm sorry, but I'd like—"

"No need to explain," he said. "No need to humor your poor, single nephew; I'll eat alone, despondent, in my hotel room."

"Harry," she protested. The notion of Harry despondently alone was ludicrous. But what did she know, really?

"I'm only joking. Have your romantic dinner and I'll be back tomorrow," he said with a grin.

"Thank you," she told him firmly.

After the door closed behind Harry, she called.

"So?" Bob said. "How was it?"

"It was something," she said. "It truly was. I'll tell you all about it later. But about dinner—my nephew wants me to join him, alone." She lowered her voice as if Harry was still nearby. "I'm sorry, but he's only in town until tomorrow, and he's being quite insistent."

"Oh," Bob said with audible disappointment. "I would like to meet him, you know."

"I know," Rose said, and she felt a pulse of regret. Bob was a good man. He wasn't Thomas, but he was a good man. Why was she pushing him away? "After everything today, I just can't tonight," she finished, honest in sentiment if not in fact.

After she got off the phone, she went straight for the kitchen cabinet with the bottle of Ardbeg—Thomas's favorite. She loaded a coffee mug with ice cubes, tipped in a generous measure of the whiskey, and settled into the armchair with her Dick Francis mystery. This was what she needed, she thought. She read and she drank and she nodded off.

THE LIGHTS WERE ABLAZE WHEN Rose awoke, her heart careening, her limbs stiff. Where was she?

It was long dark by the time they had gathered in the field behind the station, the cold air biting. Mutti and Papi and Gerhard and Rose had taken the tram together and walked the last several blocks to the train station. The field was packed with people, children and parents and representatives from the Jewish organization. Dim lights bobbed up and down, flashlights carried by officials providing paltry illumination.

"We need to check in," Papi said. His wool overcoat hung loose on his frame. His face looked haggard in the shadowy light, but he also seemed strangely energized, more talkative than he had been in months. "Where do we do check in?" he asked aloud, before flagging down a representative with a flashlight, who pointed to a thick cluster across the field.

They pressed through the crowds and finally reached a red-faced woman carrying an armload of materials. "Yes," she said, consulting her papers. "Rose Zimmer, you are 163, and Gerhard Zimmer, 171." She thumbed through and pulled out two stiff placards with strings attached. "You must wear these around your neck. Attach the corresponding tags to your luggage. In a little while, we'll walk to the platform in groups. You two are in the same one, group C, 151 to 199."

"They're together," murmured Mutti. "Thank God."

"You can see the posts now with the placards," the red-faced woman continued. "You should make your way to your group soon." She looked past them. "Next," she called.

They moved to the side. Mutti put the placard around Rose's neck, freed her hair from the string. Gerhard put on his own. The string was itchy against Rose's skin. She yanked at it.

"You must leave it," Papi warned. "You don't want it to fall off."

Rose nodded, silent. What would happen if it did fall off? Would anyone know where she was supposed to go? What if she were separated from Gerhard?

Mutti pulled at the shoulders of Rose's plaid coat, inspecting the seams. "This isn't all that big. I hope it'll still fit you in a few months' time."

"That's all we need," Papi said, and Mutti nodded fast.

"Of course," she said. "*Mausi,* I packed my blue scarf with the birds that you like. And Gerhard, there's a diary for you. It's leather-bound, a fine book, and I want you to fill it with lots of details from your English adventure."

"Thank you, Mutti," he said. "I promise I will." Why did he get the diary? What was Rose supposed to do with a scarf? She had always thought it pretty, but on her mother, not herself.

Gerhard looked so mature, so serious, that Rose couldn't help but say: "I would have liked a diary instead. I'm old enough."

"Really? You want one now?" Gerhard said. "When have you ever wanted a diary before?"

"Just because you have one doesn't mean I can't," Rose said.

"Please, children," Mutti said, burying her face against Papi's overcoat.

He barked: "For heaven's sake, not now."

Gerhard was murmuring, "I'm sorry, so sorry," and Rose was sorry too, but she felt chilled into silence. She was terrified of what she might say: *I'm not leaving, I'm not.*

Mutti turned back to Rose, her face mottled and flushed. "I'll send you one tomorrow morning, just like Gerhard's. First thing. How does that sound?"

Rose nodded in assent. Why had she ever asked for it? The hollow feeling in her stomach was expanding by the moment. She couldn't imagine wanting to write anything down.

"It's time," they heard a man call out. "Line up. Please check your number and make sure you are in the correct line." Representatives were waving big signs attached to sticks listing groups of numbers. The numbers swam in the dim light. The four of them, Gerhard carrying his suitcase, Papi carrying Rose's, made their way through to their group.

Their names were checked off again, this time by a man so short that Rose nearly mistook him for a child. Papi handed Rose's suitcase to Gerhard, clapped his son on the back. "Write a letter as soon as you arrive—even before you arrive. And take care of your sister. I am counting on you."

"I will. I promise," Gerhard said. Rose didn't want to hear it. She moved closer to her mother, slid her hand into hers.

"We will take care of each other," Gerhard said, wiggling his eyebrows at his sister, and for the first time that night, Rose felt a slight leavening.

"I only wish they were going to be in the same house," Mutti said.

"It can't be helped," Papi said.

"I know," Mutti said with desperation, "I know."

A ginger-haired girl ahead of them in line clung to her father. She looked about Rose's age. "I won't go," she cried. "I won't." Rose watched her.

"You are very brave," Mutti whispered close to her ear.

"I'm not crying," Rose said. This was a statement of fact. She felt too numb to cry. Mutti and Papi said it should only be a few months, six at most. She knew precisely four words in English: *toilet, day, jam,* and *yes*. How was she supposed to live with a family she didn't know? How would she talk to them? Who would take care of her? What would happen when she got those cramps in her legs at night that only Mutti knew how to make go away? She had seen a picture of the couple she was going to live with, and they looked very stern. They had no children. *But they must be good,* Mutti had said. *For they are taking you in.*

I can't go. I won't, she wanted to cry. But she needed to make Mutti proud. "I *am* glad for your scarf," Rose whispered, flinging herself at her mother's hip. "I truly am."

"I know you are. You are my brave strong girl," Mutti said with unaccustomed fierceness.

All too soon the baby-faced man who headed their line cupped his hands together. "We need to go to the platform. Please, remain orderly." The crowd surged forward as he strode down the line, assessing. "Carry your own suitcase and remain in line!"

Gerhard gave Rose her suitcase, who strained to lift it.

"Why can't he help her? How in the world is she supposed to carry that?" Mutti asked Papi.

"Charlotte," he said. "She has to."

Rose struggled, her arms shaky with effort, but she managed. Her nose stung from the cold; her chest felt hot. As the lines wound through the field and to the platform, Mutti walked beside her in silence, holding her hand. Neither wore gloves. Mutti's fingers were slick with sweat, entwined with her own. "Look," Mutti said, "see the moon?" It was a bright inhospitable shard, emerging through the knitted clouds. "You will see the moon in England, and I will see the same moon here in Vienna. You see? We will not be so far away from each other." Rose gripped her mother's fingers tighter, said nothing. She did not want to think about the moon in England.

All too soon they arrived at the train platform. So many people jostling, so much noise—crying, reaching for each other, weeping. "Don't forget there are cheese sandwiches in both of your rucksacks," Mutti said as a pair of SS men strode past. "And I want to hear that you are working hard on your schoolwork, harder than you would at home. And you must be polite, no matter what. You are good children." A boy tripped, fell onto Rose's suitcase. "What did you do that for?" he cried accusingly, but Papi scooped up Rose—his wiry arms, his smoky smell, his rough cheeks, Papi hugging her so hard that it didn't feel like a hug at all but something more. And yet it wasn't enough; it would never be enough. Then Rose was clinging to Mutti, burrowing her head at her chest, in the warmth of her wool coat, stroking her rabbit-fur collar. "We will see you soon," Mutti promised, her cheeks aflame. "We will see you in no time at all."

This was not good-bye. Rose held on to her mother. She didn't want an English adventure. She didn't care if it was safer. Why were they sending her away?

A mittened hand tunneled into hers. "Rose," Gerhard said as he tugged at her. "We have to get on."

"We will be here, watching the train," Mutti said, pressing her hot cheek against her daughter's, desperately kissing her brow, her lips. "We will not leave."

Blindly Rose followed her brother. They stepped inside the train. The group leader pointed them into a compartment where several children were already gathered, including the ginger-headed girl who had been weeping earlier, now calm, and a pair of older boys, playing a card game. Gerhard moved close to the boys. Rose went to the big window beside the girl.

"I'm Anita," the girl said, tugging at the window. "I'm twelve."

"Rose," Rose said. "Eleven."

"Can you help me, Rose?" And the two of them pushed the window as high open as it would go, letting in a swoop of cold air, and used the leather sash that hung from the ceiling to secure the window into place.

She and Anita leaned out. Rose saw a pair of SS men conferring near the train door on the platform. Anita saw them too. "Soon we'll be leaving them behind," she said. Rose nodded. No more Nazis, this was true. This was good. But where were her parents? She scanned the crowded platform. They had promised that they wouldn't leave. There! She alighted on their worried faces, carved out and distinct from the others. "Mutti, Papi!" At the sound of her voice, they rushed toward her, waving furiously.

"Papa!" Anita called. Her father pushed his way through the knots of people to a spot beneath the train window. Anita leaned out more and her father grasped her hands. "My baby," he moaned.

The engine coughed and began to shudder. It was happening, they were leaving, Rose thought, shocked. They could not be leaving. How could her parents do this? "Mutti! Papi!" she cried.

Lights flooded the platform—Mutti's face was an awful purplish hue. "We are coming." Mutti choked the words out. "We are."

Slowly the train began to move. The crowd along the platform moved with it. Anita's father hurried alongside, held on to her hands. "No, I can't let you go," he moaned. "No."

"Papa," Anita cried.

"No, no." He grasped at her elbows, tugging, yanking. "Papa, no!" she shrieked as he pulled her torso through the window. Suddenly Anita was neither in the train nor out of it. Rose watched in horror as she tumbled onto the platform. Adults rushed over as Anita's father, weeping, hugged her tight. Out the window, Rose leaned, frozen, the air lashing against her face, her neck—*Take me,* she wanted to cry out. *Grab me too!* But the train picked up speed, and the platform and everyone on it—Mutti's contorted face, the heap of Anita—was receding. "No!" Rose cried. She felt pressure on her legs, a tugging at her waist. "Rose!" Gerhard, pulling her back.

"I don't want to go," she cried inside the warmth of the train. Gerhard jammed the window closed as she scooted feral-like to the farthest seat on the bench, away from the others. The train clanked and careered down the tracks and her brother was hugging her and she wanted none of it. "No," she howled as she buried her face against her brother's side.

"I know," Gerhard kept repeating, "I know," as the train chugged west and left everything they cared about behind.

BY THE TIME ROSE WOKE up a second time that day, it was late morning in Los Angeles. It took her longer than usual to get herself dressed. She made an egg scramble—slowly, over a low flame, just as Thomas taught her. She sat down to eat it with buttered toast and coffee, surprised at how hungry she was. She tunneled the food into her mouth automatically, with little pleasure.

The images kept shuttering through her mind: her mother's slick fingers grasping her own, the chaos and pushing on the platform,

Papi's rush of words, that distant chilly moon, Mutti's contorted expression, that poor girl pulled from the train. The memories tumbled forth, unbidden. That night on the platform had split her in two—everything that came afterward felt like an accident, one that she was never wholly present for.

But Rose grasped on to every shred of memory that muscled through. She was still the little girl leaning out that window, and yet she was now at least twice the age her parents had been then. She saw herself on that train, bereft, wanting more than anything not to leave, but she also saw herself standing on that platform as her parents had, her heart wrenched from her body, watching in agony as the train pulled away.

It was after dinnertime in England by the time she dialed. "I spoke to Harry already," Gerhard said, "but I want to hear it from you: Is *The Bellhop* as ugly as I remember it being?"

Rose laughed. It was a relief to hear Gerhard being Gerhard. "I will not lie to you: it is ugly, but beautiful too. Once I saw it, I couldn't stop thinking of things. Do you remember, at the train station, the girl who got pulled out?"

"Of course," Gerhard said, with unmistakable impatience. "That was nothing you can forget."

Alone in her apartment, Rose blushed. "What do you think happened to her?"

"What do you mean? Mutti wrote that the girl was bruised and a little cut up, but basically okay. It was a miracle that she didn't fall to the tracks, die on the spot. Bloody madness, pulling her out like that."

"No," Rose ventured. "I meant—what happened to her during the war? Do you think she survived?"

"Oh," Gerhard said, and sighed. "I don't know, who knows. The odds aren't good." He paused and she wondered if he too was thinking of their parents. "What made you think of that? I haven't thought of it in a very long time."

"I don't know," Rose said, and then: "I had a dream."

"Oh, dreams," Gerhard said. "Did I tell you that Isobel is now keeping a dream notebook? She's on a kombucha kick, she's convinced it's improving her memory. And her eyesight. And keeping cancer at bay. Sometimes I wake up in the middle of the night to see her scribbling away in her notebook."

"I miss Isobel," Rose said with a rush of warmth. "And I miss you too." It was true, and she didn't say it nearly enough.

"We miss you too," he said, and cleared his throat. "I can't imagine what that must have been like, to put your children on that train. I think about it sometimes. And I'm not sure I could have done it—even knowing what I know." He cleared his throat again.

"I know," she said, and it surprised her, how natural this conversation felt. This was the most she and Gerhard had talked about the past in decades. Rose was thinking about all the leaps of faith their parents had to take: that the train would not be detained, the children rounded up by the SS, that they would actually make it across the various borders and onto the boat and across the Channel to England. That once they were there, the families that said they would take care of their children, would in fact do so. Her parents were forced to make an excruciating decision—their children would be better off without them—and devastatingly, they had been right.

"We were fortunate," she said to her brother.

"Very," he agreed.

WHEN THE DOORBELL RANG A few hours later, Rose still felt worn out, jet-lagged, her body at war with itself. She answered it shoeless, expecting Harry. But Lizzie stood at her door, clutching a small cardboard box.

"Cookies," she said solemnly, and thrust the box into Rose's hands. "I thought you might like some."

"I never don't like cookies," Rose said, surprised. "Come in."

"I'm sorry I didn't call," Lizzie said, "But I thought it might be better if I just came by."

"I'm glad you did," Rose said, and led her into the living room. "I'm sorry I ran off yesterday."

"You don't need to apologize."

"Well then. How about some coffee with these cookies?"

"That sounds lovely." Lizzie was wearing a long dark top over dark leggings, curly hair loose over her shoulders. All that darkness conspired to make her pale skin look luminous. Had she always looked this young? Yes, Rose told herself. She was at least forty years younger—another creature entirely. But there was something else at work, Rose decided: she had gained weight. It suited her.

In the kitchen, Rose opened the box: "Linzers!" she exclaimed. "Wonderful."

Lizzie smiled shyly. "There are two kinds, raspberry and black currant."

Rose started the coffeemaker, arranged the cookies on a plate. "You know, we never had Linzer cookies growing up, or if we did, I don't remember them. I only started having them here, in America," she said as she brought the plate back into the living room.

"I'm glad you like them," Lizzie said, and lapsed into silence. Rose broke a cookie into two.

"Delicious," she said after taking a bite. "Sometimes Linzers are too sweet, the filling can overwhelm, but these are done right. Thank you for bringing them."

Lizzie was gazing toward the entry hall, where Joseph's masks still hung. "I'm so sorry, I still can't believe that my father—" She stopped. "He did this."

"He had his reasons," Rose found herself saying. It disturbed her to think of those lunches with Joseph, all those times he had talked to her about the supposed investigator on the case, but after seeing the painting, after all that she remembered . . . well. Things were different now.

"That's bullshit," Lizzie said, her dark eyes fixed on Rose's own, no longer tentative, and Rose heard an echo of Joseph in her tone.

"It's not," Rose said, and she felt this was essential to impart. "I didn't say they were good reasons. I said they were particular to him."

"What does that even mean?" Lizzie said.

"Look, what if I had known that your father had engineered the theft of the painting years ago? If I had gotten it back, that would have meant something, of course. But it wouldn't have meant everything. Not to me." Such a simple truth but it hurt to articulate it. There was nothing she could do to change what had happened.

"I know," Lizzie said, "I *know.*" Her voice cracked on the last word. "But it would have meant something to you. You can't tell me it wouldn't."

Rose gave her a short nod. What would be the point in lying? That would help neither of them.

This wisp of an admission seemed to soothe Lizzie. She swiped a few errant cookie crumbs into her napkin, her face calmer. Finally she spoke. "I'm sorry I was out of touch for so long. So many times I thought about calling. But I felt so guilty. I didn't know what to say."

"You don't have to explain," Rose said. "It's not necessary."

"I'm going to help you get *The Bellhop* back," Lizzie said. "The situation with the insurance company is only temporary—"

"I know."

"I've already made phone calls. There's Ciparelli, who I told you about before. But there's also Michael Zalman in New York, who won the Schiele case. And I've heard that Roger Yannata here in L.A. is terrific, tenacious and surprisingly pleasant, at least to his clients—"

"Lizzie, stop."

"I know, you hate talking about this. But this time it's different," Lizzie insisted. "You can't ignore it."

"I'm not ignoring it. My brother and I are handling it. And I'm grateful for your help, truly." She meant it. *The Bellhop*'s reappearance didn't solve everything, but its absence wasn't to blame for everything either.

"I should be the one thanking you," Lizzie said, picked up another cookie. "This might sound strange, but some of the things you said to me last year—they resonated. You have no idea."

"I see," Rose said, because she was beginning to. She studied Lizzie openly now. It wasn't Rose's imagination; Lizzie had gained weight. "So, out with it. How far along are you?"

A speckled pink spread across Lizzie's cheeks. Rose was right, she knew she was. "I'm due in June. I'm just over four months now." Lizzie held her palm to her stomach, smiling an inward but unquestionable smile. "I can't believe you noticed."

"Of course."

"Not *of course*," Lizzie said with frank admiration. "So many people don't—or are too afraid to ask me. But you never miss a thing."

Rose shrugged. "It suits you." It was more than just the changes to her body, it was the way she carried herself, more confident. "You look good."

"Thank you," Lizzie said, and blushed some more.

"You won't be able to be able to hide it for long, you know."

"But I'm not," she said. "I'm not trying to hide a thing."

Of course not. Lizzie had no need to hide anything. Rose caught her breath. She thought back to her miscarriages. What would have happened if they had tried sooner? What would have happened if she simply let herself live? But she could hear Thomas in her head: *There you go again. You did live. You* are *living.*

Thomas would have liked Lizzie, Rose thought with a strange but unmistakable fierceness. The two of them would have gotten along splendidly. Rose reached across the coffee table and patted Lizzie's hand, a light gesture that did little to reflect the emotions roiling inside her. "A summer baby, how nice," she murmured.

Lizzie held on, her fingers moist. "It's just me. I'm having the baby alone. I have no idea what I'm doing."

"Oh, you're going to do just fine," Rose said, and she stroked her palm. She was certain of it.

"Maybe," Lizzie said, with a half laugh. "I don't know that at all."

"But you do," Rose said, looking at her with steadiness, and she was thinking of Thomas as she said it, trying to channel his generosity. He could calm like no one else she knew. "I know you do."

Lizzie rubbed her eyes with her fists, almost childlike, and then she exhaled sharply. "Okay, then," she said. "If you say so."

"I do," Rose said, remembering: coffee. She went into the kitchen, reached for the delicate green teacups Thomas had loved, and poured. Back in the living room, she handed Lizzie a cup and asked: "Do you know if you're having a boy or girl?"

"I don't know."

"It's too early."

"No, it's not. I've decided not to find out," Lizzie said shyly. "I would have thought I'd want to know, but I decided—so much of this was planned, and you can't know everything."

Rose's hand felt shaky, and she worked to steady her cup on the table. "That's right," she said. She nearly whispered it. "You cannot." Just like that, she was sitting by the Embankment with Thomas when they first met, the meager lunches they had on those overcast spring days when the oyster-colored sky and the water of the Thames seemed to be one and the same. She wasn't dead and she mattered to someone and these plain facts fueled a giddy promise. The possibility alone had been enough.

Rose wished she could tell Thomas what happened on that train. *I wanted to jump too,* she would say. *I wanted my parents to pull me out of the train.*

But you didn't. And they didn't, Thomas would tell her. *And I for one am so very glad.*

"You know," Lizzie said. "I live here now, in Los Angeles. I moved back."

"No, I did not know that." It came out sharply but that wasn't how Rose meant it. "How nice," she added, more softly.

"Maybe I can come over every once in a while," Lizzie said. "Bring the baby when the time comes."

"I would like that. But you should know that I know nothing about babies."

"That makes two of us." Lizzie offered her a small cracked smile.

And perhaps it was just the haze of the afternoon light filtering through the window, but the contour of Lizzie's stomach suddenly seemed more pronounced. Rose tried not to stare. She remembered that feeling. She thought of Mutti, the impossible choice she and Papi had to make, and she wished more than anything that she could have told her she understood.

"These teacups are beautiful," Lizzie observed. "Didn't you tell me they were from Thomas's family?"

"No, he bought them here," Rose said, sipping the coffee that was good and hot. "Not long after we moved. It's a funny little story, actually."

"I want to hear it," Lizzie said.

And Rose began.

AUTHOR'S NOTE

THE LITHUANIAN-BORN CHAIM SOUTINE MOVED to Paris in 1913, where he indeed became friends with Modigliani, and struggled to eke out a living as a painter. In 1923, Dr. Albert C. Barnes arrived in Europe on an art-buying spree. He saw a painting of Soutine's in a Montparnasse gallery—a portrait of a young pastry chef—and fell in love. He snapped up dozens of works by Soutine, giving the artist much-needed funds and igniting his career.

In the 1920s, Soutine painted numerous portraits of people who often went unnoticed—waiters, cooks, and hotel employees—including several bellhops. The portrait described in *The Fortunate Ones* is an amalgam of Soutine's bellhops, but the owners depicted in the novel are purely fictional.

I first came upon Soutine's work years ago in a wonderful exhibit at the Jewish Museum, and I'm grateful to its curators, Norman Kleeblatt and Kenneth Silver, as well as to Maurice Tuchman and Esti Dunow for their extensive Soutine scholarship.

While this is a work of fiction, a number of books served as key resources and inspiration, including: *Austerity Britain,* by David Kynaston; *London 1945,* by Maureen Waller; *London War Notes,* by Mollie Panter-Downes; *War Factory,* by Inez Holden; *The Tiger in the Attic,* by Edith Milton; *The Rape of Europa,* by Lynn Nicholas. Lore Segal's clear-eyed *Other People's Houses* is both a terrific novel and an invaluable testament. I spent fruitful hours at the Center for Jewish History, and the memoirs and oral histories contained in its archives were indispensable.

Mark Jonathan Harris and Deborah Oppenheimer's vivid documentary, *Into the Arms of Strangers*, and its accompanying volume, opened my eyes to the *kindertransport* experience and was a crucial reference. I'd like to offer a special thank you to Lory Cahn; her memory of being pulled through the window and off the train has haunted me for years, and I'm grateful to her for sharing it, as I am to all those who told their stories.

ACKNOWLEDGMENTS

This book was many years in the making, and many people were instrumental along the way. Thank you to Al Filreis, Deborah Treisman, and Sarah Burnes for early encouragement. I'm especially grateful to Helen Schulman, who cheered me on from the start.

Thank you to Merrill Feitell, Halle Eaton, Jennifer Cody Epstein, Lizzie Simon, and Sarah Saffian, all of whom read early versions and were full of good advice and unstinting support. I owe an incalculable debt of gratitude to the talented and ever-inspiring Joanna Hershon, who read countless drafts and offered astute suggestions at every turn. Her faith, friendship, and wisdom kept me going; this book would simply not exist without her.

For ideas, advice, and support of all kinds, I'm grateful to David Boyer, Sam Zalutsky, Ed Boland, Sara Pekow, Karen Schwartz, Emily Nussbaum, Hana Schank, Lewis Kruger, Dorian Karchmar, Rebecca Gradinger, Yona McDonough, Cathy Halley, Cassie Mayer, and Ruth and Enrique Gutman. To the Millay Colony of the Arts, where I took the first steps in writing the novel, thank you. I'm lucky to have a coterie of literary-minded cousins, and I'm grateful to Sara Mark, Kate Axelrod, and Sam Axelrod for their suggestions and encouragement, and to Marian Thurm for leading the way. An enormous thank you to Jen Albano, who suggested the title.

I'm deeply indebted to my stellar agent, Lisa Grubka, for her enthusiasm, wise counsel, and unwavering commitment. Kate Nintzel shaped this book and had faith in its potential; I am hugely appreciative of her vision and sharp editorial eye.

To my family, I owe more than I can ever say: my excellent brothers, Eric Umansky and David Umansky; my wonderful parents, Michael Umansky and Sherry Weinman, and Gloria and Allan Spivak, all of whom believed in me from the beginning and unfailingly supported me throughout. I wish more than anything that my mother was here to read these words.

Lastly, especially, to my husband, David Gutman, who encouraged me throughout the long writing of this book, and whose intelligence, humor, and keen sense of character were a boon to this narrative, but more important, to my life. I am forever grateful for his love and partnership. He and our daughters, Lena and Talia, are my greatest pieces of luck and true fortune.

THE NIGHTMARE GARDEN

CAITLIN KITTREDGE

Delacorte Press

 Published in the United States by Delacorte Press, an imprint of Random House Children's Books, a division of Random House, Inc., New York.

Delacorte Press is a registered trademark and the colophon is a trademark of Random House, Inc.

Visit us on the Web! randomhouse.com/teens

Educators and librarians, for a variety of teaching tools, visit us at randomhouse.com/teachers

Library of Congress Cataloging-in-Publication Data
Kittredge, Caitlin.
The nightmare garden / Caitlin Kittredge. — 1st ed.
p. cm. — (The iron codex ; bk. 2)
Summary: "Aoife Grayson continues to discover hidden secrets about herself as she journeys to find the Nightmare Clock, fix the gates she's broken, and save her missing mother"—Provided by publisher.
ISBN 978-0-385-73831-6 (hardback)—ISBN 978-0-385-90721-7 (glb)—
ISBN 978-0-375-98569-0 (ebook) [1. Magic—Fiction. 2. Fantasy.] I. Title.
PZ7.K67163Nig 2012
[Fic]—dc23
2011038306

The text of this book is set in 11.5-point Berling.
Book design by Trish Parcell

Printed in the United States of America
10 9 8 7 6 5 4 3 2 1
First Edition

Random House Children's Books
supports the First Amendment and celebrates the right to read.

Man rules now where They ruled once;
They shall soon rule where man rules now.
After summer is winter, and after winter summer.
They wait patient and potent,
for here shall They reign again.

—H. P. LOVECRAFT, "The Dunwich Horror"

Innsmouth
N
W
E
S
Smuggler sub
landing

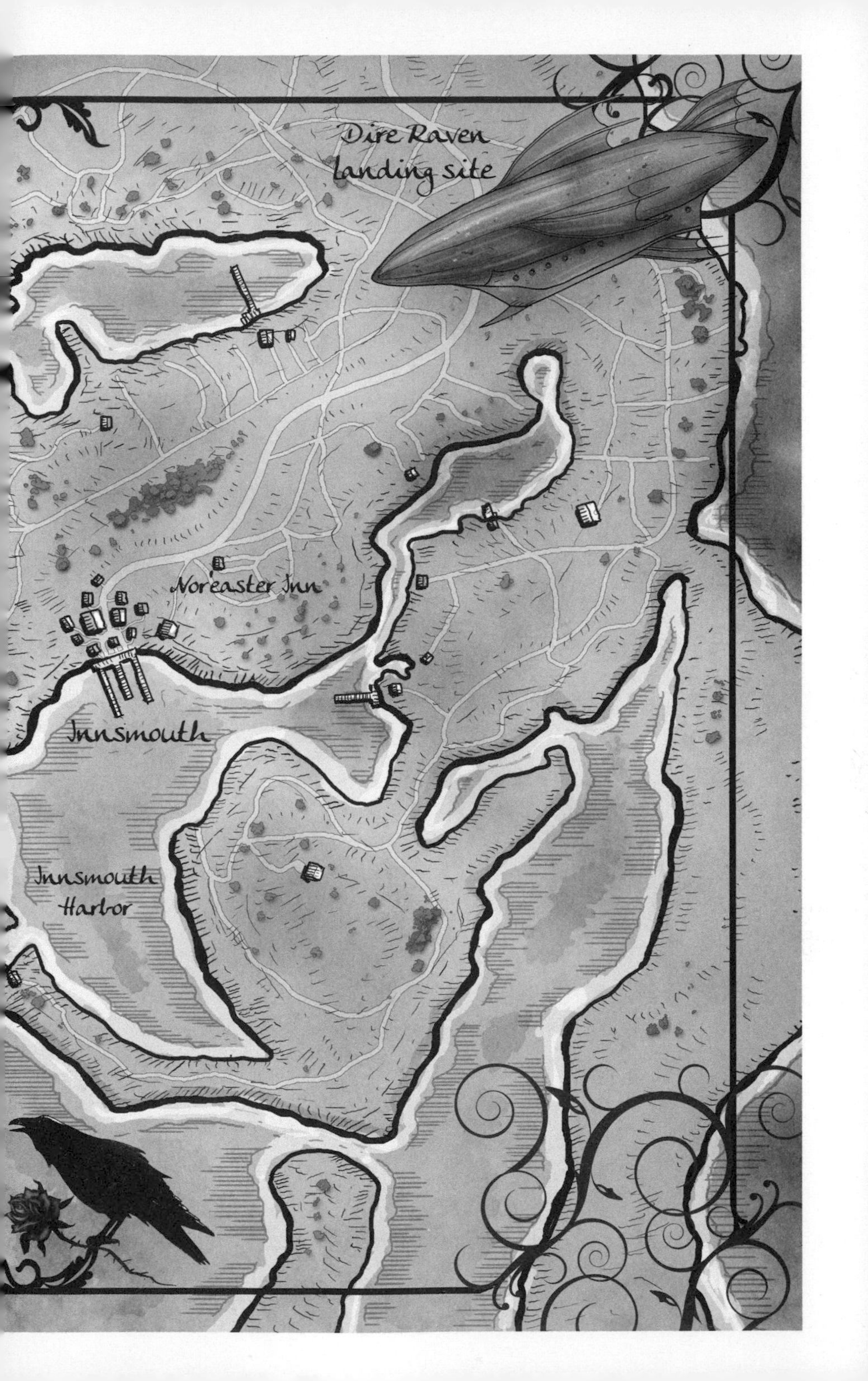
Dire Raven
landing site
Nor'easter Inn
Innsmouth
Innsmouth
Harbor

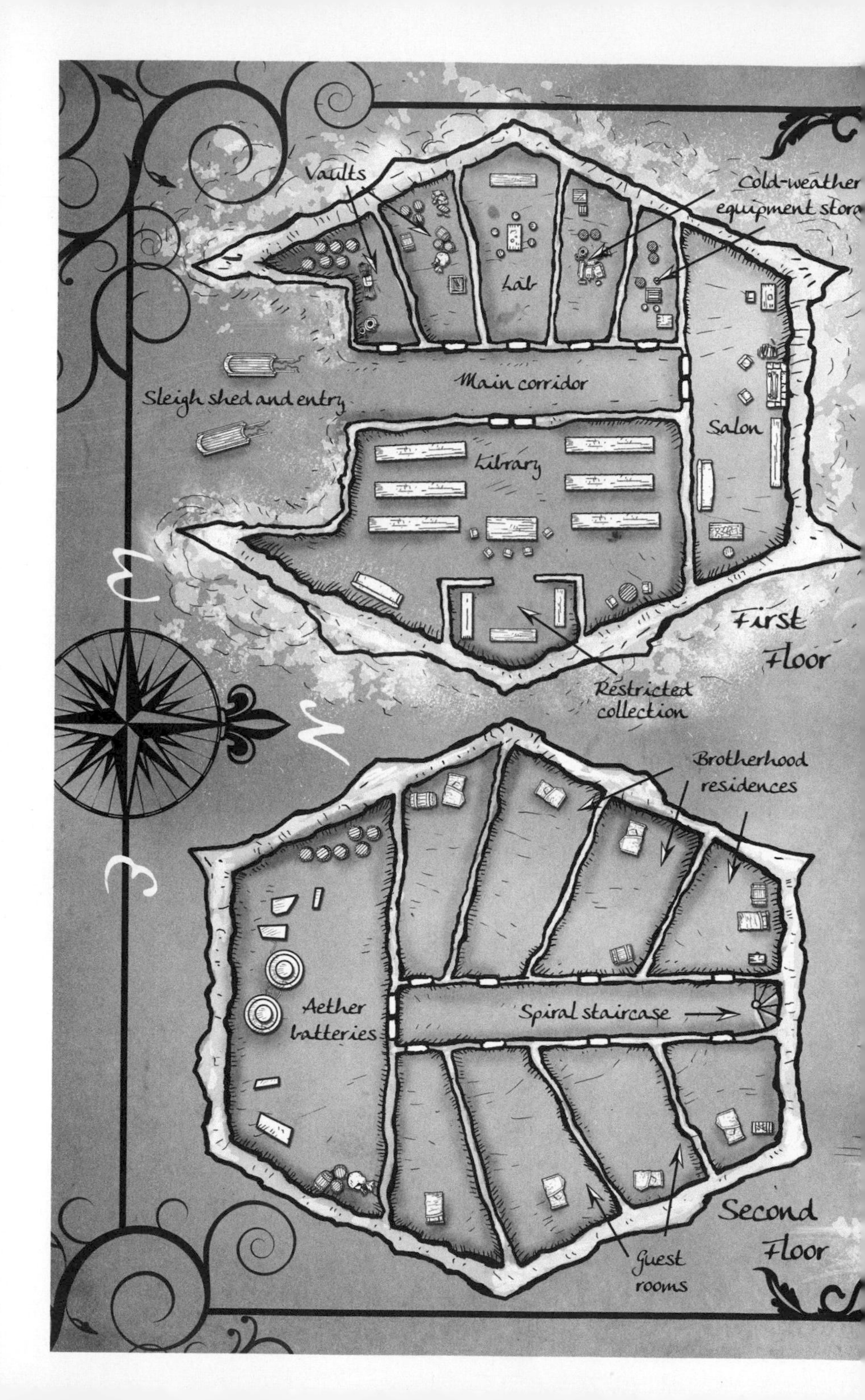
Vaults
Cold-weather equipment stora
Lab
Main corridor
Sleigh shed and entry
Salon
Library
First Floor
Restricted collection
Brotherhood residences
Aether batteries
Spiral staircase
Second Floor
Guest rooms

Closed-off lab
Broken staircase
Aether conductor
Telescope / observation deck
Third Floor
The Bone Sepulchre

The Dark City

IN MY DREAM, I am alone.

The spires of a ruined city reach for gunmetal clouds, the horizon a wound in the belly of the sky.

Acrid chemical smoke burns the insides of my nostrils, and all around, sirens wail, banshees made of iron, steel and steam.

A road stretches out before me, and I must walk. Walk toward the dead city, under the red sky stained with the black taint of fire and smoke.

Something breaks under my boot, and I know before I look down what I'll see.

Bones. Human skulls, femurs, ribs. The bones of other things as well, things that starved once the humans rotted away. Twisted spines, elongated jaws. Teeth.

I am alone. Alone except for the sirens, alone except for the burning, empty city on the edge of a rotting, polluted river green with algae, host to rubber-skinned, gibbous-eyed things with mouths large enough to swallow me whole and protruding stomachs ready to digest me.

Not even a ghoul remains to send up a howl. The city is dead. *My* city is dead.

My mother was in that city.

My mother is dead.

I am alone.

And I know that this city, this disaster, this spreading disease of flame and death, is all my fault.

I woke up with my head pounding and the rest of my body fever-hot. My thin blouse stuck to my skin, while the frozen air that swirled through the broken walls of the farmhouse raised steam off my bare legs. The Mists, this place where I'd found myself, so far from my home, was unforgiving in every way, including the predawn temperature.

Kicking back the blankets from the half-rotted mattress, I pulled on my coat and shoes and stepped through the door. It was held in place by only one hinge, which let out a rusty shriek. I froze, but no one sleeping inside stirred.

We were all tired. Tired to the bone.

Outside, unfamiliar stars stared down impassively from a crumpled velvet sky. The horizon was silver now, not red like the sky of my dream, and I felt the pounding of my pulse and the sickness of the nightmare subside.

"Couldn't sleep?"

"I had a bad dream," I said to Dean. He leaned against the clay wall, a Lucky Strike jammed between his lips, his hair falling in his face.

Dean blew out a blue cloud that blended with the sky.

"I'd offer you one, but it's my last pack. Somehow I doubt there'll be a filling station around the next bend in the road."

"I don't think so," I said quietly. I went and leaned against the wall next to him. I was shivering, and my stomach snarled at me. We hadn't exactly been eating regularly since we'd run away from Lovecraft. Away from everything.

From what I'd done, and from the city that poisoned me with its very existence. As long as I avoided the Iron Land, I could stave off the madness the world of men injected into my blood. I'd managed to escape the fate shared by my mother and brother—a descent into madness that took hold of every member of our family when we turned sixteen—but I'd be safe only as long as I stayed away from the one place I'd ever thought of as home. If I went back, the clock would begin ticking again. I'd had less than a week when I left. Every minute I spent there shortened the span of my sanity.

But how long could I stay away? How long until the people who wanted me to pay for what I'd done in Lovecraft caught up and hauled me back there? Once they did, I'd be gone. I'd be as crazy as my mother, poisoned by the city.

If my mother was still alive.

I couldn't think through this circle of frantic worry anymore. It was practically all I'd thought about since the night I'd run away with Dean, my friends Cal and Bethina and my brother, Conrad. No matter how I tried, I couldn't silence the voice: *Eventually, they'll take you back there.*

Dean dropped his cigarette butt and stomped on it, then collected the filter and tucked it away. He was adept at moving through a place and leaving no trace. Dean was a lot of things.

His arm went around me and pulled me close. "It's gonna be all right, Aoife. We're gonna get out the other side of this, somehow."

Sixteen years of listening to how I should act like a proper lady tugged at me—I should have told him to take his arm off me, but I moved closer instead. Dean smelled like Dean, like tobacco and old leather and that boy smell of sweat and hair grease. He was practically the only familiar thing in this place, and I was clinging to him with all my might. "You can't possibly know that," I mumbled into his jacket, sliding my arms inside and feeling the warmth of his skin and his body.

"No," Dean agreed. "But men are supposed to say things like that to the womenfolk. Right?"

"I wouldn't know," I said. "I'm not very good at being *womenfolk*."

"I promise, then," Dean said. "From me to you: nothing is going to happen to you while I'm around." He pressed his face against my hair, stirring up the already unruly nest of crow's-feather black atop my head. All the Graysons had black hair and gray eyes; even my mother's fair hair and complexion hadn't changed that.

My mother, whom I'd abandoned in Lovecraft. When I'd left Lovecraft in shambles, burning and destroyed because of what I'd done to its Engine, the heart that drove the city, I'd promised to come back for her. That was before I'd realized the scale of what had happened. Rip out the heart of something and it will die. I'd been a fool, and I'd listened to the wrong whispers, and now my mother could be dead and Lovecraft was a wasteland.

“Dean, what am I going to do?” I whispered. “I can’t go back there.”

He sighed. “Princess, I haven’t the faintest idea what’s coming next. But you’ll think of something. You always do.” He planted a kiss on my hairline and straightened. “You’re the brains of this operation, remember?”

The sun was almost up, and the silver line was turning blue and gold. Sunrises were different here in the Mists, the unknowable land between lands, the thin place where things that didn’t like the light hid. The sun never shone, not really. It was a dull silver flame rather than a fireball. Just another strange piece of this strange land we’d all fallen into.

I could admit it, alone with Dean.

I was lost, and I had no idea how to find my way home. And now, I didn’t even know where home might lie.

2

In the Mists

BEFORE THE OTHERS woke and after Dean had gone to check that the road was clear, I got my battered composition book out of my bag and opened it on my knees. The book was half full of my engineering homework. It was from my other life, from when I was a schoolgirl who thought that magic was a lie and that a virus was responsible for things like inhuman creatures and uncanny abilities, ghosts and prophetic dreams.

That girl was gone. The Aoife writing was a new girl, one who'd discovered that the necrovirus was a hoax perpetrated by men who sought the magic for themselves. Who were hunting me, even now. The old Aoife wanted to panic, felt the tightening in her chest even now, watched ink dribble from her pen as her hand started to shake. How was I ever going to stop being a fugitive, knowing what I knew?

But the new Aoife didn't have the luxury of curling up in a ball and pretending the outside world didn't exist. She had to learn how to be strong and unbending, how to evade the men chasing her and the disease that was eating her mind away from within. Had to, because she had no other choice.

I wrote it all down. I had to write. It was my duty now, because the person who should have been writing this account, my father, was long gone and my brother wasn't interested. I was the last Grayson still able to record her strange life, as all Graysons before me had. Still, I felt like a fraud the moment I put pen to paper.

First entry:

My name is Aoife Grayson, and I am the last person who should be writing this account, but know I am the only one left who can.

Others like me and my family, the Gateminders, who watch the thin spots known as Gates between the Iron Land, the Mists and the land of Thorn, have the confidence of those who have come before. They know how to navigate the Gates, how each different type works, from the Fae hexenring *to the mechanical marvels of the Erlkin. I know nothing.*

I have nothing. I am the Gateminder by default, due, I believe, to chaos and chance. It sometimes feels like I'm being punished for uncovering the hoax of the necrovirus, as my father did. For daring to question the Proctors, the order of things. Gateminders before us labored in secret, but at least the rest of the world was not actively encouraged to believe they deserved death.

The Proctors told us that the strange creatures, my family's madness, everything in the world that could not be explained by science and reason, was a virus. A powerful virus with no origin and no cure. They never hinted that its origin was inhuman and that the cure was to embrace my Faerie blood, the inhuman, immortal side of me, and to stay far away from iron.

At the time, all I saw was that my mother was one of the mad, that my brother was a fugitive and that I was about to follow in their footsteps and go mad. I would be locked up, another victim of the "virus."

It was all a lie. I was trapped in the stone and iron of Lovecraft, trapped by my own mind and by the lie I believed. And now Lovecraft lies ruined. Ruined because I was stupid.

I scratched out that word, stupid, *so many times, writing this. But it's the right word. I believed the Fae creature Tremaine when he came from Thorn and told me I was the heroine who would free the Fae from bondage, curing my iron madness in the process. He set me up, and I fell, harder than I ever could have imagined.*

I should have listened to the words my father left behind, in his own diary: as a Gateminder, you should trust only yourself. Only you stand between the Iron Land of men and what lies beyond. And in that role, you have only your own mind to rely on, your own wit and intellect.

I should have listened to Dean, too. He said it—you can't trust the Fae. They lie. And Tremaine did lie to me. I destroyed the Lovecraft Engine, in a great cataclysm of magic. I broke down the barriers my father and his Brotherhood of Iron were so careful to construct, over hundreds of years, before the lie of the necrovirus. Barriers the evil things of Thorn had never broken.

I left my mother in Lovecraft.

I can forgive myself, possibly, for being the gullible little girl Tremaine thought I was, but I can never forgive myself for abandoning my mother.

The only way I can sleep at night is by promising myself that I am going to find her and help her escape the city and the iron madness, as I have escaped it, at least temporarily. Conrad, my brother, said that as long as we stay out of the cities, and out of the Iron Land entirely, with its train tracks, iron pipes, steel conveyances, we might stave off madness. In his case, spending months away from the Iron Land meant total remission. In my case, the progress has slowed; I avoided the full psychotic break that usually occurs around age sixteen, and suffer only the occasional headache, visual disturbance out of the corner of my eye and bad dream.

But nothing I'm doing now seems any saner than the dreams I started having weeks ago, before my birthday and the inevitable onset of madness. The dreams are the first sign of acute and chronic iron poisoning, the warning bell. Though I'm still reasonably sane because I fled, the dreams haven't stopped. I don't know now if they come from madness or from another source. From something worse.

I do know we're running, me and Conrad and Dean, Cal and Bethina, too. It seems like there's no one we aren't running from. The Proctors and Grey

Draven, who has some bizarre notion I'll lead him to my father, his true target.

The Fae, who did not exact their full price from me after I woke their sleeping queens and ripped the thin, thin barrier between our worlds. Tremaine has more for me to do. He said as much. Opening the Gates between Thorn and Iron was only the beginning.

It was like knocking aside a spiderweb. How could breaking something so huge feel like less than nothing?

These things I do have: My brother. Dean and my friendship with Cal, and I suppose with Bethina, too—she was loyal to my father before I came along, even though she's only human and the law dictates she should have turned me in. But Bethina is steadfast, and stubborn to a fault; plus, it's good to have another girl along.

Things I don't have: A plan to hold off the iron madness and keep ahead of the Proctors and Grey Draven. A way to get to Lovecraft. Anything to go home to if I can get to the city, because the Lovecraft Academy sure isn't my home any longer. I don't know what is.

I meant what I said—I'm the last person who should have taken over my father's burden, recording my life for the next Gateminder. Yet I continue to write in the books that the Brotherhood calls witches' alphabets, grimoires of power and experience that are supposed to help me along, to keep me safe.

Fat lot of good my father's records did me. And he's not here, even though I've never needed him more and his absence makes me want to sob or scream.

The one thing he asked of me was to be strong, willful and resolute, and I couldn't do it.

All I can truthfully say now is that my name is Aoife Grayson, and I have my freedom, and my sanity. I could at least temporarily cure my mother, if I could take her from the Iron Land and the poison that's clouding her mind.

But I don't know how much longer she'll survive in ruined Lovecraft. And if I go back to the iron, I don't know how much longer I'll have, either.

After the days of walking, of little food and less sleep, of cold and wet and none of the comforts of the human world—like, say, beds, bathrooms and hot food—the Mists had lost their charm.

The Mists weren't exactly the world as humans understood it. Humans saw a single world with no others sitting beside it. Really, the Iron Land sat beside all the others like marbles in a sack. But at least the Mists weren't Thorn, home of the Fae. We'd run here from my father's house, Graystone, in Arkham, in a desperate bid to escape both the Proctors and my iron madness. The Mists were where the tides of reality ebbed and flowed, and the edges of other places knit and then split apart like wounded skin held by poorly stitched thread.

Austere and alien as the Mists were, though, they were largely devoid of iron, and that was important. Iron made me sick, made me see things. This endless windswept wilderness at least wouldn't drive me insane, according to Conrad. If Conrad was sane. He certainly hadn't appeared that way the last time we'd met, when he'd shown up and dragged me here with little preamble. That was the extent of his plan—the part he'd shared with me, anyway. Asking him questions just got silence or grumbling.

Really, I had only his word that he even *had* a plan other than hiding in the Mists for the rest of our lives, and I hadn't been able to trust the word of anyone in my family in years.

And despite the lack of iron, I was still dreaming.

I'd fallen to the back of the group, my steps leaden and my thoughts heavier, and Dean slowed down to let me catch up.

"You all right?" He nudged my hand with the back of his and then wound our fingers together.

"No," I said. "I'm hungry and I feel like my feet are going to fall off." I'd taken sturdy boots from Graystone, but they were mud-spattered now, and one of the heels was starting to come away. My legs felt like logs, and my mind was fuzzy from lack of sleep. I'd felt this way before, during finals at the Academy, when I'd slept maybe two hours a night and crammed my brain so full I thought it would burst, but I'd never had to trek through a swamp on top of that. More than anything I wanted to shut my eyes and lie down in a patch of soft moss.

"I could use a break myself," Dean said. "Hey, Connie!"

Dean had taken to calling my brother Connie, and I could see from the twitch of Conrad's shoulders how much he hated it.

"Yes, Dean?" He turned his head slightly, but he didn't slow his pace.

"Looks like the group's voted for a sit-down," Dean called.

Conrad turned fully to face us but continued walking.

He'd always been quicksilver graceful, my brother, in a way I'd never been and never would be. It just wasn't in me. I tried not to let it bother me as my holey boot filled up with water when I misstepped and put my foot in a soft patch of moss and muddy water. Back in Lovecraft, Conrad was the handsome one, the smart one, and I was, well, the shy, plain younger sister who was never quite as good at anything. Even according to the lore of the Gateminders, he was first in line, being the eldest son of the current Gateminder. I was just the girl. The second choice. The replacement, if neither my father nor Conrad could perform the duties, after all this was said and done—despite my being able to pass between Thorn and Iron, my being able to communicate with the Fae when Conrad had never even seen them. Still just the girl. It stung, and just once, I wanted him to figuratively fall on his face.

"I don't care what the group wants," Conrad said to Dean. "We stop when I say we stop, and we need to get through these woods before nightfall. You don't know the Mists, Dean, despite what you are. You've spent your entire life in the Iron Land. I've spent almost a year here. The Mists aren't Thorn or Iron—they're treacherous, and I don't want to get caught in an ambush because my baby sister's feet hurt, so why don't you two toughen up and accept that I know what I'm talking about?"

Dean snarled under his breath. To look at him, you'd never know he was only half human, but he was, and his other, Erlkin half had a bad temper when it was crossed. Conrad was like me, human blood poisoned with a drop of Fae. More than poisoned—saturated. But at least we weren't like our mother, struck mad simply by virtue of living in the Iron Land, as all full-blood Fae like her would eventually be. Conrad and I, with our human father, were hopefully all right as long as we steered clear of iron. More than that, though, Conrad thrived and never seemed bothered by much. With his charm and force of will, Conrad could say anything and make it so. It merely annoyed me, but it made Dean furious, and to head off the fight that had been brewing for days, as the fog got thicker, the ground wetter and the food scarcer, I dropped Dean's hand and jogged to catch up with my brother.

"We're all tired," I told him. "If you keep up this pace we're just going to stop following you. We can't run from the Proctors and the Fae if we're dead of exhaustion." My brother listened to me very rarely; I hoped this would be one of those times.

Conrad's jaw twitched, and my hopes fell. "It's not your call, Aoife," he snapped.

"You're right," I agreed, through gritted teeth to avoid outright angry shouting. "It wasn't my call to leave Lovecraft looking for you, it wasn't my call to run here when the Proctors came for us. But I followed you, Conrad. I've done what you said without complaining for almost a week, and now I'm telling you I'm tired. You can walk." I stopped and plopped down on a mossy stump. "I'm not going another step."

The old Aoife would never have dreamed of disagreeing with anyone, but this new Aoife had no such compunctions. Her feet hurt, and I was glad she'd spoken up. She didn't even care that Conrad was puffing up his chest, getting ready to chastise her like the father we'd never had. We stared at each other while the throaty call of a crow echoed from a nearby thicket. I wasn't going to be the one to look away. I'd been glad of Conrad's protection in our care-homes and at the Academy, but since he'd left, I'd realized I didn't need him. He needed to see it now too. He was my brother, and I loved him, but the closeness of our old relationship had blown away with the ash from the ruined Lovecraft Engine.

"Well?" I said at last. Dean, Cal and Bethina, who'd been a chambermaid in my father's house before a few days ago, stopped and clustered around me. Conrad had elected himself group leader, but so far they'd stuck with me. Not that I knew where we were going, or where we were going to stay when it got dark again. These were ancient forests, night forests, and who knew what was lurking in the shadows? In Lovecraft, things like nightjars, shape-shifting blood drinkers and springheel jacks, terrifying long-toothed predators, ruled the night along with the ghouls. And those were just the creatures who'd managed to slip through from Thorn and other places. Here in the Mists, this native land of theirs so far from Iron, if they caught us we'd be so much lunch meat. I felt a small, traitorous prick of pride at that and tried not to show it on my face. I'd managed to get us as far as the Mists. I tried to believe I could see us through to wherever we ended up, but I wasn't very convincing, even inside my own head. Conrad *did* know the Mists, and I had no idea how to even find my way out of this wood.

Conrad folded his arms. "Aoife, you're being a child."

"I left her there, Conrad," I said quietly, voicing what had been bothering me since the morning dream. "I left her to whatever might happen."

Conrad sighed, shifting his feet. "Listen, when we get

somewhere safe we can talk about this. Right now, we're exposed and we need to keep moving." He started walking again, until my words distracted him and he tripped.

"She's *our mother*."

My brother turned back to me, and his face was colder than I'd ever seen it. "Nerissa hasn't been a mother to me for ten years, Aoife. To you either. She left us to the mercy of people who'd just as soon burn us alive, or cut us open and study us. She didn't even try to keep us from that when she knew she couldn't take care of us. Some kind of *mother* to do that."

"I said I wouldn't leave her there," I told him. I'd promised her. No matter what she'd done, I'd promised that I'd keep her safe because she couldn't do it for herself. That was what you did, when you had a mother, and I hadn't managed to do anything except put her in more danger. Guilt made my stomach roil. "This is my fault," I said, "all of it, but most of all Nerissa, and I have to—"

"Dammit, Aoife!" Conrad bellowed. The crows took flight in a ripple of glossy black against the silver sky. "Going back to the Iron Land and risking your neck won't change what happened! You're going to have to accept that so we can all stay alive."

I wished he'd just slapped me. The hole that opened in me at his words was a hundred times more painful than any blow would have been. Because I knew he was right. My guilt was like a chain around my ankle, attached to a weight the size of my mother. If I couldn't put the thoughts out of my mind until we'd reached safety, I'd drag them with me. But I didn't know how. I swiped at my eyes, telling myself my face was damp only with cool fog, not hot tears.

"All right, now," Dean said. "I think we've established neither of you is giving up this ghost, so why don't we agree to disagree?" He helped me off the stump and put his arm around me. "And Conrad—how about shutting your big trap and not making your sister cry before I knock your teeth in?"

Conrad blinked once. "What did you just say to me?"

"Hey!" I clapped my hands. Boys could be like unruly dogs. Where was a bucket of water when I needed one? "I'll keep going," I told Conrad quietly. "But I'm not going to forget about this. I *am* going to get her back."

"I'm not saying forget it," he said. "Just focus on staying safe until our father comes back and can help us settle things."

He started walking again, his stiff-shouldered posture evidence that he was dismissing Dean and me—and the straggling Cal and Bethina—so I spoke my last thought to his back: "You know, Archie coming back and saving the day is about as likely as a snowball surviving the heart of the Engine." It was harsh, but it was true. Conrad was the only one who refused to see that.

Second entry:

What can I say about my father? I knew him as only a story for the first fourteen years of my life, a figure both larger and smaller than any real father could hope to be.

I know that he stayed just long enough to watch Conrad take his first steps and see me born before he returned to the city of Arkham, to Graystone, his family home, and then had nothing more to do with us.

Nerissa never mentioned it, but I knew they weren't married, and that a family like the Graysons didn't need bastards running around. It made me angry, made me feel small and worthless, like a trinket rather than somebody's child. Usually I pretended I didn't have a father at all.

I only saw him once: when the Proctors scooped me up and Grey Draven told me the truth about the necrovirus, that it was a lie and that he planned to use me to lure in the insurgents my father was running with. My father showed up and helped me get out of Ravenhouse, the bastion of the Proctors in Lovecraft, and run to Arkham, back to my brother and into the Mists.

We spoke maybe ten words to each other.

So you can see why I don't have a lot of faith in Archibald Grayson showing up and saving the day, even though Conrad thinks he'll solve everything. People relied on the Proctors to solve everything too—to keep them safe from the necrovirus—and look what happened. The world is going to burn. Maybe not all at once, but what happened in Lovecraft is surely worldwide news by now, and who knows what's already crossed over from the Thorn Land to make a picnic of the human race? I can't even think about it without feeling like I want to cry, scream, or simply lie down, let the guilt eat me alive and give up.

I don't know if our father is coming back. I don't know if he'll help us if he does.

I don't know anything except that Conrad's wrong about me, and about our mother when he says that she's a lost cause, and that if I want to survive, I have to cast my lot with a father I barely know. If I can go back, if I can at least make sure she's alive and see what condition the city is in from what I did—if it still exists at all—then I'll know.

I'll know exactly what I did and what the damage was, the number of deaths and exactly how many tons of guilt should press on me. I'll know if there's anything I can do to make it right, because the plain fact is, innocent people shouldn't pay for my stupidity. That, nobody had to teach me. That's just the truth.

And maybe if I know what happened, I can stop dreaming about it.

I'd stopped keeping track of how many miles we'd walked days ago, but not of the day. My birthday had come and gone, and so far, I still had my mind. But I wasn't cured. Periodically I felt the scratches and whispers of the madness, and I waited for the iron poison to awaken it fully in my blood and plunge me down an endless hole of insanity.

The road disappeared for a time, and we relied on the dim sun to navigate until it came into view again. Well, Conrad did. The rest of us were so tired we mostly just trudged. Cal had barely spoken since we'd come through from Arkham to the Mists, and finally, when I looked back and saw him stumble, I dropped back to walk with him.

"How are you holding up?"

Cal grunted. He was a head taller than me, and I watched his knobby Adam's apple bob up and down.

Of all of us, Cal was the least what he appeared to be. I

should have been afraid of him—after all, the Proctors had filled my mind for years with warnings about the ghouls that lived in the old sewer tunnels below the streets and surged up to hunt when the moon was full.

But they'd also told me my mother was crazy and had to be locked away, and that a bloodborne virus was responsible for my abilities and my madness dreams, so there you were. Cal might have been a monster before he'd come to the Academy, a ghoul who'd hunted people like me, but he'd stuck by me when everything went wrong. Draven had sent him to spy on me, threatened to burn Cal's family alive if he rebelled, and Cal had still helped me get out of Lovecraft. Cal was loyal. I trusted him a lot more than Conrad at that moment.

Which made me feel lousy, like I was betraying my own blood in favor of someone who wasn't even human, but the fact remained that Cal had been there for me when Conrad hadn't. And he didn't have potential madness lurking in the dark corners of his mind, ready to spring forward and sink its teeth in the moment he got too close to the Iron Land. I loved Conrad, but I'd never forget that in his worst moment, he'd hurt me, and hadn't hesitated to do it. I had a scar to ensure I'd never forget.

"Cal?" I said when he didn't answer me.

"How do you think I'm holding up, Aoife?" he snapped, thin face growing a deep frown. "Being in this place isn't going to get us into any less trouble, and it just might get us into more."

Regardless of the shape he took, Cal had a nearly endless capacity for worrywarting. I was just glad he'd decided to keep his human shape for the time being, though that was a credit more to Bethina than to me. Cal was sweet on her, and she thought he was a regular boy. I just hoped she wouldn't try to light him on fire when she figured out the truth. Bethina was bubbly and sometimes flighty, but she wasn't stupid, and eventually all the strange bits of Cal's personality would fall into place for her.

I'd decided at the outset that I'd cross that bridge when we came to it. Besides, how was I supposed to pull her aside and tell her the nice boy with the city manners was actually a flesh-eating beast? *That* was a conversation I couldn't even fathom how to start. It would come up one way or another—Cal wasn't always good at hiding his true nature. None of us were, I guessed. Dean snarled when he was angry, and I got blinding headaches when I was too close to iron. Conrad was the only one among us who could appear effortlessly human, and I was really starting to resent him for it. He'd been out of the Iron Land long enough that his madness had largely receded. I hoped it would be the same for me, but sooner or later, I'd have to go back, and if he went with me we'd both be in trouble.

"Fine," I grumbled.

"If you say so," Cal said, and I could tell I'd played on his last nerve. He could tell I was wishing I could just leave the lot of them, aside from Dean, in the woods and go home.

Not even that. I wished I could wind time backward until none of this had ever occurred. And if I could live that time over again, I would ignore what was happening to me, go on being a good student, a good girl, good little Aoife Grayson, who adored her brother because he was the strong one, the charming one who could do no wrong. He was a brother she could trust, implicitly. A brother who'd never hurt her.

But then I'd also be insane from the iron of Lovecraft, locked up with my mother, and who knew what would have happened to Conrad. I could never have that little girl's imaginary version of my brother back, and I was just going to have to live with it. If I'd done it sooner, I might not have been so easily swayed by Tremaine, or so quick to dismiss my mother's ramblings. If I'd been more willing to accept reality, my mother would be safe and alive, instead of alone in a city overrun with creatures of Thorn.

If she'd survived. I didn't let myself think that my mother might be dead too often, because the very idea was a physical pang in my chest. Nerissa had managed to survive for seven years in the worst madhouses in Lovecraft. She couldn't be dead. I kept repeating that, with all the dedication of a fanatic. My mother couldn't be dead. She had to be waiting for me when I went back.

I became aware that Cal's skinny shadow no longer loped next to me, and I turned back. Cal was frozen, quivering, his nostrils flared and his chest vibrating like a plucked string.

"Cal?" I said with soft alarm, motioning to the others to stop.

His lips drew back from teeth that razored out of human gums, leaving thin red trails of blood and spittle on his lips. They disappeared just as quickly, when Bethina turned toward him, but the wire-tight tension didn't leave his skinny frame. "Someone else is here."

Dean cut his eyes toward the brush and back to me. "Get off the road."

"What's going on?" Bethina called tremulously from behind Cal.

"Get off the road *now*!" Dean bellowed, and grabbed me by the arm, dragging me into the brush. I gasped in pain as thorns snagged my sweater, rending skin and finding blood beneath.

I saw Cal, Conrad and Bethina go into the ditch on the other side of the path as Dean pulled me down. Mud soaked into my stockings and through the holes in my boots, and freezing water numbed me.

"What—" I started, but Dean pressed his finger against my lips.

A second later, I felt something unfurl in my mind, like a flower opening under the light of the moon. It prickled across my forehead, over my scalp and down my spine, fingers of feeling scraping across my every nerve.

Please, I thought as panic pressed on my chest, slowing my breath to almost nothing, *not here. Not now.* I knew the sensation bubbling up from the recesses of my brain, knew it the same way I knew my own heartbeat. My blood was reacting to iron, iron that whoever Cal had scented carried, iron worked into an unseen machine. And with the machinery came something else: the power that my father, in his journal, had called a Weird. And on the heels of the Weird, because machines and iron were inexorably intertwined, the madness would bloom.

My Weird had been quiet since we'd been walking through the Mists, but not now. Now it was pushing against the inside of my skull, threatening to crack it. I pressed a palm against my forehead and dug the heel in, willing myself to stay quiet as my thoughts went wild, clamoring for me to scream and let my Weird free. Behind them was something blacker, something that crawled and giggled as it picked at the scars on my psyche. *Let me in, Aoife. Let me show you. . . .*

I saw a sharp stone protruding from the embankment, and I ran my hand against it, dragging it down my palm. Blood dribbled down my wrist and the sharp, clear prick of pain pushed the whispers back. When all else failed, physical hurt would quiet the voices in my head. For now, anyway.

The Weird still pressed on my skull, and I pushed harder against the stone, focusing only on the pain.

On the road, the trees parted ahead of us and disgorged two tall, thin figures. They weren't Fae—I could tell that much from their lack of silver eyes and pointed teeth—but they weren't human, either. They moved too smoothly for that, like the fog all around us glided between the trees, and their forms were too slim and angular.

The Erlkin had found us. The people of the Mists, the other half of Dean's bloodline, had found the intruders in their domain and were coming to exterminate us. At best. At worst, they were Erlkin working for Grey Draven, and we were about to be shackled and taken back to Lovecraft. I pressed my forehead down into the dirt. That couldn't happen. It would be the end of even a faint hope that I could remain free and sane.

Dean squeezed my arm, each finger carving a groove that would leave purple marks behind. He was telling me to stay quiet. Stay still. Not to give us away.

I wasn't the one, as it turned out, who screwed up—a

splash came from the ditch on the other side of the path and I knew it could only be Cal.

"Oh, iron *damn* this day!" I hissed, breaking free of Dean's grasp, trying to reach Cal before the Erlkin did . . . something. I'd use my Weird, keep them from taking us, keep us free of imprisonment for one more day. Honestly, I didn't know what I was going to do. The new Aoife moved without thinking, summoning the scream of the Weird into the front of her mind.

Conrad erupted from his side of the ditch before I could fully leap from my hiding spot, entrapped my arms and took me to ground, my knees crashing into the gravel with sharp, hot blossoms of pain as he smothered me.

The Erlkin shouted at us in a guttural language I didn't understand, but I knew when someone was yelling at me not to move. And Conrad was muttering to me as the ground shook with their approaching footsteps, a single word over and over.

"Stupid, stupid, stupid. So stupid, Aoife."

"We know there are more of you skulking in there!" the Erlkin shouted in English. "Show your faces!"

"I'm going to let you up and we're going to run, all right?" Conrad whispered into my hair. "Fast as you can. Just run. The others will be all right—the Erlkin don't want them, just us."

I struggled, trying to get out from under his weight. "Get off me, Conrad!" I hissed. "You're not making this any better."

"Show yourselves," the Erlkin ordered. "Or we open fire into the bushes and drag your bodies back to the dirigible!"

"Wait!" Conrad shouted, raising his head. "We aren't Fae spies. We're just traveling through. There's no need for all this, I promise you."

I heard the lock and snap of a weapon, and my Weird pounded against my skull at the proximity of a complex machine, a machine it wanted to bend and twist to its will. *My* will. But that couldn't happen. The Erlkin couldn't know about my ability, so I held it back, until I thought I'd burst. I threw Conrad's arms off me, feeling as if I'd suffocate if he touched me for another second.

"I'm Conrad Grayson," Conrad announced. He stood above me now, hands out to the side, the long, clever fingers we shared splayed in deference to show his empty palms. "I've been here before, and I've always been a friend to the Erlkin, just like my father, Archibald Grayson. Maybe you've heard of him?"

To my right, Bethina and Cal climbed slowly from the ditch they'd thrown themselves into, Bethina clutching Cal's arm. He was doing an all-right job of not losing his form, but it wasn't good enough. I could see long teeth, and yellow eyes, and claws. I jerked my chin at him and he swallowed his ghoul face, features rippling until he was human again.

Now that we'd been caught, all I could think about was how we could convince the Erlkin we weren't a threat. I wasn't leaving Dean and Cal and Bethina, that much was certain. Conrad could run if he wanted to. I'd already left enough people behind.

"You," the Erlkin said to Conrad. "Oh, we know all about *you*, Conrad Grayson."

I took the chance to examine the Erlkin while he was

focused on my brother and his big mouth. He was tall, thin, with hollow cheeks and stringy black hair pulled back with a leather thong at his neck. He looked like a human who'd been dead a few days, whose skin, tinged blue, had begun to tighten. In another life, when I'd been a student, some of us freshmen had been dared to go into the anatomy room in the School of Hospice. The cadaver on the table, dead of a ghoul attack, had looked much the same.

The thing he held in his hands was about the size of a crossbow but had a bulbous end, a glass ball that enclosed a coil of copper piping running back to a bulky gearbox near a trigger. Putting together what I'd learned at the Academy, I guessed it was a stun gun, with a windup static charge.

"You think you can hire slipstreamers to smuggle you back and forth across our borders any time you please?" the lead Erlkin snarled. "You think we don't know every time your sack of meat walks through the Mists? We're not stupid, human, nor are we savages. We see you. We know that someone breached the Gates, and we know that our borders aren't safe. You're not welcome here, by any true citizen of the Mists who's not just out to take your money and leave you to die in a swamp."

I looked up at Conrad in alarm. I'd thought the Erlkin who'd helped us escape Graystone, our father's house, had been, at the very least, not criminals. Honestly, I'd hoped they'd been in some kind of authority, that Conrad had used his charm to sway the Erlkin to his cause, but I saw now that I was wrong. Slipstreamers, Dean had said, were Erlkin who used the Gates on the sly, for illicit purposes, caring nothing for what might happen if they misused the Gates or allowed something unwanted to come through along with them. It was horribly dangerous—slipstreamers didn't really know what they were doing, and often as not, their charges disappeared into a void.

In short, I thought we'd been invited to the Mists. But knowing Conrad as I did, I should have guessed he'd done something underhanded. I could have strangled him in that moment, and I doubted Dean or Cal or Bethina would have stopped me, judging from the looks on their faces.

"Listen," Conrad said, making a smoothing motion in the air between the Erlkin and himself. "I'm sure we can work this out."

"You're a wanted man," the Erlkin snarled. "And the rest of you are trespassers. Every time you cross from the Iron Land or anywhere else to the Mists, you raise the chance of the Fae finding a way in and crossing over with you. This may be an in-between place, but it's *our* place. And we don't want you. Breaching borders without permission of the Erlkin is a grave offense." He moved his leather-clad finger to the trigger of his weapon. "For the danger you've caused our lands, I could put you down right here, by law."

Conrad took another step forward. I wanted to yell at him not to be an idiot, but I couldn't make myself talk. I wanted to grab him like he'd grabbed me, foolish and frantic, and run, but the trees rustled behind us and two more Erlkin with similar weapons stepped onto the road. Who knew how many more might be in the trees? I stayed still, my heart pounding, hating myself for hesitating.

"We can work this out," Conrad said again. "I have money."

"We're soldiers—we work for the people of Windhaven.

We don't want your money." The Erlkin nodded to the weapon in his hands. "This is a shock rifle. Might not kill you, but it'll knock you out. Now stay put before I prove it to you."

"I say we shoot him here," said the other. "Lowlife consorting with slipstreamers, and probably a human criminal himself. We don't need that kind in our land."

Both Erlkin raised their rifles. I opened my mouth to shout. Conrad might have been a complete idiot for using criminals to get him into the Mists and escape the Proctors, but he was my brother, and if I had to throw myself into the line of fire, I would.

Before I could do more than stumble to my feet, Dean's shape appeared between us and the Erlkin. "Don't shoot."

The Erlkin looked at Dean, then each other. The pair behind us shifted uncomfortably, but at a gesture from the leader, they lowered their rifles.

"Is it . . . ?" said the one who'd wanted to vaporize Conrad.

"I think it is," said the leader. He cocked an eyebrow at Dean. "You've grown a foot or two, Nails, but I'd know that smug face anywhere."

I cut a glance at Dean. I knew that he was half Erlkin, but I'd had no idea he was known to the Erlkin at large. I stayed quiet, waiting for him to say something and praying that it wouldn't be one of the smartass comments that usually came out of his mouth.

Dean bristled, his shoulders going up the way they did when he got insulted. "That's not my name. It hasn't been for years, and you of all people, Skip, should know that."

"*That's* his name?" Cal said, surprised. "Skip? Kinda lighthearted."

"Cal," I said, trying not to move my lips or my body in any way that could be interpreted as threatening. *"Shut up."*

"I forget what you're running under these days," Skip said. "Dave or Dale or something, right? While you pretend you're flesh-and-blood human?"

"It's Dean," Dean gritted out. "And I'm a hell of a lot more human than you."

For a breathless second, I thought Skip was going to shoot Dean, and then move on to Conrad and the rest of us. His cadaverous brow furrowed, and his body language tightened so much I was surprised he didn't break. Then he dropped his rifle and laughed.

Dean laughed too, but he didn't drop his shoulders. Neither did Skip, although he pasted a great big smile on his face, one that looked about as out of place as I'd have looked at a formal tea party.

"Hell, man," Skip said. "How long has it been?"

"Ten years, at least," Dean said. "We were both still playing with toys, for sure."

"Yeah, except it looks like you never stopped playing around," Skip said, gesturing at us. "What on the scorched earth is going on here? You still running humans around in circles and calling yourself an underground guide?"

Dean's shoulders tightened another notch. "Why are you asking, Skip? You keeping tabs on me?"

"Not me." Skip shrugged. "But someone up there is keeping an eye on you, boyo, a close and watchful eye, at that."

Dean didn't stop smiling, but he dropped back to stand next to me. The implicit meaning wasn't lost on me: he was with us, even though he shared Erlkin blood, just like Conrad and I shared the Fae's. None of us was one thing or the other. We were caught in the middle, just like we were caught between the four Erlkin with their rifles.

"We're not here to make trouble," Dean told Skip. "We're just passing through."

Skip shook his head. "Don't even try to sell that one to me, Nails. Dean. Whatever. You know we've got to take you up. That one's a wanted criminal, and the others, well." He sighed. "We know what's happening in the Iron Land."

"I really doubt that," Dean muttered, but he nodded to Conrad and the rest of us. "Fine. Take us up to the city on Windhaven. Can't say I missed that flying junkyard at all, so let's get this over with."

Skip gestured at Conrad. "We're going to arrest him and put the cuffs on."

Conrad bristled. "The hell you are."

"Conrad," I snapped at him, jabbing him on the arm. "You've done enough to aggravate these gentlemen, don't you think?"

He looked at me like I'd slapped him with my hand rather than my tongue. I felt a pang in return. I used to be a good girl, a nice girl, who never so much as raised her voice. Who would never have scolded her brother for only doing what he thought he had to.

Well, she was gone, along with the life she'd lived. Conrad had led us back into the Mists as a wanted criminal, and he'd gotten us into this mess. I loved my brother, but he could be a prize idiot.

Skip gestured to his fellow soldier, who pulled out a pair of old-fashioned skeleton-key shackles. I flinched when I saw the gleam of polished, oiled iron. I just hoped Conrad would be out of them before the madness started to creep in. The last time he'd had a fit, back in Lovecraft, he'd attacked me and tried to slash my throat. I tried not to think about it, the feel of the knife against my skin, the curious warmth of blood loss, but the memories crept in and I flinched as the Erlkin snapped the cuffs shut around my brother's wrists.

Skip gestured to the group, and we fell into a loose line, bracketed by the four Erlkin.

Dean grabbed my arm and leaned close enough that his lips were against my ear. "When he asks—and he will—you and I met somewhere that didn't involve guiding, you're here because your brother got you mixed up in a scheme, and for the love of all that's iron, don't mention the Fae stuff unless you want your head hung out as a warning to anyone else who'd wander into the Mists. Got it?"

"Got it," I murmured, keeping my eye on the back of Skip's head. Dean had made it evident there was no love lost between Fae and Erlkin, but I had the sinking impression that I'd gotten into a swamp much deeper and more dangerous than I could have conceived. I wasn't as good a liar as Dean or Conrad, and I couldn't lie inside my own mind at all—I was scared of what we'd find when we reached this Windhaven, whatever it was.

"Knew you'd catch on, princess," Dean muttered, and brushed a kiss against the top of my ear before he let go of me.

I put aside the way his touch made my thoughts jiggle out of alignment. It wasn't the time for crushes and weak knees, even if I wanted nothing more than to have everything be right again, and my biggest concern to be what to wear on a date with Dean, a real one with no Proctors and no specter of their lie. I raised my voice instead and spoke to Skip.

"Where are we going?"

"Windhaven," he said. "And to get to Windhaven, we're going to fly."

3

The Dance of the Air

We walked perhaps half a mile, to a clearing down a gravel path off the main road. Skip and his friends kept in tight formation around us. I found it a bit ludicrous—they had no idea who the real threat was. Conrad, presumably, had a Weird like I did, some kind of elemental magic that allowed the Graysons to conjure wind and flame and everything in between. But he had never shown it to me, and I hadn't brought it up.

It'd be much better if Skip kept thinking of Conrad as criminal but basically harmless, just a stupid human overstepping his bounds. This goal in mind, I walked with my head down, the same ache in my feet that had been there all day twinging in my worn-out boots.

"There's going to be a weight issue," said Skip's short friend. "The dirigible wasn't built for nine. Or more like ten, including the portly dame."

"Excuse you!" Bethina snapped. "I'm not an ounce overweight!"

"You're too heavy for the sky," Skip said bluntly. "That's just simple math."

"Better than being a walking cadaver, like some of us," I piped up. Skip looked at me, then at Dean.

"Keep a gag on your girlfriend, Deano, unless you want me to do it for you."

Dean looked at me and, no doubt seeing the murder in my eyes, brushed his hand against mine. "Not the time," he muttered.

I took a deep breath and then leaned a bit closer to him, so that the sides of our hands stayed in contact as we walked. Dean caught my eye again and gave me a sideways smile.

"You three can walk back to the pickup zone," Skip told the other Erlkin. "I'll stay with the prisoner."

"That's fifteen miles!" his friend protested.

"You don't like it, go live in the woods with the slipstreamers," Skip snapped. "You have your orders."

We came within range of the dirigible, and surprise made me stop and stare. Far from the metal-walled zeppelins I was accustomed to, the Erlkin's dirigible looked like it shouldn't fly at all. It consisted only of a metal cage slung under a balloon with bronze-colored ribs holding it in place, the red skin of the balloon rising and falling like the sides of a sentient creature.

The cage looked delicate, the wire thin and woven intricately, and Skip opened the retractable door with a crank handle. "Get in," he ordered, shoving Conrad. My brother fell to the floor of the cage, and Skip kicked him hard in the gut.

"Hey!" I shouted, lunging for Skip. Dean grabbed me by the sweater and yanked me back.

"*No,* Aoife," he hissed through gritted teeth. I struggled against him for a moment before going still. I'd always had a temper, and it was coming out more and more now that I didn't have the admonition to be a "proper young lady" hanging over me, as I'd had at the Academy. I gave Skip the worst look I could muster, but I smoothed my hands over my skirt and stood down.

"I'm fine," I told Dean. "He's not worth it."

"You're a firecracker," Skip sneered. "Time was, Dean knew just what to do with a girl like you."

I crouched next to Conrad, cradling his head in my lap as Skip got Cal and Bethina on board and reeled in his mooring lines. "Bastard," I said to him, stroking my brother's hair. Seeing Conrad hurt brought back the old feelings, the feelings of the girl who'd do anything for her strong, loyal brother. Conrad coughed weakly.

"I'm fine, Aoife," he said. "We'll get this fixed. Just a misunderstanding."

Once we'd all boarded, the craft rose from the forest floor with a bump. I looked at the ground drifting away below my feet and tried to focus on the construction of the Erlkin's craft to still my temper and the fear that once we reached Windhaven, we'd be in even worse trouble. The cage was made of fine silver mesh and iron bones that echoed in the wind, giving an empty *bong* when I tapped my knuckle against it. Hollow bones, like a bird's, light and strong. The Erlkin were better engineers than the Fae, that was for sure. The Fae feared anything with moving parts, treated it like it was some object from beyond reason if it mimicked their magic in any way.

Except I was in an iron cage, and even now I could feel it pressing on my mind, stirring in my blood and bringing on light-headed fits.

I tried to breathe, to think of orderly numbers and figures, the physics that allowed us to rise from the ground and drift above the treetops. Tried not to think of my dreams or my mother, as impossible as that might be.

"How far?" I asked Dean.

"Not much longer," he announced. "The faithful of the fold never venture too far from Windhaven. Isn't that right, Skip?"

Skip said nothing, just kept his hand lightly on the rudder of the dirigible, until we were far enough off the ground that all I could see were the tops of trees, rising through the fog like the blackened fingers of dead hands.

"Not far now," Skip said, but his tone didn't fill me with hope.

When Windhaven came into view, it wasn't a sight that anything in my life, including my visit to the Thorn Land, the home of the Fae, had prepared me for.

The fog parted like the sea before the prow of an old-fashioned ship, and I saw gleaming towers of iron suspended high above the ground.

The distinctive burnt-paper scent of aether reached my nostrils, and as Windhaven got larger, I realized it wasn't merely suspended—the entire city was flying along before us, moving above the Mists like a great raven casting its shadow across the ground. Iron didn't poison the Erlkin, I knew—Dean had been just fine spending his life in an iron city surrounded by machines. Good for Dean and the Erlkin. Bad for Conrad and me. My stomach dipped along with the craft.

As we drew closer, I saw that Windhaven's structures were built on an oval platform supported at the thinnest and widest points by giant fans whirring so loudly that even now, hundreds of yards off, they overwhelmed my ears. At the base of the city a giant aether globe hung by flexible cables, supplying Windhaven with light and communications. It looked small as a marble, or a twinkling star in a vast sky, against the grand scale of the flying city.

A mass of radio aerials flew from the highest tower at the apex of the buildings, which were largely curved but didn't look as if they'd come together in any particular order. It was, for lack of a better description, a flying scrapyard, albeit one held aloft by engineering that made me dizzy with its genius.

I saw a cluster of spindly docking arms radiating from the back of the flying structure, in the dead spot for drag near one of the giant fans. Some were already occupied by crimson-sailed dirigibles similar to ours. Skip steered us toward an empty berth.

The arm extended toward us, long, flexible cables seeking out the iron ribs of the balloon.

"Magnets," I said to Cal, analyzing how everything worked out of habit. We'd both been students at the School of Engines before I'd found out he was actually a ghoul and I was actually, in the eyes of the Proctors, an abomination.

"It's boss," he murmured, distractedly keeping one hand on Bethina's where it clutched his arm in a death grip.

The magnets clamped on and reeled us in, safe against the docking arm. A thin ladder that looked like it couldn't support even its own weight locked onto the outside of the dirigible's cage.

"I'm not climbing that," Bethina said instantly.

"You're welcome to stay here," Skip said shortly. "Once the city climbs up to night flying altitude, the temperature will drop enough that you should freeze to death in an hour or two. You probably won't feel a thing."

Cal put his hand on Bethina's shoulder. His stringy body was vibrating, and I could tell it was taking everything he had not to change and launch himself at Skip's throat.

I was thinking it would be a toss-up who clocked Skip first—Cal or me.

"Come on," Cal soothed Bethina. "It'll be okay. I'll be right behind you." He opened the door and helped her out onto the ladder. She was sheet white, her knuckles the color of bone where she held on to the metal, and I didn't envy her. I wasn't afraid of heights, but I had plenty of other fears to fill that void, and being so close to iron was making every one of them stir and raise their heads.

Skip turned to Conrad and pulled a key on a flexible chain from his belt. "I'm going to unlock you to climb up. There are more of us at the top than you could hope to overpower, and if you pull anything you're going off the side." He smacked the cage for emphasis, and it rattled. "It's a long way down."

"You can lay off the lanternreel-villain talk," Conrad told him. "I'll be a good boy."

Skip curled his lip and looked at Dean. "And what about you, Nails? You going to be a good boy?"

"Doubt it," Dean told him. "Never managed it before."

Skip snorted before he manhandled Conrad onto the ladder and followed him up.

Dean helped me out, his hand warm on mine even though the breeze whipping along the docking stations was icy cold. "Why does he call you Nails?" I asked.

"Long story," Dean said. "Not one I'm going to waste time telling, either."

I looked up the ladder at the dark, arched mouth of the entrance to Windhaven. The lump of fear in my chest hadn't dissolved, and in fact felt like it had grown. "Is this in any way a good idea?"

"No," Dean said. "Probably the opposite, as a matter of fact, but I don't see that we've got much of a choice on this one."

I didn't either, so up I went. As we climbed, we went from breathless open space to a tiny tunnel. Skip was waiting at the top of the ladder, snapping the cuffs back on Conrad, and as soon as we were all on our feet on the platform, we marched down the tunnel to a hatch leading to Windhaven proper, marked with a symbol in the shape of a wheel and spokes with wings attached.

More Erlkin dressed in uniforms like Skip's waited at the hatch, and he handed Conrad off to them before turning to me. "We'll keep your friends in holding until we determine their status. You too. Nails, you're free to go." He gave Dean a look I couldn't identify. Not anger, not contempt, but not pleasure, either. "I'm sure Shard will want to see you."

An Erlkin even taller than Skip took my arm. "You come with me, girlie."

I glanced back at Dean as they led me away. I was smart enough to know that I had to stay calm and passive with this many edgy Erlkin around, so I didn't fight, but it was hard to take my eyes off Dean. Dean was constant, and he was safety. Separated from him, I didn't know how long I could hold off the madness dreams. Besides, I didn't want to leave him and the gleam of his silver eyes, the blush that sat on his lips, full for a boy's, and the feeling of his strong hands gripping mine.

Dean didn't look at me. He was staring into the middle distance, and I could tell he was seeing something I couldn't see at all.

I didn't get to view much of Windhaven as the Erlkin marched me to my cell. They kept me belowdecks, and we passed through a series of hatches lit by spitting aether globes, the walls pitted with rust and painted with more of the strange pictograms like the wheel-shaped symbol that marked the entry. I reasoned it was the Erlkin language, and these must be shorthand for directions to the various levels of the city-ship. I tucked them away in my memory to write out and puzzle over later. I was good at symbols and riddles, and the sooner I didn't have to rely on an Erlkin to translate, the sooner I'd be able to escape Windhaven if I had to.

I hoped it wouldn't come to that, but I had the bad feeling it was going to, and rapidly. The Erlkin didn't seem overly friendly now, when they thought Conrad and I were only human. Who knew what would happen if they ferreted out our secret?

The cell wasn't nearly as cell-like as the one the Proctors had shoved me in when they'd caught me, after I'd escaped Lovecraft. It was more like a deserted classroom, plain metal tables with stenotypes arranged around the perimeter of the room, and a chalkboard with numbers—latitude and longitude—written on it. It looked as if the room's rightful occupants had just stepped out.

The Erlkin pulled out a chair for me and sat me in it with a hard push. He dropped my bag next to me, after searching it and removing my engineer's toolkit and anything else I could use to escape. Luckily he didn't find my notebook, which I'd tucked away in a hidden pocket.

"Stay put," he said. "Someone will be in after a while."

"How specific," I muttered. "Will it be before my hair turns gray?"

The Erlkin sneered at me and closed the hatch. I heard a rumble and saw the rods at the top and bottom lock into place. It would take a blast to dislodge the door now. I was stuck in here until they decided to let me out. If they ever did. Unless I used my Weird.

I had discovered in Lovecraft that I could move machines, that they responded to my blood as my blood responded to iron. But to use my Weird was to invite pounding headaches, hallucinations and nosebleeds. I drummed my fingers against the nearest desk. The Erlkin hadn't actually hurt anyone yet. I had to save my strength for when we were really in danger. Being on the run had taught me that, if nothing else.

Windhaven moved slowly, but it did move. I could feel the barest vibration of motion from where I sat at the bare desk, spatters of ink coating the pale surface.

I searched the drawers and found a mechanical pencil. It would have to do. I flipped open my battered notebook and sketched out the symbols I'd seen from memory. Underneath I scribbled *Erlkin symbols as seen at Windhaven.*

My father had never run into the Erlkin, except once. They'd taken him into the Mists, like they had Conrad, before the Fae could get to him.

But were they the same smugglers who had gotten Conrad into trouble? Or had it been someone else, someone who had allowed my father to escape the Fae? I didn't know, nor did I know where my father was now.

I started an entry on the next page. Writing at least gave me something to occupy my mind, rather than fretting over what would happen when the door opened again. Fretting rarely did anyone any good.

Third entry:

The Erlkin seem hostile at best, but they helped my father escape so the Fae couldn't force him to do what they eventually made me do—break the Gates, allowing the Fae and their nightmare creatures to flow freely through the Iron Land and attempt to eradicate the iron, then annex the land to the Thorn. And they helped Conrad, or at least a certain group of them did.

They don't love the Fae any more than they love humans or other trespassers, that much Dean told me. The enemy of my enemy is my friend. Straight out of Proctor propaganda, when it encouraged us to inform on each other, to collude to send heretics to the castigator for punishment.

Who's worse? The Proctors or me? They fought the power beyond their understanding with lies and terror. On the other hand, I've read enough from my father's books about the Brotherhood of Iron to realize that at least I'm not entirely alone in my struggle. The Brotherhood was my grandfather's cadre of scientists, magic users and scholars. They fought that same power by keeping their society absolutely secret, accepting the occasional casualty and adhering to ancient rules that neither the Fae nor the Proctors are playing by any longer. My father himself fought it . . . or did he? I still don't know why he broke with the Brotherhood, only that Draven has a score to settle with him.

And then there's me. I didn't even try to fight the power. I set it free, and in the process I shattered the world.

Not shattered—cracked. I've cracked the mask, and the true face is showing from underneath, and it is horrible, ugly and crawling with maggots, something no human eye should be forced to look at.

Where is my father? He got me out of Lovecraft, but he could be dead now, for all I know. If he didn't get out before the blast, before the cataclysm, he could be gone, like all the other poor souls.

Gone. My mother can't be gone. I can't have unwound things that badly. I'll get out of Windhaven and go back and find her, no matter what Conrad says. I'll do what I have to.

Somehow.

* * *

The sound of the hatch wheel spinning alerted me, and I jammed the pencil back into the drawer and my notebook back into my bag. When the hatch opened, I was sitting primly, my ankles crossed and my hands folded, like the star of any comportment class.

A single Erlkin entered, and I tried not to stare. She was nearly as tall as Skip, with twin braids running from her temples down her back, thin and tight as bullwhips. Her clothes were a simple olive drab jacket with a double row of silver buttons and tight military pants tucked into steam ventor's boots like the ones Dean wore, steel toes gleaming and the leather spit-polished.

"Aoife Grayson, I gather," she said. She gestured at me with a long-fingered hand. "Stand up."

I raised an eyebrow at her, more in surprise that she was being so businesslike about taking me prisoner than anything else. "Why?"

Her lip twitched, and I could tell she wasn't used to being questioned when she gave an order. "Get up, you wretched girl," she said, and grabbed my arm, hefting me easily out of the chair. I wasn't big, and she was, and strong besides. "I just want to get a look at you." She took my chin between her thumb and forefinger and turned my head from side to side. "Skinny," she said, "but not too skinny. Not a pale-faced wreck, either. That hair—that hair is most definitely human."

I flushed, even though my grooming or lack thereof should have been the furthest thing from my mind. My black curls had been a gift from my father—my mother had hair as sleek and golden as a lion's pelt. Back at the Academy, my hair had been one of my primary worries. Things sure did change. "I've been in the wind."

"And a sense of humor," the Erlkin marveled. "You pass very well. If I didn't know better, I'd say you were a sweet little human." Her grip on my chin tightened, and I felt her fingernails dig into my skin. "But you're not, are you? You're a filthy quicksilver-blood changeling."

"I'm sorry, I don't think I caught your name." My voice rose on the last word, but I tried to keep the fear there and not let it creep into my face. She knew what I was. Who I was. And I had no idea what the Erlkin did to people like me.

The woman smiled. It was cold, like watching the steel of a switchblade pop out. "I'm Shard. Dean's mother."

I stayed frozen, not making eye contact. After a time, Shard tilted her head. "Got anything to say for yourself, Aoife?"

The first thing that came to mind made my stomach drop out, as if Windhaven had begun to plummet from the sky. It was a horrifying thought, but it was entirely possible, seeing as Dean shared half his blood with the Erlkin, just as I shared mine with the Fae. "Dean told you about me. What I am."

"Hmm?" Shard shook her head, her smile softening a degree so that she no longer looked like she was about to eat me. "He didn't tell me a thing, dear. I smell it on you, like sewer filth."

I twitched back a step from Shard. She could have passed for human. Though her features were sharp and ethereal, she didn't have the predatory quality shared by most of the Erlkin I'd seen, with bones jutting from their faces like they'd been specially made to frighten anyone who looked at them. But she was more terrifying than Skip and his cronies by an order of ten. "I . . . smell? Strange?"

"I was a tracker, dear," Shard said. "I spent my days chasing down fugitives and slipstreamers. You stink like a Fae, but you don't look like one. You're a changeling. *Half-breed* is probably the right word."

"I don't like that word," I told her angrily. How dare Shard pass judgment on my family? She didn't even know us. I was guilty of being gullible and trusting, it was true, but I wasn't the enemy. Shard let go of my face, giving my cheek a pat that stopped just shy of being a slap. I flinched, and felt like the worst sort of frightened, shrinking girl.

"I don't give a damn what you like, dear. You brought the shadow of the Fae here. You and that brother of yours." She folded her arms and regarded me. "You're lucky Nails is taken with you. Otherwise, you'd be over the side of Windhaven without a second thought."

With that, she opened the door and gestured me out of the makeshift cell. "Come on," she snapped, when I hesitated. "We're not barbarians. Get moving and clean yourself up. That Fae stench is bad enough without your generally unwashed state on top of it."

Shard led me up another ladder, down another set of halls and to a hatch that was less rusted, and painted with a number rather than one of the cryptic symbols. "You should be comfortable here." She appraised me. "You're the size of one of my lieutenants. I'll have some clothes sent over for you."

She opened the hatch and waited until I was inside, when she promptly shut and locked it again.

It was a better class of cell, but I was still a prisoner, and I had no idea what was happening to Dean, Conrad and the others. I slung my bag down and took in my new surroundings, sitting on the carpet and wrapping my arms around my legs. I was alone—I felt I was entitled to have a few seconds of pure panic and shaking before I got myself together and tried to find a way out.

Shard hadn't outright condemned me, but it was clear Conrad and I weren't welcome. The sooner we were away from these hostile Erlkin, the better.

I breathed in, breathed out and willed my heartbeat to slow down. After a moment, I stood up and examined the room. I would cope. I'd use my brain and get us out of here. It was what I did. Iron or not, I had to keep myself together for just a little longer.

The room was cramped, the ceiling following the curve of Windhaven's hull, the base of the floating city that held up the spires above, and the bunk barely looked long enough for me to fit into. There was one empty closet and a desk barely larger than a single sheet of paper. A thin door opened onto a water closet with a steam hob and copper covering the walls in one corner, sloping down to a drain so that I could wash standing up.

Otherwise, it was only me and my things.

First things first—I took out my notebook and pried the cover off the air-shaft vent above the door, standing on the desk to reach it. I slipped the notebook inside and slid the vent cover back in place. Knowing that no one would happen upon my writing if they searched the room while I was gone made the tightness in my gut relax a little. I'd gotten very good at hiding things, living under the Proctors—

searches for contraband had been practically weekly at the Academy, and with a brother who was a wanted heretic, who sent me letters that I couldn't bear to throw away, a foolproof hiding place in my dorm room had been essential.

Next thing—I had to find a way out of here under my own power. I wouldn't be at the mercy of the Erlkin when they so clearly mistrusted me. Besides, I couldn't waste time at Windhaven—I had to keep my plan in motion. Evade my pursuers, go back to Lovecraft and get my mother.

Once she was safe, I could come up with a cunning plan, like the heroine of some adventure play, to set right what had happened in Lovecraft. I could find a way to outsmart the Fae and reverse the shattering of the Iron Land's Gate, the only protection ordinary humans had. I might even find a way to stave off iron madness a little longer.

I wished Dean were in the room with me. He was good for telling my ideas to, no matter how far-fetched they were. Dean was a believer in doing the impossible, which he was usually convinced needed only a little push from my brain and his charm to become possible. He had more confidence in me than I did, most days. I could have used his hand in mine, his wiry arms around me, the shine of his silver eyes. I could have used a moment pressed against his chest, smelling leather and tobacco.

I had begun to need Dean. But he wasn't here. So I was going to have to do this one on my own.

Portholes were an obvious choice. I checked the one above the bed. It was latched but not locked, yet when I looked I saw only the slick riveted side of the hull above and below and small pieces of iron to the side, on flexible springs. Designed, I thought, to increase or decrease drag and enable Windhaven to turn. It really was a miraculous thing, this flying city. Not my city, though. Not where I needed to be.

At any rate, the small rudders were too far away to be of any use. The wind would peel me off the side of the craft and toss me to the swampy ground of this place before I could even think of grabbing for one.

That left the door. The idea made sense on paper, but in reality, the place was lousy with Erlkin on the other side. Plus, I had no idea about the layout of the underside of Windhaven, the myriad tunnels and hatches that comprised the bulk of the flying fortress, so if I did manage to get out, I'd be running blind.

Still, I went to the door and eased my forehead against it. My Weird responded to the locks and the mechanisms in the wall, to the gears that vibrated throughout Windhaven.

It would be easy to slip the lock, and I splayed my fingers against the metal. Pressure built in my skull, my mind aligning itself with the thing that lived in my blood, which could talk to machines and make them its disciples.

When the hatch wheel unlocked and started to turn, I let out a small sound and jumped back onto the bed just as the door swung open.

An Erlkin about my size came in, holding a uniform over her arm. "You Aoife?"

I nodded. "Who are you?"

She curled her lip at me. "Captain Shard told me to bring you clean clothes." She tossed them onto the bed next to me.

"Thank you," I said, with a game smile. I really wanted to return her glare, but I was the prisoner, and I wanted the

Erlkin to think I was harmless. Well, less harmful than Conrad, anyway. At least until I figured out how much trouble we were actually in.

"Half-breed," the Erlkin spat at me, and then left, the hatch slamming shut behind her retreating back.

I slumped on my bed next to the clothes, shoving them aside to give myself space. The hull vibrated gently, and I leaned into it. I was exhausted, and being in a place that wasn't an abandoned farmhouse or the crook of a tree was lulling me to sleep.

I tried to stay awake and think of more plans to get Conrad out of trouble, but sleep stole my senses, and soon I was deep under the waves of dreaming.

4 The Sea of Dreams

IN MY DREAM, I was still alone. But this time, the skyline of Lovecraft had faded into the distance, and I saw it like a mirage on the horizon, shimmering. I stood in a room, the floor inlaid with silver, a star map of constellations I had never before laid eyes on. Alien stars, from an alien sky.

Before me stood a figure twice as tall as I, only a shadow, smooth and without feature. I stayed still, unsure of my footing in the dream. I always felt only vaguely attached to my dream-body, as if my mind were floating free in the void of outer space and my body were waiting back on Earth.

Behind the figure, a great gear rose, half of it above the platform on which we stood. Above us, a hundred skies turned by, sunrises and sunsets, skylines and the blackness of space. And in those skies things twisted and writhed, great tentacles of darkness coming down to merge and mingle with the shadow figure before me.

I found I could speak, which wasn't always the case in

these madness dreams—for that was surely what this was, brought on by the iron of Windhaven. "Where am I?"

The figure stared back impassively. I knew he was staring, despite his lack of eyes or any features at all. I could feel his gaze, hot and penetrating. Beyond him, beyond the gear and the platform, the skies spun faster. They were more than skies now—it was as if we were inside a giant dome and lanternreels in the thousands and millions were projected onto the glass sides.

"Where am I?" I asked again.

The figure reached out a hand. It was fathomless, black smoke in the shape of a human thing, and I felt cold emanate from the shadow as it drew closer to me. The tentacles writhed faster, lashing, and from all around us came a great moaning, which vibrated the dome to its core and came up through my feet into my bones.

Who are you? the figure hissed. *Why did you come here?*

"You tell me," I whispered, my lips barely able to move from the frozen air of the dream and my own fear. This felt too strong, too real, to be purely a result of the iron around me. The madness was getting worse. I was starting to believe my own dreams. I dug my fingers into my palms, but in this dream place, I felt no pain. That didn't soothe my worries any.

"I don't know where *here* is," I said. The great gear behind the figure began to turn, and as it did the tentacles retreated, the black figures floating in the skies shrinking away. In my ears, and through the dome, a thousand screams echoed.

You shouldn't be here, the figure told me. *This isn't your dream. This isn't a dream at all.*

Then, as if I'd fallen from a great height, I snapped awake.

* * *

My head was throbbing, and it was dark in the room when I opened my eyes. For a moment I didn't know where I was, and then it all came back to me. I slumped against the pillow. My clothes, none too clean to start, were soaked with sweat. That had been a bad one. Usually my encroaching madness didn't talk back to me in my dreams.

I fumbled around until I found the aether lamp above the bed and turned the valve, the blue glow filling the tiny room. I took the uniform the Erlkin had left for me and stripped out of my filthy skirt and sweater, all the way down to nothing. I took my underthings into the water closet and ran hot water into the basin, washing them and leaving them on the towel bar to dry. While they dripped I stepped into the copper stall and let the trickle from the pipe above wash the grime off my skin.

The Erlkin didn't skimp on amenities for their guests, and I wrapped a fluffy Turkish towel around myself and a smaller one around my damp hair in an effort to keep it from blowing up like a thundercloud.

I looked out the porthole again, but there was nothing now except night, a row of running lights on the hull streaming away from me like fireflies in the blackness.

When the hatch rattled again, I shrieked and spun, pulling the towel up to my chin. "Who's there!" I demanded, casting around for something to throw or prod the intruder with.

"Whoa, princess," Dean said, ducking through the hatch and shutting it. "Shhh. Nobody knows I'm here."

"Dean," I breathed in relief. Dean took in the scene, and me. Wrapped in a towel.

"Oh," he said. "Sorry about that."

"Do you knock?" I demanded, tightening my grip on the towel.

A slow smile grew on Dean's face. "Don't make a habit of it." He cleared his throat, making a visible effort to keep his eyes fastened on my face. "This isn't exactly going to convince me to start, you know."

"You're terrible," I said, trying to collect the clothes the Erlkin had left for me and slide into the water closet, while at the same time hiding the warmth his stare brought to my cheeks.

Dean smiled wider. "Isn't that why you like me so much?"

"Right now I'm not sure I like you at all," I teased, shutting the door but for a crack, so Dean and I could still talk.

"You sure riled my mother," he said, his shadow falling across the opening. I unfolded the clothes—brown pants with a wealth of pockets and a plain white high-collared shirt and dust-colored uniform jacket. They were patched and smelled of a cedar chest, but they fit when I slipped them on, and they were clean. By my standards lately, bliss.

"I don't think she liked me very much," I said, opening the door again. "Or at all." I met his eyes. "Did you say something to her about Conrad and me? Is she going to let us go? I'm not angry, if you did. I understand she's your mother, but I need to know." Needed to know that Dean was as loyal as I'd always thought, and that he wasn't the reason I was locked up in Windhaven with Shard looking for an excuse to jettison me out a hatch.

Dean was a good liar. He had eyes the color of silvery thunderheads, changeable and unpredictable and impossible to truly fathom. But he'd never lied to me. Not when it mattered.

"Course I didn't, princess," he said easily. "My mother is just sneaky that way—I could never put anything past her either. She's also calculating, and she's not dumb. She'll realize you're not a Fae spy and your brother isn't a criminal. She's our best tracker and the captain of Windhaven—she answers to the Wytch King only. She and a few other generals are just under him in terms of who bosses around the rest of the Erlkin. Everything will be all right once she gets her nose back into joint."

He couldn't even look at me when he said it. Well, I supposed there was a first time for everything—first kiss, first touch against bare skin, first lie. At least I could hope the part about him not ratting us out was true. I thought it probably was—Dean hadn't seemed overly fond of his mother when we'd talked about her, and I certainly didn't tell my mother everything. Or anything, because it didn't matter to Nerissa in her madness anyway.

When I didn't reply at once, Dean put his index finger under my chin and raised my face to his. "Hey. You believe me, don't you, princess?"

"Sure," I lied right back, amazed at how easily it came to my tongue. "It'll all get straightened out, I guess."

"That's what I like to hear," Dean said with a forced joviality that wasn't like him. Dean didn't smile when there was no reason to smile, and he didn't lie to me—except now. Before I could decide whether to confront him or hold off until I'd discovered a sure way out of this flying iron hellhole, Dean drew me into his arms and pressed his lips to mine. "It'll be okay, Aoife," he murmured against my mouth. "I promise, all right? No matter what happens, I've got you."

I kissed him back, because even when I was frustrated and wary, Dean had an effect on me I couldn't fully explain. He made me light-headed and dizzy, wanting nothing but to taste him and keep tasting him until I'd had my fill. He made me need him, with his taste and his scent and his beautiful eyes, and I realized I had to just not think about what had happened for a few minutes and be with him.

Outside in the corridor, footsteps and voices stopped us from doing more than lying back on the narrow bunk. "I'm going to bug out. I really don't want to play the scene with my mother if she catches me in here." He looked for a moment as if he'd kiss me again, but then he rolled off the bed and stood, the usual edgy tension stringing back into his body. "I'll see you later, Aoife."

"Dean," I said, as he put his hand on the hatch. "Tell me the truth. What's going to happen to Conrad and me?"

Dean raised his shoulders, and I could tell that he was done stretching the truth. "It's not good, Aoife. The Fae and the Fae-blooded don't have any friends here." His eyes darkened. "But I won't let them hurt you. I'll take Windhaven to the ground first."

"I hope it won't come to that," I said as he spun the hatch open. We both jumped when we were confronted with Skip's ever-sneering face.

"Well, look at you, Nails," he said. "Still sniffing around the henhouse, are ya, even though the bird's been naughty?"

"Go jump off a high spire," Dean snapped. "I can talk to Aoife any time I want."

I blushed, sure Skip could tell exactly what had been happening before Dean opened the door. His smirk didn't argue with my assumption.

"You sure can," he said, "but you'll be doing it during an audience with the king." Skip reached past Dean and grabbed me. I yanked against him reflexively and I fought the urge to punch him.

Skip overpowered me easily, giving a laugh when Dean snarled at him. "Come on, *princess,*" he said in a pitch-perfect mockery of Dean's voice. "The Wytch King wants to speak with you."

He dragged me off by the arm before either Dean or I could object, and all I could see when I looked back were Dean's worried eyes, cloudy and uneasy as wind-driven storm clouds.

After a nerve-racking minute, Dean caught up with us. My feet barely touched the metal plates that comprised the floors of Windhaven. Skip's stride was long and quick, and my arm burned where he grabbed it. "You're a lucky little human," he told me. "One of the few to ever lay eyes on the Wytch King."

I managed to keep my voice steady, though I was terrified beyond belief. Even Dean had seemed afraid of the Wytch King when he'd finally told me the truth about being half Erlkin and about his people, and Dean wasn't afraid of anything, that I could see. "What does he want with me?"

"I imagine you interest him," Skip said. "Or he's hungry. Erlkin like live meat." He grinned at me, every tooth like a carving knife.

"Stop it," Dean growled from behind us. "Right this red-hot second." He pried Skip's viselike grip off my arm and slid his hand into mine. "The Wytch King doesn't eat people," he said to me.

I squeezed his hand. Whatever would happen between us, at least he was here now. I was relieved—without Dean, with my exhaustion and the weight of memory constantly on me, I was about an inch from being a blubbering mess.

"You used to be a lot more fun, Nails," Skip muttered as we mounted a broad set of steps. The double doors at the top were flanked by two Erlkin in uniform sporting shock rifles.

"And you used to be a lot less of a jerk," Dean muttered back.

The doors swung back of their own accord, and I was distracted from the imminent fistfight between Dean and Skip by what lay beyond. I'd been expecting a throne room, the sort of thing Cal's fantasy-story heroes like Conan and Lancelot would enter, hair flowing and swords gleaming. Some grand hall covered in silk from floor to ceiling and emblazoned with noble crests.

Instead, the room was bare, containing only a broad metal table and a long swath of black velvet curtains covering the back part of the vast, echoing chamber.

The Wytch King himself sat in a swivel chair with his back to us, pale hands with pale fingers tapping against the dark, rough leather of his chair. He turned to face us, and I felt my stomach drop as if Windhaven had plummeted from the sky.

The Wytch King's gaze was silver and pupil-less, glossed over with a mercury sheen that seemed to slip and slither across the surface of his eyes. His lips were black, and his teeth were filed to sharp points. He wore a high-necked black uniform that looked eerily like those the officers among the Proctors wore. He sniffed the air with flattened nostrils, and those silver eyes locked on me. They were the same color as Dean's, but where Dean's burned with life and warmth, the Wytch King might as well have been made from clockwork.

I felt a million things in that moment—fear, disgust, the urge to scream. Those were the initial tidal wave of panic, and then my engineer's brain kicked in. The logical, impassive side that didn't get scared or confused. I tried to assess how much danger I was actually in, and what I could do to get myself out of it. *Not much,* came the rapid answer, which started the panic all over again.

"Sir," Skip said. "The human girl."

The Wytch King stood, extended his hand to me, and smiled. "Hello, Aoife. I've been waiting to meet you."

I looked at the hand, the nails blackened at the edges with some foreign substance I couldn't identify. I recoiled at the thought of touching him, but I knew I couldn't risk angering the Erlkin further. I put my hand in his and gripped it firmly.

His fist closed around mine like a bear trap, and while I struggled, all my fantasies of being resolute and a good ambassador for the Iron Land slipped from my mind and were replaced with the same low-frequency hum of panic that had been present since I'd left my father's home.

"You aren't soft," he said. "Your hands are calloused. Not what I'd expect from a Fae spy."

"I'm not a spy!" I said hotly, nearly at a shout. Skip's hand dropped to his weapon and I turned my eyes on him, raising my voice to a real yell. "You want to shoot me, you pasty-faced freak?" I yelled. "Go ahead. Go ahead and do it so you can tell your friends how you stopped the dangerous Fae spy who hasn't done a thing except try to stay alive."

I ripped my hand from the Wytch King's grasp, and his nails left tracks of blood across my palm. My chest was heaving, my vision was tunneled in black, and I could hear my heartbeat roaring in my ears. I didn't even realize I'd balled up my fists and started for Skip until Dean caught me and spun me into his arms.

"Aoife," he said against my ear. "Aoife!" again, louder, when I reflexively fought back against his embrace. "You're bleeding," Dean murmured. He released me and uncurled my hand to show three long furrows in my skin, oozing blood. "Let me take care of that for you," he said softly. "Just cool your jets, all right? This is *not* the place. I know how you feel. But it just isn't."

"You know and I know we're not leaving here," I said, trying to still the shakes running through me. "They've already made up their minds that Conrad and I are working against them."

The Wytch King began to laugh. It was an eerie sound, more like static crackling over the aether than a sound borne from a living throat. He wheezed for a moment and then slapped his knee. "I like your girl, Nails. Like her very much." He turned those flat doll's eyes on me, and once again I felt the chill of something cold and older than I could imagine sweep over me. The Erlkin might not have had the iron affliction or cruel, spiteful streak of the Fae, but they weren't human, and things like me were prey to them. I was acutely aware of that as the king stared at me.

"It doesn't change the fact," he said, "that your brother consorted with slipstreamers, smugglers who weaken our borders by bringing your kind through. And I will not let that go unanswered. I can't. My people rely on me to keep them safe, just as you rely on Nails."

"I keep myself safe," I said, steel creeping into my tone. "I've been doing it for a long time." How dare he imply I was some helpless, sappy girl, cowering in fear unless she had a boyfriend to protect her? The more time I spent with the Wytch King, the more his unpleasantness reminded me of Grey Draven's. The former Head of Lovecraft, the man who'd tried to use me to lure my father into a trap, had the same single-minded coldness as the Wytch King. I didn't know if that made the Wytch King more human or Grey Draven less so.

"You welcome some humans," I challenged the king, spurred by the memory of Draven and his cold-blooded threat to find and exterminate my father, Conrad and anyone else of the Grayson line he could get his hands on when I wouldn't cooperate with him. "You helped my father." Maybe if I could convince the Wytch King I wasn't his enemy, I could wheedle my father's location out of him. The thought made me stand a little straighter and try to act as if I weren't a knock-kneed mess. During my life at the Academy, I'd gotten good at pretending such things.

"I did," the Wytch King agreed. "I helped Archie Grayson, because the enemy of my enemy is my ally, and Archie has never crossed an Erlkin widdershins, which is more than

I can say for most of your kind." He took his seat again, leather and springs creaking under surprising weight. "But you're not your father, little miss. And if the Fae and that human-shaped stain on the world who calls himself Grey Draven have their say, you're never going to follow his footsteps through the Gates either."

This time, the chill I felt had nothing to do with his stare. "How do you know him?" I demanded. Were we in even worse trouble than I thought? Had Draven somehow snowed the Erlkin into an alliance to bring me in, use me as the bait he needed to lure my father?

"We do not voluntarily shut ourselves in a cocoon of superstition like the Fae, Aoife," said the Wytch King. "Don't look so alarmed. I've heard of what happened in that iron city, the one called Lovecraft. Draven's made sure your face is plastered across every newsreel there is, and your name spoken hourly on the aether waves. Your disappearing act has become something of an embarrassment to him now that he's used the disaster to rise through the ranks, according to my spies."

I had never imagined that Draven would use the destruction of his own city, the city he'd been responsible for, to leverage a promotion with the Proctors, but in retrospect I felt stupid for being so naive. Of course Draven would seize the chance—a supposedly mad terrorist attacks his city, and he, stalwart, picks up the pieces and puts on the brave face. Of course the Proctors would promote him, give him all the power he needed to hunt down the person responsible: me. It fell into place like the worst sort of war machine, efficient, sleek and deadly.

"Draven's in charge of the Proctors now?" I whispered.

The Wytch King chuckled. "The director, from what I hear. Head of the whole business, making sweeping changes. There's chatter that he'll be president someday."

I felt numb, dizzy, as if I were plummeting. Draven had the ear of the current president of the War Council. Only Inquisitor Hoover, who'd founded the Bureau of Proctors, stood above him.

If I'd thought getting back to Lovecraft would be hard before now, it had just taken on a whole new dimension of impossibility. Never mind the city—I wouldn't be safe anywhere in the Iron Land where the Proctors had eyes.

Dean squeezed my hand gently, and I could tell by the lines between his eyes that his thoughts had followed the same track. I just felt worse—not only had I destroyed Lovecraft, I'd catapulted Draven into a position of even more power.

Somewhere, that ugly Fae Tremaine was laughing himself sick, I just knew it.

"So, my dear," said the Wytch King. He raised his fingers and licked my blood delicately from his nails. "I wouldn't be so anxious to escape Windhaven just yet. Once your brother has had his day in court, you'll be free to go. Until then, well . . ." He tilted his head. "Silver-tinged Fae blood or no, it will be very interesting to have humans aboard. Very, very interesting."

He gestured us out, and with prodding from Skip, we exited the king's chamber.

Back in the hall, I looked at Dean and asked a question I already half knew the answer to, hoping he'd say something different. "Do we want to be interesting to the Wytch King?"

"Hell no," Dean said. "Not one little bit."

"I didn't think so," I told Dean with a sigh, before we separated, the brush of his fingers on my cheek the last thing I had to remember him by before Skip took me by the arm.

I let him take me back to my room, playing the part of the good little human girl, even though I was more determined than ever to be anything but. Anything but the Fae spy the Erlkin believed me to be. Anything but the simple, pliant girl Grey Draven wanted to think I was. That wasn't going to fix anything, wasn't going to find my father and free Conrad. And it wasn't going to save my mother.

After I calculated that enough time had passed for most of Windhaven to be asleep, I tried the hatch of my room again. Using my Weird here was rolling the dice—the madness could find a way in as easily as my gift—but I felt the lock give quickly when I applied the force of my mind to it. My nose didn't even start bleeding, as it had been wont to do in the past. I felt a brief boil of nausea in my guts, and thankfully, that was all. I was relieved. Knocking myself down would defeat the whole purpose of using my gift in the first place.

I didn't know precisely where I was headed, I just knew I couldn't let the Erlkin treat me like a prisoner any longer. And the more of Windhaven I saw and mapped in my mind, the easier it would be for me to get Conrad and escape when the time came.

I was sure it would come to that. I had a feeling, heavy in my chest, that arriving under the purview of the Erlkin had irretrievably left me in their web.

Windhaven's lower decks appeared to be constructed like those of a seagoing ship, with layers of hulls and corridors stacked next to one another, like a heart with chambers too numerous to count. Brass ladders led from one level to the next, and I began to see repeats in the Erlkin symbols—numbers or levels, in diminishing order as I climbed, fewer and fewer spokes filling in each wheel.

The highest landing I could reach was blocked by a brass hatch, a skull and crossbones stamped straight into the metal. Not a fool, I pressed my hand and ear to the hatch and heard the howl of the wind from the other side. I wagered if I opened it, I'd be swept off Windhaven and meet the ground quickly enough, so I turned and went back down the stairs to the corridor. A series of arrows marked a symbol shaped like a lotus flower, and I followed them as the corridors narrowed around me, until only one hatch remained straight ahead.

It opened before I could put a hand on it to test what was on the other side, and I found Shard's thin, elfin face and burning eyes glaring down at me. I flinched. This was the exact opposite of what I'd had in mind when I snuck out.

"It took you long enough," Shard snapped. "How did you get out?"

I backpedaled a step. Her glare felt like a slap. "You were watching me?"

Shard pushed the hatch wider. "We can see all of Windhaven from here."

I stepped into the room and gasped. Below my feet, the ground fell away, and clouds drifted below the belly of

Windhaven. The walls and floors of the room were glass, bulbous petals of glass riveted to the walls along brass veins.

Rising from the glass in the center of the room like the stamens of this odd frozen flower was a pilot console replete with dozens of dials and four rudders that steered the four great fans. To one side sat a bank of dials and knobs marked with more of the strange symbols, and to the other was a wall filled with screens that twitched and danced with images.

Like the lanternreel screens back home in Lovecraft, but writ small. Dozens of them, showing rooms and halls and the exterior hull of Windhaven.

"The aether feeds images from all over Windhaven," said Shard, "and sends them to the screens here. So yes, we saw you escape, and yes, I saw you with my son."

She turned to me, but I refused to look away. "And?" I asked her, brash as the criminal she believed me to be. "Have you decided that I'm not a Fae spy? Or are you going to toss me off Windhaven without a parachute? Either way, make up your mind soon. I'm bored being locked in a tiny room on this floating lug nut."

Shard moved her hand lightning quick and smacked me across the face. It wasn't hard enough to draw blood, but my cheek stung where she'd struck. I flinched, feeling all my bravery disappear with the pain. I'd tried to act like Dean, but I didn't have his nerve. Most of my bravery was like fast-burning aether—a bright flame with a quick flare, and then nothing except ashes.

"I hear you managed to impress the Wytch King," she said. "So you're probably not a Fae spy, I'll give you that much. But what you are is a rude, impetuous little girl who can still bring the Fae to us, and for that alone, we're not letting you leave."

"'We'?" I said. "You speak for all of the Erlkin?" I wasn't sure exactly how much power Shard wielded aboard Windhaven, and she certainly didn't seem to agree with the Wytch King's assessment of me. This could go either way.

"You're important to my son," Shard said, her voice softer. She looked out the front of the bubbled glass, at the fog drifting back from the prow of Windhaven. "And Nails is important to me. I already lost him once when he chose his father over me." Her eyes drifted back to my face, and I could tell by the coldness in them I was no more substantial to her than the fog outside. "I won't let it happen again. Not now."

"I—" I started, but Shard waved her hand.

"Go back to your room, Aoife. Nobody but Windhaven crew is supposed to be up here."

"I care about Dean," I blurted. That was a truth I didn't have to question, ever. Dean, aside from Nerissa and Conrad, was always first in my thoughts. "Just as much as you do. He saved my life. I'm not trying to lead him astray or get him in trouble, but he should be able to have his own life in the Iron Land if he wants it."

"No, he should not," Shard said shortly. "Saying that just proves how young and unsuited for *Nails* you are." She gestured at one of the Erlkin arrayed around the deck, checking gauges or watching the rudders and the aether screens. "Take Ms. Grayson back to her room. If she won't stay in it, move her to a holding cell."

"Yes, Commander," said the Erlkin, and moved for me. Before she could close her hands around my arm, an alarm began to whoop from the flight console.

"Commander!" the pilot shouted. "Contact on the aether waves! Bearing one-zero-two!"

"Show me," Shard said tensely. The Erlkin she'd snapped at darted back to her station.

"This ping," said the pilot, pointing to a radio screen. A large, wavering blob appeared and disappeared under the stroke of the aether detector. "Huge." She flipped another switch. "And closing in fast."

I felt the fear return, smooth and cold as an iron ball in my stomach. Whatever was out there in the fog, I knew from the prickles all over my exposed skin that it wasn't going to be a friendly encounter.

"We're being hailed!" another Erlkin at the side console shouted.

"Put it through the aethervox," said Shard. A moment of static blanketed all other sound, and then a voice I thought I'd only hear again in my nightmares barked out of the cloth-covered speakers mounted at the apex of the glass bubble.

"This is Grey Draven, Director of the Bureau of Proctors. You are an enemy vessel, carrying fugitives. You are ordered to heave to and surrender any wanted criminals on board."

I froze. I couldn't have moved for anything in the world, no longer able to pretend that Draven wouldn't find me. Before I'd spoken to the Wytch King, I'd fervently hoped that Draven had died, like so many in Lovecraft, when the Engine was destroyed. Failing that, I'd simply hoped to run forever and never have to look at his face again. But he was out there, in the fog, inexorable, and I was never going to escape.

Draven, while he was alive, was never going to leave me be.

Shard cut her gaze to me, then shoved the radio operator out of the way and depressed the return switch, a finely wrought ebony knob. "You're out of your depth, Mr. Draven. The Proctors don't rule here, and no humans are wanted by the likes of you once you cross the borders of the Mists. Go home."

"I know you have her." Draven's voice was precise and flat as a scalpel blade. "Don't play games with me, you goblin bitch."

I watched Shard's back stiffen, but she was all calm as she responded. "Go home, Mr. Draven. I don't know how you got to the Mists, but leave. There's nothing for you here."

Draven laughed. "I came through the Gates, of course. The gates Miss Grayson so kindly ripped asunder when she destroyed the Engine in my city." A pause, while Shard turned to stare at me. "Oh, I'm sure she didn't tell you that," Draven purred. "That she's the reason for all of this misery. That with her unnatural talents, she sent a pulse of power from the Engine to the Gates so great that it shattered the very fabric between our worlds and all the others, that she destroyed countless innocent lives, that she's a traitor to her kind, prey to the honeyed words of the Fae."

Shard took a step toward me, another. Her eyes weren't flat now. She'd been proven right. I was nothing but a criminal, something foul that had contaminated her little flying world. I was in deep trouble, and began to consider where I could run to. Nowhere good.

"Commander," said the pilot. "We have visual contact."

Shard let her gaze wander from me, and we both stared as a dirigible hove out of the mists. It was the largest I had ever seen, a zeppelin with its rigid balloon painted matte black and embossed with the gold seal of the Proctors, raven's wings stamped just underneath the gear and sickle, the symbol of the Master Builder, the false god Draven and his kind had created to replace magic and religion.

The dirigible was running red lanterns, a color aether took on when it was treated with other chemicals to burn brighter or hotter or longer. The hull was silver and looked like the body of a beast that lived deep under the ocean and only surfaced in legend, when it feasted on what floated above.

Gatling guns swiveled toward Windhaven from the hull, their cylinders turning slowly, and the dirigible was so close I swore I could count the individual bullets waiting to stream forth and puncture the glass bubble we stood in.

Shard swore, a coarse, barking word I didn't understand but recognized instantly as a curse. "Evasive action," she snapped. "Get us out of their fire zone!"

"Headwind, Commander," the pilot said. "We can't."

"Do it!" Shard screamed.

"You have a choice, Erlkin," Draven's voice purred. "It's an easy one. Give me Aoife Grayson or I blow that floating scrap heap out of the sky."

I backed toward the door, desperate to get away from Draven's voice and the view of his great dark shadow of an airship. If I couldn't see or hear him, I could pretend this wasn't happening. Shard wasn't paying attention to me now. She was screaming orders, and her crew was scrambling to obey.

"I guess you've made your choice," Draven said. "Too bad." With that, tracers of orange fire streaked across the distance between the zeppelin and Windhaven. One shell shot through the glass of the pilothouse and embedded itself in the far wall. Wind screamed through the opening, and cracks like spiderwebs spread from the hole. Windhaven appeared to be well armored, but Draven's gunners had been lucky, and the glass fell away in jagged slices as the negative pressure fought with the bullet holes.

"Return fire!" Shard bellowed. "Don't let them get another shot like that!"

I bumped into the hatch and reached behind me to spin the wheel. My heart was hammering in time with the rounds from the Gatling guns on Draven's airship. I couldn't think beyond the cold fact that we had to get off Windhaven before Draven boarded it and found us. If he'd already tracked us here, there was nowhere I could truly hide from him. Draven was relentless. Eventually he'd board Windhaven, and then we'd be, as Cal would put it, screwed up like sugar in the gearbox.

I'd known Draven was depraved and possibly insane, but obsessive enough to track me into a foreign land full of hostile Erlkin? I shuddered to think what he'd do if he actually caught me again.

I slipped out through the hatch, unnoticed by any of the crew, and fled down the corridor, back the way I'd come. Windhaven jolted and swayed under round after round of fire, and there was a shriek followed by a thump that rocked me off my feet, sending vibrations through the entire hull.

Some kind of antiaircraft projectile. Windhaven righted, but I felt a change in the tenor of the turbines. We'd been hit, and a dip in my stomach told me the craft was losing altitude.

Hands took me by the arm and tried to right me, and I swatted at them reflexively.

"Relax!" Dean shouted over the whooping alarms and thudding of projectiles as Windhaven and the dirigible exchanged fire. "It's me. Just me."

"Thanks be for small favors," I said, slumping. "We have to go, Dean. Now."

His face was grim, and his jaw twitched when he nodded. "Yeah. Figure no good's going to come of me staying here. My mother can take care of herself."

I let him pull me to my feet. "Where are Conrad and the others?" I said.

"Cal and Bethina are in the regular cabins like you," Dean told me. "My mother put Conrad in a holding cell down near the engine room."

"Of course she did," I muttered. Nothing could ever be easy on me and my family. "Is there a way we can tell Cal and Bethina how to meet us at the balloon bay?"

"There's aethervox between the rooms, yeah," Dean said. We stopped at a red iron box with a symbol stamped on the outside, three lines rising from a triangle. Dean picked up the handset and cranked a knob to bring up power, then turned two dials, one for deck number and one for room.

Erlkin were beginning to fill the corridor around us,

rushing to and fro. Nobody paid any attention to me, since I was with Dean and they had more pressing matters, like the ever-increasing tilt of the floor beneath our feet. The hit to the bridge must have been worse than it looked. We were falling, and at a rate of speed that made my stomach float slightly off center, a sick reminder of the impact that awaited us. I'd brought Draven here, and now I'd destroy Windhaven like I'd destroyed Lovecraft—unless I got off the ship and directed Draven's rage away from the Erlkin. I'd honestly rather be back under his thumb than have the weight of more lives on me.

"Cal!" Dean yelled. "Get the milkmaid and meet us in the balloon docks." He paused and then rolled his eyes at me. "Why do you think, dummy? Get your ass moving!" He slammed down the handset and turned to me. "I swear, that kid's thick as two boards. Let's go."

"I'm sorry," I said as we ran against the tide of Erlkin moving toward the bridge and the doors to the outside. "This is my fault."

"This is no more your fault than mine," Dean said. "Draven's the one shooting shells at our hull."

As if to punctuate his point, an explosion rocked us against one of the curved walls and debris sprayed from a direct hit, filling the air with dust. The fine paneling and polished copper that made up the walls of the corridor and the section of hull beyond bowed and broke, and a shriek of cold air snatched at my hair and cheeks. A smoking hole reaching down into nothing stared back from where I'd been about to place my foot, half the floor and wall gone. Draven was using heavy shells—it took more than mere bullets to punch through inches of iron and rivets.

Dean's forehead was cut, and blood ran from one of his ears. My own were ringing, like I'd stuck my head inside a bell, and wetness trickled into my left eye. "You're bleeding!" Dean shouted at me, though I read his lips more than heard him speak.

I swiped at my face and my entire palm came away coated red. "I'm fine!" I shouted back. Whatever had hit me, I could still walk, and that was the important thing. I could panic about the amount of blood when we were away from Windhaven.

We struggled to our feet, and Dean went first along the narrow span of corridor that hadn't been blown away. To the side was open air, and below I could see down at least four decks, sparks and escaping aether mingling to create tongues of short-lived blue fire amid the twisted wreckage.

"This way," Dean panted. His voice came to me sounding flat and far away, like a bad connection over the aether.

We reached a stairwell, and looking over the railing dizzied me. We were at least twenty levels up.

"No lifts," Dean said. "We're in one and another shell hits . . ." He clapped his hands together.

"I hope Conrad's all right," I said. He had to be. My dazzlingly clever brother, who could escape any trap. He'd be fine. If he wasn't, I'd lost my only other family and was totally alone. I couldn't let myself contemplate that right now. I could only run.

Dean didn't say anything, but he did move faster, taking the stairs two at a time.

The downward journey seemed interminable, especially when I was alone with my own heartbeat and the faint screech of the alarms. Every time Windhaven bounced violently, I had to stop and grab the rail or risk being pitched headfirst off the landing.

"Here," Dean said at last. "Prison level."

"Thank stone you know your way around here," I panted, slowing at last. Dean shrugged.

"I grew up here. Skip and I used to sneak off all the time."

I tried not to look too surprised. I'd always thought Dean hated the Erlkin side of him, and had pictured him absconding to Lovecraft as soon as he could toddle. But maybe it had been later. Shard's pain over Dean's return certainly seemed to indicate that.

By the cells, two Erlkin in uniform carried the same sort of guns Skip and the other soldiers had carried slung across their backs when they'd caught us in the forest. The cells themselves were plain gray doors, each marked, mercifully, with a number rather than a foreign symbol.

"We should evacuate," one Erlkin was insisting, gripping his gun so tightly I could see the white of his bone through his papery skin. They hadn't spotted us yet, and I waited in the curve of the corridor with Dean, sharing his breath and smelling the salt of his sweat and the sweetish odor of tobacco that permeated his clothes.

"And do what with the prisoners?" the other Erlkin demanded.

"Hell, I don't care!" the other said. "Leave their asses behind. Filthy Fae and slipstreamers, the lot of them."

"Fine," said the other as another artillery blast shook Windhaven. "Let's get to the balloons."

I pulled Dean into an alcove as they passed, but they were beyond caring about a couple of teenagers wandering around. Dean picked up a left-behind manifest hanging on a clipboard and skimmed the sheet of vellum, pointing down the corridor. "Cell nine."

Relief coursing through me, I ran down the hall and stopped at number nine, peering through the barred window in the top half of the door. Conrad had braced himself against the far wall of the cell, and his face slackened in relief when he saw me.

"Oh, thank stone," he said. "Get me out of here."

The lock was a tumbler and a bolt, nine pins, too complicated for me to try to shove with my mind at a time like this. If I had an episode and knocked myself out, I'd be useless, and we'd be sitting ducks for Draven. "Dean!" I shouted. "Keys!"

"They're not here!" he yelled back. "Guards must've taken 'em." He came down the corridor, looking up as Windhaven shuddered like an animal in the throes of a death rattle. The aether lamps flickered, throwing us from bright to black and back again. "We need to move," he said. "Before all the evac balloons are gone."

"Leave me," Conrad said. "There's no help for it."

"No," I snarled. "We're not splitting up again—that's what got us into trouble the first time." When he opened his mouth to protest, I played my ace. Conrad and I could be equally stubborn, but I was better at changing his mind than he was at changing mine. "Draven is out there, Conrad. He'll torture you. Throw you in some dark hole." I'd already lost Nerissa. I couldn't abandon Conrad to Draven and ever expect to sleep again. If he survived the crash of Windhaven at all.

"Yeah," Dean said. "Nobody here is going to be your friend if you stay, man. It's time to motor."

"Aoife," Conrad said. "Don't listen to him. Get out before it's too late and we're both back in Draven's cells."

"Don't," Dean started, pointing at Conrad. "Don't make your sister feel any worse than she already does."

"*I'm* making her feel worse?" Conrad came to the bars, looking for all the world as if they were the only thing preventing him from wringing Dean's neck. "You little grease monkey, it's *your* mother who locked me up in here!"

"Both of you shut up!" I shouted, sick of their arguing. My head throbbed, warning me that all the iron on the prison level was building up in my blood. "Let me think!"

Dean and Conrad stared at me for a moment and then went quiet. They both knew me well enough. I pressed my palm against the door lock and tried to tamp down the panic inside me, control my heartbeat and breath. It wasn't easy. I felt fragile, as if the frantic racing of my pulse would shatter the delicate vessel of my body.

My Weird came as intolerable pressure against my skull. My vision skewed and filled with the glow of the aether lamps, but I pushed the pain back. I grabbed the pressure and squeezed it out through my pores, my tear ducts, my nose and mouth, funneled the thing in my blood into the lock. It popped open, dead bolt flying back so violently it bowed the iron of the door, which in turn swung back and hit the cell wall with a sound like a gong.

"Come on," I said, reaching for Conrad, who stood still and glassy-eyed, and grabbing his arm. This was the first time he'd seen me use my Weird, and much as I wanted to know he didn't think I was a freak, we just didn't have the time to talk now. He stumbled as I yanked him.

"Jeez, Aoife," he said. "I'm coming, I'm coming."

Dean leading the way, we ran toward the balloon bays as fast as the jostling, tilting vessel would allow.

Just before we reached the outer catwalks, which sprang away from Windhaven like a collection of spindly antennae, we ran into Cal. Bethina was with him, clinging to his arm as Windhaven shuddered under our feet, the death throes of the city feeding through the soles of my boots.

"It's no good in the balloons," Cal said. "Some got off, but they got shot down. They're trying to slag the docking arms."

Indeed, many of the catwalks were wrecked and smoking, just twisted memories of what they'd been. My heart sank to my feet. Draven was going to make me his prisoner again. Torture and interrogate me. Use me to bring in my father.

No.

I dug my fingers into my temples, determined to stop the clawing and whispering of the iron poisoning that tried to seduce me into the frantic, illogical thoughts of end-stage madness.

"Is there another way off?" I demanded of Dean. He nodded.

"There's emergency craft for the crew and the security force. The last ones off the boat."

"Good," I said, already moving. "Let's get there before somebody else has the same great idea."

"I don't know if they're anything you want to try to escape a hail of gunfire in," Dean said. "Took one out once when I was a kid and damn near pasted myself against a mountain."

I kept moving. "We don't have a choice." We could either

risk dying while getting off the ship or be condemned to something worse when Draven caught us. In my mind, the course was obvious, no matter how slim the chance we'd all survive in one piece might be.

"Agreed," Conrad said. "We have to run. However we can. If we stay here we're dead for sure."

"Okay." Dean nodded. "Better than no damn plan at all. Come with me."

Cal grabbed Bethina's hand, and Conrad brought up the rear. I followed Dean, and we made our way back toward the top of Windhaven so we could fall toward the ground, and freedom.

Through the Mist Gate

BEFORE LONG, WE ran into clots of Erlkin in the corridors, and Dean cursed. "We can't get down to the bay."

"Where is it?" I said. Dean pointed his finger at the floor.

"Below the pilothouse," he said. "They can reach it by evacuation tube."

I bit my lip. The idea that sprang to mind just then was insane, but it was less of a danger than passively waiting for Draven to catch us again.

"Come with me," I said, hoping the others wouldn't ask too many questions, because I didn't have a lot of answers. That was the problem with on-the-fly plans—sometimes you fell. I turned and started toward the room where Shard had kept me, hoping now wouldn't be one of those times.

Dean shook his head as I crossed the room and opened the porthole. "Oh, no, Aoife," he said, realizing what I had in mind.

"We're not moving," I said. "We can make it."

"Yeah, and the next time we take a direct hit we're going to get shaken off like so many pieces of dust," Cal said, gesturing at the porthole and the ledge beyond. "This is crazy, Aoife."

"You of all people have something real to lose when Draven boards us," I told him, giving him a cutting look. Bethina glanced between us.

"What's she mean?"

"Nothing," Cal snarled. "Nothing."

Above us, I heard the whirr of powerful turbines and a knocking against the hull.

"Boarding ladders," Dean said. "The Proctors are coming onto Windhaven. We don't have any more time."

I levered my leg out the porthole. "I'm going."

"Me too," Bethina said, squaring her shoulders. "It couldn't be any worse than here."

Clinging to the metal skin of a vessel floating in midair was not my idea of a pleasant experience. I reached out and grabbed the nearest rudder, and for a breathless moment before my foot found the ledge, I swung free.

Dean followed, then Cal. He helped Bethina, and Conrad came last. I allowed myself a small moment of relief that everyone had gone along with me with minimal arguing. We might have a chance after all.

"I changed my mind!" Bethina shrieked above the wind howling around us. "I want to go back!"

"No!" Cal shouted. "No going back now! I'm right behind you."

I crawled down the side of Windhaven, gripping the rudders and the rungs of a maintenance ladder, feeling the shudders of Draven's boarding under my hands. But as the bottom hull curved, holding on became harder, gravity pulling my weight away from the hand- and footholds.

"You okay?" Dean grunted as we climbed.

"No," I gritted out. I couldn't see him where he hung above me, just heard his ragged breathing. "Okay is not what I am at the moment."

"Hang on, princess," he said. "This is nothing. This is a walk in the park."

"You have a very strange idea of a park," I panted. Two plump blue balloons were tethered at the bottom of Windhaven's hull. I reached the first and risked taking one hand off the hull to open the basket door. My hands and arms were on fire, and I could feel tremors starting in my shoulder and working down to my fingers.

"Go on," Dean said. "Start untethering this thing and I'll help the others."

To get into the basket, I had to turn myself around and crawl in upside down and practically headfirst. Spinning with vertigo, I let go and dropped onto the wire mesh. I pulled myself to my feet and went to the balloon's tether, a flexible metal arm that was attached to the evacuation tube above us.

Dean landed on the mesh next to me, then stood and pulled Cal into the basket after him. He reached out for Bethina, who shook her head, copper curls hanging free in space. "I can't let go!"

"Foul the gears, Bethina!" Dean shouted. "You can't stay plastered to the bloody hull for the rest of your life!"

"If I let go, I'll fall!" Bethina cried. Tears were streaming down her face, streaking like rain in the wind.

"You won't fall, doll," Dean promised, his voice changing to a soothing tone. "I've got strong arms. I'll catch you."

"Go!" Conrad snarled at her from where he clung to the ladder behind her. "I could have climbed up and down this ship twice in the time it's taking you."

"Conrad!" I snapped, horrified at how he could be so insensitive at a time like this. "That is really not helping!"

Bethina extended one trembling hand to Dean, and he caught her and hauled her aboard. When she stood up, shaking, she cast Conrad a look that could have stopped traffic. Cal wrapped his arms around her, and she buried her face against his collar. I almost wished she'd just slapped Conrad. Maybe then he would have learned that he couldn't say whatever he wanted whenever he wanted to whoever was within earshot.

I finished untethering the balloon and the craft floated upward, bumping gently against the underside of Windhaven.

"At last," Conrad breathed, and moved to close the gap and jump aboard from where he hung.

But before he could, Windhaven groaned, the propeller blades spinning to life high above us, and the floating city listed sharply to one side.

Conrad missed the balloon cage and lost his grip on the hull, pitching off the edge of the cage. He caught the mesh with two of his fingers, slipping down toward the nothing of the mist below.

"Conrad!" I shrieked, diving across space and catching his hand. He flailed and latched onto my sleeve, and with horror I felt myself sliding out of the balloon cage. Bethina screamed, sounding very far away, and Dean shouted something at Cal, but all I could see was the fear in Conrad's eyes as he hung over the gently roiling cauldron of fog. Everything else was sucked away; there was only the knowledge that I had to save him, and the resolute stone in my stomach saying it wouldn't end this way. Not after everything we'd been through.

I scrabbled for hold and grabbed the bar at the foot of the balloon's door, hanging on with all my strength. Conrad grappled for purchase on my other arm. The pain was worse than anything I'd ever felt, and it radiated through me. But I couldn't let go—I wouldn't. Conrad's fingers found my skin, digging furrows in my wrist.

"Aoife!" Dean shouted, dropping to his stomach as the balloon swayed wildly, free of its restraints. He grabbed me by the wrist with one hand and the shoulder of my jacket by the other, trying to haul me back into the basket. "Cal, get over here!" he bellowed. Cal left the rudder of the balloon waving wildly and joined Dean, reaching out his lanky arm and catching Conrad's free hand. With heaving and straining and a lot of swearing, they finally hauled us back in.

Conrad collapsed, shaking, and I lay perfectly still, unable to move. My right arm, the one Conrad had grabbed, felt boneless and disconnected from the rest of my body. I could feel blood from scrapes dribbling across my skin, turning cold against the air. My forehead had begun bleeding again, sending stinging red spots into my vision. All of it was from far away, though, as if I were attached to my body by nothing more than the air we were floating in.

Dean's face drifted into my tunneled vision. "You all right?" he said. "Let me get a look at you, princess."

Cal helped Conrad to a place in the corner of the basket while Dean turned my head from side to side. "Don't check out on me," he murmured. "You're fine. We're all fine."

"We might not be!" Cal shouted, pointing ahead of us. The balloon was trapped beneath Windhaven's hull like a butterfly beneath a glass bulb. The brass finial at the top of the harness holding the balloon's gas bag in place squealed along the underside of the floating city, trying desperately to gain altitude.

I followed the sight line of Cal's finger along our route and felt panic rise in my chest, unfreezing my body from the shock of finding myself still alive.

The great propeller fan on the rear of Windhaven pulled us closer and closer as it sucked air into its blades, turning the city at a bank so steep that metal screeched and rivets popped and flew like bullets around us. One punctured the silk of the balloon, but we didn't drop clear of the fan.

"We're going to get chopped up!" Cal shouted. "We need to lose altitude!"

"And how exactly do you propose we do that?" Dean asked him.

"Steer us out of here, then!" Cal cried as the balloon bounced harder. Conrad twined his fingers in the mesh of the passenger cage. Bethina grabbed me around the shoulders and held me still so that I wouldn't get thrown around in my fragile state.

Dean snatched the rudder, straining so hard the cords of muscle in his neck stood out like the cables of a suspension bridge.

"It's too strong," he panted. "I can't turn it." Conrad got

up shakily and tried to help him, but even their combined efforts weren't moving us quickly enough.

I crawled to the front of the passenger cage, curling my fingers in the mesh and using it to pull myself to my knees.

I focused my senses on the fan. It was the largest thing in my mind, a great mechanism of gears and blades, harnessing power from the wind and using it to hold up a device that was never supposed to fly.

My Weird wanted to touch the fan, wanted to connect with it, like reaching into a flame because it burns so brightly you have to feel it against your flesh even though you know it will sear your skin.

I pushed, with all my strength, pushed against the fan, willed it to reverse its direction and allow us to escape Draven.

My head throbbed, heat blossoming across my skin as if my blood were molten in my veins. Then the wind changed direction, blew so hard that it knocked me backward, and I lost my grip on my Weird, falling out of touch with my body and into the dark of unconsciousness.

I came to on a bed of moss that was the delicate blue color of a summer sky. I inhaled its dry, earthy scent and waited for my eyes to focus. There was a bit of dried blood crusted in the corner of my eye, and I swiped at it as I took in my surroundings. We were in a dead forest, gray spindly trees reaching twisted, bare branches into fog. Everything was gray and blue and white, as if we had fallen into a world with all other color leached out.

I rolled onto my other side and caught a more vivid slash of blue: the balloon, deflated. The cage was half sunk in the black muck of a swamp, and nobody was inside.

I sat up, alone for a moment in the drifting grayness, and called out. "Dean? Conrad?" My voice didn't actually form words, just came out in a croak. What if something had happened? What if I was the only one left? My stomach clenched.

"Miss?" Bethina materialized from the fog, and I collapsed back onto the moss in relief. I wasn't alone.

"Oh, stones! She's awake!" Bethina called back into the nothingness. The others came running, and Dean crouched beside me.

"Easy," he said. "You've been out for a while."

Conrad crouched on my other side and pulled my chin so I was facing him. "Pupils are the same size," he announced. "The bump on the head is superficial. We can move her."

"I've got it under control," Dean snapped. "Aoife isn't going anywhere if she's not in shape to walk."

"Excuse me, but you're not in charge here," Conrad said. "Nor are you my sister's keeper. I took care of her for fifteen years, I think I know when she's fit to walk."

"You call leaving her all by herself taking care of her?" Dean snorted. "Attacking her, putting a mark on her she can never wash off? Please. Aoife's better off with me."

"Listen, Erlkin," Conrad snarled. "I know exactly what your idea of *taking care* of my sister entails, and that's gonna stop right now. She's a good girl and she doesn't need your paws all over—"

"Stop it!" I shouted, and every one of my injuries throbbed, but I bit the inside of my cheek to stop myself from flinching. "You are both," I enunciated carefully, so there would be no mistake, "behaving like complete idiots."

I stretched out my hand to Cal. "Can you please help me up? We should get moving before Draven sends out men on the ground to track us."

"Sure thing," Cal said quickly, easing between Dean and Conrad and taking my hand. I left them crouched on the moss, glaring at each other. I wasn't a shiny brass trophy, and I wasn't in the mood to be batted back and forth in Dean and Conrad's little contest to see who was the biggest, baddest boy in our group. Right now, Bethina would do a better job of leading us to safety, and she'd scream a lot less too.

There was no path through the fog, just spongy ground punctuated by vernal pools that seeped into my boots whenever I mistakenly splashed down in one. The dead forest was endless, as if a blight crept ahead of us through the fog, washing all life out of the world. This was even eerier than the ancient forest we'd come to when we crossed from Lovecraft. The creeping sensation up my spine told me we shouldn't be here.

"What happened to this place?" I asked Dean, when he caught up with my limping steps.

"Fire," he said. "Long time ago, before I was born. Maybe before my mother, too."

"Big fire," I said. The fog swirled back and forth, thinning to lace. The dead forest went on as far as the eye could see.

"The Fae set it," Dean said. "They were looking for insurgents, some of my kind who'd set off an explosion in the silver mines in the Thorn Land. They burned the entire forest to the ground. Killed thousands."

"I'm sorry," I said quietly. I understood then why Shard

had looked at me with such coldness. It didn't excuse her locking me up and refusing to believe a word I said, but it at least explained it.

Dean shrugged. "Not my world. I left as soon as I was able."

"Shard and Skip," I said, "they both call you Nails. Why do you have two names?" Cal had two names, but he was a ghoul—wholly other. Dean was more human by a mile than he was Erlkin, from what I could see, and I wanted to know what his name in the Mists meant. I wanted to know everything about him, not that he'd tell me without a lot of effort on my part. But I was willing to try.

"Nails isn't my name," Dean said tightly. He fished in his pockets and pulled out a pack of Lucky Strikes, crushed beyond recognition. "Dammit," he muttered, shoving the twisted cardboard back into his jeans.

"Your mother seems to think it is," I said. Dean shook his head.

"You have to understand, the Erlkin are a slave race. Way back in the primordial ooze they lived underground, and when the Fae dug down looking for silver, they enslaved the creatures they found. They wouldn't give us real names, names with meaning and magic, so they called us after scraps—glass and silver, drill bits and rock crushers."

"Nails," I offered.

"Yup," Dean said. "When the first generation of free Erlkin named their children, they gave them slave names as a way to tell the Fae they didn't own us anymore. It's tradition now." His mouth twitched. "But I'm not Erlkin, and I don't need to be reminded that I was ever anyone's slave."

"I noticed your mother doesn't have any problem with

your being a half-breed, unlike her problems with me," I muttered.

"Oh, she has plenty of problems with it," Dean said with a laugh drier than the dead trees all around us. "But she knows that I'm her fault, too. Stealing away and meeting a human—tsk, tsk and all that. I know it was a lot easier for her in her position at Windhaven after I lit out for Lovecraft and decided to live with my old man. She got that nice shiny captain's promotion the minute I left." Bitterness tinged his voice like unsweetened tea on the tongue.

"You really have a brother?" I asked. Dean had only mentioned him in passing, but I was realizing that in spite of spending nearly all my waking moments with him since we'd met, I still knew virtually nothing about his family or his life before me.

"Half-brother," Dean said. "One hundred percent pure boring human. Older than me by a good few years—my pops had a wife before Shard bewitched his poor dumb self. The woman ditched him and Kurt—that's my brother. Kurt was never too fond of me, even though his old lady was long gone. Didn't blame him except when he and I were slugging it out. I wouldn't be itching to bond with the bastard child of my father's new girlfriend if I were him either."

"And where's Kurt now?" I prompted, racking my brain to remember what else Dean had told me about his past.

"Hell if I know," Dean said. "He went MIA fighting the Crimson Guard, 'bout a year before you and I crossed paths." He sighed, and I could tell from his twitchy gait and fingers that he wanted a cigarette. "Truth is, Aoife, I never really felt like I was part of the family. I was a wayward kid and I wasn't at home much. But it beat the pants off staying in Windhaven and marching in lockstep like my good little Erlkin relatives."

"I'm sorry," I said. "About Kurt."

"It's all right," Dean said. "Like I told you, we were never close. Not like you and Conrad."

"Conrad and I haven't been that close for a while," I said quietly. "And we've been apart since he ran away a year ago."

"You'll get it back," Dean said. "He looks out for you, and even if he's a cranky bastard, he cares about you. I can tell by the way he's giving me the hairy eyeball right now."

I glanced over my shoulder and saw that Conrad was indeed staring a hole into the back of Dean's head as we walked. I sighed and dropped back to match my stride to my brother's.

"Will you quit glaring? You're embarrassing me."

"I don't like your friend, Aoife," Conrad told me. "Not one bit. He's too familiar with you."

"He's familiar because I want him to be familiar," I snapped. "Stop acting like you're our father, Conrad, because you're not."

He flinched, and I felt as if I might as well have smacked him across the face. "I know that," he muttered. "But he's not here, is he? Nobody knows where he is or if he's even alive."

I stayed quiet for few steps, our feet squashing into the bog the only sound besides the faint murmur of Cal and Bethina's conversation. Conrad was right—we didn't know. None of the Erlkin would admit to knowing where Archie had gone. And he'd made no attempt to contact us. Not that he could, even if he was in a position to. After the Engine exploded Conrad and I had effectively vanished from the Iron Land without a trace.

No matter how much I wished Archie would appear again and make it right, as he had when I'd been in Draven's prison, he wasn't going to, and it was time I accepted that. I bit down hard on my lip to hold back my tears. "We know where Nerissa is," I said after a time, when I could speak without a break in my voice.

"No," Conrad said instantly. "Don't even think of that, Aoife. We can't go back there."

"Draven already found us," I said. "He'll find us no matter where we go, and I have to get Nerissa out of Lovecraft." Or what was left of Lovecraft. I imagined a wasteland overrun with ghouls and pockets of vicious survivors barricaded in their homes while black-clad Proctor squads roamed the streets and their clockwork ravens swooped overhead, watching every living thing left in the desolation.

"Why?" Conrad demanded. "She was locked up in a madhouse when everything went sideways. Those places are fortresses. She's probably safer there than on the run with us anyway. And honestly, Aoife—that woman never did one bit of good for us our entire lives. She's crazy."

"She's *not* crazy," I snarled, feeling my teeth draw back over my lips. My anger flared bright and I felt the insane urge to strike out at Conrad. I'd never wanted to actually hit him before, beyond a light smack when we were arguing over something minor. "She's poisoned by iron, like we were. She'll be fine if we can get her out of the city."

"You don't know that," Conrad said. "She's been exposed to iron for years longer than us, Aoife. And she's full-blood

Fae besides. Her mind could be punched full of holes, just like the doctors always said it was." He stopped and folded his arms, brows drawing together. "Why do you care so much, Aoife? You were always more angry at her than I was for leaving us, making us wards of the city."

"Because," I said softly. "I *left* her there, Conrad. *I* did this, and when everything went wrong and the city got destroyed I had to leave her." A sob bubbled out of my chest and I didn't try to stop it. Crying was better than screaming or collapsing and refusing to go on. "I have to go back and try to fix her," I whispered. "Fix her and try to fix what I did to Lovecraft. Mend it somehow, the Gates and the Engine and all of it."

"People aren't machines, Aoife," Conrad said softly, and reached for my hand, squeezing all my fingers by wrapping his thumb and forefinger around them like he had when we were very small. "Some, nobody can fix."

"I have to try," I whispered. My dreams would never cease, and the weight of my guilt would never be lifted, until I was able to look at what I'd done to Lovecraft with my own eyes, until I had at least tried to get my mother out of the iron city that had turned her into someone my brother and I didn't recognize.

Conrad sighed and then dropped my hand, shoving his through his unruly black hair, so much like mine.

"All right," he said at last. "Say I was insane enough to go back to the Iron World—where I can't even remember my own name once the poison takes hold—risk using the Gates now that they've been breached by the Proctors and stone knows what else, travel overland with ghouls on the loose, and go back into the *very same* city I barely escaped from a year ago—what then? How are we even going to find Nerissa if she's not still in Christobel Asylum, never mind get her in shape to walk out of there on the kind of rough journey we've had? How would we evade the Proctors and Draven?"

I chewed on my lip for a moment. The sting wasn't worse than the pain through the rest of my body, but Conrad's questions were. "I don't know," I told him. "But I will by the time we get to Lovecraft."

I filled Dean in on the plan—if you could call it that—while we walked, and to his credit, he reacted better than Conrad had. "I can't say what I'd do if Shard and I were in the same situation," he said.

"You are," I said. "Draven was boarding Windhaven. He's not inclined to be kind."

Dean sniffed. "My mother can take care of herself. And a city full of Erlkin is a far cry from some scared, sniveling humans hiding in a basement."

"I hope so," I said. "You know I feel terrible. I thought he'd never find me in the Mists."

"Not your fault," Dean said shortly. "Draven's a pit bull. He'll hold on till he's dead or somebody else is."

"He doesn't want me dead," I muttered. "He doesn't want me at all. He just wants bait for my father."

Dean stopped us at the crest of a hill, behind a half-collapsed stone wall. We had come out of the dead forest and were standing on the outskirts of a ruined village, small white stone cottages topped with rotting thatch, the only thing stirring in the breeze.

"Wait here," Dean said. I looked down the slope toward where the cottages disappeared into the ever-flowing mist.

"Why? Where are we?"

"The Mist Gate," Conrad said, nearly making me jump out of my skin. Cal joined us, and his nostrils flared.

"Humans are down there," he muttered, out of Bethina's hearing.

"Draven's, likely," Dean said. "He'll have guards to make sure his bread crumbs don't dry up and blow away."

"How did he even come through?" Conrad said. "Humans can't pass into the Mists, not even members of the Brotherhood. Not without help." He shifted, obviously remembering the "help" the Erlkin slipstreamers had given him, crossing him over like so much contraband.

"He might have it," I said

He jerked his thumb down the hill. "So what do we do about them?"

Cal's tongue flicked out. "Leave that to me."

"Cal, no," I hissed, glancing behind me at Bethina. "What about her?"

"Keep her busy," Cal said, shrugging. "We need to get out of here, and this is the quickest way."

"*Cal,*" I snapped. "Don't be ridiculous." I turned and pointed at Conrad. "You and I." We were the only ones besides Cal who had the ability to defend ourselves, even if my Weird was unreliable and my fighting skills nonexistent. At least I didn't have to turn into a long-clawed, fanged monster to tap into my particular talent. I didn't relish confronting the Proctors again, but I had to think of the group, not just myself.

"Me?" Conrad squawked, but I grabbed his arm and

tugged him along, keeping to the shadows of the ruined cottages.

We crept down the hill, and before long I could hear low conversation in human voices.

"You better at least have a plan," Conrad hissed. "These guys will have guns."

I stopped in the archway of what had once been a barn. Peering around the corner, I could just make out two shapes standing in the fog.

I'd seen the *hexenrings* the Fae used to travel between the Iron World and their own, circles of simple stones or mushrooms wreathed with enchantments that could bend space and time, but the Erlkin's Gates were a mystery to me. I'd watched Conrad use them only once, when he'd helped us escape from the ruins of the Iron World. Not even him, really—the slipstreamers had opened the way.

After I'd broken the Gates . . . and presumably allowed Draven to manipulate them somehow, without Erlkin aid.

That bothered me. If the Mists were open, what was to stop a free-for-all, beings crossing every Gate between every land? The fact that we'd seen only Draven so far in the Mists made me think there was something larger going on, possibly worse, but I hoped with everything I had that what I'd done to the Gates to Thorn hadn't rippled to the rest of the lands.

That would be worse than one destroyed city. That would be worse than anything.

Now is not the time, Aoife. I steadied my breathing, and with it, my racing thoughts.

Two Proctors stood beyond the last of the ruins, in front

of a tumbledown iron structure that was hard to make out distinctly through the mist.

I crouched down and hefted one of the stones that had fallen from the cottage wall.

"Whistle," I told Conrad. He raised an eyebrow.

"Whistle? Are you cracked?"

"Will you just trust me for once?" I hissed. I might not have had a grand and daring plan for sneaking into Lovecraft, but I could at least handle a couple of Proctors. All students in Lovecraft learned how to get around guidelines and curfew, and uniformed Proctors weren't usually the best and brightest of the crop anyway.

Conrad's face was marked deeply with skepticism, but he put his fingers in his mouth and let out a piercing whistle.

Instantly the Proctors snapped alert, and the closer one started toward us. "Hey!" his partner shouted. "Draven said we were supposed to stand on this spot!"

"That could be him now," the other insisted.

"No," the first said. "He told us to stay put."

"You really want to be the one who kept him waiting?" said the first Proctor. "You've seen how he gets. Especially since he got to be a bigwig in the Bureau."

The other sighed, but then jerked his head in assent. "Make it fast, will ya? This place is the worst. Creepy as all hell."

"Hello?" the first Proctor shouted. "Any virals lurking, show yourselves!"

I blinked, momentarily surprised that the Proctors still believed in the necrovirus. But how could they not? I wondered what excuse Draven had come up with to bring them all here, to a place that wasn't supposed to exist and could get you burned for heresy for suggesting that it did.

The Proctor passed the stone wall, so close I could have reached out and plucked at the sleeve of his black uniform. Once he'd passed out of sight of his friend, I stepped out from cover behind him and swung the rock swiftly and surely, connecting with the back of his skull.

Conrad gaped at me, then at the sprawled Proctor on the ground, who lay unmoving. "Well?" I said to Conrad, hefting the rock. "Whistle again."

"Stone and sun, Aoife," Conrad muttered. "You're not the sister I left behind, that's for sure."

"You're not the brother who left, Conrad," I retorted. That brother wouldn't have looked at me like I was crazy for doing what was necessary, and it made me sad. But that was for another time, when we weren't surrounded by Proctors and who knew what other dangers. "It's a natural progression, as far as I'm concerned."

Conrad rolled his eyes at me as if I were unbearably childish, but he stuck his fingers back in his mouth. The second Proctor fell in much the same way as the first.

Once Cal and Dean had helped Conrad tie the Proctors up, using their own belts and some rope in Cal's backpack, we approached the Gate.

"All right," Dean rubbed his hands together. "Conrad, get this bad boy up and running, and get us far away from Draven and his jackbooted blackbirds."

"Me?" Conrad pointed at Dean. "You're the Erlkin, you get us out of here."

"Brother, I know less than nothing about those

contraptions," Dean said. "I've lived most of my life in the Iron Land, just like you. 'Sides, you need a technician or a slipstreamer to work the Gates, if you don't want just anything getting in."

"Yeah, you're the one who's been going back and forth like he knows a magic trick, according to Bethina and Aoife," Cal piped up. "How'd you do it, Conrad?"

"I didn't, all right!" Conrad answered, clearly irritated. "I paid Erlkin to take me back and forth. Just like that square deal Skip said." He kicked a clump of muddy earth with his shoe. "I don't know how to work the Gates. Is that what you want me to say? It's the one thing I'm supposed to do as a Gateminder, besides have a Weird, and I can't. I tried, I can't, and I never could. And now that the Gates are so screwed up even people like us can't always use them, I'll never get the chance to try again. You happy now?"

"Damn, man," Dean said after a moment. "You don't have to put your dukes up. We were just asking a question."

"Yeah," Cal said. "I didn't know. And it doesn't matter," he added quickly. "You just haven't gotten the hang of it yet."

I hadn't known either, and I looked at Conrad with a new light shining on him, surprised that he'd admitted to all of us he wasn't perfect. I'd assumed Conrad had found his Weird, and more importantly, learned how to manipulate the Gates, long before he'd sent me the letter that started me looking for him. I had no way of knowing he'd found someone to smuggle him. That he'd never touched his Weird.

That it was all up to me.

While Conrad sighed and paced away from the group, I turned in the opposite direction and went to examine the Gate. Conrad needed his space when he got in moods like this. He always had. Bethina looked for a moment like she was going to try to speak to him, but Cal laid a hand on her arm and shook his head.

Gates were, from what little I'd gleaned from the Fae, tears in the fabric between the Lands. Call it physics, or magic, or heresy, barriers kept humans, Fae, Erlkin and the older, darker things apart. Erected after the great Storm, when magic ran unbidden through the Iron Land and nearly caused a catastrophe on a global scale, the Gates had been a human idea first, but the Fae had taken them, twisted them. The Erlkin's physical markers for their Gates were a far cry from the stone circles of the Fae and the simple thin spaces in the fabric of the Iron Land that a Gateminder felt as a tingle down the spine. This Gate was an iron structure, a plinth that tapered to a point at the top. A network of iron lattice filled the center, and in it a small tube of aether glittered, held at either end by spindly iron arms. That much aether could flatten the land for half a mile if it made contact with the air. I drew back my hand from the iron. I had better not screw this up.

"What do you think?" Dean asked at my shoulder. I jumped and let out a small noise.

"Sorry," he said. "But can you get us out of here?"

"I'm not sure," I said, tentatively placing my hand against the iron marker of the Gate. My Weird responded immediately, opening a vast void in my head, through which I could feel the mechanism of the Erlkin's Gate—a machine, here, rather than a spell like the Fae's stone circle—churning and wide open. "Holy . . ." I jerked my hand away. The skin was hot and pink, and I felt the telltale dribble of blood down my upper lip. "Darn it," I said, swiping at it.

Dean handed me his bandanna. "So," he said carefully, "not good?"

"It's a machine," I said. "So that's . . . better, I guess, than Fae magic. But it's open."

One of Dean's dark eyebrows arched above his silver eye. "Right now?"

"Wide open." I sniffed and tasted metal in the back of my throat. My Weird was far more of a pain than a gift most of the time. And how could the Gate be open, with no one controlling it?

Because you didn't just open the Gates to Thorn, my thoughts whispered. *You broke something, some fundamental backbone, and now it's just a matter of time until another Storm.*

No. I couldn't let my thoughts spin off track. It was just the Weird, or residual echoes from being on Windhaven and close to so much iron. That was all. I hadn't kick-started a disaster of apocalyptic proportions.

Now if I could just believe that.

"Well, hell," Dean said. "I'm taking the leap, then. We need to move—those two are going to wake up and Draven's going to come back sooner or later." He braced himself to run at the Gate. "I'll go first, make sure it's safe."

"No!" I cried. Dean's impetuous lack of forethought was one of the things that had appealed to me when we'd met, but now he was just acting insane, and it wasn't helping anything.

I grabbed for his arm, but his leather jacket slipped

between my fingers as he took a run at the Gate. "We don't know what's on the other side!" I shouted, frantic. Dean couldn't get hurt. Couldn't leave me alone. I couldn't let him put himself at risk.

A split second later, Dean smacked into the metal lattice with a loud clang.

"Shit!" he bellowed, sitting down hard on the spongy ground, clutching his nose, which leaked a velvety trickle of blood down his square chin.

"Dean!" I cried. I ran to him and crouched at his side, using the tail of my shirt to stanch the bleeding.

"You said it was *open,*" he groaned.

"It was." I fluttered my hands helplessly, wishing more than anything that I could stop his pain, but there was nothing I could really do.

"*Man,* that smarts," Dean said, muffled against my shirt. He closed his hands over mine. "It's okay, princess. Not your fault. I'll be okay."

I reached out from where I crouched and passed the tips of my fingers over the cold, mist-kissed iron of the Gate. It was dead now—nothing pricked my Weird as working. As quickly as it had opened, it had shut again. Which lent even more credence to my theory that something was deeply wrong.

Later, I could puzzle it out, worry and fret over what I'd done, but for now, Conrad's statement remained true—we had to go before Draven found us here.

I focused my attention fully back on the Gate. I opened my mind, just as I had on Windhaven, not able to control a slight wince at the anticipation of skull-shattering pain.

I felt the machinery of the Erlkin Gate respond to my

Weird, the aether blazing across my mind. I cracked one eye and saw the lattice begin to move. The arms were mechanical, and they moved like spider legs, crimping and rearranging themselves into new formations as gears within the Gate begin to grind. For a moment I felt the Gate slipping open again, responding to the blood of a Gateminder as it should, and then all at once it was too hot, too bright, and I couldn't feel anything except furnace-warm air. I was burning alive, turning to ash, and I think I screamed before the world fell away.

The room had turned from sunset to night, the skies replete with a million stars. On one horizon, a faint blue line of dawn flared, while above my head triple moons, in phases from swollen full to the hunter's horns, turned and waxed and waned in time.

"It's not just gears and aether," said the figure standing before me in a black cloak. "It's those things, but it's more. It's the same thing that puts uncanny power in your blood, and it's what allowed the Gates to come to exist in the first place." He turned to watch the moons, cloak swirling. "And it can't be harnessed and controlled. It's a wild force, Aoife. It must be bargained with."

I looked at the spinning clockwork palace and voiced the thought echoing in my head. "Am I dead?"

"Dead?" the figure snorted. "Knocked out, perhaps. Far from the Deadlands as you are from anywhere else, in this place."

"Then why are we talking?" I said. "I haven't been exposed to enough iron to trigger a madness dream."

The figure smiled at me, the darkness of its face shifting. "You don't know, Aoife?"

"No," I said frankly. "I have no idea who you are or where we are." This time, it felt even more real, more present, *than when I'd first dreamed of the place, and it made me want to scream. I couldn't be mad. I'd been doing so well, trying to hold on until Conrad and I found a more certain cure than simply hiding in the woods.*

The sunrise beyond the dome was growing in intensity, but it wasn't the sun of the Iron Land—it was green and flared around the edges with sunspots. It was a dying sun, looking down on a dying universe.

Above, the black tentacles lashed and writhed in the green light, and the figure turned back toward the great gears that churned before us.

"You're dreaming, Aoife," he said. "Not seeing the product of iron poisoning, but really dreaming. And it's time for you to wake up."

"Fantastic," I mumbled. "Not only do I visit this place every time I close my eyes, I have to leave it and go back to the real world."

"You don't give your world enough credit," said the figure. "I've seen them all. Yours is beautiful."

"It's awful," I said. "And I made it that way."

"No, Aoife," said the dream figure. "What you did to the Engine was not as terrible a thing as you think. The worlds were never meant to be gated. At least, not your worlds. The Fae and the Iron . . . they need one another."

The figure turned away from me again. "Now it really is time for you to go." He turned the great gear, and I saw the green sun begin to spin out of its orbit, and the tentacles to recede with it.

"By the way," said the dream figure. "Don't try to use your handy little magic trick on a Gate in the Mists. The Erlkin are much better at keeping your kind out than the Fae."

He moved the gears again, and I watched as the green sun began to go nova, burning out in a flash so bright that it seared my vision.

I came back to the world with a gasp, and the worst spike of pain in my head that I'd ever endured, save the one when I touched the Lovecraft Engine with my Weird. "Did I faint?" I demanded of Cal, the first face I saw leaning over me with an anxious expression. It was embarrassing, but better than blacking out from a madness-induced hallucination by miles.

"You just kind of keeled over," he said, and upon seeing my mortified expression hastened to add, "You were only out for a few minutes."

"You fell like somebody cut your strings," Dean said, frowning. The bloody mark across the bridge of his nose made him look savage, but his eyes were filled with pure worry. He put his hands under my shoulders and helped me sit up. Touching Dean calmed the throbbing in my skull a bit, until Conrad cleared his throat.

"You were mumbling," he said, reaching out his hand for me and then pulling it back like touching me might pass the fainting spell. "Your eyes were twitching in their sockets too." He swallowed. "I've never seen you do that. Are you okay, Aoife?"

"Not really," I said. I managed to stand up by myself, so that was something. When your friends and brother could disappear at any moment, every small thing a girl like me could do for herself was monumentally important.

"I really don't like this place," Bethina piped up. "I feel like something is watching us."

I had to agree with her. This ghost-colored bit of the Mists was eerie, even by the standards of the things I'd seen recently, and my skin crawled as the drifting moisture kissed it.

"Don't worry, Bethina," Dean told her. "Nothing's going to jump out and bite you." He patted me on the shoulder. "Aoife will get us out of here."

I didn't say that with my spinning head, I wasn't going anywhere in a hurry, but I grasped Dean's hand in return. He was something solid to cling to, and I was so glad he was there.

Conrad's lips compressed in a straight line. "If this is what's going to happen, I'm not letting her touch the Gate again." He fished in his jacket pocket, pulled out a dirty kerchief and handed it to me. "Clean yourself up," he muttered to me, pressing the cloth into my hands. "Don't like to see you bleeding."

I swiped at my face and then shoved the kerchief into my own pocket.

"Thanks," I whispered to Conrad. He shrugged—a gesture of kindness I thought we'd forgotten how to exchange. I felt a little less strained in that moment.

Planting my feet carefully until my balance came back, I returned to the Gate, but this time I examined the plinth itself. The Erlkin were engineers, I was an engineer. Surely

I could make their machine work without my Weird. I still had a brain, at least until I fetched up against that much iron again. The plinth, not iron itself but some kind of smooth black stone, revealed a hinged door in the side, which opened into a small space studded with dials and gauges.

The symbols stamped next to each were similar to what I'd seen in Windhaven, and I called Dean over to translate. "There've got to be instructions for this thing."

Dean whistled. "There's just markings for places like the black forests, the dry wastes—not that I know why anyone would want to head there—and there's one marked *Iron*." He fingered the burnt edges of the panel. "But this thing is dead, princess. No way we're turning it on manually."

"The Gates are made of magic," Conrad said. "This is just their physical manifestation. The rift between here and the Iron Land is still there."

I gave Conrad a look with a raised eyebrow, a private look that said *Can you feel the Gate?*

Conrad coughed and looked away. "I mean, according to what I read at our father's house."

"Right, of course," I said quickly, turning the dial Dean had pointed out to us.

The next dial asked for directionality in pictograms, incoming or outgoing, and I turned it. All that remained was to complete the circuit, but they were all fried.

Reflexively, I put my hand against the panel and felt a flutter of life from my Weird. The figure's words came to me, but from far away. This could be our only chance to get out of here. I put both hands against the panel and fervently hoped this wouldn't be the last thing I ever did.

"Here goes nothing," I murmured so that only Dean could hear. Best case, the Gate worked for me and we got to go home. Worst case, I got electrocuted.

I wasn't nearly as strong and capable as Dean and Bethina and Cal seemed to think I was, but I could do this. I could be brave, like they needed me to be.

I grabbed the lever with my hand, and my Weird with my mind, and flipped the metal circuit to the *On* position.

For a moment, there was nothing, just the sweet ache of the Weird coursing through me and into the circuit board. I didn't try to push forward into the mechanism of the Gate, but I felt the void drop away again as the rift within the mechanism opened.

I felt a rumble under my hands and feet and heard the subtle swoop of aether rearranging itself inside the vacuum tube, and then I felt the hairs on the back of my neck prickle and stand up. I jerked my hand away from the lever and stepped away from the Gate. The row of gauges below the dials vibrated to life, needles climbing toward maximum.

Above us, I saw a bright flash of lightning and heard a crack of thunder nearly directly above my head. The ionized air all around made my skin crawl, and my Weird ran frantic circles in my mind as it sensed the wondrous, terrible machine that controlled the incalculable power of the world rift.

The lightning flashbulbed again, brighter than anything, leaving whorls on my vision, black clouds gathering over us like ghost crows, swooping down and making my head ring with a thunderclap so loud my teeth shook.

I gasped, drawing back from the Gate, which had become a lightning rod, making sure the others were clear as well. Nature and magic were beyond anyone's control, even someone with a Weird. I didn't feel ashamed of being wary of them.

The third flash snaked a bolt of electricity from the boiling clouds and hit the Gate, punctuated by a thunderclap so loud it deafened me instantly. Dean grabbed his ears and Bethina let out a scream, though I couldn't hear it, could only see the panicked pink O of her lips.

Before me, in the center of the Gate's iron arch, stood the same shimmering mirror that I'd seen when Conrad had transported us into the Mists, a wavering image of the Iron Land on the other side. It flickered, spiderweb cracks running across the glassine surface and then retreating. I could tell that the Gate still wasn't stable, but it was open, and that was all that mattered.

I'd kept us safe from Draven. I'd gotten us home.

"Well, what are you waiting for?" Dean shouted at the others. "Go!"

One by one, they hurried through the flickering hole in reality, Conrad bringing up the rear, until only Dean and I remained.

"Now or never, princess," he told me. I looked back at the Mists, the ruined village, and the swirling white fog that hid Draven and his men, growing closer by the second.

"I hope this is the right thing to do." I hadn't meant to say anything, just step through the Gate, but it came out. I felt if it hadn't, I might have exploded.

Dean looked into my eyes. "I don't know that. But I trust you, princess. You've got a good head on your shoulders and you haven't steered me wrong yet."

I reached out and put my hand on one of his slightly

rough, stubble-covered cheeks. I pressed my lips to the other, and tasted the warmth and salt of his skin. "Thanks, Dean."

He flashed me half a grin and skimmed his thumb across my lips. "Thank me when we've got your mother with us and we're out of Lovecraft for good." Motioning to the Gate, which had grown increasingly fractured and jumpy, he dropped his hand. "Go on, now. I'm right behind you."

I touched the opening of the Gate with my fingers first. It was an absence of feeling in the shimmering space the aether had created. Holding my breath, and still thinking I could possibly be making the worst mistake I ever made, I stepped through, back along the line of travel to the last location, the one the Proctors had used. Back to Lovecraft, and whatever awaited me.

6

The Ruins of Lovecraft

TRAVELING BY GATE was unpleasant, a fact that I had forgotten in the whirl of more pressing problems since Conrad and I had escaped Graystone.

I was reminded violently as I passed into the Gate and felt as if I'd been jerked by a string implanted in the center of my chest, down and sideways, spinning end over end, out of control. I caught flashes of other places, other skies not my own, mountains of a shape that no horizon of the Iron Land bore.

It was like seeing a tiny slice of the world the shadow figure from my not-dreams occupied, spinning by at a speed a human eye couldn't hope to process.

I wished I knew how the Gates truly worked, how they folded in all the worlds between Mists and Iron and shot my matter across incalculable distances to reassemble it on the other end. But the only ones who knew that were the

Brotherhood, and the Fae, and neither one was a group I relished asking.

I landed on a patch of burnt earth when my journey ended, and pain stabbed up my right arm as my wrist twisted under my full weight.

"Dammit!" I shouted, cradling my arm. I had just recovered my equilibrium when Dean came flying from the Gate and landed on me, sending me into the dirt again.

"Sorry," he mumbled, face buried in my hair. "Not much in the way of navigation through that thing."

"It's okay," I managed, looking back at where we'd come from. There was no Gate on this side, nothing physical—just a weak spot that nobody except a Gateminder or a Fae would ever notice.

Dean raised his head and smiled down at me.

"All in one piece?"

I managed a smile in return. It was hard not to smile at Dean when he turned the full force of his eyes and his slow, full grin on you. "More or less."

"Excuse me," Conrad said loudly from above. His voice broke into the warm place I was drifting in within Dean's eyes like a jangling chronometer alarm. "But if it's not too much trouble for you, please get off of my sister."

Dean dropped me a wink before he rolled up to his knees and then his feet and offered me a hand. I took it and stood, brushing ash and dirt from my clothes. "Where are we?"

"Somewhere around Nephilheim, looks like," Conrad said. The slumped gray row houses and treeless vista did look like the factory town attached to the Nephilim Foundry, whose belching smokestacks I'd looked out at my entire life in Lovecraft. Now the sad little houses were shuttered and deserted, and the brick factory buildings in the distance were blackened with long streaks of soot. One of the foundry's smokestacks had partially collapsed, and reached for the brown-tinged clouds like the jagged end of a broken spoke.

I'd expected it to be bad, but the fact that this much ruin had spread across the river, right into Nephilheim, made my stomach drop. How far had the destruction of the Engine reached? How many people had been in its way?

"Aoife?" Dean said, touching my shoulder. "You want to get moving?"

"Yeah," I said, blinking back what I told myself were tears from the ash drifting through the thick, acrid air. "The bridge isn't far past the foundry. We should go that way."

We walked, keeping in a tight group, Conrad at the head and Dean at the back. I nudged him in front of me—if something jumped out at us, Dean could protect Cal, Bethina and himself. Conrad and I would just have to fend for ourselves. Dean took it with good grace, and winked at me.

"Don't worry, princess. I'm fine."

I tried to smile back, but the farther we walked and the more wrecked homes we passed, the sicker to my stomach I felt.

"Where is everyone?" Bethina turned in a wide circle, taking in the dirt street and the empty houses.

No one else was in evidence, and the only movement I saw was a white curtain in an open window at the far end of the block, fluttering in the intermittent breeze. It was November and the beginning of winter in Lovecraft and the surrounding towns, and I tucked my hands under my arms to warm them. I didn't get the eerie prickle of being watched by live eyes as I had in the Mists, but that didn't mean nothing was watching. The Proctors had plenty of ways to keep eyes all around Lovecraft without any flesh and blood involved.

"Not here," Cal said. He sniffed discreetly. "There's nobody within a mile of this place."

Which just made me wonder where everyone in Nephilheim had gone. Foundry workers, jitney drivers, their families. There was really no good train of thought running down those tracks. I bit my lip hard, hoping the pain would distract me from my racing thoughts. It was just the iron. Whispering treacherous things to me, that I'd done this, that my stupidity with the Fae had made these people disappear.

Just the iron. Not the truth.

I walked a few steps away from the group and looked down the broad avenue. It ended at the west gates of the foundry. Beyond was the Erebus River, which I'd crossed for the first time a little more than two weeks earlier, fleeing the city where I'd spent my entire life.

Now I was willingly going back, into the jaws of the Proctors and who knew what else, things that had slipped through the tears appearing and disappearing in the Gates.

Reassuring myself that I wasn't already insane was getting harder and harder. And with every step I took back toward Lovecraft, the iron of the city and the land around me whispered louder in my blood.

On the horizon, across the river, columns of black and silver smoke rose, as if souls were drifting up from the broken cityscape, trying to find a hole in the overcast sky. The clouds were blood-red, and lightning danced between them as the smoke from burning aether formerly trapped in the Lovecraft Engine drifted into the atmosphere.

I could hear sirens faintly, the constant warning of an air raid. Those sirens were supposed to warn us of Crimson Guard attacks, but now they were screaming senselessly, echoing back from the smashed walls of the foundry.

Something crunched under my boots, and I looked down to see what it was. The street, in addition to being covered in ash, was peppered with shards of glass—silvery window glass and also crockery, as if everything had been flung and shifted in the Engine's great spasm.

As we trudged on, block after block with no human in sight, and as the wreckage grew worse, some of the houses window- and doorless, merely yawning maws covered in smoke marks, I pulled Cal aside. "I think you and Bethina should stay here."

"No," he said, shaking his head vigorously. "I need to be with you. I have to stay close."

"Cal," I said. "You know what's over there. You know what the Proctors will do if they catch you." Never mind Cal's own clan of ghouls, who regarded siding with humans as an offense serious enough to get you torn limb from limb and cooked in a stew.

I gestured toward Lovecraft. The sirens were louder with every step we took, and I imagined that on the same wind, I could hear the howling of the tribes of ghouls that had populated Lovecraft's sewers. "You know all that," I repeated to Cal. "And if you go across that bridge you're not going to be able to hide what you are from her."

"It'll be fine," Cal insisted.

"Calvin," I hissed, anger at his stubbornness bubbling up. "It will not be *fine*. It will be a disaster. You're my friend and I love you, but those ghouls over there aren't all your family. You said it yourself when the Engine got destroyed—the ghouls in Lovecraft are on a Wild Hunt. I don't know exactly what that means, but it can't be good."

Cal swallowed, his lumpy Adam's apple scraping at his pale throat. "A Wild Hunt is what we do when we mean to cleanse a place of all prey. It means that everything not a ghoul is fair game, and ghouls who refuse to hunt become the hunted."

"Then that includes Bethina," I said. "And you, by extension. You don't want to do that to her, Cal. If you insist on lying to her, don't put her in danger on top of it. Please. I like her, and I don't want her hurt."

He sighed, raking a hand through his stiff, oily blond hair. "I hate this, Aoife. I've never met anyone like her. I do want to be . . ." He dropped his hand, ungainly and too big for his wiry frame. "I want to be Cal, sometimes. Cal all the time. If my nest heard me say that . . ."

"I know," I murmured. "Trust me, I know the wanting to be something you aren't. I want it too." I stopped and faced him, reaching up to put my hands on his shoulders and meet his eyes. Those eyes could be stone cold, animal and vicious, but they'd also provided the only kind gaze I'd known in all my time at the Academy. "The best thing you could do for Bethina right now is not let her come to any more harm. And when this is over, the next best thing you can do is tell her the truth."

Cal's shoulders drooped at that, and he opened his

mouth, probably to tell me how crazy I was to even suggest that he reveal his true nature, but he straightened again and went quiet when Bethina caught up.

"This place is spooky, huh?" she said, linking her arm with Cal's. I moved away and let her have the closeness. From having Dean, I knew how important that could be.

"It's not so bad," he said, trying to stand and push out his chest to look bigger. "Besides, I'm here with you."

"Like I was saying to Cal," I told Bethina. "I think it's best if the two of you wait here, in Nephilheim. Cover our retreat, sort of."

Cal nodded now that Bethina was listening, but his jaw was tight. I knew how much Cal lived for adventure, in fictional form and in the cheesy aether plays the Bureau of Proctors broadcast over the tubes. Being told he had to stay behind might grate on him, but if he went into Lovecraft, he'd be eaten alive. That was, if the Proctors didn't capture and torture their former informant to death first.

It was the truth, and Cal knew it just as well as I did.

"Stay here?" Bethina trilled, loud enough to reach Dean and Conrad. "But this is an awful place to stay! Stone knows what's hiding in these houses."

"No, this place is good," Cal soothed. "It's fine, Bethina. We'll be fine."

"Well, of *course* we'll be fine," she said. "I'm not a shrinking violet, but I don't relish fightin' off viral creatures with my bare hands, either."

"Probably best," Dean chimed in before Bethina could read the flinch on my face. I hadn't told her about the Proctors' lie. Escaping the Mists was already more than she could handle. In a way, I guessed I was just as guilty as

Cal. "We'll move quicker that way," he added. "No offense, Bethina."

Cal pointed to a cottage that was in relatively good shape. "We'll wait in there, okay? I've got a pack of cards. It'll be like no time at all."

Bethina cast a wary look back at me as Cal escorted her into the cottage. I smiled and waved, feeling not one iota of the cheerful expression plastered across my face.

"Thank goodness," I muttered, once they were inside without more protests. Bethina wasn't stupid—soon Cal's and my carefully constructed tower of falsehood was going to collapse like so many blocks, and when it did, I wouldn't blame her one bit if she smacked us both across the face. Repeatedly.

"Yeah," Conrad agreed. "That girl's sweet, but she's dead-weight."

Dean shot me a look, but I waved him off, hoping to avoid yet another contest to see who could puff his chest out farther. Conrad didn't know about Cal's little skin-changing trick either, and right now that was best. I wasn't up to explaining to my brother, especially considering how he'd been acting lately, exactly why we were running around with a ghoul to watch our backs.

We approached the foundry gates, which hung open at odd angles, as if something large and out of control had smashed them in its mad dash for freedom.

Dean pressed a finger to his lips, moved along the iron of the foundry fence and peered around the gate without letting anything that might be on the other side get a look at him. I pressed against his back, curling my fingers in the leather of his coat, and followed his eyes.

Great tread tracks led to the gate from the innards of the foundry, where the forge and the assembly sheds lay, and one side of the nearest sheds was smashed, bricks lying in piles. The automatons that worked in the hottest, most dangerous parts of the foundry had vanished.

"I don't like this at all," I said in Dean's ear. So much destruction, and now the foundry was so quiet.

I was close enough to Dean that I could smell his hair cream, like a hint of sweetness on my tongue, when he turned to reply.

"Me either," he said. "But like they say, princess—only way out is through. No other road to the bridge on this side of the river, and swimming's going to get us a nice case of hypothermia and not much else."

"Forward, then," I said, and I slipped my hand into Dean's as we walked, making Conrad snort as he brought up the rear. "Grow up," I muttered at him, but he pretended not to hear me. Brothers didn't make life easier, not even the jinxed sort of life we'd found ourselves in, I decided. They were tailored by evolution to be annoying.

The foundry grounds were as quiet as the town behind us, but unlike that of the town, this wasn't the silence of abandonment. It was more like walking along a darkened street at night, with the pressure on the back of your neck that let you know something was watching you from the shadowed places along the way.

Conrad pointed to a bright spray of paint splashed along the walls, overlaying the wing-and-crucible logo of the foundry. The paint was red and black, violent slashes that depicted blood pouring from the crucible, great arrowheads through the wings. The sort of things the Proctors would have had scrubbed away immediately, before.

"We're gone two weeks and this place goes full-on anarchist?" Dean said. "This is nuts."

"Maybe we should be quiet," I suggested nervously. The foundry was silent and felt wrong. No smoke belched from the stacks, and the resounding clang and clank of cooling ingots that used to echo across the river and into my dormitory room had ceased.

Dean, Conrad and I formed a sort of line, Conrad at the rear and Dean at the head. I wanted to tell them I didn't need the press of a boy's body to keep me safe—whatever was running loose here would just as soon chew on their flesh as mine.

We passed through the smaller wooden outbuildings, several of which had been crushed to matchsticks, presumably by the vast weight of runaway automatons. One such machine slumped in its tracks near the last shed, the aether globe in its chest that had kept it powered smashed and a broad burn mark scorching its metal torso. The scent of burnt paper was still in the air.

Conrad approached the thing and touched one of its tracks, which had come off the wheels. Each tread was twice the span of his arm.

My eye was caught by movement from behind the automaton. Just a flicker, but my heart clenched with surprise and fear, and I tapped Dean on the arm, pointing. "Something's over there."

He followed my finger, and we both saw the flicker of red on the unbroken gray brick of the foundry walls.

"Son of a bitch," Dean growled, jamming his hand in his pocket and pulling out his switchblade. "Hey!" he bellowed at the moving shadow. "Hey, you!"

"Dean . . . ," I started, thinking that perhaps shouting at the figure wasn't the best idea.

"I see you!" Dean shouted. "No point in hiding."

"Dean, we don't know what it is," I whispered, worried that if he made a move, whoever or whatever lurked beyond the automaton would take it badly. Dean shook his head.

"Relax, princess. It's a kid." He advanced on the shadow. "Aren't you?"

"Up yours, mister!" the shadow shouted back. I pressed a hand over my mouth, both to stifle a laugh and from relief. To find another person in this wasteland was ten times more unexpected than finding a creature like the nightjars and ghouls that populated Lovecraft's underground.

"Say," Dean drawled, brows drawing together. "I know you, kid."

"I know your mother!" the kid retorted. "And she has some disappointing things to say about you." The kid's brassiness didn't worry me half as much as his actually wandering around out in the open, but Dean's lip curled back and he balled up his hands.

Before Dean could swing a fist, I closed distance, reached out and grabbed the boy's red scarf, jerking him into the light.

"Tavis?" Dean said.

The boy and I gaped at one another for a moment. I realized that Dean did know him, and so did I. Tavis, the peddler boy in the Nightfall Market. I'd met him the same night I'd met Dean, when Cal and I had run away from the Academy. Tavis had steered me to a guide who wasn't a guide at all, but a man who sent people to be devoured by ghouls in exchange for free passage and scavenging rights in the old Lovecraft sewers.

"Oh, cripes," Tavis sighed, relaxing a bit. "The wags in the Market said you were long gone, Dean."

"No such luck for them," Dean told him. "What are you doing all the way on this side of the river?"

"Live here now, don't I?" Tavis squirmed in my grip. "Come on, girlie. Give a guy a break."

I let go of him, and his bright red scarf fluttered to the crushed gravel. I picked it up and ran it through my hands. Soft wool, dyed and still smelling of woodsmoke. "This is an Academy scarf," I said, the unexpected appearance of an object from my former life making my voice barely a whisper. "Where did you get this?"

Tavis shrugged, but his gaze darted away from mine as he tried to disguise the lie. One end of the scarf was darker than the other, stiff and soaked in blood.

I let the scarf fall from my hands. "What happened over there?" I asked Tavis. "In Lovecraft? After the blast."

"Hey," he said, ignoring my question and looking back and forth between Dean and me. "Are you two going steady? Harrison, you sly dog."

"You're way too young to be throwing that kind of talk around," Dean said. "You still dealing in piss-poor information and tonics that are mostly rusty tap water?"

"Nightfall Market's gone," Tavis said, kicking at the broken bricks with the toe of his boot. "Proctors raided the Rustworks right after the big blow. Rounded up everyone they could find. Ghouls got the rest. Monsters've been crazed lately—even springing out on folks in broad daylight."

Dean rubbed his chin, a calm gesture, but I saw the thunderheads of anger steal into his eyes. "Figures."

I dropped my gaze to the vicinity of Tavis's boot. The people in the Rustworks might have been rough and dishonest, but they hadn't deserved the blame for the Engine. The Proctors were all too eager to name scapegoats for every little thing that went wrong in their city.

"Some of us came here," Tavis said. "Foundry workers ran when the automatons went nutty and started smashing things. It's safe here. For the most part."

Conrad waved at us from near the wrecked sheds and mouthed *We should go.*

"Good seeing you, kid," Dean told Tavis, ruffling his hair. "Keep yourself safe, you hear?"

Tavis gave Dean a smile, and it was as sly and slippery as the tongue of a snake. "Oh, I don't gotta worry about that," he said. "I kept you talking. I'll get my cut."

My heart sank. Dean pulled his knife again. "What did you say?"

A low rumble started from behind the sheds, the gravel around my feet jumping. With it came the clamor of voices and the clatter of an automaton's tread.

I grabbed Tavis by the front of his shirt. "What did you do?"

"Can't have you tipping off the Proctors!" he squeaked. "And we need food! Weapons! Cash!"

"Do we *look* like we'd tip off the Proctors, you weaselly

little bastard?" Dean snarled. His switchblade gleamed in the low gray light coming down through the smoke.

"Rules of the Rustworks," Tavis said. "You're gone a little while and you forget. Every man for himself."

A foundry automaton rolled around the corner of the shed, surrounded by a dozen men and women wearing identical red scarves and carrying weapons, from pump-action shotguns and the sort of electric rods the Proctors carried to simple tools like axes and pitchforks and, in one case, a baseball bat with rusty nails driven into the business end. I stared, rooted to the spot by both shock and the hungry look in their eyes. Hungrier than any ghoul, and twice as frightening.

The man driving the automaton had a scar that closed one eye, a gray beard, and white hair flying out from under a ratty top hat. He wore evening clothes, wildly mismatched, and his high-collared shirt was so blood-soaked that it was the color of Tavis's scarf.

"Throw down your weapons!" he bellowed at us through the automaton's vox system. The things weren't meant to be driven, but I could see where a torch had cut away the chest plate to make a spot for a man to sit and manipulate the controls in real time, rather than having an engineer program the thing and send it on its way. I might have admired the wild-eyed man's ingenuity if he hadn't clearly been about to crush us with his metal appendages.

"Screw off!" Dean shouted back. "You're not getting a damn thing from us!"

"Not that we have anything to give, anyway," I murmured so only Dean could hear.

"Don't be so sure, princess," he said softly. "Those boots and my coat will get fought over down in the dirt by types like this."

I realized he had a point—the refugees from the Rustworks were starving, likely freezing as winter set in, and clean clothes and sturdy shoes would be worth as much as fine steel or aether. They didn't appear to be reasonable, so I braced myself to either fight or run, waiting for Dean's cue.

The man grinned, showing several prominent gaps in his teeth. "This here is my town now. Nephilheim, the city of the angels. And I'm the voice on high!"

Crazy talk wasn't exactly rare among people in the Rustworks—it was why most of them were fugitives. They said things the Proctors deemed heretical and thus were condemned to lives in madhouses, at best, or execution at worst. But the conviction with which the man shouted reminded me of my mother, utterly sure her iron-induced nightmares were true and happening before her eyes.

"He's not going to back down," I said to Dean.

"Perfect. Got a plan, then?" he asked, not relaxing his grip on his knife.

"Yeah," I said, sliding my foot backward and shifting my weight. It was the same plan I always had when I was outnumbered by people much crazier and meaner than I was, from schoolyard bullies to these rust rats. "Run."

Conrad got the idea, and the three of us bolted. The ground under my feet shook as the automaton rumbled to life and the group of scavengers gave chase. One of the women let out a battle cry, which the rest quickly took up.

"Were people in the Rustworks always this unfriendly?" I shouted at Dean.

"This is above and beyond, princess!" he shouted back. "Don't know what's gotten into them!"

Personally, I thought sanity was a thinner thread than most people realized. And I knew the thread could snap quicker than you could take a breath.

My own breath sawed in my chest; it seemed as if the narrow foundry avenues ran on forever, one folding into another.

Dean skidded, his ankle twisting under him, and he fell and rolled. I reached down without breaking stride and grabbed him by the shoulder of his leather jacket, yanking him along. A bottle shattered on the ground where his head had just been, and I looked back to see the fastest of the scavengers closing in.

"Run them down," the automaton's pilot bellowed. "Run those devils straight to Hades!"

A serrated horror of a blade whizzed past my face and embedded itself in the wall of the nearest building.

I stopped, spinning to face the person who'd thrown it. It was a woman—wild eyed, red hair bound up with gears and bolts that clanked and clacked when she moved. "I've had just about enough of this," I snarled, my fear having been burned away by indignation. We weren't a threat. We were just like them—wanted by the Proctors, just trying to survive. How dared they think they could run us down like prey? I looked forward to showing this girl she'd underestimated me.

The girl raised another blade. "Make your move, demon!" she screamed.

I didn't think; I just scooped up a stray brick from near my feet and flung it at her. It thumped her in the chest and she staggered, dropping her knife. I snatched up another brick and waved it at the encroaching crowd. "Who's next?" I yelled.

The automaton pilot bore down on me, causing the crushing pincers that made up the thing's hands to scissor open and shut.

Too furious to even think of running, I pushed back with my Weird. I'd never tried to move something without touching it, or at least being within a few feet, but I pushed with all my strength, and with a great rattle and scream of rivets the tracks of the automaton seized, steam and smoke rising from the thing along with the smell of tortured metal. It shuddered to a stop.

I stood where I was, my heart pounding, my blood roaring. Far from feeling the falling-away sensation using my Weird usually brought on, I felt inexplicably alive, all body and blood rather than that detached piece of myself that floated around inside my mind. It was exhilarating, and yet I sort of wanted to scream.

Before I could do anything about either screaming or holding it in, Conrad grabbed me and abruptly broke the spell. "Are you *crazy*?" he shouted over the death throes of the automaton, which had started to shoot sparks and jets of flame from its innards as all its mechanisms failed in turn. Acrid steam blanketed the scavengers, and us.

The scavengers milled nervously a few yards away, and then one by one they bowed their heads in my direction, nodding rhythmically and drawing toward Conrad, Dean and me in a tight knot. Behind them, the automaton pilot fell from his vehicle, beating at the flames on his jacket.

I realized as all the scavengers' eyes looked at me what

I'd done: I'd shown my Weird to perfectly ordinary people. People who were already on edge, and would likely just as soon burn me alive as a Proctor would for my unexplained trick. I pressed my lips together, my heart throbbing with anxiety. After everything I'd done, I'd shattered it with one thoughtless move. *Stupid, Aoife. So stupid.*

"We're sorry," the woman I'd hit with the brick wheezed. "We didn't know."

I blinked at her, my rage and dread replacing itself with confusion. "Didn't know what?"

"That it was you," she said. "You are Aoife Grayson? The destroyer? The one who made the big blow?"

I was speechless for a moment, then answered hesitantly. "I'm Aoife, yes. But the Engine . . ." I stopped myself, unsure what to say next. "This isn't important. Are you going to let us go?" I shouldn't have been shocked that my name was known on the other side of the Erebus River. The Wytch King had said Draven was painting me as a radical, a heretic terrorist responsible for the senseless destruction of Lovecraft. What was more shocking about the girl's words was that she seemed happy about what I'd done, the wreckage and the ruin. What was *wrong* with these people?

"Anything you say, Destroyer," the woman murmured, bobbing her head. She was only a few years older than me, I could see now, but her face was streaked with grease and painted up with blue woad.

"Don't call me that," I said. The shakes were starting, and the familiar light-headedness of my nosebleeds. The iron was creeping in, inexorably, and fraying my emotions. "Don't you ever call me that again." Such a hateful name, said with such reverence. I was no better than the Crimson

Guard and their aether bombs. *Destroyer* wasn't a name that would ever pass my lips without making me cringe.

"But you saved us," the girl insisted. "You freed us from the Proctors and you rained down destruction on their world." She stretched out her arms to point to the world around her. "You saved *all* of us. The ones ground under the heel of the Proctors," she said, and the other scavengers murmured assent.

"I didn't do a damn thing," I snarled at the girl, knocking her hands away from me, "except do what I *thought* was right." Her reverence just reminded me all over again of my mistake, how I'd let myself be manipulated by Tremaine. I wasn't a hero. I wasn't even clever, I was gullible.

"You'll have no more trouble from us," the girl promised. Then she tried a different approach, sticking her hand straight out to shake, like an eager schoolboy. "I'm Casey."

"Apparently you already know who I am," I said, and sniffed, not interested in making friends with someone who'd been ready to stick a blade in me not five minutes before.

"We all do," Casey reiterated. "You're a hero."

"How's the bridge?" Dean cut in before I could open my mouth and start screaming incoherently at the word *hero*. "We need to make tracks into Lovecraft."

"You don't wanna do that," Casey told him. "The Proctors got the bridge locked down tight. And in the city, well . . ." She shivered, her braids clanking again.

"You've been getting in all right," I pointed out. "You have Academy and Proctor gear. I seriously doubt you carted all that with you while you were running for your lives."

Casey reddened a little, her freckles standing out against

her pink cheeks. "I guess there's one or two of us who make the run, yeah. Mr. Angel tells us what he needs and we go in after dark. Nephilheim is stripped bare—those people evacuated. They were the smart ones."

"Is Angel the cracked nut with the automaton?" Conrad said, pointing to where the hunched old man sulked at the back of the crowd.

Casey nodded. "He was a street heretic—he preached down in the Rustworks. When the big blow happened, he said it was a sign. That we were to go and form a new city on the ashes of the old."

"A new city based on raiding and pillaging? History is on your side, for sure," I said. Casey raised her skinny shoulders, missing my sarcasm.

"He's kinda cracked, but I don't have anywhere else to go. My parents were transported as heretics and my trade was smuggling. Nothing to smuggle now, is there?"

I sighed. Much as I wanted to dislike her, I couldn't. She was skinny and starving and pathetic, more like a kitten nipping at your ankles than a junkyard dog. "Yeah, I get not having anywhere else to go," I told her.

"If you need supplies, you can show us how you get in and out of the city," Dean said to her. "We can pay you."

I gave Dean a hard look when he mentioned payment, and he shook his head minutely at me, which I took to mean he must have something the girl wanted that wasn't cold, hard cash. Because cash was in very short supply among our trio.

"You really want to go?" Casey directed her question to me rather than Dean.

I nodded. "My mother is in there. I need to get to

Christobel Asylum, near Old Town." If I could just get there, then at least I'd know. Know if she'd survived, or if I'd really done the worst thing a daughter can do, even worse than leaving the city without her.

Casey instantly made a negative gesture. "If your mum was in Old Town, she's gone. That place was the first to go full-on chum bucket. Ghouls up to your ears, and worse. You could hear the screaming for days."

"I have to go," I insisted, although there was a roaring in my ears. *Madhouses are fortresses,* I reminded myself. They weren't connected to sewers, were surrounded by thick granite walls topped with razor wire. Christobel was the most secure of them all, the place for dangerous lunatics, said to be escape proof. What kept the infected and the heretical inside could keep ghouls out. Maybe. The alternative I couldn't handle thinking about without curling up into a useless ball.

"I have to go," I repeated. "I left her there."

Casey sighed and fidgeted. She looked back at the rest of the mob; they had put out the automaton fire and were scavenging usable parts off it like a particularly efficient swarm of fire ants. Angel stood to one side, his hair singed away, muttering invective that was no doubt directed at me.

"Well?" I said, folding my arms and hoping my bluff of heroic toughness passed muster. "If I'm such a hero, you should trust that I know what I'm doing."

"Of course you do," Casey said. "It's just . . . you ain't scared? Of what's over there?"

"Not a bit," I lied, crisply and without pause.

I was becoming a good liar. I realized that without any surprise, just like you notice that your hair has gotten longer and that your clothes are hanging off you because of the miles of walking and only intermittent food.

Of course I was scared. I never wanted to go back to the city. I didn't want to see the dour spires and the cold gray edifice of Ravenhouse ever again. I didn't want to see the crater the destruction of the Engine had left, or the wreckage of the places I'd once walked through with my school bag slung over my shoulder and, relatively speaking, not a care in the world.

I was scared. I was more scared than I'd ever been. But I was learning to hide it, to become as smooth and facile as any of the Fae I'd encountered.

And that scared me most of all.

7

The Lair of Monsters

CASEY CARRIED A pack from the Lovecraft Academy, the kind issued to boys, with two shoulder straps. She gestured to it proudly. "Those little Uptown brats cut and ran like nobody's business. Left a treasure trove behind."

Those "brats" had been my fellow students. I hadn't called any of them my friends, but the thought of them meeting a fate normally reserved for the worst of criminals turned my stomach a bit.

"So what's the plan, Casey?" Dean asked her as she tromped ahead of us, red hair swinging almost gaily.

"The Boundary Bridge is the only way in or out, but the Proctors have set up quarantine checkpoints. Regular boat patrols too. We gotta cross under the span, and we gotta do it fast, before they spot us."

"What do people know?" I blurted. "About the Engine, and the city? What have the Proctors been saying?"

"That you acted alone," Casey said. "That you're some

kind of radical. Your picture went in all the papers. Reporters came from New Amsterdam to poke around the foundry, with cameras and such. Proctors are claiming the big blow was your fault, and there was a huge ceremony when they made that fink Draven director of the Bureau." Her brows drew together. "They ain't said much about what came out of the ground afterward. That'd mess with their big old lie of a story."

That figured. Any fabricated explanation for the "viral creatures" never before seen would strain the credulity of even the dumbest citizens of Lovecraft. And Draven, only the city Head then, was doubly in control now, had the whole machine of the Proctors to back up whatever story he cared to spin like the venomous spider he was. He was a big man now, bigger than everyone except the president and a few other men who were equally cruel and conniving. He had somebody to blame—me. As long as he had my face to put to the disaster, uncomfortable truths could be swept aside, the way uncomfortable truths often were when the Proctors got involved.

"So, you're a wanted criminal now," Dean said, grinning. "I'd be lying if I said that didn't make me like you even more, princess."

I tried to smile back but mostly just felt sick at the thought. My picture would be in every paper in every part of the world that didn't belong to the Crimson Guard. *Terrorist. Heretic.* Lies. But there was nothing I could do, unless I could turn back time. And that was about as likely as Draven asking me out for tea.

Casey led us off the main road and down an access path. I could hear the ice creaking in the river as we drew closer.

Wind cut into me, and I was glad for the jacket Shard had given me in Windhaven. "The trusses on this side aren't too heavily guarded," she called. "We just gotta be quick."

"And then getting to Old Town?" I asked. Casey chewed her lip and cut her eyes to the river below.

"Getting to Old Town means you're gonna have to be even quicker," she said. "You're not bleeding, are you? Any of you? Ghouls'll sniff blood a week old."

"We're square," Dean said. "Nobody's cut so's it'll bleed freely."

Casey bit her lip. "For the record, I still think this is a stupid idea."

"Duly noted," I told her.

Ahead of us, I saw one of the great trusses of the Boundary Bridge planted in the riverbank like the resting foot of an iron animal.

The supports traveled down into the bedrock, but from here at the base they looked impossibly thin and high, the span above creaking in the harsh wind.

Casey cast a look at my hands, which I'd tucked as far as they'd go into my sleeves. Exposure to the cold air felt like scraping my knuckles across a brick wall. "Here," she grumbled, shoving a spare pair of fingerless leather gloves at me.

"I'm fine," I insisted, though the idea of clinging to a piece of iron with my bare skin above a hundred-foot drop was about as far from fine as I could conceive.

"You'll be fine until you get about halfway across," Casey said. "Then either your hands will freeze to a piece of iron or they'll get so cold they can't grip the iron at all. Best case, you lose the skin off your palms. Worst case, you go swimming."

I looked out at the river, the surface a rumpled canvas of ice floes and black water. I put the gloves on.

Casey went first, climbing the support as quickly and surely as a pirate from Cal's adventure stories going up a mast. I followed, using the massive rivets as foot- and handholds, as she had. Conrad came next, and Dean was last.

I knew exactly how high and wide the bridge ran, of course. Every engineering student in the world probably knew its dimensions, marvel that it was. Joseph Strauss's masterwork, along with the Cross-Brooklyn Bridge in New Amsterdam. The Boundary Bridge was one hundred twenty feet high. Just shy of one-half mile across. Two hundred lengths of wrist-thick cable suspending it above the river.

As we climbed, I could feel the bridge humming. My Weird didn't crackle like it did when I encountered a machine with moving parts, but I could feel the river's force running through the iron, the never-ceasing current working to push the bridge aside and be free. Working through me, into the cracks and crannies of my mind, working at the madness, trying to pick the lock and set it free.

The higher we climbed, the worse the wind got, until it was a trial to even breathe when a gust blew straight at my face.

I just kept going. Hand up, foot up. Muscles crying out, every fiber straining. Grab rivet, test for ice, pull myself to the next. I had to get into the city, had to find Nerissa, get her out of there. Then, I knew, and only then, I could rest.

Hand up, foot up. I couldn't feel my cheeks or the tips of my fingers. Up ahead, Casey reached the span, the metal lattice that supported the roadbed, slick with ice. With one last tug I joined her and slumped, panting, in the crooked embrace of the iron while we waited for the boys to join us.

"See that?" She pointed at a small black launch with a prow shaped like a blunt battering ram that was working its way through the river below. "Proctors patrolling in an ice-breaker," she said. "We'll have about three minutes before they get down to the point and start to come back."

I looked to the next support lattice, at least six feet away across open space. "Am I supposed to sprout wings?"

Casey pointed up, grinning. "Those wires will hold us. You just lace your legs above it and then pull hand over hand and you're over in no time."

The idea of hanging upside down over certain death didn't exactly appeal to me, but I wouldn't be any kind of hero if I balked. I followed Casey's lead and grabbed the wire. She slung herself up easily, muscular legs encased in men's dungarees wrapping around the thin line and holding her weight.

The wire jiggled as Conrad followed me, and bowed a bit as Dean joined him. I couldn't see them, but knowing they were behind me gave me the nerve I needed to edge along after Casey.

Casey tracked the progress of the ice breaker, which had nearly reached the tall stone lighthouse at Half Moon Point.

"Scoot," she hissed. "And keep it quiet. There's men up there on the bridge."

Clinging to that wire was one of the most singularly miserable experiences of my life. The cold cut straight through my trousers and my gloves everywhere I touched the wire. My skin was rubbed raw, and my hands ached so much I hoped they wouldn't simply break off and fall away.

Casey was nearly all the way across, and I close behind her, when I felt a shudder in the bridge and heard an explosive cracking of ice in the river below.

My shoulder began to throb with a vengeance. When I was in Arkham, a shoggoth, one of the mindless creatures made up of mouths and eyes that roamed outside the city, had latched onto me and left a bit of itself in a black and puckered scar flushed with venom even now. I gasped at the pain, losing my grip on the wire. I dropped rather than try to hold on, my feet landing on the edge of a support beam.

"There's something down there!" Conrad shouted from his vantage above, and I looked down to see the ice churning and the water foaming as something fought its way out of the depths.

"Shut up!" Casey hissed at us. "Keep moving!"

My shoulder throbbed so badly it caused black whirlpools to grow in my field of vision. I looked at Dean frantically as he dropped down to stand beside me. "This is wrong . . . ," I said, my throat raw from cold. I sounded like I was floating far above myself, my voice a hollow and metallic echo. Something was rising out of the river. I could see through the fog that it had yellow, lidless eyes, lanternlike beneath the dark ice, and rubbery green limbs extending from a bullet-shaped body.

Ice shattered when it broke the surface, sending shards and spray in all directions. The creature wrapped its tentacles around the bridge, battering the solid parts of its body against the supports and nearly shaking all four of us free.

"What *is* that?" The shout came not from any of us but from the roadbed above. A cluster of Proctors peered over the side of the bridge, rifles at the ready.

"Leviathan!" one shouted. "Shoot that bastard before he shakes the bridge down!"

Dean lost his grip as the thing battered itself against the bridge again, and I reached out and grabbed the back of his jacket before he could fall.

"Never seen one that close before," he panted. "Must've picked up the vibrations from the explosion. Gotten turned around."

Leviathans were abominations of the deep supposedly caused by the necrovirus, but really, who knew where they came from? Its tentacles were spiraling up the supports of the bridge even as the Proctors opened fire, bullets zipping past us too close for comfort. My stomach lurched as the bridge rattled under its assault, and I abandoned all pretense of bravado. This was not good. Not at all.

"We should move!" Casey bellowed. "While they're distracted."

Dean nodded at me. "Get back on the wire. I'll help you." He put his hands on my hips without any more preamble and lifted me like I didn't weigh a thing.

The wire swayed and bounced under the assault of the leviathan, and I screwed my eyes shut, focusing on the sting in my palms as the wire bit into them.

I moved forward, concentrating so hard that I started when hands grabbed me and Casey pulled me onto the last support. We were below the elevated section of Derleth Street, the gray half-light shining through the slats of the river walk. There was a gaping hole in the boards, and Casey pulled herself up.

"We owe that old deep water bugger a thank-you,"

she panted. "He distracted those blackbirds right and proper."

"I'll feel better when everyone's across," I said, squinting against the ice glare to make out the others where they clung tightly to the great structure. The leviathan roared as the Proctors shot at it, then battered its entire weight into the bridge. There was a groan and the iron vibrated under my feet, and then everything stilled as the leviathan slid back into the river, causing violent waves of ice and black water to crash into either shore.

The sound was small in comparison, but it was high and close—a light ping as the rusted bolts holding the wires of the suspension assembly in place snapped in half, one by one, like aether bulbs blowing on a circuit. The wires whipped free like the tentacles of a second, metal leviathan hanging in the air above the first.

Dean dropped and caught himself by the elbows on the support where Casey and I were crouching. Casey grabbed Dean's arm, and I reached out for Conrad, but just like when we'd been in the balloon, I grasped only air.

My heart stopped and I watched helplessly as Conrad plummeted, a scream ripping from his throat, until the wire he was clinging to reached the end of its arc and snapped. Conrad swung a good thirty feet below us, small above the vast expanse of the river.

I locked my arm through the iron lattice to brace myself and grabbed the top of the wire with my free hand. "Help me!" I screamed at Dean and Casey, the icy air tearing my throat raw.

"No!" Conrad yelled up to us. "Just go!"

I shook my head, trying to pull the wire up and bring Conrad with it. I wasn't leaving him.

Casey, on the other hand, made a move to crawl up to the roadbed.

"What's that for?" she hissed when she saw Dean's reproachful look. "He said leave him, and we gotta move before that boat sees us!"

Dean just grunted and grabbed the wire along with me. Between the two of us, we hauled Conrad up, and the three of us climbed after Casey to the roadbed, leaving the Proctors and the bridge behind us.

Once we stood on Derleth Street, behind the arcade of the river walk to hide us from the Proctors, I ran and caught up to Casey, leaving Dean to walk with Conrad, who was swaying like a tree in a hurricane. He was pale, but I knew he'd be all right. Conrad was tough in ways you couldn't see. He didn't let fear or panic ever get their hooks into him. I wished I could be more like that.

"That was way closer than I like to cut things," Casey told me. "From now on, Miss Grayson, you need to listen to me and do as I say."

I had only intended to talk to her, but her comment sliced through my patience, and all the frustration and horror of the last few days exploded to the front of my mind. I balled up my fist, hard and sure like Conrad had taught me, and smacked Casey in the face.

She reeled, and there was already a fat red bruise growing near her lip when she turned back. "What on the scorched earth is your malfunction?"

"The next time you suggest leaving *any* of us behind," I snarled at her, "that'll be the last suggestion you ever make to anyone." In that moment, I meant it entirely. I couldn't recall a time I'd ever felt such pure, hot rage before.

"Aoife, whoa." Dean appeared at my side. He squeezed my shoulder. "Take it easy."

Casey touched her lip and winced. "I'm just doing what you asked me to do. Gee whiz."

"You know who else just does what they're asked? Proctors," I snapped back.

Casey yanked her blade from her belt. "Okay, girlie, I respect you, but that crosses the line. I ain't in bed with the Proctors."

"Why don't we all calm down?" Dean suggested. "You two girls want to slug it out later, I'm not going to stop you."

I uncurled my fist. My palm was red and raw, rubbed bloody from holding frozen metal. "He's right," I told Casey. All the rage ran out like so much water, and in its place was just embarrassment. I was supposed to fix problems with my mind, not my fists. I was the smart girl, the civilized one, who didn't resort to what my female teachers at the Academy would have called "tawdry emotional displays."

At least, I had been, until all of Tremaine's lies and everything that had gone on since then. "I'm sorry about that," I said to Casey, feeling my cheeks heat. "I think we can take it from here."

"Nah, look," Casey said. "*I'm* sorry about saying we leave your brother to go in the drink. I got piss-scared."

"Fine," I said shortly, glad she wasn't going to try to turn things into a real brawl. I wasn't much of a hand-to-hand fighter unless the element of surprise was on my side. "Let's just get going, all right?"

"Hell of a right cross," Dean muttered as we started walking again. "Remind me never to get you testy."

"Consider yourself warned," I said, nudging him with my elbow and flashing a grin. Despite where we were and what had almost just happened, I felt a little lighter for the first time since I'd walked out of the Academy and away from the life I'd had there.

We were going to get my mother back, take her far away from the iron that made her mad, and have our family, me and her and Conrad, together.

And then I would find some way to make everything in Lovecraft and the worlds beyond all right again.

Walking through Lovecraft was like walking through the dream I'd kept having in the Mists, except I was awake. Awake enough to see the wrecked shops and burnt-out houses. To know, finally, the toll of having destroyed the Engine and broken the Gates to the Thorn Land. I was awake enough to feel the cold bite against every inch of exposed skin, and awake enough to taste the smoke rising in the south on the back of my tongue.

South was where the Engineworks had been.

The people who had worked in the Engine had evacuated. As far as I knew, I hadn't killed anyone outright. But how many had died afterward, as a result of what I'd done?

And how many of them deserved exactly what they got? whispered a dark retort inside my head. Part of me, the part who'd kept quiet for fifteen years while her mother went crazy and the Proctors lied to her—that Aoife wasn't sorry for what she'd done to Lovecraft at all.

Old Town was silent, the crumbling brick storefronts and row houses painted all the colors of the rainbow now pale and faded, deserted and, in many cases, destroyed beyond recognition or repair.

Christobel Charitable Asylum had been a convent a long time ago, when there had still been such things as nuns and people who believed in gods and not the reason-based Master Builder or the Great Old Ones, drifting through the outer stars in their endless, frozen sleep. You could still see the spire poking above the sharp Victorian rooflines, and I angled toward it, up Derleth Street.

I'd walked here so many times as a student, on my way to and from the madhouse. I'd hated the walk then, the obligation to go visit my mother almost a physical weight. I'd never noticed how alive the street was, bustling with life in a way the Academy and Uptown weren't. Now that it lay silent, windows staring at us with our own reflections, old newspapers caught against the fences and lampposts flapping like wounded birds, I missed the activity acutely.

"I don't like this at all," Casey murmured. We walked in a loose, staggered line, choosing whichever side of the street kept us clear of shadows and alleyways. "It's way too calm," she elaborated. "No sirens, no screaming, no Proctors." She inhaled deeply. "Something bad in the air."

"Could you be any more doom-and-gloom?" Conrad complained. "I'm already sour enough on this whole idea without your naysaying, all right?"

I agreed with Casey. I could feel the iron of this place tickling the back of my mind, and its whisper didn't even cover the snuffling and scraping I could hear in every patch of darkness, tangible reminders that we could be set upon at any moment by nightjars, ghouls, or worse things that had made it through the cracks from the Thorn Land.

Nothing made a move, which only ratcheted my nerves tighter as we reached the gates of the Asylum. In the distance, I could hear the dull tolling of the bells in St. Oppenheimer's, as I always used to when I'd visited. Only now they were discordant and hadn't stopped ringing, as if a giant funeral were going on.

In a way, I supposed it was.

The gates in the fence surrounding the asylum were off their hinges, one bent nearly in half, as if a giant had folded it like a piece of paper. That didn't bode well, but I tried not to panic. Just because the gates were open didn't mean anything had breached the asylum itself. Everyone in there could still be fine. Likely agitated, as they wouldn't have had sedatives in close to a week, but fine. I hoped.

I could see from where we stood that the main doors were shut, yet the massive clockwork locks that kept the place from spilling lunatics into the street were open, and the steps were covered with paper files and office supplies. I looked up. A few papers were still caught in the bars of the upper-floor windows, flapping sadly like dying doves.

That doesn't mean anything, I insisted to myself again. Surely the doctors and nurses had fled. There might have even been a patient rebellion. The doors were shut. I didn't see any corpses or hear any screaming. In this situation, crazy as it sounded even in my own head, the silence and desolation were good signs.

"Well?" Dean stood beside me. "We going in?"

I didn't reply, not able to articulate what I was thinking without sounding as crazy as the patients beyond the walls.

I took one step through the wrecked gates, then another, and let that be my answer. I half expected them to slam behind me, even in their ruined state. Going into the asylum never felt like anything other than walking into the jaws of a beast.

"I'll watch your backs," Casey said. "I ain't going in there with the loonies."

I waved her off, not surprised. Casey was a survivor, and survivors knew when to hide rather than rush ahead. That much I'd learned from Cal.

I stopped on the first step, patients' charts and photographs crumpling under my boots. I'd waited so long to come back here, and now I could feel myself shaking inside my clothes. The truth about what had become of Nerissa was just beyond the doors, and yet I wanted nothing more than to turn and run. Where, I didn't know. Just away. I didn't, though, because Conrad was staring at me, daring me to admit this was a bad idea, and because I didn't want to show Dean just how scared I was of finding out the truth. Good or bad, I was going to have to own up to my mother about what I'd done when I let Tremaine trick me into breaking the Gates, and I couldn't imagine her reaction. Just that it would be bad and would probably involve a lot of screaming at me.

If she was even in there.

If she was even alive.

Panic like this hadn't clutched me since I'd first left the city. My shoulder began to throb again—as it had when the leviathan had appeared.

The shoggoth venom was reacting to something beyond the doors.

I froze in place as the doors yawned open seemingly on their own. A dozen pale white paws, puckered and with a greenish cast like the skin of a corpse, gripped the walls. The ghouls' snouts were long, longer than Cal's when he wasn't wearing his human shape, and their claws were pure black. They were part of another nest. One that was a lot more comfortable in daylight than most ghouls I'd run into who weren't Cal.

I wanted to swear, or scream, but all that made it out of my mouth was a light squeak, like a mouse's. I didn't even dare look to see if Conrad and Dean were still with me. Any movement could provoke a ghoul.

"Mmm," the ghoul in the lead purred. *"A delivery. I love it when the meat walks right up to your front door."*

Before I could move, the ghoul tucked its legs and sprang, clearing the steps in one bound. I barely had time to flinch in expectation of its weight on my chest and its teeth in my skin before Dean tackled me, slamming me out of the way.

We landed in the gravel at the foot of the stairs as the rest of the ghouls burst forth from the asylum, howling in anticipation of a meal.

Dean hauled me up. "Run," he growled in my ear. "For your life."

Out of the corner of my eye, I saw Conrad and Casey head the other way, toward Uptown. There was no argument from me. I snatched Dean's hand. In the face of horrors, he'd thrown himself into the line of fire with no regard for his own safety.

I didn't have time to even hope Conrad would be all right. The ghouls were hot on our heels, their screaming bringing more and more of them out of hiding, spilling out of broken shop windows and shadowed alleys and an open sewer grate in the center of the street.

We ran. We ran until it felt like there was fire and razors in my chest in place of air. Ran so fast that my feet didn't even catch in the pockmarks left by missing cobblestones.

Dean whipped his head back, then forward again. "Shit" he gasped, and when I looked I saw that the entire street had become a churning, rushing mass of bodies, white and blue and corpse-gray all the way down to rotted, decomposing greenish-black. There were hundreds of the ghouls, fighting and clawing to be at the front of the pack, and their screaming was the only thing I could hear over my own heartbeat.

We hit the top of Dunwich Lane, the center of despicable goings-on back when Lovecraft had been the Lovecraft I knew. Now Dunwich Lane's red-light district was a smoking, ash-gray ruin. Fire could have started in any one of the dive bars or brothels by the river, and it had chewed on the shabby neighborhood's bones as surely as the ghouls were going to chew on ours if they caught us.

Still we ran, until I couldn't feel myself, except for my straining breath, and could barely see except for a tiny tunnel straight ahead.

We weren't going to make it. I could smell the foul, orchid-sweet stench of the ghouls, and before me I could see the flash of the river. We would have a choice in a moment: jump in and freeze, or stand on the bank and be torn limb from limb, turned into dinner for the horrific and hungry citizens of this new Lovecraft.

The last houses on the street were on pilings out over the river, listing dangerously and plastered with warnings that they were condemned. The street ended at a crumbling wall, and beyond there was nothing but the river. My heart sank.

As Dean and I ran toward the wall, I heard a great whirring from overhead, the sound of a zeppelin's fans. I looked up, thinking Draven had finally caught up with us. That would be the grand finale to this wretched day.

It wasn't Draven's black craft, though—it was a smaller ship, the balloon a dark green and the cabin underneath made of polished wood trimmed with brass that gleamed even in the smoky sunlight. The craft banked sharply over the river and a ladder extended from the cabin hatch.

"You!" bellowed a voice made sharp and metallic by the horn of an aethervox. "You two on Dunwich Lane! Grab the ladder and get on board!"

The ladder drifted into range. I looked to Dean, and he nodded vigorously. Whoever was in the dirigible, he was better than what was closing in on us, no question. I grabbed the ladder's wooden rungs and leather straps and climbed as best I could while it swayed in the wind. Dean jumped on behind me, and the dirigible rose into the air, away from the ravening horde of ghouls.

"Any others alive in the city?" the voice bellowed at us.

"North!" I shouted, gesturing in the direction Conrad and Casey had run.

Another ladder dropped from the other side of the dirigible, and we swooped over the grounds of Christobel Asylum in a hard turn, toward what had been Uptown and the Academy grounds. From above I could see that the back wing of the asylum had been gutted by fire, and ghouls were scampering across what had once been a garden where the patients could walk in warm weather. Half-chewed bodies in the asylum-issued gray pajamas lay like discarded toys on the flagstones, but from what I could see, my mother wasn't one of them.

That was it, then. The truth I'd known in the back part of my mind, the black part that only understood logic and odds, fell home with a hammer blow.

My mother wasn't there. Nobody human was. If she'd managed to survive, she was alone in the city, adrift.

We swooped low across the mazelike streets leading to Banishment Square and Ravenhouse, the Proctors' headquarters in Lovecraft.

Conrad's movements were easy to pick out among the stately granite buildings. He was alone, cornered near Ravenhouse's back wall.

My stomach flipped from the abrupt change in altitude as the dirigible lowered, and I waved frantically at him. "Grab the ladder!"

Conrad jumped, then did as I'd said and clung tightly as the dirigible rose. The ladders clanked against the metal parts of the hull as they retracted into the hatches of the craft, and I scrambled into the cabin along with Dean.

"You all right?" I asked Conrad, who'd climbed in from the other side. He nodded, patting himself down.

"Mostly. That was a hell of a close call."

"Where's Casey?" I asked.

"Dunno," Conrad panted. "Lost her in the back alleys. She was rabbiting back toward Nephilheim last I saw. Not ghoul food yet."

He rubbed his arms, shivering. "I tried to stay with her, Aoife. . . ."

"It couldn't be helped," I reassured him. "Nobody expects you to be ghoul lunch." I patted him awkwardly on the shoulder. "Don't worry, Conrad."

"And why not? This is a Proctor ship isn't it?" he grumbled. "We're under arrest."

"I have no idea who picked us up," I said. "But I doubt they're Proctors."

He managed a weak smile, which I returned. Never mind that I had less than no clue who this airship belonged to and why the pilot had rescued us.

I examined our surroundings, hoping to make a guess on that score. We were in a narrow cargo bay at the aft of the dirigible, and there were no hints, just a few boxes tied down in a corner, devoid of any markings.

"Aoife's right. I don't think it's Proctors," Dean said. "Proctors probably would've just left us to get eaten. Less work for them that way."

"Good point," Conrad said. He got up and brushed himself off. "Come on. Let's see what kind of degenerates we've hooked up with."

I went to the hatch that led to the rest of the dirigible to see what I could find out. Best case, we'd been picked up by pirates or smugglers who also hated the Proctors. Worst, we'd been picked up by pirates or smugglers who didn't hate the Proctors enough to turn down a quick buck they could earn by handing us over.

I tried the hatch, which swung open easily enough. At least we weren't locked in. I stepped through it before Dean or Conrad could protest. A ladder led up one level to a deck, swaying aether lamps lighting my way as the airship climbed at a steep angle, passing through turbulence in the clouds.

The passenger deck was richly appointed, like the interiors of the private craft wealthy families in Lovecraft once used to fly from their mansions to New Amsterdam or their vacation homes in Maine. Lush velvet covered the corridor walls, and all the fittings were brass. When I peeked above deck I saw rich wood and bookshelves lining the room. Furniture bolted to the floor creaked gently as the craft banked, and I saw a plethora of charts spread out on the wide dining table. I'd never seen anything like it in real life—the only airship I'd been on previously was a repurposed war buggy, stripped to the bare bones. This was the sort of craft I'd always dreamed of flying on when I was just another girl at the Academy. I was sad I couldn't explore it now, but I did take in all the details to remember later, when I had the time.

"Hello?" I said cautiously, braced for a confrontation.

"Hello!" A blond woman stuck her head in from another compartment and hurried over to me. "We're so glad you're all right!"

"We?" I said, backing up in surprise when she reached out her hand. She went with the cabin—immaculately curled hair, a traveling skirt and boots that probably cost more money than I'd been given to live on in an entire year as a ward of the City. Her ivory blouse was pressed, and a blue stone brooch sparkled at the collar.

"You don't have to be afraid of me, Aoife," she said, attempting a friendly smile that looked slightly out of place on her perfect porcelain features. She wasn't much taller than I was, but there was a sureness to her posture and a set to her delicate face that told me she was used to being listened to and obeyed.

"How do you know who I am?" I started casting around for a weapon. Something not good was definitely happening here.

"Aoife . . . ," she started, but I snatched an animal leg bone from its display hook and waved it at her.

"You stay away from me!" I didn't know how the woman knew my name, but her perfect facade didn't inspire trust. Beautiful things were usually ugly under the surface, in my experience, and I wasn't about to trust this one.

"Aoife!" Another voice called from above, and I looked up to see a tall, rangy figure with a shock of white at his temples standing on a balcony.

I felt my body go slack, and the bone tumbled from my hand as I stared at the figure, shocked. "Dad?"

My father looked much different from when I'd glimpsed him in the jail cell. There he'd been masked, with deep half-moons under his eyes and his hair wild. Now he wore a natty safari outfit similar in color and style to the blond woman's clothes, canvas pants held up by leather suspenders, a linen shirt open at the collar and boots shined within an inch of their lives. He looked every bit the wealthy gentleman my mother had always told me he was.

"Yes, it's me," he said. He descended the curving brass staircase that led from the bridge. He held up a hand, as if to still a temperamental child. "Calm down."

"I . . ." I took a second look around the airship. It really was a marvelous craft, the cabin more like a stately apartment than the interior of an airship. "What's going on?" I said. It was a lame response, but it was the only one that came to mind.

"I'll explain it all as soon as we're clear of the city and those damn Proctor sweeps," my father answered. "Now I've got to get back to the helm." He gestured to the blond woman. "Val, make sure Aoife is comfortable, and tell her friends they can come up from the hold, will you?"

The woman stooped and picked up the bone I'd liberated, setting it gently back in its display rack. "Of course, Archie."

I stood awkwardly in the center of the dark night sky–blue carpet, feeling both underdressed and acutely aware of how filthy I was after the two days of hard travel from Windhaven. I didn't know who the woman was or why she was being instructed to take care of me. I had no idea what was going on, and I didn't like that. Confusion was my least favorite state.

The woman—Val—gestured me into a leather wing chair, which was bolted to the floor, like everything else. "Would you like some tea?"

"All right," I said, a bit in shock. The two of them were acting as if rescuing Dean, Conrad and me from a horde of ravening ghouls was the most usual thing in the world. Or at least, not strange enough to interrupt afternoon tea.

I watched quietly as Val went to an aethervox panel in the far wall and pressed one of the intricately worked silver-and-brass buttons. "You two can come up now," she said sweetly. "Aoife is fine and we're not going to hurt you."

She went over to a steam hob built into the bookcases and set a silver teakettle on it. "You've had quite a journey," she said to me. "You must be worn out."

"I'm sorry," I answered, shutting my eyes briefly in an attempt to reconcile what had almost happened in Lovecraft with my new opulent surroundings and the gentle hum of the airship's fans. "Who are you, exactly?"

"Oh, how rude of me!" She fluttered her hands around that brooch. "I'm Valentina Crosley. I'm an associate of your father's."

"And this?" I gestured at the airship cabin as Dean and Conrad poked their heads through the hatch. Dean relaxed visibly when he saw that I was in one piece. His hand came out of the pocket where he kept his knife, but he trained a wary eye on Valentina.

"This is your father's craft, the *Munin,*" said Valentina. "It belonged to my father, but now it's Archie's."

"It's very . . . nice," I said cautiously. It was too nice—I clearly didn't belong here, and neither did Dean. Conrad was the only one who appeared at ease. I wondered if his composure would last when he saw our father. Conrad had always taken it harder that Archie had left us with our mother.

"I'm pleased to meet you," he told Valentina, seeming calm enough. "There were some letters in my father's house from you. Archie and I never spoke about you, but I'd hoped we'd meet someday."

Valentina blinked at him, staring for a moment, and I stared as well. Where was Conrad's sullen rage at being abandoned? The outrage that Archie had clearly taken up with another woman? I was feeling both in spades, but my brother seemed pleased as punch to be here.

Valentina recovered inside of a second and held out her hand. "And it's really a pleasure to meet you at last, Conrad.

Your father has told me so much about you and your sister both."

I shot a glance toward the bridge while pleasantries were being exchanged. My father stood alone, silhouetted against the glass. I rose and climbed up the brass steps and stood at the lip of the bridge, feeling awkward but needing to see him, to speak to him again and convince myself this was really happening. How to start a conversation like that? *Why did you save me from the Proctors? Where have you been? Why did you leave our family behind?*

"Two of my friends are still in Nephilheim," I said at last. "Cal and Bethina." I figured he'd at least appreciate my being to the point.

"Bethina, really? My maid? She's come a long way." He looked over his shoulder at me. The *Munin* was flown standing up, with a half-moon brass wheel for the rudder and two controls for the fans. It was really a beautiful craft in every way. If I hadn't been put so off guard by how I'd come aboard, I would have been excited to see something that was this much art along with its function. And would have been doubly excited that my father was at the helm and I was face to face with him for only the second time in my life.

"We need to get them," I said. "Or you need to let me off there so we can go somewhere safe together."

Archibald locked the rudder in place and turned to me, folding his arms. He was taller than I remembered from meeting him in the interrogation room in Ravenhouse, and his eyes held none of the warmth they'd had then. "And what if I said no?"

I kept his gaze and adopted the same icy tone. "Then I suppose it's been nice to see you again."

Archibald shook his head, dropping his arms. "I swear, you're even more stubborn than your mother." I flinched. It was strange to think of his spending time with my mother before Conrad and I were born, learning her expressions and her moods and seeing them in me.

My father banked the craft, dropping us over the dour gray roofs of Nephilheim. "Don't think I don't know," he told me, "that your little buddy Cal Daulton is a ghoul. And don't think I'm going to welcome him aboard."

"He saved my life, Dad," I said, folding my arms to mimic his earlier posture. "He's not like the other ghouls."

"I know," he said. "That's why I'm picking him up." He spun the wheel and we crossed the river, drifting up the far bank, over the foundry and into the village, which from this vantage looked like a ruined toy, stepped on by an angry child.

"There," I said, pointing to the broad avenue where we'd left Cal and Bethina. My father throttled back the fans, hovering, and the *Munin* shivered as the thin, delicate ladders unfurled from its hatches. I saw figures emerge from the nearest ruined cottage, and mere moments later, Cal and Bethina were in the main cabin with the rest of us.

"Mr. Grayson!" Bethina shrieked, running to my father and wrapping her arms around him. She'd been his chambermaid; he probably knew her better than he'd known me, before all this happened. I was just relieved they were both all right, and didn't begrudge her the reunion.

My father smiled at her and patted her on the back. "Glad to see you in one piece, Bethina. Didn't I dismiss you, though?"

She shrugged. "I didn't have anywhere else to go. Someone had to keep your house in order."

Cal sidled up to me. "That's your father?"

"In the flesh," I said, still barely able to believe it myself. Every time I looked at Archie, he seemed like he should shimmer and vanish like an illusion, rather than be standing not ten feet from me, pouring Bethina a cup of tea.

"Something to sweeten it?" he asked, reaching for a cut-glass brandy decanter in the sideboard.

"Oh, no," said Bethina primly. "You know I don't do that sort of thing, Mr. Grayson."

"Seems nice enough," Cal muttered to me. "Certainly not the raving lunatic Draven was always yelling about."

"Jury's out on the first part," I said, just as Cal's eyes lit on Valentina.

"Who's the dame?" he said, brows going up. "She looks like a lanternreel star."

I spread my hands. "I've been here about ten minutes longer than you have, Cal. Her name is Valentina. Aside from that, your guess is as good as mine."

Valentina bubbled up to us, carrying a tray holding two delicate china cups painted with briar roses. "Tea?"

I took it and pointed to the brandy. "I think I'll have something in mine." My old teacher, Mrs. Fortune, would give us tea with brandy when we had the flu at the Academy. I could use the calming effect just then.

"No, you won't be having any brandy," my father returned crisply. "The rest of you, make yourselves comfortable. Conrad and Aoife, we need to speak privately."

He gestured to a small hatch that led to the room

Valentina had appeared from and waited until we'd followed him in before shutting and latching the door. I felt as if we'd been called on the carpet for passing notes during class, not as if we were having the first real meeting with our father, ever. His expression was stern and his eyes betrayed no emotion beyond annoyance.

This was not how I'd imagined my first conversation with Archie going, and I could tell from Conrad's fidgeting and his frown that he felt the same way.

"First of all," Archie said, "what the *hell* were you two thinking, going back into Lovecraft?"

"I—" I started, but Archie pointed his finger at me and focused his eyes on my brother.

"I'll get to you. Conrad?"

Conrad spread his hands as if to ask what was the big deal. "It wasn't my idea. I was actually against it."

"Oh, come on, Conrad!" I shouted, furious that now we were actually caught, he was trying to wriggle out of getting in trouble. "You were the one who ran off in the first place! It's because of *you* that I'm even here! You and that *stupid* letter!"

"I wrote that letter to get you out of Lovecraft, not rip apart space and time and destroy the entire damn city!" Conrad shouted back.

Rage overwhelmed me and I cocked my arm back and whipped my teacup at Conrad's head. He ducked and the cup hit the wall, sending tea and china shards spattering across the cream-colored damask wallpaper.

"Enough, both of you!" Archie bellowed. He stepped between us, pointing at the door. "Conrad, give us a minute."

"You always overreact," Conrad muttered at me. "That's why we're in this mess."

"*You're* an idiot," I returned, too angry to watch what I was saying. Conrad could treat me like I was still his excitable little sister, but I'd managed on my own for over a year after he'd run off. I'd managed after he'd nearly killed me. He didn't get to talk to me like that any longer.

Archie thumped him on the side of the head with his knuckles. "I said enough. This is not your sister's fault. Not entirely. Go."

Conrad turned and stormed out, slamming the hatch behind him hard enough to rattle the framed paintings on the walls. In the silence that followed I looked anywhere but at my father's face: A bunk in the corner immaculately made up with cream linens and rows of clothes neatly hanging in the wardrobe. A brass globe swaying from the ceiling, lit from the inside by aether. Outlines of continents and seas glowing softly against a ceiling painted like the night sky, constellations spelled out with silver thread. Finally, I ran out of things to stare at and had to look at my father again and see his shoulders slumped with fatigue, the dark circles under his eyes and the new lines along the sides of his mouth. I felt horrible for screaming at Conrad, for breaking my father's things. What must he think of me after that?

Archie sighed, sitting down in one of the two small, overstuffed chairs by the cabin's porthole. "Have a seat, Aoife."

I stayed where I was and fidgeted. Being around him was still too new for me to sit and act comfortable—as if we were actually father and daughter. Besides, if I sat, I couldn't study him while we talked, look for the similarities in our faces that I wanted to be there. I wanted to be a little bit like Archie—otherwise, my only fate was to end up like Nerissa.

Archie's eyes were an eerie reflection of my own when we locked gazes, dark green and glittering, like something that had waited for light a long time in a dark place.

But his held none of the uncertainty mine did, just a calculating hardness that seemed to measure me up and dismiss me as wanting. I'd always hoped that Archie would be warm, like the fathers in books and lanternreels who came home every evening, hung up their hats and kissed their wives and children hello. But I'd known I was probably just fantasizing. His hard eyes weren't really a surprise, just a disappointment.

"It's good to see you," he said at last, more quietly than I had expected. "It's been a really long time."

This I hadn't expected. A lecture, maybe, or a punishment for making him rescue us from the city, but not the sadness that hung on his frame like an ill-fitting coat. "Yes," I said at last, matching his soft tone. "It has."

"Aside from when I got you out of Ravenhouse, I mean," he said. "And that's not exactly a family memory I'm looking to cherish." He sighed and raked a hand through his hair, disturbing his carefully groomed coif into something that was closer to my own unruly cloud. "I'm glad you're all right, Aoife, but you have to promise me never to do something that stupid again—and I mean both times, when you let Draven pick you up and this time, when you were doing whatever the hell it was you were doing down there in that wasteland."

I had a feeling he wouldn't be so forgiving when he found out why I'd come back, especially after he'd helped me escape the Proctors' cells when I'd turned myself in to Draven as a means to get to the Engine. But I was done lying to everyone. Done pretending everything was fine, when even now the iron told me that the clock had started ticking on my madness again.

At least up here on the *Munin*, made of wood and brass, it had quieted to an insidious whisper rather than a scream. I looked out the porthole while I formulated my answer carefully. The country passing beneath us was blank now that we'd left the outskirts of Nephilheim, gray and white with patches of bare trees and snow. The coastline cast gentle lace on the frozen beaches, and I could see the red buoys of the shipping channel we followed bobbing like tiny beacons in the vast Atlantic.

"I was looking for Ner—for my mother," I told Archie. "What happened . . . I left her there."

"Nerissa isn't in the madhouse," Archie said. "She'd know the ghouls would come up when everything went to pot. That ghouls or something worse would be after her. Nerissa is a survivor, Aoife. She knows to go to ground and wait for things to blow over."

"How can I possibly know that for sure?" I snapped, shocked and angered that he was brushing off my mother's fate. Archie hadn't seen Nerissa for nearly sixteen years. She wasn't a survivor. She was fragile. Exposed to the world, the open air and the creatures in it, she'd wither like a hothouse bloom. "Is that supposed to make me feel any better about what I saw down there? Should I get back to tea and scones with your friend Valentina and leave all my troubles behind me?"

"Don't you speak to me that way," Archie snapped back.

"You have no idea what went on between your mother and me. Like it or not, Aoife, I know her better than you do."

I felt tears press up against my eyes, hot and traitorous. I couldn't cry in front of my father. Couldn't show him how I was panicking over not being able to find Nerissa, and over everything else that had come out of my one misguided moment of trusting the wrong person. I covered the panic with anger instead. "Oh, really?" I whispered, because that was all I could say. "Where were you, up until a few weeks ago? Oh, that's right, you left your bastard children to rot in Lovecraft and went on your merry way. You didn't even care that Conrad and I existed until Draven decided to use me to get at you." I breathed hard, feeling the anger heat my cheeks and quicken my heart, burning away the tears. "You left us, *Dad*. You left us to whatever might happen. So no, I don't believe you, and I don't think of you as my father. Not in any way except by blood." I had to get out of the close little room, which was hot and smelled cloyingly of rosewater, no doubt Valentina's doing. I scrabbled at the hatch.

Archie jumped up and slammed the door shut before I could fully yank it open. "You are a *child*, Aoife," he said, color rising in his face. "You're a smart child, and a resourceful one, but there are things you don't yet understand about your mother, or me."

"Then tell me," I said. My heart thumped in time with Archie's ragged, angry breaths. "Tell me, or I have no reason to trust you and never will." The simple truth coming out lightened me to a surprising degree. I'd been waiting, consciously or not, a long while to say that to Archie's face.

My father slumped, like someone had opened a valve

and let the air out of him. "That's fair," he said. "That's honest. Look, sweetheart. I know I wasn't any kind of father to you. Not in any way that mattered." He pointed at the second chair again, and this time I joined him. Hearing him admit it so easily had extinguished my rage like a bucket of ice water. I'd imagined telling Archie off in so many different ways, and now I just felt like a petulant, spoiled brat, whining because her father hadn't bought her a pony.

I'd never expected him to admit it. And I'd never expected the deep ache in my chest when he did. I'd *wanted* a father. I could pretend I only hated him for leaving, but I'd always wanted him back, as well. And every day and month and year he didn't come had made the knife cut a little deeper into the wound.

I didn't hate Archie anymore, I realized. He'd screwed up. So had I. But maybe I didn't have to be a child. Maybe I could be a girl who tried to forgive him.

"Look, I was really mad . . . ," I started, but Archie held up his hand.

"Don't you start apologizing for speaking your mind," Archie told me. "That's a dangerous habit to get into." He glanced at the door for a second, then went to the wardrobe and pulled an old, dusty evening jacket from its hanger, fishing in the pocket for a pack of cigarettes. "Open the porthole, will you?" he said. "If Valentina smells this I'll catch hell."

I did as he said, too drained to do much else, and sat back. He was being remarkably calm. I could have misjudged the hardness in his face—maybe Archie wasn't unyielding. Maybe he wore the face as a shield. I did the same thing, when I was hurt and angry.

"I didn't know you smoked," I said. It was all I could think of.

Archie pulled a silver lighter from his pocket and lit the cigarette, exhaling with a sigh. "I have a lot of bad habits. Is that all right for a father to admit?" He shrugged. "Too late now." He tapped ash into my empty saucer and sat forward. "I know you don't believe me that Nerissa is safe, but you have to trust me—if anyone can outrun the ghouls and the Proctors, it's your mother." He squeezed my shoulder—not a long gesture, or a gentle one, but solid. "I know you're worried about her, and that you came back for her, but you need to trust me when I say this: We need to be a family, to get through what's happened. And what's coming. If you can just take me at my word, I promise we will get Nerissa back." He inhaled once, sharply, then stubbed out the cigarette and slid the unburned portion back into his pack. "Can you give me that? Just until we get where we're going?"

I thought, really, it was a pretty simple thing to ask. Archie had rescued me, after all. Let himself tell me how he really felt. I could wait to interrogate him with the million questions I had, about the Brotherhood and my Weird and the Fae, just a little longer.

"Aoife?" he said, his expression begging me to just go along with him.

"Okay," I said. "But you and I really need to talk when we get— Where *are* we going?" I asked, peering out the porthole. I saw that we'd been following the coast as the land got narrower and narrower. I figured we were tracking over Cape Cod, and could see two small islands in the distance.

"Valentina's summerhouse," Archie answered. "Can't go back to Graystone—the Kindly Folk—the Fae, whatever you call them—and the Proctors both'll be crawling all over it."

"Are her parents expecting us?" I said, and immediately felt inane. Who cared about manners at a time like this?

Archie snorted. "Hardly. The elder Crosleys live down in New Amsterdam. Where it's safe." His lip twitched, just the barest flicker of scorn, but I caught it, and it dawned on me that Archie didn't feel any more comfortable with the money dripping off the *Munin* and Valentina herself than I did.

"I suppose Valentina's home is all right," I offered. It had to be safer than Lovecraft, even though small towns and villages didn't offer the protection of big cities. Then again, the lack of iron would keep me from getting sick a little longer, so I supposed the mortal danger balanced that.

Though with things like Tremaine around, what good had protection done?

"Thank you," Archie sighed. "And I meant it—I'm glad you're all right."

I felt my first real smile in what seemed like years flicker. Just a spark, but it felt good to know that *somebody* other than Dean and Cal cared if I turned into ghoul food. "I know you're angry that I went back to Lovecraft," I said. "And I know it wasn't that bright, but I'd do it again. It's my fault Nerissa is . . . is . . . out there."

"Hey," Archie said, squeezing my shoulder again, longer and harder this time. "None of that. Your mother isn't a fool. She will have found a place to hole up. It's how she survived as long as she did, when the Fae were after her." He shoved a clean handkerchief into my hands, and I was embarrassed he'd even noticed my tears. "We'll find her eventually, or she'll find you. I know you blame yourself, but you're going to have to stop trying to find her and set things right all by yourself. You're going to get yourself killed."

I looked at him, knotting the handkerchief between my fists. The fine linen turned to a wrinkled lump in my grasp. "You don't seem all that worried about her. About any of this."

"Of course I am," Archie said. "But tearing out my hair and running straight into a herd of ghouls isn't going to help anyone. Not Nerissa, not you." He opened the hatch. "Nerissa is smart, Aoife. She always was. Smart and a survivor. She'll be fine. I'm more worried about you."

I squirmed under his scrutiny. "I'm fine."

"You're not fine," Archie said. "Aoife, you can't beat yourself up about what happened with Tremaine. The Fae trick you. It's what they do. How they survive. You did a terrible thing with the Engine, but your mother— It's not your fault. You did it, but the blame doesn't lie with you."

"He tricked me," I whispered. I swiped viciously at my face with Archie's handkerchief, hating that I was showing weakness at all, never mind to my father. "Tremaine tricked me, but I shouldn't have left her."

Archie looked as if he was going to reach for me, then drew back when another guttural sob came out. I was glad. We weren't at the point where we could touch each other like a normal father and daughter. "Listen," he said. "I guarantee, the minute no one was around to pump her full of sedatives, Nerissa was over that fence," Archie said. "She's a firecracker." He smiled, as quickly as he'd glared before, and I wished that I could add another question to my list, about what Nerissa was like before Conrad and I were born.

Before all the badness that came down on us after Archie left. "You're a lot like her."

I handed back the handkerchief, now a stained and soaked mess. "I'm going to be as crazy as she is if I stay in the Iron Land, I know that much." I sighed.

Archie shrugged. "Probably. I don't know you that well, strange as that is to say about your own flesh and blood, but I hope that changes." He took a step from the cabin. "I've got to get back to the bridge. If you need something before we land, Valentina can get it for you."

I looked back at the wardrobe. One side was my father's jackets. The other side held dresses and skirts, rows of shoes lined up neatly on the bottom and hatboxes stacked along the top shelf. Archie knew Nerissa, but there were no signs of her here. Here, it was Valentina's domain, and I wasn't sure I could accept that. "How long?" I asked Archie. He blinked at me in surprise.

"Valentina? I . . . Well. A few years, I guess."

I looked past his broad shoulder out into the main cabin, where Valentina sat with Bethina and Conrad, sipping tea. Dean paced from one porthole to the next, never sitting still.

"My mother asked for you," I told Archie. "Over and over, all the time I visited her. She kept talking about you and asking for you." I stared him down, waiting for something. I wasn't sure what. Guilt? An admission that I wasn't the only one who'd left Nerissa behind?

I got nothing except the inscrutable mask once again, the frown lines and the cold glance of my father's glittering emerald eyes. "Aoife," he said. His tone was as heavy as an iron door. "I'm sorry, truly, that you feel that way. But what went on between Nerissa and me is complicated, and my being with Valentina is my business. Not to put too fine a point on it."

He might as well have slapped me. Although he and Nerissa hadn't even talked since just after I was born, the idea that he'd managed to find himself someone new didn't sit well with me. Maybe it was a selfish way to think, but whenever I thought about my father and Valentina, my stomach twisted involuntarily. "Are you going to marry her?" I asked bitterly, loudly enough to make Dean look up from where he was examining the antiques and curiosities on the wall.

"I'd like to," Archie said, pulling back from me a bit and looking surprised at how forward I was. "But Valentina doesn't believe marriage is necessary." The *Munin* shuddered in the wind and he turned and left, making his way back to the bridge. From where I sat I could see him take the wheel again. Valentina stared at me for a moment before leaning over to refill Bethina's teacup, and I flushed hot, looking away.

I couldn't say that if Dean and I were separated, after years and years I wouldn't move on. Find somebody new, especially if they cared about me as much as my father clearly cared about Valentina. The way his features softened when he talked about her made me almost jealous. They weren't soft at all when he talked to me, so far.

But I doubted I'd be able to forget Dean. I doubted I'd be able to say our being apart was for the best. And for that, I found my father's attitude callous. I decided that I wouldn't ask him any of those questions that were burning me up about him and Nerissa after all. I couldn't hear him talk about my mother while Valentina was here, safe and alive.

I went into the main cabin and over to a porthole away from the others and stared out at the passing landscape, trying to let the hum of the *Munin*'s machines calm my mind and take me away from my racing, angry thoughts about my father, Valentina and everything else.

The ship, under Archie's guidance, flew on, over the spindly arm of Cape Cod, past stately white-painted mansions hugging the coastline. The destruction was less here, but I could still see creatures moving among the low scrub, darting and jumping from place to place. An overturned jitney on the side of the road lay smoking, steam wafting from under the crushed hood like spirits escaping into the cold air. No people.

Dean came and stood next to me at the porthole. "So, your old man. He going to chase me with a shotgun?"

I had to smile. All family unpleasantness aside, I *did* have Dean. He wasn't gone, and I wasn't going to have to make the choice my father had. At least, not yet. "Don't worry, I didn't tell him about us," I said. "Anyway, he doesn't really have a lot of room to talk, what with his little friend over there."

Valentina smiled at me as she got up and began clearing the tea things. It was a forced smile, and it didn't reach her eyes. Good. I didn't like her any more than that smile and those fake pleasantries pretended to like me.

"Maybe you should give your old man a break," Dean said, brushing his thumb over my cheek. "Sixteen years is a long time to be lonely."

"I know that," I said grudgingly. But the fact that Archie must have been lonely didn't make Valentina's presence—and my mother's absence—sting any less. "And it's not like he ever made it legal between them. I guess I just thought he cared more than that." I felt my mouth twist down, and an answering twist in my guts. "He doesn't even seem that worried that Nerissa's missing."

Dean sighed and pressed his lips against my forehead. "You know, my dad was a decent guy," he said. "But like I said, he and my mother never would've worked out. It was better they went back to their own people. Maybe it's the same for your folks."

I had to admit, he had a point. Who was to say they'd still be together? My mother was impossible to get along with on her best days, and on her worst she'd scream and throw things at your head. Still, the fact that Archie had never given us a chance to be a family grated on me. "Maybe my father should stop giving the eye to girls who are closer to my age than his," I grumbled. Dean snorted.

"Oh, come on. She looks all right to me. Hardly an evil stepmother."

"Oh, I bet she looks good to you," I told him before I could bite the words back, acid etching them onto my tongue. Jealousy tasted ugly and bitter, like bile and spoiled fruit, but I couldn't stop the surge.

Dean shook his head. His dark hair brushed across his pale forehead like an ink stain. He looked inhumanly beautiful in moments like this, when the light hit him just so and brought his Erlkin features to the forefront. "Aoife, don't be that way. You're not one of those girls, and that's why I like you."

"Do me a favor, Dean," I said. "Don't tell me what I am and what I'm not. You don't know me that well yet."

He drew back from me, hurt replacing the tender look

in his eyes. "I want to, dammit," he murmured. "But you won't let me. There's a wall around you, princess, but I'm not going to stop trying." He squeezed my hand and then stepped away from me. "I know this is hard," he said. "And I'm here for you, but you've got to stop shoving me back every time I try to get in."

I searched for the words to tell Dean that I was sorry, and that if anyone was close to me, it was him. He knew things about me that nobody else did, and he wasn't put off by them. But Archie's voice drowned out my reply of *I'm sorry*. Which was fine with me, really. Banality like that could never show Dean how I really felt.

"We're landing, and it's rough wind!" my father bellowed. "Strap yourself in if you don't want to be dumped on your ass." Dean and I both scrambled for seats and safety harnesses. I'd survived one airship crash, on the way to Arkham, and I had no desire to even come close to the experience again.

Valentina sighed as she hurried to an armchair, drawing a pair of leather straps with brass buckles from beneath the cushion. "Archie, your language. Honestly."

Dean looked over at me and mouthed *You all right?* I nodded as the wind buffeted us. Conrad looked distinctly green around the edges, which I couldn't help feeling a little smug over. Flying had never been his favorite thing. I saw Cal reach over and squeeze Bethina's hand as the *Munin* drifted back to earth, and in that moment I envied her. Her life was easy, with someone who loved her unconditionally. Mine was becoming anything but.

8

The Frozen Shores

THE CROSLEY HOUSE was a great white thing, clothed the whole way around in porches, all the way up to the third floor, like lace wrapped around bleached bones. It sat on a spit of land poking into the Atlantic, and on the rocky point beyond sat a lighthouse, its crimson band of paint the only color in the winter landscape.

It wasn't as grand as Graystone, Archie's huge granite mansion in Arkham, but was imposing in its own way, clinging to the rocks, crouched above the sea as if the house were waiting for something, or someone, to come in from the horizon.

My father set the *Munin* down on the vast expanse of dead, snowy lawn behind the house, amid ice-dripping statues and drooping topiary animals. He looked to Conrad. "Well, that shaved about ten years off my life. You know how to tie down an airship, boy?"

Conrad spread his hands and shook his head, but Dean

took off his straps and jumped out of his seat next to me. "I do."

"Good man," Archie said. "Usually it's just me and Valentina to keep her steady, and it can get hairy with this much wind." He went down the ladder to the lower deck, and Dean followed.

"Be careful," I called, before his gleaming raven head disappeared belowdecks.

He turned back and threw me a wink. "You know me, doll."

I felt the heat start again in my chest. Dean had an effect on me with just a look. I was glad he'd gone back to smiling after I'd snapped at him. Later, I'd have to try to find a way to really apologize.

"We can disembark," Valentina said, knocking me out of my Dean-induced daze. "I'll lock the wheel while you kids go inside." She pressed a brass key into my hand. "That opens the back door."

I was surprised at how casually she handed over the keys to her home, especially when I'd made it glaringly obvious I didn't like her. Dean's voice echoed in my head, reminding me to give her a chance.

But I remembered the emptiness in my guts when I'd seen the ruined madhouse and realized Nerissa was still gone, and I just couldn't do it. I snatched the key and went ahead of Conrad, Cal and Bethina down the ladder and across the lawn. Up close, the house was even more foreboding, like it had been emptied out and was only a skeleton, a dead insect left on the lawn after warm weather had gone. Salt-rimed windows glared back blankly at me as I crossed the frozen grass, crunching blades under my boots, and I looked at the vast expanse of empty beach and dune and rock around us. There were no ghoul traps here, nothing to thwart some kind of creature lying in wait for a fresh meal. My shoulder wasn't throbbing, so I walked on cautiously, but my every nerve sang with alertness, and looking too long at the skeletal house gave me a chill.

"So," I said to Conrad as we mounted the shallow weather-grayed steps to the wide, faded blue back door. "Valentina is something else."

"She seems swell," Bethina piped up. "A real classy lady." Of course Bethina would think that. She expected the best from people until they showed her otherwise. I wished I could do the same, sometimes, but now I couldn't help being a little annoyed. Just because Valentina had fancy clothes and good manners didn't make her good all over.

Conrad sighed and rolled his eyes in consternation at my annoyed expression.

"Aoife, don't be naive. People in the real world don't sit around and pine for the rest of their lives when their wives get committed to madhouses. And you know they were never legally married, anyway."

"Why don't you strip your own gears, Conrad?" I suggested, glaring at him.

He flung his hands in the air in response to my insult, looking for all the world like someone who had reached the end of his rope.

"I can't even talk to you these days without getting my head bitten off. I'm done."

"Fine by me," I told him. "All you ever do when you open your mouth is try to make me feel stupid."

"Hey!" Cal shouted, when Conrad opened his mouth

again. "Me and Bethina are freezing. You think maybe we could take the family fight inside?"

I turned away from Conrad. I wasn't embarrassed for losing my temper this time, but I was infuriated that Conrad seemed to be sticking up for Valentina just to be contrary.

I shoved the key in the lock and opened the rickety wooden door to Valentina's house, following Cal and Bethina inside, away from Conrad and that disapproving line between his eyes.

The remainder of the afternoon was taken up with my father turning the aether feed to the house on and getting hot water flowing while the rest of us checked the pantry and returned to the *Munin* for provisions. Conrad and Dean carried in wood to stoke the fireplaces; various other household tasks like making up beds and washing plates and cups fell to Valentina, Bethina and me. The work did absolutely nothing to stem the tide of fierce resentment growing in my chest.

Valentina flitted around taking dust catchers from the furniture and asking if everyone had had enough to eat or wanted tea and biscuits, and everything else well-bred young ladies were supposed to check up on when they entertained guests. I didn't know how she could be so calm in an unprotected house, with no reinforced doors, shutters, or traps—ghouls could burst in at any moment, and then the tea party would be over.

I finally cornered my father when he came back from the basement, cleaning soot from the boiler off his palms. "Are we safe here?"

"Sure," he said, frowning. "The house is in Valentina's father's name. The Proctors have no reason to suspect we'd come here."

"I meant . . ." I lowered my voice as Valentina passed, carrying a tray of sandwiches into the dining room. Dean, Conrad and Cal fell on them like, well, starving teenage boys. My stomach grumbled. I couldn't remember the last time I'd had a real meal. "Are we safe from, you know . . ."

Archie raised one eyebrow. "From the Fae? Yes, Aoife." He put his hand on my shoulder, surprising me, and gave a half smile. "There may not be ghoul traps outside, but the bones of this house were built to protect the people inside. There's no iron, but that's not the only way to keep out Fae." He patted me, in what I'd call a fatherly gesture from anyone else. From him, I wasn't sure what to call it yet, but it still calmed me. "When we're settled in, I'll tell you all about it. It's stuff you need to know anyway."

"And Conrad," I reminded him. Archie's eyes darkened into an expression I couldn't identify as he looked past me to where Conrad was shoving roast beef into his mouth.

"Right," he said. "Conrad. Of course." He shoved the dirty rag into his back pocket and gave me another of those enigmatic half smiles. "Get some sleep, kid. You look exhausted."

I was exhausted, so I didn't argue, just went up to the room Valentina had told me was mine when she was running around playing hostess. I didn't understand how she could take the time, considering what was going on. Valentina definitely seemed as if she was showing off—her grand house, her skills at hospitality. Wasn't it enough that she was stunningly beautiful and rich? Did she have to be perfect at everything else too?

I huffed as I flopped backward on the creaky bed, examining the room to which Valentina had exiled me. Maybe *exiled* wasn't the right word. Removed. I was rooms away from Dean, my brother and my friends, never mind the master suite. Just like at the Academy—stick the charity case up under the rafters and forget about her.

My room was in a corner so small that the ceiling formed a pyramid where the sides of the roof met. The furniture was mismatched and clearly picked from other parts of the house. A chipped mirror over a dressing table told me I was dirty, tired and really in need of a change of clothes. I got back off the carved wooden bed, which was covered with a crazy quilt and a long-forgotten family of porcelain dolls, and went to the wardrobe to look for some clean underthings, at the very least.

Cal and Bethina were still downstairs—I could hear them laughing. They could enjoy Valentina's house with none of the resentment the place triggered in me. Dean's whereabouts were a mystery, and if I knew Conrad he was probably hanging off my father and Valentina, determined to play the part of the good son.

If my mother had been safe, I would have tried to give Valentina a chance to be my stepmother and my father a chance to be happy. I would have forced myself to at least be polite to her, even if we'd never be the best of friends.

But the world was turning to ashes, and Archie didn't seem nearly as concerned with that fact as he did with his pretty blond doll.

I'd feel better if I were clean. That was the only thing I was sure of. I rooted around in the wardrobe and found a robe made of silk so old it crumbled in places under my hands. It was the only thing remotely resembling night-clothes that fit, though, so I pulled it around me and let the musty, sharp scent envelop my skin.

The bottom of the wardrobe held a stack of old composition books, so old the pages breathed dust when I smoothed one open. Searching the drawers, I found a pencil with a little lead left. My bag and my original journal were gone, but I needed to write. Maybe if I got all these racing, swelling, screaming thoughts out of my head, I'd be able to make a new plan.

I dated the corner of the page and began.

Fourth entry:

I failed. I had a plan, I executed it, and I still failed.

My mother is not in Lovecraft and the city is gone. Lovecraft is an abattoir filled with ghouls. My father has a girlfriend who could be my sister and he doesn't think I should have any problems with that fact. He just says I have to "trust" him, that he has the answers that will let us fix the Gates and find Nerissa. I want to trust him. I want a father, a family. I want people I can trust. But everything that's happened since I destroyed the Engine makes it close to impossible.

The world is burning, and all I can do is watch and feel the flames on my face. I don't have a plan to put the fires out. I don't even know where to look for water.

I didn't only fail my mother. I failed as a Gateminder.

There has to be a way to stop Draven and put

things back like they were. To stop ghouls from roaming free, to stop the Gates from being thrown open to allow whatever can find them to make their way from world to world and cause more destruction. To restore the order the Brotherhood of Iron worked so hard to protect.

I think of the way my life was. I was so afraid of the Proctors, of going crazy, but also of getting bad grades and whether my hairstyle would get me teased. Such small worries now. Of course, that was a life built on lies, but innocent people weren't in harm's way.

A life of lies or a life of nothing except this vast feeling of loss inside me.

Is there another way?

I threw down the pencil and slapped the book shut. How was scribbling maudlin little thoughts supposed to save the world? Was the whole Brotherhood of Iron indolent and/or insane? Where were they? Why wasn't Archie contacting them, trying to find a solution to all this?

What was he waiting for?

In the middle of my worrying, a knock sounded at my door, and I jumped, tearing my robe at the shoulder. I shoved the notebook under the threadbare pillows on my bed and got up to answer it.

Valentina stood on the other side, a dress draped over her arm.

I let my distaste show in my posture, something I'd learned from Dean. "Can I help you, Valentina?"

In her other hand she held a quilted ditty bag, which she held out to me. "Peace offering?"

I looked at the thing askance. Valentina didn't have to try to befriend me—she already had my father, and Conrad was clearly smitten with her presence. What could she possibly gain from kissing up to me?

"What is it?" I didn't take the bag.

"Let me in and I'll show you," Valentina told me, attempting a smile. It looked about as real as the creamy, note-perfect platinum tones in her smooth, glowing hair, which was to say, not at all. In my old life, friendly faces bearing gifts were usually just looking to trick or mock me, or make me look stupid for the other students' amusement. I'd learned a long time ago not to trust them, so why should Valentina be any different?

A tiny, doubtful part of me whispered that I was being awfully hard on Valentina, but I told it to be quiet. "I'm very tired," I said aloud. "I think I'm going to bed." I started to shut the door, but Valentina stopped it with her foot. She and I exchanged polite stares for a moment, before she sighed and dropped her gaze. I was surprised—she was in charge here, the lady of the house, and she could just as easily have demanded Archie make me behave as tried to reason with me.

"Look, Aoife," she said, and her voice was no longer the pleasant trilling of a well-trained bird. All at once, she just looked tired. "I know you don't like me. It could hardly be more obvious, really. But I love your dad, and because of that, I want the two of us to get along. Can you give me five minutes to make my case?"

I felt a tightening in my chest. Five minutes with Valentina would feel like betraying Nerissa the entire time.

"I'm not asking you to take a side," Valentina said quietly.

"I just want you to know I'm not as awful as you seem determined to make me out to be."

I had some doubts about that, but she looked so defeated I felt the resolve to hate her washing away like the dunes outside under heavy seas. She really wasn't much older than me—if I'd been in her shoes, I'd have been at my wits' end trying to deal with somebody so openly hostile.

"Fine," I said, and pulled the door all the way open. "You can come in, I guess."

"Well, thank the stars for that," Valentina said. "You're even more stubborn than your father, you know that?"

"No," I told her, sitting on the bed again and pulling my knees to my chest. "I barely know him, never mind whether he's stubborn or not." It made me happy to know she saw *some* similarity between my father and me. I felt a bit less like we'd simply been thrown together as father and daughter by fate. Maybe something other than the Weird tied us together after all.

"He is," Valentina assured me. "Stubborn as an old goat." She pulled a hanger from the wardrobe and put the dress she'd brought in on it, placing it on a hook inside the door and smoothing it with her neat, manicured hands. "It didn't look like you had any clean clothes," she explained. "You and I should be around the same size, though I'm a bit larger in the bust." She drew a packet of hairpins from the ditty bag and put them on the edge of the dressing table. "You'll get there. I can already tell you're going to be a true beauty."

I chewed on my lip, not able to think of anything to say, so I just settled for blushing furiously and staring at my feet.

"You don't hear that much, huh?" Valentina said, raising

an eyebrow. "Well, take it from me—when you grow into your face, you're going to stop traffic."

"You're the only one who thinks so, I'm sure," I mumbled. "Not even my mother ever said I was pretty."

"Neither did mine, unless I was doing as she commanded," Valentina said, with a crackly, dry-paper laugh. "My family places a great deal of value on beauty," she continued, then shook her head. "That's not exactly right. They put a lot of value on appearances. For instance, my father detests Archie, really. Can't stand him. But they're part of the same cause, working for the Brotherhood to protect the Iron Land from the Fae and anything else out there, so he pretends they're great friends to keep the other members thinking he's a genial old man, when really, it couldn't be further from the truth." She sighed. "What you must think of this place—a kid who grew up like you did. You must find me unbearably bourgeois."

Valentina was making it harder and harder to completely dislike her, and that just made me feel even crankier and more exhausted than I already did. I wanted things to be simple—she was the evil stepmother, I was the neglected daughter. Her being nice and friendly and normal made things much less cut and dried. "My father's family isn't poor," I said. "But I don't think my father is like yours."

"The Graysons have family money," Valentina said. "But your father and your uncle Ian didn't do much besides working with the Brotherhood, so Grayson money's not the fat stack of cash it once was. Another mark against him, from the Crosleys' perspective. They've got that Rationalist work ethic, even if they don't believe in any of the teachings."

"It's really strange," I blurted, unable to think of a polite way to say it, "hearing about my family from you."

Valentina drew a hairbrush from the bag as well. "Come over here," she said, patting the seat of the dressing table.

I drew my brows together, suspicious of her again. "What for?"

"Just come," Valentina said. "And trust me a little. I may not be an ace engineer like you, but I know what I'm doing here."

I sat, but slowly.

Valentina sighed. "I'm not going to bite you, Aoife."

"Maybe I'm just not ready to be best friends yet." I kept one eye on her in the mirror as she opened the bag and pulled out a Bakelite case.

"Just as paranoid as your dear old dad too," Valentina said. "For two people who never talked but once before today, you have a lot in common."

I dropped my eyes at that, unaccountably pleased that someone had confirmed what I'd been thinking—Archie and I were alike, if only in that we were both stubborn and cranky. But it made me feel warm inside, warmer than the cool air of the house could make me.

Valentina opened the case top, revealing twin rows of ceramic rollers, with a connector in the back to allow a small steam hob to heat them. "Your hair is a travesty," Valentina said. "I'm going to fix it, and we're going to talk."

"Do I have a choice?" I asked. I wasn't entirely opposed to the idea of a makeover, but talking seemed like it might be strained. What could someone like Valentina possibly want to talk about with me? I wasn't rich and I wasn't cultured. I didn't even know the right fork to use at a fancy dinner party.

"No," Valentina said as she picked up the hairbrush and a small tin tub of pomade and tilted my head down so I was looking at my lap. She yanked the brush through a section of my hair, and I hissed at the sting.

"Where did you meet Archie? You seem a little young for him." If she was going to push and pull at me, I decided I could at least control the talking part.

"We met when he came to consult with my father on a matter of importance regarding the Brotherhood," Valentina told me. "I was seventeen then—and yes, that's very young. Archie was a gentleman, and he waited for three years, until I could return his affections freely."

"You didn't like boys your own age?" I asked, looking up at her from under my eyelashes. She didn't blink, just laughed lightly, as if nothing I said could bother her.

"Your brother told me downstairs you had a smart mouth." She'd separated my hair into a dozen or so sections, each a sharp tug and sting on my scalp. She tested the rollers with her finger. "Nearly heated. And no, Aoife. Boys my age bored me, although there was no shortage. I was pretty, and my father was rich. That's how it goes. But they were fools, and I'd never met a man I could love until I met Archie."

I swallowed, and then decided this might be my one chance to get an honest answer, even if it wasn't the one I wanted. "Are you and my father going to get married?"

"Marriage is an antiquated construct," Valentina said. I tucked that away—no straight answers on that score from her. That made me like her a little bit more. Under her manners and clothes, she was just as out of place as Conrad and me.

"What about you and Dean?" she asked, changing the subject.

My face flushed, and the heat of the rollers didn't have much to do with it. What about me and Dean? *He makes my heart beat faster. He makes me feel alive.* Neither was a sentiment I was comfortable sharing with my brand-new pseudo-stepmother. I stayed quiet while Valentina carefully rolled and pinned one, then another and then a third section of my hair. It stung, like hot water droplets on my scalp. I bit down hard on my lip to hold in a yelp.

"Do you like him?" she tried again. "You two seem very fond of each other, from what I saw."

"You know, it's not very polite to ask me questions and not answer mine," I told her, almost smiling. It was nice to know that Dean's feelings for me showed.

Three more rollers and three more hot spots. Valentina's hands were much stronger than their delicate bones implied. My head in the mirror was rapidly becoming a beehive of black and silver.

"When you're a little older, Aoife, you'll understand that answers aren't always black-and-white or easy," she said, as if she were confiding in me. "I feel like I live two lives a lot of the time. Good, demure Crosley girl, who'll marry someone appropriate, who plays piano and knows how to fix hair in the new fashions and wears all the right clothes."

She had used up the rollers, and she handed me a rubbery pink cap emblazoned with cabbage roses. "Put this on. In the morning you'll have a good proper set, and we can style it."

I pulled the cap over my head, hiding the mountain of hair sausages that my usually unruly mane had turned into. My scalp felt a bit itchy and claustrophobic under it, but I kept still and pretended my head wasn't stinging, for Valentina's sake. She *was* trying, that much was obvious. "What's the other life?" I asked. Valentina was gathering up her things but paused for a moment and turned to answer me.

"A member of the Brotherhood," she said. "Even if I don't have an ability like you and your father do, I can do my part. Now more than ever, with what's happened."

She must have seen her words hit home, though I tried not to flinch.

"Oh, I don't blame you," Valentina said. "You were manipulated. It happens more than you'd think, among those who know the truth about the Gates and the Thorn Land. The Fae are very persuasive."

"I didn't do it for them," I whispered, my face hot with the kind of shame unique to being misunderstood. "I did it for—"

"For your mother, I know. Try not to drown yourself in your guilt, Aoife," Valentina said. "We've all done things we wish we could take back." She looked at her shoes for a moment, then back at me, as if she'd decided to confess. "I used to have terrible nightmares about the things I saw after I joined the Brotherhood. Some choices I had to make for the greater good."

"And now?" I whispered. I had to admit Dean was right—I had misjudged Valentina. The pain written across her face mirrored my own in that moment.

"Now I don't dream at all," she said, and smiled. It was

genuine, but sad. "It does get better, Aoife. Try and get some sleep. Things will seem brighter tomorrow." She started to shut the door and then leaned back in. "And try not to squash your rollers in your sleep. You'll look so grown-up tomorrow."

I didn't want to burst her bubble on that score, but I knew my unruly hair. I just nodded. "Good night. And . . . thank you."

Valentina gave me another one of her sad smiles before she backed out and closed my door, the latch catching with a click. So different from the clanging doors of Graystone and the heavy, creaking hinges of the Academy. A normal house sound, for a house full of normal people. What a joke.

I sat for a long time, listening to the house tick and settle. There was a draft coming through the windows, and I burrowed under the covers of the tiny bed. It was like being back at the Academy, in my drafty dormitory under my threadbare school-issued coverlet. Not exactly comforting, but familiar.

What was I supposed to do now? Sit and wait for my father and Valentina to solve things? If I was going to be the daughter Archie had asked me to be, the trusting one, the answer was probably yes.

If I was being honest with myself, that sounded like trading in one set of rules designed to keep me passive and sweet for another designed to keep me obedient and not asking questions.

But before I could debate any more, my mind decided that I'd been awake for enough days in a row, and I fell asleep hearing the wind worm its way through the cracks and hollows of the house.

* * *

In the morning, I realized that I'd slept dreamless and dead to the world for the first time in weeks. My neck was cramped from lying on the rollers. I unpinned them and pulled them off my head, combing the curls with my fingers. I wrapped my head with a rag while I took a bath and then wiped the mirror free of moisture to see what I looked like.

Valentina had been right. I hardly recognized myself. My dark hair set off my skin—which until this moment I'd always lamented as too pale—as it fell in gentle waves to just below my shoulders, swooping low across my brow to partially shadow my gaze.

I'd almost call myself pretty. Almost.

I tried not to let my shock at how I looked distract me while I got dressed. I was still here, in Valentina's house, and still had no idea what my father wanted from me beyond shutting up and doing as I was told.

The dress Valentina had left for me was plain blue wool, with a straight skirt and mother-of-pearl buttons up the bodice. It was a lady's dress, not a full-skirted thing with a wide, round collar made for a child. This dress required stockings, a garter belt and pumps, not a petticoat and stiff, flat shoes.

I put it on gratefully. Now that I'd distanced myself from them, the clothes I'd gotten in Windhaven really did stink.

I found underthings in the wardrobe, rolling on stockings that smelled of mothballs, and when I ventured outside my door, a pair of tan leather pumps with low, practical heels sat next to my doorway in the hall. Valentina and I had the same size feet, it turned out, and the pumps gave me height that I loved, even if I did wobble crazily until I learned how to balance on the narrow heel.

All right, I admitted. *She's not my favorite person on the face of the earth, but she's not an evil stepmother, either.* In time, maybe I could accept the fact that my father had replaced Nerissa with her. After all, it wasn't really Valentina's fault. That lay wholly with my father, and meant an entirely different unpleasant conversation we would have to undertake at some point.

But not now. Now, my stomach growled and reminded me that real food was nearby, and I hadn't had nearly enough of it lately. I headed for the stairs.

In daylight, with a chance to look around undisturbed, I saw that the Crosley house wasn't in much better shape than my old, mud-stained clothes. Everything was clearly expensive, overstuffed and velvet-covered and practically oozing out the money it had cost, but it was all curiously faded and dusty, as if nobody had come to the house for a long time and the house preferred it that way.

I followed the smell of bacon into the kitchen, which was vast and modern, both icebox and range a pale pink I'd only seen over a makeup counter in a department store. All the latest gadgets to mash and peel and open cans under the power of clockwork rather than doing it yourself sat on the countertops, covered in a thick layer of dust.

My father stood at the stove with his back to me, and I watched him for a moment. I tried to see myself in him, as I had the day before, and as I'd done with his portrait at Graystone before that. His posture wasn't mine—he stood feet apart and shoulders thrown back, even as he chopped onion and turned eggs in a frying pan.

Our hands moved the same way, though, sure and quick. Our hands knew what to do even if we didn't. You needed steady hands and a delicate touch to be an engineer. It was the one way being smaller than everyone else in the School of Engines had come in handy. In those days, I could always fix what was broken.

"How long are you going to stand there?"

I ducked away reflexively at being caught and then looked at the toes of my shoes, my face heating. "I'm sorry. I didn't mean to sneak."

Archie didn't respond. He scooped up the onions and dropped them into a second frying pan, covering them with egg mixture from a pink porcelain mixing bowl. He tossed in a few lumps of soft white cheese and then wiped his hands on a blue-checked towel and turned to face me, sizing me up with those stony eyes once more. And once more, I felt like a squirming specimen under a microscope.

"How did you know I was here?" I said finally, to break the unbearable silence.

"Basic situational awareness isn't a magic trick," Archie said. "At least, not a very good one. And it's something you're going to have to learn, if you want to stay alive by more than pure luck."

I bristled. He could at least give me a tiny bit of credit for staying alive this long. "It's not just luck. I know things."

Archie raised an eyebrow and then turned back to the stove, flipping the omelet in the pan with an expert hand. "You can't fight. You don't know wilderness survival. You know nothing about the Fae or the Erlkin, or even the Gates. You've spent your whole life safe in Lovecraft." He slid the omelet onto a plate and cut it into sections, placing them on several dishes along with potatoes and bacon and toast. "Tell me, Aoife—exactly what great feat of skill or strength kept you out of the clutches of the Proctors besides pure, blind luck?"

He turned back, set a plate on the table in front of me and folded his arms, awaiting an answer with the tilt of his head.

I stared at him for a moment, stared at the plate, and then, unable to contain myself, shoved the plate back at him, scattering food everywhere. "If you feel that way, Dad, why'd you ever pull me out of Lovecraft on your stupid, prissy airship and let your stupid, prissy girlfriend act like you two actually wanted me here? If I'm such an idiot, you should have just abandoned me to the damn ghouls."

I turned and left the kitchen, my ridiculous shoes clacking on the wood floors, raising tiny hurricanes of dust in my wake. I snatched an overcoat from a tree by the wide French doors leading to the back deck and ran across the lawn, past the *Munin*, all the way down to the shore. My breath sawed in my chest, pushing the urge to scream to the surface.

I'd been right the first time. My father didn't care about me. All he wanted to do was hold me up as an example of how he could do everything so much better.

As if I'd ever had a chance, with him leaving. He was a hypocrite, and he was cruel.

The waves were higher than my head on the beach, breaking with vibrations that raced up through my feet where I stood on the sand. The heels of my shoes sank in, and I yanked them off viciously and threw them, along with my stockings. The freezing sand bit into my bare feet, and my toes went numb. Good. My whole body could have gone numb for all I cared in that moment. I wanted to smash up against something, like the surf, vent my rage on something tangible, but there was nothing there. I settled for staring furiously at the waves, tears blinding me as I faced the wind, breath coming in short, hot, razor-sharp gasps.

The ocean was gray, and far off I could see the wobbly horizon line, the promise of a larger storm to come. I stayed, relishing the sting of cold and salt on my face, waiting for the wind and rain to roll in and blanket me in their fury, so much larger than mine that it was the only thing that might erase how I felt right then.

"Aoife!" My father's voice cut straight through the wind and the roar of the surf, and when he appeared at the top of the dune, he sounded as if he were right next to me. "Where the hell do you think you're going?"

He came down the rickety weathered steps from the dune two at a time and crossed the sand to grab me by the arm. "It's not safe out here by yourself! Anything could be wandering around!" His brow furrowed. "And where on the scorched earth are your shoes?"

I looked down at his hand, back at his face. Suddenly I couldn't even muster the energy to be angry. He'd told me how he really felt, and that was that. Now that he'd been honest, I had no reason to be angry, or hopeful, or confused any longer. Just numb, like all the exposed bits of my skin. "Let go of me," I said, flat as the wet sand around us. Far down the beach, some kind of aquatic mammal had beached itself, white skeleton picked over by a horde of gulls.

"I . . ." Archie dropped his hand from my arm and stuck it in his hair instead, his face a mask of confusion and upset. The dark strands were laced with white and stood out from his head, toyed with by the wind. "I'm no good at this," he said. "It's not gonna do any good to sugarcoat it, Aoife—most Gateminders grow up learning how to do the job. And for various reasons, you didn't. It's going to be hard to teach you what you need to know in so short a time. But it doesn't mean I'm . . ." He spread his hands, at a loss for words.

"Disappointed," I finished for him. "And you are. I can see it." Why wouldn't he be? He was a Gateminder and I was his daughter who had destroyed everything he and the Brotherhood had tried to build up. Build up and keep safe for hundreds of years. I was a failure as a Grayson. There was no sugarcoating that, either.

"I'm disappointed in a whole hell of a lot," Archie said. "I'm disappointed I couldn't tell my daughter not to trust the first Fae who fed her a good story. I'm disappointed her mother went so crazy even I couldn't fix her. I'm disappointed we live in a world that's so full of lies it seeps poison like a snakebite. But I'm not disappointed in you, Aoife." He reached out as if to cup my cheek, but then detoured to my shoulder, patting it awkwardly. I felt like I should pull away after what had happened, but I didn't. I allowed myself the tiny hope that maybe things would turn out all right after my tantrum. "You're my child," Archie said. "We're kinda stuck with each other."

"I do have my Weird, you know," I told him, drawing my brows together in reproach. "You act like I need rescuing, but I can be useful." I wanted my father to believe that more than anything.

Archie's mouth curled into a smile. "Yeah, they seemed pretty excited about that in Ravenhouse when they caught you. It works on machines, huh?"

I nodded, adding my own smile. "Anything with moving parts. Some things are easier than others."

Archie leaned down, and his expression was conspiratorial, like we were the same age. "Wanna see mine?"

His enthusiasm was infectious, and I thought I caught a glimpse of the boyish side that had entranced Valentina, and likely my mother. So different from his perpetual frown and judgmental gaze. I wanted to see more of that, so I said, "All right. I'd like that." I stood back, excited, but not sure what to expect. Better to be out of the danger zone, as I'd learned when Cal and I had taken a welding class and he'd lit not one but three of his aprons on fire with his torch.

My father winked at me, then trained his eye on a pile of driftwood and dried seaweed that had washed up a few dozen feet farther down the beach. He opened his palm and blew on it, just the smallest touch of air to skin.

A split second later, the driftwood ignited with a *whump*, a jet of crimson fire rushing toward the sky.

Archie let out a whoop, and I clapped my hand over my mouth. I'd figured out from his journal that my father could conjure fire, but seeing it in reality was a whole new dimension of thrill. I stared, unable to stifle a grin that matched my father's miles-wide one.

I wasn't alone. We could both do things that would be considered heresy by any Proctor.

But it wasn't born of anything evil. It was magic, pure and simple.

"So?" My father was breathing hard from the effort, his face flushed. In the warmth of the nearby fire, my skin was no longer numb.

"Pretty neat," I admitted. My father looked so animated, I couldn't resist teasing him a bit. "I've seen better."

"'Pretty neat'?" Archie shook his head. "You kids today. What do I have to do to get your attention, dance a jig?"

I shook my head rapidly, trying not to giggle. "Please don't. Really. It's not necessary."

Archie reached out and messed up the top of my hair. I didn't care—Valentina's beautiful curls were lost to the wind anyway. "Who taught you manners?"

It was like walking a tightrope—I took one step at a time and hoped I wouldn't fall into a chasm. Archie was behaving like a father, me like a daughter, and I decided to just keep going until something did go wrong. "Certainly not you," I teased.

"True enough," Archie agreed. "Can't say I'd have done a much better job if I'd been around. My manners are shit." He squeezed his eyes shut for a moment and then looked at me, pained. "See? You're not supposed to swear in front of your teenage daughter. I'm hopeless."

"Trust me," I said. "I've heard worse." I knew that sooner or later, we'd run into another roadblock, have another fight, and things would go back to being strange and strained. But right now, I wanted to keep taking the tiny steps, keep swaying on the rope and enjoy a few minutes alone with my father.

The way things were going, they might be the only ones I'd get.

I pointed to Archie's pocket watch, tucked into the front of his vest. My father's clothes were nice, but they were also out of fashion by about ten years and clearly ripped and repaired dozens of times over. He was always just a bit too unkempt to maintain the appearance of a gentleman of his station. He looked more like a professor or a clock maker than somebody who lived in a grand house and could call flame out of thin air.

Then again, I supposed I looked more like the daughter of the same than what I really was.

"My turn," I said. "Give me that and I'll show you what I can do."

Archie frowned, turning the silver watch in his hands before he gave it over. "Be careful. That watch was your grandfather's."

I popped open the top. The face was mother-of-pearl, and the hands were black, the numerals painted on in a fine hand and intertwined with vines hiding tiny forest creatures. It was a work of art. Inside the lid was an engraving, almost worn away with age: *There is no rule but iron, and no balm but time.* The date was 1898.

Pushing a little of my Weird to the forefront of my mind, I let the smallest tendril touch the watch. Here, away from the city and in Valentina's iron-free house, the whispers and the pain weren't nearly so bad. I could probably stay here for years before I started to go truly insane.

My Weird responded eagerly, unmuted by iron, and in the space of a heartbeat, the hands began to turn backward, still ticking off time. The dates in the face also turned back, and once I'd ensured they would stay that way as long as I held a bit of the watch in my mind, I handed it back to Archie proudly. "I can do that with anything. Came in handy when we were on the run."

"Pretty neat," he told me with a grin, and this time I didn't hesitate to return it.

"What's the inscription mean?" I asked.

"It's the motto of the Brotherhood," he answered. "Or was, at least. Back when the Brotherhood actually did some good."

I started to ask what he meant but thought better of it when his smile dropped and the stone-faced expression I recognized returned. He shut the watch and shoved it into his pocket. When he looked up, he was smiling again. "But enough about that. Want to take another crack at breakfast?"

"Sure," I agreed, and followed him inside. The hundred questions I had about Nerissa, the strange comments about the Brotherhood and my Weird could wait. I *did* trust my father, and I just hoped that sooner rather than later, he'd be in a mood to give me answers.

The next two days at the Crosley house passed uneventfully. Things with my father were all right when it was just the two of us, but when Valentina was around he got gruff and awkward and had a hard time looking me in the eye. I wasn't sure how to act either—yes, I was his daughter, but in reality he barely knew me, and the last thing I wanted was a spat with my de facto stepmother over territory she had clearly already claimed.

Valentina wasn't completely bad, as long as we avoided serious subjects. She showed me how to apply rouge and paint my nails without getting the enamel everywhere. We sipped tea in the sunroom and everyone gathered around the piano to hear her play thunderous classical music that sounded like the ocean had broken down the dunes and come rushing through the music room.

It was a break from running, that was for sure, and there was decent food and a warm bed. Still, every time I looked toward Lovecraft and saw the orange glow against the night sky from still-burning fires, my guts churned with guilt and worry.

On the third morning, I couldn't take it anymore. My patience caved, and with it went my placid veneer. "Are we going to stay here forever?" I said to Archie. He and I were washing up from breakfast, a task I'd taken away from Bethina by force. She thought as long as she was in Archie's presence, she had to revert to her old job of maid, but I'd bribed her with some leftover scones and cream and sent her away with a suggestion of taking Cal for a walk along the dunes. She wasn't a maid any longer, and I wanted her and Cal to be able to relax.

"It's safe here," Archie said. He was scrubbing while I dried. "Relatively so, anyway. We're not behind walls like in New Amsterdam and San Francisco, and there are things roaming out there, but no Fae is going to risk coming within spitting distance of this house and not one but two members of the Brotherhood of Iron."

"Is the Thorn Land trying to invade us?" I asked bluntly, setting the plates in a pile. They clacked like ghouls' teeth. I hadn't asked yet because I didn't really want the truth, but I couldn't avoid it any longer. If I'd done more than wake the queens of the Thorn Land, if I'd opened not just a crack but an actual channel for invasion, I needed to know.

"You sure are good at picking the one question I don't have an answer to," my father said. He shut off the hot water and dried his hands, wincing. I noticed that his knuckles were cut, like he'd driven his hand into something hard and unforgiving.

"Tremaine said—" I began.

"Tremaine lied to you," Archie snapped. "That's what he does. He's a snake, even among his own kind. He told you exactly what you needed to hear so you'd wake the queens, and then he told you exactly what you needed to hear so you'd stay good and scared and not try to put anything right once you saw what you'd done."

He had a point—I'd seen the extent of Tremaine's lies firsthand. But his lies always held a grain of truth, and that terrified me.

"You're with the Brotherhood of Iron!" I cried in frustration. "You all saved the world when Tesla made the Gates. You're supposed to know what to do."

"The Brotherhood is not some magical cavalry that rides out of the smoke and hellfire and saves the poor, innocent humans from the menace of the otherworlds," Archie said. "No matter how much Grey Draven and his cronies might want to change us into that very thing."

He gestured me outside to the kitchen steps, and despite my irritation I followed him. He stood quietly for a moment and then furtively drew out one of his cigarettes. "Truth is, Aoife, the best we ever were was a police force that was too small and spread too thin to do all the good we could against encroachment from Thorn, the Mists and wherever the hell else nasty monsters crawled up from. And that was in my grandfather's day. Now the Brotherhood has . . . Well. They've lost sight of the endgame, to say the very least, and there's a lot of things the leadership and I don't agree on."

I sat next to him, pulling my skirt down over my legs to keep out the cold. I'd wanted the Brotherhood to be the knights, to have the knowledge in their collection of Gateminder's diaries to fix what I'd done. But the image of squabbling men, and only a handful of men at that, didn't inspire much hope. "So they can't help us?" I was only half surprised. Most hope these days died a quick death the moment I got close to it.

"Oh, they're trying to shut the broken Gates, and keep the Fae and the Mists at bay while they do it," Archie said. "Avoid Draven and his plans to turn them into his own personal shock troops while they're at it. But when Tremaine came after me and started this whole mad plan that ended with you, I couldn't ask the Brotherhood for help."

"Why not?" I said, confused. I wasn't naive enough to think the Brotherhood would come and set everything right, but I'd at least thought they could be an ally and that, as members, my father and Valentina counted among their number and were to be aided no matter what.

"Because they'd have negotiated," Archie said softly. "They'd wheedle and cajole, try to get something for themselves out of the deal and use me like a damn trading chip. The Grayson family has done a lot for the Brotherhood, Aoife, but we are *not* in charge. Gateminders are guard dogs. Dogs have masters. If you have the idea that you can go and ask them to help you now . . ." He reached out and squeezed my hand, hard and all at once, with bruising strength. I hissed in pain, flinching under his touch, but he held fast and stared into my eyes.

"Promise me, Aoife. Promise me you will not throw yourself on the mercy of the Brotherhood. They know it was a Grayson who broke the Gates, because it couldn't be anyone else. I don't think they've figured out which one yet, since they haven't tried to haul me in for questioning, but listen—they won't take you in with open arms and they won't fix anything, because despite acting as if they're all-knowing, they can't. Tesla was the only one who really understood how the Gates on our side work, and he's long gone, along with his research."

"Dad . . . ," I began, trying to ease his grip on me and reassure him I wasn't going to go running off, but he squeezed harder, wringing a droplet of sound from me at the pain. "I can't promise," I whispered. "You don't understand. My mom . . ."

"I told you, Nerissa is going to be all right for a little while longer," Archie said. "Stay with me, let me show you the ropes, make it so you don't end up like you did in Lovecraft. Let me help you, Aoife. Stay here for a month or so and promise me you won't go to the Brotherhood, and then I'll do what I can about Nerissa, all right?"

"I can't . . . ," I started. My mother didn't have that kind of time, no matter what he said. I couldn't waste a month learning whatever it was Archie wanted to teach me. If the Brotherhood had actual answers, I had to seek them out, no matter what they thought of my father or he of them.

"Promise me," my father ground out. Pain flared in my fingers.

"I promise!" I cried, because I could tell by his expression I wasn't going to change his mind.

I didn't change my own mind, either, though.

My mother didn't have a month.

Crunching footsteps over the icy grass made my father finally let go of me, putting his hand back in his lap, and when Dean rounded the corner, Archie looked like himself again. I breathed a sigh of relief, glad it was Dean and not Conrad or Valentina.

"Hey there, Aoife," Dean said. "Mr. Grayson." He was smoking the very end of a Lucky Strike, which he stamped out under his steel-toed boot. "Am I interrupting something?"

"No," I said, jumping up. "We were just finishing our talk." Honestly, I didn't think *that* talk would ever be finished. The revelation that the Brotherhood might blame me for what had happened, might actually refuse to help, was almost more worrying than thinking about my mother's fate.

Archie stayed where he was, smoking and running his other hand absently up and down his temple, his index finger leaving a small red mark. He didn't look strong and self-assured just then, more small and lost, like I felt a great deal of the time. I wanted to do something to make him feel better, but I knew from my own bleak moods there was nothing for it except time.

Before I could say anything else, Dean laced his fingers with mine and was leading me away. The motion aggravated my already sore hand, and I jerked loose without thinking.

"Whoa," Dean said as we rounded the corner of the porch. "You hurt? Did he hurt you?" Quick as a cloud scudding across the moon, darkness dropped into his eyes. "I'll beat his hide so hard your granddad feels it."

"Dean," I said as he started back toward Archie, realizing what he'd read into the situation. "He didn't do anything."

Dean looked down at me, his nostrils flaring and his lips parted so I could see his teeth. In that moment he looked more Erlkin than human, and I took a step back. "You've been quiet and glum since we got here, and now I see you looking tore up. Is he—"

"No!" I shouted. "Stones, no. He's my *father,* Dean. He's not hurting me." The very idea that Archie would be physically abusing me was sort of laughable. To me. But Dean's life had been very different, and I knew he was just trying to look out for me.

Dean settled back inside his leather jacket, like a predator retreating back into its cave. "Well, okay. Why are you so gloomy, then?" He brushed his thumb down my cheek. "I miss you, princess. I miss your spark."

I didn't speak, just leaned in and wrapped my arms around his torso under his jacket. I loved the feel of his ribs under my fingers, the warmth of his skin through his shirt. I put my cheek against his cotton-wrapped chest and let out a breath for what felt like the first time since the *Munin* had touched down.

"I miss you too" was all I said. All my anger at the Brotherhood and all the worry about my father deflated, and I felt exhausted.

Dean pressed his lips to the top of my head. "Is it that bad?"

"Yeah," I whispered. "We're stuck here. And everyone in the world wants my head on a spike."

"They can't all," Dean said. "Though it is a very pretty head."

I laughed, even though it felt like swallowing a mouthful of ash. "You're the only person who thinks so, I guarantee."

Dean moved his lips to touch mine. "Only one that matters, aren't I?"

I nodded, and stood on my toes to kiss him in return. After a minute I tilted my head toward the metal hulk of the *Munin*. "We could be alone in there."

Dean's smile came slowly, but it warmed me from the inside out. "I like the way you think, princess."

"I am the brains of this operation," I said, and then shoved him lightly and took off across the grass at a run.

"Oh, you are gonna get it when I catch you," Dean called as I darted away from his grasp, feeling lighthearted for the first time that day. He followed me until we'd climbed the ladder into the *Munin*, both of us out of breath and shivering from the cold.

Dean snapped his lighter and illuminated our way into the cabin, where he shut the hatch and then turned to me, stripping off his jacket. I sat on the edge of the bunk, feeling the satiny brush of the fine linen on the backs of my legs. Valentina had given me fresh stockings and a garter belt to replace the ones I'd destroyed on the beach, and suddenly I could feel every inch of them against my skin.

I couldn't leave the Crosley house, I couldn't fix what was happening outside it, but I could be myself with Dean. Never mind that my hands shook when I gripped Dean's biceps, his wiry muscles moving under my hands as he lowered me to the mattress, the length of his body pressing against mine. I could feel his weight and smell his smell—cigarettes and leather and woodsmoke. It covered me and pushed away all the helplessness and the choking feeling of being caught in a spiral of events that I had as much control over as an oak leaf over a hurricane.

"I like being this close to you, Dean," I whispered.

"And I you, princess," he whispered back. "What do you want to do?"

"Honestly?" I propped myself up, looking into his eyes, and bit my lip.

"Honesty is good," Dean said.

"I want to take a nap," I confessed. "I'm exhausted, and that house is so echoing. I can never really drift off." I was self-conscious all of a sudden. Would he get mad that I didn't want to just make out until we either got caught or had to go in to supper? Would he go find someone who would, when we left here, if I kept putting him off? "Or we could just go inside," I rushed. Dean stopped me moving.

"Don't do that," he said. "Don't leave."

"I-I'm sorry," I stuttered. "I just . . ."

"Hey, calm down," Dean said, and I managed to stop my frantic babbling long enough to look into his eyes. As always, the calm gray seas within soothed me. He stroked my hair, pulling me back to his chest so that I could hear his heartbeat. In that moment, I never wanted to move. "So lay yourself down and sleep." He grinned at me. "How many guys get to sleep next to somebody who looks like you?"

"Just you," I murmured, eyelids already fluttering now that I knew he wasn't upset with me.

"Damn right," Dean said, pulling a blanket over us. "And in my book, that makes me the luckiest guy on this messed-up planet."

"Good night, Dean," I whispered. I planted a light kiss on his chest before nestling my head against him. His arms went around me, and I was so warm and calm that I never wanted to get up.

"Good night, princess," he said softly. "Sweet dreams."

The figure didn't seem surprised to see me, and I wasn't as shocked as I had been in the past to see him.

All the skies were red, bleeding sunsets and throbbing, bruise-colored sunrises. The black things that drifted above were close now, close enough to cast shadows.

I no longer even bothered asking what he wanted from me. I just stood, watching the great gear tick off the heartbeats of this place.

"You are unhappy," the figure said.

I shrugged, watching absently as, one by one, the suns winked out, replaced by stars, and listening to the glass bell that made up the figure's domain vibrate as the great shapes passed back and forth overhead.

"You have regrets," the figure said. He reached out a hand to me. His robe fell back, and it was a disappointingly common hand, pale but not too pale, as if it had once been a darker shade and had spent a long time in the dark, leaching pigment into the nothing around it. "Please don't look that way," he said. "I do like your visits, you know."

"Unless you can bring back my mother, mend my father's life and turn the world back to how it was before it got ripped

apart," I told him, "then you'd better get used to this expression on my face."

The figure withdrew like I'd burned him, hand disappearing into the black miasma of his body. Eyes glittered at me from under his hood. "I shouldn't," he said. He looked at the shapes overhead. "But it's a new day, not an old day. This is a day never before seen by the universe, by any spoke of the wheel."

"What are you talking about?" I sighed. "I hate your damn riddles."

"This is the day and the night and the place in between," the figure told me. "You can see it when you sleep. You cannot cross into it via magic or machine, but you can dream your way into it. Dreams are in every world, Aoife. In everything. Time. Dust. Your blood. The things you can't remember when you wake."

"Meaning?" I spread my hands.

"The nightmare clock can find your dreams," said the figure. "It can weave them and unravel them. It can make your dreams real and allow you to cross not just worlds but time. If you can dream it, the nightmare clock can give you the ability to make it a reality, no matter where or when or how impossible your dream may seem." He stretched his hand out once more and grabbed mine, and I realized that he was as cold as I knew the airless space outside the glass was. "Aoife," he whispered. "The nightmare clock can undo what you have done, what plagues your dreams. The nightmare clock can set you free."

Footsteps woke me, all at once, like breaking the surface of icy water. I sat upright and knocked Dean's arm off me in the process. He grunted and scrubbed a hand across his face. "Not awake yet," he muttered.

"I heard something," I insisted. Before Dean could respond, the hatch swung open and Valentina appeared, aether lantern in hand. The sky had gone dark while we'd been asleep, and the blackness inside the *Munin*'s cabin was near absolute.

"There's that mystery solved, then," Valentina said, lowering the lantern. "We thought you'd been devoured by something."

"No such luck," I said sarcastically, trying to cover for my embarrassment at being found here. Valentina looked me up and down, and I could see her eyes pause on my mussed hair. Never mind the fact that Dean was lying next to me.

"Get up," she said shortly. "Your father is in a mood, and I have a feeling none of us wants to have this conversation."

Dean got up, grabbing his jacket and pulling it on. "We weren't doing anything you need to be worried about," he told Valentina. I nodded vigorous agreement, glad it was mostly dark in the *Munin* and she couldn't see that my face was on fire.

"Fine, but I doubt Aoife's father will believe that," she told him. She didn't look angry, but she sure wasn't happy, mouth compressed into a thin line. She jerked her free hand at me. "Come along, Aoife. Your father is waiting."

I made sure the buttons on my dress hadn't come unfastened and the seams on my stockings matched. I slipped my shoes back on and went as far as the hatch, drawing even with Valentina. I knew she was doing me a favor, letting me know she wasn't going to tell my father how she'd found us, even if we hadn't been up to anything. I couldn't help wondering, though, what I was going to have to do in exchange for her silence. "Thanks," I mumbled.

"I swear I wasn't doing anything." Not entirely true, but not entirely a lie. Half-truths seemed to be the order of the day.

Valentina sighed. "Aoife, I was sixteen once. Just go find your father. And quickly. He's terribly worried."

Worried that I was dead or worried that I wasn't doing exactly as I was told, even if he hadn't told me yet? I decided it didn't matter right now—I'd gotten away with sneaking off, and if Archie wanted to yell and rant at me a bit, I'd take it.

I crossed the lawn back to the main house and found Cal sitting at the table in the sunporch, playing a game of solitaire, his greasy hair falling in his eyes.

"You might want to check a mirror," I told him. "Before Bethina figures out you aren't just afraid of bathing and that patchy skin is hiding something."

Cal looked up and gave me a glare. "Nice mouth. What's gotten into you?"

"I've been summoned by Mr. Grayson," I told him. "I'm pretty sure he's going to read me the riot act."

Cal grimaced. "Yeah, he was stomping around the library a minute ago, before he went out with Valentina to find you. He's pretty steamed."

"Of course he is," I said, feeling the heavy dread of a punishment, a holdover from my days at the Academy. Meals, things like hot water and clean clothes, even our shoes, were taken away sometimes, for the smallest things. I didn't think Archie was going to switch me, but the residual twinge of fear was still there.

I walked as slowly as I could, following the irregular lamplight to the library. It wasn't anything like Graystone's magnificent collection of books, not even close. This was small and cozy, stuffed with the sort of reading material wealthy people like the Crosleys put on display to prove they were educated. The potboilers and cheap romances were probably tucked behind the Proctor-approved classics and the fashionable novels.

"You think you can just run off whenever it suits you?" My father was sitting in one of the twin leather armchairs, the oxblood deep and slick by the glow of the fire in the grate. He was drinking, a bottle half empty and a glass more than that.

"I'm sorry," I said, figuring contriteness was the first and easiest route to take. My father looked much angrier than Valentina, all the lines in his face deep and stark.

"I told you how dangerous the world is now," my father said. "And I know you're not stupid enough to not listen to me about that. So what is it, Aoife? Typical teenage willfulness? Or something else?" He picked up the glass, drained it and slammed it down. "I've got enough problems without my daughter sneaking off to canoodle with some useless greaser and letting me think she might be nothing but rags and bones in a ghoul's nest for hours on end." He poured and drank, and the glass landed again. *Clank*. "Maybe if we were a regular family we'd have the luxury of learning boundaries and setting rules. But we don't, Aoife." Pour, drink, *clank*. "Let me make this perfectly clear—disobey me again, go outside these four walls without letting me or Valentina know it, or sneak off with *Dean* again, and I'll tan your hide." He examined the bottle, now within a millimeter of empty, and gave a regretful sigh. "Do we understand each other, child?"

I stayed where I was until he glared at me. "Something you want to add?"

I chewed my lip for a moment and then decided he couldn't get any angrier if I just asked. "Do you know anything about the . . . something called the nightmare clock?" I said softly.

Archie stopped moving, glass halfway to his mouth. "Where did you hear that?" he asked, in the same soft tone I'd used.

"It's not important," I said quickly, seeing his alarm. At the same time, though, his alarm told me this was real, or that I wasn't the only person who'd had the dream. Not the only one the dream figure had talked to, not the only one to visit the strange room. With my father's reaction, I couldn't write the bleak figure off as a product of iron poisoning, the human world making the Fae blood in me boil with insanity. The dreams were more than my own fancies. The figure's words echoed in my head. *Set you free.* A device I could use to cross not just space but time—one that would set me free. I could return to the moment when I'd destroyed the Engine. I could stop that Aoife from listening to Tremaine's lies.

I could go further and make a reality my oldest dream, awake or asleep—that my father had never left us. That he, Nerissa, Conrad and I were a family, together.

"Well, I never heard of such a curious phrase," Archie said, and tossed back the last of his drink. "No idea what you're talking about. Sounds like some story in a cheap magazine."

That was one way Archie and I weren't alike, I realized. He was a terrible liar. He couldn't even look at me, and fidgeted uncomfortably in his seat, as if a colony of ants had taken up residence under his shirt.

"All right," I said. "I suppose I'll say goodnight, then." I started to walk out, then stopped and looked back. "And I am sorry. For going off like that and worrying you."

I sped out of the room before Archie could reply. His lie had told me a lot.

He had heard of the nightmare clock. And what my father knew about it scared him enough to make him lie to me about it. If he knew, someone else knew. Someone who might be willing to tell me the whole story, explain the cryptic riddles of my dream figure.

His knowing about the clock also meant that I'd been right: the dreams, the black figure and the endless skies, the great gear, all of it—they were at least partly real.

I felt a swell of happiness in my chest like a soap bubble, fragile but there. As I climbed the stairs to my room, my thoughts were racing. The nightmare clock could set me free—if the dream figure was telling the truth. Could I use it to undo what I'd done in Lovecraft? I had to think so. Otherwise it was just another dead end, another dashed hope. It was like a Gate, but with the power to move time and events already set. That, I could use. That would set me free, free of everything I'd let Tremaine make me do.

While I got ready for bed and crawled under my blankets, I decided I needed to find out, and fast—because if I had a chance to set everything right, I was taking it, no matter what.

* * *

My father was quiet at breakfast, holding his head in his hands. Valentina was by contrast unusually sharp and impatient for someone who prided herself on decorum. She slammed a coffee cup down at Archie's elbow, and he winced.

"Do you have to?"

"Your own fault," she returned, and went and sat at the other end of the table. Conrad raised his eyebrow at that, then went back to sulking over his notebook. Dean and my father were engaged in some kind of glaring contest, and Bethina was focused on her food. Only Cal seemed to be in a good mood.

"Say, Valentina," I said in a voice that was gratingly perky to my ears. "I'm a bit bored. I was wondering if I could use the library on the *Munin* to do some reading." I widened my eyes in innocence. "I wanted to ask permission, after yesterday, of course."

"Sorry, no," Valentina said. "I have more important things to do today. You're just going to have to entertain yourself in the house with the others, where we can keep an eye on you."

"Good grief, Val," Archie snapped without looking up. "This isn't a reform school. Just let her go get some books that don't insult her intelligence. If she stays on the *Munin* and doesn't wander around, she'll be fine."

"Oh, of course," Valentina said, and the acid in her tone could have etched the teacup she was holding. "Because you have the final say in all things, Archie, don't you?"

"As far as the people at this table are concerned, I do," Archie said.

"Right," Conrad said, pushing back from the table. "I'm going . . . somewhere else."

"Yeah," Cal said hurriedly, also jumping up. "Thanks for breakfast, Miss Crosley. I mean, Mrs. Grayson. Uh . . . I mean . . . just thanks."

Bethina took that as her cue to start clearing plates, and Dean pulled out his pack of Lucky Strikes, practically waving them under Archie's nose before he went out to the back steps to smoke one. I rolled my eyes.

"Looks like it's just you and me, then," Valentina said in the same tone she'd used on my father. "Let's get you fixed up with something a girl like yourself finds stimulating." She snatched my hand and practically dragged me outside and to the *Munin*.

I had prepared this lie carefully, so that it would practically drip sincerity. "I am sorry about yesterday," I told her as we climbed the ladder into the main cabin. "I really didn't mean any disrespect."

"Aoife, I'm just going to say this once," she told me when we were inside. "Because I'm not your mother, and not trying to be, but I am older and I've been around. From what I've seen these past few days you're a sweet, bright girl. You don't want to waste yourself on somebody like Dean Harrison." She flipped the switches in the main cabin to turn on the aether lamps and then folded her arms, looking for all the world like a miniature, younger version of one of my professors at the Academy. "You want to wait for someone who's marriage material. Lifelong material. Don't sell yourself short just because a boy gives you a wink and a smile. I've seen too many smart girls take that route and end up stuck in the mud."

"You're not married," I said, feeling reflexive anger when Valentina insulted Dean. She didn't know him, and she'd admitted she didn't know me. Four days didn't qualify her to give me parental advice. "And don't worry about filling in for my mother. You're barely old enough to be my big sister." I knew it was mean, but she'd fired the first volley.

Valentina smiled, a tired and sad smile. "I know that your back will get up no matter what I say about that boy. But maybe in a few months or years you'll realize I'm not just trying to be a snob. I want to help you." She went back to the ladder to the outside. "I have mixed feelings on marriage, but I do believe that were things different, did we not lead these lives, I would marry Archie. In a heartbeat."

She sounded sincere, her face softening and her voice dropping, and looked so happy at the prospect that for a moment I felt almost guilty about what I was going to do. Almost. It seemed Valentina could be your best friend one minute and then in the next instant be as cold and hard as the brass that kept the *Munin*'s hull intact. I knew I couldn't predict which Val I'd be getting, and after a lifetime as a charity ward, with new families and new mothers every few months, I couldn't trust someone like that.

"So, when you worked with the Brotherhood," I said, deliberately pulling down a stack of blue cloth–covered boys' adventure novels and trying to act casual, "did you use this ship for traveling and battles with eldritch creatures and things?"

Valentina laughed softly. "It's not as exciting as you'd think. A lot of chasing, a lot of frustration and dead ends. A lot of time cooped up with musty books, learning the lore. The only exciting part was combat training. I liked that."

"But some excitement in the field, surely? It sounds a lot better than the Academy," I said. If Valentina wanted to talk about the Brotherhood, I was happy to encourage her.

Valentina went over to a map of the world painted on the wall, in the spaces between the bookshelves and curio cabinets, and traced her fingers over it. "Oh, yes," she said. "It's a wondrous life. If you have the strength for it."

While she wasn't looking, I grabbed a few books from the section of the library filled with handwritten volumes and shoved them under my coat. They were what I had come for—the diaries of the Brotherhood members, whose knowledge was compiled into the vast Iron Codex, the go-to guide for fighting things like the Fae. Hundreds of diaries, like Archie's and like mine, collected into a single volume. That volume was watched over by the Brotherhood. These were the next likeliest place to look for the knowledge I needed—about both the Brotherhood and the nightmare clock, if it existed at all outside of the sort of fear-tinged whisper it had caused in my father.

"Thank you," I said loudly to Valentina, holding up the adventure novels. "This should keep me."

"Good," Valentina said. "Let's run along, then. I've got a busy day." We got as far as the ladder to the lower deck before she turned, blocking my way like a little blond fireplug. "Are you going to give them back?" she asked.

"What do you mean?" I said, heartbeat picking up to a frenetic pace. Just because Archie was a bad liar and not as perceptive as he liked to think when it came to me didn't mean I should have assumed the same of Valentina. She was sharp. "The dress and shoes? You said they were for me to keep."

"Don't insult both of us," Valentina said. She reached out and undid the buttons on my jacket. The books slid to the floor, making soft plops on the carpet.

"Now what?" I said, refusing to drop my eyes.

"You want to tell me why you're poking in my father's journals, for a start?" Valentina said, folding her arms.

I bent down and picked up a book, brushing off the cover. "Nobody will tell me what I need to know," I said bluntly, passing it back to her. "And when nobody will help me, I'm used to helping myself." I raised my chin, refusing to be cowed.

"Helping yourself to other people's things, more like it," Valentina said. She put the books back where they belonged and then gestured to one of the chairs in the reading nook. "Sit."

I did, knowing that anything else would just rile her more and make her more likely to report what I'd done to Archie. "My father lied to me," I said. "I asked him a simple question and he wouldn't tell me the truth, so what am I supposed to do besides find the answers on my own?"

"Maybe I wouldn't have lied if you'd asked me," Valentina said. "Ever think of that?" She sat and folded her hands. "What did he lie to you about?"

"The nightmare clock," I said plainly. "I asked him what it was and he said he didn't know. That was a lie."

I got the same reaction from Valentina that I had from Archie. She twitched, but the freezing of her expression and the stiffening of her posture were identical to Archie's. "Where did you . . . ," she started.

"I had a bad dream," I said, and left it at that.

Valentina sighed. "Yes, he lied. But I don't blame him for not wanting to give you crazy ideas," she said. "Not at all."

"You both know what it is," I insisted. "What is so horrible that you have to keep it from me?" I sat up straighter. "I'm not a little kid. I can handle the hard truth."

Valentina sighed, then ran her hands over her face. "Only the Brotherhood is supposed to know—at least, as far as the Iron Land goes."

She traced lines on the fine inlaid wood of the table between us. "Imagine that Thorn and the Iron Land and the Mists—all of them— are spokes in a wheel, and in the center of the wheel . . ." She sighed. "This is just a theory, mind, and it has a lot of holes. But some people believe that at the center of the wheel is a place that isn't entirely whole—an in-between place. A place made of dreams, which no Gate or magic can access—only the people who have the abilities to make dreams real, the ability to travel between the other worlds that have Gates and such."

"People with the Weird?" I guessed.

Valentina was far from maintaining her usual composure. She looked strained, as if every word were being drawn from her under duress. Her pretty round face crumpled with frown lines, making her look a lot less angelic. "Yes, people with the Weird," she continued quietly. "In this dream place, these same people believe that there exists a machine, a machine that can grind the fabric of space and time and remake it—can permit time travel, cross-world travel, the ability to transport things, or people, from one place to another, in time as well as space. Can spin the spokes on that wheel so that they rest in any order the clock chooses. It's a clock that measures off dreams, and nightmares, and everything else. Anything you imagine, it can be. It's different for everyone who sees it. So the Brotherhood scholars believe." She leaned back and sighed. "Of course, a lot of the same people who believe the nightmare clock is real believe the Great Old Ones will return to the Iron Land from the stars and that you can summon the dead to do your bidding with Erlkin rituals, so, you know, for them, time travel and transporting yourself across the vast dimensions of space must not seem so far-fetched." She waved a hand in a circle. "Crazy as bedbugs in a burning mattress, most likely."

"But it does exist," I said, excited. My dreams weren't just madness and poison. Somewhere out there, the dream figure was seeing me—dreaming of me? I wasn't sure—while I dreamed of him. He was reaching out to me, trying to save his small slice of world from what had happened when the Gates ruptured as I was trying to save mine. Those figures outside his dome would scare me, as they'd clearly scared him. I didn't know why he couldn't fight them off, but I thought of how helpless I'd be in the jaws of a Fae like Tremaine. Perhaps it was the same for the dream figure. And he had in his possession a device I was going to use to send myself to the moment when this had all gone wrong, and stop it from happening.

"Of course not," Valentina said, much too quickly. "At least, not in my opinion, it doesn't. I mean, the Gates are real. Tesla made them, and the Erlkin built theirs, and the Fae enchanted their *hexenrings*. That's science as much as it is sorcery. It's tangible. But a place that exists between sleeping and being awake? That you can only dream yourself into? A device that can turn whoever uses it into a virtually unstoppable time traveler? That's a fairy tale."

She was a better liar than my father, but the way she practically ran back to the house and slammed the door behind her told me that if Valentina didn't believe that the nightmare clock actually existed, she at least worried that it might.

9

The Weight of Blood and Bone

I SPENT THE AFTERNOON trying to compose an entry in my journal about what had just happened with Valentina, then crumpling the pages one by one and tossing them across my bedroom to land in a corner like a drift of downed birds.

I was almost relieved when someone knocked at the door, and I opened it to see Archie and Conrad. "Oh," I said. I'd been hoping it was Dean. Even if we couldn't slip away to the *Munin*, he would have been someone to talk to.

"Don't get too excited," my father said dryly. He looked me up and down. "Get changed and meet us down at the beach steps," he said. "Pants and a blouse—something you can get dirty."

I cocked my head, confused. "What are we . . . ," I started, but my father was already walking away, that stiff-legged stalk I'd noticed he adopted, the one that warned all before him to get out of his way.

"What's happening?" I asked Conrad, catching him by

the sleeve before he could follow. "No idea," he said, and tugged free of me. His face was a thunderhead, which made me think he *did* know, but I figured if something was upsetting Conrad maybe it wouldn't be so bad for me. We were getting more different, in every way, but rather than dwell on it, I changed and hurried down to the beach steps to meet my father and brother.

Conrad stood with his hands shoved in his pockets, wind whipping his hair back and forth. Archie stood a little way off, smoking, but he extinguished his cigarette when he saw me. My steps slowed, but I forced myself not to look nervous, even though my stomach was in fits.

"All right, you two," he said. "It's time both of you learned how to handle yourselves. Aoife showed me her Weird, but it's obvious she can't hold her own in a stand-up fight. So you, Conrad—let's see what you've got."

I let my gaze rove between Archie and my brother.

Conrad's face had flushed, two bright flowers in his cheeks that had nothing to do with the wind. "You want me to what, do a trick?"

"I want to see your Weird," Archie said evenly. "If there's a problem there, then there's a much bigger problem with this whole plan. If we're going back into the city in a few weeks to take another crack at finding survivors, I need you both in fighting form."

Of course I'd wondered when I'd found out Conrad had used slipstreamers to get himself into the Mists. I'd wondered when he hadn't offered to open the Gate back to the Iron Land. But he had to have a Weird—he was the firstborn Grayson of our generation, the only son. Heck, my father was only Gateminder at all because his older brother, our uncle Ian, had died young. I didn't know *how* I was able to manipulate the Gates. There hadn't been time to really think about it when the Proctors had chased us, or when Tremaine had been watching me, threatening to hurt my family. I might have thought of myself as a Gateminder in my lighter moments, but I wasn't really sure *what* I was.

But either *both* of us were Gateminders or Conrad had been skipped and it was me. Had always been meant for me.

I wrapped my arms around myself and prayed that Conrad was just a late bloomer.

"There's no problem," Conrad said evenly, but all his muscles were tense. He looked like he did right before he was going to fight somebody, a kid at school who'd made a remark or a foster sibling who'd gotten too pushy with me. I sincerely hoped he and Archie weren't about to come to blows, because then I'd have to jump between them, and nobody wants to break up a fistfight between members of their own family.

"Then do it." Archie took a step closer to him. "Show me, son."

Conrad looked at the ground, looked back at Archie. Veins stuck out in his neck and at his temples, and his face turned crimson. I took a step toward him, to try to calm him down, but he beat me back with a glare.

Archie sighed and then went over and patted Conrad on the back. "That's enough. Don't hurt yourself."

Conrad let out his breath in a rush, white mist meeting the freezing air. "I can't do it, all right?" he shouted. "I've waited and waited and tried every damn thing—fire, water, wind, even machines, like Aoife—and I can't do it. I'm useless."

He stormed past us and back toward the house. I ran after him without thinking. "Conrad, wait!"

I caught him by the arm as he reached the steps, and he shook me off. "Why should you care?" he growled. "You're the one he wants, aren't you? You've got the gift."

I reminded myself he was angry and probably didn't mean it as cruelly as it came across. I grabbed his arm when he tried to run off again, harder. "You think this is a gift?" I whispered. I could barely hear myself over the wind. "Conrad, all it means is I have something in my blood that can kill me, that can split my skull apart if I try to control it, and that makes me a target for everyone in the Thorn and Iron Lands who wants a pet Gateminder. It doesn't make me better. It doesn't make me not your sister. Forget about what Archie thinks. *You're* my family. You're the only one I've known until now." I stopped talking, but held on. I wanted the distance between us to stop. I wanted this painful chasm of bad feeling and resentment to close.

Conrad snarled for a moment, looking for all the world as if he was going to slap me across the face, but then he collapsed, wrapping his arms around me so tightly I couldn't breathe.

I hugged him back, as hard as I could. Relief flooded through me. This was the Conrad I knew, the one I'd grown up with.

I realized amid my pounding heart and the wind that Conrad was saying something to me, and I pulled back to listen. "I'm sorry," he said. "I'm so, so sorry, Aoife."

"For what?" I said, confused. "Neither of us has been very nice lately, but that's not—"

"No." Conrad tugged my scarf down. I flinched when he touched my scar but squeezed his hand between my own.

"It wasn't your fault. The iron madness—"

"Nothing will make my attacking you all right, Aoife," he said. "Not the fact that I was crazy, not the fact that I'm in remission. Nothing will make this mess with me making you come find me all right. Just let me say I'm sorry."

I dropped his hand and nodded, pulling off my scarf on my own. "I forgive you, Conrad." After everything that had happened, the words that had once stuck in my throat at merely thinking them came without any effort at all.

Conrad didn't say anything; he just buried his face against my shoulder. We stayed that way for a minute, until Archie came up and coughed softly. He looked almost ashamed to be intruding, and I thought it sort of served him right. He was trying to teach Conrad to be a survivor, but calling him out had been cruel. I held on to my brother protectively as Archie spoke.

"I think that's enough for today, son. You can go on back to the house." He gave Conrad an awkward tap on the shoulder, the sort of male gesture that somehow conveyed it was all right, that he wasn't really mad.

Once my brother had gone out of earshot, Archie turned to me and shook his head. "This is going to cause an epic uproar, I hope you know. There has *never* been a female Gateminder, not in the hundred and twenty years since Tesla made the damn things in the first place. If you turn out to be my heir with the Weird—and let's face it, we both know it's likely after your brother's performance just now . . . Well. There's going to be some hurt feelings in the Brotherhood."

I didn't particularly care what sort of uproar I'd cause. By now, I was pretty used to being the one who made everything go sideways for the people in charge. "Are you mad at me?" I asked my father. He gave me a look as if I were going crazier than I already was.

"Of course not. I'm damn proud of you. You're smart, and your Weird is something to behold. Once we toughen you up, you're going to do a much better job of this whole thing than me."

I blushed a little. Inspiring pride in Archie was a new sensation, and I liked it. "But without the Brotherhood, what good are the Gateminders?" I asked. "What will it matter if it passes to me?"

"We're still the only humans who can open Gates," Archie said. "In this world or any other. As long as that's the case, we have a duty to police what comes through, whether or not those fat cats who've taken over the Brotherhood have a say."

I kicked a furrow in the sand with my foot. It was a lot of responsibility. But it certainly wasn't more than what I'd already decided to shoulder myself: to find the nightmare clock. That was what I had to do, above all else.

"I'll do my best," I said to my father. I felt lousier than I admitted about lying to him, even partially. But his falling-out with the Brotherhood wasn't mine, and I needed a look at the Iron Codex, now more than ever. I needed a way to find the nightmare clock and use it, and Archie couldn't do that for me.

I was as ready as I was ever going to be, I realized. And I was going to have to disobey my father to do what I needed to do—only, now there was at least the small hope that he'd forgive me after the fact for running off on my own.

Archie pulled me in with one arm and gave me a squeeze. "Thank you," he said.

I frowned in confusion. "For what, Dad?"

"Trusting me," he said. "I know it was a lot to ask. All I ask now is that you keep being smart, and strong, and trust yourself." He held me at arm's length, and for the first time the expression in his eyes softened when he looked at me. I wouldn't have called it fatherly, but it was no longer calculating. "Trust yourself, Aoife. And never stop fighting."

Trusting other people doesn't come easily to you when you've never had someone who trusts *you*. But I had to tell someone about my dreams of the dark figure and the spinning worlds beyond his glass prison, someone who wouldn't tell Archie or Valentina in turn. Or let it slip to the girl he was infatuated with.

Dean shook his head when I finished, and lit a cigarette. "Hell of a story, Aoife."

"They're not regular dreams," I said. "I'm sure of that. They *feel* too much. I can taste the air and hear the gears clacking, feel the vibrations under my feet."

"I've had some doozies of dreams," Dean said. "Bourbon and bad diner food will do it. But not lately." He slid closer to me and draped his arm around my shoulder. "I sleep nice and tight here, princess."

"It's different," I said, blushing at his reminder of the day before. "If the nightmare clock actually exists, and I think it does, Valentina said it can . . . change things. Reality." I swallowed, hoping it didn't sound insane when I said it aloud. "It could put the world right again. The Engine, the Gates, everything."

"Right." Dean exhaled. "You mean back like it was, with Proctors and secret prisons and burnings? Because that was top-notch, I gotta say." Venom dripped from his words.

"Back to where I know why my mother is sick, and I can help her," I whispered, feeling tears prick at the corners of my eyes and hating my weakness. "And where the Proctors don't exist at all."

Dean ground out his cigarette against a porch post. "You've got that look, Aoife. Like all the gears are seized. What crazy thing are you thinking of?"

"Someone who knows more than Archie could be a big help," I said.

"True, but you're stuck here with dear old Dad," Dean said. "He's got his eye on you, to make sure you don't . . ." He trailed off and rubbed his chin, not meeting my eyes.

"Blow up an Engine and break the Gates?" I supplied. It was the truth. It shouldn't have hurt. But it did, and I pulled back.

"It wasn't your fault," Dean said. He drew me close again. "I know you feel like you have to put things right. I just don't want you to get hurt. Besides, who knows more than your old man about this stuff?"

"The Brotherhood," I said instantly. "They have the Iron Codex—all the knowledge this world has of any other."

"I thought Archie said we couldn't trust them," Dean

said. "People who think they know everything are usually pretty good at hiding stuff, Aoife."

"But I don't know anything right now," I said, all the frustration I'd been feeling earlier cropping up again. "I don't know if my dad's right or just paranoid. I'd just like the chance to ask them myself."

"Well, if you insist," Dean said. "Let's bust out of here and go ask 'em. Where do they bunk?"

I shrugged. "No idea." I looked back at the house, where off-key piano music floated out through the glass. "But I bet Valentina knows all about it."

Valentina and Archie shared the master bedroom in the Crosley house. The four-poster bed was unmade, and bottles of ink and papers bearing my father's jagged handwriting were scattered across the writing desk in the corner.

I stood still for a moment, taking in the details of the room. A negligee hung from the door of the wardrobe, and one of Archie's shirts was crumpled on the floor.

A creak from below reminded me that I was on borrowed time, and I went over to the dressing table, which was covered with rows of makeup pots and perfume bottles and a powder puff, all the tools Valentina had shown me how to use to put my face on. She'd really tried to make this easier on me, and a small part of me felt rotten for snooping now and deceiving the both of them.

But in the greater scheme, if I fixed things, if I used the clock the way Valentina had said some believed it could be used, wouldn't it justify what I was doing now?

I sure hoped so.

While Dean kept watch on the door, I dug into the drawers, beneath the underthings and the odds and ends of old hairpins and mostly empty bottles.

Valentina had to have something—a letter, her own witch's alphabet—that would tell me how to connect with the Brotherhood of Iron.

My fingers brushed paper—good, thick vellum paper—and I moved aside a stack of slips to see several oversized envelopes tied with a blue silk ribbon. *Finally.* Elated, I pulled them from the drawer and flipped through them one by one. They were all addressed to *Miss Valentina Gravesend Crosley* in the same precise hand.

I slipped the letters—six of them—out of the envelopes and retied the parcel sans the pages inside the envelopes. That would buy me a little time before Valentina and Archie discovered what I was up to.

What I was up to could be mad; I'd considered that. The iron of the Iron Land could be poisoning me—more slowly than before, it was true—but then, my particular brand of madness had always shown itself first in dreams.

Still, if there was a chance I could put things right, I was going to take it, no matter what the odds might be. I knew myself well enough to know that.

Shoving the letters into the waist of my skirt, I pulled the pin-neat white cardigan Valentina had lent me over the bulge and went back to my own little room.

I propped a chair under the doorknob to avoid being interrupted. I'd hit the jackpot. The letters, all but one, were from Valentina's father, and he'd signed them *Herbert*

Gravesend Crosley, which just solidified the image I had of Valentina's parents as stuffy, unappealing sticklers.

Lastly, I unfolded a letter in familiar handwriting—the jagged slanted scrawl of my father. It was old, the ink worn away at the crease, and written on cheaper paper than the rest; it was beginning to fray at the corners.

Dearest Valentina,

I shut my eyes and sucked in a breath of the stale air in my room. A love letter. A love letter written when I was still in Lovecraft, when my mother was locked away, when Conrad and I were in some orphanage.

That couldn't matter now. Shaking my head to clear it, I read on.

It's cold here, and I'm getting more frustrated by the day.

The Brotherhood as it is now is a disgrace. They sit, fat and content here at the top of the world, and they scheme and argue, but they never do anything. Not about the Thorn Land, not about the Proctors, not about the instability of the Gates.

They don't realize that with every bargain they cut with the Fae, they bring us an inch closer to another Storm. They are weakening the very world that they helped build. The tenet of never trusting the Fae has fallen by the wayside, and nobody listens to anything I have to say on the matter. They sit and scribble in their damn notebooks, natter on and on about the glory of the Iron Codex, and never admit that things are worse now than they ever were when the Storm was raging.

Too late, I thought. I gripped the letter hard enough to make tiny tears in the edges of the paper. There was a second Storm now—a slow-moving plague that was pouring from the shattered Gate into the Iron Land, a Storm I'd had a hand in causing when I'd broken the Gates to Thorn.

This is not about protecting the human race anymore. This is not even about balance, about living in harmony with the eldritch things that crawl out of Thorn. This is a shell game to see who can grab the most power and influence from under the cup before the whole thing collapses and we all realize we've grabbed a fat handful of nothing.

Or until the Proctors burn every last reasonable person on earth alive. I don't know which we'll get to first.

Archie's handwriting started to skid off the page, his pen blotting and leaving long dribbles of ink that obliterated entire words.

Coming home. That's what I want. I want to see green hills and blue skies again. Even that vile smoke over Lovecraft would be preferable to the endless days cooped up here with these old men in the Bone Sepulchre. I want

After that, the words were blotted out, until the very end.

> hold you again, smell you and feel you next to me.
> I love you, Valentina. I hope you understand why I can't be a part of this farce the Brotherhood has become anymore. Say you'll stay with me. Please.

I crumpled the letter and tossed it across the room. It landed in the corner, with a flutter rather than a satisfying bounce.

I'd found out something useful. The rest of it shouldn't matter.

My resolve had hardened.

The Brotherhood was going to help me, whether they knew it or not. The Iron Codex would have answers, and I was going to have to go and find them.

I laid out my plan to Dean, Cal, Bethina and Conrad, because I needed their help. They took it about as well as I expected.

"You're cracked," Conrad said. "You heard what Dad said. We have to lie low, and we have to wait until there's more of us together to try and fix the Gate. In the meantime, there are Proctors everywhere, and creatures coming through the broken Gates. Have you thought about how you're even going to *get* to this . . . what'd you call it?"

"The Bone Sepulchre," I said, matching his testy tone. "And stop calling me nuts, Conrad."

"I'm sorry, but when you say something that's nuts, I'm not gonna lie," he said. He looked at Dean. "Please tell her she's being crazy."

"It's a bad idea," Dean said. "But if you're going, I'm going with you."

"No," I said firmly. "I don't know how they'd react to you, Dean. It's bad enough that I have Fae blood. I can't put you in that position."

"Have you ever thought that your father might be right?" Bethina spoke up. "The world isn't the same at all. Ghouls everywhere, stone knows what crawling out from under every rock." She shivered. "Mr. Grayson has good sense, miss. Maybe you should listen to him for once."

Cal nodded agreement, and I shot him an annoyed glance. He was only doing that to impress his girlfriend, and I kicked him under the table when he glared back. Boys *and* girls got silly when crushes and love came into play. I hoped I didn't come across as that irritating when I was with Dean.

"I'm going to try," I said. "So don't even attempt to change my mind."

Cal grumbled, and I spread my hands. "If it were *your* mother missing in this mess . . ."

"All right, all right," Cal said, throwing me a murderous *shut up* glance. As if I'd spill his secret in front of Bethina. "We'll help you, but for the record, I think this whole plan is going to come to a bad end."

"Well, I'm not helping," Conrad announced. "Your running away is just that—running. You're afraid of what might happen if you let Archie be in charge and fix this the right way."

"And what exactly are you doing besides nothing,

Conrad?" I asked. "What exactly did you do before, besides pant after Archie's trail like a puppy and almost get yourself killed? Thank goodness you had your Weird," I said, and then snapped my fingers. "Oh, that's right—yours hasn't shown up yet."

"You're being a bitch, Aoife," Conrad said, his brows lowering and his eyes going angry.

"And you're being a dunce if you think we can just sit here and expect everything to be fine," I snapped back. I shouldn't have picked on Conrad's lack of a Weird, but he could be so infuriating. "Archie's not perfect, Conrad, and he doesn't always have a plan. He *did* just leave us in Lovecraft."

"You know our mother, Aoife," he cried, slamming his hand on the table in frustration. "I would have left too."

"You leave wives," I said. "Not children."

"She's got a point," Dean murmured.

Conrad stood up, shoving back his chair. "Fine. You two run off like delinquents, and drag poor Cal and Bethina with you. I'm out of this." He left, and I stood up to go after him, to do what, I wasn't sure, but Dean pulled me back.

"Forget it," he said. "You're not changing his mind."

I sank back in my chair and pressed my face into my hands. I thought I'd lost Conrad over a year ago when his iron madness made him go for my throat with a knife, but to find him alive and sane and now to see the gulf between us getting even wider—that, I couldn't handle.

Nor could I blame Conrad entirely for being such a jerk. I wanted a father again as badly as he did. He was just more willing to accept Archie's demands for obedience.

"He's right, though," I muttered. "I don't have a plan for

how I'll get out of here, never mind how I'll get to the Brotherhood. We don't even know where the Bone Sepulchre is."

Cal cast a look back at the door. As a ghoul, he had much better hearing than Dean and me, and I'd entrusted him with keeping watch. "Is there some way we can figure it out?"

"Well, Archie's letter talked about the top of the world," I said. "The Arctic Circle somewhere would make sense. The Proctors steer clear of there." The accepted story was that great viral creatures flourished under the polar ice, but I didn't know the real truth. Regardless, there was something there that kept the Proctors out of the cold, unclaimed waters and led them to keep everyone else out too, with blockades and patrol boats. It made as much sense as any other location on earth.

"Not to put a damper on the party," Bethina said, "but you can't just grab a skiff and row up to the Arctic Ocean. That's a long journey, and you need an ironside boat. I saw a lanternreel on the subject when I was a girl. About the expeditions and such."

"I guess I'll figure it out when I get to the Bone Sepulchre." I shrugged, feigning a confidence I didn't feel in one iota of my being.

"There's a submersible that runs from Innsmouth," Dean spoke up. "Usually up to Nova Scotia and beyond, ferrying fugitives into Canada." He took out his pack of cigarettes and tapped it against the table. "But I wager that for the right price they'd go all the way to the top. The captain's a tough nut—not afraid of going under the ice."

I looked at Dean, pained. "You know I don't have any money."

"There's things other than money," Dean said. "But they're not pirates. They won't take you unless I vouch for you. And if I vouch, I'm coming." He took out a Lucky and stuck it behind his ear, and I could tell by his posture I wasn't going to get to argue.

I didn't want to appear scared, but I *did* want Dean along. Without him, I'd be alone, at the mercy of whatever cropped up between here and the Bone Sepulchre. "That's fine."

"Getting out of the house isn't going to be easy," Cal said. "Neither your dad nor Valentina is exactly asleep at the wheel." He cocked his head and then jerked a thumb at the door. "Speaking of. Someone's coming."

"Don't worry," I told all three of them. "That part I've got covered."

Valentina was in the library, and for a minute I thought Archie was with her before I realized she was seemingly talking to herself.

"No, I don't know when." A pause. "Stop it. Stop *pushing*. It will happen when it happens."

I knocked twice, softly.

There was a clatter from inside, and then Valentina yanked the door wide. "What, Aoife?"

"Listen," I said. "I'm sorry about what happened before. I shouldn't have fibbed. But I really would like to use the *Munin*." I wrapped my arms around myself and shivered in the ever-present drafts that ran through the Crosley house like the vapor trails of dirigibles. "It's kind of dreary in here."

"I know," Valentina sighed. "It's meant to be a summerhouse. Open windows, cool ocean breezes and all that."

"Maybe just for an hour or two a night?" I wheedled. "You can even watch me if you want."

"You're a big girl, Aoife," Valentina said. "I trust you've learned your lesson?"

"Oh, yes," I said. "I won't touch the journals. I just want a little peace and quiet and space."

"Fine," Valentina said. "Honestly, I'm glad to see someone so enamored of the old bucket. Always hated the damn thing when my father would pile us all in it for family trips."

"It's a beautiful craft," I said. It was a relief to say one thing, at least, that wasn't a lie.

"You know what it means, *Munin*?" Valentina asked. She absently straightened a few books on the shelf before her. "Before the Storm, the Vikings and such worshiped a father-god, a man who put out his own eye for the wisdom of the world." Valentina brushed a stray curl behind her ear and looked past me, to something only she could see. "To replace the eye, the Allfather had two ravens named Hunin and Munin that flew out into the world every day and brought back what they had seen. *Hunin* and *Munin*—'thought' and 'memory.'" Valentina smiled. "My father always did have a flair for the dramatic."

"So does mine," I murmured.

"Anyway, the dusty wisdom of that particular bird is all yours," Valentina said. "But you and that boy are not to canoodle in there. You get me?"

"Yes, ma'am," I said. "Loud and clear."

"I thought you were a brat when we first met," Valentina said. "Sheltered and petulant. I'm glad I was wrong."

"Me too," I said as she brushed past me and left the library. When I turned back to take stock of the books, I was startled by a gleam of metal from the shelf where she'd stood. I pulled out a few volumes, then a fat handful. I recognized the simple brass box, the aether tube and the speaker and receiver. It was an aethervox, a long-range variety, wired into an antenna on the top of the house. Valentina hadn't been talking to herself.

I turned the dial, watched the aether swirl inside the clear glass tube at the top of the vox for a moment as it warmed up, but only static greeted me when the speaker clicked on. The vox was tuned to a dead channel.

Whoever Valentina had been speaking to, she didn't want anyone else to know.

I covered the vox again. It couldn't help me now, and I knew I couldn't afford to accuse Valentina of anything; I'd just lose all the credibility I'd gained with her and my father, and I'd never be able to slip away and find the Brotherhood.

After I'd hidden the vox, I went up to my room to pack a few things and meet Dean before I lost my nerve.

Despite Conrad's naysaying, running away went pretty smoothly. Dean and I slipped out separately to the *Munin,* where I made sure to turn on all the lights and find a station on the aether tubes to send noise back toward the house. Cal and Bethina waited in the shadow of the boxwoods by the porch. The hard part was up to me.

The Crosley house had bright arc lamps mounted on

the four corners, a standard precaution against ghouls in unprotected areas. Dean glared at them. "You got an idea for those? Your old man is gonna see us the minute we make a break."

I hefted the small ditty bag I'd picked up from Valentina's dressing table. "I've got it covered. Help me find the transformer box."

We crept around the house, keeping below the windows. Valentina was at the piano again, Archie was sitting near her scribbling in his journal, and Conrad was sitting across from him doing the same. The very image of the good son. I guessed that left the black sheep role for me.

Dean helped me get the cover off the box that controlled the aether flow to the exterior lanterns, the transformer hissing as it converted the elemental gas to electrical impulses.

I pulled a handful of Valentina's hair curlers out of the bag and, using a careful, delicate touch, shoved them one by one between all the circuits. The ceramic protected me from an electrical current, and the fat rollers pushed the wires off the contacts.

There was a shower of sparks, the snap of aether against air, the scent of burnt paper, and then the gardens all around the house went dark. Only the glowing hulk of the *Munin* was visible in the shadows, like a lamprey floating in a black sea.

We crept back to the ladder. My heart thudded. We didn't have a lot of time before Archie noticed the house was dark outside and came to see what had happened.

Dean started to climb after me, but I stopped him. "No. It'll be less dangerous if there's only one of us."

We'd gone over the plan, all four of us, again and again that afternoon, but I was still nervous. Dean stayed behind, grumbling. "Be careful, all right?"

I nodded my assent as I scrambled up the ladder and across the cabin into the pilothouse. I flipped the switches to turn on the fans and felt the *Munin* strain against its ties.

Now it was a race against time and physics. Almost sick to my stomach, I skidded back to the ladder and slid down it, skinning one of my knees. I hit the ground as the first tie-down snapped, a whip crack that echoed through the black night like a bullet.

Dean ran to me and helped me up, and together we ran.

As far as distractions went, a runaway airship was a pretty good one. We were already a hundred yards from the house when the outside lamps came back on. I could hear Archie and Conrad shouting.

I felt one last stab of guilt for what I'd done, and then it was washed away by the cold night air stinging my chest. Dean and I moved, holding hands, our feet striking the frozen earth. The branches of the topiary animals tugged at my jacket as we ran through the darkness.

I knew it was only my imagination turning every rasp and rustle of icy branches and wind into prowling ghouls and hungering nightjars, but I still gripped Dean as hard as I could.

We'd arranged to meet Cal and Bethina beyond the grounds, and we stayed quiet until we were well down the road. Not only because of my father, but also in case anything else was watching. Traveling at night was dangerous, but it was our only chance to make it to Innsmouth unobserved by either Archie or Proctors.

I just wished Conrad hadn't been so stubborn. I wished he could have been here with me.

But what I wanted rarely came to be, so I just hunched deeper into my jacket, shouldering the small bag of things I'd taken from Valentina's house, and ran.

The house already seemed infinitely distant, and I turned back to the gravel road, lit to a white ribbon by moonlight, spotted with black where the ice had melted and formed reflecting pools for the stars above us.

We came to a signpost, CAPE COD and GLOUCESTER and INNSMOUTH written in faded lettering on its crooked arms. It creaked in the wind, swaying back and forth.

I didn't bother looking behind me again as the four of us took the fork to Innsmouth. Archie would be furious, Conrad would be irritable, and Valentina would probably hit the roof, but it didn't matter to me.

In my mind, I was already on my way to the Arctic.

10

Ravens over Innsmouth

DEAN, CAL, BETHINA and I dozed for a few hours in a barn, taking turns sitting watch with Dean's lighter trembling between our palms both for warmth and to ward off the night-dwelling creatures we could hear hooting and crying in the darkness beyond. Fire would keep them at bay—for a while, anyway.

When the sun was just a stain on the horizon, we resumed walking. I was numb everywhere, especially in my heart and mind, but the horrible weight I'd been carrying since we left Lovecraft had lessened a little. Just to be *doing* something, instead of sitting and waiting for someone else to figure out the plan, was freeing enough that I actually hopped over an icy puddle.

Dean gave me a crooked grin. "You're in a good mood."

"Better than the last few days," I agreed.

He kicked a pebble ahead of us down the road. "You ever been to Innsmouth?"

"No," I said. "Conrad and I didn't exactly get seaside vacations."

"Nice little town," said Dean. "Quaint, I guess you'd call it. I ran a few fugitives up there to catch the boat for Canada."

Sometimes it was easy to forget Dean's life before we met. He had been a guide to fugitives and those wanted by the Proctors; he'd lived every day of his life with danger. Because of that, I tried to stay in the good mood he was seeing. I didn't want him worrying.

"Tell me more about the places you've been."

"Favorite place ever was San Francisco, hands down," Dean said. "They have the walls, not like Lovecraft, and inside it's like a million cities compressed into one, piled on top of each other, like layers you could dive down through. They have a Chinatown there, and men who can breathe fire if they drink a potion, and women who can swallow knives. It smells like steam and smoke and gunpowder, and since it's a modern city the Proctors don't pay any attention to the poor folks and we have the run of the place without much risk of getting burned."

All I really knew about San Francisco was that it was home to one of the three great Engines in the States—now two, I supposed—and that off the coast was Alcatraz Island, where the worst heretics were confined to a hospital run by the Bureau of Proctors, like Ravenhouse in Lovecraft, only a hundred times worse.

"At night you can see weird blue lights out on Alcatraz," Dean said, as if reading my thoughts. "Everyone says the Proctors have got secret experiments going on out there."

He looked at me. "Knowing what I know now, I gotta wonder."

I'd wondered too: if there was no necrovirus, what had the necrodemons everyone had so feared during the war really been?

"Maybe someday we'll know," I said to Dean.

"Maybe," he said, "but I doubt it. I don't think the whole truth's ever really going to get out."

Before I could give that too much thought and just depress myself all over again, we came over a hill and saw the sea, with a cluster of gray and blue buildings huddled at the water's edge.

"Innsmouth," Dean said. "Doesn't look like much, I know."

"No," Cal agreed. Bethina wrinkled her nose.

"Smells like fish."

"We need a plan," I said. "Dean and I will go ahead and try to find the captain of the submersible, and you two wait here for him. If something happens, you need to get word back to my father. All right?"

Cal instantly shook his head. I knew he wouldn't like staying behind again, but Cal was the only one I trusted to be wily enough to get back to the Crosley house if we ran into trouble in the village. Plus, he could protect Bethina, which was more than I could do at the moment. I was so jittery and nervous I could feel myself vibrating, even standing still on the hilltop.

"Please," I said to Cal softly. "I promise we'll either send word or we'll be back in a few hours and this will all be a wash." The last part was a lie. I *had* to go north.

Bethina took Cal's hand. "I think Miss Aoife is right," she said. "If there's trouble, they'll need someone to light out and send help."

"There won't be," Dean assured them, but I saw worry lines in his forehead that usually weren't there. I wondered if he knew something about Innsmouth that I didn't.

"As long as there's someone down here who can get me out of this place," I said aloud.

"I'll introduce you around," Dean said. "If the boat I'm thinking of hasn't been sunk yet, they can get us to the Great Old Ones themselves. Crackerjack crew, every one." He shoved a hand through his hair, a nervous gesture that I'd come to recognize as Dean getting ready for trouble. "But antsy," he said. "So move slow and stay quiet in the village, and don't say anything stupid to anyone."

I squeezed his hand to reassure him I could handle it. "I trust you, Dean."

We walked in silence until we came to the village outskirts.

Even as early as it was, I'd expected some movement, but there was nothing. No jitneys, no steam carriages. Not even the horse-drawn variety was in evidence, though far away I heard some sort of livestock bray and then quiet. The place felt as if it were holding its breath—not abandoned, but staying perfectly still, waiting for something.

The curtains on the rows of pitch-roofed cottages were drawn, down to the last one; passing the houses was like passing a line of faces with blind eyes staring into nothing. I shivered, not entirely from the brisk sea air.

I got close enough to Dean so I could whisper. "Is it supposed to be this quiet?"

"No," Dean said in the same tone, his hand going into his pocket for his knife. "Something's wrong."

I reached deep for a little of my Weird, but nothing unusual prickled, just the usual sorts of machines and locks and clockworks that a village at the edge of the ocean would possess.

There was a small town square, like a hub in a wheel, and a fountain in the center of it frozen solid, plumes of ice erupting from the mouths of a trio of metal leviathans.

A scream came, then cut off as abruptly as a needle skipping off a record. I started down the narrow side street it had come from, placing my feet carefully and silently on the bricks.

Dean caught up with me. "I'd say we should get to the docks, but I don't know that I want to be that exposed right at the moment," he whispered.

I nodded silently and reached back for his hand. Dean squeezed it and then let it drop, and we crept ahead in matched steps, until we'd gone away from the sea and the center of town and come upon a farmhouse set a little back from the street. A sagging red barn beyond held the source of the scream.

Something else, softer and more terrifying, drifted on the wind. Sobbing. Human sobbing, coming from a human throat.

"Aoife . . . ," Dean started, but I shushed him and continued toward the barn, keeping myself out of view of the barn door.

Through a slat in the side, I saw three people in nightclothes on their knees on the dirt floor of the barn, two Proctors in black uniforms brandishing shock rifles at them.

The girl, the one sobbing, had a split lip, and blood dribbled down her white nightgown. One of the Proctors drew back his hand again.

"We've been flying up and down the coast looking in every rathole they could duck into," he snapped. "We know everyone in this filthy town harbors fugitives. Now tell me where they are—at least two, boy and girl, dark haired. One calling herself Aoife Grayson."

"We don't *know,*" the girl sobbed. "If that terrorist were here, we'd turn her in real quick. Please. We don't *know*."

I almost shrieked when Dean clapped a hand on my shoulder. I'd been transfixed by the scene in the barn, and enraged. "Aoife," Dean whispered.

"I'm not leaving," I hissed at him. "We have to do something."

"Not that," Dean insisted, his mouth practically pressed against my ear. "Look. Past the barn."

There was a long field that sloped down to cliffs above the water, probably half a mile away. And there, moored at the edge of the cliff, was a familiar black hulk of an airship with the spiky Proctor insignia painted on the side.

Draven's. I'd been so preoccupied with the people in the barn I hadn't even looked beyond. It wasn't just regular Proctors in there, but Draven's elite troops. How had he known I'd be coming to Innsmouth?

"What do we do?" Dean muttered. His voice was still as soft as a flick of silk, but his grip on my shoulder betrayed panic as he squeezed hard enough to bruise.

"I don't know," I said in the same voice. Inside the barn, the girl screamed again.

"I can't tell you what I don't know, sir! Please stop hitting me!"

"Just . . . something," I said to Dean, and wrenched free of his grasp.

In Cal's stories, heroines usually carried bullwhips or daggers, flew their own airships, swung in on ropes. They always had a daring plan. Or even a stupid plan. Never no plan.

Inside the barn door, I grabbed up a disused axe handle and swung it at the nearest Proctor, catching him across the back of the skull. He went down with a grunt, and the other swung his rifle toward me.

Dean grabbed him from behind and threw him into the nearest wall. The Proctor rebounded off it with a clatter but held on to his shock rifle and got off a wild shot. The sizzling electric bolt clipped the older woman in the trio—the girl's mother, I guessed—and she cried out as she fainted.

"Mother!" the girl screamed.

Dean caught the Proctor across the jaw with a hard punch, and the man went down for good.

I took the girl by her shoulders. "You're strong," I told her. "Help your father carry her inside. Trust me, you need to get out of here."

Her eyes widened as she got a good look at my face. "You're . . . ," she started, then slapped my hands off and scrambled away.

She didn't have to say it. I knew. Aoife Grayson, terrorist. *Destroyer of the Engine.*

As the girl and her father got her mother up and out

the back door of the barn, I saw black shapes approaching from the front. My chest clenched. I'd hoped we could escape unnoticed, but I should have known better when Grey Draven was involved.

I could tell, even from my distance, that the weapons were new. The guns were copper, and midway along the barrel was a green glass bulb in which some kind of substance churned. The end narrowed to a point, like a needle. Some kind of fine ammunition, or perhaps gas, or . . .

"You like my toys?"

Grey Draven walked through the row of Proctors and into the barn as if it were perfectly usual for him to be walking through a field in the first hours of the morning in full dress uniform. "Hello, Miss Grayson," he said, tipping his head at me. "And the infamous Dean Harrison. It appears I get two for the price of one today. Already worth getting out of bed for."

They hadn't found Cal and Bethina. My stomach plummeted in relief. Cal would be dead if Draven got his hands on him. But my friend knew how to hide, and I knew he'd keep Bethina safe. He fancied her too much to let anything happen to her. They'd get away and tell my father what had happened, so at least he wouldn't always wonder.

"You sure came a long way from your cushy new job in Washington to chase a couple of kids," I said to Draven. *Keep him talking. Keep him thinking it's just the two of you.*

"Oh, I think we both know you're no innocent child, Aoife," Draven purred. "As for my new job—one of the perks is I get to do exactly as I wish. Including kit out my men with the best." He extended his hand to the two men at the head of the troop. "A little something I've been working on. I call it the needle pistol." He took one from the Proctor standing nearest and aimed. A thin bolt of light arced from the pistol to the barn wall, leaving a smoking hole. "Pretty impressive," he said. "And I'm not even a genius. Imagine what your father could do for us."

"Is that what this is about?" I asked. "My father?"

"You've got me wrong, Aoife," Draven said. "I don't want to hurt your father. I never wanted to. I want to use him, his knowledge of the Thorn Land and his uncanny mind, for my own ends."

"Against his will," I countered. Draven shrugged, as if I'd caught him out in a white lie.

"One way or another. We need him, now more than ever."

I shook my head. Draven could sugarcoat it any way he liked, but at the end of the day he'd still be a brute, a kidnapper and a liar. "I'm not helping you, Mr. Draven," I said. "Either let me go or try to take me to jail again. We all remember how well that worked last time."

Draven stepped forward and raised his hand as if to slap me across the face. I didn't flinch from his dark gaze. I wasn't afraid of him anymore, I realized in surprise. I'd seen so much worse, Grey Draven didn't even rate at this moment.

Dean made a move toward Draven, and two Proctors jumped at him and held him back. Draven waved the pistol. "Now, now, Dean. Don't get hotheaded. Your little girlfriend here needs to learn how to speak to her betters."

He dropped his hand. "This is hardly the place I wanted to have this conversation. Come. We'll retire to the ship, where it's warm." He smiled at me, and it was worse than anything he could hit me with. "I do enjoy a few creature comforts, don't you?" He brushed the backs of his knuckles down my cheek and I shivered in disgust.

"I can take them or leave them," I said. The Proctors shackled Dean while Draven took me firmly by the arm.

The airship grew bigger and bigger as we approached, until it blocked all but the barest edge of the sun. I could see scrolling letters along the prow—*Dire Raven*.

"Beautiful, isn't she? I had her specially built," Draven boasted. "She's triple armored, with two pressurized hulls. Her balloon is ultralight. Five bladders inside, and backup batteries so we never lose power." He touched the hull lightly as we climbed the folding steps to the hatch, unctuously opened by yet another uniformed Proctor.

"Much better than that hulk your father flies," Draven said. "What's he call it, again? The *Bad Memory*?"

"You know damn well what it is," I said. Draven pursed his lips.

"This little rebellious act you've got playing now is not amusing," he told me.

The *Dire Raven* was enormous in comparison to the *Munin*, and we passed through two decks before we reached a small room wrapped with windows. We were in the prow of the craft, just under the helium bladders, in a sitting room done in black, red and gold. Even more patriotic than Draven's old office, when he'd only been Head of the City and not one of the most powerful men in the country. Dean glanced around, and I could tell he was as nervous as I was. I hoped Cal and Bethina knew to run as soon as they spied Proctors, to not wait for us. I knew they'd be safe in Innsmouth, especially when Draven was distracted with us, but I still worried.

Draven sat in an armchair and put one foot up on an ottoman, drawing my focus back to him. He pulled over a rolling metal cart and poured himself a drink from a metal decanter. All metal, I realized, so that nothing would shatter during a rough ride. The *Dire Raven* was full of iron, and I could already feel it starting to eat away at my edges. If I stayed here for more than a few hours, I was going to be out of my mind. *Calm down, Aoife,* I told myself. *Don't panic over the disaster that hasn't happened yet.* "It's early, but you understand how hard my job has become these days," he told me, placing the decanter back on the cart.

"I still don't know what you want from me." I stood straight and tried to appear calm. Inside, I was trembling worse than a bare twig on one of the trees outside. Draven could kill me, torture me, or do worse to Dean while he made me watch, and I couldn't do a thing except beg. Using my Weird inside this iron ship would be suicidal, and trying to fight off the Proctors and escape would be suicide, period. The Proctors might all have been part of a lie, but they were still men, men with guns, and Draven gave them orders.

"I don't think you're that stupid, so do us both a favor and drop the ingénue schoolgirl act." Draven tossed back his drink. "Your father had a little spat with the Brotherhood, and I don't blame him. They're unrecognizable from the stalwart society my grandfather helped found. And I don't care about them—right now I exist to put the status quo back in place. And you're going to help me." He narrowed his eyes over the top of his cup. "You and that clever little trick you do."

Draven refreshed his cup, this time filling it to the brim

with hot tea to cover the amber liquid at the bottom. "At first I thought another Grayson with uncanny powers would just complicate my life. But you had to be too smart, too bright a penny. So I adapted."

"Like the reptile you are," I spat.

Draven raised his cup to me. "Too right. To Mr. Darwin, and his proof that a clever creature like me will always survive." He blew on the tea. "And you too, Aoife. If you're as clever as you think you are."

"Is this going anywhere?" I sighed.

Draven sipped and set the cup aside, never taking his eyes from me. "You are going to fix the Gates. Convince your father to help. Or I'll cut your friend Dean's throat so that his blood pools all over this lovely carpet. That's how strongly I feel about this, Aoife." His tongue flicked out over his lips like a lizard's while I shot a glance at Dean. His face was pale, his expression mirroring the panic I felt.

Draven sat back and raised one eyebrow. "Don't mistake my current civility for a lack of conviction."

For a moment I just listened to my heart raging, my blood boiling through my ears with an enraged thrum. I knew that Draven didn't want to fix the Gates the way I did. I knew that he didn't want my father and me for anything except the power over Thorn we could grant him. He could act like we had the same motives, but we didn't.

And threatening Dean was the last damn straw. I reached out and smacked the hot tea into his lap. Draven yelped, leaping out of his seat. "Don't think that because I'm standing here quietly you can threaten me or the people I love," I said in return, moving back to stand next to Dean.

Draven bared his teeth as he grabbed a monogrammed

tea towel and swiped the hot liquid off his pants. "You're just like your mother, you know that? A stubborn bitch."

Hearing Draven actually swear made me realize I was probably about five seconds from being tossed into a deep, dark hole, no matter how reluctant he'd initially seemed to harm me. Draven was normally immaculate in both speech and appearance, but something more than me had cracked his demeanor. Now that I was looking, I saw that the buttons on his black jacket were crooked, and his dark hair had been yanked back with a comb rather than carefully smoothed into place. Lines of sleeplessness had appeared under his eyes, and he hadn't shaved.

"Then I guess this is pointless," I said. "You better just clap the shackles on me and drag me right to Banishment Square to burn the wickedness out of me."

"Don't think you're getting off that easy," Draven gritted out. He went to his desk and pulled out a small brass box, flipping it open and stroking his thumb over whatever lay inside.

My curiosity allowed the words to sneak out. "What's that?"

"Nothing much," Draven said. He came over and held it out to me. I strained to look and was surprised by the simplicity of what I saw: it was a compass, just the usual kind they gave out to the Expedition Club at the Academy, only in the center the compass rose had been removed and instead of needles I saw a tiny globe of aether churning inside the device. It emitted a strange sound, a high-pitched tone I could feel in my teeth, while the arrows of direction constantly shifted.

"From the *Dire Raven* and her instruments, I can find

anyone holding this compass, anywhere in the world," Draven said. "Take it."

"I don't think I want you knowing where I am," I said, shrinking from his gift. "In fact, I know I don't."

"Take the damn thing. Or do I have to remind you of what happens to Dean if you sass me?" Draven snapped.

I took the box, which prickled my Weird fiercely. I set it as far away from me as possible, on the arm of my chair. "Why give this to me if you already have me?" I whispered.

"I have you, but I want what you want," Draven said. "You're going to the Bone Sepulchre, to the Brotherhood of Iron. You're going to continue your journey north, Aoife." He tapped the box with one slender forefinger. There was some kind of black dirt or engine grease under his nail. "And this little box is going with you."

As if a map had unfurled behind my eyes, I saw all at once where this was going. "No," I said. "No, I won't."

"You will convince the Brotherhood of your intent to betray your father and become one of them, toe the party line, and you will guard this box as if your life depends on it. If not your life, than certainly the unlucky Mr. Harrison's." Draven gave me a wide, sharp grin. "He'll be staying here."

"The hell I will!" Dean spat. Draven turned one cold eye on him.

"Don't even pretend you have any say in the matter, boy. I could gut you like a fish and have somebody clean up the mess, and no one would ever know. So stay. Quiet."

I shook my head at Dean. He felt things strongly, and that could make him reckless. A rash move was the one thing we didn't need right now.

Draven turned away from us and went to the portholes

in the side of the *Dire Raven*. He breathed on a spot and polished it with his sleeve. "I've tried for a long time to find the exact location of the Brotherhood," Draven said. "Not to exterminate them, mind. I want them to answer to a single law, as it was in the old times. The law of humanity. Not the law of magic or any other creature. Especially not those Fae they're so enamored of."

"And get a private army of magicians in the bargain," I added.

Draven came back to me and squeezed my upper arms with an intensity that would leave bruises. "You're so smart, Aoife. And because of that, I know you'll make the smart call, to save your friend and your own hide. I thought it would be your father who'd redeem this world for me, whether he knew it or not. But no. It's going to be you. Scared little Aoife." He exhaled against my ear, and I could feel the scrape of his stubble as he smiled. "Fail and I kill your friend. Then I come for your mother, your brother and everyone you've ever spoken to, friend or enemy, in your life. You think even I can't be that ruthless? I can. Make no mistake, Aoife. I can, and will, if you fail." He drew back, brow furrowed. "You believe me?"

My throat was so dry and my heart thudding so fast in that moment that I didn't think I could make a sound. But a squeak emanated from me. "Yes."

"Yes what?" Draven snapped.

"Yes, Mr. Draven," I whispered. "I believe you."

And I did. One hundred percent.

Draven tucked the compass into my bag with a pat and then guided me to a lower level of the *Dire Raven*, where three cells were set into the hull, bolted directly to the ultralight steel. He instructed the Proctors to put Dean in the farthest one.

Dean turned back and looked at me when he was inside, and I pressed my fingers against his through the bars. "Aoife," he said, his voice rough with panic. "Aoife, don't do this."

I grabbed his hands and held them around the iron, inches away but separated by miles. The Proctors and Draven watched us, unblinking. "I'm so sorry," I whispered, pressing my forehead against the bars. "It's the only way either of us will get out of this alive." That was true, I knew—I'd at least partially failed in my mission to reach the Brotherhood on my own. If I refused Draven, he'd lock me up next to Dean and hold me there until my father was forced to comply in my place, to go back to the men who regarded him as a traitor and would certainly simply lock him up as well. Draven had me over a barrel, and for now, I had to take his compass and play his game. "I'll be back for you," I told Dean. "Please don't ever doubt it."

"Don't worry about me," he muttered. "Just get out of here. Get as far away as you can. I'll be fine." He moved as close as he could, like he was trying to kiss me, and muttered, "The captain's name is Rasputina Ivanova. The Nor'easter Inn, on the docks, is where she usually picks up passengers. Tell her I sent you, and ask about the Hallows' Eve in New Amsterdam to prove you really know me."

Draven grabbed me by the back of my collar before I could reply. "Time is up, young lovers. Aoife has work to do."

Dean held on to me for as long as he could, and when our grasp was broken his fingers left faint marks, like the memory of a burn.

The same pair of Proctors escorted me to the hatch of the *Dire Raven*.

"One last thing," Draven said. "I know that you might be tempted to ditch my compass the moment you're out of my sight, but if it stops moving—if I get any hint that you've tried to rid yourself of it—then I'll kill Dean without a second thought." He patted my cheek, and I couldn't draw back this time, hemmed in by Proctors as I was. My stomach heaved.

"I know you'll complete your mission," Draven continued. "And just think—if you do, if you help me seal the Gates and fix this world, you may even be able to sleep at night."

I glared at him as the Proctors prodded me back down the gangway and into the farmer's field. "You're a vile person," I told Draven when I was at a safe distance. "You're no better than a ghoul crawling up from the sewer."

Draven tapped his chest. "Words will never hurt me, Aoife. Now get moving. Safe travels, don't get devoured, all that usual sentimental nonsense."

I could feel his eyes on me until I reached the road and turned the corner.

Walking back to Innsmouth, I was numb. I'd had to leave Cal and Bethina behind for their own safety, but I'd never planned on being separated from Dean. I'd never felt so alone. Dean had been the one constant in my life since I'd met him—he'd *saved* my life.

I steeled myself. Grey Draven was not going to beat me again. I was going to keep Dean alive, no matter what it took. Alone or not, I was smarter than Draven. And he was going to learn, by the time this was over, just how big a mistake it had been to cross me.

11

Journey to the Sea

THE NOR'EASTER INN was as deserted as the rest of Innsmouth, at least from the outside. All of the residents seemed to fear the Proctors as much as the farmers we'd rescued did. I nudged open the front door with my foot and peered around the jamb to the inside while trying to keep the sun behind me. Backlit, I could get a look at the interior of the tavern before anyone inside got a look at me.

I gazed back at the street once more. A few Proctors moved in groups, Draven's new needle pistols at the ready. One of them met my eyes and quickly looked away as he passed on the other side of the street without a second glance. No Proctor would touch me now; that much was clear. Not while I was marked as Draven's agent.

The weight of the compass in my bag increased, or I imagined it did. The complicated clockwork within was driving my Weird crazy, like the tickle of a feather on my skin.

I was going to find a way to defy him, of course. There was no possibility of doing as he asked, allying myself with the Proctors. Draven might think he owned me by threatening to hurt Dean and my family, but hadn't Tremaine threatened the same thing? I'd obeyed him out of what I thought was a lack of choice, and the results had been horrific. This time I had to fight. Had to be the girl my father told me I was—strong and smart. A Grayson, not a scared child.

Besides, Draven hadn't discerned my entire mission in finding the Brotherhood. They were welcome to slug it out, but I had one goal in going north, and that was to find the nightmare clock. And once I did, the clock, if it worked, would set things right.

That was the promise I made to myself as I turned back and edged into the Nor'easter, letting the shadows dip across my face. It was oddly quiet and, as far as I could tell, empty. Dust motes were suspended in the gray midwinter light streaming through the broken windows. They cast jagged kaleidoscopic patterns on the dirty floor and showed just how shabby the place was.

"Hello?" I called.

Nobody answered me. I wandered a circuit of the small room, glass crunching under my shoes. The Nor'easter was beyond shabby, but that gave me a little hope. A place this run-down wasn't likely to be harboring the law-abiding types who'd take one look at me and scream for a Proctor.

I determined that nobody was around, then pushed into the back room. Somebody screamed, and I raised my hands reflexively, until I realized it was the farmer's daughter I'd seen at the barn.

"Great Old Ones return," she hissed. "You do have a habit of popping up on people, don't you?"

"Why are you here?" I said, shocked. The girl had changed from her nightclothes, but her face was still bruised and swollen. She gestured to her apron and the broom she held. "Proctors or not, if I don't show up to work, I get fired. We can't afford that in my house."

"You seem all right," I offered hesitantly.

"Yeah," she said. "Thanks to you." She stuck out her hand, awkwardly, and I shook it, just as awkwardly. "I'm Maggie," she said. "Maggie Fisher."

"You seem to already know who I am," I said.

Maggie blushed. "I'm sorry about that stuff I said. I weren't thinking. You did save me from the Proctors."

"Forget it," I said. I would have done the same in her position. I didn't hold it against her. "Your mom all right?"

Maggie's face fell. "She's in and out, but the doc said she'd be okay. Might be in bed for a few weeks."

"I'm sorry to ask you this now," I said. "But do you know a woman named Rasputina Ivanova? Apparently she comes in here a lot."

"Sure." Maggie snuffled. "She's always with this group of shady Russians. Hate 'em. They never tip." She pointed back to the main room, to a round table in the corner. "She sits there and never talks, least not to decent types."

I took a breath. "I don't have a lot of time, so I'm just going to be frank. They smuggle people out of Innsmouth, don't they?" I couldn't exactly hop aboard a commercial steamer bound north, not with the sort of place I was heading for. And I didn't want to run into any more Proctors if

I could help it. My encounter with Draven had been more than enough.

Maggie stared at me, and I could see the struggle taking place behind her eyes.

"Do they pay you to point desperate people in their direction?" I lowered my voice, drawing closer, hoping to impress on her how serious I was. "I'm desperate, Maggie. Desperate as they come. I know you don't trust me, but the sooner you point me in the right direction, the sooner I'll be out of your village."

One hand crept up to touch the bruises on her face, and Maggie flinched. "The submersible comes up out past the jetty, eleven-thirty or so on nights with a new moon. Tonight, I don't know. So many Proctors out there . . . but there'll be desperate folks too. There always are, and Captain Blood out there never turns down a quick buck."

"I thought her name was Ivanova." I shouldered my bag and prepared to go find a place to lie low until midnight.

"Yeah, it is," Maggie said. "But we all call her after that old pirate story, because that's exactly what she is. A bloody pirate."

I looked out at the angry ocean, past the jetty to the clanging buoy that signaled the start of deep water. "Terrific," I said. More pirates. More people out for my blood. Just what I needed.

Maggie told me how when the sky was dark, the submersible would creep into shallow water, past the jetty, and signal those hiding beneath the pier. Sometimes they sent a boat, but I doubted they would with the *Dire Raven* crouched over Innsmouth like an ill omen.

I spent the time as the sun set in the back room of the Nor'easter, where Maggie had agreed I could stay. I found an old vulcanized raincoat and turned it into a rubber sack for my journal, the compass and anything else vulnerable to seawater. I sealed it with a little glue and wrapped it tightly with rope, shoving it back into my satchel.

The hours as the clock crept toward midnight were agonizing. Nobody came into the pub, and Maggie paced restlessly, sweeping up broken glass, washing dishes and mopping the floor, chores to occupy a restless mind. In times past I had done math to keep my thoughts quiet, but I couldn't focus that much tonight.

At last, the nautical clock chimed the quarter-hour, and I shrugged into my jacket and picked up my things. I couldn't miss the sub.

"Hey," Maggie said as I pushed open the door to the main room. "Be careful." I stuck my head out the front door and checked the deserted street. "Those Russians on the sub ain't exactly friendly."

"I think it's a little late for careful," I told her. "But thanks all the same."

The temperature had dropped from merely chilly to agonizingly cold, sea wind cutting across my bare cheeks like animal claws. I snuggled into my jacket and walked down to the end of the dock, scanning the dark-capped waves for any sign of life.

Nothing stirred except the wash of the waves against the dock, and as my chronometer crept past midnight, I began to lose hope. *They have to come,* I thought; even though I didn't relish the journey, it was the only way I was getting north. The only way I could get far enough from Draven to figure out how I was going to outsmart him.

Heights didn't bother me, but I didn't like water. It was black, and cold, and the rocking made me feel as if I'd lost my grip on both the earth and gravity. I couldn't think about that now, though. I could only think about the nightmare clock, the one thing that could help me.

The clanging of the buoy reached my ears again, and clouds scudded above my head. Lit only by faintest starlight, they were black hulking things, like the creatures that strove endlessly through the hundred skies above the black figure's dome in my dreams.

Just then, far off in the shipping channel, I saw a single blue spot glow, slowly joined by others as something long and sleek slid from the depths. It bobbed to the top of the water with a knocking groan, the sound of rivets and iron rather than soft, slippery flesh. That was the only hint I had that it wasn't something entirely of the sea.

The submersible floated where it was for a moment, and then a hatch clanged faintly. A red light joined the blue, the pinpoint of a lamp. It flashed Morse code, a simple sequence asking if there was anyone on shore. My Morse wasn't the best, but I grabbed one of the dock lanterns and flashed back, using the blue glass filter in place for just such a purpose.

Come quickly, the red light said.

I was about to flash back that I didn't have a boat and they'd have to come closer when I picked up another sound over the buoy bell and the waves. A powerful spring-wound motor, the kind that could move a craft along at tremendous speed. I caught the movement of blacker on black, a craft with no running lights.

Proctors. I swore under my breath.

Though Draven had surely told them to steer clear, the crew of the submersible didn't know that, and one of the faceless crew opened fire on them with some sort of gun that rattled fast and loud, striking sparks against the patrol boat's metal hull.

I cried out, even though they couldn't hear me, but then realized I had both an advantage and a much bigger problem. I wouldn't be marked as one of Draven's agents if the Proctors engaged the Russians. But then again, I wouldn't have a ride in another minute, if the sub crew was being shot at.

The submersible was barely a hundred yards offshore. I could do this. I could reach the ship and be gone from this place, on my way toward fixing everything I'd broken. My fear couldn't stop me. Not this time.

I stepped to the edge of the dock, wriggled out of my shoes and coat, strapped my satchel across my back and jumped into the ocean.

At first, when the water hit me, I felt nothing. It was like burning myself on an acetylene torch—my nerves simply went dead, and a great envelope of unfeeling covered me.

I surfaced and swallowed a mouthful of salt water, choking and sputtering as I tried to keep my head above the waves. I wasn't a horrible swimmer—everyone at the Academy had had to take a swimming unit—but I wasn't a great one either, and with my clothes and satchel weighing me down, I wasn't making much progress.

I stroked against the aching cold, straining toward the

row of lights on the side of the submersible, the tracers of light from the guns as they exchanged fire with the Proctors. I didn't hear any screaming—the Proctors were aiming wide, their shots splashing on the sub's hull and coming nowhere near the crew. Draven really wanted me on board the sub, wanted me heading north to the Brotherhood.

The cold came to me by degrees and was heavy as any lead. It compressed my lungs and dulled my nerves, until I knew that I was freezing, sinking, and I couldn't do anything to stop it. I was so close. I could almost touch the sub, could see its running lights dazzling my salt-stung eyes, but I would never get there on my own. I was swallowing more water than air, and I could feel the cold tugging my numb body down.

Light engulfed me, bizarrely, as if the moon had at last shown its face. I had the absurd notion I was in the grip of one of the creatures said to live under the waves, enfolded in clammy, webbed hands. And then there was the brightest flash of all, a searing, stabbing pain through my chest, and everything went dark.

The glass dome of dreams was black now, smoke and thunderheads swirling outside. The gear ticked frantically, sending spiderweb cracks through the glass. Lightning illuminated the dark figure, and he looked at me in profile. His nose was sharp, his skin the gray of something long dead and buried. It was the first time I had glimpsed anything of him besides his eyes, and I was frightened by what I saw.

"You shouldn't be here," he rasped at me, hands buried in the mechanism of the great gear, fiddling with bolts and tiny

components that even my hands weren't delicate enough to manage. Lightning flashed over the dome again, and I realized that I stood on fresh-turned earth rather than transparent glass. All around me, flowers bloomed, their buds opening to reveal skeletal hands reaching toward the dark sky.

"What happened?" I asked. It seemed a question far too small to encompass the destruction all around me.

"You happened," the figure snarled. "You stole into my world, and you were the first I'd seen in so long, I was careless. You listened to me whisper secrets and now the barriers have broken, because you were never supposed to come here."

"I . . . I did this?" I whispered in confusion.

"You will," the figure whispered as the glass began to shatter and fall, slicing through the stems of the bone flowers as it rained around us. "When you die."

The flowers oozed blood, red and wet, that stained the dirt. I stood rooted where I was. "I'm dying?"

"Not yet," the figure said. "Go away. Stop dreaming about this, or do like the others you care for and stop dreaming at all. Stop stealing into my world, Aoife. Or you'll be here much sooner than you think."

Something bright and hot cut through me when the lightning flashed again, and the dome cracked completely, vanishing from before my eyes.

"There's a good girl," a cigarette-tinged voice boomed in my ear. I rolled away from the voice, from the blinding light in my dazzled eyes, and vomited what even in my delirious state I could tell was an impressive amount of seawater.

I blinked the sparks from my vision while I coughed. I

was lying on a brass walkway, mesh digging into my legs through my soaked stockings. The walls around me were curved, riveted, and painted a humorless gray. Iron pierced my brain, all around me. Lettering spun before my eyes until I realized I wasn't delusional but was merely seeing a language I couldn't read.

"Am I . . . ," I gasped. Breathing, never mind talking, embedded a cluster of small knives in my chest when I tried it. The light dazzled me again, and I slumped. Strong hands caught me, and my nostrils were invaded by the smell of pipe tobacco.

"Take it easy," said the same voice. "Back from the dead and trying to walk so soon. Tough little thing."

"Or desperate," said another voice, strongly accented and female.

"Or that," the smoker agreed.

"I made it," I gasped as I lay staring at the round ship's hatch above me. "I'm on the submersible." I was honestly surprised not to be dead. I remembered the suffocating feeling of the water, the hands of the sea tugging me down, and shivered uncontrollably.

A face came into view, wavering around the edges as my eyes worked to dispel the ocean's tears. "You are indeed aboard," agreed the female voice. "And that brings us to the thorny question of who you might be."

The face, when my eyes focused, belonged to a woman, her rich brown hair woven into two meticulous braids. She wore a coat the same gray as the walls, with red trim at the collar and cuffs and two spots on the breast pocket where insignia had been ripped off.

"I'm Aoife Grayson," I said. "Dean Harrison sent me to

meet Rasputina Ivanova. He told me to ask her about the Hallows' Eve they spent in New Amsterdam."

The woman flushed bright pink and then drew back out of my line of sight. She snapped a few orders in Russian, and before I knew it I was on my feet, being helped down a walkway by a bear-sized man in an undershirt, red suspenders and filthy, oil-stained pants. "Easy, sweetheart," he rumbled, in an accent twice as thick as the woman's. "You'll be walking on your own in no time." We came to a galley where a half-dozen sailors stopped eating and stared at me. Another command from the woman and their eyes dropped back to their plates.

The man shoved a ratty blanket at me, along with a steel cup full of tea.

"Drink," he ordered. "Or you'll never get warm."

Now that I wasn't seeing things or drowning, I became aware that I was shivering so violently my muscles were spasming. Still, I hesitated to take a drink from a stranger.

"Drink," he insisted, shoving it at me again and slopping a little on my skin this time. I could see every vein, every freckle and every scrape on the back of my hand painted in stark relief. It was as if the sea had sucked every drop of blood from me and left icy water in its place.

I grabbed the cup and drained it. The tea burned my tongue, but the pain reassured me at least that I was thawed enough to feel something. I wrapped the blanket around myself, still shivering hard enough to rattle the bench I sat on.

"You weren't in the water very long," said the man, refilling the cup, "but you might still have the hypothermia. Keep warm and keep drinking, if you please." His English was good, but each word was as heavy and precisely formed as an ingot, and he fidgeted, as if he was afraid of saying the wrong thing.

The woman came back into the galley and barked something at him in Russian, and he bobbed his head at me apologetically and left the room.

The woman took his place across the table from me. She moved like a man, taking up a lot of space. She folded her arms so that her elbows hit the table. "I am Rasputina Yelena Ivanova," she said. "Captain of this vessel."

I tucked deeper inside the blanket, wilting under her gimlet gaze. She didn't look much older than I was, but her eyes were older by decades. Eyes that had seen and absorbed too much. I couldn't hold them.

"Nice to meet you," I murmured, staring down at my hands.

"Yes, whatever," Rasputina said brusquely. "So. You know Dean Harrison."

"He said you'd get me where I need to go." I forced myself to meet her eyes again and found them now full of cautious curiosity. "Was I wrong?"

"A girl comes from a village full of Proctors, we'd be suspicious on a good day," said Rasputina. "But a girl who jumps into freezing water to get away from that village, well." She shoved my waterproof satchel across the table at me, along with a pair of utilitarian black shoes to replace what I'd left on the dock. "I suppose I can at least hear you out."

Rasputina wasn't particularly pretty, in the sense of delicate features, ruby pouts and pleasant smiles. She had a broad mouth that looked like it wouldn't know a smile if it bit her, cheekbones that stood out from her face like they were trying to escape and wide black eyes that felt like drill bits boring into the center of my forehead. They were the eyes of a crow, a primeval thing that missed nothing and knew every lie before you told it.

"All right," I said, deciding a mostly true story would get me further with her bull-like directness than an outright lie. "Those Proctors were after me. I'm a fugitive, and I'm going to the Arctic Circle. A place called the Bone Sepulchre."

Rasputina's eyes widened, and her hard face split into an expression of shock. "Maybe you aren't cracked," she muttered. "I knew that kid Harrison had a taste for the strange, but this . . ." She shook her head and stood. "Even if I knew how to get there, I wouldn't."

"Why not?" I insisted, determined not to let her put me off. "Dean said you'd take anyone anywhere, for a price."

"I plucked you out of the sea, girl," Rasputina told me. "At great personal risk. You have no proof that you are who you say you are, and you have no money. I don't have to do a damn thing for you besides not stuff you into a torpedo tube and shoot you back to the surface."

"That's fair," I said. "But please, hear me out. I swear I do know Dean, and he's in a lot of trouble."

Rasputina pulled a bottle of clear liquor over and poured herself a glass.

"If you spend enough time with Dean, you'll learn he's always in a lot of trouble," she said, tossing back the shot. "So, here's the situation: you'll ride with us until we get out of territorial waters, and then we'll drop you at Newfoundland or somewhere like that, and you can tell Dean that I said I hope like hell I get the chance to meet him again so I can smack him in his smart mouth."

I didn't have the strength to argue. I was shivering too hard, and my teeth clacked when I tried to talk. Rasputina softened a bit and offered me the bottle.

"No," I said. "I feel like I could pass out as it is."

She stood and pointed down the corridor. "Take one of the empty bunks. We'll be running underwater until we clear Maine. Then we'll find a place to put you off."

"I can pay you," I said to Rasputina. "I have money." I don't know why I lied. Desperation, most likely, but I shouldn't have worried, because she saw right through me.

"No amount of money could convince me to tangle with what lives under that ice," Rasputina told me. "Get some rest."

She was probably right. I was exhausted, and I had a little while before they dumped me off. I could figure out how to change the captain's mind, but not when I was exhausted and half frozen.

I went into the small, curved cabin Rasputina had pointed out. Something on the other side of the wall hummed, and the bunks, though steel framed, looked like the most comfortable things on earth at that moment. I crawled into one and pulled both blankets over me.

I didn't sleep, though. I listened to the engines churn and tried to ignore the sharp pain in my skull reminding me that the longer I was trapped inside an iron tube, the worse I was going to feel.

After hours of staring at the rust spots on the ceiling and listening to the engines, the entire ship shuddered, and the tilting in my stomach that let me know we were moving ceased.

Footsteps rang in the corridor outside, and I swung out of my bunk and peered into the hallway. "What's going on?" I asked a passing crewmember. He growled something in Russian and shoved past me, slamming me into the bulkhead, hard.

"Ow," I muttered, but it was lost as sirens blared and the light in the corridor changed to red.

Rasputina barreled past me, and I caught her arm. "What's wrong?"

"Another sub," she snapped. "You might as well come up to the bridge."

Heart sinking, I followed her up a ladder and into a room similarly lit with red warning lights, stuffed with controls, a wheel and a periscope at the center. Rasputina grabbed a floppy rain hat and then leaned into the periscope, icy seawater raining down from the seal that led to the top of the sub.

She spat out a curse and put the periscope up. "You," she said to me. "Who are you? Really?"

Before I could blink, I found the thin barrel of a pistol leveled at my face. "Answer me," Rasputina said. "Or I'm going to paint the dive controls with your brain."

"I'm Aoife Grayson," I whispered, wondering what on earth Rasputina had seen through the periscope to make her react in such a way. Nothing good, clearly. "I haven't told you one lie since you brought me on board." That in itself was a lie, but I'd told the truth where it counted, hadn't I?

Rasputina pointed behind her, at a young girl, younger even than me, sitting at a radar station. "Explain that," she said to me. She snapped at the girl in Russian, and she took off her earphones and spoke to us in English.

"Ping bearing one mile off port side, visual range in fifteen seconds. Border Guard destroyer. Seems to be holding its position, ma'am."

The Border Guard—the Proctors who patrolled coastal waters to keep out Crimson Guard spies and heretics of all stripes—were notorious for their black ships, their silent gliders and their brutal interrogations of anyone who crossed their path. We'd watched a few reels on them at the Academy.

"We are six miles off the coast of Maine," Rasputina told me. "They have us dead to rights, and they aren't moving. No torpedoes. Not even a screw turning. Now, were I a Proctor, I wouldn't hesitate to blow us right out of the water and into the sky like the pirates we are." She pressed the pistol against my forehead until it bit into my flesh. "The only thing that's different on this trip is you. The only reason those bastards haven't opened fire on us is you. Who are you?"

"I'm Aoife Grayson," I repeated. My shivering now had nothing to do with being frozen.

"All right, Aoife Grayson," Rasputina snarled. "If that's who you are, what's so special about Aoife Grayson? Why is she so precious and dear to those squawking blackbirds?"

"Captain," said the old man. "We're on a full charge. We can outrun them."

"And drain our batteries halfway to land and drift around like a piece of garbage until we sink, suffocate, or run aground," Rasputina told him. "No. We're getting to the bottom of this now."

"I destroyed the Engine," I blurted. Rasputina snapped her gaze back to me, and the pistol wavered away from my head. The barrel was as black and endless as the space outside the dome in my dreams, and when it dropped to her side I let out a breath I hadn't been aware I was holding.

"Good lord," Rasputina said. "I knew you looked familiar."

"The Proctors are keeping Dean hostage until I get to the Bone Sepulchre. I have to . . ." I kept my eyes on the gun. My heart was thumping so loudly I could barely hear my own words. "I have to do what I did to the Engine. I have to destroy the heretics who live up there, where the Proctors can't reach, or they're going to kill the person I care about most."

That sounded plausible to me, and left out both the nightmare clock and Draven's compass, ticking away like a tiny evil bomb in my satchel.

Rasputina holstered her pistol. She looked at the blinking blob on the radar screen and back at me. "So you're not a spy. You're an assassin."

"Look," I said. "I'm doing what I have to, for Dean. I'm not happy about it, but if either of us wants to survive long enough to try to find a way out of this, you better get the hell away from the coast while they're holding their fire."

Rasputina's mouth set in a hard, long line, like the blade of a knife. "You better be telling me the truth."

"I am," I said quietly.

"Dive," Rasputina said to the old man. "Ten degrees down. Make your depth one-zero meters."

The dive officer grumbled his assent in Russian, and a bell rang three times, short and sharp. The sub dove, the rivets of the hull creaking and groaning all along its length. Rasputina straightened her cap and jacket after she removed the rain gear, then touched me on the arm. "Come with me, Aoife."

She took me to the captain's quarters this time, a small, curved room like the one I'd tried to sleep in, but paneled with real wood instead of rust-bubbled steel. The insignia of the Crimson Guard was inlaid in the wall above the bed. Someone had hacked a thick slash mark through it.

Rasputina got a bottle of clear liquid out of her footlocker, along with two glasses. She poured an inch into each and pushed one at me. "I suppose I should apologize," she said. "For holding a gun to your head."

"You had a good reason," I said. I would have done exactly the same in her position, and I knew it. I wasn't angry that she'd threatened me, just terrified that she'd realize that the story I'd come up with about destroying the Brotherhood was bunk. If she found out Draven was tracking me, using her ship as a pilot fish, I'd be out a hatch faster than I could blink.

"We're going to be dead in the water after that dive, unless we put in at Newfoundland," Rasputina said. She let the words hang between us, regarding me as she swirled her drink in her glass.

I sniffed at mine. It smelled faintly like the incendiaries rioters tossed at Proctors during the every-other-day upheavals in Lovecraft. "I'm going to the Bone Sepulchre one way or the other," I told Rasputina. "I won't let the Proctors hurt Dean."

"And to protect your love, you will destroy another's life? All of the Brotherhood?" Rasputina asked.

"It's not . . . ," I started, my face heating. Was *love* the right word to describe what Dean and I had?

"A woman after my own heart," Rasputina said. She tossed her drink back. *"Na Zdorov'ye."*

I drank mine. It burned my throat and made me cough. Rasputina chuckled. "You can walk around the boat, but don't get in the way. We'll be a few hours yet up the coast."

"So you'll take me to the Arctic Circle?" I said, refusing to budge. Rasputina waved me away with an annoyed gesture.

"I can't very well leave Dean Harrison to rot, can I? Damn that boy." She stood and opened her door, the signal for me to leave. I started to obey, then stopped. "Why do you trust me? Just like that?"

"Because," Rasputina said. I didn't know if the drink had made her more expansive, or outrunning the Proctors, but her iron-hard face softened. "Once, I was a girl who believed in the Crimson Guard above all else. I signed on to the navy at fourteen. And I served, until the day our engine batteries ruptured and the commander abandoned ship. The batteries were leaking toxins, and we were left to die. Expendable to the cause." She cleared her throat. "A few of us made a lifeboat, but it sank in the freezing waters, and I washed ashore near Lovecraft. A heretic boy took me in, fed me, got me clothes. And when I found the commander who'd left us all to die for his own ends, I took his new ship and I never looked back, at his cause or any other."

She moved aside to let me out then, her stony expression falling back into place. "Dean Harrison is a good boy, Aoife. And if he'd risk his neck for you, I'll help you risk yours for him. I just hope you have a plan of your own and not just the Proctors'."

"Oh, yes," I said, though I was sure it wasn't the kind of plan Rasputina was thinking of. My secrets were still my own. That was Dean's only real chance. "It's a good plan," I assured her. She looked like she doubted me, but before she could say anything, there was a great clanking groan, and the entire sub vibrated beneath us.

"What *now*?" Rasputina snarled, shoving past me. The old man with the beard met her halfway down the corridor.

"Captain, the main rotors on the starboard propeller are jammed," he said. "The jam is tearing the entire screw assembly apart. We're bleeding power."

"Then have someone fix it, chief," she snarled. "What do I have Jakob and Piotr for if they're not going to fix the damn ship when it breaks down?"

"They're trying," the chief said. "But it's a complicated problem."

I could fix their problem. At what cost, I didn't know. Being inside iron was already starting to make me feel woozy, see flickers of light and shadow at the corners of my eyes. But if we didn't get moving, Dean would be doomed for sure and I'd never reach the Brotherhood. I went to Rasputina and lifted my hand. "I can fix it."

Rasputina and the chief both scoffed at me. "You?" Rasputina said. "You can't even fix that bird's nest you call hair."

"I'm good with machines," I insisted, ignoring her jab. "If your engineers can't fix it, then what do you have to lose by letting me try? I was an engineering student in Lovecraft. I can't make things any worse."

"You could blow up the boat, and all of us with it," the chief snapped. "Get back to your bunk, little girl."

"Look," I said, glaring at him. "I'm not an idiot. I can fix your propeller without blowing up your submersible. So you can accept that the *little girl* might know what she's talking about, or we can all sit here until this bucket rusts through and we sink to the bottom."

"She's right," Rasputina said, heading off what was sure to be a shouting match between the chief and me. "We're dead. Never mind that the Proctors, the Canadian Coast Guard, or another rogue sub could pick us up at any moment."

"Fine," the chief snapped. Rasputina cocked her head.

"Yes, it is fine. I'm the captain, and I give the orders, and you nod."

The chief muttered a slew of Russian, and I watched Rasputina's brows draw together. "If my father were here, he'd give the same order. But he's not here. This is my boat now, so take the girl to the engine room, get her a suit and a set of tools and get her working." She pointed a leather-gloved finger at me. "Fix my ship, Aoife Grayson."

I felt the urge to salute but quashed it. "Yes, ma'am." I just hoped fixing the propeller would actually be a feat of engineering, rather than a feat of magic that caused my brain to short-circuit from the pressure of my Weird.

The chief grabbed me by the arm and dragged me toward the rear of the boat, despite my protests that I could walk on my own. "Aoife, eh," he grunted. "What kind of name is Aoife?"

"It means 'radiant,'" I said. "At least, that's what my mother always told me."

The chief snorted his obvious derision. "Why?" I demanded. "What's *your* name?"

"Alexei Sorkin," he grunted. "Dive chief of this boat. And medical officer, since we have no real one. I am the one who restarted your heart when the cold water stopped it."

"And what's the boat's name?" I asked. I was chattering a bit, trying to keep my mind focused outside of myself so that I couldn't think about the slowly blossoming flower of a headache just behind my eyes.

Not a headache, I knew. *Madness.*

"Her name is the *Oktobriana*," Chief Sorkin answered. "After the warrior heroine of the Crimson Guard."

"You were one of them?" I asked. "Like Captain Ivanova?"

"You ask a lot of questions for such a little girl," Sorkin said curtly, and ducked through a hatch into a steamy space that smelled of oil and metal shrieking against metal. When I hesitated, he grabbed me by the wrist and pulled me along with him. "I thought you said you knew your way around engines."

"I do," I said curtly. I didn't know why I expected a bunch of grouchy Russian sailors to treat me like a lady, but it was starting to irritate me that they didn't at least treat me like I had a brain. "I like engines better than people, most of the time. I definitely do right now," I added, and Sorkin surprised me by barking a laugh.

"Ah, so you are little but you have sharp teeth! I like it." We delved farther into the engine room, and steam all but obscured my vision, giving me uncomfortable memories of the Mists.

"Who's there?" said a voice from the white world beyond.

"Jakob, this is Aoife," said the chief. He mispronounced

it "Effie" instead of "Ee-fah," but I didn't bother correcting him. "She claims she can fix our boat."

When he finally came into view, I was surprised to see that Jakob was as thin as Cal and about my height. He was practically miniature, and his ocean-blue eyes shone from his grease-streaked face with an eerie brightness. "Huh" was all he said.

"Have at it. Piotr will be forward if you need him," Sorkin told me, and turned around to stomp back to the main part of the sub.

Alone and suddenly out of my element, I stared at Jakob for a long, awkward moment, and he stared back. "Do you speak much English?" I asked at last.

"Just a little," he admitted. His accent wasn't the rich, rounded syllables of Rasputina's or the bear's growl that Sorkin had. I couldn't quite put my finger on it, but I wouldn't have called it Russian. Well, they were a pirate crew. Jakob could be from anywhere. I had the niggling thought I'd heard that sort of accent somewhere before, but I put it aside.

"That's better than no Russian, which is what I speak," I said to him. "What happened here?"

Jakob extended a handful of what looked like limp rubber noodles, nipped neatly at the ends. "Somebody cut the coolant lines. Batteries, they power the propellers. We recharge in port, but the batteries need coolant or they can overheat and then . . ." He made a *boom* motion with his hands. Rasputina's story came back to me with new, stark reality. Overheated batteries could rupture and start leaking acid, causing toxic fumes. A sub trapped below the waves with no power to surface and no fresh air would have a dead crew in a matter of hours.

It was imperative I get this boat working again, not just for the sake of our journey, but for the sake of all our lives, not to mention my sanity. My head throbbed a bit and the pain warned me not to get overexcited or I'd speed the passage of the iron through my system.

"That's bad," I said.

"We don't start the starboard propeller again, we go in circles, but nowhere else," Jakob said. He twirled his finger to demonstrate.

"But if somebody sabotaged the boat . . . ," I said. What on earth could be going on? Even if Draven had a spy on board, he *wanted* me to reach my destination. Sabotaging the *Oktobriana* accomplished nothing.

"I said, we can't worry about that right now," Jakob said. "Unless we want to drift where the current takes us, what matters now is getting the boat started again."

"All right, all right," I told him. "I'm working on it." I wasn't used to being so easily dismissed, but Jakob was right. What mattered now was fixing the boat.

I put my hands on the casing of the rotors, the whole assembly of the motor that drove the sub, feeling out the gears and pistons and letting my mind get a sense of the machine within. "Will you be able to replace the coolant?"

Jakob nodded. "I'm working on it now."

I nodded back and placed my forehead against the engine case. My Weird whispered to me, and I looked at Jakob. "You have some tools I can use?"

I didn't have the control to fix the broken bits of the *Oktobriana* purely with my mind. It was different from picking a lock or starting an aethervox. And my Weird was better at destruction, anyway.

We worked in silence for a while, Jakob's taciturn grunts when I asked him to pass me a tool the only sounds. My sweat soaked through every layer of my clothes, and I stripped down to my undershirt. Jakob took off his shirt, period. His upper torso was smooth and perfect, not a scar, not a mark. For a pirate mechanic, he was in remarkably good shape. He saw me looking and his blue eyes sharpened. "What?"

"Nothing," I said, blushing furiously. "I'm sorry."

Jakob drew closer to me, and his pale, almost translucent skin caught the aether lamps lighting the engine room, making him look as if he were carved from stone. I backed up, banged into the side of the rotor assembly and realized too late I had nowhere to go.

I was totally alone with Jakob. It was doubtful anyone at the other end of the *Oktobriana* would hear me if I screamed. *Stupid, Aoife,* I berated myself. *Stupid, stupid, stupid.*

My shoulder began throbbing, as if someone held a hot iron to it, and I gasped as I cringed from Jakob's hot breath in my face. His hand landed on my shoulder, and a thin blade found the soft spot on my neck, under the jawbone, pressing tight and causing me to suck in my breath lest it nick my skin. "Don't move," Jakob purred in my ear. His strange, musical accent filled my ears, even more than my panicked, pounding heart, and all at once I placed the voice, the too-bright eyes, the unearthly alabaster skin.

"Fae," I said, my voice strained as I tried not to move against the knife. "You're Fae."

He didn't reply, just pressed the knife harder against my flesh. It didn't make any sense. Why try to leave us helpless in the water if all he wanted was my death, in the end? Was he an agent of Tremaine's? How was he surviving, trapped in an iron tube, when I was already getting the first symptoms of poisoning?

Jakob still didn't say anything. The pain in my shoulder was dizzying, and I felt tears squeeze from the corners of my eyes from fear. "Who are you?" I choked out. "What are you going to do to me?"

"I got you alone to deliver a message," Jakob said. "You always have to be the clever one, Aoife. The one to fix things." He kicked the door to the engine compartment shut, never moving the blade from my throat. Thin, and made from pure hardened silver—Tremaine had a similar knife. He'd also held it to my neck, and it hadn't made me any more inclined to listen to him than I was to listen to Jakob. "Nobody can break in here. Nobody will hear you scream." The knife pressed, and I felt a thin line of blood trickle down into the hollow of my throat. "The message is this, Aoife—the Brotherhood can't help you. The nightmare clock can't help you. Your only chance to find your mother is to come back to Tremaine and beg for forgiveness."

A pounding started up outside the door. "Effie! Effie, girl! What is happening in there?"

Jakob cut his eyes toward Chief Sorkin's voice, but he was immovable, and quick as a cat besides. I stood no chance of trying to get away on my strength alone. My father's words came back to me: *You're not much in a stand-up fight.*

“Shut up, Dad,” I grumbled. Jakob cocked his head, then smiled, a thin smile. He turned his wrist to dig the knife in more, and I caught a flash of a flaw in the skin of his wrist, a brand of some sort, which surrounded a small metal rivet. My Weird responded, frantic and hot against my mind in my panic. I had an idea, just a germ of one. I might not be a fighter, but I was smart. And Jakob hadn’t counted on how badly I wanted to live.

Rasputina’s voice joined the clamor outside. “Open this door, Jakob! What’s happening in there?” Something heavy hit, and Sorkin shouted.

“Jammed, Captain! Something is wrong!”

Rather than focus on Jakob, his pointed features, his now-pupil-less blue eyes, I focused on the door. Using my Weird felt like driving a drill through my temple, and blood gushed from my nose, but the wheel that opened the door turned, ever so slowly, and then, with one last push, flew back and dented the bulkhead with a clang like a coffin lid.

Rasputina and Sorkin stood there, and Jakob spun me to face them, arm clamped across my shoulders, knife at my neck. I was closer to this Fae than I’d ever been to anyone, even to Dean, and I could feel his heart beating. “You little sneak,” he hissed in my ear.

I snarled, not willing to be afraid of his blade or the fact that a Fae was here, alive, aboard an iron ship. “What? Did Tremaine fail to mention that?”

Rasputina drew her pistol and aimed it at us. “Jakob,” she said softly. “Your eyes. What’s wrong with your eyes?”

Jakob’s laugh was short and harsh as a seal’s bark. “*My* eyes? Nothing, you idiot woman. My eyes are open. Yours are closed. You are ignorant to everything around you, especially me."

I twisted my neck a bit while he ranted, trying to see if I had any give with the knife. There wasn't much. Jakob's skin felt cold and clammy where his bare torso pressed against me, and I caught a glimpse of his eyes, which had so alarmed Rasputina. Fae eyes gleamed with an inner light. If I were Rasputina, I'd have been losing my cool staring into them as well.

"Speak," Rasputina said. "You've been loyal crew for months, Jakob. What are you going to do to this girl?"

"Cut her throat if you don't lower that crude weapon and leave us to our business," Jakob snarled. "And also if she declines to obey my terms."

Fury flared in me. Tremaine still thought he controlled me, either via an agent or directly, through my fear of the Fae catching up to me. Now it had happened, and strangely, I wasn't panicking. I was just furious. "It wouldn't be the first time," I told Jakob. "My brother sliced my throat. He almost killed me. I was bleeding all over myself. I'm not going to scream and beg."

"You mad bastard," Rasputina said, lowering the hammer on her pistol. The click echoed in the closed space, and I swallowed in fear, acutely aware that I was in the way of the bullet.

"Let the girl go." Her voice had gone soft, placating, more like that of a kindly teacher than that of a captain. "This can still end with everyone alive, Jakob."

"She's a destroyer," Jakob snarled. "When she turns the wheel and opens the kingdom, they will come and come and come, come from the stars and cover this world, and the next, and the next. . . ."

Finally, my opening. I recognized those ramblings—iron madness, eating into your brain until you just rambled endlessly, about the things only you could see. My mother had talked about the same things.

I snapped my head back into Jakob's face, feeling something give—something nose-shaped. Jakob yelped, the knife skidding down my neck and over my collarbone as he windmilled.

Rasputina's arm never wavered; she didn't even blink. The gunshot was impossibly loud, stole all sense of sound from me, and I felt the bullet fly through the air next to my face.

She missed Jakob by inches, the bullet digging another dent in the bulkhead, and he bared his teeth. They weren't pointed like Tremaine's, but they were white and sharp, ready to tear flesh.

I didn't know for sure that it'd work, but I didn't hesitate. I grabbed Jakob's wrist, above the brand surrounding the curious metal rivet. Fae couldn't survive in iron. I dug my fingernails into the spot and accessed my Weird.

Jakob groaned and swiped at me with the knife, but Sorkin darted forward and pinned his arm to the bulkhead with a roar. I felt skin, blood and metal beneath my nails, and Jakob's screams spurred me on. I yanked on the piece of metal—silver, I saw now, carved in the shape of a tapered screw, going all the way down to Jakob's bone—with my fingers and my Weird together.

Splitting pain in my skull, a shattering scream from Jakob, and he collapsed, still, on the floor of the engine room.

I looked down at my bloody hand, which gripped the silver screw. My shoulder throbbed at the contact with it. Powerful Fae enchantments were wound around this piece of silver—powerful enough, I thought, to keep a Fae citizen alive in the Iron Land for months.

"Jakob," said Rasputina, bending down and feeling for his pulse. Jakob thrashed and screamed when she touched his skin, as if her touch were flame, and I darted back, into the arms of Sorkin, who held me steady.

"It's all right, little girl," he rumbled. "It's going to be all right."

I tried to pull away, to get to Jakob and make sure he was really finished. Rasputina had no idea what she'd let onto her boat, and as she shook Jakob by the shoulders, I wanted to snatch her away, to scream that she wasn't nearly as afraid as she should be.

Jakob was even paler than he had been, all his veins standing out, as he grabbed for Rasputina.

"Burn, witch!" he shrieked. "You burn! Bright as the red fire they put into your blood!"

Rasputina jerked her hand back. "What are you saying?" Her face had gone from flushed to pale in an instant, and she drew away from Jakob's twitching body.

He giggled, and I flinched. It wouldn't be long now. This much iron around a full-blooded Fae . . . I didn't want to think about what would happen when the poison took full effect.

It would be too much like looking into my future.

"The fire and the ice," Jakob hissed. "The beginning and the end. The waking dreamer there, Aoife Grayson, will end you. She'll drown the whole world, and she'll do it with a smile." His laughter turned into a shrill scream. "I don't want the clockwork inside me! I don't want the dreams!" His hand lashed out again, and he snatched Rasputina's pistol from her belt.

"No—" she started. Not a shout, not an exclamation, just the softest beginning of a plea, before Jakob put the barrel to his chin and squeezed the trigger.

I immediately tucked my head down against my shoulder, and the force of the gunshot slapped me like a hand. Rasputina screamed, and I stayed perfectly still, with my eyes screwed shut, until she stopped. I didn't want to look.

Footsteps raced, and other crewmembers who'd heard the shot from outside came spilling in. There was yelling, in Russian and French and half a dozen other languages, and still I stayed where I was, until Rasputina got off the floor, scraping the fine spray of blood off her cheeks, and grabbed me by the arms. I braced myself to be hit. The rage and confusion on her face were plain, and those feelings only led to one place, in my experience.

But after a long moment, she let go of me. "You better be worth it" was all she said before she picked up her cap from the floor and put it back on her head, sweeping past the crew and out of the engine room.

I stayed. I had to see, to make sure Jakob was really gone. Crewmembers bundled his body into an oilcloth sack and hauled it away, and only then, as they brought a mop and bucket to scrub up the blood, did I open my hand.

The enchanted silver had bitten deep divots into my flesh, but the thing was dead now, no more magical than a bread box.

Tremaine had known where I would be before I'd known

myself. Had sent an agent ahead to retrieve me. Had willfully put close to fifty lives in danger just to get me alone, to deliver his message to me. And I wasn't surprised at any of it. That was Tremaine's way—destroy an Engine, destroy a city, destroy my life. Nothing mattered but the agenda of the Fae, and his agenda in particular.

I made my way back to my bunk, past crew who gave me a wide berth. I looked down at myself and saw that I was covered in Jakob's blood. I was as numb as I'd been when Sorkin and Rasputina had pulled me from the ocean—all that mattered was that the Fae knew where I was.

My legs were rubbery and my heart was thudding as I collapsed on my bunk, listening to the *Oktobriana*'s screws come back to life and feeling the slight sway in my stomach that said we were under way. At least I'd accomplished that much. We were still headed north. Draven wouldn't take out his wrath on Dean just yet.

Having come that close to being taken to Tremaine again made me nauseous. Draven was malicious, but I could outthink him, outmaneuver him. I knew I was smarter, and that I could make a plan that both kept Dean alive and got me what I wanted from the Brotherhood.

With Tremaine, I had no such assurances. He'd fooled me before, made me a virtual puppet, and now he'd gotten close enough to draw blood, all without my seeing it. I'd done what he wanted, I thought, with the same burning rage I'd felt when I'd fought off Jakob. I'd started a slow hurricane that would eventually sweep the entire Iron Land bare. And yet he still wanted me. For what?

The only answer I could muster was that it was more important than ever for me to find the nightmare clock. It could deal with Draven, with the Fae, with all my mistakes. Find it, use it, set things right. That was my only course now, no matter what the cost.

Being resolute helped me calm down a little, but only a little. I wiped the blood off myself as best I could with the single towel Rasputina had provided and shut the door. I got back into bed, and pulled my legs up to my chest and a blanket around my shoulders. Draven might have given me passage that kept me safe from the Proctors, and Rasputina had agreed to carry me, but the journey to the Bone Sepulchre was turning out to be anything but easy.

Rasputina knocked on my door after a time. "Join me in my cabin," she said, and gestured me into the corridor. I was too tired to argue, or even to wonder what she was going to do to me. Nothing she could come up with would be worse than Draven or Tremaine.

We took the same seats, the two small chairs, but there was no offer of a drink this time, and Rasputina didn't stare a hole in me as if she could read my thoughts. "Are you going to tell me what happened to Jakob?"

"You wouldn't believe me if I did," I said. I could have put my head down and slept there—Rasputina's cabin was warm and smelled faintly of cinnamon. It reminded me a bit of our old apartment in Lovecraft, the last we'd had before Nerissa was committed.

"You looked scared when he talked to you," I said. "He knew things about you nobody does, right? Things you never told anyone?"

Rasputina took off her cap and rubbed her forehead in

distress. She'd washed most of the blood off, but a faint line of pink lingered at her hairline. I looked down at my own rust-streaked hands and shuddered. The gunshot seemed to echo in my ears.

"And *how* do you know *that*?" Rasputina asked at last.

"Jakob isn't a man," I said, and then amended it. "*Wasn't*. He was a creature from a world that's close to ours, but isn't ours. He was poisoned by iron in the ship. He was here to spy on me." That was as simple as I could make it. The Crimson Guard didn't deny magic and the other lands as heresy like the Proctors did, so I thought maybe Rasputina would be willing to believe me. I hoped she was, because otherwise she was sure to think I was insane, just as all those people back in Lovecraft did.

"I grew up in a village called Dogolpruydny," Rasputina said softly. She tipped her head back and shut her eyes. "A wild place, mostly run by crime lords. The Crimson Guard press-gangs children to serve as grunts in their army, but otherwise, the people there are less than cattle to those in the capital." She sighed. "There are things roaming the streets at night. Halfway between men and dogs. They feed on your blood, and they are deathless. Not even bullets can stop them."

My mouth felt dry. I remembered some of the creatures that lurked below the surface of Lovecraft. Even Cal's family, the only ghouls I'd met not out for my blood, was unsettling. I couldn't imagine how Rasputina had survived.

"One caught me one night," Rasputina said. "I was small, and slow. Sick much of the time. It bit me, but it didn't like my taste." She opened her eyes again and went to the steam hob, rattling a teapot. "I found out in that moment that my blood is poison to the deathless creatures that come from that dark place, the place your Proctors insist doesn't exist." She turned on the water and watched it hiss from the tap with great concentration. "I just don't know what they want with you."

"They want me to do something," I said. "It's part of why I'm going north. I can't do what they ask, and I can't escape them, as you saw." I wrapped my arms around myself. Since I'd come aboard the *Oktobriana,* I hadn't been able to get warm. I didn't know if it was from having been frozen or from my creeping apprehension that I was making a huge mistake.

But I couldn't think that way. This was my only choice.

"And the other part is Dean?" Rasputina poured the hot water over a tea strainer and swirled the pot a bit, steam rising to obscure her face.

I looked at my hands, not able to meet her eyes. "I don't know if we should be talking about this, seeing as you two have history. Dean tends to make me say things I don't mean to."

Rasputina choked on the tea she'd poured and then started to laugh. I flushed and blinked at her, surprised. I wasn't sure what I'd said that was so funny.

"Oh," she said, "he does, does he. Rest well, Aoife—we are friends, and I am grateful to him for saving my life, but Dean is not my type, not in age and not in the sense that he's . . . well, a boy."

"Oh," I said, realization dawning. "*Oh.*"

"See? You are smart," Rasputina told me. "And loyal. And fearless. Dean is damn lucky to have you." She checked her chronometer, a wrist style that I'd always wanted but could never afford. "We'll be at Newfoundland in a half hour or so. Try to keep out of the way until then, all right? My crew will be busy."

I got up and managed to smile my assent, but at that moment all I could think of was that I might never see Dean again. There was a chance I wouldn't even make it back to the United States, never mind free him from Draven and tell him I thought Rasputina was right but the reverse was also true—I was lucky to have Dean.

At least I knew it in my heart, even if I never got a chance to tell him.

Below the Ice World

Fifth entry:

This boat, and Rasputina, made me realize something important: even if I never see him again, I'll never forget Dean Harrison. He's quiet and strong, and he doesn't fuss and worry over me like every other man I've known. I could see myself standing next to Dean for the rest of my life.

I don't know anything about love. I don't know what it's supposed to feel like. I don't think birds swoop down and bells chime, like in those stupid romances other girls at the Academy loved to giggle over. I think it might be more like the Gothic novels our house matron, Mrs. Fortune, read when she wasn't looking after us—if two people are in love, you may be torn apart by circumstance, but you're always together, at least in your hearts.

Of course, it's not a scheming stepmother keeping me

and Dean apart. It's someone much worse. Draven knew exactly where to cut me to draw the most blood. I hate that he's not willfully ignorant like most Proctors. I hate that if I'm honest, he's as smart as me, if not smarter. I hate him, in the way that spreads poison through a mind. The more I think about Dean being under his control, the more I hate Draven. Hatred is not what my father would choose in this situation. He'd stay calm. He'd figure out some horribly clever solution. He'd fix everything.

There's Draven. There's my father and Valentina. There's the Brotherhood. Three directions, all pulling at me, like I'm the magnet in a compass. All wanting different things, all wanting to use me for different things. And now Tremaine, letting me know he hasn't forgotten, that he wants more from me than everything I've already given. He's the worst, because I know that he will be unceasing until I bend to his will.

I'm so tired of being shuttled from one place to another like a ball in a maze. I want to stand up, but I can't. I have to pretend to work for Draven, for Dean's sake. I had to lie to my father to find my mother. And I have to face the Brotherhood, with more lies, for everyone else in the world, at the same time avoiding being pulled back to the Fae and whatever new scheme Tremaine has for me to take part in.

So many lies. I don't even know how many layers deep they go any longer. I don't think I'll ever be who I used to be after this is over. The Aoife Grayson who left Lovecraft is dead. And I don't know who's taken her place.

* * *

Once we'd recharged the batteries and cast off from Newfoundland, the routine on the submersible was unceasing and unchanging. The crew slept in shifts, and everyone had a job to do. I was frequently in the way, so I took to spending a lot of time sitting in the mess, playing backgammon or checkers with off-duty crewmembers, many of whom didn't speak a lick of any language I knew. The mood was bleak—everyone knew what had happened to Jakob, if not the details leading up to it, and that I was somehow involved, and many of the crew wouldn't even make eye contact, never mind try to talk to me.

Not that I minded much. I was busy turning over every piece of information I'd gleaned about the Brotherhood, and planning how I'd approach them. I had to appear to be on their side, which wouldn't be too hard. I didn't have any love for the Fae, certainly. I just had to keep the compass hidden and figure out a way to put off Draven until I'd found the clock. Then his plans to ensnare everyone in his web wouldn't matter.

When Rasputina wasn't busy, she taught me a few snippets of Russian and told me about living in her childhood village, which sounded, if it was possible, even worse than life as a charity ward in Lovecraft.

"There are secret societies as well as press-gangers," she said one day as we were playing backgammon, "and they recruit children from poor neighborhoods. They make them runners, get them in trouble, and if they want to survive the gulag they have to join the society, get official tattoos and be bound to them forever." She moved a piece across the board. "It's that or the Crimson Guard. Don't know which is worse."

She looked up at me with that black bird's gaze. "So what are you trying to find up there, in the Bone Sepulchre? It's supposed to be haunted, you know. A place built centuries ago, with engineering not of this earth. They say you can only see it if you're about to die."

"I told you," I said. "I'm trying to stop what's happening back in Lovecraft. All the chaos and monsters everywhere. Sooner or later, it's going to cover the entire world, like the Storm did. The Brotherhood makes deals with the Fae and other creatures. They're the problem that needs destroying. And I'd . . ." I took a breath—I had to avoid saying too much. "I'd really like to have a good night's sleep," I finished.

"Wouldn't we all," Rasputina muttered, moving another piece. "I win," she announced. "You're horrible at this game."

"I'm better at machines than games and puzzles," I said. "My brother always beat the pants off me when we played backgammon."

"He's dead?" Rasputina said, with only the barest interest.

"No!" I exclaimed, alarmed that she'd automatically assume everyone I knew met a horrible end. "I mean, no, he was alive when I left. Angry at me, but alive."

"Hmph," Rasputina said. "Take it from me—family is like having a hundred pounds strapped to your legs."

"I take it you have one, then." Though I couldn't completely disagree with her about the weight, my life had certainly been simpler when I'd only been responsible for myself.

"I did." She shrugged. "My father was a drunk who had

only his boat, and my mother barely survived an attack by the deathless creatures that roamed our village. She was bedridden, and her medical bills cost us everything except the shack we lived in. They're probably dead now. I haven't seen them since the Crimson Guard took me." She collected the backgammon pieces and shut the board with a hard snap, her face rigid and carefully expressionless. "We're going under the ice in a few hours. We'll surface to scrub the air and then we'll be under until we get to the Arctic."

"How will we know when we're there?" I asked, surprised by her abrupt change of topic, but not willing to push her about her family. I knew how much that could sting.

"Stories go that the Bone Sepulchre can be seen under the aurora borealis," Rasputina said. "There's a launch for journeys over the glacier that pirates carved out a few hundred miles along once we go under the ice. We can come up there and look at the northern lights, see what we see." She sighed. "And I cannot believe I'm navigating to some place that I've only heard stories about on the say-so of a teenage girl."

"You're nineteen," I said with some indignation, having learned this fact during our earlier conversations. "Three years hardly makes me a girl in comparison."

"It's not the years," Rasputina said. "It's how you spend them." She waved me away. "I'll call you when we're under the ice. If you want a look at the sky before we dive, go up when we replenish our air. It'll be the last you'll see of it for a few days."

* * *

Diving under the ice was nerve-racking, even more than I'd imagined, and what I'd imagined wasn't pleasant. The sub scraped the underside of the glaciers, and chunks of what Sorkin told me were free-floating ice bumped the hull with alarming regularity. Once, we came upon a pod of whales and kept pace with them while Oksana, the radar officer, played their song through her speakers.

I distracted myself from the fact that one wrong turn could bring thousands of tons of ice down on the *Oktobriana*, pushing us deep into the lightless depths of the Arctic sea, by learning everything I could about how she worked.

The Crimson Guard had built the boat, but she'd been modified to run on aether batteries rather than a steam furnace that meant diving for only a few hours at a time. There was German tech in the sub too, salvaged from the war—air scrubbers and depth gauges and torpedoes. Its periscope had come from a Proctor vessel Rasputina had found stranded on the Outer Banks off North Carolina and salvaged ahead of a hurricane.

The batteries were running down, but they could still power the propellers and basic life support for days at a time, creeping along under the ice at a pace that seemed to be even slower than that of the glaciers above us.

The closer we got to the Arctic Circle, the less I slept. My dreams were tangled and terrible, no longer visits to the dream figure but often just writhing, screaming black masses that exuded the same kind of cold I imagined I'd feel in outer space, a cold that froze me in place so I couldn't run, couldn't even scream. Nobody else was dreaming, though—Sorkin remarked to me once that he was sleeping like a baby, deep and dreamless.

I knew what was happening—the iron was creeping into me. I realized after I woke up screaming for the third day in a row that I probably had less than twenty-four hours left before I started raving like Jakob. I had to get off the boat before then. I just hoped Rasputina knew what she was doing, and that the launch she'd talked about was where she thought it was.

That afternoon I was drinking some of the sludgy black Turkish coffee the crew swilled by the quart, trying desperately to keep my thoughts in order and not fall asleep again, when the screws of the *Oktobriana* slowed and then stopped. Rasputina stuck her head into the mess a moment later and jerked her chin at me. "Get your cold-weather gear and come topside. We're here."

13

The Spine of the Earth

NOTHING COULD HAVE prepared me for the cold outside the submersible, or the strange half-night sky that confronted us, bright on the horizon but fading to velvet black at the top, much like the ever-shifting sky of my dream place. I'd thought the wind was bad back home, that the ice and snow that enveloped Lovecraft from Hallows' Eve to spring thaw most years was as cold as anything could be, but it wasn't.

Even wrapped in a thick coat as I was, mask strapped over the lower half of my face and fur-lined goggles over my eyes to protect them from the wind, the cold crept in through all the cracks and stole my breath. Rasputina, wearing a navy greatcoat and a similar mask and goggles, gave no indication she even noticed it, and I envied her fortitude.

It was so cold that I felt like I might shatter, drop off the top of the *Oktobriana*'s conning tower, and become part of the ice, forever staring at the empty sky. Beyond the boat launch the sub rested in, which was only a small hole carved into the glacier allowing ocean water to surface, I saw nothing. The whiteness was gleaming and absolute, as if we stood atop the skeleton of a great beast of incalculable size.

"That's strange." Rasputina gingerly held a pair of binoculars. It was so cold that any spots of moisture clung to her gloves and ripped out tiny chunks of leather. She aimed the glasses at a tiny wooden shack at the edge of the launch. It barely hung on to the ice along with a ramshackle dock.

"What's strange?" I tried to shrink deeper into the coat and fur-lined pants and boots I'd been given, which wasn't hard since everything was at least two sizes too large. Another kind of cold crept in, that sixth sense I was developing that said things had gone horribly wrong. I was getting it now, and I hoped I was mistaken.

"There's no moon," Rasputina said.

"New moon," I said with a shrug, trying to seem unconcerned even though my heartbeat had picked up and my shivering was no longer entirely from the bone-deep cold.

Rasputina shook her head. "Half-moon. I checked the chart."

I turned my face up and scanned the sky. More stars than I had thought existed scattered the silver-black field of the sky, turning their unearthly white light on the glacier, which glowed as if alive.

But no moon. Not even the pockmarked slice Rasputina had said should be there. Not a sliver.

"That is strange," I agreed, because saying anything else would come across as either silly or panicked. Celestial bodies were constants. They did not change.

This was unnatural, and I wondered what had happened to make the sky so foreign here.

"I don't like this at all," Rasputina said, echoing my thoughts aloud.

I turned a slow circle. We were alone. I had never felt so exposed as I did at that moment, certain the great eye of something as ancient as the starlight was turned on the boat, the same something that was blotting out the moon and causing the dead, chill atmosphere that wrapped the *Oktobriana*.

"We're leaving," Rasputina said. "This launch has always been a bad spot. The captain who told me about it got his throat cut a week later. It's a cursed place."

"You don't seem like you'd believe in curses," I murmured.

"I believe in a lot of things," Rasputina snapped. "We're diving. Get below." She climbed down the conning tower, the thump of her boots against the ladder amplified in the ice field until each footstep was the thump of a coffin lid.

I stayed outside for a moment longer, hearing only my own breath against my mask.

At first I found the night around me silent except for the wind, but slowly I realized it wasn't. The launch was about the size of a soccer pitch, ridiculously small when you thrust a military submersible into it. Displaced water sluiced against the hull, and out in the night I could hear the ice cracking and knocking, over and over. It was an endless rattle, the sound of bone against bone.

Bone against bone.

My Weird tingled, and I gasped at the sharp pain against the front of my skull. I fumbled at my goggles, yanking them off, trying to get all the metal off my body to relieve the pain. As the filtered glass came away from my eyes, a thin finger of violet light unfurled in the sky above me, like pale blood in dark water. It was joined by greens, blues, yellows, dancing in concert.

I'd seen lanternreels of the aurora borealis, but these lights were nothing like that. The violet streak moved with a pattern, a purpose, with none of the randomness that indicated true northern lights. It flowed toward a point directly to the east of me, where the moon should have been.

The purple light gathered into a starburst, and it touched the very top of something growing out of the ice, the same color as the glacier and nearly invisible in the low light. Something so large that, from my vantage on the tower of the *Oktobriana*, it was blotting out the moon. Something that was reflecting starlight, like the ice and the sky, invisible until the aurora touched its spire.

It *was* ice and sky, I realized as I stared, forgetting that I was cold and ignoring the tears the wind sparked in the corners of my eyes. The aurora illuminated the massive shape by degrees, gleaming against its translucent ice walls. It was a palace, the kind you'd see in lanternreels of faraway lands or read about in forbidden fairy tales.

Or maybe it was a giant tomb, the kind that held the kings and princes of old, before the Storm or any of this at all. . . .

The Bone Sepulchre. My breath hitched, and I was helpless to look away as the violet light illuminated the surface. It was beautiful.

"Effie!" Sorkin bellowed from below. "We're diving! Get yourself below!"

"Just a minute!" I yelled back over the wind, unable to tear my eyes from the great edifice before me. I could pick it out of the glacier easily now. Smooth surfaces I'd taken for natural flaws became columns and balconies and a tower that reached so high it became part of the night sky.

The aurora flashed and vanished, all its energy running in lines down the Bone Sepulchre like an electric current through a living thing, lighting every window, every rampart, every spire. Shocked and overjoyed, I shouted for Rasputina and Sorkin to come topside and look, pulling aside my mask to scream until the cold stole my voice.

They came rushing up the ladder. The dive siren sounded below, but they ignored it, as transfixed as I was by the glowing sight before us.

Rasputina stared, her face slack with disbelief. "I'll be damned. It's real."

"It was the ice. The—the sound it makes," I stammered. "The sound like breaking bones. It made me think, and then I saw the lights. . . ."

"It was right here all this time," Rasputina muttered. "I could have been making a fortune doing this run."

I swung my leg over the conning tower and grabbed hold of the ladder leading down the outside, knowing what I had to do. I was so close—just a jump to the ice and a short walk to the dock.

"Where in this frozen hell do you think you're going?" Rasputina shouted at me. "You'll die out there with nothing but your coat!"

"Going where I meant to when I got on this boat!" I shouted back. I couldn't risk waiting around for more trouble in getting where I was going. I could make it. The

Bone Sepulchre was so close, I had to tilt my head back to see the top spire.

"You can't trek over ice!" Rasputina bellowed. "The snow could be six feet deep, and who knows how far away that thing really is!"

"Thanks for everything," I shouted, jumping from the bobbing boat to the ice. I turned back to wave to Rasputina and Sorkin. They'd taken me far enough. This part I could do on my own. The thought warmed me a bit. My satchel was under my coat—I had barely let it out of my sight since I'd boarded the *Oktobriana,* because if Rasputina or her crew found the compass or my diary . . . well, it didn't bear thinking about. I had everything I needed, minus a plan, but I'd deal with that when I actually reached the Brotherhood.

"Dammit, girl!" Rasputina shouted, leaning over the railing of the tower. "I am not responsible for you any longer! You are insane!"

My feet dug into the ice for balance, and I stood for a moment, staring at the Bone Sepulchre. I couldn't argue with Rasputina—the *idea* of trekking across ice and knocking on the Brotherhood's door unannounced was insane—but off the boat, in the open air with no iron close to me, I felt more lucid than I had in days.

I started walking, Rasputina's voice and the *Oktobriana*'s bulk fading behind me, until I was alone on the glacier, with only the stars for company.

The Bone Sepulchre was much farther away than it had looked under the glow of the aurora, and I felt as if I'd been walking for hours when I heard the bells. Not the dull tolling of the bells at St. Oppenheimer's back in Lovecraft, but a light tinkling that traveled to my ears across the windswept waste.

A shape came into view, whiter than the starlit ice field: a low conveyance of some kind, pulled by another hulking white shape.

The shape stopped, and something that at least *looked* human tugged at reins hung with sleigh bells. "Whoa."

The shape was alive. I stood perfectly still in surprise, wind buffeting the empty bits of my too-large coat and pants, as it huffed a puff of dragon's breath at me. Horns curled behind the creature's ears, and its fur hung shaggy and white. It stamped its black hooves and returned my stare with glowing gold eyes. I couldn't think of anything to say, so I just put up my hands in surrender. Better to let them think I was harmless, at least to start with.

Despite my gesture of surrender, the human in the sleigh pointed a very businesslike gun at me, which I found to be a bit extreme. "State your business," the man snapped. His eyes were covered by goggles like my own, and his winter gear was completely white, down to the fur on his collar, which looked suspiciously like the coat of the thing that pulled the sleigh. I didn't like talking to faceless people, be they Proctors or the Brotherhood, but I backed up a step and raised my hands higher.

"I'm Aoife Grayson," I said, over the howling wind. "I'm here to—"

Before I could finish, the faceless man vaulted from his seat and grabbed me, pressing the gun into my side and shoving me toward the sleigh. "Get in and get on the floor. Facedown."

I tried to comply, but he shoved me and I fell. My bulky coat saved me from smashing my ribs on the bench, but I landed on the satchel, and Draven's compass dug uncomfortably into my side. That was fine. As long as this man didn't think I was a spy, he could shove me around all he wanted. I'd do what I'd always done back in Lovecraft when faced with a bully: keep my head down and try not to draw attention.

The man holstered his gun and turned the sleigh around, clucking loudly at the creature pulling it until it broke into an awkward gallop.

"Boy oh boy," the man muttered to himself. "Wait until they see who I've got here." He let out a surprisingly high-pitched cackle for such a big, gruff type. I stayed quiet not so much because he scared me, but because I was finally sheltered from the wind, which was a relief.

The ride was bumpy, at least from where I lay on the floor. The ice looked smooth, but we jittered and bounced, and the thing pulling us panted in a harsh rhythm in sync with my heartbeat.

When we slowed, I chanced a look up. We had passed through a carved archway, and doors slid shut behind us—doors of ice that blurred the outside world but didn't cause it to disappear entirely. If I hadn't been being held at gunpoint, I would have been thrilled by the engineering skill it took to carve an entire room and working mechanical doors from a glacier.

"Get up," the man ordered, and I did as he said. The cold wasn't so paralyzing indoors, but it still sliced straight through my coat. I wrapped my arms around myself protectively to keep the bulge of the satchel hidden as he shoved me down from the sleigh.

"Goggles and hood off," the man ordered, and snatched them off my head before I could comply on my own. I chewed on my lip and waited for his reaction, my stomach knotted with apprehension.

He looked at me and then snorted behind his own mask. "You know, for all the flap about you back in the world, you're still just a kid."

"And you're not a gentleman," I responded. "What of it?"

He raised his free hand and pointed a scolding finger at me. "Destroyer of the Engine or not, Gateminder heir or just Grayson's bastard—you don't get to speak to me like that, and I'll put you in your place next time you do."

I bristled at the mention of my father. The destroyer label was going to stick to me—I accepted that now—but my family was off-limits.

"Now, now, Bruce," someone said before I could slap the man across the face. The voice was full and resplendent, as if it should have been echoing from a pulpit somewhere. "That's no way to talk to the favorite child of the Gateminder."

I turned to look, curious about my rescuer. The man who'd spoken wore a white padded coat trimmed in fur, like the first man's, but suit pants protruded from beneath, along with shoes shined to a high gloss. Not clothes for the outside, and not the clothes of someone low on the totem pole. His hood was down, and I took in a full head of white hair gleaming under the violet-tinged light that still danced through the ice walls all around us. "Well, well," he said.

"Aoife Grayson, in the flesh." He frowned at me. "Do you know who I am?"

I recognized the blunt nose, not nearly as attractive on a man, and the snapping eyes. I tried to sound as if I knew what I was talking about, as if my being here having this conversation were normal. "You're Valentina Crosley's father."

"Ah, very perceptive," he said. "I see you've met my dear daughter. Tell me, how is she faring on her own, with your . . . father?"

I pretended not to notice that he evidently would much rather have used another word in place of *father* and put a smile I wholly didn't feel on my face. "She's well. They both are."

He held out his hand, and his smile was also false. So we were going to be achingly polite rather than confrontational. That suited me just fine—I wanted the Brotherhood to like me. "My name is Harold Crosley, and I hope that you and I will get along *very* well indeed, Miss Grayson. It's such a relief to have you among the fold."

I didn't take his hand. It was crucial that I choose the right response, if I was going to make the Brotherhood trust me. Or trust me for long enough that I could find the nightmare clock and figure out how to use it, at any rate. "Really?" I said. "A relief? A happy occasion? Do you think I'm stupid, Mr. Crosley?" I took a breath and kept going, even though I was quaking with the fear that they wouldn't let me finish my performance and the big jerk with the gun would just shoot me for insolence. "You know what I did in Lovecraft," I told Crosley. "You should want to throw me in a deep, dark hole and never let me see daylight again. Not only did I destroy the Engine and break the Gates in the Iron Land, I weakened all the others. Plus, I'm Archie Grayson's daughter. The Archie Grayson who stole your darling daughter Valentina away." I folded my arms across my chest in an imitation of Dean's posture, hoping I looked tough. "And yet you're *happy* to see me at your doorstep? Why is that, Mr. Crosley?"

"Why are you here?" he countered with a smile. It wasn't the false smile he'd shown before—this one told me he'd been proven right about something he'd suspected. "If we're so bound to do you wrong and you're such a villain," Crosley continued, "I'd have to conclude you're only here because you want something from us, and that you're going to try to use deceit to get it. I'd hate to think such a thing of a Grayson, young lady. Even if Archie and I are no longer civil."

"You have something my father doesn't," I said. For once, I could tell lying wasn't going to get me anywhere. Crosley was a lot more accomplished at it than I was.

"And what's that?" His mouth twitched with amusement. He must have loved having somebody from my family need something from him.

"I need to look at the Iron Codex," I said. My father's journals had told me a little when I'd read them back in Massachusetts, but not everything. Not much of actual use. Short of being knocked unconscious, I didn't even know how to reach the dream room, with its dark figure. I had no idea how to manipulate the clock should I make it there. I needed the Codex.

"That's interesting," Crosley said. "You need my Codex and I need somebody with a Weird, which we're fully aware that your brother does not possess."

Valentina's hushed and frantic conversation came back to me. Now it made sense. Mr. Crosley wanted my Weird, and she hadn't wanted to give me up. "Then you'll let me look at it?"

"Maybe." Crosley shrugged. "If your Weird can help us as much as I think it can."

He didn't trust me, that was obvious. "I don't know how much my Weird can help anyone," I murmured. "You've seen what it can do."

"You'll come to understand, Aoife," Crosley said quietly, "we don't revile you for what happened. We know how the Fae can be, and that it wasn't your fault, the incident with the Gates. We're glad you came to us." He put a hand on my shoulder, snaking me into his grasp. "What say before we continue this conversation we get you warmed up somewhere a little more comfortable. Are you hungry?"

"Famished," I said truthfully. Relief coursed through me. I was in.

Crosley smiled even wider when I assented. It was a sweet trap of a smile this time, the kind designed to entice little girls who wanted to show they were clever.

"I'm glad you found your way home, Aoife. It's good work we do here, and the Gateminder and future Gateminders like you are needed for every bit of it. We're glad to have you."

"I'm so very glad to be here," I replied, and let him lead me through the doors.

* * *

Beyond the doors lay a great hall, at least thirty feet from floor to ceiling. Icicles dangled from the roof. "Is this whole place made of ice?" I asked in wonder. I couldn't conceive of such a feat.

"It is. And never more than thirty-two degrees," Crosley said proudly. "Don't worry, we'll get you out of that outfit and into something that'll keep you warm." He marched straight through the hall, ignoring the stares of the other occupants. There were a fair number of people in the room. Reading tables lined the gleaming ice walls, along with workbenches, and there was even a depression in the ice where a pair of mechanics bent over the innards of a clockwork jitney.

"Why do you use those sleighs if you have mechanicals?" I asked. I figured the more inane questions I asked of him, the less suspicious he would be of any ulterior motives I might have.

"Engines seize up in low temperatures," Crosley said. "That critter that pulled you in here with the sleigh—it's a yetikin—bred for the cold."

"I see," I said, and forced a ladylike smile. I couldn't care less about what pulled the Brotherhood's sleighs, but Crosley seemed content to chatter while we walked, and as long as I acted like a simpering schoolgirl, nothing I said would give him a second's pause.

"This way, my dear," he said, and ushered me into what looked like a men's clubroom: all dark furniture, distinguished suits and jackets on the occupants, and air full of their cigar smoke and heavy, hushed conversation. A carved bar took up the back portion, a bartender in a natty white jacket and scarf hard at work.

"Would you like a cup of tea?" Crosley asked, sitting me in one of the engulfing armchairs. I sank so deep that I wouldn't easily get out again, especially in my bulky cold-weather clothes.

"A cup of tea would be lovely, please," I said. "Thank you so much." I didn't like being backed into a corner, in this chair, unable to gauge what was happening around me, but I forced myself to stay calm. Crosley wasn't going to try to cut my throat, at least not yet. He didn't know I was really after the nightmare clock.

"Well, now that I can get a proper look at you, you're quite lovely," Crosley said. "You remind me of Valentina, before her unfortunate decision to leave her place in society and take up a . . . front-line position in the Brotherhood, doing things unsuitable for a well-bred young woman like her." The way he said it, lips pursing, left no doubt how he felt about his daughter's allegiances. Apparently I, not being of the same breed of rich jerk, was exempt from such disapproval.

He excused himself to the bar and claimed a silver tea service with two cups and saucers. I watched him until somebody flopped into the chair opposite me. "Hey. You made it."

I nearly choked when I recognized the face. "*Casey*? You're alive!"

"You act like you're surprised," she said. "Takes more than a few ghouls to keep me down. Also, you trust people way too easy when you're getting what you want. Your old man's right—you need to learn if you're gonna live to be seventeen."

Rage flamed in me, and for a moment I forgot that I was supposed to be acting harmless. "You . . . you . . . *backstabber,*" I spat. "You're not a street kid! You're not even from Lovecraft!"

Casey wagged her hand. "I was *born* there," she said. "I've been working for the Brotherhood for a long time, keeping tabs on the Rustworks and anyone who might be useful to the cause."

"The Brotherhood was *spying* on me?" I was flabbergasted. I expected this sort of thing from the Proctors, but not from people who knew the truth about the world. "For how long?" I asked. Another, darker possibility was creeping through my mind like a hungry ghoul—if Casey had been following me, had she seen what happened in Innsmouth? Was I about to be thrown under the train before I'd even had a chance to find the nightmare clock?

"Until I lost you in Old Town you took off from the Crosley house for Innsmouth," Casey said. "Lost you. Too many damn ghouls running around."

My breathing started again, fast and full of relief. Casey hadn't seen me with Draven. She hadn't dipped below the first layer of my reason for coming to the Bone Sepulchre.

"So, this place is pretty crazy, right?" Casey said. "I can see it in your eyes. You're bugging out."

Glad of any topic except her following me around for stone knew how long, I nodded. "More than pretty crazy," I said. "It's beautiful."

Casey sat forward in excitement, eyes lighting up as she talked. "We pull aether right out of the air. There's a device in the tower that they say was designed by Tesla himself. You don't need to refine it; you can pull a full charge and disperse it into a feed just like normal. That's why it's purple, not blue. No refining chemicals."

That explained the "aurora borealis" I'd seen. Not light. Aether. The energy of the cosmos ripped directly from the air. A machine like that, especially one built by Tesla, would normally be something I'd be eager to see, but not now. Now, I was fishing. "Seems kind of boring around here," I said. "No lanternreels, no books that I can see."

"Oh, you're wrong. There's a giant library," Casey said. "I know you're a bookworm."

I narrowed my eyes. "Exactly how long have you been watching me?"

"Me personally? Only since you rabbited from the Academy," Casey said. "Before that, I couldn't say if Mr. Grayson or someone else had an agent watching you." She sat back in the chair and regarded me. "Nobody else can do what you do, Aoife. You're important to a lot of people for that reason, and a lot of things that aren't people at all. But I'm glad you chose us and not the Proctors."

"Of course I did," I said, shrugging as if there were no question at all. "I believe in what you're doing. Draven and the Proctors are vile." True. I knew it was always best to put a little truth in your untruths. It made you believable.

"Ah, Miss Casey," said Crosley, returning with the tea. "So good of you to take Miss Grayson under your wing." He grinned at me. "Casey is a very capable girl, much like yourself. She can show you to your room, order you some supper, and explain to you the kinds of tests we'll be running."

I paused, the teacup halfway to my lips. "Tests?" I said,

pulling back from Crosley warily. Nothing that started with "running a few tests" ever ended well, in my experience.

"Relax!" Crosley boomed genially. "We just want to see what your Weird can do, and how much we can still teach you. We must use the Gates for good instead of as instruments of disaster going forward, and to do that we have to see where your talent lies."

His hand landed on my shoulder, and the weight pushed me deeper still into the armchair. "Does that sound all right to you, my dear?"

That sounded just the opposite of all right. "I'll prove to you I have my Weird," I said. "But I don't relish being poked at like a laboratory rat."

Crosley folded his fingers together in a motion I recognized from when my professors were trying to make a pop quiz appealing. "Terrible what happened to your mother, Aoife. Just terrible. And young Conrad showed symptoms as well before he removed himself from the Iron Land. We know that if you stay away from iron, out of cities and such, the onset is slower, and comes not at all in Thorn, but if you stay in the Iron Land, you'll inevitably go mad, and I think it's a crime that Archie would never allow me to help him with his children's . . . unique bloodline. I'm confident that with time, we can find a way to help you. So you won't have to risk iron madness every time you go into a city."

That all sounded, to put it mildly, just a bit too good to be true. "How do I know you won't just chain me up and force me to use my Weird to do whatever you want with machines and the Gates?"

Crosley laughed. It was deep and wet, from the lungs of a man, I realized, who was gravely ill. His face turned crimson, with amusement or lack of air, I couldn't tell. "Aoife, if we wanted to imprison you, wouldn't doing so immediately after you'd arrived have made more sense than offering you a conversation and a nice cup of tea?"

I set the teacup back down and looked him in the eye. "There are all different kinds of prisons, Mr. Crosley."

"Smart girl. So there are," he said, "but this is not a prison, it's a promise. You let me run my tests and cooperate, and I will not only give you access to the Codex, I will find a solution to your iron madness. A permanent one. You won't have to end up like poor lost Nerissa."

I twitched at my mother's name crossing his lips. He didn't know anything about us, spies or not. Nerissa had done the best she could. In our small apartment, before she was committed, we'd at least been free.

I didn't let any of that come across to Crosley, and he spread his hands. "I ask again—does this sound equitable to you, young Miss Grayson?"

I looked into his eyes and found the same falseness there I knew I was showing in my own. "Sounds fantastic," I said dryly, but Crosley didn't pick up on my sarcasm, just grinned again and left me in the care of Casey.

She sat with me while I drank my tea, chattering about the great cause of the Brotherhood of Iron, Tesla and his prototype Gate, and how she'd personally seen two Fae! In the flesh! "They were creepy," she said, and shuddered. "Had hollow spaces where their eyes should be, and fangs."

I didn't bother telling her that she'd most likely seen something that had crawled from the Mists rather than full-blooded Fae. Besides, perfect faces with gleaming beauty and dead, unblinking eyes weren't really any less terrifying.

After I finished my tea, she guided me to a guest room, where a cot piled high with furs and lit by the same eerie purple aether lamps greeted me. The Brotherhood, for all their status as fugitives, had means far beyond even the Proctors. Clean clothes waited for me, thick woolen socks and silk pajamas that trapped the heat next to my skin, and I burrowed under the blankets, some of the hides nearly as thick as carpets.

It was pure luck, burrowed as I was, that I heard the door lock from the outside. I'd probably been meant to fall asleep, warm and dry and full of soporific tea, lulled into a false sense of security by Casey and her uncomplicated nature.

That jibed a bit with what Archie had told me. I didn't think his view of the Brotherhood of Iron was entirely fair, but I also knew my father wasn't stupid. If he'd broken with the Brotherhood, there was a good reason. At the very least, I was the daughter of the man who'd stolen Harold Crosley's own daughter, and I'd broken the Gates besides. Nobody, no matter their nature, was that forgiving.

And now I was locked in, and even if I wasn't, they'd taken away my cold-weather gear. If I went back onto the ice dressed as I was, I'd be dead inside of ten minutes.

With that cheerful thought ringing in my head, along with a dozen considered and discarded plans to find information about the clock, I managed to fall asleep, but too lightly for any dreams except the dark things, writhing and twisting through an empty, starless sky.

* * *

The next day, I was woken by a white-clad servant. He gave me breakfast in my room, and soon after, Casey appeared. After I'd dressed in more brand-new clothes, smart trousers and a black jacket this time, we went together to a sort of laboratory, just a long table and a few microscopes and other scientific instruments arranged along the wall.

Crosley and a panel of stern-faced men waited for me. A single chair sat before the table, and in front of me was a machine with a variety of needles for scratching data onto a roll of paper.

The other end of the machine had wires running out of it, and one of the anonymous men taped two of the electrical leads to my temples. They were cold, and I flinched, but I tried to act as if everything were all right.

"It's just for a few readouts," Crosley assured me, placing his hand on my shoulder. "We need to quantify your Weird scientifically."

I turned to look at him. "Did you do this to my father?"

"Of course," Crosley said smoothly, not missing a beat. "All Gateminders go through these tests when they ally themselves with the Brotherhood of Iron." His grip tightened, his nails digging in beneath my collarbone just a fraction, and I bit my lip. *Don't react. Don't give him any reason to doubt you.*

I sighed, trying to focus on my Weird. There was virtually no metal in the Bone Sepulchre, and my headaches and the shadows I glimpsed from the corners of my eyes had all but ceased. That, at least, was a relief. "What am I supposed to do for these tests, then?" I asked Crosley.

He took his pocket watch off the fob and placed it before me. "Can you wind it?" he asked. "Destroying things isn't terribly useful in the long run, Aoife. The best weapon is one that you can carefully aim and fire."

"Is that what I am to you?" I asked him, examining the watch. It was heavy, gold-plated, overdone. Much like Harold Crosley himself. "A weapon?" That was a stupid question. I already knew the answer.

"It's what we'd like you to be," Crosley said, with that clasp on my shoulder that was becoming all too familiar. "We're not the Proctors, Aoife. We won't force you to do anything. But we'd very much like you to choose to use your gift for the good of all, not just the few the Proctors deem worthy." He leaned down as if to share a secret. It was a ploy that hadn't worked on me when I was eight, and it didn't work now. I was actually a bit insulted that he'd patronize me so. Maybe I'd overdone it on the simpleton act.

"Wind the clock, Aoife," Crosley murmured. "Use your Weird for us. Show me that you'll use it for the Brotherhood and be the loyal soldier your father refused to be."

That was it, I realized. I had to tell the truth now, and then I could lie with impunity. I had to let the Brotherhood see the full extent of my skill with my Weird, and then I would be home free, because if they knew what I could do, they'd think they owned me, that only they could keep me from another event like the Engine. They'd believe that I was being honest with them, and I'd be free to do what needed to be done.

I put my fingers on the edge of the table and slid them forward so the tips just touched the pocket watch. My Weird gave a tickle, an itch I couldn't quite reach. The watch was complex, and I breathed in and out, shallower and shallower, focusing on the mechanism that would make the tiny hands spin backward. The only time I'd managed this was with my father, and then I hadn't been a virtual prisoner, being stared at like a curiosity by a cadre of men who could keep me locked up indefinitely. The pressure didn't help.

After one tick, two, three, four, the hands finally stopped. After another breath, they began to run in reverse, my Weird sending the gears spinning back and back until they stood at exactly midnight.

More. I had to do more. I had to show them the earth-shattering power waiting in the dark places of my mind.

The watch was spinning so fast now it vibrated on the table, and I picked out each individual gear and cog as my Weird flowed, not a trickle now but a flood, one that could drown me if I let it have too much more rein. I could feel every bit of clockwork in the place now.

I was the machine. And the machine was me. Just as it had been in Lovecraft.

The glass face of the clock cracked open and the hands went flying, embedding themselves in the far wall. I picked it apart piece by piece, until every bit of the watch was turning around my head, spinning of its own accord.

As quickly as it had come, the flash flood of power vanished, as I knew it would. My control wasn't that good yet.

The gold case dropped to the floor, smoking, and a few heartbeats after that I lost my grip on the clockwork and it too fell, raining gears and brass.

Murmurs, and an excited but subdued round of applause

broke out among the Brotherhood members. My mind still itched, and I felt the familiar trickle of blood from my nose. The needles on the machine I was hooked to danced wildly.

"I'd like to be excused," I told Crosley. My head was spinning, I was sick to my stomach, and I was *not* going to faint in front of these men if I had any say.

"Of course, of course," he said, and rang for Casey to take me back to my room.

"You're bleeding," she said, but made no move to offer me a handkerchief or a rag. I wiped the blood on my sleeve, where it stood out damp and dark.

"I'll live," I said. The walls of the Bone Sepulchre wavered in front of me. The ice appeared to shimmer in the low light, and with the way my head was pounding, I wasn't sure I could make it out of the room. I scrabbled against the slick walls, vision blurring, and Casey caught me.

"Whoa!" she said. "You don't look so good, Aoife. Are you all right?"

My shoulder began to throb again, ten times worse than it had on the submarine. Tears squeezed from my eyes, and I saw that they were red when they landed on the backs of my hands.

"This is wrong . . . ," I choked out, my tongue feeling too large for my mouth. My heart kicked into overdrive with fear, and it exacerbated the pain in my shoulder. Hot pain, searing pain, bone-deep pain that clutched at every bit of me, held me and didn't let me go.

The sensation of falling gripped me as well, beyond the pain, the displacement of gravity acting on my stomach, and then the vertigo of being in two places at once, neither quite here nor there.

Fae magic. The kind that could rip me from one place to the next as quickly as I breathed.

I braced myself to land, but when I opened my eyes, I was in the same spot, standing just outside the door of the library, heart pounding and my breath coming not at all.

The Fae magic hadn't reached out to grab me, but had thrust another figure into my path.

Tremaine smiled at me, his pointed teeth gleaming silver.

"Hello, Aoife. You have no idea how glad I am to catch up to you."

14

The Fate of Thorn

FOR THE LONGEST of heartbeats, I simply stared at Tremaine. It couldn't be. There was no way he could have found me again after Jakob had killed himself.

Well, my mind whispered, *there was no way Jakob could have survived for any length of time aboard the sub, and he did that.*

Casey stared at Tremaine, slack-jawed, but she stayed crouched protectively over me. "Who in the hell are you?"

"I think Aoife can tell you," Tremaine purred. He extended his hand and put it on my cheek. "I think she's even been dreaming of me. Is that right, Aoife?"

I swatted weakly at his hand. It was all the energy I could muster. "Don't you dare touch me."

Casey shrank back a step, staring at Tremaine still. "Is he . . ."

"Get away, Casey," I said. My voice sounded faint, feeble.

I felt the same—I couldn't have moved even if I'd had the chance to stab Tremaine in the heart where he stood.

She hesitated, and I gritted my teeth, tasting blood. *"Go,"* I snarled.

Casey backed up a step, her gaze never leaving Tremaine. "I'll go get help," she said softly, then turned and bolted down the corridor.

I rotated my heavy, dizzy head to look Tremaine in the eye. "What do you think you'll do when you have me? What more could you possibly need? I broke the Gates, is that it? Are you looking to fix what you started now, and be a savior?"

"I already am a savior," Tremaine said. "I woke the queens, you know. I broke Draven's curse. And I used you, darling of the Brotherhood, to do it, which makes me not only a hero, but a clever hero." He touched my face again, his sharp white nails scraping narrow lines in my skin. "And now I believe that I'll be able to do whatever I want to do with you, Aoife, because we both know you can't stop me."

Tremaine took me by the hand, almost gently. His skin was cooler than the icy air around us, and it shot a bolt of nausea straight to my core. "It's time to come back, Aoife." He leaned down and whispered to me in the voice of a wind across a vast, empty wasteland of ice. "You are half in my world, you know. Your blood is half Fae. Did you really think getting away from me would be as easy as pretending you're human?"

I glared up at him. In that moment, I wasn't scared of Tremaine, only infuriated that he'd outsmarted me yet again. "I'd hoped it would be, you glassy-eyed monstrosity."

"Hope isn't a real thing, Aoife," Tremaine said. "It's a lie that desperate souls cling to as comfort."

"You would know, wouldn't you?" I snapped. "You're full to the brim with lies."

Tremaine just smiled in return, a smile that said he'd already won.

The world began to fall away around me, and this time I was moving, moving with the raw power of the *hexenring*, the Fae magic that bent space and time the same way Tesla had when he'd made the Gates. I wanted to scream, but nothing came out, not even air.

I fell, and then snapped back to myself on a white marble floor, choking, with blood gushing from my nose. The pain in my shoulder and the numbness in the rest of my body were gone, and I was gasping for breath. My nose still gushed, but now the droplets landed on fine marble instead of rough-carved ice, and the light around me was mellow and amber, oil lamps rather than aether. "Of course," I sighed, watching my blood stain the stone under my knees. I was back in the Thorn Land. It was the last place in all the worlds I wanted to be, so of course I'd landed here. It was just my rotten, nonexistent luck.

"I've waited a long time to be standing here with you," Tremaine said, sweeping his arm to take in the whole of the area.

This *hexenring*, rather than an arrangement of mushrooms or rocks as Fae rings usually were, was carved directly into the stone underneath me. I stood up, feeling the blood trickle down my face, but I didn't move. I knew from experience that I needed Tremaine's permission to leave the ring.

He extended his hand and smiled. It was a smile of cold, dead places and white bones, polished to points, that speared me and pinned me to the spot. "Welcome to the court of the Winter Queen, Aoife. She's been waiting to show you the gratitude she owes you for freeing her. We all have."

I left the *hexenring* with the greatest reluctance. Staying in the vortex of magic so strong it bent space and time was preferable to getting one bit closer to Tremaine.

I only took his hand because I didn't have a choice. I fought off a shiver, and he just grinned wider. Tremaine knew exactly the effect he had on me, and delighted in it. I wanted to smash his perfect face in when he looked at me like that.

To distract myself from my anger and growing fear, I examined my surroundings. The court of the Winter Queen was solid, gleaming marble veined with bronze and gold and scarlet. I swore the walls were pulsing, like a living thing, and that the floor was vibrating beneath my feet with the steady *lub-dub* of a heartbeat. Of course, it could also have been my spinning head and the residual effects of the shoggoth venom in my shoulder getting stirred up. At least here in the Thorn Land, there was no toxicity, no iron madness to plague me. Which was fortunate, because I'd need every speck of my brains to outsmart Tremaine and whatever new scheme he had in mind.

As we walked, snow—actual snow—drifted through the air around us, and the only color came from sprigs of holly growing directly from cracks in the walls and the red berries adorning the heads and clothing of some of the passing Fae. The other Fae were skinny and wan-looking, bones jutting out underneath their richly dyed woolen clothes. Their lips were white, their veins standing out beneath the skin; they looked like some of the victims of the camps I'd seen lanternreels of when the war ended. The poisoned sleep of the queens had taken its toll on the Thorn Land and the Fae.

Only Tremaine looked fat and healthy. He was a shark among tadpoles, and I wasn't surprised. He was the consummate survivor. Looking at the other Fae in comparison eased my panic a bit, though. They weren't frightening. They were more pathetic than anything else.

"Why did you bring me here?" I asked Tremaine. "I did what you wanted," I insisted, when he only gave me another maddening, cryptic smile. "I woke up the queens. And I ripped the Gates to shreds doing it. I'm guessing I'm here to clean up your mess. Am I right?" I risked a sidelong glance as we walked down the endless, curving hallways and caught the full brunt of Tremaine's glare.

"How do you think Thorn existed before the Gates, you simpleton?" he snapped. "We passed freely between worlds without any sort of gadget. *We* had the power. Not the Erlkin, and certainly not anyone with human blood in them. We were the shining people, Aoife, and the last thing I want is for the Gates to be repaired. Now stop trying to fish information out of me. Your attempts are ham-handed at best."

I stopped and returned his glare. Tremaine might be frightening and terrible, but I was through with his game of pushing me around for his own amusement. "You'd think you didn't learn anything from the Iron Land. Like it or not, when you woke up the queens, you fractured something between our two worlds. The Proctors have already found a way into the Mists. How long do you think it will be before they use the broken Gates to come here?" I put my hands on my hips, not budging, and refused to look away from him.

Tremaine bared his teeth in anger for a split second. "I've been alive much longer than you," he said. "Men have tried to breach Thorn before, and they have failed. This so-called fracture is a side effect of breaking Draven's mechanical curse, nothing more."

"You and I both know that's not true," I insisted. "You wouldn't have sent Jakob to try and kidnap me back if it were. You wouldn't have risked coming into the stronghold of the Brotherhood." I jabbed my finger into the blue velvet lapel of Tremaine's jacket. "You wanted a destroyer and you got one. It's only going to be a matter of time before another Storm, unless we put the Gates back to how they were."

Tremaine reached forward and grabbed me by the chin, squeezing hard enough that he wrung a whimper from me. I forced myself to stay still, to not struggle. Then, just as abruptly as he'd grabbed me, he let go and brushed the hair out of my eyes with an almost tender gesture that made me recoil. "Or perhaps you'll simply stay here, and I won't have to take the blame for a thing," he said softly. "After all, I am not the half-breed who destroyed the Gates. In Thorn, you'll age faster than a full-blooded Fae, but you'll be alive long enough to see everyone in your precious, wretched Iron Land grow old and die while you still look the same. So don't cross me, Aoife. And give up this ridiculous talk of fixing the Gates."

He took me by the arm and we started walking again,

approaching a pair of white doors in which there was carved a great tree, leafless and dripping with icicles, which were diamonds set into the marble, glittering as faintly as far-off stars. At the base of the tree sat two carved white wolves, and at the top was a dove, pierced with an arrow, a single droplet of blood, picked out in rubies, resting on its breast.

"The Winter Court," Tremaine said, as if that would tell me everything I needed to know about what lay beyond the doors.

They swung back, pulled open by two girls who looked about thirteen years old, though who knew how old they were, really. Fae aged at an infinitesimal rate compared to humans, or even to half-bloods like Conrad and me. The girls wore identical blue dresses, of a type about eighty years out of style. Fine corsets with the whalebone exposed trimmed their waists so they looked like bare branches themselves, as if they'd sway with every breeze. Heavy blue velvet bell sleeves hung from their slender arms, and their skin was so white I could see every vein, every bone, in sharp relief. The white of the flesh was beyond corpse pallor—it was otherworldly. That fit—this was not my world.

Tremaine urged me forward, toward a dais at the far end of the room. It was not the showy spectacle I'd come to expect from the Fae, but a simple raised platform carved from a solid block of marble, etched with bare branches and dead vines migrating down to a litter of rust-colored fallen leaves gathered around the base, which crackled and crunched as emaciated Fae walked about the room. From the stone platform rose a throne woven from long, curved bones and crowned with the three-inch pointed teeth of some predatory animal. I stared, unable to look away. Atop this vicious creation, on a pale blue silk pillow, sat the small, fair-haired figure I recognized as Octavia—the Winter Queen.

When I'd last seen the queen, lying in her cursed glass coffin, she'd looked around my age, but with her eyes open she looked like some sort of alien creature, eyes ancient and fathomless as a piece of meteorite. She had the same unearthly skin as the girls, and hair so fine it looked like spun wire. It trailed from a high pompadour to hang down her back in a long braid woven with some sort of thorny vine. Her crown was more bones, bones and blackened teeth that were not pointed, but rather, looked human. I elected to stare just behind her instead of looking at that unearthly oval face for one more second. If I stared into the queen's eyes much longer, I knew I'd simply start screaming, as mindless as anyone locked in a madhouse.

She raised one delicate hand and beckoned me closer. Her nails were pure white and clawlike. Her teeth, like Tremaine's, were needles, and a droplet of silver sat on the end of her tongue when she smiled wide at me. Her tongue was shockingly red in comparison to her complexion; the whole effect made me think of a sleepy predator that had just woken and scented blood. *My* blood. I didn't move—there was no way I was getting closer than I absolutely had to.

The same kind of silver jewelry ran up both ears and sat in her delicate white eyebrows as she raised them in displeasure at my insolence. "Tremaine," she said, and though we were at least twenty feet away and she wasn't shouting, I heard her bell-clear. She beckoned with one talon-tipped finger. "Bring her here."

Tremaine shoved me forward, hissing, "When the queen calls, you obey."

It was the last thing in the world I would have done willingly, but having been commanded, I walked to the end of the dais, drawing the stare of every Fae in the cavernous room. Whispers went up among them, but I focused on the Winter Queen. Those terrible eyes never blinked, not once. Her lips were the only color on her face, stained to the exact red of blood. When her silver-crowned tongue darted out and licked a spot of the color away, I realized that at least some of it *was* blood.

Fear was something I was getting used to pushing away, to be felt later, when I could deal with it on my terms. But I couldn't push this away. What I felt looking at the Winter Queen wasn't like a cut or a scrape but a mortal wound.

I'd never felt such a vibration rolling off a living creature—if Octavia was alive. She didn't look it, not really. Something was filling up the beautiful vessel sitting before me, making it walk and talk and gesture, but I couldn't shake the feeling that it was only renting the space, not inhabiting the flesh.

"I'm not going to hurt you, Aoife," Octavia said. One slippered foot poked from under her voluminous, airy white, black and red skirts. The foot shoved a silken floor pillow toward me. "Sit."

This seemed more like exposing my throat as if I were a vulnerable animal than sitting, but I did as she said. I didn't want to find out what would happen if I was openly defiant.

The pillow silk felt cool, and the marble against the backs of my legs nearly burned with cold. I looked up at Octavia, who was even more terrifying from this vantage point. "I know what you said, but I have to ask: are you going to kill me?"

"Kill you!" she exclaimed, and let out a laugh like the croaking of a crow. "Why would I do such a thing?" She looked at Tremaine. "You haven't been nice, have you? You're never nice."

"Aoife is only a changeling, Your Majesty," he said. "I'm not required to be nice."

"She's a beautiful present, is what she is," Octavia said. "And you've done well by bringing her here. But if you lay a hand on her again, Tremaine . . ." Her perfect, frozen face moved into a frown that made her look like a wild animal. "I won't be happy. Do you understand?"

Tremaine tensed, leaning away from her anger. "Yes, madam."

All at once, she was back to being regal and expressionless. "Good."

I watched the exchange, fascinated. So there *was* something Tremaine was afraid of, someone he had to take orders from. I didn't blame him for his fear—Octavia would be intimidating no matter what the context, never mind when she was perched on her throne like a carrion bird atop a tombstone.

Octavia turned to me once more. "My dear, you must be calm. You saved my life, and I have no intention of harming you in return. Contrary to the stories, my sister the Summer Queen is the one who keeps changelings as pets."

I must have frowned, because she let out another laugh. "Oh, you didn't know that, did you? Yes, the Summer Court builds wonderful things that gleam and glitter in the sun. But to do that you need silver and gems, and to get them you need slaves." She gestured at the room. "Do you see one goblin—pardon me, Erlkin—enslaved here?"

"No," I said softly, not knowing where this conversation was going, but fairly sure it was nowhere pleasant.

Tremaine rapped his knuckles against the back of my head. "No, *Majesty,*" he snarled. "Show some bloody respect to your betters."

I whirled on him, furious, but Octavia beat me to it, rising to her feet with a sound like a dozen crows taking flight. *"Enough,"* she growled at Tremaine. "Your temper is your undoing. Every time."

Tremaine scrambled back, dipping his head. "Forgive me, Majesty. I was only thinking of your position."

I saw my chance to perhaps buy myself a little goodwill with the queen, here where Tremaine was cowed and couldn't smirk or talk over me. "I know Tremaine told you I broke the Gates on my own," I said. "That I screwed up when I destroyed the Engine and sent the power to Thorn to break your curse." I stood as well, even though Octavia towered over me when she was upright. If I was going to meet my fate, it would happen while I was standing. "But I didn't know," I said. "And all I know now is that if they aren't fixed, soon the Proctors will have control of the Gates, and complete supremacy over all the Iron Land. They're already figuring out how to use them. How long until they start trying to conquer Thorn? As it is," I said, realizing that this, more than anything, might get me out of Thorn, "any of your people, your creatures who come through the cracks, will be trapped there."

Octavia raised one of those almost invisible, perfect eyebrows, but she didn't make a move to shut me up, so I kept talking. From the corner of my eye, I saw Tremaine's face heating to crimson with rage, but I ignored him. Octavia was my chance to get out of the Thorn Land unscathed.

"Permanently," I rushed on. "Forever. The Proctors and the Brotherhood of Iron used to work together, and if another Storm happens, it'll unite them again. They'll close the Gates for good and trap whoever is still there, and the creatures of the Mists besides. Your *hexenrings* won't work, because the Proctors are smart enough to lace all their vulnerable spots with iron. Your people wouldn't be able to travel anywhere. You'd have Thorn and Thorn only." I stopped, my heart thudding, and waited for Octavia to either rip my throat out or pass her judgment.

Octavia cut her eyes to Tremaine. "Truth?"

"Of course not!" Tremaine sputtered. "Majesty, nothing of this nature is certain. The problems with the Gates, the issues we've had casting *hexenrings*, they're almost certainly aberrations that can be fixed." He jabbed a finger at me. "Besides, I know for a fact this little half-blooded bitch lies as easily as she breathes."

I glared at him. Nothing he said could touch me now. I'd taken the leap off the cliff, and I'd either fly or fall. Name-calling didn't matter.

"This 'half-blooded bitch' saved my life," Octavia snapped at Tremaine. "She saved all of Thorn from devastation. Or have you forgotten so quickly the very wheels you set in motion?" She pointed one of her bony fingers at him. "And when you talk of half-bloods, Tremaine, you are talking of the offspring of my dear sister. The loss of whom, as you know, I mourn every day. I look harshly on those who would criticize her."

"You can't only take the word of this—" Tremaine started.

"I am the queen!" Octavia jumped from the dais in a fluid motion and advanced on Tremaine, who scuttled backward faster than any bottom-feeding ghoul exposed to light. "And you, while loyal, are nothing more than a servant. Do you understand me, Tremaine? You got Aoife to help us, and therefore you are responsible for what she's wrought."

Abruptly, she turned from Tremaine and moved toward me, folding her arms and looking almost conciliatory. I just stayed as still as possible, the way I would have if I'd been faced with a hungry wolf.

"Are you telling me the truth, Aoife?"

I willed my voice not to shake. "Yes."

"And I suppose," Octavia said, running one of those talons down my cheek, "that you wish something in return for setting things right." Before I could jerk away, she moved again, mounting the dais and settling back on her throne. Her movements were so liquid, it was like watching water flow under ice. "Name it, then," Octavia said, tapping her nails against the bone arms of her throne. "All the knowledge of Fae and Thorn is at your disposal. One thousand years of magic and wisdom. I won't have it destroyed and sealed off like a tomb. Name your price."

I shut my eyes. I wanted to sob with relief, but I had a feeling that here, the tears would only freeze against my face. If this didn't work, I'd likely die. I'd be just another Gateminder who'd played against the Fae and lost.

Strangely, I wasn't afraid. I knew this was how it had to be, deep down and with certainty. I was more upset that I'd never see Dean again, never get to tell Conrad I was sorry for how our relationship as brother and sister had faltered, never get to thank Archie for trying to protect me, even if he'd done it in the most backward way possible.

I swiped at my eyes and then faced Octavia. "I want the location of the nightmare clock."

Octavia tilted her head but didn't speak. For once her face wasn't impassive, and I got the idea I'd shocked her, if such a thing was possible. "And why, pray," she said, "does a sweet half-blood girl need such a horrid thing as the dreamer's great gear?"

"I need it to fix the Gates," I said. "Stop the leaks, stop the disasters. Tell me how I get there."

Octavia grinned at me. "You're the Gateminder, Aoife. You figure it out."

I did what was anathema to every screaming instinct then. I turned my back on Octavia, on Tremaine, and started to walk. I cringed with every step, waiting for the blow or the bolt of magic, until I reached the door; then I turned around. "I guess we don't have a deal."

"Wait a minute," Octavia said, her voice echoing down the room. "You don't just get to walk out of here, Aoife. The Fae can find you anywhere. Your blood calls to us."

She came to me, across the throne room, and I watched her advance the way I imagined a mouse felt watching a hawk swooping down. "You have something I want, it's true," she said. "But then, I have something *you* want. Plus, you're my prisoner until I say otherwise. So, Aoife, here are *my* terms."

She reached into a pocket in her dress and pulled out a photograph. It was a tintype of a human, and I gasped when I saw the face, faded and water stained but so familiar.

"My sister, Nerissa," said Octavia as I stared at my mother.

She was young there, flowers in her hair, far too young to have even met my father yet. "And my terms: The nightmare clock for my blood. Your blood. You and your mother will return to the Thorn Land once you've fixed the Gates. I get my sister back, I get my Gateminder, and you get to know you didn't destroy that filthy, smoke-ridden iron world you insist upon calling home." She tucked the photograph away again. "It's a good exchange, Aoife. Take it."

I couldn't breathe. Couldn't think. Nerissa . . . ? She was *full*-blooded Fae? It was possible. She and Octavia had the same narrow faces, the same burning gazes. Octavia was fair and Nerissa was dark, but it was possible . . . Same father, different mothers? How had I not known from Tremaine that Octavia and Nerissa were related? *Because if you had known, you'd never have done as he asked,* the maddeningly logical part of me whispered.

Tremaine appeared at Octavia's shoulder, smirk firmly back in place. "Good effort, Aoife. But your human half is always going to get in the way of striking a true bargain."

I ignored him. I couldn't let Tremaine lord it over me that I'd lost again. There were more important factors to consider. I wasn't leaving Thorn unless Octavia let me—that much was plain. There wasn't a machine here that I could trick into getting me home. My Weird was useless. Draven would kill Dean, my mother would be devoured by the wreckage of Lovecraft, and the rest of the people I cared about would fall under martial law put in place by the Proctors as the Storm slowly encroached upon the rest of the world. People like Rasputina couldn't fight back, even with the Crimson Guard's acceptance of magic. The world would wither and die like poison fruit.

Or I could accept Octavia's offer, and then nothing would happen to any of them. The same uneasy balance would exist between Proctors and Brotherhood, humans and Fae. The world would go on exactly as it was. All I had to do was take myself out of the equation, agree to become Octavia's servant and return with my mother. It wasn't the choice a Gateminder would make, but in that moment, I wasn't a Gateminder. I was Dean's love, I was Conrad's sister, I was Archie and Nerissa's daughter. I was a half human who cared about the Iron Land even though it was sometimes dark and desperate beyond compare.

Octavia's voice pulled me back. "Well, Aoife?"

When I thought about it, it wasn't a hard choice at all. "I won't fight you," I said. "You can have me and my Weird, to do with as you like. But the only way you're getting Nerissa is if you tell me how to find the clock and send me back to do what needs to be done to stabilize the Gates."

Octavia looked upward, clearly thinking. It was like being regarded by a hungry, unblinking owl. "Very well," she said at last. "And of course I can trust you, because if you attempt to void our deal, there will be nowhere you can hide from us. Closed Gates, open Gates, we will find you, Aoife Grayson, and we will pick the flesh from your bones if you betray us."

I raised my chin. Octavia had to think she didn't scare me, though the opposite was true. If I was going to spend my time in the court of the Winter Queen, it wasn't going to be as a pet. "You can trust me. Unlike you, I know what that word means."

Octavia gave another croaking laugh. "Good. As for the nightmare clock, the mad inventor Tesla didn't just build

Gates between physical realms. He started the Storm, and it will end with him." She snapped her fingers. "Tremaine, take her back to the *hexenring*."

He dragged me out of the room, his mouth set in a grim line. I hadn't seen Tremaine angry often before, but it had always led to explosive results. "I bet you think you're terribly clever for pulling that little stunt, ratting me out. Rest assured, when you're back in the fold, I'm going to teach you some manners."

I jerked my arm from his grasp and stepped into the *hexenring* on my own. After hearing Octavia's revelations, after being taken from the Bone Sepulchre, I was worn out. I didn't have the capacity for any more emotion. "I'll never be afraid of you again," I told Tremaine as my body began to separate from my mind, the awful vertigo of magic sinking its claws into me once again. It might not always be true, but after what had happened, I couldn't let him think he'd won. "I've seen what else is out there. You're nothing."

Tremaine laughed, throwing his head back. "I'll be everything to you, Aoife. You'll see, when you return. If I can't take the Winter Throne as a regent, then marrying its heir will do nicely."

I stared at him, feeling a chill when I realized that he'd once again managed to outmaneuver me, but then the magic of the *hexenring* took me and I was flying. I caught the brief, dreamlike flashes of the other places, dark and light places, bloody places and empty places, before I landed back in the same corridor of the Bone Sepulchre from which I'd left.

15

The Machinery of Magic

THE FIRST PERSON to see me was a woman in a smart suit, who screamed loudly and promptly fainted. Girls didn't appear out of thin air every day, apparently, even in the lair of the Brotherhood of Iron.

Casey came running, followed by Crosley and a few of the men in white. Crosley crouched down, turning my head this way and that, his flabby hands all over me. "What happened? Casey told us the most outlandish story. Are there Fae in the Sepulchre?"

Even in my dizzied state, I knew Crosley couldn't know what had transpired between Tremaine and me. I still needed Crosley and the Brotherhood's help, and if he knew the Fae had managed to infiltrate his base, any trust I'd earned would crumble.

"She's crazy," I said. "I just fainted. I'm exhausted. All those tests have taken it out of me."

I cut my gaze to Casey, praying that she'd go along with

me. She owed me—she'd been spying on me ever since we'd met. She didn't say anything, and after a moment Crosley and one of the men in white helped me up. Crosley fussed, dabbing under my bleeding nose with a handkerchief. "I blame myself," he said. "I've pushed you too hard, and you're such a delicate little thing."

I leaned against him dramatically and held the kerchief to my nose. "I'm just so tired." It was harder than anything to act normal for the Brotherhood after what had just happened, but my entire plan relied on it.

"Casey," Crosley said, handing me off. "Help her to her room, please?

"Of course, sir," Casey murmured, putting her arm around me. As we walked away she leaned in close and whispered, "What the hell is going on? Who was that?"

I shook my throbbing head, acutely aware of Crosley watching us retreat down the hall. "Not here. In my room."

We stumbled in an awkward dance into the room Crosley had had prepared for me the previous evening, where I collapsed on my bunk. Someone had left a tea tray, and Casey poured me a cup. It warmed me up a little, but it couldn't erase the memory of the cold, fathomless eyes of the Winter Queen boring into mine.

"You look really terrible." Casey sat on the edge of the bed and pressed her hand to my forehead in a motherly manner. More motherly than Nerissa had ever been, for sure.

Nerissa. I'd promised Octavia we'd both come back. Did Nerissa even remember she was from the Thorn Land? Did she even know her sister's name?

"Fae will do that to you," I said. Casey's face crinkled in alarm.

"I *knew* I wasn't imagining things," she said. "Mr. Crosley said I was, but I knew something had happened to you—that a Fae was in the Bone Sepulchre." She stood, her braids clanking, echoing her excitement. "Maybe we can still catch him!"

"Casey," I sighed, irritated at her innocence in matters of the Fae. "Forget it. He's long gone."

"But Mr. Crosley will be furious with us if he doesn't know the truth. . . ." She worried her lip and sat back down. "What did the Fae do to you? Are you hurt?"

"Not physically," I said, waving her off. I didn't want Casey worried about me—I needed her, I realized, and I was going to have to tell her the truth.

As briefly as I could, I outlined what had happened with Tremaine, why he'd come for me and how Octavia had revealed the location of the nightmare clock.

"Tesla built this place," I finished. "He built the Gates. I need to know what else he might have here—plans nobody ever saw, secret things like the clock he built for the Brotherhood. Then I think I can set everything right."

Casey stayed quiet, not looking at me, and I grew nervous. "Please don't think I'm crazy," I begged. "I'm not. All of this is true, and it's the only way I know to stop what's going to happen to the world."

Casey finally spoke, barely above a whisper. "I told Mr. Crosley when you came here what you'd been doing with your father—practicing your Weird, getting ready to take over as Gateminder. I told him I couldn't be sure, but I had a feeling you'd run into Proctors in Innsmouth. And you know what he said?"

"What?" I said. My stomach was knotting uncomfortably.

Calm down, Aoife. I just had to act innocent of whatever Casey was going to reveal.

"He said to leave you be," Casey said. "He said that in time, you'd either serve one purpose or another for the Brotherhood. He told me that if you can't fix what you've done, you'll at least be incentive for Mr. Grayson to come back to the fold." Casey wrapped her arms around herself. "I'm sorry, I know I should have told you before, but if he ever found out we talked . . ." She began to shake.

I felt bile creep up my throat, felt the thick, knobby hand of fear grasp my neck. I itched to run back out into the snow, anywhere but here, but I forced myself to remain perfectly still, my body's only movement the beating of my heart. I would not panic. Would not crack. Everything depended on it.

"Look," Casey said, "I know what happened in Lovecraft wasn't your fault. I know how tricky the Fae can be." She lowered her voice. "I lied to you when I said I'd only seen two. They took my sister, when we were both tiny. They left a creature in her crib, this squalling thing with double rows of teeth and no eyes. I know Crosley and those men can't possibly understand what they're dealing with when they make those bargains." Her mouth quirked. "Besides, I know you, and I know you're not some simpering pushover. That act didn't fool me."

"I'm actually a bit glad of that," I said, managing a tiny smile. "It's getting tiresome."

"So what now?" Casey sighed. "Seems as if we're over a barrel."

I rubbed my temples. They ached, like everything else

in me ached, including my thoughts. There were so many pieces, so many lies I'd stacked on top of lies, until they threatened to topple and crush me. Well, the lying was over, at least with Casey. I was sick of it anyway, sick nearly to death.

"The nightmare clock," I said. "My life and yours, and everyone's, depends on us getting to it."

Casey nodded. "Okay," she said. "You need Tesla's notes and diaries, right?"

"That would be a start," I agreed. Despite Octavia's orders, despite Draven's encroachment and what was sure to be an ugly confrontation, I felt the tiniest grain of hope.

"They don't exactly trust orphaned errand girls with that kind of information," Casey said, "but fortunately, I'm no dummy either." She leaned in and whispered. "Tesla's private papers are in the locked collection in the library."

My hope faded again. "I'm guessing that's not easy to get into."

Casey shook her head. "Oh, no. Mr. Crosley keeps those books personally guarded by his handpicked men. The last person who tried was your father."

I sat up in shock. "Seriously? My father?"

"It was awful," Casey said. "I've never seen Mr. Crosley so angry. He threatened to throw Mr. Grayson in the brig, but Miss Crosley intervened, and then the two of them snuck out in the middle of the night. Mr. Crosley *hates* him," she said. "Taking his daughter like that."

The story redoubled my determination. I could succeed where Crosley had foiled my father. Harold Crosley was right—I was going to fix things. But not for his sake. For mine, for my mother's, for the entire world, innocent and caught in the path of what I'd started when I broke the Gates.

"You get me into the library," I said. "We can take care of the guards together."

"He's got powerful locks on the room too," Casey said nervously. "And alarms."

"Don't worry," I told her, laying my hand on her shoulder the way Archie had done to me. "I'll take care of those."

After Casey left, I changed out of my bloody clothes, into a loose blouse and cigarette pants that had been left folded on my bed. I curled onto my side on the bed, and I opened my satchel. Draven's compass was still blinking as implacably as ever.

How close was he? Airships as large as the *Dire Raven* could only fly in the warmest part of the day this close to the North Pole, lest they risk ice building up on their iron parts and weighing them down.

He was coming, though. If Harold Crosley had been the only one we were talking about, I would have been happy to leave him to Draven. Crosley was keeping me prisoner—there was no denying it now. And if I didn't prove to be a useful weapon, then I'd be bait in a trap for my father. Again.

But if Draven came after the Brotherhood, eventually he'd be led back to my family. He had a vendetta against the Graysons, that much was obvious. I had to find the clock—find it physically, not just in dreams—before he showed up so I wasn't just a limp body for him to snatch.

The day crept by with agonizing slowness, and I tried to

sleep, tried pacing, tried staring at the shimmering ice walls, but nothing worked. I just kept thinking of Octavia and Nerissa. Sisters. I truly hoped my mother wanted to return to the Thorn Land when this was over. But if she had run away from it once, was I returning her to a worse fate than the one she faced now? If she was even alive. And if I could find the clock and make it work.

After the aether lamps had dimmed for the night, Casey unlocked my door and came in. "Mr. Crosley is playing checkers with some of the other brothers. He'll usually get into the gin and go to bed early."

I stopped her from turning on the lamp; we couldn't alert anyone that we were wandering around together. It was cold and silent, just us and the shadows dancing against the ice. "I know you're scared of him, Casey," I said. "I can't thank you enough for trusting me."

"I've seen what you can do," Casey murmured. "That kind of power shouldn't be under anyone's control but your own. And I wasn't always an orphan. If it were my family, I'd do anything to help them. Anything."

We walked quickly through the halls, passing only a few other members of the Brotherhood, most of them in nightclothes or just starting their shifts in the mechanics' bay. No one paid us the slightest bit of attention; we were two faceless girls meekly going on our way.

The library wasn't locked, although a sign on the door noted that it was closed and would reopen at eight a.m.

We slipped in and Casey stopped me inside the main doors, pointing back through the stacks. The library was massive, shelves curving far over our heads, bolted to the ceiling and the floor, and reading tables every few feet. With the lights off, the library was eerie, shelves crouched like lines of sentinels waiting for the signal to come to life and march forward.

We crept through the stacks, toward a flare of light near the back wall. Every footstep seemed magnified, every breath Casey and I took echoingly loud. But the two guards watching the small iron cage didn't seem to notice, and I breathed a little easier—that is to say, I breathed.

The two men in white sat on hard metal stools on either side of the cage. One leafed through a magazine and the other dozed, his head tilted back.

Casey looked at me and I examined our options. The men had weapons—short truncheons on their belts—and there could have been more hidden. *Can you take one?* I mouthed at Casey.

She nodded, knotting her hands into tight, knobby fists. I sucked in a breath. I was shaking. Once I took this step, there was no turning back.

Still, I didn't hesitate before I called up my Weird and burst the bulb of the aether lamp on the wall next to the guards. A bit of smoke curled, and the scent of burnt paper permeated the air.

I didn't have any more time to worry. The guards were up, shouting, stumbling into one another, and I saw the flash of Casey's metal hair decorations as she flew past me and laid the first guard out with a right cross. She fell on the man, kicking him and hitting him, letting out small huffs of rage.

I grabbed my guard by the front of his tunic and used the one fighting move every girl knows: I drove my knee hard into the spot between his legs. The guard buckled and fell, and I hit him once more in the temple to make sure he was out.

Casey was still punching her guard, atop him, her face gleaming with sweat. "Casey!" I hissed, horrified. These men had done nothing to us—they were just obstacles. "Casey, *stop!*"

She blinked at me, as if she'd forgotten I was there. "Yeah. Sorry," she said.

I helped her up, watching her wipe blood off her knuckles onto the tail of her shirt. "What happened?" I said softly. The pain on her face echoed in me. "Not just now. I mean, why did you do that?"

She shook her head, not looking at me. I brought a portable aether lamp from one of the tables and turned it on low so I could look into her eyes. Casey remained sullen. "It's not easy being an orphan the Brotherhood plucks off the street," she finally said with a sigh. "Any more than it is being a ward that the Lovecraft Proctors get their hands on."

She didn't meet my eyes, and I didn't push the issue. I knew the rage that could boil up when you least expected it. I knew it all too well. "Let's take a look at these locks," I suggested.

Casey looked crestfallen. "Mr. Crosley has the only copy of the keys. There's no way I'm getting my hands on them."

At least here, I was in my element. I could do something about Casey's misery. "Good thing I don't need his keys, then, eh?" I said, placing my hands on the door to the cage. Casey was right—the locks were strong, complicated, not the sort of kid stuff I could break open easily with my Weird.

But it could be done. Was going to be done. I laid my forehead against the iron. I didn't have much time, and the pressure didn't help my concentration, but I let the locks speak to me, let my Weird speak to them, allow the meshing of two machines, one ethereal and one iron, to occur.

After a moment, the locks popped open, and Casey gave a small squeak. "I'll never get used to that," she explained when I gave her a questioning look. "Closest thing to magic I'll ever see."

I thought of my father trying to teach me control back on the beach and felt a small pang. I did want to see him again, to give us a chance to spend more than a few days together, to really be father and daughter.

But for the sake of everything else, I shoved the tightness in my chest aside and pointed into the cage. "I probably shouldn't spend too much time enclosed in all that iron," I told Casey. "Can you get the Tesla stuff and bring it out here?"

"Sure can," she said, seeming relieved to have a task. I looked back at the guards, wondering how we were going to explain them. While Casey collected diaries, blueprints, journals and bound papers, I rooted through the librarian's desk until I unearthed a flat bottle of whiskey.

Perfect. I upended it over the unconscious guards' clothes, then left the bottle lying near the outstretched hand of the one Casey had beaten up. Not that whiskey would explain the bruises, but it would at least cast doubt on the story that two grown men had been beaten by two teenage girls—if they admitted such a thing at all.

When Casey had finished stacking a table high with archived documents, I took a seat before them, pulling the aether lamp close while she kept a lookout. I figured I had a few hours at most—the Brotherhood never truly slept, and sooner or later somebody would notice that I wasn't in my room, nor was Casey in hers. I had to be fast, to focus, even though my mind was still spinning from Tremaine's visit and felt like it might never stop.

Just think, I cajoled myself. *You're holding the same plans in your hand that were once in Nikola Tesla's. How many Academy students would crawl over broken glass to do the same?* Then again, I doubted most students of engineering realized that when he wasn't building coils and finding the alternating current, Tesla was building magical devices to keep a race of predatory Fae at bay.

His plans weren't anything special to look at—his handwriting was precise, his drawings meticulous, but they didn't glow or catch fire beneath my fingers, as would seem to fit such a portentous occasion. And there were lots of plans and diaries—hundreds at least. Tesla was prolific, and I'd heard that, unlike his competitor Edison, he recorded most ideas, even the wholly impractical ones. "This is going to take forever," I muttered. Casey shrugged.

"The ones Mr. Crosley thinks are particularly special are bound up in that big blue book," she said, shoving toward me a ledger that was almost too large for me to turn the pages of. It was full of blueprints, most of them for terrestrial inventions that I'd seen back in Lovecraft—the prototype steam jitney engine, a Tesla coil, an aether feeder that became the system everyone in the world whose home was piped with the stuff was familiar with.

I set the book aside. Crosley's ego display didn't interest

me. I tried a few of Tesla's personal journals, and then started looking through loose plans, some folded and faded so that the machines were almost unrecognizable. But the clock wasn't among them. There were no notes to even indicate Tesla had entertained the idea of such a machine.

I had a terrible sensation in my stomach that I might have gone about this all wrong, but I persisted. The nightmare clock had to be here. For so many reasons.

Casey looked back at me, chewing on her lip. "I can hear people moving around out there. We should probably get going soon."

"If we do get caught," I said, opening another bound volume, the paper so decayed the corners turned to dust in my hands, "blame me. Crosley needs me—I'll be punished less."

Casey gave me a tentative smile. "Thanks. But I don't want you punished either."

I shrugged. "I'm not scared of Harold Crosley. You helped me, now I'll help you. That's how it works."

Casey lowered her eyes. "Maybe in your world. I'm not used to it."

"What do you . . . ," I started, but was distracted by the spidery handwriting at the top of the last blueprint in the bound journal. *Arctic Gate—Transportive Device for Interdimensional Travel, commissioned by Raymond Crosley, 1899.*

I felt my mouth drop open in surprise, and I flipped the book around so Casey could see. "There's a Gate? Here?"

Casey nodded, looking as if she'd done something wrong. "But it never worked right. Mr. Crosley won't let anyone use it—there've been folks who've lost limbs and horrible stories about people who got shot out into the vacuum of space and whatnot." She chewed her lip. "Said it was just a prototype Tesla fiddled with. He locked that whole wing. Nobody goes there."

I heard Octavia's whisper. *The man who built the Gates. It started with him, and it will end with him.*

I carefully tore the blueprint from the book, tucking it under my shirt. My heart was pounding again, but this time it was from excitement and urgency at finally being so close to what I needed. "We're going there. Right now."

16

Tesla's Lost Gate

THINGS WERE WAKING up in the Bone Sepulchre as the short day—only a few hours of light, this time of year—got under way. Casey took me to the blocked-off staircase that led to where she said the Gate rested.

This had to be it—not a Gate, but the clock Tesla had conceived. I couldn't think of anywhere else Tesla could have hidden a doorway into the very dreams of the world. Faulty it might be, but I'd cross that bridge when I came to it.

"Are you sure about this?" Casey whispered as I performed my lock-picking trick again. It hurt more this time. My Weird had been making me suffer more and more with even the smallest exercises. I didn't know what that heralded—iron madness, fatigue, or something worse—but I had to sit down for a moment and catch my breath when the door sprang open.

"No," I told Casey, swiping at my bloody nose. "I have no idea if this will work. But I have no other options."

"I hear you there," Casey murmured, and then whipped around at the sound of approaching footsteps. "Inside!" she hissed, the fear back in her face. Later, when this was over, when things were back to how they should be, if I still knew her, I needed to ask Casey exactly what the Brotherhood had done to her, why she feared them so much.

They wanted to keep me locked up and use my talents as a weapon, and had tried to do the same to my father, so I doubted her story would be pleasant.

We crouched inside the stairwell, which was icy cold compared to the rest of the Bone Sepulchre, shivering and watching our breath form thunderheads as it escaped our mouths. The footsteps approached, passed and retreated. Casey doubled over, gasping with relief. I looked up, cringing when I saw the broken steps in the ice-covered spiral staircase leading up into nothing. "At least we're not afraid of heights," I said.

Casey shoved her hands into her armpits, shivering. I already couldn't feel my exposed skin. If Crosley didn't catch us, the Arctic chill might. This wasn't a cold you could shake off—it could stop your heart, freeze your skin and kill you between one breath and the next. We had to be quick and get back to where it was warm.

Casey and I climbed, clinging to the railing that remained in a few spots. Wood, like metal, would peel the skin off your palms at these temperatures. The steps groaned beneath our weight, the same bone-cracking sound the ice had made around the *Oktobriana*. It was almost a relief to have a tangible fear, something concrete I could concentrate on rather than Tremaine and Draven. Fear of plummeting to your death was a lot easier to cope with than fear of being exiled to the Thorn Land and having your boyfriend killed.

Casey's foot slipped through one of the gaping holes in the ice, and she grabbed at me. I grabbed the railing in turn, but the bolts ripped free from the wall. I let out a scream that was choked off when I hit the floor. Casey clung to my leg, dangling in space through one of the concentric holes, as if the floor had been burned away. I felt myself sliding backward and grabbed for a ridge, which mercifully held. I tried to pull us up, gasping. It felt as if I were being ripped apart. My fingers slipped, slicking the ice with blood, and I knew I was going to lose my grip, and then we were going to fall. The thought didn't make me particularly panicked—it was just a fact, a hard fact.

"Aoife," Casey gasped. "Don't let go!"

"You're going to have to climb over me," I gritted out. "Use me to get to the next step."

To Casey's credit, she didn't argue. To mine, I didn't scream when her weight increased exponentially and I felt a sick, wet popping in one of my elbow joints.

Her foot hooked in my belt, and then her weight was off me and her hands were around my tingling wrists, pulling me up by any bit of shirt or skin she could grasp. We both sprawled on the icy floor atop the spiral staircase.

I couldn't remember when I'd been in more pain. Though, on the bright side, I wasn't cold any longer.

Once I'd gathered my breath and my wits, I rolled onto my back and looked up at the ceiling. I couldn't stand just yet, and my arm was on fire, but I was alive, and I decided that for the time being, that was enough.

I saw we were at the top of the Bone Sepulchre, in a spire barely large enough for four people to stand shoulder to shoulder. I poked Casey with my good arm. "Are you all right?"

"More or less," she panted. "Can't stop shaking."

"We're lying on ice," I said, and giggled. There was no rationality behind laughing—I was just glad to be alive, even with a busted arm, trapped at the top of a frozen spire. I tried sitting up and found it wasn't an entirely impossible feat.

The spire room wasn't polished like the rest of the Bone Sepulchre. The ice was rough here, icicles dripping from the ceiling, as if we were standing inside a pincushion. The walls were covered with black marks, and the floor, when I managed to clamber to my feet, was jagged and uneven.

"This is nuts," Casey said. "We're never going to get back down those stairs, and Mr. Crosley will skin me alive for sure." She looked ready to cry. I held up a hand.

"It's going to be all right, Casey. With any luck, we won't have to climb down anywhere." I hoped, at least. I really didn't have the faintest idea.

But then I saw Tesla's Gate. It sat in a corner, almost as if it had been shoved against the wall and forgotten, like unwanted holiday decorations in someone's attic. Spindly and wholly unlike the Gate the Erlkin had constructed in the Mists, the whole thing rested on three squat legs, like a hat stand. A pair of metal arms arched overhead, a giant circuit connected at the top to a Tesla coil, which was attached in turn to a bulb of aether, sickly opalescent white with age and disuse, that barely moved any longer.

Two dials were attached to either side, just waiting for somebody to activate them, and I shivered, a shiver born not of cold but of pure excitement. This was the experience I'd hoped for, when I'd been holding Tesla's journals. This connection, across time, to a man who'd envisioned such a thing, such a delicate piece of machinery that had the power to move whole bodies between worlds.

I couldn't waste any time, I knew. Casey was right—by now, somebody had to have discovered we were both missing from our quarters. I checked for a power source, but the coil was it. I activated it and was rewarded with a spark of electricity before the thing began cycling. I was elated, but Casey shrank back.

"I don't like the look of that thing," she said. "Lots of faulty machines back in the Rustworks would kill you if you touched 'em. And that one looks rickety."

I approached the Gate slowly, reaching out with my Weird. The coil was snapping and the ancient aether was drifting around inside its teardrop-shaped globe, but nothing pricked my Weird. The machine was, for all intents and purposes, alive but dead. It didn't function, not even a whisper beyond the ions of electricity I could taste on the back of my tongue.

My hopes sank. A faulty Gate I could fix. But one that was simply dead, a lump of iron where a vortex into other worlds should be? I had no idea how to fix that, and my Weird wouldn't help me if I did.

I tried both dials and was rewarded with electricity writhing across the ground as the Tesla coil released its pent-up energy, but there was still no flutter in the fabric of the space around us. Nothing. My Weird felt nothing. The machine was as dead and cold as the ice field outside.

I wanted to sob, scream, to kick at the Gate until it fractured, but the destruction all around us put me off. At one time or another, the Gate to the dreaming place had worked. I was missing something.

Be smart, Aoife, I told myself. *Be an engineer.* The Gate had both a power source and enough power in the aether to transform the dimension around us, but what did it lack? What, if I turned in this schematic in an Academy class, would I get marks off for?

Tesla. It began with him, it ends with him. Tesla was the connection. Tesla connected the Iron Land with all the others. Controlled the wild energy of the vortex between worlds. Beat back the Storm he'd caused even as he'd opened us up to unimaginable horrors.

He connected worlds, and his Gate needed a connector. Something to close the circuit that arced energy all around the spire, making Casey shriek with each new bolt, even though the offshoot of the coils was harmless.

"Don't be frightened," I told her. Maybe if I said it to someone else, I could take my own advice. It wasn't very far to step into the rain of castoff electrical charge, to stand myself between the two iron bars that made up the main part of the Gate.

"What are you *doing*?" Casey shrieked as the coil amped up to a roar. I felt a spark of life in the machine, just the faintest one. I opened my Weird, hoping it wasn't the last time I would do so.

This time, though, it didn't hurt at all. It felt as if I'd always been meant to be here, standing in the center of the only Gate to reach past Iron, past Thorn, and directly into the dreams of everyone in every world. This wasn't a machine I was touching. This was the fabric of reality itself. I nudged gently, and I felt the vortex grip me.

Just one more step.

17

The Dreamer's Domain

When I stepped into the center of the Gate as it came to life, power humming through its every mechanism and rivet, I felt it close around me. The energy snapped off my skin and sent blue streams of electrical fire arcing toward every corner of the small room. "Don't worry!" I shouted at Casey, who was plastered against the wall, eyes as wide as they would go. "I'll be all right!"

Of course, I really had no idea. But I didn't care. My Weird filled my mind, cool and deep as diving into a bottomless pool.

My vision turned into endless light as the coil arced brighter and brighter. The Gate was too powerful, no longer part of me but a tide pulling me under and replacing what made me Aoife with the unrelenting strength of the Weird.

I spread my arms, embracing the ride, feeling electricity arcing from my fingers, my hair, my eyelids. The violet light of the aether whirled around me, obscuring the ice tower, obscuring everything.

The falling sensation gripped me, and it was far stronger than the *hexenring* or the Gates in the Mists. This was being pulled into a vortex, not transported from place to place.

Fading, the light bleeding away into blackness, I saw the thousand skies above me again and was frozen for a moment before I felt the breath sucked from my lungs and the stars blinked out, one by one, as I passed into unconsciousness.

I felt something brush across my face. Not a hand. Something more like a feather or a cobweb, light and insubstantial as breath on my cheek.

Opening my eyes was a tremendous effort. Everything about me was heavy, most of all my thoughts, which were moving at the pace of sluggish snails.

Was I lying unconscious somewhere, or dead? Was any of this real?

It was my dream, I realized, but tethered to the painfully real, as every part of my body could attest. Above me, I saw a glass ceiling looking out onto a gentle blue sky studded with a few white clouds, delicate as spun sugar. A wind blew them apart and re-formed them into new shapes. Pink sunset blushed at the edges, and for a moment all I could do was stare through the spiderweb cracks in the glass.

"I like this time of day."

I rolled my head to the left and saw bare white feet surrounded by the hem of a black robe, moth-eaten and nearly gray from wear.

The figure in black was no longer shadowed and covered by illusion and my own mind's dream projections. His chest was bare, plain black trousers hidden under the robe, which he shrugged off and let fall to the floor. His hair was slicked back from his face, curls gathering at his neck. His eyes were strange, not silver like a Fae's but white and ever-changing, like smoke under glass. I couldn't stop looking at him. The dream figure was one of the most beautiful creatures I had ever seen.

"You're the first person besides me to see it in a very long time," he said. "It happens in the winters of the worlds, the same sunset all at once, when things are desperate and broken and on the verge of cataclysm everywhere else."

The sky darkened to blood-red, blood dried to puce, turned to crumpled blue velvet and then darkness, studded with winking stars. The figure sighed. "And it's over."

I swallowed. My throat was tight and sore, as if I'd been screaming for hours. My voice, when I found it, was barely a rasp. "Am I dreaming?"

"No," the figure said sadly. "You're awake, Aoife."

Then I'd made it. The Gate had worked. I felt like screaming for joy and sobbing with relief all at once. "I'm . . . This isn't my dream?"

"No. You're here, in the center of all worlds, the place that is not a place," the figure said. "The real here. The here that can no longer hide under the veil of sleep."

"I've been here before, though, and thought it was real," I said as the ticking of the great gear reached my ears. I was still unwilling to believe that after all I'd been through, I'd finally done something right. "I've dreamed exactly this a lot of times. Standing here and talking to you."

"I know, but dreaming you're here isn't the same," said the figure. "People dream their way here sometimes, or at least they used to. They put their images up on that glass there, make this place what they want, not what it is when you actually exist in it or when you come to it through a Gate. Except you. You could see most of what was really here in your dreams, but not all. Part of you still saw what you wanted to." He gestured at the place. "Does it really look anything like you wanted? Now that you're standing here with your body and not just a fragment of your mind?"

I swiveled around to take in my surroundings from my vantage on the floor. The floor itself was thick with dust and grit, and covered in the skeletons of small birds and mammals, feathers and bones decaying under my hands and feet, which I could feel with the realism of the waking world. It was as if things had been trapped behind the glass of the dome and never escaped. The throne and the great gear so prominent from my nightmares were in reality dilapidated, the seat propped up under one broken leg by thick cloth-bound books, the regalia flag tattered beyond recognition. It blew back and forth in an invisible wind. Actual cobwebs swam from the ceiling in thick banks like rain clouds. The gear itself was rusty, and it ticked with a sonorous groan each time it moved. The air had changed when I stepped through the Gate, was stale and sour and ancient against my face.

In the light, in reality, it was as far from what I'd expected as a true face was from a blurry photograph. I felt crushing disappointment. This place couldn't help me. Nothing here was more than a poor imitation of my dreams of setting things right.

"You're disappointed," the figure stated, as if he could read my mind. I didn't deny it.

He sighed, moved away from me, and sat at an ornate dining table hidden in a shadowed corner, large enough to seat twenty. A tarnished candelabra was at his elbow, candle wax flowing across the surface. The single chair wobbled under even his slight weight. "It's been unseen for a long time," he said. "I used to have a place across every world, even if it was only in people's dreams. But when they put gates and guards at all the entrances and exits . . ." He sighed, his breath kicking up some dust from the tabletop. "Those things are broken now. The dreams have stopped coming."

I flashed on Dean. *I sleep tight beside you, princess.* Valentina, Cal, my father and even Draven had all made mention that they hadn't been dreaming.

How could I not have seen it? The broken Gates were fracturing not just all the physical Lands, but the metaphysical one as well. This dream place was drying up. That fact left me with one burning question.

"Why do I still have dreams?"

The figure shrugged, as if the answer should be obvious. "You're not dreaming when you visit me. You're touching something you can't quite grasp. Like the man who built that contraption you used to get here, you can lift the veil, the perceptions put in place by space-time, and you can see the worlds as I see them from here. It's your gift, both of you."

"Tesla? Tesla came here?" My voice came out a high squeak, and I felt an impending sense of panic of the worst kind. This was all wrong. My dreams were dreams. Reality was reality. Without that, I might as well be mad.

The figure nodded. "Nikola was a troubled man. A man who thought he was going insane, until his science helped him realize he wasn't having visions. He had a gift, and where some controlled fire or water or air, he controlled reality itself. His gift was trying to show him what he could do, but unfortunately he never believed that what he'd done was a worthy thing. When he realized that he could use his gift to build those Gates, he thought he'd brought about the end of the world."

He stood up again as I stared at him slack-jawed, trying to process what he'd just told me, and moved to stand in front of the great gear. The skies outside changed in time with its agonized, rusty ticking, becoming stormy and dark. Lightning arced from place to place, and the ground under my feet vibrated with thunder. I wasn't scared of what was outside, but I was terrified at the implications of this man's words.

"He didn't destroy the world," I said in a whisper. "The Storm made it a bad place. A hard place. But the Iron Land still exists." This couldn't be true. My Weird was machines. It was iron, steam, aether. Gears and wheels, turning in time with my mind.

My Weird was not this, not this power to rend reality. I'd already done enough of that.

But how else to explain how I'd come here? I hadn't fixed the Gate with my Weird—it hadn't been broken to begin with. It had come to life at my very presence. Almost as if it had been waiting for me.

I started shaking, and knotted my hands together to hide it. Fixing the Gate in the Bone Sepulchre hadn't hurt. Not one bit. My Weird usually crushed my brain, compressed and remade it, every time I tried to use it, but this time . . . this had felt right. I had to consider that the man from my dreams could be right. Maybe machines weren't my Weird. Maybe manipulating machines was just a side effect. Maybe, really, Tesla and I were the machines, made of bone and blood and magic rather than iron. Machines able to open the doorways between worlds with our thoughts.

It wouldn't be the strangest thing I'd heard of since I'd left Lovecraft. I looked back at the dream figure. "Tesla wasn't afraid of the Gates," I said. "He made them for a reason—he made them to keep people safe. Maybe what grew up around them was bad, the Fae and all the creatures creeping into the Iron Land, but . . ." I trailed off, frustrated and confused by the whole conversation. I'd come here to make things better and I'd only found more questions.

"It's not the Gates Tesla was afraid of," the figure said. "He was afraid of *them*." He pointed out at the storm, which billowed across all the skies now, blanketing us in iron-gray violence and bright white lightning. Rain began, spattering patterns across the glass, and every time the lightning flashed, I caught a glimpse of things with blind eyes and long tentacles, writhing and racing and fighting among the clouds, growing closer and closer with every heartbeat, every boom of thunder. I drew back, even though, exposed inside a glass dome, there was nowhere to hide.

"What are they?" I whispered, feeling my shoulder begin to throb with a vengeance the closer the great creatures came. "Who are *you*?"

"I'm nothing," the figure said. "I'm everything. Depends on how you look at dreams." He looked back at me, silhouetted in the lightning. His face was handsome, not young and not old, taut skin over sharp bones, a hawkish nose and those blind eyes that nevertheless stabbed me with a visceral feeling of vulnerability when he turned them on me.

"I think dreams can be real," I said softly. "In part."

"Then if I'm real, and they're real, at least in part, I'm the one who looks after them," he said. "The king, the keeper, the weaver and the destroyer. There are a lot of names that spin out all across the skies. Some say I'm a trickster and some that I'm a demon. Depends on who you ask."

"What should I call you?" I said, unable to stare at the skies outside any longer without giving in to the urge to scream. "You know my name. I need yours." Names had a lot of power, at least with the sort of people I dealt with. It would make me feel a tiny bit more in control if I could name the dream figure, give the darkness substance.

"I don't have one. I'm just a shadow," he said. "A shape on your wall, when a little light comes under your door at night. You can call me whatever you like."

"You remind me of the crows," I said. "They followed me from place to place, back home. My friend Dean says they're clever watchers. They see everything. Like you."

"They're psychopomps," said the figure, the same thing Dean had said to me when I'd been frightened of the crows following me in Arkham. "Not agents of mine." When I cocked my head in confusion, he elaborated. "Psychopomps are the heralds of the dead. They go to and from the Deadlands with souls that have escaped the notice of both Death and the living." He tilted his face up and frowned in concern as raindrops worked their way through the cracked glass at the apex of the dome. I watched as well, but the glass appeared to hold, so I looked away rather than watch the writhing black shadows beyond.

"I'll take that name you want to give me," the figure said. "It's as good as any."

"Crow," I agreed. "You're bad tempered and squawk like one, anyway."

Above us, again the great figures clashed and retreated. This storm wasn't moving, despite the rapid pace at which everything moved here, the endless sunsets, sunrises, storms and clear skies of all the worlds that spun around this place. The thunderheads, and the shadows, were staying still, right overhead. It wasn't normal, and I looked at the dream figure for confirmation. Crow rubbed his left hand over his right, and I noticed for the first time, in the stark relief of the lightning, that a network of white scars, whiter than the dead-colored skin underneath, webbed his entire body, his face and his eyelids, up to his hairline and down to his fingernails.

"What are they?" I repeated, and pointed upward. I had an idea, but it seemed so fantastical. I'd never believed in the stories of great alien beings who drifted endlessly through space. Worshipped by some, they were forecasted to return someday and restore the wisdom of the cosmos.

I was part Fae, and even I could recognize a fairy tale when I heard one.

"You know what they are," Crow said, and my heart dropped. He continued, "They travel through space and time, from star to star. They create, they send magic and madness and the spark of invention into the primitive beings they encounter." He sighed. "But sometimes, they also devour. They can be the beginning of a golden age or the end of everything." He touched one of the great spiked gears protruding from the floor. The nightmare clock, in the flesh. "The power of my gears keeps them close to me, because I'm protected. I keep them occupied and prevent them from visiting one world too often. There's always the possibility that it will be a visit of destruction. But you see their children everywhere, in what you call the Iron Land. You have ghouls and things like the Erlkin, yes, but some of those abominations that feed on your flesh don't come from Thorn and they don't come from the Erlkin. They creep and crawl and pretend all they're interested in is food, and little by little they're paving the way for a return visit from those creatures out there beyond the glass. They journeyed to your world once before, left behind the sort of magic in the human blood that leads to things like the Gates, but this time, this return, I couldn't guess their motives."

Crow turned and looked at me full on, and even though his eyes lacked pupils his stare was penetrating. "It takes millions of years for a dead star to send its last light across the cosmos. It'll take them millions of years to devour the universe, but I believe they'll do it eventually, Aoife. They came from another place, another wheel and spoke of a world much like ours, where they've done the same." He rubbed his scars harder, the white lines standing out like brands and gradually fading to pink under his nails, as if he were having a reaction to the very idea of the creatures outside.

"Those . . ." My mouth dropped open, and the confirmation of my fears made me sick and dizzy all over again. "Those are the Great Old Ones. They're real."

"Perhaps the realest things in the universe," said Crow. "And the most unreal as well. They bring a vortex of madness and creation with them, and to power it, they expend enormous energy. So they are always hungry."

He came to me and offered his hand. I took it with trepidation and then gasped when he yanked me against him. His chest was hard, unyielding as granite. He was warm, though. I was surprised—I expected that a being such as him would be not warm, but cold as outer space. Crow didn't look as if he should have any blood in him at all, but I stopped struggling when I felt the warmth of his skin. It calmed me, and I had the strangest urge to cling to him.

"I know why you're here," he said, lips nearly against my ear. It didn't feel like a violation, though—it felt as if he was trying to keep me safe. "The same reason Nikola came." Crow grabbed the back of my neck with his other hand and drew us together so that we shared breath. "You both came here because you both lost something," he whispered. "And you're going to use the clock to turn it back and make it right. Nikola tried to turn it back to the time when he was young, before he ever conceived of bending reality to his whim. Before the Gates were even a spark. To avoid the Storm, and all the destruction it caused. I think you're here for very similar reasons."

"I have to use it," I whispered back. "I wouldn't be here if I didn't need it, Crow." I felt tears slip down my cheeks, warm and wet and alive. "I need it," I repeated, unable to articulate all the reasons why over my sobbing.

"The clock is what keeps them at bay," said Crow, turning me to face the writhing shapes outside the glass. "The gears hold power that even they covet, and they're wise creatures. They fear it a little too. Only the clock. Nothing else." He let go of me. "That's how it is."

"But you don't *know,*" I told him. "They could be coming not to devour. You said it yourself." The Great Old Ones could create as easily as destroy, according to Crow. Who was he to decide that they were only on a mission to end the Iron world?

Crow shook his head, his features less sad now than set, with no way for me to change his mind. "I can't take that chance, do you understand? I'm not the power I once was, Aoife. Humans don't believe in dreams as anything but fancies, Fae think they are invincible, and the Erlkin dream only of machines, clanking and steaming and tearing this place apart. Nobody fears me, and nobody believes I truly exist."

He pressed his forehead against the glass, so close to the things outside that I swore he could have embraced them. I'd never given the Old Ones more than a passing thought. In their way, they were placebos for the sort of people who bought wholeheartedly into Proctor propaganda. Great alien beings, bringers of wisdom and knowledge.

Except the Proctors were wrong. Because Crow was afraid of these vast beings. In my dreams I would have thought nothing could scare Crow. He was ancient, after all. The king of dreams.

I didn't know how I felt. There was a chance the Old Ones could break free, but there was also a chance they didn't care about our world at all. Crow was too scared to see clearly, that much was plain. I had to make the choice this time. No Tremaine whispering in my ear, no Draven holding me hostage.

My choice, I realized as I stood at the center of the dome, was the same as it had always been. No choice at all. I had to set right what I'd done. I had to use the clock.

"I need the clock, Crow," I repeated. "I have to go back and stop myself, find my mother and come back. I *have* to."

Crow shook his head, and my panic redoubled. Not now, not when I was so close. "Please," I whispered. "If I don't, the world won't ever recover. It'll be worse than the Storm."

"This is all I have left," Crow muttered. "Protecting the rest of the lands from the Old Ones is all I have. But as long as I exist, as long as the gear turns, this is what I must do."

I felt fresh hot tears sprout in my eyes. "I'm not like you, Crow. All *I* have is my family, and Dean, and I need them to be all right." I made myself move despite my fear of the Old Ones. I went to Crow at the glass and reached out. I touched the very tips of my fingers to his skin. The scars were ridged and warm, and I fought the urge to run my hand over them.

"You're not special," he said. "You or Nikola. You're just a girl, and he was a troubled young man who made terrible mistakes. What gives you the right to unleash the Old Ones just to put right a single error?"

His words were a hammer blow, but I didn't let myself crumble. "I did something really horrible," I told him. "But if you're so worried about protecting the worlds, well—there won't *be* a world much longer, not if I don't stop what I set in motion."

What I said next would likely decide whether I ever got to touch the nightmare clock or Crow simply shut me out of his domain, as everyone else in the world was slowly closing off from their dreams. "You can't hold them back,

Crow." I looked up at the things outside, watched their tentacles and their great cloudy eyes rove from sky to sky, world to world, hungry. "They know it too," I said. "They know you're weakening every night, every hour, that human and Fae and Erlkin don't dream. Every minute that the Gates are broken, keeping your dreams from reaching anyone except me."

I don't know what I expected, but it wasn't for Crow to close the space between us, grab me by the throat and slam the back of my head into the glass hard enough to make tiny cracks. I gasped in pain, my vision blurring and my skull ringing.

"I walked the spheres with gods, you speck of flesh," Crow growled, his tone no longer soft and measured. "And you call me weak?"

"That's what I said," I agreed. "Your only chance is to let me use the clock."

Crow glared down at me. His features really were beautiful, in the way that something terrible is also beautiful—a silver-plated straight razor, a fireball, or the trapped fury of aether under glass.

"You can't be happy here," I continued. "Cut off. Nobody dreaming. It'll only get worse."

A small shudder passed through Crow's narrow shoulders. It could have just been wind, but inside the dome, it was as still as a calm afternoon in midsummer, so I knew I was getting somewhere. "Let me turn it back," I said. "Or I'll use my Weird to do it without you." I could already feel the clock in my mind, as if it had always been there. Maybe it had—I'd touched it in my dreams and it had waited patiently in my subconscious until my brain caught up with what my dreams had always known. Of course, I had no idea if I could manipulate it. That wasn't my gift, after all. But I had to try.

Crow gave a startled laugh. "Your Weird? You mean the magic trick your blood trots out when your higher brain can't take it another second and asks the lizard to jump in the driver's seat? You can't use that on this. This isn't a machine. And your *Weird* is so much more than that. Your mind would break from the strain."

"Watch me," I snapped, and pushed. It felt natural, no pain, no struggle and not even any pressure in my skull. I married my mind with the nightmare clock so perfectly it might have been made of flesh, or I of iron.

But nothing happened. The gear ticked on, the storm continued to rumble, and outside the bodies of the Great Old Ones pressed ever closer.

I pushed harder, because it was easy now, and then all at once I was felled by the worst pain I had ever known. Worse than when I'd destroyed the Engine. Worse than when I'd plunged into the icy Erebus River afterward. It was so bad I couldn't even think of it in terms of my own body; the pain was a separate and distinct being, sharing my skin and filling me to the brim with agony, until it overflowed into a scream.

Flashes. Light. Pictures. A dizzy lanternreel on a torn screen, projecting from the Edison box, out of focus and saturated with blood colors.

My father on his knees, a dark head cradled in his lap. My mother standing in front of great iron walls that run on and on. Cal halfway between a ghoul and a boy, the seam stitched with wire, listening to faraway screams while smoke roils around him.

Crow grabbed me and shook me, and I let go of the clock. The pain stopped, leaving me trembling and soaked in freezing sweat. I felt as if I wanted to throw up, but none of my muscles would respond to do anything more than spasmodically tremble. I had been electrified, and was now burned.

"I warned you," he said, without a modicum of sympathy. "If you were really good with machines, you'd have me over a barrel, but you're not. That's not where your true gift lies."

He *had* told me, and I should have listened. Crossing worlds didn't hurt, but the nightmare clock wasn't responding to me. Machines had always been a fight, but coming here had felt natural. "I guess . . . ," I began, but talking hurt. I tried again. "I guess you'll just have to kill me to stop me, then. Because otherwise I'm not going to stop."

"I told you," Crow sighed, using the hem of his robe to blot the blood from my face. "Sacrificing yourself won't change what you did. You have a gift. You owe it to yourself to try rather than throw yourself on your sword."

I tried to sit up, but I was too spent, too wrung out. I wanted to scream in frustration. "But I destroyed the Engine," I croaked.

Crow sat back on his heels. "You can cross worlds, Aoife. Without a Gate, without anything but your own mind. Explain to me how you can have such a gift, believe in it and not believe you can fix this?"

I didn't have a good answer for him. I just lay there

watching the top of the dome, the Old Ones growing larger and closer.

"Machinery and magic in the same mind." Crow shook his head. "World crossing, right there." He reached out and ran his thumb along my cheekbone, through the blood. "Amazing. Humans can still surprise me."

I curled up in a ball, away from him. I wanted to be smaller and smaller, until I disappeared. Having a Weird that Draven and Tremaine would kill for was bad enough. If they, or the Brotherhood, knew what I could truly do, create Gates out of thin air, I'd never be safe again. They would all converge, fight over who got to use me or murder me. Depending on their outlook, I was a savior or a destroyer.

I would never be free, and neither would anyone I cared about.

"I have to . . ." I sat up, even though it hurt almost as much as trying to manipulate the nightmare clock. "I have to put things right."

Crow worried his lip and looked at me. His teeth were small and square, not pointed like the ones I'd come to associate with most inhuman things. "I can't let you," he said. "The Old Ones—"

"I'll put them back." I grabbed his arm and made it fruitless for him to pull away. His forearms, on the insides, were snaked with black marks, ink tracing the scars to form words, though they were in a language I couldn't decipher. I held on. "You told me I can do it. I can cross worlds. I can make them stop ever coming to you again. I can put them back where they belong, out in the cold, empty space where they can never escape."

"Nobody knows what I go through, keeping them from

the rest of the worlds," Crow said, looking up. "When they talk, it's in riddles. To hear their voices would melt your eyes out of their sockets."

"Then you'll have to tell me what to do," I said, holding on to him as he stood up, falling against his hard chest. The warmth of his skin made my cheek flush.

"I don't think you understand what you're willing to do," Crow said. "I don't think you can."

"I think you want things to be set right as badly as I do," I said. "I think you're scared of those things."

"If you fail," Crow said, "you're going to set them loose. On everything. The Gates and what's happening to the Iron Land will be a tiny dot of misery on history's time line of pain if they're allowed."

"That's a chance I'll take," I said. I could do it. I had to. In the back of my mind, I recognized the same sort of desperation that made people in Lovecraft do insane, suicidal things like hurl firebombs at Ravenhouse and attack Proctors in gangs, dragging them off to be hanged from old machine skeletons in the Rustworks.

And I didn't care. I would get what I needed from Crow.

"Even if I have faith you can deliver on your promise," Crow told me, "you would have to face the clock. And it's not a clock, not really. It's a vessel holding in the past and the future and the dreams that tie them together." He held up his palm, bloody from where he'd touched me. "That's what it is, when you look into the heart of it. The nightmares of everyone you love. A machine made of bad dreams that you must walk through to use the clock. Nobody can weather that storm, I don't think. Not Tesla. Not even you."

I pressed my palm against his, taking the blood back onto

my own skin. "I can," I said. I didn't even bother to hope Crow couldn't see the lie. He had known what I'd say before the words left my tongue. But at last, to the greatest relief I'd ever felt, he pretended to believe me, and folded his fingers over mine.

"Then so be it."

18 The Nightmare Machine

TOUCHING THE NIGHTMARE clock didn't hurt this time; it just took up residence in my mind as surely and swiftly as a thought. There was no sensation of falling, no pulling apart as vast mathematical distances compressed like accordioned paper to accommodate my body.

I was simply there, in another place, as if I'd fallen asleep and forgotten where I was.

Crow stood next to me, looking singularly unhappy. "How long this lasts is up to you," he said. "The clock is a harsh master. I'll be here, but I can't interfere. If you can weather the machine grinding your mind, you may use it. But you won't."

I didn't argue. I had no idea what was coming, except that it wasn't going to be pleasant.

Crow looked around at where we were, which was nowhere special. We stood on a brick sidewalk in front of a blue house, shutters sagging and paint a thing more of memory than of fact. "You know this place?"

"Yes," I said, feeling a hard lump in my chest. I did know it, too well. Here, I was eight years old. Here, in our first care-home, Conrad and I were in a dark closet, sitting with our knees pulled to our chests, smelling musty winter coats. Here, we were locked in, because we'd been bad.

Not bad. *Evil*. That was the word our care-mother had used. She thought it would be worse for Conrad to see me punished, because I cried all the time. Our care-mother thought I was a brat.

But I knew the closet was worse for Conrad. He hated small spaces. He had gotten himself stuck in a dumbwaiter in our old flat once and nearly stopped breathing before the landlord fished him out and returned him to our garret. My mother had barely noticed he'd been gone at all, lost as she was in her fancies.

That had been the beginning of the end. The landlord called the care-workers. The care-workers called the Proctors. The Proctors took her away.

Conrad would shift next to me in the dark during those times, and I would hear choked breathing. I would pretend he wasn't silently sobbing into his knees. I'd squeeze whatever part of his arm I could find in the dark and whisper it'd be okay.

It wasn't okay, for months. Finally our neighbor noticed we were rail thin and still wearing the same clothes we'd arrived in. We were rushed out, to another care-home, which I now knew was because Archie was trying to make sure we were all right while he was off with the Fae, chasing the specter of harmony of a world without Proctors. He'd greased the Lovecraft care-workers well enough that if we were being abused in any flagrant way, we got moved to a new care-home and never got separated.

But for those months, there was the closet. I didn't mind it after a while. At least we were out of our care-mother's sight, and even if we had to sleep in there, she didn't bother us.

Conrad, though, stopped sleeping, stopped eating, jumped at every sound. He thinned out in more ways than physically, and spent long patches of time just staring at things like the aethervox or the hole in the front hall carpet, waiting. Waiting for the next time he'd go up into the hot darkness and be locked in.

And in his nightmare, I was right there with him.

Couldn't breathe. Couldn't see. Couldn't tell my sister it was going to be all right. I was weak. That horrible fat woman made me weak, no matter how hard I tried to stand and be the man of the family. I wanted to grab the scissors she used to chop off all of Aoife's hair and jam them into her fat back so far they disappeared, up to their pearl-handled hilt.

"No!" I screamed, Conrad's anger feeling like acid in my guts and throat.

His claustrophobic rage was like a tide, and I swam away from it, trying to define my own memories of that horrible house. It didn't help much, but the thing did begin to crumble, collapsing on its foundation like I hoped it had years ago.

Then it was over and we were gone, and in an entirely new kind of darkness. This one was alive, rustling, stinking of wet dog. Old sewer pipes dripped above me, water landing on the back of my hand, brackish and black like blood in a no-color lanternreel.

This dream I didn't recognize from my real life, but I knew who it had to be and I didn't want to have to see it.

Cal watched as light appeared, half in and half out of his ghoul shape.

The light was carried by a girl, plump and buxom, with rosy cheeks and bouncing curls. Bethina stopped and looked at him, and her pretty face crinkled in disgust.

"*I . . . ,*" Cal rasped, but all that came out was the ghoul voice, his true voice, and Bethina screamed.

As I occupied his view in the dream, I saw what he wanted to tell her, so badly it ached. He wanted to tell her, and knew he never could, that eventually he'd either break her heart or reveal himself as a monster, to her disgust and terror.

"Bastard!" Bethina shrieked, and all around her Cal's nest came to life, ghouls pawing and clawing at her, tearing her clothes. I choked, doubling over, but the air of the sewer wasn't any better and I couldn't breathe.

"*I want you . . . ,*" Cal croaked, and then he couldn't speak. *I want you to see me,* he'd tried to say, but it was an obscene parody of that, and Bethina dropped her lantern, the aether globe shattering open.

"Burn!" she screamed. "Right to cinders!"

The fire caught impossibly fast. Smoke filled the tunnel, obscuring Bethina, who sobbed, naked and covered in soot. Cal listened to the screams of his nest dying, Bethina crying, choking on smoke, and he couldn't move.

I couldn't either, tied to his mind until the horrible recurring nightmare played itself out. I couldn't push on from this. This wasn't memory, this was pure overwhelming fear manifesting itself like poison in Cal's subconscious. His senses made it visceral, until I was screaming too, and then choking, until I thought I was going to pass out.

When the smoke cleared, Crow and I were someplace much worse.

I recognized the flat where Conrad and I had last lived with Nerissa. It hadn't been in a good part of town, sitting on the edge of the Rustworks near South Lovecraft Station. Conrad slept on the sofa, and I slept on a small Murphy bed that came out of the sitting room wall. It might once have been an ironing board, but it was just the right size for an eight-year-old girl.

I wasn't inside the flat, however, but rather was looking at it from the outside, up at the yellow glow of the window, since the building was so old that it didn't have an aether feed, just oil lamps that coated everything we owned with a fine layer of soot.

A shape passed in front of the glass, then another. Boy and girl, racing back and forth, yelling in some sort of made-up contest.

"Archie." The view rolled to the left, and I saw a younger Harold Crosley. Gray still shot through his white hair, and he carried considerably less weight in his jowls. "We need to keep moving," Crosley said. "Patrols are tighter than ever."

Archie waved his hand, his breath steaming in the cold. "In a minute."

"Now," Crosley insisted. "We can't stand staring up at a window forever, Grayson."

Archie rounded on Crosley. "That's my family in there, Harold." He ignored Crosley's huff of irritation and turned back to the window. He stared intently, all his attention on the children inside, hearing them laugh through the thin single-paned glass.

The sense of loss as he stared at the window was so intense, so profound, that I felt myself starting to weep. It was the opposite of being full—when Archie looked up at our flat, he was totally empty. He felt so far from us he might as well have been on the opposite side of the globe.

He knew he had to protect us from the silver-tongued, sharp-toothed Fae. Knew that for that reason, he could never be with us. Must never draw attention to his family. Never expose them to danger.

Nerissa came to the window. She was too thin, her hair lank, her cheeks flushed and feverish. She wouldn't last much longer here in Lovecraft, Archie knew. I could feel the bank book he carried with him everywhere, an account left over from when his father was alive, secret from the Brotherhood. It wasn't much, in the scheme of the Grayson family's formerly vast wealth, but it would be enough to pay off the right city officials to make sure his children were safe.

Archie knew in that moment that he would have chucked his upbringing, his travels to the four corners of the globe, his massive house in Arkham and all the fine things within, to be able to go up the stairs, open the door and sweep Conrad and Aoife into his arms. To kiss Nerissa's too-warm forehead and tell her it was all going to be all right.

But he couldn't, so he turned his back on the flat and followed Howard Crosley, pretending it was only the icy winter wind that had caused the moisture in his eyes.

19

The Gears of All Things

AND THEN I was back in my own head. I was on my knees in Crow's space, at the heart of all things. I was sobbing, my face soaked, and I was trembling. I'd known the dreams would be bad, but I'd never expected the darkest hearts of everyone I cared about to be marched across my mind.

Outside the dome, there was no sky around me now, none of the endless worlds. The places I'd seen, the nightmares of Conrad and Cal and Archie, whirled around me instead, and beyond them, I saw a thin pinpoint of yellow light, like a candle bobbing above the black waters of a river leading away into a secret place.

I knew on some level that I wasn't really hearing the voice that came out of the dark; rather, it had planted itself deep in my mind, where my Weird came from, where the memories of my oldest ancestors were stored.

Did you dream? the Old Ones whispered.

"Yes," I whispered.

We have dreamed. We have dreamed stars and suns. The before time and the after time. Dreamed your world into being.

"I want you to turn it back," I said. "Stop all this from ever having happened. Stop me from having met Tremaine, having destroyed the Engine, all of it."

Is that what you truly wish? the voices hissed, like the burn of steam against my mind. *The before time of blood and entrapment? We are trapped. We are trapped so long, dreaming.*

Crow stood next to me, staring at the pinpoint as it grew larger and larger, and I saw all at once that it wasn't a light but an eye, nearly as large as the dome itself, staring down at us from a fathomless distance. The Old Ones, linked inexorably with the nightmare clock. Now that I'd found its heart, they were speaking to me, letting me know what would happen if I turned the thing keeping them prisoner to my own use.

"I want what I did to have never happened," I repeated.

But the world is bleeding, the voice replied. *And the flow can never be stanched. You are a destroyer, and even the great gear of the worlds cannot turn back what has already been done.*

My mouth dropped open in shock and anger. "No. I stood up to those horrible things I had to see. Now I get to use the clock."

Who are you to change the course of history? the Old Ones whispered. *You have torn the world. For that there is no cure. Not in your lands, and not in this device. Some things cannot be unmade, Aoife Grayson. Some things simply are.*

I snapped my gaze to Crow, furious and unbelieving. "You lied to me," I snarled.

Crow spread his hands, helpless. "I told you the clock

can't simply turn time around. I thought maybe it would work for you, but there are some things nothing on earth or in the heavens can move, Aoife. The clock can't undo time and knit the past back together—not like Tesla thought, like he told others it could. But maybe it can set things differently, allow you to see things in a new light." He took my hand, even though I fought him. My skin was ice. I could feel the clock as a part of me, and saw that Crow and I were both limbs of a greater organism, while below us the Great Old Ones churned, a sea of things so ancient they didn't even feel alive, only constant and cold, like the stars they traveled.

"Your life before," Crow whispered. "Was that really a life you wanted? The world was sick long before the Gates shattered, Aoife." He ran his free thumb down my cheek. "You can't go back. You can go forward, though."

Ever onward through the cold of space, the voices agreed, tickling my mind.

I realized that ever since I'd learned about the nightmare clock, I hadn't really been meaning to reset the world. I'd really just wanted to make things with my mother okay. Crow was right—the Proctors, the Brotherhood and their war had broken it long before I'd ever been born. Tremaine and his trick of forcing me to open the Gates were merely symptoms, not problems. And as long as the worlds sat side by side, bleeding into one another, the boundaries slowly fracturing, no mere mortal was going to be able to change a damn thing.

There would always be Fae to entice mortals; there would always be mortals to protect those who couldn't resist the temptation, mortals like my father.

There was only one mistake I was directly responsible for, and only one I could set right, because of that.

You know your heart's blood and your heart's desire, the Great Old Ones intoned. *You know what you have allowed to slip through your fingers.*

"My mother," I whispered.

Lost little lamb, the Old Ones hissed. *Changeling child, fragile as glass.*

"I want my mother back," I said to Crow. "I left her behind," I said. "I should have made sure she was all right."

Then the great gear is yours, said the voices. *Let us go. Let us free, let us roam and devour the four corners of the universe, and all you desire can be yours, not just your mother.*

When I reached out to touch the nightmare clock, it didn't hurt at all. I felt the gears turn smoothly, erasing something from one world while they drew something from another.

The pressure in my mind finally eased and the voices disappeared.

I had gotten my wish.

And in the process, I had set the Old Ones free.

When I came back to myself in the spire of the Bone Sepulchre, Casey was shaking me frantically. The Gate had shut off, leaving just a hum to indicate it had ever been alive. From far below, sirens whooped.

I couldn't process anything beyond blinding pain, so I rolled onto my side and vomited. Casey pointed out the window and shouted something I couldn't hear over the roaring in my head.

Had I really seen any of what I thought I'd seen in Crow's realm? Had I done anything at all besides pass out and throw up?

"I said, we gotta run!" Casey shouted. I managed to pull myself together and follow her gaze, and when I saw what had her in such a panic I was truly back in reality, cold and hard as the ice around me.

A black blot appeared against the white of the horizon as I watched from the tower window, wobbling and wavering against the last of the light, dipping dangerously close to the white wasteland below as it struggled against the extra weight of ice.

Reflected light from the glacier caught the blob, and it grew a shape: the slim, sharp hull of a dirigible. I stared, hoping that I was wrong.

The dying sun illuminated the black wings on the balloon, and my heart sank through the floor.

The *Dire Raven* had found me.

I watched them land from the tower. Draven's shock troops were well outfitted for winter, and they didn't meet much resistance from the Brotherhood. I heard them yelling, the Brotherhood screaming, the sizzle of Draven's guns. I waited. He'd find me soon enough. I didn't want to put up any overt resistance. Not until I knew Dean was all right.

"What are we going to do?" Casey whispered, crouched next to me at the window.

I sat, wrapping my arms around my knees to keep warm. "Wait," I said. "Trust me, Draven wants me alive."

While we listened to the Proctors make their inexorable way toward us, I thought about what I'd seen inside the nightmare clock. Could Crow have been right? Could Tesla and I have shared a gift, to bend reality rather than machines? Could he have gone through the same trials I had, when he made the Storm in the first place?

Had anything I'd done actually helped Nerissa?

Casey looked up, alarmed, as footsteps crunched toward us, spiked boots eating chunks out of the ice steps, grappling hooks that they'd no doubt used to mount the tower hanging from their belts. The half-dozen Proctors who appeared in the tower entrance covered us with their guns. They were coated in snow.

"Hands up!" one barked.

I didn't move. Just waited. I was so numb and exhausted that I wasn't scared.

"Hands *up*!" the Proctor screamed. "Or we shoot!"

"Knock it off." Draven's voice was muffled by the wool mask over his face. It hid everything but his eyes, turning him into the dark figure of nightmares that so many people in Lovecraft thought he was. "She's no threat to you," he told the Proctors. "Not while I've got her precious Dean."

He snapped his fingers and the Proctors lowered their guns. "Go help with prisoner counting and transport," he said. "Anyone puts up a fight, shoot them."

"We can't take off until it warms up again, sir," said the lead Proctor. "The *Raven* will freeze up and we'll crash from the extra weight."

"Thank you so, so much for educating me on the laws of physics, Agent McGuire," said Draven. "Now get the hell out."

The Proctors filed out, using their hooks one by one to rappel past the gaps in the stairs. Draven glanced around the tower, then lifted his mask up and grinned at me. "You're such a good spy, Aoife. That guileless little face and those big green eyes of yours. I bet I could send you into the headquarters of the Crimson Guard in Moscow and you'd have them eating out of your hands."

"Where's Dean?" I snapped.

"Now, that's not very civil," Draven said. "I'm trying to pay you a compliment and all you care about is your little greaser friend."

I clenched my jaw, fighting not to scream. "I did everything you said. To the letter. You found the Brotherhood. Now tell me where Dean is, and let him go."

Draven gestured to the ice where the *Dire Raven* sat. "He's on board. I haven't harmed one Brylcreemed hair on his precious little head." He took off his gloves and smacked them together. "But by all means, say the word and I'll throw him out onto the ice. It's only about thirty-five below out there. He'll have a good ten minutes before he starts to lose fingers and toes."

"You're a bastard," I told him.

Draven smiled at me. "I'd be careful how you toss that term around. I both knew my father and know that I come from a wedlock. Can't really say the same for you."

He looked at the Gate, kicked at the iron arch. "One of Tesla's science projects? Pathetic." He edged closer, his boots treading on the copper and crushing the outer border of the Gate. "You know what you and that rabble-rouser Tesla will be remembered as? When the Brotherhood of Iron works for me? The name Aoife Grayson will be a new fairy tale, one parents tell their daughters when they stray off the path and think that they can change the world."

He took another step toward us, then planted his feet. "I'm going to take you from here, Aoife, and I'm going to put you in an iron box, where you can never, ever hurt anyone else. You'll think I'm a monster, but what I really am is a man. A normal man, without any gifts, a man who protects his world and the people in it by any means necessary. I thought in Innsmouth we could come to an understanding, but that blood of yours will always betray you." Another step.

"Fine," I said. "But I'm through letting you threaten the decent people, who don't know the truth."

He sneered at me. "You think you're meant to stop me, be a heroine who casts aside the darkness? You're the opposite. It's you who is the bringer of darkness and damnation, Aoife, and I'm the cleansing fire."

His hands flashed out and one closed around my arm, the other around Casey's. "Now you come with me. We're going to put you where I should have in the first place."

Casey stared at me with panicked eyes, but I shook my head. Draven had found the Brotherhood, but he hadn't found the truth, and the sooner we got out of this room, the better. Before he realized how close he was to the unimaginable power he craved.

We made our way to the ground, where two Proctors thrust us into our cold-weather gear. Casey was shuffled off with the other line of prisoners. I caught sight of Crosley, the side of his head bleeding red droplets onto the ice, handcuffed in a row of men waiting to board the *Dire Raven*.

He glared at me as I passed by under Draven's protection. "I hope you're happy," he snapped. "I know you brought him here. I knew I shouldn't have trusted you."

"I'm not remotely happy," I told him, and meant it. Draven huffed and pulled me along.

"You're about to get unhappier still," Draven said. "And believe me, the only reason you aren't shackled with the rest of them is because you agreed to help me."

We rounded the corner of the dirigible, and my heartbeat picked up. I had one chance to get away from Draven, one chance to hope that I hadn't accepted his vile compass and doomed everyone in the Brotherhood for nothing.

I'd visited the nightmare clock. I'd done what I'd come back to the Iron Land to do. *Now where the hell was he?* He'd always had a flair for the dramatic.

Draven pounded on the hull, and a black-clad Proctor slid open a small hatch, extending a set of steps that I guessed ran straight to Draven's personal quarters. The Proctor shivered in the harsh wind sweeping across the glacier. "W-w-welcome back, sir."

Draven reached back to pull me inside, and I decided all was lost, just before the vertigo gripped me and I fell to my knees.

Another gust blew snow across my eyes, and when they cleared, Tremaine stood before me. "Aoife . . . ," he started, and then his eyes fell on Draven and the gaping Proctor. "Oh."

I stayed still, watching. Waiting to see what would happen. Draven stared, absolutely still, as did Tremaine. The Proctor was the first to move. He raised his rifle and aimed it at Tremaine, but the Fae was too quick. I watched, almost awed at his fluid movements as his silver knife slipped from its hiding place in his sleeve. He ducked behind the Proctor and drew the knife soundlessly across his throat.

The man dropped to the snow, a fan of crimson spreading from under his body and freezing on the ice. I stared, shrinking away from the corpse. Tremaine's savagery always came as a shock—his face was so beautiful, you couldn't see the cruelty in it until you looked into his eyes.

Draven raised his chin. "Am I supposed to be afraid of you, silver-blooded freak?"

"I don't know," Tremaine said with a grin. "Are you a smart man or a stupid one, human?" He wiped his knife on his sleeve, twice, and tucked it back into his sheath.

"Oh, come on, Draven," I said, sensing my opening. "Surely you're not going to let this Fae get away with that. After all . . ." I looked to Tremaine, hoping he'd pick up my cue. "The Head of the Proctors would never be worried by one Fae."

Tremaine grinned at that, thin and cruel. "Oh," he said. "So clever, Aoife, well done."

Draven pulled his pistol, but it was already a losing proposition. The Fae was faster, stronger, angrier, and I watched the same way you'd watch a frog strike a fly. Tremaine pulled Draven close, disarmed him with a wet cracking sound in his wrist and spun him around, front to back. "I think we're going to have a fine time together, Grey Draven," he hissed. "My queen will be so pleased to meet you."

"No. . . ." I watched Draven struggle, all the color draining from his face. "No, you can't. . . ."

"See?" I told him. "I told you I wouldn't help you. You should listen to me, Draven." I stepped closer, looked into his eyes. "Maybe you'll actually stay alive for more than a few minutes when I see you in the Thorn Land."

Tremaine laughed when I stepped back from Draven, showing every one of his pointed teeth. "You're more Fae than you admit, Aoife. And pursuant to that, you'd better get moving." He gestured at the *Dire Raven*. "Go south and find your mother. The two of you belong at home." He pointed to the sky, and far off, I saw a great blackness surrounded by a crimson corona, as if a blot had appeared on the surface of the faint Arctic sun.

The Old Ones. I hadn't expected what I'd done. But I was also elated as I watched the tiny black dot in the sky. That meant the clock had worked. Somewhere, my mother was safe.

I looked back at Tremaine. "I told you, you'll get us when I'm finished." I could see from his frown this wasn't what he wanted to hear, but I didn't care. Everything Crow had said had been true. I did matter. I had the gift of the Gates, and all that implied. And it was a truth as vast as the encroaching objects in the sky, a truth that I was going to need time, possibly all the time I had left, to accept.

Now, however, I had to find Dean.

Tremaine dragged Draven back into the swirling vortex of magic that led to the Thorn Land, but I didn't stay to watch. I didn't need to be told twice that I'd made a miraculous escape from Draven. Feeling the soft *whump* of displaced air as Tremaine used the *hexenring*, I ran through Draven's quarters toward the bowels of the ship, toward the cell where I'd last seen Dean.

Draven had gotten what he deserved. I didn't feel sorry for him, and I never would.

"Aoife?" Dean stuck his hands through the bars when he saw me, and I ran up to him, clasping them in mine. "Hell, I thought I might never see you again," he said.

"Course you would," I said. "Don't be silly."

"I'd try for a snappy comeback, but I've waited long enough," Dean said, and pulled me to him, kissing me through the bars. I took my time, the relief at seeing him alive and well making me feel like a puppet with its strings cut.

"You're freezing," I said when we finally broke apart.

"Funny, what with this being the Arctic and all," Dean said. I searched the small brig until I found a spare set of keys for the cells, and a pair of mittens, goggles and a coat for Dean. He raised an eyebrow when I unlocked the cell.

"No magic tricks?" he asked.

I shook my head, tucking the keys into my coat. "It's a long story. I can't do the things I used to." At least, not without possibly scrambling my brains like an egg, and that was a chance I'd be just as content not to take.

"Are you all right?" Dean said, staring at me anxiously until he pulled down the goggles over his eyes and obscured his gaze behind reflective glass.

"I think I am, actually," I said, and reached out to take his mittened hand. I didn't know how we were going to get home, and I didn't know what we'd find when we got there, but for once I'd done something right.

"Good," Dean said. "Can we please get the hell out of here? I've been in that cell for days."

"Yeah," I said. "I think that's probably a good idea."

Dean flicked a glance at the sky when we were outside.

"You hear that? The droning? It's been going on for a while now." He turned his eyes back to me. "What in stars is going on here, Aoife?"

"I'll tell you everything, I promise," I said. "As soon as we're away from here." When the sun came up, the *Dire Raven* could probably fly. Probably. It was a big ship, and getting enough lift in the freezing air would be a trick. I wasn't too worried about the remaining Proctors. Whoever was still alive would just be grateful to be headed away from this terrible, barren place and away from the slowly spreading stain in the sky. I would be, if I were them.

"Not soon enough for me," Dean said, and shivered. I tugged at him.

"Come on. Let's at least get back inside the ship, until it's warm enough to try and fly out of here."

"Right behind you," Dean said. "Just glad to be breathing free air again."

Nobody in the prisoner line paid us much attention, nor did the Proctors, who were all running around trying to find Draven. *Good luck on that one,* I thought, not without happiness. The Iron Land was a better place without Grey Draven in it.

Harold Crosley saw me again, pointed at the sky with his shackled hands and screamed, "Do you have any idea what you've done? You stupid girl! You've killed the world! All the worlds!"

It happened so fast that I wouldn't have had time to react, even if I'd known what was coming. I played it over and over in my head during the next few days, but I could never find any other conclusion.

Crosley snatched a gun from a nearby Proctor with his manacled hands. He aimed at me, screaming wordlessly. A weight hit me from the side, throwing me down onto the ice, and there was a blinding green flash as the pistol spoke. I screamed, thinking I'd been shot, but when I looked down expecting a burnt hole in my guts, there was just my dingy white coat, my mittened hands clutching the fabric.

"No . . . ," I whispered, looking to Dean.

He said, "Aoife," and I turned to see him fall, not all at once but first to his knees, and then to a curious, folded position, his mittens pressed against a dark, wet spot on his stomach. I screamed again, and kept screaming as I rushed to him and tried to cradle his head. Behind us, the Proctors disarmed Crosley and beat him savagely with their truncheons, but it didn't matter. Dean was still bleeding, and I was still screaming.

Dean coughed, a small sound against the wind, and I pushed his goggles up before pulling off my mitten with my teeth to stanch the bleeding. Dean had gone white, and a thin line of blood so dark it was nearly black dribbled from the corner of his mouth.

"You'll be all right," I said desperately. He had to be. Had to be all right, despite the ghostliness of his features and the blood that had made his parka sodden and was now spreading into the snow around us. I started to unzip my own coat as he shivered, his teeth rattling.

He stopped me, squeezing my wrist. "Don't," he whispered.

"Don't be silly," I said. "I'll get you back on the *Dire Raven* and everything will be fine."

Dean swallowed and tried to smile, but he was shivering too much. "Don't think so," he muttered. "Not this time."

"Dean . . ." My face was hot despite the icy wind, and my eyes were wet. Dean couldn't be mortally wounded. My mind wouldn't accept it, even as the evidence stained the snow under my knees. "Don't leave me," I begged.

"Sorry, princess," Dean whispered. "Looks like this is the end of the line."

"No," I whimpered, feeling gut-shot myself. "No. . . ."

"It's not so bad," Dean murmured, his face going slack. "It doesn't hurt. Doesn't really feel . . . like anything."

"You're cold," I insisted, my mind flying a thousand miles an hour. He was cold. I had to get him warm. If I could just get him warm it would be all right. "I have to get you inside."

"No," Dean said, fumbling to get my bloody mitten back on my already numb hand. "Don't waste your strength . . . on me. I'm not going any farther. Aoife . . ." He struggled with his own mitten until I pulled it off, and he put his hand against my face. "Aoife . . . I don't want you to think this is your fault. . . ."

"It is," I said. I was crying in earnest, and could feel the glassy half-frozen tears sliding down my cheeks. "If you hadn't pushed me—"

"No," Dean said forcefully. "You make your own luck in this life, Aoife, and my luck was to be here with you." He brushed away the tears with his thumb. "I love you, Aoife Grayson, and that's what I want you to remember. The rest . . ." He coughed again, and more blood trailed down his chin. "The rest doesn't matter one good damn."

"Things can't end this way," I said, although all the

desperation had run out of me. I wasn't very good at lying to myself, when it came down to it. Dean's eyelids fluttered, and his hand dropped away from me.

"Just say it back to me," he said. "Even if it's not true."

I grabbed up his hand again and pressed it against my lips. "It is true," I whispered. "It is, Dean." It was painful to voice, but I figured I'd always known Dean was it. Dean was for good. He deserved everything I had to give him, so I did the best thing I could think of to do. After the truth, I told him one more lie.

"It's going to be all right, Dean," I whispered. He looked up at me, and I could see that he knew. He squeezed my fingers once with his, light and fast, like a heartbeat.

"Yeah," he whispered. "It is, isn't it?"

Dean's eyes slid closed, and he stilled. He didn't go limp or convulse, he just went perfectly still, and except for the red stain still spreading beneath us, he could have been part of the ice.

I bent my head over his chest and sobbed until it felt as if my lungs were frozen, and then I too went still. I couldn't have moved even if I'd wanted to. I stayed where I was, clutching Dean until ice had grown on my exposed skin, and I would have stayed there until I was completely frozen, while the Proctors loaded the prisoners and ignored one dead boy and one frozen girl, probably thinking her dead as well.

She might as well have been. After a time, the *Dire Raven* took off, and my hope of escape along with it, and I still didn't care. Dean was here, and I couldn't leave him. I'd failed him, just as I'd failed Nerissa the last time I'd tried to do what I thought was right and destroyed the Engine.

I'd tried to save everyone, and I'd saved nobody, nobody in this entire world.

I would have stayed crouched in the snow until I *did* freeze to death, except that after it had grown dark, a spotlight framed me as turbines whirred above my head, and an airship blotted out the aurora borealis as they danced above me, wild and free.

Ladders lowered and two figures dropped down, the crampons on their boots throwing up spikes of ice. One of them raised his goggles and I saw my father's eyes. I stared back numbly. How had he found me? Why did it matter to him whether I lived or died? I was worthless to his cause now.

"Aoife!" he shouted, above the wind and the whirr of the *Munin*'s engines. He came and crouched by me, his breath hot on my ear. "Thank stone you're all right. When Conrad told me what you'd done . . ." He saw who I held, and trailed off. "Oh, gods." He felt for Dean's pulse beneath his coat, and then he gently put his hands over mine. "Aoife, you have to let go now," he told me. "Let him go and we'll take care of him."

I knew that I couldn't let go of Dean, but I was so cold and weak I couldn't resist as Archie hauled me to my feet and slung me into his arms, carrying me like a tiny child as the ladder lifted all of us into the *Munin*.

While we floated off the glacier, I felt as if I were staring at myself from down a long tunnel, or through a spyglass, watching a thin-faced girl with dark hair poking wildly from under her cap letting herself be taken aboard an airship, leaving behind nothing but blood on the snow to mark that she'd ever been there.

20

Aboard the Munin

ONCE I'D BEEN settled in blankets aboard the *Munin* by my father, I pressed my forehead against the porthole and watched the true aurora borealis as we turned south. It was bright and sharp and unpredictable, like Dean. I could almost think he was out there, rather than strapped in the hold of the *Munin*.

Someone sat down across from me and pressed a mug of something warm into my hands. Eventually I looked up and saw my brother.

"So," Conrad said. "It looks like despite your best attempts, you didn't manage to kill yourself. Dad says you have some frostbite but you weren't out there long enough to get hypothermia." He took a sip from his own mug. "I know you probably hate me for ratting on you, Aoife, but . . ." He sighed. "I'm your brother, and I'm not going to stop looking out for you just because things change."

"How are we flying?" I said, because it was the only thing

I could think of to say. "We should be icing up and crashing and dying."

Conrad blinked. "The *Munin* has a deicing system. Valentina designed it, I think."

"Oh," I said. Dean was dead. Dean was dead and cold and it was my fault.

Archie came and stood by Conrad, putting a hand on his shoulder. "You doing all right, kiddo?" He shook his head. "Stupid question. Of course you aren't. You going to be okay to go back down the coast, or do we need to set down once we're out of the Arctic Circle?"

"She's covered in blood," Conrad pointed out.

"It's not mine," I said. The words came out flat and toneless. It was how I felt, as if something had stepped on me and stopped my heart from beating right along with Dean's.

Archie squeezed my hand. "I'm furious with you for running off like that, and for running *to* the Brotherhood," he said quietly. "But that doesn't matter now. Are you going to be all right, at least?"

I couldn't muster the energy to outline the many ways in which I was not, so I just turned my face back to the porthole.

I couldn't reverse the mistakes I'd made. Crow had taught me that much. But I could make up for them. From that moment on, I vowed, I would. Dean wouldn't have died for nothing. I wouldn't be remembered as Aoife Grayson the destroyer. I'd be Aoife Grayson the girl who tried with every bit of herself to put right what she'd made wrong.

That Aoife Grayson might have a chance. Not the liar or the deal maker or the dutiful daughter, but the Aoife Grayson who took it upon herself to move ahead, rather than trying to reverse the present into the past—that Aoife Grayson I could live with.

"Do you want anything?" Conrad asked me as he took away my stone-cold tea.

I kept looking at the dancing lights and saw how, bit by bit, they were being blotted out by the encroaching storm I'd called forth. I shook my head and made myself look at my brother, my interfering brother, who was only trying to help me. "I want to go home."

21

Return to Lovecraft

I STOOD ON A street in front of a tumbledown flat near the Rustworks, a streetlamp with a faint aether leak hissing above my head. Cal stood next to me, shifting nervously from foot to foot. He wasn't my first choice to accompany me on this outing, but I trusted him to keep his mouth shut.

In the building before us, the only flat lit was on the third floor, where we could see the yellow glow of an oil lamp. The aether feed was long dead.

Ghouls keened not far away, but I didn't let them worry me much. The ghouls had been quieter since the advent of the Old Ones, and the howling skies had replaced the howling ghouls. Even the lunatics in the madhouses around Lovecraft—the ones the Proctors had managed to round up, anyway—had grown quiet.

It was obvious, once I'd thought about it after we'd touched down in Lovecraft. Crow had said the clock couldn't remake time, but it could make me see things in different ways, make parallel lines cross, help a mother and daughter find one another again amid the chaos of a ruined city.

"Light's new," Cal said, pointing. He cast a look back at me, at the small satchel I carried. Just some clothes and my notebook. "What's the deal with the luggage?"

Seeing the lamp made my heart beat faster. "I'll tell you later," I said, starting across the street. I'd come every night to the flat Conrad, our mother and I had shared, come alone and occasionally with Cal, and I knew that sooner or later, the lights would be on. The Old Ones had promised it. Just as they grew ever greater in the sky, their advancing mass now nearly the size of the moon, they had promised when I'd been in Crow's world that sooner or later, I'd find Nerissa.

I just hoped that trusting them hadn't been my last, worst mistake. I stepped off the pavement into the cobbled street, careful not to turn my ankle in the holes left by missing stones.

"Hey." I turned back to Cal. "You're my best friend. And no matter what, you're a good guy."

Cal frowned at me, clearly knowing he was missing something. "Thanks? I think?"

"Don't be afraid, Cal," I said. "If Bethina finds out, she won't love you any less. I know, and I love you. She will too."

I was across the street. I was at the stoop where I'd sat and waited for Conrad on so many afternoons.

"Aoife!" Cal hissed as I mounted the cracked steps. "What's going on?"

I waved at him, feigning a happiness I didn't feel. That

had died with Dean. "Take care of Bethina," I said. "Tell my father and Conrad not to worry. And that I love them. But not about this."

The street-level door of the building was half off its hinges, and every other tread of the stairs was a gaping hole. "Goodbye, Cal," I whispered, and stepped inside, mounting the rickety staircase.

I climbed the stairs and made my way to the end of the hall. The wallpaper, yellow with blue blossoming violets, had peeled and now hung in long strips like seaweed washed up on a dead shore.

There was no number on the door anymore, but I knew it by heart. Number Seven. I raised my hand and knocked twice. I waited, holding my breath. I was prepared to hold it forever, to be suspended in this moment for as long as it took, but in reality it took no more than a few seconds.

The door opened a crack. "Yes?"

She was even thinner than the last time I'd seen her in the Christobel madhouse. Her hair was stringy and drooped in her face, and her eyes gleamed more brightly than the lamp. But she recognized me, and that was more than I could have said for her in the madhouse on her best day.

"Aoife," she said, her face cracking into a grin. She pulled open the door and threw thin arms around me. "Oh, Aoife." She held me in a firm grip, and whispered against my hair. "They said I should come back. The dreaming voices. They told me to go to the old places and look out the old windows and I'd see you just as I'd see you coming home from school when you were a little one."

"They were right," I whispered back. Nerissa let me go and stepped back to regard me.

"Baby," she said. "What's wrong? You look so sad."

"Nerissa, I . . ." I swallowed, and willed my tears not to spring forth again. I hadn't cried since I'd held Dean in the snow. "Mother. I paid a lot to see you again."

"The Old Ones," she said instantly. "The great gods, turning the gear of the world to their own ends."

I stopped, realizing for the first time how much truth was hidden in her seemingly irrational words. Could Nerissa have a gift as well? Could Fae possess the Weird?

"We have to go," I said. "I need to take you away from here. We need to go . . ." The word hitched in my throat, unfamiliar and terrible. "We need to go home."

"Home, yes. To Thorn. I expected as much. That's not why you're sad, though," Nerissa said matter-of-factly. "There's a shadow of a soul on your eyes. Through glass, you're looking at another place but you can't touch it."

"A boy," I whispered. "His name was Dean."

Nerissa took my face in her hands, turned it this way and that. "I know what brought me back here," she said. "I know what you could be, child, given time to hone your gift in a place without iron. You don't have to be like me, you know. You don't have to go mad."

"How?" I muttered. "I know I have to try and send the Old Ones back, but I don't know how."

"There's a way," Nerissa said. "You think the gear only works between our two worlds? That there are only two sides to everything? The universe is shapes and spaces, Aoife. It flows and moves like bubbles through water. Your Dean has gone, it's true, but where?" She brought us so close our noses were nearly touching. "You know the wheres. You know how to move between. You can have him again, and in that place, you can find what you need to send the Old Ones away, not just to the stars, but forever."

I stared at my mother, willing the light in her eyes to be inspiration and not insanity. I thought of what Crow had said to me, when I'd asked him if the dome of dreaming was the afterlife. "The Deadlands," I said aloud. "You can't visit them if you're alive. Crow said . . ."

"The king of dreams has his rules and we have ours, and we rewrite them with the ink of our blood," Nerissa said, fast and in a monotone, as if she were reciting a prayer. "You can go anywhere, Aoife. Anywhere that dreams can see, you can go. You can make the dream king point the way."

I stayed very still for a heartbeat or two. I was determined that I was going to be a Gateminder in the way the Brotherhood had meant for me to be, before Crosley and Draven had split it apart and allowed the world to fracture. I was determined that I would stop the Old Ones before they spread their madness and destruction across all the worlds I could visit. But in that moment, the only determination I cared about was the small, slender, flickering flame of a chance that I could have Dean back. That I could journey not to the Thorn Land or to the empire of the Old Ones, but to a land that no living thing, be they human or immortal, could visit.

"I can get Dean back," I repeated to Nerissa, slowly and carefully, as if we were just learning to speak the same language. In a way, I supposed we were. I was learning to decipher her madness, and she was learning to extrapolate from my Weird. "I can go to the Deadlands and get him, and I can push back the Old Ones at the same time." I swallowed, throat tight and dry. I wanted to hope, but I didn't dare. "I can get Dean back."

"Oh, yes," my mother said, her eyes glistening like beads in the lamplight. "You can go. To the Deadlands and beyond, and what you meet in the Deadlands can be the end of anything you choose. Including the Old Ones. There is a way."

"How?" I said. "How can you be alive and bring someone back from the dead?"

My mother stepped outside and shut the door firmly. "Walk with me, until we get to the *hexenring*," she said, "and I'll tell you."

Final entry:

So here I sit, in a spot where no Gateminder ever expected to find herself. The court of the Winter Queen is nothing like the life I knew, but it's not unbearable. At least, I tell myself that, because I only have to endure the stares of the full-blooded Fae and the glares of Tremaine for a little while longer.

My mother is well, and getting stronger, although I don't know if she'll ever be the same after the years of iron poisoning, locked up in Lovecraft.

Octavia spends hours talking to her. I know too well the agony of having a sibling you can't reach, the almost primal desire to make them well.

Tremaine is just as he has always been, conniving and cruel, although of late, his cruelty is mostly directed at his new human pet, Grey Draven, and I personally feel that's the way it should be.

So no, I didn't beat back the Storm. I didn't fix

what I broke. I am the destroyer, and it's a name that'll follow me for the rest of my life. But I do have a plan, a new plan. I am living for the plan, because if it fails, I'll truly have nothing. I'll just be a mostly human girl trapped in the Thorn Land while everyone she knows and loves back home grows old and dies.

This will be my last entry in this journal. I am not a member of the Brotherhood. I'm never going to be. And my Weird doesn't work like my father's, like my family's. My gift is so much stronger, so much worse than theirs. I'm not going to keep writing about it for some future Brotherhood member to pore over and dissect and use to their advantage.

I don't know what will happen now, but I have a plan, and my plan is simple: I am going to the Deadlands. I am going to use my gift to get there. I am going to find Dean, and I'm going to bring him back. And when I do that, I am going to kill the Old Ones and make the world safe again.

Or I am going to die trying.

ABOUT THE AUTHOR

Caitlin Kittredge is a history and horror movie enthusiast who writes novels wherein bad things usually happen to perfectly nice characters. But that's all right—the ones who aren't so nice have always been her favorites. Caitlin lives in western Massachusetts in a crumbling Victorian mansion with her two cats, her cameras, and several miles of books. When not writing, she spends her time taking photos, concocting alternate histories, and trying new and alarming colors of hair dye. Caitlin is the author of two bestselling series for adults, Nocturne City and the Black London adventures. *The Nightmare Garden* is her second book for teens. Look for her first, *The Iron Thorn,* available from Delacorte Press. You can visit her at caitlinkittredge.com.